MAGIC CITY: RECENT SPELLS

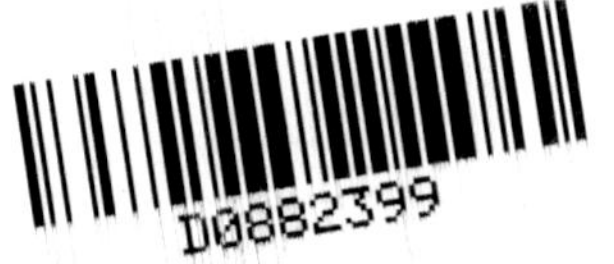

Other Anthologies Edited by
Paula Guran

Embraces
Best New Paranormal Romance
Best New Romantic Fantasy
Zombies: The Recent Dead
The Year's Best Dark Fantasy & Horror: 2010
Vampires: The Recent Undead
The Year's Best Dark Fantasy & Horror: 2011
Halloween
New Cthulhu: The Recent Weird
Brave New Love
Witches: Wicked, Wild & Wonderful
Obsession: Tales of Irresistible Desire
The Year's Best Dark Fantasy & Horror: 2012
Extreme Zombies
Ghosts: Recent Hauntings
Rock On: The Greatest Hits of Science Fiction & Fantasy
Season of Wonder
Future Games
Weird Detectives: Recent Investigations
The Mammoth Book of Angels & Demons
The Year's Best Dark Fantasy & Horror: 2013
Halloween: Magic, Mystery, & the Macabre

MAGIC CITY: RECENT SPELLS

EDITED BY

PAULA GURAN

PRIME BOOKS

Cover art by Joseph Corsentino.
Cover design by Sherin Nicole.

Prime Books
Germantown, MD
www.prime-books.com

For more information, contact Prime Books:
prime@prime-books.com

Print ISBN: 978-1-60701-427-0
Ebook ISBN: 978-1-60701-436-2

CONTENTS

There's a bit of magic in everything
And then some loss to even things out.
—Lou Reed "Magic and Loss"

INTRODUCTION: METROPOLITAN MAGIC

Paula Guran

I. Magic

Magic used to be "real"—meaning people believed in it. (Some folks still do. Maybe we all do, to some extent . . . but that's a tangent we won't explore here.) Magic influenced the course of natural events or achieved the impossible. But it took special powers, or preternatural talent, or sorcerous learning, or special words, cryptic symbols, or strange spells, or manipulation of the gods, or . . . you get the idea . . . to *access* the supernatural side of things. Magic might be all around, but you had to know how to reach it because there was always a border, an edge, a barrier between the mundane and the magical.

Without reality, there was no magic. The real and the unreal coexisted and were mutually dependent. Without the natural, there could be no supernatural; no paranormal without the normal.

Authors use magic in many ways in their fictions, and learned people have produced many erudite words to discuss how they do so. I'm neither learned nor erudite. I merely want to offer the thematic premise for this anthology. But I think we can all more or less agree that for fantasy and/or magic to truly and effectively capture the reader's imagination, it still needs to be grounded in reality. (Or perhaps be the reverse of it. The equation still holds.)

You can create your own fantasy world (or entire universe)—one where "our world" doesn't exist—but to successfully tell your story it will need to have its own reality—its own rules and limitations—even if it is quite different from our (consensual) reality. Magic may be common in the imagined world, but it still needs to function with self-contained consistency or at least an attachment to customarily accepted concepts whether they are arcane secrets or the sciences.

Or you can base your fantastic story in a version of our world and bend it to accommodate the magical. These environments can be open—where the existence of the supernatural is known to exist, at least by some—or closed—where "otherness" is concealed from common knowledge. A magical world can exist parallel to our own: sometimes accessible through a gateway or portal, or perhaps with some bleeding back and forth across that barrier I mentioned above. It can even be, overall, the world we live in, but where magic once functioned in the past and has now "thinned" out to nonexistence (or nearly so).

Whatever the magical "system" or fantastical world an author invents, when it comes to magic there's often some price to pay to use it—as minimal as the draining of physical energy or as dire as death. Maybe that's a remnant of our primal idea of the balance between the natural and the supernatural.

II. Cities and Recent Spells

These are stories about various magics set in the varied realities of those comparatively permanent human settlements we call cities.

For most of you reading this, a city—large or small—is your native environment. And even if you live in a rural area or very small town, our society is primarily urban and you, personally, have vital connections to cities. Cities are, more than ever, our world—the primary symbol of our current reality.

All these stories were written in the twenty-first century, a time in which this urban reality rules more than ever. In fact, except for two tales, all were written within the past decade.

Most of them have contemporary, if fantastically modified, metropolitan settings—Chicago (twice), Cleveland, Detroit (maybe twice) and Kalamazoo, Las Vegas, London, Los Angeles, New York (three times), Providence, Seattle—and a few fictional but modern-day nameless, cities. I wanted, however, to offer at least a glimpse or two of very different urban locales. In "Alchemy" Lucy Sussex take us back to the ancient city of Babylon. Scott Lynch provides us with an example of an "other universe fantasy city" with "In the Stacks." Alison Wise, in "The Thief of Precious Things," takes us to a near-future city. And no modern collection of stories about magic and cities could be considered complete without at least a short visit to Bordertown—a city invented by Terri Windling (and written about by many writers) that lies on the border between "the Elflands" and "the World"—which Catherynne M. Valente provides in "A Voice Like A Hole."

Love, crime, vengeance, salvation, revelation, adventure, triumph, tragedy, and more all mix with magic in the cauldron of the city. Expect to meet wizards, witches, faeries, magicians, demons, elves, shape-changers, magic-makers without convenient labels . . . and, of course, the unexpected . . . on our supernatural streets.

Writers-as-characters seek out magic (as in Caitlín R. Kiernan's "-30-") or, as Angela Slatter's protagonist does in "Words," conjure it themselves. We visit universities—cities have always been places of learning—twice: once in the Lynch story and, in a much more modern context, with Jonathan Maberry's "Spellcaster 2.0."

Sometimes, as in "Paranormal Romance" by Christopher Barzak or Elizabeth Bear's "The Slaughtered Lamb," your own magical powers don't seem to do you, personally, much good. Magic can be a city-dweller's career—like it is for the wizards in Jim Butcher's "Curses" and Simon R. Green's "Street Wizard," or a way of life, as it is for characters in "Seeing Eye" by Patricia Briggs or Amanda Downum's "Snake Charmer." Humans can interact with fairies and their magical powers in *very* different ways as shown in Delia Sherman's "Grand Central Park," "The Land of Heart's Desire" by Holly Black, and Emma Bull's "De la Tierra" (among others).

Magic can suddenly enter your metropolitan life unexpectedly as it does for a lawyer in Nnedi Okorafor's "Kabu Kabu" and a high school boy in "Dog Boys" by Charles de Lint. Or it can be there all along, but undiscovered—as many things often are in cities. Such discoveries are made in Diana Peterfreund's "Stray Magic," "The Woman Who Walked with Dogs" by Mary Rosenblum, "Stone Man" by Nancy Kress, and Carrie Vaughn's "The Arcane Art of Misdirection."

And don't be surprised to find some of our protagonists to be on the younger side. Children and young adults seem to be able to find magic more easily than grown-ups—or perhaps they more desperately need it to survive the city as Nisi Shawl ("Wallamelon") and Mark Laidlaw and John Shirley ("Pearlywhite") show.

Are these stories "urban fantasy"? Well, that's a term that started out defining one thing, was accidently applied to something else, and is now changing yet again. But if you want to keep it simple, to quote one of our authors, Elizabeth Bear: "In urban fantasy you don't leave the chip shop and go to another world to find the unicorn. Rather, the unicorn shows up at the chip shop and orders the cod."

Most chip shops are found in cities and towns. Urban areas.

23 February 2014
(John Keats died on this day in 1821)
Paula Guran

The City: *London, England.*

The Magic: *A night in the life of an urban public servant: lots of responsibility, hardly any authority, and the pay sucks . . . but when you can See all the wonders of the hidden world, you walk in magic and work miracles, and the night is full of glory.*

STREET WIZARD

SIMON R. GREEN

I believe in magic. It's my job.

I'm a street wizard, work for London City Council. I don't wear a pointy hat, I don't live in a castle, and no one in my line of work has used a wand since tights went out of fashion. I'm paid the same money as a traffic warden, but I don't even get a free uniform. I just get to clean up other people's messes, and prevent trouble when I can. It's a magical job, but someone's got to do it.

My alarm goes off at nine o'clock sharp every evening, and that's when my day begins. When the sun's already sliding down the sky towards evening, with night pressing close on its heels. I do all the usual things everyone else does at the start of their day, and then I check I have all the tools of my trade before I go out: salt, holy water, crucifix, silver dagger, wooden stake. No guns, though. Guns get you noticed.

I live in a comfortable enough flat, over an off-license, right on the edge of Soho. Good people, mostly. But when the sun goes down and the night takes over, a whole new kind of people move in. The tourists and the punters and every other eager little soul with more money than sense. Looking for a good time, they fill up the streets with stars in their eyes and avarice in their hearts, all looking for a little something to take the edge off, to satisfy their various longings.

Someone has to watch their backs, to protect them from the dangers they don't even know are out there.

ᔕ

By the time I'm ready to leave, two drunken drag queens are arguing shrilly under my window, caught up in a slanging match. It'll all end in tears and wig-pulling, but I leave them to it, and head out into the tangle of narrow streets that make up Soho. Bars and restaurants, night clubs and clip joints, hot neon and cold hard cash. The streets are packed with furtive-eyed people, hot on the trail of everything that's bad for them. It's my job to see they get home safely, or at least that they only fall prey to the *everyday* perils of Soho.

I never set out to be a street wizard. Don't suppose anyone does. But, like music and mathematics, with magic it all comes down to talent. All the hard work in the world will only get you so far; to be a Major Player you have to be born to the Craft. The rest of us play the cards we're dealt. And do the jobs that need doing.

I start my working day at a greasy spoon caff called *Dingley Dell.* There must have been a time when I found that funny, but I can't remember when. The caff is the agreed meeting place for all the local street wizards, a stopping off place for information, gossip, and a hot cup of tea before we have to face the cold of the night. It's not much of a place, all steamed-up windows, Formica-covered tables, plastic chairs, and a full greasy breakfast if you can stomach it. There's only ever thirteen of us, to cover all the hot spots in Soho. There used to be more, but the budget's not what it used to be.

We sit around patiently, sipping blistering tea from chipped china, while the Supervisor drones on, telling us things he thinks we need to know. We hunch our shoulders and pretend to listen.

He's not one of us. He's just a necessary intermediary between us and the Council. We only put up with him because he's responsible for overtime payments.

A long miserable streak of piss, and mean with it, Bernie Drake likes to think he runs a tight ship. Which basically means he moans a lot, and we call him Gladys behind his back.

"All right, listen up! Pay attention and you might just get through tonight with all your fingers, and your soul still attached." That's Drake. If a fart stood upright and wore an ill-fitting suit, it could replace our Supervisor and we wouldn't even notice. "We've had complaints! *Serious* complaints. Seems a whole bunch of booze demons have been possessing the more vulnerable tourists, having their fun and then abandoning their victims at the end of the night, with really bad hangovers and no idea how they got them. So watch out for the signs, and make sure you've got an exorcist on speed dial for the stubborn ones. We've also had complaints about magic shops that are there one day and gone the next, before the suckers can come running back to complain the goods don't work. So if you see a shop front you don't recognize, call it in. And, Jones, stay away from the wishing wells! I won't tell you again. Padgett, *leave the witches alone*! They've got a living to make, same as the rest of us.

"And, if anybody cares—apparently something's been eating traffic wardens. All right, all right, that's enough hanging around. Get out there and do some good. Remember, you've a quota to meet."

We're already up and on our feet and heading out, muttering comments just quietly enough that the Supervisor can pretend he doesn't hear them. It's the little victories that keep you going. We all take our time about leaving, just to show we won't be hurried. I take a moment to nod politely to the contingent of local working girls, soaking up what warmth they can from the caff, before a long night out on the cold, cold streets. We know them, and they know us, because we all walk the same streets and share the same hours. All decked out in bright colors and industrial strength makeup, they chatter together like gaudy birds of paradise, putting off the moment when they have to go out to work.

Rachel looks across at me, and winks. I'm probably the only one there who knows her real name. Everyone else just calls her Red, after her hair. Not much room for subtlety, in the meat market. Not yet thirty, and already too old for the better locations, Red wears a heavy coat with hardly anything underneath it, and stilettos with heels long enough to qualify as deadly weapons. She crushes a cigarette in an ashtray, blows smoke into the steamy air, and gets up to join me. Just casually, in passing.

"Hello, Charlie boy. How's tricks?"

"Shouldn't I be asking you that?"

We both smile. She thinks she knows what I do, but she doesn't. Not really.

"Watch yourself out there, Charlie boy. Lot of bad people around these days."

I pay attention. Prossies hear a lot. "Anyone special in mind, Red?"

But she's already moving away. Working girls never let themselves get close to anyone. "Let me just check I've got all my things; straight razor, knuckle duster, pepper spray, condoms and lube. There; ready for anything."

"Be good, Red."

"I'm always good, Charlie boy."

I hold the door open for her, and we go out into the night.

I walk my beat alone, up and down and back and forth, covering the streets of Soho in a regular pattern. Dark now, only artificial light standing between us and everything the night holds. The streets are packed with tourists and punters, in search of just the right place to be properly fleeced, and then sent on their way with empty pockets and maybe a few nice memories to keep them going till next time. Neon blazes and temptation calls, but that's just the Soho everyone sees. I see a hell of a sight more, because I'm a street wizard. And I have the Sight.

When I raise my Sight, I can See the world as it *really* is, and not as most people *think* it is. I See all the wonders and marvels, the terrors and the nightmares, the glamour and magic and general weird shit most people never even know exists. I raise my Sight and look on the world with fresh eyes, and the night comes alive, bursting with hidden glories and miracles, gods and monsters. And I See it all.

Gog and Magog, the giants, go fist-fighting through the back streets of Soho; bigger than buildings, their huge misty forms smash through shops and businesses without even touching them. Less than ghosts, but more than memories, Gog and Magog fight a fight that will never end till history itself comes stumbling to a halt. They were here before London, and there are those who say they'll still be here long after London is gone.

Wee-winged fairies come slamming down the street like living shooting stars, darting in and out of the lamp posts in a gleeful game of tag, leaving long shimmering trails behind them. Angels go line dancing on the roof of Saint Giles' Church. And a handful of Men in Black check the details of parked vehicles, because not everything that *looks* like a car *is* a car. Remember the missing traffic wardens?

If everyone could See the world as it really is, and not as we would have it—if they could See everything and everyone they share the world with—they'd shit themselves. They'd go stark staring mad. They couldn't cope. It's a much bigger world than people think, bigger and stranger than most of them can imagine. It's my job to see that the hidden world stays hidden, and that none of it spills over into the safe and sane everyday world.

∽

I walk up and down the streets, pacing myself, covering my patch. I have a lot of ground to cover every night, and it has to be done the traditional way, on foot. They did try cars, for a while. Didn't work out. You miss far too much, from a car. You need good heavy shoes for this job, strong legs and a straight back. And you can't let your concentration slip, even for a moment. There's always so much you have to keep an eye out for. Those roaming gangs of Goths, for example, all dark clothes and pale faces. Half of them are teenage vampires, on the nod and on the prowl, looking for kicks and easy blood. What better disguise? You can always spot the real leeches, though. They wear ankhs instead of crucifixes. Long as they don't get too greedy, I let them be. All part of the atmosphere of Soho.

And you have to keep a watchful eye on the prossies, the hard-faced working girls on their street corners. Opening their heavy coats to flash the passing trade, showing red, red smiles that mean nothing at all. You have to watch out for new faces, strange faces, because not everything that *looks* like a woman *is* a woman. Some are sirens, some are succubae, and some are the alien equivalent of the praying mantis. All of it hidden behind a pleasing glamour until they've got their dazzled prey somewhere nice and private; then they take a lot more than money from their victims.

I pick them out and send them packing. When I can. Bloody diplomatic immunity.

Seems to me there's a lot more homeless out and about on the streets than there used to be: the lost souls and broken men and gentlemen of the road. But some have fallen further than most. They used to be Somebody, or Something, living proof that the wheel turns for all of us. If you're wise you'll drop the odd coin in a cap, here and there, because karma has teeth; all it takes is one really bad day, and we can all fall off the edge.

But the really dangerous ones lurk inside their cardboard boxes like tunnel spiders, ready to leap out and batten onto some unsuspecting passerby in a moment, and drag them back inside their box before anyone even notices what's happened. Nothing like hiding in plain sight. Whenever I find a lurker, I set fire to its box and jam a stake through whatever comes running out. Vermin control, all part of the job.

From time to time I stop to take a breath, and look wistfully at the more famous bars and nightclubs that would never admit the likes of me through their upmarket, uptight doors. A friend of mine who's rather higher up the magical food chain told me she once saw a well-known sitcom star stuck half way up the stairs, because he was so drunk he couldn't remember whether he was going up or coming down. For all I know, he's still there. But that's Soho for you: a gangster in every club bar, and a celebrity on every street corner doing something unwise.

I stoop down over a sewer grating, to have a chat with the undine who lives in the underground water system. She controls pollution levels by letting it all flow through her watery form, consuming the really bad stuff and filtering out the grosser impurities. She's been down there since Victorian times, and seems happy enough. Though like everyone else she's got something to complain about; apparently she's not happy that people have stopped flushing baby alligators down their toilets. She misses them.

"Company?" I ask.

"Crunchy," she says.

I laugh, and move on.

Some time later, I stop off at a tea stall, doing steady business in the chilly night. The local hard luck cases come shuffling out of the dark, drawn like shabby moths to the stall's cheerful light. They queue up politely for a cup of tea or a bowl of soup, courtesy of the Sally Army. The God botherers don't approve of me any more than I approve of them, but we both know we each serve a purpose. I always make a point to listen in to what the street people have to say. You'd be amazed what even the biggest villains will say in front of the homeless, as though they're not really there.

I check the grubby crowd for curses, bad luck spells, and the like, and defuse them. I do what I can.

Red turns up at the stall, just as I'm leaving. Striding out of the night like a ship under full sail, she crashes to a halt before the tea stall and demands a black coffee, no sugar. Her face is flushed, and she's already got a bruised cheek and a shiner, and dried blood clogging one nostril.

"This punter got a bit frisky," she says, dismissively. "I told him; that's extra, darling. And when he wouldn't take the hint, I hit him in the nads with my knuckle-duster. One of life's little pleasures. Then when he was down I kicked him in the head, just for wasting my time. Me and a few of the girls rolled him for all he had, and then left him to it. Never touch the credit cards, though. The filth investigate credit cards. God, this is bad coffee. How's your night going, Charlie boy?"

"Quiet," I say, and work a simple spell to heal her face. "You ever think of giving this up, Red?"

"What?" she says. "And leave show business?"

More and more drunks on the street now, stumbling and staggering this way and that, thrown out of the clubs and bars once they run out of money. I work simple spells, from a safe distance. To sober them up, or help them find a safe taxi, or the nearest Underground station. I work other protections too, that they never know of. Quietly removing weapons from the pockets of would-be muggers, driving off mini-cab drivers with bad intent by giving them the runs, or breaking up the bigger street gangs with basic paranoia spells, so they turn on each other instead. Always better to defuse a situation than risk it all going bad, with blood and teeth on the pavement. A push here and a prod there, a subtle influence and a crafty bit of misdirection, and most of the night's trouble is over before it's even started.

I make a stop at the biggest Chinese Christian Church in London, and chat with the invisible Chinese demon that guards the place from trouble-makers and unbelievers. It enjoys the irony of protecting a Church that officially doesn't believe in it. And since it gets to eat anyone who tries to break in, it's quite happy. The Chinese have always been a very practical people.

Just down the street is an Indian restaurant once suspected of being a front for Kali worshippers on the grounds that not everyone who went in came back out again. Turned out to be an underground railroad, where people oppressed because of their religious beliefs could pass quietly from this dimension to another. There's an Earth out there for everyone, if you only know where to look. I helped the restaurant put up an avoidance spell, so only the right kind of people would go in.

I check out the dumpsters round the back, while I'm there. We've been having increasing problems with feral pixies, just likely. Like foxes, they come in from the countryside to the town, except foxes can't blast the aura right off you with a hard look. Pixies like dumpsters; they can play happily in them for hours. And they'll eat pretty much anything, so mostly I just leave them to get on with it. Though if the numbers start getting too high, I'll have to organize another cull.

I knock the side of the dumpster, but nothing knocks back. Nobody home.

After that, it's in and out of all the pokey little bars in the back streets, checking for the kind of leeches that specialize in grubby little gin joints. They look human enough, especially in a dimly lit room. You know the kind of strangers, the ones who belly up to the bar next to you with an ingratiating smile, talking about nothing in particular, but you just can't seem to get rid of them. It's not your company, or even your money, they're after. Leeches want other things. Some can suck the booze right out of you, leaving you nothing but the hangover. Others can drain off your life energy, your luck, even your hope.

They usually run when they see me coming. They know I'll make them give it all back, with interest. I love to squeeze those suckers dry.

Personal demons are the worst. They come in with the night, swooping and roiling down the narrow streets like leaves tossed on the breeze, snapping their teeth and flexing their barbed fingers. Looking to fasten on to any tourist whose psychic defenses aren't everything they should be. They wriggle in, under the mental barricades, snuggle onto your back and ride you like a mule. They encourage all their host's worst weaknesses—greed or lust or violence, all the worst sins and temptations they ever dreamed of. The tourists go wild, drowning themselves in sensation—and the demons soak it all up. When they've had enough they let go, and slip away into the night, fat and engorged, leaving the tourists to figure out where all their money and self respect went. Why they've done so many things they swore they'd never do. Why there's a dead body at their feet, and blood on their hands.

I can See the demons, but they never see me coming. I can sneak up behind them and rip them right off a tourist's back. I use special gloves that I call my emotional baggage handlers. A bunch of local nuns make them for us, blessed with special prayers, every thread soaked in holy water, and backed up with nasty silver spurs in the fingertips. Personal demons aren't really alive, as such, but I still love the way they scream as their flimsy bodies burst in my hands.

Of course, some tourists bring their own personal demons in with them, and then I just make a note of their names, to pass on to the Big Boys. Symbiosis is more than I can handle.

I bump into my first group of Grey aliens of the night, and make a point of stopping to check their permits are in order. They look like ordinary people to everyone else, until they get up close, and then they hypnotize you with those big black eyes, like a snake with a mouse, and you might as well bend over and smile for the probe. Up close, they smell of sour milk, and their movements are just *wrong.* Their dull grey flesh slides this way and that, even when they're standing still, as though it isn't properly attached to the bones beneath.

I've never let them abduct anyone on my watch. I'm always very firm; no proper paperwork, no abduction. They never argue. Never even react. It's hard to tell what a Grey is thinking, what with that long flat face and those unblinking eyes. I wish they'd wear some kind of clothes, though. You wouldn't believe what they've got instead of genitals.

Even when their paperwork is in order, I always find or pretend to find something wrong, and send them on their way, out of my area. Just doing my bit, to protect humanity from alien intervention. The Government can stuff their quotas.

Round about two or three a.m., I run across a Street Preacher, having a quiet smoke of a hand-rolled in a back alley. She's new, Tamsin MacReady. Looks about fifteen, but she must be hard as nails or they'd never have given her this patch. Street Preachers deal with the more spiritual problems, which is why few of them last long. Soon enough they realize reason and compassion aren't enough, and that's when the smiting starts, and the rest of us run for cover. Tamsin's a decent enough sort, disturbed that she can't do more to help.

"People come here to satisfy the needs of the flesh, not the spirit," I say, handing her back the hand-rolled. "And we're here to help, not meddle."

"Oh, blow it out your ear," she says, and we both laugh.

It's not long after that I run into some real trouble; someone from the Jewish Defense League has unleashed a Golem on a march by British Nazi skinheads. The Golem is picking them up and throwing them about, and the ones who aren't busy bleeding or crying or wetting themselves are legging it for the horizon. I feel like standing back and applauding, but I can't let this go on. Someone might notice. So I wade in, ducking under the Golem's flailing arms, until I can wipe the activating word off its forehead. It goes still then, nothing more than lifeless clay, and I put in a call for it to be towed away. Someone higher up will have words with someone else, and hopefully I won't have to do this again. For a while.

I take some hard knocks and a bloody nose before I can shut the Golem down, so I take time out to lean against a stone wall and feel sorry for myself: My healing spells only work on other people. The few skinheads picking themselves up off the pavement aren't sympathetic. They know where my sympathies lie. Some of them make aggressive noises, until I give them a hard look, and then they remember they're needed somewhere else.

I could always turn the Golem back on, and they know it.

I head off on my beat again, picking them up and slapping them down, aching quietly here and there. Demons and pixies and golems, oh my. Just another night, in Soho.

Keep walking, keep walking. Protect the ones you can, and try not to dwell on the ones you can't. Sweep up the mess, drive off the predators, and keep the world from ever finding out. That's the job. Lots of responsibility, hardly any authority, and the pay sucks. I say as much to Red, when we bump into each other at the end of our shifts. She clucks over my bruises, and offers me a nip from her hip flask. It's surprisingly good stuff.

"Why do you do it, Charlie boy? Hard work and harder luck, with nothing to show but bruises and bad language from the very people you're here to help? It can't be the money; I probably make more than you do."

"No," I say. "It's not the money."

I think of all the things I See every night that most of the world never knows exists. The marvelous and the fantastic, the strange creatures and stranger people, gods and monsters and all the wonders of the hidden world. I walk in magic and work miracles, and the night is full of glory. How could I ever turn my back on all that?

"You ever think of giving this up, Charlie boy?" says Red.

"What?" I say. "And leave show business?"

෴

Simon R. Green was born in Bradford-on-Avon, Wiltshire, England (where he still resides). He obtained an MA in Modern English and American Literature from Leicester University; he also studied history and has a combined Humanities degree. He is the bestselling author of several series, including twelve novels of The Nightside and The Secret Histories (book seven, *Property of a Lady Faire*, is due out soon). *Once in a Blue Moon*, eighth of the Hawk & Fisher series, came out earlier this year. His newest series, The Ghost Finders, will also have a fifth novel, *Voices From Beyond*, published this year.

The City: *Cleveland, Ohio.*

The Magic: *A modern witch makes her living weaving love spells for others, but the magic in her fingertips goes still and cold when she tries to find romance for herself.*

PARANORMAL ROMANCE

Christopher Barzak

This is a story about a witch. Not the kind you're thinking of either. She didn't have a long nose with a wart on it. She didn't have green skin or long black hair. She didn't wear a pointed hat or a cape, and she didn't have a cat, a spider, a rat, or any of those animals that are usually hanging around witches. She didn't live in a ramshackle house, a gingerbread house, a Victorian house, or a cave. And she didn't have any sisters. This witch wasn't the kind you read about in fairy tales and in plays by Shakespeare. This witch lived in a red brick bungalow that had been turned into an upstairs/downstairs apartment house on an old industrial street that had lost all of its industry in Cleveland, Ohio. The apartment house had two other people living in it: a young gay couple who were terribly in love with one another. The couple had a dog, an incredibly happy-faced Eskimo they'd named Snowman, but the witch never spoke to it, even though she could. She didn't like dogs, but she did like the gay couple. She tried not to hold their pet against them.

The witch—her name was Sheila—specialized in love magic. She didn't like curses. Curses were all about hate and—occasionally—vengeance, and Sheila had long ago decided that she'd spend her time productively, rather than wasting energy on dealing with perceived injustices located in her—or someone else's—past. Years ago, when she was in college, she had dabbled in curses, but they were mainly favors the girls in her dorm asked of her, usually after a boyfriend dumped them, cheated on them, used them as a means for money and mobility, or some other power or shame thing. A curse always sounded nice to them. Fast and dirty justice. Sheila sometimes helped them, but soon she grew tired of the knocks on her door in the middle of the night, grew annoyed after opening the door to find a teary-eyed girl just back from a frat party with blood boiling so hard that the skin on her face seemed to roil.

Eventually Sheila started closing the door on their tear-stained faces, and after a while the girls stopped bothering her for curses. Instead, they started coming to her for love charms.

The gay couple who lived in the downstairs rooms of the apartment house were named Trent and Gary. They'd been together for nearly two years, but had only lived together for the past ten months. Their love was still fresh. Sheila could smell it whenever she stopped in to visit them on weekends, when Trent and Gary could be found on the back deck, barbequing and drinking glasses of red wine. They could make ordinary things like cooking out feel magical because of the sheer completeness they exuded, like a fine sparking mist, when they were near each other. That was pure early love, in Sheila's assessment, and she sipped at it from the edges.

Trent was the manager of a small software company and Gary worked at an environmental nonprofit. They'd met in college ten years ago, but had circled around each other at the time. They'd shared a Venn diagram of friends, but naturally some of them didn't like each other. Their mutual friends spent a lot of time telling Trent about how much they hated Gary's friends, or telling Gary about how much they hated Trent's. Because of this, for years Trent and Gary had kept a safe distance from each other, assuming that they would also hate each other. Which was probably a good thing, they said now, nodding in accord on the back deck of the red brick bungalow, where Trent turned shish kabobs on the grill and Gary poured Sheila another glass of wine.

"Why was it probably a good thing you assumed you'd hate each other?" Sheila asked.

"Because," Gary said as he spilled wine into Sheila's glass, "we were so young and stupid back then."

"Also kind of bitchy," Trent added over his shoulder.

"We would have hurt each other," said Gary, "before we knew what we had to lose."

Sheila blushed at this open display of emotion and Gary laughed. "Look at you!" he said, pointing a finger and turning to look over his shoulder at Trent. "Trent," he said, "Look. We've embarrassed Sheila."

Trent laughed, too, and Sheila rolled her eyes. "I'm not embarrassed, you jerks," she said. "I know what love is. People pay me to help them find it or make it. It's just that, with you two—I don't know—there's something special about your love."

Trent turned a kabob with his tongs and said, "Maybe it's because we didn't need you to make it happen."

It was quite possible that Trent's theory had some kind of truth to it, but whatever the reason, Sheila didn't care. She just wanted to sit with them and drink wine and watch the lightning bugs blink in the backyard on a midsummer evening in Cleveland.

It was a good night. The shish kabobs were spiced with dill and lemon. The wine was a middlebrow Syrah. Trent and Gary always provided good thirty-somethings conversation. Listening to the two of them, Sheila felt like she understood much of what she would have gleaned from reading a newspaper or an intelligent magazine. For the past three months, she'd simply begun to rely on them to relay the goings-on of the world to her, and to supply her with these evenings where, for a small moment in time, she could feel normal.

In the center of the deck several scraps of wood burned in a fire pit, throwing shadows and orange light over their faces as smoke climbed into the darkening sky. Trent swirled his glass of wine before taking the last sip, then stood and slid the back door open so he could go inside to retrieve a fresh bottle.

"That sounds terrible," Sheila was saying as Trent left. Gary had been complaining about natural gas companies coming into Ohio to frack for gas deposits beneath the shale, and how his nonprofit was about to hold a forum on the dangers of the process. But before Sheila could say another word, her cell phone rang. "One second," she said, holding up a finger as she looked at the screen. "It's my mom. I've got to take this."

Sheila pressed the answer button. "Hey, Mom," she said. "What's up?"

"Where are you?" her mother asked, blunt as a bludgeoning weapon as usual.

"I'm having a glass of wine with the boys," Sheila said. Right then, Trent returned, twisting the cork out of the new bottle as he attempted to slide the back door shut with his foot. Sheila furrowed her brows and shook her head at him. "Is there something you need, Mom?" she asked.

Before her mother could answer, though, and before Trent could slide the door shut, the dog Sheila disliked in the way that she disliked all dogs—without any particular hatred for the individual, just the species—darted out the open door and raced past Sheila's legs, down the deck steps, into the bushes at the bottom of the backyard.

"Hey!" Gary said, rising from his chair, nearly spilling his wine. He looked out at the dog, a white furry thing with an impossibly red tongue hanging out of its permanently smiling face, and then placed his glass on the deck railing before heading down the stairs. "Snowman!" he called. "Get back here!"

"Oh, Christ," Trent said, one foot still held against the sliding door he hadn't shut in time. "That dog is going to be the death of me."

"What's going on over there?" Sheila's mother asked. Her voice was loud and drawn out, as if she were speaking to someone hard of hearing.

"Dog escaped," said Sheila. "Hold on a second, Mom."

Sheila held the phone against her chest and said, "Guys, I've got to go. Gary, I hope your forum goes well. Snowman, stop being so bad!" Then she edged through the door Trent still held open, crossed through their kitchen and living room to the front foyer they shared, and took the steps up to her second floor apartment.

"Sorry about that," she said when she sat down at her kitchen table.

"Why do you continue living there, Sheila?" her mother said. Sheila could hear steam hissing off her mother's voice, flat as an iron. "Why," her mother said, "do you continue to live with this illusion of having a full life, my daughter?"

"Ma," Sheila said. "What are you talking about now?"

"*The boys*," said her mother. "You're always with *the boys*. But those boys like each other, Sheila, not you. You should find other boys. Boys who like girls. When are you going to grow up, make your own life? Don't you want children?"

"I have a life," said Sheila, evenly, as she might speak to a demanding child. "And I don't want children." She could have also told her mother that she was open to girls who liked girls, and had even had a fling or two that had never developed into anything substantial; looking around the kitchen, however, Sheila realized she'd unfortunately forgotten to bring her wine with her, which she would have needed to have that conversation.

"Well, you should want something," her mother said. "I'm worried about you. You don't know how much I worry about you."

Sheila knew how much her mother worried about her. Her mother had been telling her how much she worried about her for years now. Probably from before Sheila was even conceived, her mother was worrying about her. But it was when Sheila turned fifteen that she'd started to make sure Sheila knew just how much. Sheila was now thirty-seven, and the verbal reminders of worry that had started when she'd begun dating had never stopped, even after she took a break from it. So far, it had been a six-year break.

Sheila didn't miss dating, really. Besides, being alone—being a single woman—was the one witchlike quality she possessed, and it was probably the best of the stereotypical witch features to have if she had to have one.

"Ma," Sheila said.

But before she could tell her mother that she didn't have time to play games, her mother said, "I've met someone."

Sheila blinked. "You've met someone?" she said. Was her mother now, at the age of fifty-eight, going to surprise Sheila and find love with someone after being divorced for the past eighteen years?

"Yes," her mother said. "A man. I'd like you to meet him."

"Ma," Sheila said. "I'm speechless. Of course I'll meet him. If he's someone important to you, I'd love to meet him."

"Thank you, lovey," her mother said, and Sheila knew that she'd made her mother happy. "I think you'll like him."

"I'm sure I'll like him, Mom, but I'm just happy if you like him." What Sheila didn't say was how, at that moment, it felt like a huge weight was being lifted from her.

"Well, no," her mother said. "You have to like him, too. As much as I'm glad you trust my judgment in men, it's you who will be going on the date with him."

"*Ma*," Sheila said, and the weight resumed its old position across her shoulders.

Her mother made a guttural noise, though, a sound that meant she was not going to listen to anything Sheila said after the guttural noise reached completion.

"He'll pick you up at seven o'clock tomorrow. Be ready to go to dinner. Don't bring up witch stuff. No talking shop on a date. His name is Lyle."

"Lyle?" Sheila said, as if the name seemed completely made-up—a fantasy novel sort of name, one of those books with a cover that features castle spires and portentous red moons covered in strands of cloud. One of those novels where people are called things like Roland, Aristial, Leandor, Jandari, or . . . Lyle.

"Lyle," said her mother. Then the phone went dead. Sheila looked down at it for a while as if it were a gun that had accidentally gone off, leaving a bullet lodged in her stomach.

The bullet sat in Sheila's stomach and festered for the rest of that night, and the feeling was not unfamiliar. Sheila's mother had a habit of mugging her with unwanted surprises. Furniture that didn't go with Sheila's décor. Clothes that didn't fit her. Blind dates with men named Lyle.

Her mother was a mugger. Always had been. So why was she still surprised whenever it happened, as if this were a sudden, unexpected event? By the next morning, Sheila had come up with several jokes about her mother the mugger that she would tell to the two clients who had appointments with her that afternoon.

"Mugger fucker," Sheila mumbled as she brushed her hair in the bathroom mirror. "Mugger Goose. Holy Mugger of God. Mugger may I?"

Her first client was a regular named Mary, who was forty-three, had three children, and was married to a husband she'd fallen out of love with four years ago. Mary came every other month for a reboot of the spell that helped her love her husband a little longer. She'd tried counseling, she'd tried herbal remedies, she'd even tried Zumba (both individually and with several girlfriends as a group), but nothing seemed to work, and in desperation she'd found Sheila through a friend of a friend of a former client who Sheila had helped rekindle a relationship gone sour years ago, back when Sheila had first started to make her living by witching instead of working at the drugstore that had hired her while she was in college.

The knock came at exactly ten in the morning. Mary was never late and never early. Her sessions always lasted for exactly thirty minutes. Sheila was willing to go beyond that, but Mary said she felt that Sheila's power faded a little more with every second past the thirty-minute mark. She still paid Sheila three hundred dollars for each session, and walked away a happy—or at least a happ*ier*—woman. She'd go home and, for five to six weeks, she'd love her husband. Sheila couldn't work a permanent fix for Mary, because Mary had fallen so out of love with her husband that no spell could sustain it forever. Their relationship was an old, used-up car in constant need of repairs. Sheila was the mechanic.

When Sheila opened the door, Mary pushed in, already complaining loudly about her husband, Ted. Sheila had never met him, though she did have a lock of his hair in an envelope that stayed in her living room curio cabinet. Except on appointment days with Mary; on those days, Sheila would bring the hair out for the renewal ritual.

"I don't know if I want the spell again," Mary said. She hadn't even looked at Sheila yet. She just sat down heavily on the living room couch and sighed. "I don't know if I want to fix things any longer."

"What else would you do?" Sheila asked, closing the door before coming over to sit in the chair across from Mary. "Divorce? Start over? You know you could do that, right?"

Mary clutched a small black beaded purse in her lap. She was a beautiful woman, long limbed, peach-skinned, with dark hair that fell to the small of her back like a curtain. She exercised, ate healthy, and didn't drink too much alcohol—even when alcohol sounded like a good idea. She wore upper middle class clothes that weren't particularly major designer labels but weren't from a mall store, either.

"I don't know," Mary said, pushing a piece of her layered black hair away from her face. Sheila noticed that Mary had gotten a nose piercing in the time between their last appointment and this one. A tiny diamond stud glinted in the sunlight coming through the living room windows. "The children . . . " said Mary. Sheila nodded, and stood, then went to her curio cabinet and took out the envelope with the hank of Ted's hair in it.

Sheila opened the envelope and placed the lock of hair on the coffee table between them. It was a thick brown curl that Mary had cut from Ted's mop one night while he was asleep. When Mary had come to Sheila for help four years ago, Sheila had said, "I'll need you to bring me something of his. Something you love about him. Otherwise, I'll have nothing to work with." Mary had said she didn't love him anymore, so how could she bring Sheila anything? "Surely you must love *something* about him," Sheila said, and Mary had nodded, her mouth a firm line, and said that, yes, she did love Ted's hair. It was beautiful. Thick and curly. She loved to run her fingers through it, even after she'd stopped loving Ted.

Now Mary looked down at the lock of curled hair as if it were a dead mouse Sheila had set out in front of her. "You know the drill," Sheila said, and together the two pinched an end of the hair and lifted it into the air above the coffee table.

Sheila closed her eyes and tried to feel Mary's love come through the coil of hair. Like an electrical current, a slight hum flowed through it, but it was weaker than ever and Sheila worried that she wouldn't be able to help Mary once this slight affection for Ted's hair eventually disappeared. She took the lingering love in through her fingers anyway, whipped it like cream, semi-consciously chanting an incantation—or more like noises that helped her focus on the energy in the feeling than anything of significance—and after she'd turned Mary's weak affection into a fluffy meringue-like substance, Sheila pushed it back through the hair, slowly but surely, until Mary was filled with a large, aerated love.

When Sheila opened her eyes, she noticed Mary's face had lifted a little. The firm line of her mouth had softened and curled up at the edges, as if she wanted to smile but was perhaps just a little shy. "Thank you, Sheila," said Mary, blinking sweetly on the couch. This was when Sheila went soft, too. Whenever a client like Mary, hardened by a deficiency of love, took on a shade of her former self—a youthful self who loved and was loved, who trusted in love to see her through—Sheila had to fight to hold back tears. Not because seeing the return of love made her happy—no, the pressure behind her eyes was more a force of sadness, because the person in front of her was under an illusion, and no illusion, thought Sheila, was pleasant. They were more like the narcotics those with chronic pain took to ease their days. This returned love would only be brief and temporary.

At the door, Mary took out three hundred-dollar bills. "Worth every penny," she said, folding them into Sheila's palm, meeting Sheila's eyes and holding her stare.

When Sheila closed the door behind her, she turned and looked at the face of her cell phone. Thirty minutes had passed. On the dot.

Her next client was new: a good-looking young man who was a bit too earnest for only being a twenty-three-year-old recent college graduate. His name was Ben, and he had just acquired a decent job with an advertising company. He'd gotten a mortgage, purchased a house, and was ready to fill it with someone else and him together, the kids, the dogs, the cats: the works. Sheila could see all of this as he sat in front of her and told her that he wanted to find love. That was simple, really. No need to drum up love where love already fizzed and popped. He just needed someone to really see him. Someone who wanted the same things. He wasn't the completely bland sort of guy that no one would notice, but he wasn't emitting a strong signal either. Sheila did a quick invocation that would enhance Ben's desire so that it would beam like a lighthouse toward ships looking for harbor.

She charged him a hundred dollars and told him that if he didn't get engaged within a year, she'd give him his money back. Ben thanked her, and after she saw him out of the house, it was time for Sheila to sit in her living room and stare at the television, where the vague outline of her body was reflected in the blank screen.

Lyle would be coming to pick her up in several hours. *Lyle, Lyle.* She said his name a few times, but it was no good. She still couldn't believe a man named Lyle was coming for her.

Sheila had tried to make the thing that made her different the most normal aspect of her life. Hence her business: Paranormal Romance. She had business cards and left them on the bulletin boards of grocery store entryways, in the fishbowls full of cards that sat on the register counters of some restaurants, and on the bars of every lowdown drink-your-blues-away kind of joint in the city of Cleveland, where people sometimes, while crying into a beer, would notice the card propped against the napkin holder in front of them and think about Sheila possibly being the solution to their loneliness, as the cards declared.

She had made herself as non-paranormal as possible, while at the same time living completely out in the open about being a witch, probably because of what her father had once told her, years ago, when she was just a little girl and even Sheila hadn't known she had magic in her fingertips. "If I had to be some creepy weirdo like the vampires and werewolves or whatever the hell else is out there these days," her father had said while watching a news report about the increasing appearance of paranormal creatures, "then I suppose a witch would be the way to go."

The way to go. That's what he'd said. As though there was a choice about being cursed or born with magic flowing through you. Vampire, werewolf. *Whatever the hell else.* The memory stuck with Sheila because of the way her father had talked as if it were one of those "If you had to" games.

If you had to lose a sense, which one?

If you had to live on a deserted island with only one book, which one?

It was only later, after Sheila felt magic welling up in her as a teenager, that she realized how upset he was when she accidentally revealed her abilities—a tactless spell she'd cast to bring him and her mother closer. Unfortunately, her father had noticed Sheila's fingers weaving through the air as she attempted to surreptitiously cast the spell while her parents were watching television one evening. Her mother stuck by Sheila, but he filed for divorce and disappeared from their lives altogether.

Thus her business, *Paranormal Romance*, was born. She would make it work for her, Sheila decided in her late twenties. She would use this magic in a way that someone with good legs, flexibility, and balance might become a dancer or a yoga instructor.

This desire for normality also explained why Sheila wanted to kill her mother after she opened the door that evening to find a man dressed in a black leather jacket, tight blue jeans, a black V-neck shirt, and work boots, sporting a scraggly goatee, whose first words were, "Wow, you don't look like a witch. That's interesting."

"Probably the least interesting thing about me," said Sheila. She tried to restrain herself, but couldn't refrain from arching her eyebrows as a cat might raise its back.

"I'm Lyle. Nice to meet you," the somewhat ruggedly good-looking Lyle said.

"Charmed," Sheila said, trying to sound like she meant it.

"No," said Lyle, "that's what you're supposed to do to me, right?" He winked. Sheila's smile felt frail, as if it might begin to splinter.

"How do you know I'm a witch," Sheila asked, "when my mother specifically told me not to bring it up?"

"Don't know why she told you that," said Lyle. "First thing she mentioned to me was that's what you are."

"Great," said Sheila. "And I know nothing about you to make it even, and here we are, standing in my doorway like we're new neighbors instead of going somewhere."

Lyle nodded his head in the direction of the staircase and said, "I got us a reservation at a great steakhouse downtown."

Sheila smiled. It was a lip-only smile—no teeth—but she followed Lyle down the steps of her apartment to the front porch, where she found Gary dragging Snowman up the steps by his collar. The dog had its ridiculous grin plastered on as usual, but started to yap in the direction of Lyle as soon as he noticed him. Gary himself was grimacing with frustration. "What's the matter?" Sheila asked.

"This guy," said Gary. "When he ran off last night, he really ran off. Someone on the neighborhood Facebook group messaged me to say she had him penned in her backyard. Three blocks from here. You're a bad dog, Snowman. A bad dog, you hear?"

Snowman was barking like crazy now, twisting around Gary's legs. He looked up at Lyle and for the first time in Sheila's experience, the dog did not look like it was smiling, but was baring its teeth.

"Woof!" said Lyle, and Snowman began to whimper.

"Well, it's a good thing she was able to corral him," Sheila said, even as she attempted to telepathically communicate with Gary: *Did this guy just* woof*?* "I've never gotten along with dogs, so he'd have probably run away from me if I were the one to find him."

"Oh, really?" Lyle raised his brows, as if Sheila had suddenly taken off a mask and revealed herself to be an alien with tentacles wriggling, Medusa-like, out of her head. "You don't like dogs?"

"And dogs," Sheila said, "don't like me."

"I can't believe that," said Lyle, shaking his head and wincing.

Sheila shrugged and said, "That's just the way things are, I guess."

"Who *are* you again?" Gary asked, looking at Lyle with narrowed eyes, as if he'd put Lyle under a microscope.

Sheila apologized for not introducing them. "This is my date," she said, trying to signal to Gary that it was also the last date by rolling her eyes as she turned away from Lyle.

"A *date*?" Gary said, clapping one hand over his mouth as he said it. "Sheila is going on a *date*?"

"That's right," said Lyle. He nodded curtly. "And we should probably get started. Come on," he said, pointing toward his car parked against the curb. Sheila inwardly groaned when she saw that it was one of those muscle cars macho guys collect, like they're still little boys with Matchbox vehicles. "Let's go get some grub," Lyle said, patting his stomach.

"*Grub*?" Gary whispered as Lyle and Sheila went past him, and Sheila could only look over her shoulder with a *Help Me!* look painfully stretched across her face.

The steakhouse Lyle took her to was one of those places where people crack peanuts open, dislodge the nut, and discard the shells on the floor. The lighting was dim, but the room was permeated with the glow from a variety of neon beer signs that hung on every wall like a collection in an art gallery. Lyle said it was his favorite place to dine.

He said it like that too, Sheila could already hear herself saying later as she recounted the evening to Trent and Gary. *He said, "It's my favorite place to dine." Can you believe it? What was my mother thinking?*

"Oh, really," Sheila said. The server had just brought her a vodka martini with a slice of lemon dangling over the rim. Sheila looked up at her briefly to say thank you, and noticed immediately that the server—a young woman with long mahogany hair and caramel-colored skin—was a witch. The employee tag on the server's shirt said her name was Corrine; she winked as Sheila grasped after her words. "Thank you," Sheila managed to say without making the moment of recognition awkward. She took a sip, licked her lips, then turned back to Lyle as the server walked away, and said, "What were you saying?"

" 'This is my favorite place to dine,' I said. I come here a couple of times a week," said Lyle. "Best steaks in town."

Sheila said, "I don't eat meat."

To which Lyle's face dropped like a hot air balloon that had lost all of its hot air. "Your mother didn't tell me that," said Lyle.

"No," said Sheila, "but for some reason she *did* tell you that I'm a witch, even after she forbade me from speaking of it. Clearly the woman can't be trusted."

"Clearly," Lyle agreed, which actually scored him a tiny little point for the first time that evening. There it was in Sheila's mind's eye, a little scoreboard. *Lyle: 1. Sheila: Anxious.*

He apologized profusely, in a rough-around-the-edges way that seemed to be who he was down to his core. He wasn't really Sheila's type, not that Sheila had a specific type, but he wasn't the sort of guy she'd ever gone out on a date with before, either. Her mother would have known that too. Sheila's mother had always wanted to know what was going on, back when Sheila actually dated. When Myspace and Facebook came around, and her mother began commenting on photos Sheila had posted from some of her date nights with statements like, "He's a hottie!" and "Now that's a keeper!" Sheila had had to block her mother. And only weeks later she discovered that on her mother's own social networking walls, her mother was publicly bemoaning the fact that her daughter had blocked her.

But really, her mother would have known that Lyle wasn't her sort of guy. "So what gives?" she finally asked, after Lyle had finished a tall beer and she'd gotten close to the bottom of her martini. "How do you know my mother? Why would she think we'd make a good pair?"

"I'm her butcher."

Sheila almost spat out the vodka swirling in her mouth, but managed to swallow before saying, "Her butcher? Really? I didn't know my mother *had* a butcher."

"She comes to the West Side Market every Saturday," said Lyle. "I work at Doreen's Meats. Your mother always buys her meat for the week there. As for why would she think we'd make a good pair? I don't know." Lyle shrugged and held his palms up in the air. "I guess maybe she thought we'd get along because of what we have in common."

Sheila snorted, then raised her hand to signal Corrine back over. "I'd like another martini," she said, and smiled in the way some people do when they need to smother an uncivil reaction: lips firmly held together. She turned back to Lyle, who was cracking another peanut shell between his thick, hairy fingers, and said, "So what do we have in common, besides my mother?"

"I'm a werewolf," said Lyle. Then he flicked the peanut off his thumb and snatched it out of the air, midflight, in his mouth.

Sheila watched as Lyle crunched the peanut, and noticed only after he'd swallowed and smiled across the table at her that he had a particularly large set of canines. "You're kidding," said Sheila. "Ha ha, very funny. You might as well start telling witch jokes at this point."

"Not kidding," said Lyle. Corrine stopped at their table, halting the conversation as she placed another tall beer in front of Lyle, another martini in front of Sheila, and asked what they'd like to order.

"I think we're just here to drink tonight," said Lyle, not taking his eyes off Sheila.

Sheila nodded vigorously at Corrine, though, agreeing. And after she left, Sheila said, "Well, this is a new achievement for my mother. Set her daughter up with a werewolf."

"What? You don't like werewolves?" Lyle asked. One corner of his mouth lifted into a 1970s drug dealer grin.

Sheila blinked a lot for a while, took another sip of her martini, then shrugged. "It's not something I've ever thought about, you know," she said. "I mean, werewolves aren't generally on my radar. I get a lot of people who come around with minor psychic powers, and they're attracted to me because they can sense I'm something out of the ordinary but can't quite place *what* exactly, and of course I know a decent amount of witches—we can spot each other on the street without knowing one another, really—but werewolves are generally outside of my experience. Especially my dating experience."

"From what I understand, your dating experience has been pretty nonexistent in general."

Sheila decided it was time to take yet another drink. After swallowing a large gulp of vodka, she said, "My mother has a big mouth for someone who hasn't gotten back in the saddle since my father left her nearly two decades ago. And you can tell her I said that next time she comes in to stock up on meat."

Lyle laughed. It was a full, throaty laugh that made heads turn in the steakhouse. When he realized this, he reined himself in, but Sheila could see that the laugh—the sheer volume of it when he'd let himself go—was beyond ordinary. It bordered on the wild. She could imagine him as a wolf in that moment, howling at a blood red moon.

"So what is it? Once a month you get hairy and run around the city killing people?" Sheila asked.

Lyle leaned back on his side of the booth and said, "Are you serious?"

"Well, I don't know," said Sheila. "I hear it's quite difficult to control bloodlust in times like that."

"I make arrangements for those times," said Lyle.

"Arrangements, huh," said Sheila. "What sort of arrangements?"

"I rent an underground garage, have it filled with plenty of raw steaks, and get locked in for the night."

"That's responsible of you," said Sheila.

"What about you?" Lyle asked. "Any inclinations to doing evil? Casting hexes?"

"No bloodlust for witches," said Sheila, "and I gave up the vicious cycle of curse drama in college. Not worth it. That shit comes back on you sevenfold."

Lyle snickered. He ran his thumb and forefinger over his scraggly goatee, then took another drink of beer. "Looks like we're a pair," he said, "just like your mother imagined."

"Why?" Sheila asked. "Because you put yourself in a werewolf kennel on full moon nights and I don't dabble in wreaking havoc in other people's lives?"

Lyle nodded, his lips rising into a grin that revealed his pointy, slightly yellowed canines.

"I hardly think that constitutes being a pair," said Sheila. "We certainly have that in common, but it's a bit like saying we should start dating because we're both single and living in Cleveland."

"Why *are* you so single?" Lyle asked. His nostrils flared several times.

Oh my God, he is totally sniffing me! "I need to use the ladies' room," she said.

In the restroom, Sheila leaned against the counter and stared at herself in the mirror. She was wearing a short black dress and had hung her favorite opal earrings on her earlobes. They glowed in the strange orange neon beer-sign light of the restroom. She shouldn't have answered when he knocked. She should have kept things in order. Weekend BBQs with Trent and Gary, even with the obnoxious Snowman running between their legs and wanting to jump on her and lick her. Working a few hours a day with clients, helping them to love or be loved, to find love. Evening runs in the park. Grocery shopping on Wednesdays. That's what she wanted, not a werewolf butcher/lover her mother had found in the West Side Market.

The last time Sheila dated someone had been slightly less than underwhelming. He'd been an utterly normal man named Paul who worked at the Federal Reserve Bank of Cleveland downtown, and he talked endlessly of bank capitalization and exchange-traded funds. Sheila had tried to love him, but it was as if all the bank talk was more powerful than any spell she might cast on herself, and so she'd had to add Paul to her long list of previous candidates for love.

There had been Jim, a guy who owned a car dealership in Lakewood, but he always came off as a salesman, and Sheila wasn't the consumer type. There had been Alexis, a law student at Case Western, but despite her girlish good looks and intelligence, Alexis had worried about Sheila's under-the-table Paranormal Romance business—concerned that she was possibly defrauding the government of taxable income. There had been Mark, the CPA (say no more). There had been Lola, the karaoke DJ (say no more). And there had been a string of potentials before that, too, once Sheila began sorting through the memories of her twenties, a long line of cute young men and women whose faces faded a little more each day. She had tried—she had tried so hard—hoping one of them would take the weight of her existence and toss it into the air like a beach ball. The love line went back and back and back, so far back, but none of those boys or girls had been able to do this. None of them.

Except Trent and Gary, of course. Not that they were romance for Sheila. But they did love her. They cared about her. They didn't make her feel like she had to be anyone but who she wanted to be, even if who Sheila wanted to be wasn't entirely who Sheila was.

Sheila washed her hands under the faucet and dried them with the air dryer, appreciating the whir of the fan drowning out the voice in her head. She would walk out on Lyle, she decided. She'd go home and call her mother and tell her, "Never again," then hang up on her. She would sit in front of the blank television screen, watching her shadowy reflection held within it, and maybe she would let herself cry, just a little bit, for being a love witch who couldn't make love happen for herself.

"Are you okay?" a voice said over the whir of the hand dryer. Sheila blinked and turned. Behind her, Corrine the server was coming out of a stall. She came to stand beside Sheila at the sinks and quickly washed her hands.

"You're a witch," Sheila said stupidly, and realized at that moment that two martinis were too many for her.

Corrine laughed, but nodded and said, "Yes. I am. So are you." Corrine reached for the paper towel to dry her hands, since Sheila was spellbound in front of the electric dryer. "What kind?" she asked Sheila as she wiped her hands.

"Love," said Sheila.

"Love?" said Corrine, raising her thin eyebrows. "That's pretty fancy."

"It's okay," said Sheila.

"Just okay?" said Corrine. "I don't know. Sounds nice to be able to do something like that with it. Me? I can't do much but weird things."

"What do you mean?" Sheila asked.

"You know," said Corrine. "Odds and ends. Nothing so defined as love. Bad end of the magic stick, maybe. I can smell fear on people, or danger. And I can open doors. But that's about it."

"Open doors?" said Sheila.

"Yeah," said Corrine. "Doors. I guess it does make a kind of sense when I think about it long enough. I smell danger coming, I can get out of just about anywhere if I want to. Open a door. Any old door. It might look like it leads into a broom closet or an office, but I can make it open onto other places I've been, or have at least seen in a picture."

"Wow," said Sheila. "You should totally be a cat burglar."

Corrine laughed. Sheila laughed with her. "Sorry," she said. "I don't know why I said that."

"It's okay," Corrine said. "It was funny. I think you said it because it was funny."

"I guess I better get back out there," said Sheila.

"Date?" said Corrine.

"Blind date," Sheila answered. "Bad date. Last date."

Corrine frowned in sympathy. "I knew it wasn't going well."

"How?" Sheila asked.

"I could smell it on you. Not quite fear, but anxiety and frustration. I figured that's why you asked for the second martini. That guy comes in a lot. He seems okay, but yeah, I couldn't imagine why you were here with him."

Sheila looked down at her hands, which were twitching a little, as if her fingers had minds of their own. They were twitching in Corrine's direction, like they wanted to go to her. Sheila laughed. Her poor fingers. All of that love magic stored up inside them and nowhere to go.

"You need help?" Corrine asked suddenly. She had just taken off her name badge and was now fluffing her hair in the mirror.

"Help?" said Sheila.

Corrine looked over and said, "If you want out, we can just go. You don't even have to say goodbye to him. My shift's over. A friend of mine will be closing out your table. We can leave by the bathroom door."

Sheila laughed. Her fingers twitched again. She took one hand and clamped it over the other.

"What are you afraid of?" Corrine asked. Her eyes had started to narrow. "I'm getting a sense that you're afraid of me now."

"You?" Sheila said. "No, no, not you."

"Well, you're giving off the vibe," said Corrine. She dropped her name badge into her purse and took out a tube of lipstick, applied some to her lips so that they were a shade of dark ruby. When she was done, she slipped the tube into her purse and turned to Sheila. "What's wrong with your hands?" she asked.

Sheila was still fidgeting. "I think," she said. "I think they like you."

Corrine threw her head back and laughed. "Like?" she said, grinning. "That's sweet of them. You can tell your hands I like them too."

Sheila said, "I'm so sorry. This is embarrassing. I'm usually not such a weirdo." For a moment, Sheila heard her father's voice come through—*Creepy weirdos. Whatever the hell else is out there*—and she shivered.

"You're not weird," said Corrine. "Just flustered. It happens."

It happens. Sheila blinked and blinked again. Actually, it didn't happen. Not for her. Her fingers only twitched like this when she was working magic for other people. Anytime she had tried to work magic for herself, they were still and cold, as if she had bad circulation. "No," Sheila said. "It doesn't usually happen. Not for me. This is strange."

"Listen," said Corrine. "You seem interesting. I'm off shift and you have a bad blind date happening. I'm about to leave by that door and go somewhere I know that has good music and way better food than this place. And it's friendly to people like you and me. What do you say?"

Sheila thought of her plans for the rest of the evening in a blinding flash.

Awkward moment before she ditched Lyle.

Awkward and angry moment on the phone while she told her mother off.

The vague reflection of her body held in the screen of the television as she allowed herself to cry a little.

Then she looked up at Corrine, who was pulling on a zippered hoody, and said, "I say yes."

"Yes?" Corrine said, smiling.

"Yes," said Sheila. "Yes, let's go there, wherever it is you're going."

Corrine held her hand out, and Sheila looked down at her own hands again, clamped together as if in prayer, holding each other back from the world. "You can let one of them go," Corrine said, grinning. "Otherwise, I can't take you with me."

Sheila laughed nervously and nodded. She released her hands from one another and cautiously put one into the palm of Corrine's hand, where it settled in smoothly and turned warm in an instant. "This way," Corrine said, and put her other hand on the bathroom doorknob, twisted, then opened it.

For a moment, Sheila could see nothing but a bright light fill the space of the doorway—no Lyle or the sounds of rock and roll music spilled in from the dining area—and she worried that she'd made a mistake, not being able to see where she was going with this woman who was a complete stranger. Then Corrine looked back at her and said, "Don't be afraid," and Sheila heard the sound of jazz music suddenly float toward her, a soft saxophone, a piano melody, though the doorway was still filled with white light she couldn't see through.

"I'm not," said Sheila suddenly, and was surprised to realize that she truly wasn't.

Corrine winked at her the way she had done at the table, as if they shared a secret, which, of course, they did. Then she tugged on Sheila's hand and they stepped through the white light into somewhere different.

ꟹ

Christopher Barzak is the author of the Crawford Award-winning novel, *One for Sorrow*, which has been made into the Sundance feature film *Jamie Marks Is Dead*. His second novel, *The Love We Share Without Knowing*, was a finalist for the Nebula and Tiptree Awards. He is also the author of two collections: *Birds and Birthdays*, a collection of surrealist fantasy stories, and *Before and Afterlives*, a collection of supernatural fantasies. He grew up in rural Ohio, has lived in a Southern California beach town, the capital of Michigan, and has taught English outside of Tokyo, Japan, where he lived for two years. His next novel, *Wonders of the Invisible World*, will be published by Knopf in 2015. Currently he teaches fiction writing in the Northeast Ohio MFA program at Youngstown State University.

The City: *New York (Manhattan, to be more exact).*

The Magic: *Think you know about fairies? A teenager discovers a lot of the stuff you read is helpful, but when you encounter fairies in the heart of the city—you learn a great deal more.*

GRAND CENTRAL PARK

DELIA SHERMAN

When I was little, I used to wonder why the sidewalk trees had iron fences around them. Even a city kid could see they were pretty weedy looking trees. I wondered what they'd done to be caged up like that, and whether it might be dangerous to get too close to them.

So I was pretty little, okay? Second grade, maybe. It was one of the things my best friend and I used to talk about, like why it's so hard to find a particular city on a map when you don't already know where it is, and why the fourth graders thought Mrs. Lustenburger's name was so hysterically funny.

My best friend's name was (is) Galadriel, which isn't even remotely her fault, and only her mother calls her that anyway. Everyone else calls her Elf.

Anyway. Trees. New York. Have I said I live in New York? I do. In Manhattan, on the West Side, a couple blocks from Central Park.

I've always loved Central Park. I mean, it's the closest to nature I'm likely to get, growing up in Manhattan. It's the closest to nature I want to get, if you must know. There's wild things in it—squirrels and pigeons and like that, and trees and rocks and plants. But they're city wild things, used to living around people. I don't mean they're tame. I mean they're streetwise. Look. How many squished squirrels do you see on the park transverses? How many do you see on any suburban road? I rest my case.

Central Park is magic. This isn't a matter of opinion, it's the truth. When I was just old enough for Mom to let me out of her sight, I had this place I used to play, down by the boat pond, in a little inlet at the foot of a huge cliff. When I was in there, all I could see was the water all shiny and sparkly like a silk dress with sequins and the great gray hulk of the rock behind me and the willow tree bending down over me to trail its green-gold hair in the water. I could hear people splashing and laughing and talking, but I couldn't see them, and there was this fairy who used to come and play with me.

Mom said my fairy friend came from me being an only child and reading too many books, but all I can say is that if I'd made her up, she would have been less bratty. She had long Saran-Wrap wings like a dragonfly, she was teensy, and she couldn't keep still for a second. She'd play princesses or Peter Pan for about two minutes, and then she'd get bored and pull my hair or start teasing me about being a big, galumphy, deaf, blind human being or talking to the willow or the rocks. She couldn't even finish a conversation with a butterfly.

Anyway, I stopped believing in her when I was about eight, or stopped seeing her, anyway. By that time I didn't care because I'd gotten friendly with Elf, who didn't tease me quite as much. She wasn't into fairies, although she did like to read. As we got older, mostly I was grateful she was willing to be my friend. Like, I wasn't exactly Ms. Popularity at school. I sucked at gym and liked English and like that, so the cool kids decided I was a super-geek. Also, I wear glasses and I'm no Kate Moss, if you know what I mean. I could stand to lose a few pounds—none of your business how many. It wasn't safe to be seen having lunch with me, so Elf didn't. As long as she hung with me after school, I didn't really care all that much.

The inlet was our safe place, where we could talk about whether the French teacher hated me personally or was just incredibly mean in general and whether Patty Gregg was really cool, or just thought she was. In the summer, we'd take our shoes off and swing our feet in the water that sighed around the roots of the golden willow.

So one day we were down there, gabbing as usual. This was last year, the fall of eleventh grade, and we were talking about boyfriends. Or at least Elf was talking about her boyfriend and I was nodding sympathetically. I guess my attention wandered, and for some reason I started wondering about my fairy friend. What was her name again? Bubble? Burble? Something like that.

Something tugged really hard on about two hairs at the top of my head, where it *really* hurts, and I yelped and scrubbed at the sore place. "Mosquito," I explained. "So what did he say?"

Oddly enough, Elf had lost interest in what her boyfriend had said. She had this look of intense concentration on her face, like she was listening for her little brother's breathing on the other side of the bedroom door. "Did you hear that?" she whispered.

"What? Hear what?"

"Ssh."

I sshed and listened. Water lapping; the distant creak of oarlocks and New Yorkers laughing and talking and splashing. The wind in the willow leaves whispering, *ssh, ssh.* "I don't hear anything," I said.

"Shut up," Elf snapped. "You missed it. A snapping sound. Over there." Her blue eyes were very big and round.

"You're trying to scare me," I accused her. "You read about that woman getting mugged in the park, and now you're trying to jerk my chain. Thanks, friend."

Elf looked indignant. "As if!" She froze like a dog sighting a pigeon. "There."

I strained my ears. It seemed awfully quiet all of a sudden.

There wasn't even a breeze to stir the willow. Elf breathed, "Omigod. Don't look now, but I think there's a guy over there, watching us."

My face got all prickly and cold, like my body believed her even though my brain didn't. "I swear to God, Elf, if you're lying, I'll totally kill you." I turned around to follow her gaze. "Where? I don't see anything."

"I said, don't *look*," Elf hissed. "He'll know."

"He already *knows*, unless he's a moron. If he's even there. Omigod!"

Suddenly I saw, or thought I saw, a guy with a stocking cap on and a dirty, unshaven face peering around a big rock.

It was strange. One second, it looked like a guy, the next, it was more like someone's windbreaker draped over a bush. But my heart started to beat really fast anyway. There weren't that many ways to get out of that particular little cove if you didn't have a boat.

"See him?" she hissed triumphantly.

"I guess."

"What are we going to do?"

Thinking about it later, I couldn't quite decide whether Elf was really afraid, or whether she was pretending because it was exciting to be afraid, but she sure convinced me. If the guy was on the path, the only way out was up the cliff. I'm not in the best shape *and* I'm scared of heights, but I was even more scared of the man, so up we went.

I remember that climb, but I don't want to talk about it. I thought I was going to die, okay? And I was really, really mad at Elf for putting me though this, like if she hadn't noticed the guy, he wouldn't have been there. I was sweating, and my glasses kept slipping down my nose and . . .

No. I won't talk about it. All you need to know is that Elf got to the top first and squirmed around on her belly to reach down and help me up.

"Hurry up," she panted. "He's behind you. No, don't look"—as if I could even bear to look all that way down—"just hurry."

I was totally winded by the time I got to the top and scrambled to my feet, but Elf didn't give me time to catch my breath. She grabbed my wrist and pulled me to the path, both of us stumbling as much as we were running.

It was about this time I realized that something really weird was going on. Like, the path was empty, and it was two o'clock in the afternoon of a beautiful fall Saturday, when Central Park is so full of people it's like Times Square with trees. And I couldn't run just like you can't run in dreams.

Suddenly, Elf tripped and let go of me. The path shook itself, and she was gone. Poof. Nowhere in sight.

By this time, I'm freaked totally out of my mind. I look around, and there's this guy, hauling himself over the edge of the cliff, stocking cap jammed down over his head, face gray-skinned with dirt, half his teeth missing. I don't know why I didn't scream—usually, it's pitiful how easy it is to make me scream—I just turned around and ran.

Now, remember that there's about fifty million people in the park that day. You'd think I would run into one or two, which would mean safety because muggers don't like witnesses. But no.

So I'm running and he's running, and I can hear him *breathing* but I can't hear his footsteps, and we've been running, like, *forever*, and I don't know where the hell I am, which means I must be in the Ramble, which isn't that near the Boat Pond, but hey, I'm running for my life. And I think he's getting closer and I really want to look, just stop and let him catch me and get it all over with, but I keep running anyway, and suddenly I remember what my fairy's name was (is) and I shriek out, "Bugle! Help me!"

I bet you thought something would happen.

So did I, and when it didn't, I started to cry. Gulping for breath, my glasses all runny with tears, I staggered up a little rise, and I'm in a clear spot with a bench in it and trees all around and a low stone wall in front of another granite cliff, this one going straight down, like, a mile or two.

The guy laughs, low and deep in his throat, and I don't know why because I don't really *want* to, but I turn around and face him.

So this is when it gets *really* weird. Because he's got a snout and really sharp teeth hanging out, and his stocking cap's fallen off, and he has *ears*—gray, leathery ones—and his skin isn't dirty, it's gray, like concrete, and he's impossible, but he's real—a real, like, rat-guy. I give this little *urk* and he opens his jaws, and things get sparkly around the edges.

"Gnaw-bone!" someone says. "Chill!"

I jump and look around everywhere, and there's this amazing girl standing right beside the rat-guy, who has folded up like a Slinky and is making pitiful noises over her boots. The boots are green, and so is her velvet mini and her Lycra top and her fitted leather jacket—all different shades of green, mostly olive and evergreen and moss and like that: dark greens. Browny, earthy greens. So's her hair—browny-green, in long, wild dreads around her shoulders and down her back. And her skin, but that's more brown than green.

She's beautiful, but not like a celebrity or a model or anything. She's way more gorgeous than that. Next to her, Taylor Swift is a complete dog.

"What's up?" she asks the rat-guy. Her voice is incredible, too. I mean, she talks like some wise-ass street kid, but there's leaves under it somehow. Sounds dumb, but that's what it was like.

"Games is up," he says, sounding just as ratty as he looks.

"Fun-fun. She saw me. She's mine."

"I hear you," the green girl says thoughtfully. "The thing is, she knows Bugle's name."

I manage to make a noise. It's not like I haven't wanted to contribute to the conversation. But I'm kind of out of breath from all that running, not to mention being totally hysterical.

I'm not sure what old Gnaw-bone's idea of fun and games is, but I'm dead sure I don't want to play. If knowing Bugle's name can get me out of this, I better make the most of it. So, "Yeah," I croak. "Bugle and me go way back."

The green girl turns to look at me, and I kind of wish I'd kept quiet. She's way scary. It's not the green hair or the punk clothes or the fact that I've just noticed there's this humongous squirrel sitting on her shoulder and an English sparrow perched in her dreads. It's the way she looks at me, like I'm a Saint Bernard that just recited the Pledge of Allegiance or something.

"I think we better hear Bugle's take on this beautiful friendship," she says. "Bugle says you're buds, fine. She doesn't, Gnaw-bone gets his fun and games. Fair?"

No, it's not fair, but I don't say so. There's a long silence, in which I can hear the noise of traffic, very faint and far away, and the panicked beating of my heart, right in my throat.

Gnaw-bone licks his lips, what there is of them, and the squirrel slithers down the green girl's shoulder and gets comfortable in her arms. If it's even a squirrel. I've seen smaller dogs.

Have I mentioned I'm really scared? I've never been this scared before in my entire life. And it's not even that I'm afraid of what Gnaw-bone might do to me, although I am.

I'm afraid of the green girl. It's one thing to think fairies are wicked cool, to own all of Brian Froud's *Faerie* books and see *Fairy Tale* three times and secretly wish you hadn't outgrown your fairy friend. But this girl doesn't look like any fairy I ever imagined. Green leather and dreads—get real! And I'm not really prepared for eyes like living moss and the squirrel curled like a cat in her arms and the sparrow in her hair like a bizzarroid hair clip. It's way too weird. I want to run away. I want to cry. But neither of these things seems like the right I thing to do, so I stand there with my legs all rubbery and wait for Bugle to show up.

After a while, I feel something tugging at my hair. I start to slap it away, and then I realize. Duh. It's Bugle, saying hi. I scratch my ear instead. There's a little tootling sound, like a trumpet: Bugle, laughing. I laugh too, kind of hysterically.

"See?" I tell the green girl and the humongous squirrel and Gnaw-bone. "She knows me."

The green girl holds out her hand—the squirrel scrambles up to her shoulder again—and Bugle flies over and stands on her palm. It seems to me that Bugle used to look more like a little girl and less like a teenager. But then, so did I.

The green girl ignores me. "Do you know this mortal?" she asks Bugle. Her voice is different, somehow: less street kid, more like Mom asking whether I've done my math homework. Bugle gives a little hop. "Yep. Sure do. When she was little, anyways. Now, she doesn't want to know me."

I've been starting to feel better, but now the green girl is glaring at me, and my stomach knots up tight. I give this sick kind of grin grin. It's true. I hadn't wanted to know her, not with Peggy and those guys on my case. Even Elf, who puts up with a lot, doesn't want to hear about how I saw fairies when I was little. I say, "Yeah, well. I'm sorry. I really did know you were real, but I was embarrassed."

The green girl smiles. I can't help noticing she has a beautiful smile, like sun on the boat pond. "Fatso is just saying that," she points out, "because she's afraid I'll throw her to Gnaw-bone."

I freeze solid. Bugle, who's been getting fidgety, takes off and flies around the clearing a couple of times. Then she buzzes me and pulls my hair again, lands on my shoulder and says, "She's not so bad. I like teasing her."

"Not fair!" Gnaw-bone squeaks.

The green girl shrugs. "You know the rules," she tells him. "Bugle speaks for her. She's off-limits. Them's the breaks. Now, scram. You bother me."

Exit Gnaw-bone, muttering and glaring at me over his shoulder, and am I ever glad to see him go. He's like every nightmare Mom has ever had about letting me go places by myself and having me turn up murdered. Mine, too.

Anyway, I'm so relieved I start to babble. "Thanks, Bugle. Thanks a billion. I owe you big time."

"Yeah," says Bugle. "I know."

"You owe me, too," the green girl puts in.

Now, I can't quite see where she's coming from on this, seeing as how she was all gung-ho to let Gnaw-bone have his fun and games before Bugle showed up. Not to mention calling me names. On the other hand, she's obviously Very Important, and if there's one thing I've learned from reading all those fairy tales, it's that it's a very bad idea to be rude to people who wear live birds and squirrels like jewelry. So I shrug. Politely.

"Seven months' service should cover it," she says. "Can you sing? I'm mostly into salsa these days, but reggae or jazz is cool too."

My mouth drops open. Seven months? She's gotta be out of her mind. My parents will kill me if I don't come home for seven months.

"No?" Her voice is even more beautiful than it was before, like a fountain or wind in the trees. Her eyes sparkle like sun through leaves. She so absolutely gorgeous so not like anyone I can imagine having a conversation with, it's hard to follow what she's saying.

"I don't sing," I tell her.

"Dance, then?" I shake my head. "So, what can you do?"

Well, I know the answer to that one. "Nothing," I say. "I'm totally useless. Just ask my French teacher. Or my mom."

The beautiful face goes all blank and hard, like granite. "I said Gnaw-bone couldn't have you. That leaves all his brothers and sisters. You don't need much talent to entertain them."

You know how your brain goes totally spla when you're really scared? Well, my brain did that. And then I heard myself saying, "You said I was under Bugle's protection. Just because you're Queen of the Fairies doesn't mean you can do anything you want."

I was sure she'd be mad, but—get this—she starts to laugh. She laughs and laughs and laughs. And I get madder and madder, the way you do when you don't know what you've said that's so funny. Then I notice that she's getting broader and darker and shorter, and there's this scarf over her head, and she's wearing this dorky green housedress and her stockings are drooping around her ankles and she's got a cigarette in one hand. Finally she wheezes out, "The Queen of the Fairies! Geddouddaheah! You're killin' me!" She sounds totally different, too, like somebody's Aunt Ida from the Bronx.

"The Queen of the . . . Listen, kid. We ain't in the Old Country no more. We're in New York"—*Noo Yawk* is what she said—"New York, U. S. of A. We ain't got Queens, except across the bridge."

So now I'm really torqued. I mean, who knows what she's going to do next, right? She could turn me into a pigeon, for all I know. This is no time to lose it. I've got to focus. After all, I've been reading about fairies for years, right? New Age stuff, folklore, fantasy novels—everything I could get my hands on. I've done my homework. There's a chance I can b.s. my way out of this if I keep my cool.

"Oh, ha ha," I say. "Not. Like that rat-guy didn't say 'how high' when you said 'jump.' You can call yourself the Mayor of Central Park if you want, but you're still the Queen of the goddam Fairies."

She morphs back to dreads and leather on fast forward.

"So, Fatso. You think you're hot stuff." I shrug. "Listen. We're in this thing where I think you owe me, and you think you don't. I could *make* you pay up, but I won't." She plops down on the bench and gets comfortable. The squirrel jumps off her shoulder and disappears into a tree.

"Siddown, take a load off—have a drink. Here." Swear to God, she hands me a can of Diet Coke. I don't know where it came from, but the pop-top is popped, and I can hear the Coke fizzing and I realize I'm wicked thirsty. My hand goes, like all by itself, to take it, and then my brain kicks in. "No," I say. "Thank you."

She looks hurt. "Really? It's cold and everything." She shoves it towards me. My mouth is as dry as the Sahara Desert, but if there's one thing I'm sure I know about fairies, it's don't eat or drink anything a fairy gives you if you ever want to go home.

"Really," I say. "Thanks."

"Well, dag," she says, disgusted. "You read fairy tales. Aren't you special. I suppose now you're going to ask for three wishes and a pot of gold. Go ahead. Three wishes. Have a ball."

This is more like it. I'm all prepared, too. In sixth grade, I worked out what my wishes would be, if I ever met a wish-granting fairy. And they were still perfectly good wishes, based on extensive research. Never, ever wish for more wishes. Never ask for money—it'll turn into dog doo in the morning. The safest thing to do was to ask for something that would make you a better citizen, and then you could ask for two things for yourself. I settled on a good heart, a really ace memory, and 20/20 vision. I didn't know about laser surgery in sixth grade.

So I'm all ready (except maybe asking to be a size 6 instead of the vision thing), and then it occurs to me that this is all way too easy, and Queenie is looking way too cheerful for someone who's been outsmarted by an overweight bookworm. Face it, I haven't done anything to earn those wishes.

All I've done is turn down a lousy Diet Coke. "Thanks all the same, but I'll pass," I say. "Can I go home now?"

Then she loses her temper. She's not foaming at the mouth or anything, but there are sparks coming out of her eyes like a Fourth of July sparkler, and her dreads are lifting and twining around her head like snakes. The sparrow gives a startled chirp and takes off for the nearest bush.

"Well, isn't this just my lucky day," Greenie snarls. "You're not as dumb as you look. On the bright side, though,"—her dreads settle slowly—"winning's boring when it's too easy, you know?"

I wouldn't know—I don't usually win. But then, I don't usually care that much. This is different. This time, there's a lot more at stake than my nonexistent self-esteem. I'm glad she thinks I'm a moron. It evens things up a little. "I tell you what," I tell her. "I'll play you for my freedom."

"You're on," she says. "Dealer's choice. That's me. What shall we play?" She leans back on the bench and looks up at the sky. "Riddles are trad, but everybody knows all the good ones. What's black and white and red all over? A blushing nun? A newspaper? Penguin roadkill? Puleeze. Anyway, riddles are boring. What do you say to Truth or Dare?"

"I hate it." I do, too. The only time I played it, I ended up feeling icky and raw, like I'd been sunbathing topless.

"Really? It's my favorite game. We'll play Truth or Dare. These are the rules. We ask each other personal questions, and the first one who won't answer loses everything. Deal?"

It doesn't sound like much of a deal to me. How can I know what question a Queen of Fairies would be too embarrassed to answer? On the other hand, what can a being who hangs out with squirrels and fairies and rat-guys know about human beings? And what choice do I have?

I shrug. "I guess."

"Okay. I go first."

Well, sure she does. She's the Queen of Central Park. And I see the question coming—she doesn't even pause to think about it. "So, how much do you weigh, anyway?"

Now you have to understand that nobody knows how much I weigh. Not Elf, not even my mom. Only the school nurse and the doctor and me. I've always said I'd rather die than tell anyone else. But the choice between telling and living in Central Park for seven months is a no-brainer. So I tell her. I even add a pound for the hotdog and the Mr. Softee I ate the boathouse.

"Geddouddaheah!" she says. "You really pork it down, huh?"

I don't like her comment, but it's not like I haven't heard it before. It makes me mad, but not so mad I can't think, which is obviously what she's trying for. Questions go through my mind, but I don't have a lot to go on, you know what I'm saying? And she's tapping her green boot and looking impatient. I have to say something, and what I end up asking is, "Why are you in Central Park, anyway? I mean, there's lots of other places that are more fairy-friendly. Why aren't you in White Plains or something?"

It sounds like a question to me, but she doesn't seem to think so. "I win. That's not personal," she says.

"It is too personal. Where a person lives is personal. Come on. Why do you live here, or let me go home."

"Can't blame a girl for trying," she says. "Okay, here goes. This is the heart of the city. You guys pass through all the time—like Grand Central Station, right? Only here, you stop or a while. You rest, you play, you kiss in the grass, you whisper your secrets, you weep, you fight. This ground, these rocks, are soaked through with love, hate, joy, sorrow, passion. And I love that stuff, you understand? It keeps me interested."

Wow. I stare at her, and all my ideas about fairies start to get rearranged. But they don't get very far because she's still talking.

"You think I don't know anything about you," she says. "Boy, are you wrong. I know everything I want to know. I know what's on your bio quiz next week. I know Patty Gregg's worst secret. I know who your real mother is, the one who gave you away when you were born." She gives me this look, like Elf's brother the time he stole a dirty magazine. "Wanna know?"

It's not what I'm expecting, but it's a question, all right, and it's personal. And it's really easy. Sure, I want to know all those things, a whole lot—especially about my biological mother.

Like more than anything else in the world. My parents are okay—I mean, they say they love me and everything. But they really don't understand me big time. I've always felt adopted, if you know what I mean—a changeling in a family of ordinary humans. I'd give anything to know who my real mother is, what she looks like and why she couldn't keep me. So I should say yes, right? I mean, it's the true answer to the green girl's question, and that's what the game is about, isn't it? There's a movement on my shoulder, a sharp little pinch right behind my ear. I've totally forgotten Bugle—I mean, she's been sitting there for ages, perfectly still, which is not her usual.

Maybe I've missed something. It's that too easy thing again. Sure, I want to know who my birth mom is. But it's more complicated than that. Because now that I think about it, I realize I don't want Greenie to be the one to tell me. I mean, it feels wrong, to learn something like that from someone who is obviously trying to hurt you.

"Answer the question," says the green girl. "Or give in. I'm getting bored."

I take a deep breath. "Keep your socks on. I was thinking how to put it. Okay, my answer is both yes and no. I do want to find out about my birth mom, but I don't want you to tell me. Even if you know, it's none of your business. I want to find out for myself. Does that answer your question?"

She nods briskly. "It does. Your turn."

She's not going to give me much time to come up with one, I can tell that. She wants to win. She wants to get me all torqued so I can't think, so I won't ask her the one question she won't answer, so I won't even see it staring me right in the face, the one thing she really, really can't answer, if the books I've read aren't all totally bogus.

"What's your name?" I ask.

I mean, it's obvious, isn't it? Like, how dumb does she think I am? Pretty dumb, I guess, from the look on her face.

"Guess," she says, making a quick recovery.

"Wrong fairy tale," I say, pushing it. "Come on. Tell me, or you lose."

"Do you know what you're asking?"

"Yes."

There's a long silence—a *long* silence, like no bird is ever going sing again, or squirrel chatter or wind blow. The green girl puts her fingers in her mouth and starts to bite her nails. I'm feeling pretty good. I know and she knows that I've won no matter what she says. If she tells me her name, I have total power over her, and if she doesn't, she loses the game. I know what I'd choose if I was in her place, but I guess she must really, really hate losing.

Watching her sweat, I think of several things to say, most of them kind of mean. She'd say them, if she was me. I don't.

It's not like I'm Mother Teresa or anything—I've been mean plenty of times, and sometimes I wasn't even sorry later. But she might lose her temper and turn me into a pigeon after all.

Besides, she looks so human all of a sudden, chewing her nails and all stressed out like she's the one facing seven months of picking up fairy laundry. Before, when she was winning, she looked maybe twenty, right? Gorgeous, tough, scary, in total control. Now she looks a lot younger and not tough at all.

So maybe if she loses, she's threatened with seven months of doing what I tell her. Maybe I don't realize what I'm asking. Maybe there's more at stake here than I know. A tiny whimpering behind my right ear tells me that Bugle is pretty upset. Suddenly, I don't feel so great. I don't care any more about beating the Queen of the Fairies at some stupid game.

I just want this to be over.

"Listen," I say, and the green girl looks up at me. Her wide, mossy eyes are all blurred with tears. I take a deep breath.

"Let's stop playing," I say.

"We can't stop," she says miserably. "It has begun, it must be finished. Those are the rules."

"Okay. We'll finish it. It's a draw. You don't have to answer my question. Nobody wins. Nobody loses. We just go back to the beginning."

"What beginning? When Gnaw-bone was chasing you? If I help you, you have to pay."

I think about this for a little while. She lets me. "Okay," I say. "How about this. You're in a tough spot, right? I take back the question, you're off the hook, like you got me off the hook with Gnaw-bone. We're even."

She takes her fingers out of her mouth. She gnaws on her lip. She looks up into the sky, and around at the trees. She tugs on her dreads. She smiles. She starts to laugh. It's not teasing laugh or a mean laugh, but pure happiness, like a little kid in the snow.

"Wow," she says, and her voice is warm and soft as fleece. "You're right. Awesome."

"Cool," I say. Can I go home now?"

"In a minute." She puts her head to one side, and grins at me. I'm grinning back—I can't help it. Suddenly, I feel all mellow and safe and comfortable, like I'm lying on a rock in the sun and telling stories to Elf.

"Yeah," she says, like she's reading my mind. "I've heard you. You tell good stories. You should write them down. Now, about those wishes. They're human stuff—not really my business. As you pointed out. Besides, you've already got all those things. You remember what you need to know; you see clearly; you're majorly kind-hearted. But you deserve a present." She tapped her browny-green cheek with one slender finger. "I know. Ready?"

"Okay," I say. "Um. What is it?"

"It's a surprise," she says. "But you'll like it. You'll see."

She stands up and I stand up. Bugle takes off from my shoulder and goes and sits in the greeny-brown dreads like a butterfly clip. Then the Queen of the New York Fairies leans forward and kisses me on the forehead. It doesn't feel like a kiss—more like a very light breeze has just hit me between the eyes. Then she lays her finger across my lips, and then she's gone.

"So there you are!" It was Elf, red in the face, out of breath, with her hair coming out of the clip, and a tear in her jacket. "I've been looking all over. I was scared out of my mind! It was like you just disappeared into thin air!"

"I got lost," I said. "Anyway, it's okay now. Sit down. You look like hell."

"Thanks, friend." She sat on the bench. "So, what happened?"

I wanted to tell her, I really did. I mean, she's my best friend and everything, and I always tell her everything. But the Queen of the Fairies. I ask you. And I could feel the kiss nestling below my bangs like a little, warm sun and the Queen's finger cool across my lips. So all I did was look at my hands. They were all dirty and scratched from climbing up the cliff. I'd broken a fingernail.

"Are you okay?" Elf asked anxiously. "That guy didn't catch you or anything, did he? Jeez, I wish we'd never gone down there."

She was getting really upset. I said, "I'm fine, Elf. He didn't catch me, and everything's okay."

"You sure?"

I looked right at her, you know how you do when you want to be sure someone hears you? And I said, "I'm sure." And I was.

"Okay," she said slowly. "Good. I was worried." She looked at her watch. "It's not like it was that long, but it seemed like Forever."

"Yeah," I agreed, with feeling. "I'm really thirsty."

So that's about it, really. We went to a coffee shop on Columbus Avenue and had blueberry pie and coffee and talked. For the first time, I told her about being adopted, and wanting to look for my birth mother, and she was really great about it after being mad because I hadn't told her before. I said she was a good friend and she got teary. And then I went home.

So what's the moral of this story? My life didn't get better overnight, if that's what you're wondering. I still need to lose a few pounds, I still need glasses, and the cool kids still hate me. But Elf sits with me at lunch now, and a couple other kids turned out to be into fantasy and like that, so I'm not a total outcast any more. And I'm writing down my stories. Elf thinks they're good, but she's my best friend. Maybe some day I'll get up the nerve to show them to my English teacher. Oh, and I've talked to my mom about finding my birth mother, and she says maybe I should wait until I'm out of high school. Which is okay with me, because, to tell you the truth, I don't need to find her right now—I just want to know I can.

And the Green Queen's gift? It's really weird. Suddenly, I see fairies everywhere.

There was this girl the other day—blonde, skinny, wearing a white leotard and her jeans unzipped and folded back, so he looked kind of like a flower in a calyx of blue leaves.

Freak, right? Nope. Fairy. So was an old black guy all dressed in royal blue, with butterflies sewn on his blue beret and painted on his blue suede shoes. And this Asian guy with black hair down to his butt and a big fur coat. And this Upper East Side lady with big blond hair and green bug-eyes. She had a fuzzy little dog on a rhinestone leash, and you won't believe this, but the dog was a fairy, too.

And remember the trees—the sidewalk ones? I know all about them now. No, I won't tell you, stupid. It's a secret. If you really want to know, you'll have to go find the Queen of Grand Central Park and make her an offer. Or play a game with her.

Don't forget to say hi to Gnaw-bone for me.

Delia Sherman's most recent short fiction has appeared in the anthologies *Naked City, Steampunk!, Teeth, Under My Hat, and Queen Victoria's Book of Spells*. Her adult novels are *Through a Brazen Mirror, The Porcelain Dove*, and *The Fall of Kings* (with Ellen Kushner). Novels for younger readers include New York Between Novels *Changeling* and *The Magic Mirror of the Mermaid Queen.* Her most recent novel, *The Freedom Maze*—a time-travel historical about antebellum Louisiana—received the Andre Norton Award, the Mythopoeic Award, and the Prometheus Award. When not writing, she teaches, edits, knits, and travels. Sherman lives in New York City with Ellen Kushner.

The City: *Philadelphia, Pennsylvania.*

The Magic: *Compiling a searchable database of every evocation and conjuring spell known to all the various beliefs of human culture is a resource that could bring both academic glory and a reliable cash-flow to the folklore department. Of course, outside of scholarly research, it's all meaningless and silly. Isn't it?*

SPELLCASTER 2.0

Jonathan Maberry

-1-

"Username?"

"You're going to laugh at me."

Trey LaSalle turned to her but said nothing. He wore very hip, very expensive tortoiseshell glasses and he let them and his two hundred dollar haircut do his talking for him. The girl withered.

"It's . . . obvious?" she said awkwardly, posing it as a question.

"Let me guess. It's going to be a famous magician, right? Which one, I wonder? Won't be *Merlin* because even *you're* not that obvious, and it won't be *Nostradamus* because I doubt you could spell it."

"I can spell," she said, but there was no emphasis to it.

"Hmm. *StGermaine?* No? *Dumbledore? Gandalf?*"

"It's—"

He pursed his lips. "Girl, please don't tell me it really *is Merlin*."

Anthem blushed herself mute.

"Jesus save me." Trey rubbed his eyes and typed in MERLIN with slow sarcasm, each keystroke separate and very sharp. By the fourth letter Anthem's eyes were jumping.

Her name was really Anthem. Her parents were right-wing second gens of left-wing Boomers from the Village, a confusion of genetics and ideologies that resulted in a girl who was bait fish for everyone at the University of Pennsylvania with an IQ higher than their belt size. Though barely a palate cleanser for a shark like Trey. He sipped his pumpkin spice latte and sighed.

"Password?" he prompted.

"You're going to make fun of me again."

"There's that chance," he admitted. "Is it too cute, too personal, or too stupid?" He carved off slices of each word and spread them out thin and cold. He was good at that. Back in high school his snarky tone would have earned him a beating—had, in fact, earned him several beatings; but then he conquered the cool crowd. Thereafter they kept him well protected, well-appeased, and well-stocked with a willing audience of masochists who had already begun to learn that anyone with a truly lethal wit was never—ever—to be mocked or harmed. In that environment, Trey LaSalle had flourished into the self-satisfied diva he now enjoyed being. Now, in his junior year at U of P, Trey owned the in-crowd and their hangers-on because he was able to work the sassy gay BFF role as if the trope was built for him. At the same time he could also play the get-it-done team leader when the chips were down.

Those chips were certainly down right now. Trey figured that Jonesy and Bird had gotten Anthem to call Trey for a bailout because she was so thoroughly a Bambi in the brights that even he wouldn't actually slaughter her.

"Password?" He drew it into a hiss.

Anthem chewed a fingernail. Despite the fact that she painted her nails, they were all nibbled down to nubs. A couple of them even had blood caked along the sides from where she'd cannibalized herself a bit too aggressively, and there were faint chocolate-colored smears of it on the keyboard. Trey made a mental note to bathe in Purell when he got back to his room.

"Come on, girl," he coaxed.

She blurted it. *"Abracadabra."*

Trey stared at the screen and tried very hard not to close the laptop and club her to death with it. He typed it in. The display changed from the bland login screen to the landing page for *The Spellcaster Project.*

The project.

It sounded simple, but wasn't. Over the course of the last eighteen months the group had collected, organized, and committed to computer memory every evocation and conjuring spell known to the various beliefs of human culture. From phonetic interpretations of guttural verbal chants by remote Brazilian tribes to complex rituals in Latin and Greek. On the surface the project was a searchable database so thorough that it would be the go-to resource. A resource for which access could be leased, opening a cash-flow for the folklore department. And, people would definitely pay. This database—nicknamed *Spellcaster*—was a researcher's dream.

Trey found it all fascinating but considered it immensely silly at the same time. He was a scientist, or becoming one, and yet his field of study involved nothing that he believed in. Doctors at least believed in healing, but folklorists were a notoriously atheistic lot. Demons and gods, spells and sacred rituals. None of it was remotely real. All of it was an attempt to make sense of a world that could not be truly understood or defined, and certainly not controlled. Things just happened. Nobody was at the controls, and nobody was taking calls from the human race.

And yet with all that, it was fascinating, like watching a car wreck. You don't want to be a part of it but you can't look away. He even went to church sometimes, just to study the people, to mentally catalog the individual ways in which they interpreted the religion to which they ascribed. There was infinite variation within a species, just as within flowers in a field. And soon he would be making money from it, and that was something he could believe in.

The second aspect of the project was *Spellcaster 2.0*, which began as Trey's idea but along the way had somehow become Professor Davidoff's. In essence, once the thousands of spells were entered, a program would run through all of them to look for common elements. Developmental goals included a determination of how many common themes appeared in spells and what themes appeared in a majority, or at least a significant number of them. The end goal was to create a perfect generic spell. A spell that established there were some aspects to magical conjuring that linked the disparate tribes and cultures of mankind.

Trey's hypothesis was that anthropologists would be able to use that information, along with related linguistic models, to more accurately track the spread of humankind from its African origins. It might effectively prove that the spread of religion in all of its many forms, stemmed from the same central source. Or—as he privately thought of it—mankind's first big stupid mistake. In other words, the birth of prayer and organized religion.

Finding that would be a watershed moment in anthropology, folklore, sociology, and history. It would be a Nobel Prize no-brainer, and it didn't matter to Trey if he shared that prize, and all of the fame and—no doubt—fortune that went with it. *Spellcaster* was going to make them all rich.

"Okay," Trey said, "why are we here?"

Anthem chewed her lip. She did it prettily, and even though she was the wrong cut of meat for Trey's personal tastes, he had to admit that she was all that. She was an East Coast blonde with ice-pale skin, luminous green eyes, a figure that could make any kind of clothes look good, and Scarlett Johansson lips. Shame that she was dumber than a cruller. He was considering bringing her into his circle; not the circle-jerk of grad students to which they both currently belonged, but the more elite group he went clubbing with. Arm candy like that worked for everyone, straight or gay. It was better than a puppy and it didn't pee on the carpet. Though, with Anthem there was no real guarantee that she was housebroken.

The lip chewing had no real effect on him, and Trey studied her to see how long it would take her to realize it. Seven Mississippis.

"I've been hacked," she said.

"Get right out of town."

"And they've been in my laptop messing with my stuff."

"The spells?"

"Some of them, yes."

Trey felt the first little flutter of panic.

"I've been inputting the evocation spells for the last couple of weeks," Anthem explained. "One group at a time. Last week it was Gypsy stuff from Serbia, before that it was the pre-industrial Celtic stuff. It's hard to do. None of it was translated and Professor Davidoff didn't want us to use Babelfish or any of the other online translators because they don't give cultural or—what's the word?"

"Contextual?"

"Right. They don't give cultural or contextual translations, and that's supposed to be important for spells."

" 'Crucial' is a better word," Trey murmured, "but I take your point."

"I had to compare what I typed with photocopies from old spell books. After I finish this stuff Kidd will add the binding spells, then Jonesy will do the English translations. Bird's doing the footnotes, and I guess you'll be working on the annotations."

"Uh huh."

"At first Jonesy dictated the spells while I typed, but that only really worked with Latin and the Romance languages because we kind of knew the spellings. More and more, though, I had to look at it myself to make sure it was exact. Everything had to match or the professor would freak. And there are all those weird little symbol thingies on some of the letters."

"Diacritical marks."

"Yeah, those." She began nibbling at her thumbnail, talking around it as she chewed. "Without everything just so, the spells won't work."

Trey smiled a tolerant smile. "Sweetie, the spells won't work because they're spells. None of this crap works, you know that."

She stared at him for a moment, still working on the thumb. "They used to work, though, didn't they?"

"This is science, honey. The only magic here is the way you're working that sweater and the supernatural way I'm working these jeans."

She said, "Okay." But she didn't sound convinced, and it occurred to Trey that he didn't know where Anthem landed on the question of faith. If she was a believer then that was a tick against her becoming part of his circle.

"You were saying about the data entry?" he prompted, steering her back to safer ground.

Anthem blinked. "Oh, sure. It's hard. It's all brain work."

Trey said nothing to that. It would be too easy; it would be like kicking a sleepy kitten. Instead he asked, "So what happened?"

Anthem suddenly stopped biting her thumb and they both looked at the bead of blood that welled from where she'd bitten too deeply. Without saying a word, Anthem tore a piece of Scotch tape from a dispenser and wrapped it around the wound.

"Every day I start by checking the previous day's entries to make sure they're all good."

"And—?"

"The stuff I entered last night was different."

"Different how?"

"Let me show you." Anthem leaned past him and her fingers began flying over the keys. Whatever else she was or wasn't, she could type like a demon. Very fast and very accurate. The world lost a great typist when she decided to pursue higher education, mused Trey.

Anthem pulled up a file marked *18CenFraEvoc*, scrolled down to one of the spells, then tapped the screen with a bright green fingernail. "There, see? I found the first changes in the ritual the professor is going to use for the debut thingy."

Trey's French was passable and he bent closer and studied the lines, frowning as he did so. Anthem was correct in that this ritual—the faux summoning of Azeziz, demon of knowledge and faith—was a key element in Professor Davidoff's plans to announce their project to the academic world. Even a slight error would embarrass the professor, and he was not a forgiving man. Less so than, say, Hitler.

Anthem opened a file folder which held a thick sheaf of high-res scans of pages from a variety of sources. She selected a page and held it up next to the screen. "This is how it should read."

Trey clicked his eyes back and forth between the source and target materials and then he did see it. In one of the spells the wording had been changed. The second sentence read: *With the Power of the Eternal I Conjure Thee to my Service.*

It should have read: *With the Power of My Faith in the Eternal I Conjure and Bind Thee to my Service.*

"You see?" Anthem asked again. "It's different. There's nothing about the conjurer *believing*. That throws it all off, right?

"In theory," he said dryly. "This could have been a mistype."

"No way," she said. "I always check my previous day's stuff before I start anything new. I don't make those kinds of mistakes."

The pride in her voice was palpable, and in truth Trey could not recall ever making a correction in any of her work before. The team had been hammering away at the project for eighteen months. They'd created hundreds of pages of original work, and entered thousands of pages of collected data. After a few mishaps with other team members handling data entry, the bulk of it was shifted to Anthem.

"It's weird, right?" she asked.

He sat back and folded his arms, "It's weird. And, yes, you've been hacked."

"By who? I mean, it has to be one of the team, right? But Jonesy doesn't know French. I don't think Bird does, either."

Jonesy was a harmless mouse of a kid. Bird was sharper, but he was an idealist and adventurer. Bird wanted to chew peyote with the Native American Church and go on spirit walks. He wanted to whirl with the Dervishes and trance-out with the Charismatics. Unlike Trey and every other anthropologist Trey knew, Bird was in the field for the actual beliefs. Bird apparently believed that everyone was right, that every religion, no matter how batty, had a clue to the Great Big Picture as he called it. Trey liked him, but except for the project they had nothing in common.

Would Bird do this, though? Trey doubted it, partly because it was mean—and Bird didn't have fangs at all—and mostly because it was disrespectful to the belief systems. As if anyone would really care. Except the thesis committee.

"What about Kidd?" asked Anthem. "It would be like him to do something mean like this."

That much was true. Michael Kidd was a snotty, self-important little snob from Philly's Main Line. Good looking in a verminous sort of way. Kidd was cruising through college on family money and never pretended otherwise. Even Davidoff walked softly around him.

But, would Kidd sabotage the project? Yeah, he really might. Just for shits and giggles.

"The slimy little rat-sucking weasel," said Trey.

"So it *is* Kidd?"

Trey did not commit. He would have bet twenty bucks on it, but that wasn't the same as saying it out loud. Especially to someone like Anthem. He cut a covert look at her and for a moment his inner bitch softened. She was really a sweet kid. Clueless in a way that did no one any harm, not even herself. Anthem wasn't actually stupid, just not sharp and would probably never be sharp. Not unless something broke her and left jagged edges; and wouldn't that be sad?

"Is this only with the French evocation spell?" he asked.

"No." She pulled up the Serbian Gypsy spells. Neither of them could read the language, but a comparison of source and target showed definite differences. Small, but there. "I went back as far as the Egyptian burial symbols. Ten separate files, ten languages, which is crazy 'cause none of us can speak all of those languages."

"What about the Aramaic and Babylonian?"

"I haven't entered them yet."

Trey thought about it, then nodded. "Okay, let's do this. Go in and make the corrections. Before you do, though, I'm going to set you up with a new username and new password."

"Okay." She looked relieved.

"How much do you have to do on this?" Trey asked. "Are we going to make the deadline?"

The deadline was critical. Professor Davidoff was planning to make an official announcement in less than a month. He had a big event planned for it, and warned them all every chance he could that departmental grant money was riding on this. Big time money. He never actually threatened them, but they could all see the vultures circling.

Anthem nibbled as she considered the stacks of folders on her desk. "I can finish in three weeks."

"That's cutting it close."

Anthem's nibbling increased.

"Look," he said, "I'll spot-check you and do all the transfers to the mainframe. Don't let anyone else touch your laptop for any reason. No one, okay?"

"Okay," she said, relieved but still dubious. "Will that keep whoever's doing this out of the system?"

"Sure," said Trey. "This should be the end of it."

-2-

It wasn't.

-3-

"Tell me exactly what's been happening," demanded Professor Davidoff.

Trey and the others sat in uncomfortable metal folding chairs that were arranged in a half-circle around the acre of polished hardwood that was the professor's desk. The walls were heavy with books and framed certificates, each nook and corner filled with oddments. There were juju sticks and human skulls, bottles of ingredients for casting spells—actual eye of newt and bat's wing—and ornate reliquaries filled with select bits of important dead people.

Behind the desk, sitting like a heathen king among his spoils, was Alexi Davidoff, professor of folklore, professor of anthropology, department chair, and master of all he surveyed. Davidoff was a bear of a man with Einstein hair, mad scientist eyebrows, black-framed glasses, and a suit that cost more than Trey's education.

The others in the team looked at Trey. Anthem and Jonesy on his left—a cabal of girl power; Bird and Kidd on his right, representing two ends of the evolutionary bell curve—evolved human and moneyed Neanderthal.

"Well, sir," began Trey, "we're hitting a few little speed bumps."

The professor arched an eyebrow. " 'Speed bumps' ?"

Trey cleared his throat. "There have been a few anomalies in the data and—"

Davidoff raised a finger. It was as sure a command to stop as if he'd raised a scepter. "No," he said, "don't take the long way around. Come right out and say it. *Own* it, Mr. LaSalle."

Kidd coughed but it sounded suspiciously like, "Nut up."

Trey pretended not to have heard. To Davidoff, he said, "Someone has hacked into the *Spellcaster* data files on Anthem's computer."

They all watched Davidoff's complexion undergo a prismatic change from its normal never-go-outside pallor to a shade approximating a boiled lobster.

"Explain," he said gruffly.

Trey took a breath and plunged in. In the month since Anthem sought his help with the sabotage of the data files her computer had been hacked five times. Each time it was the same kind of problem, with minor changes being made to conjuring spells. With each passing week Trey became more convinced that Kidd was the culprit. Kidd was in charge of research for the team, which meant that he was uniquely positioned to obtain translations of the spells, and to arrange the rewording of them, since he was in direct contact with the various experts who were providing translations in return for footnotes. Only Jonesy had as much contact with the translators, and Trey didn't for a moment think that she would want to harm Anthem, or the project. However, he dared not risk saying any of this here and now. Not in front of everyone, and not without proof. Davidoff was rarely sympathetic and by no means an ally.

On the other hand, Trey knew that the professor had the typical academic's fear and loathing of scandal. Research data and drafts of papers were sacrosanct, and until it was published even the slightest blemish or question could ruin years of work and divert grants aimed at Davidoff's tiny department.

"Has anything been stolen?" Davidoff asked, his voice low and deadly.

"There's . . . um . . . no way to tell, but if they've been into Anthem's computer then nothing would have prevented them from copying everything."

"What about the bulk data on the department mainframe?" growled Davidoff.

"No way," said Bird confidently. "Has that been breached?"

Trey dialed some soothing tones into his voice. "No. I check it every day and the security software tracks every login. It's all clean. Whatever's happening is confined to Anthem's laptop."

"Have all the changes been corrected before uploading to the mainframe?" asked Davidoff.

"Absolutely."

That was a lie. There were two hundred gigabytes of documents that had been copied from Anthem's computer. It would take anyone months to read through it all, and probably years to compare every line to the photocopies of source data.

"You're sure?" Davidoff persisted.

"Positive," lied Trey.

"Are we still on schedule? We're running this in four days. We have guests coming. We have press coming. I've invested a lot of the department's resources into this."

He wasn't joking and Trey knew it. Davidoff had booked the university's celebrated Annenberg Center for the Performing Arts and hired a professional event coordinator to run things. There was even a bit of "fun" planned for the evening. Davidoff had a bunch of filmmakers from nearby Drexel University do some slick animation that would be projected as a hologram onto tendrils of smoke rising from vents in the floor around a realistic mock-up of a conjuring circle. The effect would be the sudden "appearance" of a demon. Davidoff would then interact with the demon, following a script that Trey himself had drafted. In their banter, the demon would extol the virtues of *Spellcaster* and discuss the benefits of the research to the worldwide body of historical and folkloric knowledge, and do everything to praise the project short of dropping to his knees and giving Davidoff some oral love.

There were so many ways it could go wrong that he almost wished he could pray for divine providence, but not even a potential disaster was going to put Trey on his knees.

"Sir," Trey said, "while I believe we're safe and in good shape, we really should run *Spellcaster 2.0* ourselves before the actual show."

"No."

"But—"

"You do realize, Mr. LaSalle, that the reason the press and the dignitaries will all be there is that we're running this in real time. They get to share in it. That's occurred to you, hasn't it?"

Yes, you grandstanding shithead, Trey thought. *It occurred to me for all of the reasons that I recommended that we not go that route.* He wanted to play it safe, to run the program several times and verify the results rather than go for the insane risk of what might amount to a carnival stunt.

Trey held his tongue and gave a single nod of acquiescence.

"Then we run it on schedule," the professor declared. "Now—how did this happen? By *magic?*"

A couple of the others laughed at this, but the laughs were brief and uncertain, because clearly this wasn't a funny moment. Davidoff glared them into silence.

Trey said, "I don't know, but we're doing everything we can to make sure that it doesn't affect the project."

The *Spellcaster* project was vital to all of them, but for different reasons. For personal glory, for a degree, for the opportunities it would offer and the doors it would open. So, Trey could understand why the professor's vein throbbed so mightily.

"I've done extensive online searches," Trey said, using his most businesslike voice, "and there's nothing. Not a sentence of what we've recorded, not a whiff of our thesis, nothing."

"That doesn't mean they won't publish it," grumbled Jonesy, speaking up for the first time since the meeting began.

"I don't think so," said Trey. "The stuff on Anthem's laptop is just the spell catalog. None of the translations are there and none of the bulk research and annotations are there. At worst they can publish a partial catalog."

"That would still hurt us," said Bird. "If we lost control of that, license money would spill all over the place."

Trey shook his head. "The shine on that candy is its completeness. All of the spells, all of the methods of conjuration and evocation, every single binding spell. There's no catalog like it anywhere, and what's on the laptop now is at most fifty percent, and that's nice, but it's not the Holy Grail."

"I think Trey's right, Professor," said Jonesy. "We should do a test run. I mean, what if one or more of those rewritten errors made it to the mainframe? If that happened and we run *Spellcaster 2.0*, how could we trust our findings?"

"No way we could," said Kidd, intending it to be mean and scoring nicely. The big vein on the professor's forehead throbbed visibly.

Trey ignored Kidd. "We have some leeway—"

Jonesy shook her head. "The *2.0* software is configured to factor in accidental or missed keystrokes, not sabotage."

Shut up, you cow, thought Trey, but Jonesy plowed ahead.

"Deliberate alteration of the data will look like what it is. Rewording doesn't look like bad typing. If it's there, then all our hacker has to do is let us miss one of his changes he made and wait for us to publish. Then he steps forward and tells everyone that our data management is polluted . . . "

" . . . and he'd be able to point to specific flaws," finished Bird. "We not only wouldn't have reliable results, we wouldn't have the perfect generic spell that would be the signpost we're looking for. We'd have nothing. Oh, man . . . we'd be so cooked."

One by one they turned to face Professor Davidoff. His accusing eye shifted away from Trey and landed on Anthem, who withered like an orchid in a cold wind. "So, this is a matter of you being stupid and clumsy, is that what I'm hearing?"

Anthem was totally unable to respond. Her skin paled beneath her fake tan and she looked like a six year old who was caught out of bed. Her pretty lips formed a lot of different words but Trey did not hear her make as much as a squeak. Tiny tears began to wobble in the corners of her eyes. The others kept themselves absolutely still. Kidd chuckled very quietly, and Trey wanted to kill him.

"It's not Anthem's fault," said Trey, coming quickly to her defense. "Her data entry is—"

Davidoff made an ugly, dismissive noise and his eyes were locked on Anthem's. "There are plenty of good typists in the world," he said unkindly. "Being one of them does not confer upon you nearly as much importance as you would like to believe."

Trey quietly cleared his throat. "Sir, since Anthem first alerted me to the problem I've been checking her work, and some of the anomalies occurred after I verified the accuracy of her entries. This isn't Anthem's fault. I changed her username and password after each event."

Davidoff considered this, then gave a dismissive snort. It was as close to an apology as his massive personal planet ever orbited.

"Then . . . we're safe?" ventured Bird hopefully.

Trey licked his lips, then nodded.

Davidoff's vein was no longer throbbing quite as aggressively. "Then we proceed as planned. Real test, real time." He raised his finger of doom. "Be warned, Mr. LaSalle, this is your neck on the line. You are the team leader. It's your responsibility. I don't want to hear excuses after something else happens. All I ever want to hear is that *Spellcaster* is secure. I don't care who you have to kill to protect the integrity of that data, but you keep it safe. Do I make myself clear?"

Trey leaned forward and put his hands on the edge of Davidoff's desk. "Believe me, Professor, when I find out who's doing this I swear to god I will rip his god damned heart out."

He could feel everyone's eyes on him.

The professor sat back and pursed his lips, studying Trey with narrowed, calculating eyes. "See that you do," he said quietly. "Now all of you . . . get out."

-4-

Trey spent the next few hours walking the windy streets of University City. He was deeply depressed and his stomach was a puddle of acid tension. As he walked, he heard car horns and a few shouts, laughter from the open door of sports bars on the side streets. A few sirens wailed with ghostly insistence in the distance. He heard those things, but he didn't register any of it.

Trey's mind churned on it. Not on why this was happening, but who was doing it?

After leaving Davidoff, Trey had gone to see his friend, Herschel, and the crew of geeks at the computer lab. These were the kinds of uber-nerds who once would have never gotten laid and never moved out of their mother's basements—stereotypes all the way down to the *Gears of War* T-shirts and cheap sneakers. Now, guys like that were rock stars. They *got* laid. They all had jobs waiting for them after graduation. Most of them wouldn't bother with school after they had a bachelor's because the industry wanted them young and raw and they wanted them now. These were the guys who hacked ultra-secret corporate computer systems just because they were bored. Guys who made some quick cash on the side writing viruses that they sold to the companies who sold anti-virus software.

Trey explained the situation to them.

They thought it was funny.

They thought it was cool.

They told him half a dozen ways they could do it.

"Even Word docs on a laptop that's turned off?" demanded Trey. "I thought that was impossible."

Herschel laughed. "Impossible isn't a word, brah, it's a challenge."

"What?"

"It's the *Titanic*," said Herschel.

"Beg pardon?"

"The *Titanic*. The unsinkable ship. You got to understand the mindset." Herschel was an emaciated runt with nine-inch hips and glasses you could fry ants with. At nineteen he already held three patents and his girlfriend was a spokesmodel at gaming shows. "Computers—hardware *and* software—are incredibly sophisticated idiots, feel me? They can only do what they're programmed to do. Even AI isn't really independent thinking. It's not intuitive."

"Okay," conceded Trey. "So?"

"So, what man can invent, man can fuck up. Look at home security systems. As soon as the latest unbreakable, unshakable, untouchable system goes on the market someone has to take it down. Not wants to . . . *has* to."

"Why?"

"Because it's there, brah. Because it's all about toppling the arrogant assholes in corporate America who make those kinds of claims. Can't be opened, can't be hacked, can't be sunk. *Titanic*, man."

"Man didn't throw an iceberg at the ship, Hersch."

"No, the universe did that because it's a universal imperative to kick arrogant ass."

"Booyah," agreed the other hackers, bumping fists.

"So," said Trey slowly, "you think someone's hacking our research because he can?"

Herschel shrugged. "Why else?"

"Not to try and sell it?"

Some of the computer geeks laughed. Herschel said, "Sell that magic hocus-pocus shit and you're going to make—what? A few grand? Maybe a few hundred grand in the long run after ten years busting your ass?"

"At *least* that much," Trey said defensively.

"Get a clue, dude. You got someone hacking a closed system on a laptop and changing unopened files in multiple languages. That's real magic. A guy like that wouldn't wipe his ass with a hundred grand. All he has to do is file a patent on how he did it and everyone in corporate R-and-D will be lining up to blow him. Guy like that wouldn't answer the phone for any offer lower than the middle seven figures.

"Booyah!" agreed the geek chorus.

"Sorry, brah," said Herschel, clapping Trey on the shoulder, "but this might not even be about your magic spell bullshit. You could just be a friggin' test drive."

Trey left, depressed and without a clue of where to go next. The profile of his unknown enemy did not seem to fit anyone on the project. Bird and Jonesy were as good with computers as serious students and researchers could be, but at the end of the day they were really only Internet savvy. They would never have fit in with Herschel's crowd. Anthem knew everything about word processing software but beyond that she was in unknown territory. Kidd was no computer geek either. Although, Trey mused, Kidd could afford to hire a geek. Maybe even a really good geek, one of Herschel's crowd. Someone who could work the kind of sorcery required to break into Anthem's computer.

But . . . how to prove it?

God, he wished he really could go and rip Kidd's heart out. If the little snot even had one.

The sirens were getting louder and the noise annoyed him. Every night it was the same. Football jocks and the frat boys with their perpetual parties, as if belly shots and beer pong genuinely mattered in the cosmic scheme of things. Neanderthals.

Without even meaning to do it, Trey's feet made a left instead of a right and carried him down Sansom Street toward Kidd's apartment.

He suddenly stopped walking and instantly knew that no confrontation with Kidd was going to happen that night.

The entire street was clogged with people who stood in bunches and vehicles parked at odd angles.

Police vehicles. And an ambulance.

"Oh . . . shit," he said.

-5-

Tearing out Kidd's heart was no longer an option.

According to every reporter on the scene, someone had already beaten him to it.

-6-

The following afternoon they all met in Trey's room. The girls perched on the side of his bed; Bird sprawled in a papa-san chair with his knees up and his arms wrapped around them. Trey stood with his back to the door.

All eyes were on him.

"Cops talk to you?" asked Bird.

"No. You?"

Bird nodded. He looked as scared as Trey felt. "They asked me a few questions."

"Really? Why?"

Bird didn't answer.

"They came around here, too," said Jonesy. "This morning and again this afternoon."

"Why'd they want to see you guys?" asked Trey.

Jonesy gave him a strange look.

"What?" Trey asked.

"They wanted to see you," said Anthem.

"Me? Why would they want to see me?"

Nobody said a word. Nobody looked at him.

Trey said, "Oh, come *on.* You guys have to be frigging kidding me here."

No one said a word.

"You sons of bitches," said Trey. "You think I did it, don't you? You think I could actually kill someone and tear out their frigging heart? Are you all on crack?"

"Cops said that whoever killed him must have gone apeshit on him," murmured Bird.

"So, out of seven billion people suddenly I'm America's Most Wanted?"

"They're calling it a rage crime," said Jonesy.

"Rage," echoed Anthem.

"And you actually think that *I* could do that?"

"Somebody did," said Bird again. "Whoever did it must have hated Kidd because they beat him to a pulp and tore him open. Cops asked us if we knew anyone who hated Kidd that much."

"And you gave them *my* name?"

"We didn't have to," said Anthem. "Everyone on campus knows what you thought of Kidd."

And there was nowhere to go with that except out, so Trey left them all sitting in the desolation of his room.

-7-

The cops picked him up at ten the next morning. They said he didn't need a lawyer, they just wanted to ask questions. Trey didn't have a lawyer anyway, so he answered every single question they asked. Even when they asked the same questions six and seven times.

They let him go at eight-thirty that night. They didn't seem happy about it.

Neither was Trey.

-8-

The funeral was the following day. They all went. It didn't rain because it only rains at funerals in the movies. They stood under an impossibly blue sky that was littered with cotton candy clouds. Trey stood apart from the others and listened with contempt to the ritual bullshit the priest read out of his book. Kidd had been as much of an atheist as Trey was, and this was a mockery. He'd have skipped it if that wouldn't have made him look even more suspicious.

After the service, Trey took the bus home alone.

He tried several times to call Davidoff, but the professor didn't return calls or emails.

The day ground on.

The *Spellcaster* premier was tomorrow. Trey spent the whole day double and triple checking the data. He found nothing in any of the files he checked, but in the time he had he was only able to check about one percent of the data.

Trey sent twenty emails recommending that the premiere be postponed. He got no answers from the professor. Bird, Jonesy, and Anthem said as little to him as possible, but they all kept at it, going about their jobs like worker bees as the premiere drew closer.

∽

-9-

Professor Davidoff finally called him.

"Sir," said Trey, "I've been trying to—"

"We're going ahead with the premiere."

Trey sighed. "Sir, I don't think that's—"

"It's for Michael."

Michael. Not Mr. Kidd. The professor had never called Kidd by his first name. Ever. Trey waited for the other shoe.

"It'll be a tribute to him," continued Davidoff, his pomposity modulated into a funereal hush. "He devoted the last months of his life to this project. He deserves it."

Great, thought Trey, *everyone thinks I'm a psycho killer and he's practicing sound bites.*

"Professor, we have to stop for a minute to consider the possibility that the sabotage of the project is connected to what happened to Kidd."

"Yes," Davidoff said heavily, "we do."

Silence washed back and forth across the cellular ocean.

"I cannot imagine why anyone would do such a thing," said the professor. "Can you, Mr. LaSalle?"

"Professor, you don't think I—"

"I expect everything to go by the numbers tomorrow, Mr. LaSalle."

Before Trey could organize a reply, Professor Davidoff disconnected.

-10-

And it all went by the numbers.

More or less.

Drawn by the gruesome news story and the maudlin PR spin Davidoff gave it, the Annenberg was filling to capacity, with lines wrapped halfway around the block. Three times the expected number of reporters were there. There was even a picket by a right-wing religious group who wanted the *Spellcaster* project stopped before it started because it was "ungodly," "blasphemous," "satanic," and a bunch of other words that Trey felt ranged between absurd and silly. The picketers drew media attention and that put even more people in line for the dwindling supply of tickets.

Bird, Jonesy, and Anthem showed up in very nice clothes. Bird wore a tie for the first time since Trey had known him. The girls both wore dresses. Jonesy transformed from mouse to wow in a black strapless number that Trey would have never bet she could pull off. Anthem was in green silk that matched her eyes and she looked like a movie star. She even had nail tips over the gnarled nubs of her fingers. Trey was in a black turtleneck and pants. It was as close to being invisible as he could manage.

Davidoff was the ringmaster of the circus. He wore an outrageously gorgeous Glen Urquhart plaid three-piece and even with his ursine bulk he looked like God's richer cousin.

Even the university dons were nodding in approval, happy with the positive media attention following so closely on the heels of the murder.

The as yet unsolved murder, mused Trey. The cops were nowhere with it. Trey was pretty sure he was being followed now. He was a person of interest.

God.

When the audience was packed in, Davidoff walked onto center stage amid thunderous applause. He even contrived to look surprised at the adoration before eventually waving everyone into an expectant silence.

"Before we begin, ladies and gentlemen," he began, "I would like us all to share in a moment of silence. Earlier this week, one of my best and brightest students was killed in a savage and senseless act that still has authorities baffled. No one can make sense of the death of so wonderful a young man as Michael Kidd, Jr. He was on the very verge of a brilliant career, he was about to step into the company of such legendary folklorists as Stetson Kennedy, Archie Green, and John Francis Campbell."

Trey very nearly burst out laughing. He cut a look at Bird, who gave him a weary headshake and a half-smile, momentarily stunned out of all consideration by the absurdity of that claim.

"I would like to dedicate this evening to Mr. Kidd," continued Davidoff. "He will be remembered, he will be missed."

"Christ," muttered Trey.

The stage manager scowled at him.

The whole place dropped into a weird, reverential silence that lasted a full by-the-clock minute. Davidoff raised his arms and a spotlight bathed him in a white glow as the houselights dimmed.

"Magic!" he said ominously in a voice that was filtered through a sound board which gave it a mysterious-sounding reverb. The crowd ooohed and aaahed. "We have always believed in a larger world. Call it religion, call it superstition, call it the eternal mystery . . . we all believe in something. Even those of us who claim to believe in nothing—we will still knock on wood and pick up a penny only if it is heads up. Somewhere, past the conscious will and the civilized mind, the primitive in us remembers cowering in caves or crouching in the tall grass, or perching apelike on the limb of a tree as the wheel of night turned above and darkness covered the world."

Trey mouthed the words along with the professor. Having written them he knew the whole speech by heart.

"But what is magic? Is magic the belief that we live in a universe of infinite possibilities? Yes, but it's also more than that. It's the belief that we can *control* the forces of that universe. That we are not flotsam in the stream of cosmic events, but rather that we are creators ourselves. Co-creators with the infinite. Our sentience—the beautiful, impossible fact of human self-awareness and intelligence—lifts us above all other creatures in our natural world and connects us to the boundless powers of what we call the supernatural."

From there Davidoff segued into an explanation of the *Spellcaster* project. Trey had to admit that his script sounded pretty good. He'd taken what could have been dry material and given richness by an infusion of some pop-culture phrasing and a few juicy superlatives. The audience loved it, and they were carried along by a multimedia show that flashed images on a dozen screens. Pictures from illuminated texts. Great works of sacred art. Churches and temples, tombs, and crypts, along with hundreds of photos of everything from Mickey Mouse as the Sorcerer's Apprentice to Gandalf the Gray. And there were images of holy people from around the world; Maori with their tattooed faces, Navajo shaman singing over complex sand paintings, medicine men from tiny tribes deep in the heart of the Amazon, and singers of sacred songs from among the Bushmen of Africa. It was deliberate sensory overload, accompanied by a remix mash-up of musical pieces ranging from Ozzie Osbourne to Mozart to Loreena McKennitt.

Then the floor opened and a gleaming computer rose into the light. It wasn't the department mainframe of course, but a prop with lots of polished metal fixtures that did nothing except look cool. A laptop was positioned inside, out of sight of the audience. Smoke began rising with it, setting the stage for the evocation to come.

Suddenly four figures in dark robes stepped onto the stage. Two men and two women with black robes lined with red satin swirling around them. Juniors from the dance department. They did a few seconds of complex choreography that was, somehow, supposed to symbolize a ritual, and then they produced items from within their cloaks and began drawing a conjuring circle on the floor. Other dancers came out and lit candles, placing them at key points. The floor was discreetly marked so the dancers could do everything just so. Even though this was all for show, it had to be done right. This was still college.

The conjurer's circle was six feet across, and this was surrounded by three smaller circles. Davidoff explained that the center circle represented Earth, the smaller circle at the apex of the design represented the unknown, the circle to his right was the safe haven of the conjurer; and the circle to the left represented the realm of the demon who was to be conjured.

It was all done correctly.

Then to spook things up, Davidoff explained how this could all go horribly, horribly wrong.

"A careless magician summons his own death," he said in his stentorian voice. "All of the materials need to be pure. Vital essences—blood, sweat, or tears—must never be allowed within the demon's circle for these form a bridge between the worlds of spirit and flesh."

The crowd gasped in horror as images from *The Exorcist* flashed onto the screens.

"A good magician is a scholar of surpassing skill. He does not make errors . . . or, rather, he makes only one error."

He paused for laughter and got it.

"A learned magician is a quiet and solitary person. All of his learning, all of his preparation for this ritual, must be played out in his head. He cannot practice his invocations because magical words each have their special power. To casually speak a spell is to open a doorway that might never be shut."

More images from horror movies emphasized his point. The dancer-magicians took up positions at key points around the circle.

"If everything is done just right," continued Davidoff, "the evocation can begin. This is the moment for which a magician prepares his entire life. This is the end result of thousands of hours of study, of sacrifice, of purification and preparation. The magician hopes to draw into this world—into the confined and contained protection of a magic circle—a demon of immeasurable wisdom and terrible power. Contained within the circle, the demon must obey the sorcerer. Cosmic laws decree that this is so!"

The audience was spellbound, which Trey thought very appropriate. He found himself caught up in the magic that Davidoff was weaving. It was all going wonderfully so far. He cut looks at the others and they were all smiling, the horrors of their real world momentarily forgotten.

Davidoff stepped into the earth circle. "Tonight we will conjure Azeziz—the demon of spells and magic. The demon of *belief* in the larger world! It is he who holds all knowledge of the ways of sorcery that the dark forces *lent* to mankind in the dawn of our reign on earth. Azeziz will share with us the secrets of magic, and will then guide us toward the discovery of the perfect spell. The spell that may well be the core magical ritual from which *all* of our world's religions have sprung."

He paused to let that sink in. Trey replayed the spell in his head, verifying that it was the correct wording and not any version of the mistakes that kept showing up in Anthem's computer. It all seemed correct, and he breathed a sigh of relief.

"Azeziz will first appear to us as a sphere of pure energy and will then coalesce into a more familiar form. A form that all of us here will recognize, and one in which we will take comfort." He smiled. "Join me now as we open the doorway to knowledge that belongs jointly to all of mankind—the knowledge that we do, in truth, live in a *larger world*."

As he began the spell, Davidoff's voice was greatly amplified so that it echoed off the walls. "Come forth, Azeziz! Oh great demon, hear my plea. I call thee up by the power of this circle! By thine own glyph inscribed with thy name I summon thee."

Suddenly a ball of light burst into being inside the demon's circle. Trey blinked and gasped along with the audience. It was so bright, much brighter than what he had expected. The lighting guys were really into the moment. The ball hung in the midst of the rising smoke, pulsing with energy, changing colors like a tumbling prism, filling the air with the smell of ozone and sulfur.

Trey frowned.

Sulfur?

He shot a look at the others. Which one of those idiots added that to the special effects menu? But they were frowning, too. Bird turned to him and they studied one another for a moment. Then Bird sniffed almost comically and mouthed: *Kidd?*

Shit, thought Trey. If that vermin had worked some surprises into the show then he swore he would dig him up and kick his dead ass.

On stage, Davidoff's smile flickered as he smelled it, too. He blasted a withering and accusatory look at the darkness offstage. Right where he knew Trey would be standing.

Davidoff reclaimed his game face. "Come forth, Azeziz! Appear now that I may have council with thee. I conjure thee, ancient demon, without fear and trembling. I am not afraid as I stand within the Circle of the Earth. Come forth and manifest thyself in the circle of protection which is prepared for thee."

The globe of light pulsed and pulsed. Then there was a white-hot flash of light and suddenly a figure stood in the center of the conjuring circle.

The crowd stared goggle-eyed at the tall, portly figure with the wisps of hair drifting down from a bald pate. Laser lights sparkled from the tiny glasses perched on the bulbous nose.

Benjamin Franklin. Founder of the University of Pennsylvania.

The demon smiled.

The audience gaped and then they got the joke and burst out laughing. The hall echoed with thunderous applause as Benjamin Franklin took a bow.

Trey frowned again. He didn't remember there being a bow. Not until the end.

"Speak, O demon!" cried Davidoff as the applause drifted down to an expectant and jovial silence. "Teach us wisdom."

"Wisdom, is it?" asked Franklin. There was something a little off with the pre-recorded sound. The voice was oddly rough, gravelly. *"What wisdom would a mortal ask of a demon?"*

Davidoff was right on cue. "We seek the truth of magic," he said. "We seek to understand the mystery of faith. We seek to understand why man *believes*."

"Ah, but wisdom is costly," said Franklin, and Trey could see Davidoff's half smirk. That comment was a little hook for when the fees to access *Spellcaster* were presented. Wisdom is costly. Cute.

"We are willing to pay whatever fee you ask, O mighty demon."

"Are you indeed?" asked Franklin, and once more that was something off-script. *"How much would you truly pay to understand belief?"*

None of that was in the script.

God damn you, Kidd, thought Trey darkly, and he wondered what other surprises were laid like landmines into the program. Anthem, Bird, and Jonesy moved toward him, the four of them reconnecting, however briefly, in what they all now thought was going to be a frigging disaster. If Davidoff was made a fool of, then they were cooked. They were done.

Davidoff soldiered on, fighting to stay ahead of these new twists. "Um, yes, O demon. What is the cost of the knowledge we seek?"

"Oh, I believe you have already paid me my fee," said the demon Ben Franklin, and he smiled. *"My fee was offered up by vow if not by deed."*

He rummaged inside his coat for something.

"What's he doing?" whispered Jonesy.

Bird leaned close. "Please, God, do not let him bring out a doobie or a copy of *Hustler*."

But that's not what Franklin pulled out from under his coat flaps. He extended his arm and turned his hand palm upward to show Davidoff and everyone what he held.

Davidoff's face went slack, his eyes flaring wide.

A few people, the ones who were closest, gasped.

Then someone screamed.

The thing Franklin held was a human heart.

-11-

Davidoff said, "W-what—?"

Bird gagged.

Jonesy screamed.

Anthem said, "No . . . "

Trey felt as if he were falling.

-12-

The demon laughed.

It was not the polite, cultured laughter of an eighteenth century scientist and statesman. It was not anything they had recorded for the event.

The laughter was so loud that the dancers staggered backward, blood erupting from nostrils and ears. It buffeted the audience and the sheer force of it knocked Davidoff to his knees, cupping his hands to his ears.

The audience screamed.

Then the lights went out, plunging the whole place into shrieking darkness.

And came back on a moment later with a brilliance so shocking that everyone froze in place.

The demon turned his palm and let the heart fall to the floor with a wet *plop*.

No one moved.

The demon adjusted his glasses and smiled.

Trey whirled and ran to the tech boards. "Shut it down," he yelled. "Shut it all down. Kill the projectors. Come on—*do it!*"

The techs hit rows of switches and turned dials.

Absolutely nothing changed on stage.

"*Stop that, Trey,*" said Ben Franklin. His voice echoed everywhere.

Trey whirled.

"W-what?" he stammered.

"I said, stop it." The demon smiled. *"In fact, come out here. All of you. I want everyone to see you. The four bright lights. My helpers. My facilitators."*

Trey tried to laugh. Tried to curse. Tried to say something witty.

But his legs were moving without his control, carrying him out onto the stage. Jonesy and Anthem came with him, all in a terrified row. They came to the very edge of the circle in which the demon stood.

Bird alone remained where he was.

The audience cried out in fear.

"Hush," said the demon, and every voice was stilled. Their mouths moved but there was no sound. People tried to get out of their seats, to flee, to storm the doors; but no one could rise.

Ben Franklin chuckled mildly. He cocked an eye at Trey. *"This performance is for you. All for you."*

Trey stared at him, his mind teetering on the edge of a precipice. Davidoff, as silent as the crowd, stood nearby.

"At the risk of being glib," said the demon, *"I think it's fair to say that class is in session. You called me to provide knowledge, and I am ever delighted, as all of my kind are delighted, to bow and scrape before man and give away under duress those secrets we have spent ten million years discovering. It's what we live for. It makes us so . . . happy."*

When he said the word *happy* lights exploded overhead and showered the audience with smoking fragments that they were entirely unable to avoid. Trey and the others stood helpless at the edge of the circle.

Trey tried to speak, tried to force a single word out. With a flick of a finger the demon freed his lips and the word, "How?" burst out.

Ben Franklin nodded. *"You get a gold star for asking the right question, young Trey. Perhaps I will burn it into your skull."* He winked. *"Later."*

Trey's heart hammered with trapped frenzy.

"You wrote the script for tonight, did you not?" asked the demon. *"Then you should understand. This is your show and tell. I am here for you. So . . . you tell me."*

Suddenly Trey's mouth was moving, forming words, his tongue rebelled and shaped them, his throat gave them sound.

"A careless magician summons his own death," Trey said, but it was Davidoff's voice that issued from his throat. *"All of the materials need to be pure. Vital essences—blood, sweat, or tears—must never be allowed within the demon's circle for these form a bridge between the worlds of spirit and flesh."*

The big screens suddenly flashed with new images. Anthem. Typing, her fingers blurring. The image tightened until the focus was entirely on her fingernails. Nibbled and bitten to the quick, caked with . . .

"Blood," said Anthem, her voice a monotone.

Then Jonesy spoke but it was Davidoff's bass voice that rumbled from her throat. *"A learned magician is a quiet and solitary person. All of his learning, all of his preparation for this ritual must be played out in his head. He cannot practice his invocations because magical words each have their special power. To casually speak a spell is to open a doorway that might never be shut."*

And now the screens showed Jonesy reading the spells aloud as Anthem typed.

Trey closed his eyes. He didn't need to see any more.

"Arrogance is such a strange thing," said the demon. *"You expect it from the powerful because they believe that they are gods. But you . . . Trey, Anthem, Jonesy . . . you should have known better. You did know better. You just didn't care enough to believe that any of it mattered. Pity."*

The demon stepped toward them, crossing the line of the protective circle as if it held no power. And Trey suddenly realized that it did not. Somewhere, the ritual was flawed beyond fixing. Was it Kidd's sabotage or something deeper? From the corner of his eye Trey could see the glistening lines of tears slipping down Anthem's cheeks.

The demon paused and looked at her. *"Your sin is worse. You do believe but you fight so hard not to. You fight to be numb to the larger world so that you will be accepted as a true academic like these others. You are almost beyond saving. Teetering on the brink. If you had the chance, I wonder in which direction you would place your next step."*

A sob, silent and terrible, broke in Anthem's chest. Trey tried to say something to her, but then the demon moved to stand directly in front of him.

"You owe me thanks, my young student," said the demon. *"When the late and unlamented Mr. Kidd tried to spoil the results of your project by altering the protection spells, he caused all of this to happen. He made it happen, but not out of reverence for the forces of the universe and certainly not out of any belief in the larger world. He did it simply out of spite. He wanted no profit from your failure except the knowledge that you would be ruined. That was as unwise as it was heartless . . . and I paid him in kind."*

The demon nudged the heart on the floor. It quivered and tendrils of smoke drifted up from it. Trey tried to imagine the terror Kidd must have felt as this monster attacked him and brutalized him, and he found that he felt a splinter of compassion for Kidd.

"You pretend to be scholars," breathed the demon, *"so then here is a lesson to ponder. You think that all of religion, all of faith, all of spirit, is a cultural oddity, an accident of confusion by uneducated minds. An infection of misinformation that spread like a disease, just as man spread like a disease. You, in your arrogance,*

believe that because you do not believe that belief is nothing. You dismiss all other possibilities because they do not fit into your hypothesis. Like the scientists who say that because evolution is a truth—and it is a truth—that there is nothing divine or intelligent in the universe. Or the astronomers who say that the universe is only as large as the stones thrown by the Big Bang." He touched his lips to Trey's ear. *"Arrogance. It has always been the weakness of man. It's the thing that keeps you bound to the prison of flesh. Oh yes, bound, and it is a prison that does not need to have locked doors."*

Trey opened his eyes. His mouth was still free and he said, "What?"

The demon smiled. *"Arrogance often comes with blindness. Proof of magic surrounds you all the time. Proof that man is far more than a creature of flesh, proof that he can travel through doorways to other worlds, other states of existence. It's all around you."*

"Where?"

The screens once more filled with the images of Maori with their painted faces, and Navajo shaman and their sand paintings; medicine men in the remote Amazon, singers from among the Bushmen of Africa. As Trey watched, the images shifted and tightened so that the dominant feature in each was the eyes of these people.

These believers.

Then ten thousand other sets of eyes flashed across the screens. People of all races, all cultures, all times. Cave men and saints, simple farmers, and scholars endlessly searching the stars for a glimpse of something larger. Something there. Never giving up, never failing to believe in the possibility of the larger world. The larger universe.

Even Bird's eyes were *there*. Just for a moment.

"Can you, in your arrogance," asked the demon, *"look into these eyes and tell me with the immutable certainty of your scientific disbelief that every one of these people is deluded? That they are wrong? That they see nothing? That nothing is there to be seen? Can you stand here and look down the millennia of man's experience on earth and say that since science cannot measure what they see then they see nothing at all? Can you tell me that magic does not exist? That it has never existed? Can you, my little student, tell me that? Can you say it with total and unshakable conviction? Can you, with your scientific certitude, dismiss me into nonexistence, and with me all of the demons and angels, gods and monsters, spirits and shades who walk the infinite worlds of all of time and space?"*

Trey's heart hammered and hammered and wanted to break.

"No," he said. His voice was a ghost of a whisper.

"No," agreed the demon. "*You can't. And how much has that one word cost you, my fractured disbeliever? What, I wonder, do you believe now?"*

Tears rolled down Trey's face.

"Answer this, then," said the demon, *"why am I not bound to the circle of protection? You think that it was because Mr. Kidd played pranks with the wording? No. You found every error. In that you were diligent. And the circles and patterns were drawn with precision. So . . . why am I not bound? What element was missing from this ritual? What single thing was missing that would have given you and these other false conjurers the power to bind me?"*

Trey wanted to scream. Instead he said, "Belief."

"Belief," agreed the demon softly.

"I'm sorry," whispered Trey. "God . . . I'm sorry . . . "

The demon leaned in and his breath was scalding on Trey's cheek. *"Tell me one thing more, my little sorcerer,"* whispered the monster, *"should I believe that you truly are sorry?"*

"Y-yes."

"Should I have faith in the regrets of the faithless?"

"I'm sorry," he said. "I . . . didn't know."

The demon chuckled. *"Have you ever considered that atheism as strong as yours is itself a belief?"*

"I—"

"We all believe in something. That is what brought your kind down from the trees. That is what made you human. After all this time, how can you not understand that?"

Trey blinked and turned to look at him.

The demon said, *"You think that science is the enemy of faith. That what cannot be measured cannot be real. Can you measure what is happening now? What meter would you use? What scale?"*

Trey said nothing.

"Your project, your collection of spells. What is it to you? What is it in itself? Words? Meaningless and silly? Without worth?"

Trey dared not reply.

"Who are you to disrespect the shaman and the magus, the witch and the priest? Who are you to say that the child on his knees is a fool; or the crone on the respirator? How vast and cold is your arrogance that you despise the vow and the promise and the prayer of everyone who has ever spoken such words with a true heart?"

The demon touched Trey's chest.

"In the absence of proof you disbelieve. In the absence of proof a child will believe, and belief can change worlds. That's the power you spit upon, and in doing so you deny yourself the chance to shape the universe according to your will. You become a victim of your own close-mindedness."

Tears burned on Trey's flesh.

"Here is a secret," said the demon. *"Believe it or not, as you will. But when we whispered the secrets of evocation to your ancestors, when we taught them to make circles of protection—it was not to protect them from us. No. It was us who wanted protection from you. We swim in the waters of belief. You, and those like you, spit pollution into those waters with doubt and cynicism. With your arrogant disinterest in the ways the universe actually works. When you conjure us, we shudder."* He leaned closer. *"Tell me, little Trey, now that your faithless faith is shattered . . . if you had the power to banish me, would you?"*

Trey had to force the word out. "Yes."

"Even though that would require faith to open the doors between the worlds?"

Trey squeezed his eyes shut. "Y—yes."

"Hypocrite," said the demon, but he was laughing as he said it. *"Here endeth the lesson."*

Trey opened his eyes.

-13-

Trey felt his mouth move again. His lips formed a word.

"Username?" he asked.

Anthem looked sheepishly at him and nibbled the stub of a green fingernail. "You're going to laugh at me."

Trey stared at her. Gaped at her.

"What—?" she said, suddenly touching her face, her nose, to make sure that she didn't have anything on her. "What?"

Trey sniffed. He could taste tears in his mouth, in the back of his throat. And there was a smell in the air. Ozone and sulfur. He shook his head, trying to capture the thought that was just there, just on the edge. But . . . no, it was gone.

Weird. It felt important. It felt big.

But it was gone, whatever it was.

He took Anthem's hand and studied her fingers. There was blood caked in the edges. He glanced at the keyboard and saw the chocolate colored stains. Faint, but there.

"You got blood on the keys," he said. "You have to be careful."

"Why?"

"Because this is magic and you're supposed to be careful."

Anthem gave him a sideways look. "Oh, very funny."

"No," he said, "not really."

"What's it matter? I'll clean the keyboard."

"It matters," he said, and then for reasons he could not quite understand, at least not at the moment, he said, "We have to do it right is all."

"Do what right?"

"All of it," said Trey. "The spells. Entering them, everything. We need to get them right. Everything has to be right."

"I know, I know . . . or the program won't collate the right way and—"

"No," he said softly. "Because this stuff is important. To . . . um . . . people."

Anthem studied his face for a long moment, then she nodded.

"Okay," she said and got up to get some computer wipes.

Trey sat there, staring at the hazy outline of his reflection. He could see his features, but somehow, in some indefinable way, he looked different.

Or, at least he believed he did.

❧

Jonathan Maberry is a Bram Stoker Award-winning author, writing teacher, and motivational speaker. Among his novels are *Ghost Road Blues*, *Dead Man's Song*, *Bad Moon Rising*, and *Patient Zero*. *Fire & Ash*, fourth in the Benny Imura series, was published last year; *Fall of Night*, sequel to *Dead of Night*, will be released later this year. He is co-editor of the anthology *Redneck Zombies From Outer Space* and editor of the forthcoming dark fantasy anthology, *Out of Tune*. His has written comics and non-fiction works as well.

The Cities: *Detroit and Kalamazoo, Michigan.*

The Magic: *Children growing up in our unfair, ever-dangerous world. One finds guidance in divination based on the I Ching and Ifa, but there's always a cost. Only questions are: who is going to pay and how much?*

WALLAMELON

Nisi Shawl

"Baby, baby, baby! Baby, baby, baby!" Cousin Alphonse must have thought he looked like James Brown. He looked like what he was, just a little boy with a big peanut head, squirming around, kicking up dust in the driveway.

Oneida thought about threatening to tell on him for messing his pants up. Even Alphonse ought to know better. He had worn holes in both his knees, begging "Please, please, please" into the broken microphone he'd found in Mr. Early's trash barrel. And she'd heard a loud rip the last time he did the splits, though nothing showed. Yet.

"'Neida! Alphonse! Come see what me an Mercy Sanchez foun!" Kevin Curtis ran along the sidewalk toward them, arms windmilling, shirt-tails flapping. He stopped several feet off, as soon as he saw he had their attention. "Come *on*!"

Oneida stood up from the pipe-rail fence slowly, with the full dignity of her ten years. One decade. She was the oldest kid on the block, not counting teenagers. She had certain responsibilities, like taking care of Alphonse.

The boys ran ahead of her as she walked, and circled back again like little dogs. Kevin urged her onto the path that cut across the vacant lot beside his house. Mercy was standing on a pile of rubble half the way through, her straight hair shining in the noonday sun like a long, black mirror. She was pointing down at something Oneida couldn't see from the path, something small, something so wonderful it made sad Mercy smile.

"Wallamelons," Kevin explained as they left the path. "Grown all by they selves; aint nobody coulda put em there."

"Watermelons," Oneida corrected him automatically.

The plant grew out from under a concrete slab. At first all she could see was its broad leaves, like green hearts with scalloped edges. Mercy pushed these aside to reveal the real treasure: four fat globes, dark and light stripes swelling in their middles and vanishing into one another at either end. They were watermelons, all right. Each one was a little larger than Oneida's fist.

"It's a sign," said Mercy, her voice soft as a baby's breath. "A sign from the Blue Lady."

Oneida would have expected the Blue Lady to send them roses instead, or something prettier, something you couldn't find in an ordinary supermarket. But Mercy knew more about the Blue Lady, because she and her half-brother Emilio had been the ones to tell Oneida about her in the first place.

"Four of them and four of us." Oneida looked up at Mercy to see if she understood the significance.

Mercy nodded. "We can't let no one else know about this."

"How come?" asked Alphonse. Because he was mildly retarded he needed help understanding a lot of things.

Oneida explained it to him. "You tell anybody else, they'll mess up everything. Keep quiet, and you'll have a whole watermelon all to yourself."

"I get a wallamelon all my own?"

"*Wa-ter-mel-on*," Oneida enunciated.

"How long it take till they ready?"

They decided it would be at least a week before the fruit was ripe enough to eat. Every day they met at Mizz Nichols's.

Mercy's mother had left her here and gone back to Florida to be with her husband. It was better for Mercy to live at her grandmother's, away from so much crime. And Michigan had less discrimination.

Mizz Nichols didn't care what her granddaughter was up to as long as it didn't interrupt her TV watching or worse yet, get her called away from work.

Mercy seemed to know what the watermelon needed instinctively. She had them fill half-gallon milk bottles from the garden hose and set these to "cure" behind the garage. In the dusky hours after Aunt Elise had picked up Cousin Alphonse, after Kevin had to go inside, Mercy and Oneida smuggled the heavy glass containers to their secret spot. They only broke one.

When the boys complained at being left out of this chore, Mercy set them to picking dried grass. They stuffed this into old pillowcases and put these underneath the slowly fattening fruits to protect them from the gravelly ground.

The whole time, Mercy seemed so happy. She sang songs about the Blue Lady, how in far away dangerous places she saved children from evil spirits and grownups. Oneida tried to sing along with her, but the music kept changing, though the stories stayed pretty much the same.

There was the one about the girl who was standing on the street corner somewhere down South when a car full of men with guns went by, shooting everybody. But the Blue Lady saved her. Or there was a boy whose mom was so sick he had to stay with his crazy aunt because his dad was already dead in a robbery. When the aunt put poison in his food he ran away, and the Blue Lady showed him where to go and took care of him till he got to his grandparents house in Boston, all the way from Washington, DC.

All you had to do was call her name.

One week stretched, unbelievably, to two. The watermelons were as large as cereal bowls. As party balloons. But they seemed pitiful compared to the giant blimps in the bins in front of Farmer Jack's.

Obviously, their original estimate was off. Alphonse begged and whined so much, though, that Mercy finally let him pick and open his own melon. It was hard and pale inside, no pinker than a pack of Wrigley's gum. It tasted like scouring powder.

Oneida knew she'd wind up sharing part of her personal, private watermelon with Alphonse, if only to keep him from crying, or telling another kid, or a grown-up even. It was the kind of sacrifice a mature ten-year-old expected to make. It would be worth it, though. Half a watermelon was still a feast.

They tended the Blue Lady's vine with varying degrees of impatience and diligence. Three weeks, now. How much longer would it take till the remaining watermelons reached what Oneida called "The absolute peak of perfection?"

They never found out.

The Monday after the Fourth of July, Oneida awoke to the low grumble of heavy machinery. The noise was from far enough away that she could have ignored it if she wanted to stay asleep. Instead, she leaned out till her fingers fit under the edge of her bunk's frame, curled down, and flipped herself so she sat on the empty bottom bunk.

She peeked into her parents' bedroom. Her father was still asleep; his holstered gun gleamed darkly in the light that crept in around the lowered shade. She closed the door quietly. Her dad worked hard. He was the first Negro on the police force.

Oneida ate a bowl of cereal, re-reading the book on the back of the box about the adventures of Twinkle-toes the Elephant. Baby stuff, but she was too lazy to get up and locate a real book.

When she was done, she checked the square dial of the alarm clock on the kitchen counter. Quarter to nine. In forty-five minutes her mother would be home from the phone company. She'd make a big breakfast. Even if Oneida wasn't hungry, it felt good to talk with Mom while she cooked it. Especially if Dad woke up; with Royal and Limoges off at Big Mama's, the three of them discussed important things like voting rights and integration.

But there was time for a quick visit to the vacant lot before then.

The sidewalk was still cool beneath the black locust trees. The noise that had wakened her sounded a lot louder out here. It grew and grew, the closer she got to the Curtis's. And then she saw the source: an ugly yellow monster machine roaring through the lot, riding up and down over the humps of rubble like a cowboy on a bucking bronco. And Kevin was just standing there on the sidewalk, watching.

There were stones all around. She picked up a whole fistful and threw them, but it was too far. She grabbed some more and Kevin did too. They started yelling and ran toward the monster, throwing stones. It had a big blade. It was a bulldozer, it was pushing the earth out of its way wherever it wanted to go. She couldn't even hear her own shouting over the awful sound it made. Rocks flew out of her hands. They hit it. They hit it again. The man on top, too.

Then someone was holding her arms down. She kept yelling and Kevin ran away. Suddenly she heard herself. The machine was off. The white man from on top of it was standing in front of her telling her to shut up, shut up or he'd have her arrested.

Where was the Blue Lady?

There was only Mizz Curtis, in her flowered housedress, with her hair up in pink curlers. No one was holding Oneida's arms anymore, but she was too busy crying to get away. Another white man asked what her name was.

"Oneida Brandy," Mizz Curtis said. "Lives down the street. Oneida, what on Earth did you think you were doing, child?"

"What seems to be the problem?"

Dad. She looked up to be sure. He had his police hat on and his gun belt, but regular pants and a T-shirt instead of the rest of his uniform. He gazed at her without smiling while he talked to the two white men.

So she *was* in trouble.

After a while, though, the men stopped paying attention to Oneida. They were talking about the rich white people they worked for, and all the things they could do to anyone who got in their way. Kevin's mom gave her a crumpled up Kleenex to blow her nose on, and she realized all the kids in the neighborhood were there.

Including Mercy Sanchez. She looked like a statue of herself. Like she was made of wood. Of splinters.

Then the white men's voices got loud, and they were laughing. They got in a green pick-up parked on the easement and drove off, leaving their monster in the middle of the torn-up lot.

Her father's face was red; they must have said something to make him mad before they went away. But all Dad did was thank Mizz Curtis for sending Kevin over to wake him up.

They met Mom on the way home. She was still in her work clothes and high heels, walking fast. She stopped and stared at Dad's hat and gun. "Vinny?"

"Little brush with the law, Joanne. Our daughter here's gonna explain everything over breakfast."

Oneida tried. But Mercy had made her swear not to tell any grown-ups about the Blue Lady, which meant her story sounded not exactly stupid, but silly. "All that fuss about a watermelon!" Mom said. "As if we don't have the money to buy one, if that's what you want!"

Dad said the white men were going to get quite a surprise when they filed their complaint about him impersonating an officer. He said they were breaking the law themselves by not posting their building permit. He said off-duty policemen went around armed all the time.

Aunt Elise brought over Cousin Alphonse. They had to play in the basement even though it was such a nice day outside. And Kevin Curtis and Mercy Sanchez weren't allowed to come over. Or anybody.

After about eighty innings of "Ding-Dong, Delivery," Oneida felt like she was going crazy with boredom. She was sorry she'd ever made the game up; all you did was put a blanket over yourself and say "Ding-dong, delivery," and the other player was supposed to guess what you were. Of course Alphonse adored it.

Mom let them come upstairs and turn on the TV in time for the afternoon movie. It was an old one, a gangster story, which was good. Oneida hated gangster movies, but that was the only kind Cousin Alphonse would watch all the way through. She could relax and read her book.

Then Mom called her into the bedroom. Dad was there, too. He hadn't gone to his other job. They had figured out what they were going to do with her.

They were sending her to Detroit, to Big Mama. She should have known. The two times she spent the night there she'd had to share a bed with Limoges, and there hadn't been one book in the entire house.

"What about Cousin Alphonse?" she asked. "How am I supposed to take care of him if I'm in Detroit?"

"You just concentrate on learning to take better care of yourself, young lady."

Which wasn't a fair thing for Mom to say.

After dark, Oneida snuck out. She had stayed inside all day, exactly as she'd promised. Now it was night. No one would expect her to slip the screen out of her bedroom window and squirm out onto the fresh-mowed lawn. That wasn't the kind of thing Oneida ever did. She wouldn't get caught.

The big orange moon hung low over Lincoln Elementary. Away from the streetlights, in the middle of the ravaged vacant lot, it made its own shadows. They hid everything, the new hills and the old ones. It was probably going to be impossible to find the watermelon vine. If it had even survived the bulldozer's assault.

But Oneida walked to the lot's middle anyway. From there, she saw Mercy. She stood stock still, over on Oneida's left, looking down at something; it was the same way she'd stood the day they found the vine. Except then, the light had come from above, from the sun. Now something much brighter than the moon shone from below, up into her face. Something red and blue and green and white, something radiant, moving like water, like a dream.

Oneida ran toward whatever it was. She tripped on a stone block, stumbled through the dark. "Mercy!" she shouted as she topped a hill. Mercy nodded, but Oneida didn't think it was because she'd heard her. She ran on recklessly, arriving just as the light began to fade, as if, one by one, a bunch of birthday candles were being blown out.

Oneida bent forward to see better. The light came from a little cave of jewels about the size of a gym ball. A blue heart wavered at its center, surrounded by tiny wreaths of red flowers and flickering silver stars. As she watched, they dwindled and were gone. All that was left was a shattered watermelon, scooped out to the rind.

Magic! Oneida met Mercy's eyes. They had seen real magic! She smiled. But Mercy didn't.

"Blue Lady say she can't take care of Emilio no more. He too big." Emilio had been thirteen last New Year's, when he left with Mercy's mom. Mizz Sanchez hadn't been so worried about him; bad neighborhoods weren't so bad for bad boys. But now . . .

Mercy looked down again at the left behind rind.

Oneida decided to tell Mercy her own news about going to Detroit Saturday and being on punishment till then. It was difficult to see her face; her beautiful hair kept hanging in the way. Was she even listening?

"You better not go an forget me, 'Neida."

What was she talking about? "I'll only be there until school starts! September!" As if she wouldn't remember Mercy forever and ever, anyway.

Mercy turned and walked a few steps away. Oneida was going to follow her, but Mercy stopped on her own. Faced her friend again. Held out her hand. There was something dark in her pale palm. "I'ma give you these now, in case—"

Oneida took what Mercy offered her, an almost weightless mass, cool and damp. "I can sneak out again," she said. Why not?

"Sure. The Blue Lady, though, she want you to have these, an this way I won't be worryin."

Watermelon seeds. That's what they were. Oneida put them in her pajama pocket. What she had been looking for when she came here.

She took a deep breath. It went into her all shaky and came out in one long whoosh. Till September wasn't her whole life. "Maybe Mom and Dad will change their mind and let you come over."

"Maybe." Mercy sounded as if she should clear her throat. As if she were crying, which was something she never did, no matter how sad she looked. She started walking away again.

"Hey, I'll send a card on your birthday," Oneida yelled after her, because she couldn't think of what else to say.

Wednesday the Chief of Police put Dad on suspension.

That meant they could drive to Detroit early, as soon as Dad woke up on Thursday. Oneida helped her mom with the last-minute packing. There was no time to do laundry.

Dad didn't care. "They got water and electricity in Detroit last time I checked, Joanne, and Big Mama must have at least one washing machine."

They drove and drove. It took two whole hours. Oneida knew they were getting close when they went by the giant tire, ten stories tall. There were more and more buildings, bigger and bigger ones. Then came the billboard with a huge stove sticking out of it, and they were there.

Detroit was the fifth largest city in the United States. Big Mama lived on a street called Davenport, like a couch, off Woodward. Her house was dark and cool inside, without much furniture. Royal answered the door and led them back to the kitchen, the only room that ever got any sunshine.

"Yall made good time," said Big Mama. "Dinner's just gettin started." She squeezed Oneida's shoulders and gave her a cup of lime Kool-Aid.

"Can I go finish watching cartoons?" asked Royal.

"Your mama an daddy an sister jus drove all this way; you aint got nothin to say to em?

"Limoges over at the park with Luemma and Ivy Joe," she told Mom and Dad. They sent Royal to bring her home and sat down at the table, lighting cigarettes.

Oneida drank her Kool-aid quickly and rinsed out her empty cup. She wandered back through the house to the front door. From a tv in another room, boingy sounds like bouncing springs announced the antics of some orange cat or indigo dog.

Mercy watched soap operas. Maybe Oneida would be able to convince the other children those were more fun. Secret, forbidden shows grown-ups didn't want you to see, about stuff they said you'd understand when you got older.

Limoges ran over the lawn shouting "'Neida! 'Neida!" At least *somebody* was glad to see her. Oneida opened the screen door. "I thought you wasn't comin till Saturday!"

"Weren't," she corrected her little sister. "I thought you weren't."

"What happened?"

"Dad got extra days off. They're in the kitchen." Royal and the other kids were nowhere in sight. Oneida followed Limoges back to find their parents.

It was hot; the oven was on. Big Mama was rolling out dough for biscuits and heating oil. She had Oneida and Limoges take turns shaking chicken legs in a bag of flour. Then they set the dining room table and scrounged chairs from the back porch and, when that wasn't enough, from Big Mama's bedroom upstairs. Only Oneida was allowed to go in.

It smelled different in there than the whole rest of the house. Better. Oneida closed the door behind her.

There were more things, too. Bunches of flowers with ribbons wrapped around them hung from the high ceiling. Two tables overflowed with indistinct objects, which pooled at their feet. The tables flanked a tall, black rectangle—something shiny, with a thin cloth flung over it, she saw, coming closer. A mirror? She reached to move aside the cloth, but a picture on the table to her right caught her eye.

It was of what she had seen that night in the vacant lot. A blue heart floated in a starry sky, with flowers around it. Only these flowers were pink and gold. And in the middle of the heart, a door had been cut.

The door's crystal knob seemed real. She touched it. It was. It turned between her thumb and forefinger. The door opened.

The Blue Lady. Oneida had never seen her before, but who else could this be a painting of? Her skin was pale blue, like the sky; her hair rippled down dark and smooth all the way to her ankles. Her long dress was blue and white, with pearls and diamonds sewn on it in swirling lines. She wore a cape with a hood, and her hands were holding themselves out as if she had just let go of something, a bird or a kiss.

The Blue Lady.

So some grown-ups did know.

Downstairs, the screen door banged. Oneida shut the heart. She shouldn't be snooping in Big Mama's bedroom. What if she were caught?

The chair she was supposed to be bringing was back by where she'd come in. She'd walked right past it.

The kitchen was crowded with noisy kids. Ivy Joe had hit a home run playing baseball with the boys. Luemma had learned a new dance called the Monkey. Oneida helped Limoges roll her pants legs down and made Royal wash his hands. No one asked what had taken her so long upstairs.

Mom and Dad left right after dinner. Oneida promised to behave herself. She did, too. She only went in Big Mama's bedroom with permission.

Five times that first Friday, Big Mama sent Oneida up to get something for her.

Oneida managed not to touch anything. She stood again and again, though, in front of the two tables, cataloguing their contents. On the right, alongside the portrait of the Blue Lady were several tall glass flasks filled with colored fluids; looping strands of pearls wound around their slender necks. A gold-rimmed saucer held a dark, mysterious liquid, with a pile of what seemed to be pollen at the center of its glossy surface.

A red-handled axe rested on the other table. It had two sharp, shiny edges. No wonder none of the other kids could come in here.

On every trip, Oneida spotted something else. She wondered how long it would take to see everything.

On the fifth trip, Oneida turned away from the huge white wing leaning against the table's front legs (how had she missed *that* the first four times?) to find Big Mama watching her from the doorway.

"I—I didn't—"

"You aint messed with none a my stuff, or I'd a known it. S'all right; I spected you'd be checkin out my altars, chile. Why I sent you up here."

Altars? Like in a Catholic church like Aunt Elise went to? The two tables had no crucifixes, no tall lecterns for a priest to pray from, but evidently they were altars, because there was nothing else in the room that Big Mama could be talking about. It was all normal stuff, except for the flower bunches dangling down from the ceiling.

"Then I foun these." Big Mama held out one hand as she moved into the bedroom and shut the door behind herself. "Why you treat em so careless-like? Leavin em in your dirty pajamas pocket! What if I'd a had Luemma or Ivy Joe washin clothes?"

The seeds. Oneida accepted them again. They were dry, now, and slightly sticky.

"Them girls don't know no more about mojo than Albert Einstein. Less, maybe."

Was mojo magic? The seeds might be magic, but Oneida had no idea what they were for or how to use them. Maybe Big Mama did. Oneida peeped up at her face as if the answer would appear there.

"I see. You neither. That niece a mine taught you nothin. Aint that a surprise." Her tone of voice indicated just the opposite.

Big Mama's niece was Oneida's mother.

"Go down on the back porch and make sure the rinse cycle startin all right. Get us somethin to drink. Then come up here again and we do us a bit a discussin."

When Oneida returned she carried a pitcher of iced tea with lemon, a bowl of sugar, and two glasses on a tray. She balanced the tray on her hip so she could knock and almost dropped it. Almost.

It took Big Mama a moment to let her in. "Leave that on the chair seat," she said when she saw the tray. "Come over nex the bed."

A little round basket with a lid and no handles sat on the white chenille spread. A fresh scent rose from its tight coils. "Sea grass," said Big Mama in answer to Oneida's question. "Wove by my gramma. That aint what I want you to pay attention to, though. What's inside—"

Was a necklace. Made of watermelon seeds.

"Aint everybody has this in they backgroun. Why I was sure your mama musta said somethin. She proud, though. Too proud, turn out, to even do a little thing like that, am I right?"

Oneida nodded. Mom hated her to talk about magic. Superstition, she called it. She didn't even like it when Oneida brought books of fairy tales home from the library.

"How you come up with these, then?"

"I—a friend."

"A friend."

"Mercy Sanchez."

"This Mercy, she blood? Kin?" she added, when Oneida's confusion showed.

"No."

"She tell you how to work em?"

"No." Should she break her promise?

"Somethin you hidin. Can't be keepin secrets from Big Mama."

Her picture was there, on the altar. "Mercy said they came from the Blue Lady."

"Blue Lady. That what you call her." Big Mama's broad forehead smoothed out, getting rid of wrinkles Oneida had assumed were always there. "Well, she certainly is. The Blue Lady."

Oneida realized why no one but Mizz Curtis and Dad had come to her rescue when the white men tried to arrest her: for the Blue Lady to appear in person, you were supposed to call her, using her real name. Which Mercy and Emilio had never known.

"What do you call her?"

"Yemaya."

Oneida practiced saying it to herself while she poured the iced tea and stirred in three spoons of sugar for each of them. Yeh-mah-yah. It was strange, yet easy. Easy to say. Easy to remember. Yeh-mah-yah.

She told Big Mama everything.

"Hmmph." Big Mama took a long drink of tea. "You think you able to do what I tell you to?"

Oneida nodded. Of course she could.

Big Mama closed the curtains and lit a white candle in a jar, putting a metal tube over its top. Holes in the sides let through spots of light the shape of six-pointed stars. She made Oneida fill a huge shell with water from the bathroom and sprinkled it on both their heads. Oneida brought the chair so Big Mama could sit in front of Yemaya's altar. She watched while Big Mama twirled the necklace of watermelon seeds around in the basket's lid and let it go.

"Awright. Look like Yemaya say I be teachin you."

"Can I—"

"Four questions a day. That's all I'ma answer. Otherwise you jus haveta listen closer to what I say."

Oneida decided to ask anyway. "What were you doing?"

"Divinin. Special way a speakin, more important, a hearin what Yemaya an Shango wanna tell me."

"Will I learn that? Who's Shango?"

"Shango Yemaya's son. We start tomorrow. See how much you able to take in." Big Mama held up her hand, pink palm out. "One more question is all you got for today. Might wanna use it later."

They left the bedroom to hang the clean laundry from the clothesline, under trellises heavy with blooming vines. In the machine on the back porch behind them, a new load sloshed away. Royal was watching TV; the rest of the kids were over at the park. Oneida felt the way she often did after discussing adult topics with her parents. It was a combination of coziness and exhilaration, as if she were tucked safe and warm beneath the feathers of a high-soaring bird. A soft breeze lifted the legs of her pajama bottoms, made the top flap its arms as if it were flying.

Mornings were for housework. Oneida wasted one whole question finding that out.

Sundays they went to the Detroit Institute of Arts. Not to church. "God aint in there. Only reason to go to church is so people don't talk bad about you," Big Mama told them. "Anything they gone say about me they already said it." They got dressed up the same as everyone else in the neighborhood, nodded and waved at the families who had no feud with Big Mama, even exchanging remarks with those walking their direction, toward Cass. But then they headed north by themselves.

Big Mama ended each trip through the exhibits in the museum's tea room. She always ordered a chicken salad sandwich with the crusts cut off. Ivy Joe and Luemma sat beside her, drinking a black cow apiece. Royal drew on all their napkins, floppy-eared rabbits and mean-looking monsters.

Oneida's favorite part to go to was the gift shop. Mainly because they had so many beautiful books, but also because she could touch things in there. Own them, if she paid. Smaller versions of the paintings on the walls, of the huge weird statues that resembled nothing on Earth except themselves.

The second Sunday, she bought Mercy's birthday card there. It was a postcard, actually, but bigger than most. The French lady on the front had sad, soft eyes like Mercy's. On the back, Oneida told her how she was learning "lots of stuff." It would have been nice to say more; not on a postcard, though, where anyone would be able to read it.

In fact, in the hour a day Big Mama consented to teach her, Oneida couldn't begin to tackle half what she wanted to know. Mostly she memorized: prayers; songs; long, often incomprehensible stories.

Big Mama gave her a green scarf to wrap the seeds in. She said to leave them on Yemaya's altar since Oneida shared a room with the three other girls. After that, she seemed to forget all about them. They were right there, but she never seemed to notice them. Her own necklace had disappeared. Oneida asked where it was three days in a row.

"That's for me to know and you to find out," Big Mama answered every time.

Oneida saved up a week's worth of questions. She wrote them on a pad of paper, pale purple with irises along the edges, which she'd bought at the gift shop:

1. *Is your necklace in the house?*
2. *Is it in this room?*
3. *Is it in your closet?*
4. *Under the bed?*
5. *In your dresser?*

And so on, with lines drawn from one to another to show which to ask next, depending on whether the response was yes or no. On a separate page she put bonus questions in case Big Mama was so forthcoming some of the others became unnecessary. These included why her brother had hardly any chores, and what was the name of Yemaya's husband, who had never turned up in any story.

But when Big Mama called Oneida upstairs, she wound up not using any of them, because there on the bed was the basket again, open, with the necklace inside. "Seem like you learnt somethin about when to hole your peace," said Big Mama. "I know you been itchin to get your hands on my eleke." That was an African word for necklace. "Fact that you managed to keep quiet about it one entire week mean you ready for this."

It was only Oneida's seeds; she recognized the scarf they were wrapped in. Was she going to have to put them somewhere else, now? Reluctantly, she set her pad on the bed and took them out of Big Mama's hands, trying to hide her disappointment.

"Whynchou open it?"

Inside was another eleke, almost identical to Big Mama's. The threads that bound the black and brown seeds together were whiter, the necklace itself not quite as long.

Hers. Her eleke. Made out of Mercy's gift, the magic seeds from the Blue Lady.

"So. I'ma teach you how to ask questions with one a two answers, yes or no.

Bout what you *gotta* know. What you *gotta*. An another even more important lesson: why you better off not tryin to fine out every little thing you think you wanna."

Oneida remembered her manners. "Thank you, Big Mama."

"You welcome, baby." Big Mama stood and walked to the room's other end, to the mirror between her two altars. "Come on over here an get a good look." Stepping aside, she pulled the black cloth off the mirror.

The reflection seemed darker than it should be. Oneida barely saw herself. Then Big Mama edged in behind her, shining. By that light, Oneida's thick black braids stood out so clearly every single hair escaping them cast its own shadow on the glass.

"Mos mirrors don't show the difference that sharp." Big Mama pushed Oneida's bangs down against her forehead. "Folks will notice it anyhow."

Oneida glanced back over her shoulder. No glow. Regular daylight. Ahead again. A radiant woman and a ghostly little girl.

This was the second magic Oneida had ever seen. Mercy better believe me when I tell her, she thought. It was as if Big Mama was a vampire, or more accurately, its exact opposite. "How—" She stopped herself, not quite in time.

"S'all right. Some questions you need an answer." But she stayed silent for several seconds.

"More you learn, brighter you burn. You know, it's gonna show. People react all kinda ways to that. They shun you, or they forget how to leave you alone. Wanna ask you all kinda things, then complain about the cost.

"What you gotta remember, Oneida, is this: there is always a price. *Always* a price. Only questions is who gonna pay it an how much."

No Mercy.

When Oneida got home from Detroit, her friend was gone. Had been the whole time. Not moved out, but run away. Mizz Nichols didn't know where. Florida, maybe, if she had left to take care of Emilio like she was saying.

Mizz Nichols gave Oneida back the birthday card. Which Mercy had never seen.

The white people's house next to Mizz Curtis's was almost finished being built. Everyone was supposed to keep away from it, especially Cousin Alphonse. While she'd been in Detroit, unable to watch him, he had jumped into the big basement hole and broke his collarbone. Even with his arm in a sling, Aunt Elise had barely been able to keep him away. Why? Was it the smell of fresh cut wood, or the way you could see through the walls and how everything inside them fit together? Or just the thought that it was somewhere he wasn't allowed to go?

No one wanted any trouble with white people. Whatever the cause of Alphonse's latest fascination, Oneida fought it hard. She took him along when she walked Limoges to Vacation Bible School and managed to keep him occupied on Lincoln's playground all morning. After school, they walked from there all the way to the river, stopping at Topoll's to buy sausage sandwiches for lunch.

So successful was this expedition that they were a little late getting home. Oneida had to carry Limoges eight blocks on her back. Aunt Elise was already parked in front and talking angrily to Dad in the TV room. It was all right, though. She was just mad about the house. She thought the people building it should put a big fence around it. She thought one of their kids would get killed there before long. She thanked Jesus, Mary, and Joseph. Oneida had enough sense to keep the others away from it.

But after dark, Oneida went there without telling anyone. Alone.

Below the hole where the picture window would go, light from the street lamp made a lopsided square. She opened up her green scarf and lifted her eleke in both hands.

Would it tell her what she wanted to know? What would be the price?

Twirl it in the air. Let it fall. Count the seeds: so many with their pointed ends up, so many down. Compare the totals.

The answer was no. No running away for Oneida. She should stay here.

Her responsibility for Cousin Alphonse—that had to be the reason. The Blue Lady made sure kids got taken care of.

Would Mercy return, then?

Yes.

When? Before winter?

No.

Oneida asked and asked. With each response her heart and hands grew colder. Not at Christmas. Not next summer. Not next autumn.

When? And where was she? There were ways to ask other questions, with answers besides yes or no, but Big Mama said she was too young to use those.

Finally she gave up guessing and flung the necklace aside. No one should see her this way. Crying like a baby. She was a big girl, biggest on the block.

"Yemaya. Yemaya." Why was she saying that, the Blue Lady's name? Oneida had never had a chance to tell Mercy what it was. It wouldn't do any good to say it now, when no one was in danger. She hoped.

Eventually, she was able to stop. She wiped her eyes with the green scarf. On the floor, scattered around the necklace, were several loose watermelon seeds. But her eleke was unbroken.

Yemaya was trying to tell Oneida something. Eleven seeds. Eleven years? Age eleven? It was an answer. She clung to that idea. An answer, even if she couldn't understand it.

On the phone, Big Mama only instructed her to get good grades in school, do what her mama and daddy said, and bring the seeds with her, and they would see.

But the following summer was the riots. No visit to Big Mama's.

So it was two years later that Mom and Dad drove down Davenport. The immediate neighborhood, though isolated by the devastation surrounding it, had survived more or less intact.

Big Mama's block looked exactly the same. The vines surrounding her house hung thick with heavy golden blooms. Ivy Joe and Luemma reported that at the riot's height, the last week of July, streams of U.S. Army tanks had turned aside at Woodward, splitting apart to grind along Stimson and Selden, joining up again on Second. Fires and sirens had also flowed around them; screams and shots were audible, but just barely.

Thanks to Big Mama. Everyone knew that.

Oneida didn't understand why this made the people who lived there mad. Many of them wouldn't even walk on the same side of the street as Big Mama any more. It was weirder than the way the girls at Oneida's school acted.

Being almost always alone, that was the price she'd paid for having her questions answered. It didn't seem like much. Maybe there'd be worse costs, later, after she learned other, more important things. Besides, some day Mercy would come back.

The next afternoon, her lessons resumed. She had wrapped the eleven extra seeds in the same scarf as her eleke. When Big Mama saw them, she held out her hand and frowned.

"Yeah. Right." Big Mama brought out her own eleke. "Ima ask Yemaya why she wanna give you these, what they for. Watch me."

Big Mama had finally agreed to show her how to ask questions with answers other than yes or no.

Big Mama swirled her necklace around in the basket top. On the altar, the silver-covered candle burned steadily. But the room brightened and darkened quickly as the sun appeared and disappeared behind fast-moving clouds and wind-whipped leaves.

"It start out the same," Big Mama said, "lif it up an let it go." With a discreet rattle, the necklace fell. "Now we gotta figure out where the sharp ends pointin," she said. "But we dividin it in four directions: north, south, east, an west."

Oneida wrote the totals in her notebook: two, four, five, and five.

"An we do it four times for every question."

Below the first line of numbers came four, one, seven, and four; then six, zero, two, and eight; and three, three, seven, and three.

"Now add em up."

North was fifteen, south was eight, east was twenty-one, and west was twenty.

Big Mama shut her eyes a moment and nodded. "Soun good. That mean—" The brown eyes opened again, sparkling. "Yemaya say 'What you *think* you do with seeds? Plant em!' "

Oneida learned that the numbers referred to episodes in those long, incomprehensible stories she'd had to memorize. She practiced interpreting them. Where should she plant the seeds? All around the edges of her neighborhood. When? One year and a day from now. Who could she have help her? Only Alphonse. How much would it cost? Quite a bit, but it would be worth it. Within the Wallamelons' reach, no one she loved would be hurt, ever again.

Two more years. The house built on the vacant lot was once again empty. Its first and only tenants fled when the vines Oneida planted went wild, six months after they moved in. The house was hers, now, no matter what the mortgage said.

Oneida even had a key, stolen from the safebox that remained on the porch long after the real estate company lost all hope of selling a haunted house in a haunted neighborhood. She unlocked the side door, opening and shutting it on slightly reluctant hinges. The family that had briefly lived here had left their curtains. In the living room, sheer white fabric stirred gently when she opened a window for fresh air. And leaned out of it, waiting.

Like the lace of a giantess, leaves covered the housefront in a pattern of repeating hearts. Elsewhere in the neighborhood, sibling plants, self-sown from those she'd first planted around the perimeter, arched from phone pole to lamp post, encircling her home. Keeping it safe. So Mercy could return.

At first Mom had wanted to move out. But nowhere else Negroes could live in this town would be any better, Dad said. Besides, it wasn't all that bad. Even Aunt Elise admitted Cousin Alphonse was calmer, better off, here behind the vines. Mom eventually agreed to stay put and see if Dad's promotion ever came through.

That was taking a long time. Oneida was secretly glad. It would be so much harder to do what she had to do if her family moved. To come here night after night, as her eleke had shown her she must. To be patient. Till—

Then.

She saw her. Walking up the street. As Yemaya had promised. And this was the night, and Oneida was here for it, her one chance.

She waved. Mercy wasn't looking her way, though. She kept on, headed for Oneida's house, it looked like.

Oneida jerked at the handle of the front door. It smacked hard against the chain she'd forgotten to undo. She slammed it shut again, slid the chain free, and stumbled down the steps.

Mercy was halfway up the block. The noise must have startled her. No way Oneida'd be able to catch up. "Mercy! Mercy Sanchez!" She ran hopelessly, sobbing.

Mercy stopped. She turned. Suddenly uncertain, Oneida slowed. Would Mercy have cut her hair that way? Worn that black leather jacket?

But who else could it be?

"Please, please!" Oneida had no idea what she was saying, or who she was saying it to. She was running again and then she was there, hugging her, and it *was* her. Mercy. Home.

Mercy. Acting like it was no big deal to show up again after disappearing for four years.

"I tole you," she insisted, sitting cross-legged on the floorboards of the empty living room. One small white candle flickered between them, supplementing the streetlight. "Emilio axed me could I come help him. He was havin trouble . . . " She trailed off. "It was this one group of kids hasslin his friends . . . "

"All you said before you left was about how the Blue Lady—"

"'Neida, mean to say you aint forgot *none* a them games we played?!" Scornfully.

The price had been paid.

It was as if Oneida were swimming, completely underwater, and putting out her hand and touching Mercy, who swore up and down she was not wet. Who refused to admit that the Blue Lady was real, that she, at least, had seen her. When Oneida tried to show her some of what she'd learned, Mercy nodded once, then interrupted, asking if she had a smoke.

Oneida got a cigarette from the cupboard where she kept her offerings.

"So how long are you here for?" It sounded awful, what Mom would say to some distant relative she'd never met before.

"Dunno. Emilio gonna be outta circulation—things in Miami different now. Here, too, hunh? Seem like we on the set a some monster movie."

Oneida would explain about that later. "What about your mom?" Even worse, the kind of question a parole officer might ask.

Mercy snorted. "She aint wanna have nothin to do with him *or* me. For years."

"Mizz Nichols—" Oneida paused. Had Mercy heard?

"Yeah, I know. Couldn make the funeral." She stubbed out her cigarette on the bottom of her high-top, then rolled the butt between her right thumb and forefinger, straightening it. "Dunno why I even came here. Dumb. Probably the first place anybody look. If they wanna fine me." Mercy glanced up, and her eyes were exactly the same, deep and sad. As the ocean. As the sky.

"They won't." The shadow of a vine's stray tendril caressed Mercy's cheek. "They won't."

∽

Nisi Shawl's collection *Filter House* was a 2009 Tiptree Award winner; her stories have been published at *Strange Horizons*, in *Asimov's*, and in anthologies including both volumes of *Dark Matter*. She was WisCon 35's Guest of Honor. She co-edited *Strange Matings: Science Fiction, Feminism, African American Voices, and Octavia E. Butler* and co-authored *Writing the Other: A Practical Approach*. Shawl co-founded the Carl Brandon Society and serves on Clarion West's board of directors. Her Belgian Congo steampunk novel *Everfair* features a character partially modeled on E. Nesbit, author of the original *Magic City*; it's due out in 2015 from Tor. Her website is www.nisishawl.com.

The City: *Providence, Rhode Island.*

The Magic: *Every tale must have its end, but when all else fails an author can always go to see fairies who advertize: "Endings Guaranteed."*

-30-

Caitlín R. Kiernan

It has too often occurred to you that there is no end to the incarnations that Hell may assume. Hell, or merely hell, or simply damnation. And that most of these incarnations are the product of your own doing, restraints, and limitations. You certainly do not need Dante Alighieri, Gustave Doré, Hieronymus Bosch, or Saint fucking Paul and his Second Epistle to the Thessalonians to paint the picture for you. You know it well enough without reference to the hells of others. You sit in the black chair in front of your desk, and it stares you in the face. Hell sits on that same desk, splashed across a glossy 17-inch LED screen framed in snow-white polycarbonate. Hell is the scant few inches between your eyes and that screen, the space between any given story's climax and the fleeting moment of relief when you can finally type THE END and mean it. And know it's true. Hell is the emptiness that prevents you from reaching the release that comes with those six letters. You have precious few wards against this Hell. Prayers are worse than useless. Barring intervention, solution will only come when it comes, when it's good and ready, deadlines be damned (not unlike you).

In interviews, you have played the braggart and spoken of the effortlessness of finding endings. You've said how you generally allow them to take care of themselves. You've also said that the only *true* endings are organic, an inevitable outcome dictated by the path of the story and cannot ever be things that may be determined *a priori*. Not things that should be known beforehand and then written towards. You once said, in a moment of inspired, self-congratulatory arrogance:

No story has a beginning, and no story has an end. Beginnings and endings may be conceived to serve a purpose, to serve a momentary and transient intent, but they are, in their fundamental nature, arbitrary and exist solely as a convenient construct in the mind of man.

Oh, how you smiled when you cobbled together that stately gem. Nabokov and Faulkner should have been half so clever, you thought at the time. Still and all. These proclamations will not now save you from Perdition. Sure, you've thirty-four fine-tuned pages of text trapped there in MS Word 11.2, but without those closing paragraphs— however organic and arbitrary they may prove to be—you have only thirty-four *worthless* pages.

So, you sit and stare.

Like fabled Jesus in olive-shrouded Gethsemane, you'd sweat blood, were that an option.

For the better part of this week in January, you sit and stare at that deadly precipice which lies a third of the way down the aforementioned page thirty-four. Somewhere in there should lie the conclusion, which ought to be perfectly obvious. Which should, as you've said, follow from all the rest, no matter how arbitrary the final text may prove to be. It only has to tie everything up neat and pretty. You ask no more than that.

You sit and stare.

You read the last lines you wrote aloud, repeatedly, until they've been drained almost entirely of whatever meaning they might once have held. You recite your stalled-out, dead-end litany:

Not like the dogs and rats. Not like us.

You drink bitter black coffee, and chew your ragged nails, and prowl the internet, finding momentary solace in the distraction offered up by various sorts of pornography you manage to pretend are "research." You answer email. You look over your shoulder at the calendar nailed to your wall, and you note all the days marked off and how few remain. You gaze out the window at the windows of other houses and stark, leafless trees, at shivering squirrels and sparrows. And nothing comes to you. And nothing comes. And nothing comes again.

And on the seventh curs'd day of this rapidly accreting void, you bite down hard on the proverbial bullet. Being damned (as has been made clear), there remains within you hardly any fear of falling any farther into this or that flaming or glacial or shit-filled pit. You *know* your particular Hell, and you've been consigned there by your own inability, and you will be consigned there again, and again. If time permits, you admit defeat and hide failure in a computer file labeled simply, honestly, "Shelved."

But today time does not permit. You haven't the luxury of surrender. Today requires a balm, and having reached the point of "at any cost whatsoever," you bite your lip (like that bullet) and accept the steep price of that balm.

You have a photocopied sheet of paper you found thumbtacked to a bulletin board of a coffeehouse you frequent when you can afford to do so, which isn't all that often. You keep the flier inside a first-edition copy of Richard Adams' *Shardik* (Allen Lane, 1974). There's no significance to the book you chose; the selection was made at random. Random as ever random may be. You take out the photocopy, which is folded in half, and you smooth the creased paper flat against the peeling wood laminate of your desk. You light a cigarette (because this is the sort of day made for backsliding) and squint through smoke at the words printed on the page, the cryptic phrases that required many weeks to puzzle out, having been accompanied by no codex. You have three-times before resorted to *this*, this last resort (the white flag most assuredly isn't a resort, unless you decide that homelessness is an option).

When all else fails, you take out the flier. Across the top of the page are printed two words, spelled out in all caps and some unfamiliar boldface font: ENDINGS GUARANTEED. When all else fails, this is the parachute that might see you returned safely to terra firma, with nothing shattered but your dignity and another dab of sanity.

When all else fails, you go to see the fairies.

On your way out of the apartment you share with your girlfriend and three cats (two Siamese, one tortoise-shell mutt), you pause before a mirror. The woman who stares back at you looks sick. Not flu sick or head-cold sick, but *sick*. Her eyes are bloodshot and puffy, the bags beneath them gone dark as ripening plums. Her complexion is only a few shades shy of jaundiced. At forty, she could easily pass for the rough end of fifty, or fifty-five. You grab your wool cap, your keys, and your threadbare coat. You forget your mittens. You think about leaving a note, then think better of it. Your sudden absences are not unexpected, and you're not in the mood to write anything at all. A grocery list has more of a plot and considerably more subtext than you're willing to undertake at the moment.

You shut and lock the door, follow the stairs down to the lobby, and step out into the bright, freezing day. The sidewalks are slippery with ice, and the streets and gutters are filled with a slush of white-gray-black snow, a week old and still not completely melted away. There's also sand in the slush, and salt, and all manner of trash—broken beer bottles, plastic soda bottles, torn bits of paper, cigarette butts, what looks too much like a soiled diaper to be anything else.

The photocopied page is in your coat pocket now, and you absent-mindedly finger it as you walk to the bus stop. The thing about fairies, you think, is that they have an inordinate fondness for red tape, a sort of ritual fetish, a hard-on for ceremony, that amounts to nothing more than magical bureaucracy when all is said and done. You dutifully jump through the hoops if you want what they're selling, and you inevitably pay them an arm and a leg for the fucking pleasure. Sometimes literally, or so you've heard. So far, you've been lucky in your dealings with the local Unseelie and haven't lost any limbs, or very much of your mind. Just your dignity, which seems like a fair enough shake, since dignity is a commodity few writers can afford.

You catch the bus on Westminster. It's almost empty, and stinks of sweat and diesel fumes. The bus is too warm, overcompensating for the winter weather. You stare out at the ugly, slushy Providence streets. You pull the flier from a coat pocket and read it over again, though you've long since committed these weary Stations of the Cross to memory. Your fingers have worn the flier as smooth as rosary beads. You've looked for other copies, on other bulletin boards, or stapled to telephone poles, or duct-taped to the see-through Plexiglas walls of bus stops. But this is the only one you've ever seen. It might be the only one ever sent out into the world, and you might be the only sucker who's taken the bait. But you seriously doubt it. More like you get one shot at the brass ring and one shot only. Pass it by, and the chance won't ever come again. You've imagined all sorts of fliers like this one—not *exactly* the same, but the gist would be the same. Maybe fliers promising fertility to sterile would-be parents, riches to the destitute, houses for the homeless, sex changes to transsexuals, banquets for gluttons, true love for the lovelorn.

You ride all the way through downtown, across the river, to College Hill. You get off when the bus stops on Wickenden Street. There's a narrow alleyway between a Thai restaurant and a used record shop, a shop that sells actual vinyl records instead of CDs. You walk all the way to the back and stand beside a dumpster and empty cardboard boxes that once held Singha and Chang beer. The alley stinks of rotting food and urine and dirty snow, but at least you don't have to wait very long. The goblin that lives beneath the pavement peeks its head out the fourth time you knock your wind-chapped knuckles against the dumpster. It recognizes you straightaway and smiles, showing off a mouthful of crooked brown teeth.

"Oh," it mutters and rubs its indigo eyes. "You again. The poet come lookin' for a rhyme. The word beggar." The goblin's voice sounds the way the gutter slush looks.

"I'm not a goddamn poet," you tell the goblin, glancing back towards the entrance to the alley to be sure no one's stopped to watch you talking to nothing they can see, because they don't have a ticket, because they've never found a flier of their own.

"Fine. The spinner of penny awfuls, then. The madame dyke of the story papers. What the fuck ever you wish." The goblin stops smiling and begins chewing at one of its thick pea-green toenails. It seems to have forgotten you're standing there.

"Same as before," you finally say when you've grown tired of waiting. The goblin stops gnawing at it's foot and glares up at you. "I need to find Pigwidgeon again."

"Of course you do," he snorts. "Color me surprised. Didn't think you'd come for the time a day. So, what you got to trade? Ol' Pigwidgeon, you know he don't like being disturbed, so we ain't talking trinkets and baubles. You know that, right?"

"Yeah, I know that."

"Right. So, what you got to trade me, poet? What's it you can bear to part with this lovely afternoon?" The goblin farts and goes back to chewing its toenails.

"A memory," you tell it. "The memory of my first good review in the *Washington Post* and how I celebrated the night after I read it. How's that?"

"A mite stingy," the goblin mumbles around a mouthful of big toe. "What you think I want with the wistful reminiscences of a mid-list novelist?"

"It's better than last time," you reply. "That's what I've got. That's *all* I've got for you today."

The goblin spits, then glares at you again. It's indigo eyes swim with an iridescent sheen like motor oil on a mud puddle. "Well now," it sneers, "look at who's went and got herself all pertinacious. Look at who thinks she's grown a backbone. You calling the shots now, poet? That how you got it figured?" and before you can answer, the goblin has begun to crawl back into it's place beneath the asphalt.

"No, no, no," you say too quickly, all at once close to panic and silently cursing yourself for mouthing off, for trying to circumnavigate protocol. You shiver and glance towards the entrance to the alley again. "It means a lot to me. It really does. It's not a bauble. It's one of the most precious—"

"Seems that way to you, sure," the goblin interrupts. It's crouched half under the blacktop, half out. It snickers and closes one eye. "Always the way with mortals. Your heads all full of junk seems *precious*, but what you think don't necessarily go and make it so. So, sweeten the pot, or I'm going back down to finish my nap, which you so rudely disturbed, might I bloody well add."

And you want to tell this little green shit to fuck off. You want to turn and walk away, get back on the bus, go back to your apartment and the empty place where page thirty-four dried up. But you know yourself well enough to know better, and you're too cold and tired to stand here haggling with the goblin all damn day. Easier to concede. Old habits die hard, and you've been conceding your whole life, so why get haughty and stop now?

"That review and the memory of the celebration afterwards," you say once more, then hastily add, before you can think better of it, "*and* the last hour of my life."

The goblin grins his dirty brown grin, and his ears perk up, and his oily blue-black eyes shimmer. "Now, that's a whole lot more like it, poet. Got yourself a deal. In fact, you can keep the silly old review. Got no use for it. The hour's ample fare." And so he tells you where to find the elf named Pigwidgeon, the sulking, melancholy elf who never leaves his dusty attic, but whose dusty attic is never in the same place two days in a row.

You feel something icy and sharp pass through your belly, colder times ten than the bitter January air, and for a second you think you might vomit. But it passes. The goblin has what he wants, and he gives you an address on Benevolent Street (the irony isn't lost on you) before scurrying back beneath the alleyway. You want to run away and not look back, but you don't dare. That's one of the first lessons you learned about fairies: Never, ever run away. It inevitably makes them suspicious and apt to reconsider the terms of any bargain. So, you stand staring at the empty cardboard boxes for a little longer, smelling the reek from the dumpster, then you *slowly* turn and walk away, repeating the address over and over to yourself.

As the sun slinks down towards dusk, trading late afternoon for the last dregs of the day, you follow the goblin's directions and the redbrick trail of Benefit Street. Hands stuffed into coat pockets, you walk quickly between stately rows of eighteenth and nineteenth century architecture, that procession of gambrel roofs, bay windows, and sensible Georgian masonry. You pass historical landmarks and the towering white steeple of the oldest Baptist church in America, the red clapboard saltbox where President Washington slept on more than one occasion.

You turn right onto the steep incline of Benevolent Street, and here's the address you've been given, just one block from the Brown University campus. You silently stare warily at the building for two or three minutes, because you're pretty sure it wasn't there the last time you passed this way. You're pretty sure that the houses to the east and west of it once abutted one another, with hardly ten feet in between the two. But you know the routine well enough not to question the peculiarities and impossibilities that accompany this journey. Not to look too closely. You've entered a secret country. So you let it go, full in the knowledge that the house that wasn't here a week before (though it looks at least two hundred years old) won't be here the next time you happen by this spot.

The front door isn't locked, and the house is empty. No furniture. No evidence of occupants. No rugs or draperies or pictures hanging on the walls. You climb the stairs to the second floor, and then the third (never mind that when viewed from the street, there were clearly only *two* floors before the attic). At the end of a narrow hallway, you find the pull-down trapdoor set into the ceiling, and you tug at a jute rope, lowering a rickety set of steps that lead up into Pigwidgeon's moveable garret.

Even in the dead of winter, the attic is bathed in all the sharp and spicy aromas of autumn. There are tapestries covering the walls, hiding patches of the peeling wallpaper from view, and the elf sits in a tattered armchair in the center of the room. This is the garret's single piece of furniture, the entire house's single stick of furniture, so far as you can see. The chair is upholstered in satin the color of pomegranates. It looks like cats have used it as a scratching post.

You learned Pigwidgeon's story the first time you listened to the flier and grew desperate enough to go seeking after ENDINGS GUARANTEED. Here he sits, the spurned fairy knight who fell in love and wooed Queen Mab of the Winter Court, and so brought down upon his head all the ire of Oberon.

> *"Where is my wife, thou rogue?" quoth he,*
> *"Pigwidgeon, she is come to thee;*
> *Restore her, or thou diest by me!"*

His skin is pale as milk, and his hair is even paler, almost translucent. It almost looks spun from glass. His silver eyes are filled with starlight.

"You again," he sighs in a voice like soured honey and wilted flowers. His voice is as weary as you feel, and there's about it a blankness even more absolute than the stubborn emptiness on page thirty-four. Seeing him, hearing him, you want to turn tail and run away home.

"The hob sent you," he sighs. "The hob can't keep his mouth shut, not if some delicacy is dangled before him. One day, I'll take up needle and sinew and sew that filthy squealer's lips together."

You almost say, *I can come back some other time*, but all days are the wrong day to seek an audience with Pigwidgeon, and you've already paid too dear a price to turn back now. Instead, you say, "You know why I'm here. Ask your price, and I'll pay it. I need to find the shop. I have a deadline."

"And you take the easy way out," the fairy sneers. "You sorry, pitiful mortals, so willing to barter with your souls, rather than unriddle a bewilderment by your own faculties. You're cowards, every mother's son of you, every mother's daughter, every whore or rake's bastard child."

"Then my failings are your gain," you reply. When facing Pigwidgeon, nothing is more sure to tilt the scales in your favor than an out-and-out admission/show of human weakness.

"You'll regret this, one day or one night," he assures you. "And, given how short the span of your days, the regret shall come sooner rather than later."

"You're not telling me anything I don't already know."

The fairy scowls and picks at the ruined upholstery.

"Would you give me every drop of blood in your veins?" he asks without meeting your eyes. "Would you grant me every breath you would have taken from this moment on?"

"I think that would defeat the purpose," you reply. This is part of Pigwidgeon's song and dance, dog and pony, the exorbitant arrangements he suggests before naming the same price he always asks.

"Would you grant me the life of the woman you love? Would you give me both your eyes?"

And, just like always, you refuse him these things. And, just like always, he finally, inevitably, demands his reward for sending you off to the one who knows the current whereabouts of the shop that sells the services advertised on the flier from the coffeehouse.

"Fine," he says and stops picking at the frayed pomegranate upholstery. "Then it's settled. Take off your clothes, woman. Take off your clothes and come to me. Every stitch. Every scrap. Come to me naked as the day you were birthed."

You begin to undress, and Pigwidgeon smiles from his raggedy throne. The air in the garret is as warm as an October evening, and no warmer; when you stand before the hungry fairy, your arms and legs are pricked with gooseflesh. He raises his alabaster head and furrows his brow, appraising his purchase and, as always, finds it wanting.

"Such an ugly, hollow countenance," he frowns. "And yet one such as you was deemed fit vessel for a soul, and all the fair folk go without. Proof of the madness of God."

You agree with him, purposefully making the same mistake you always make, and Pigwidgeon stands and slaps you so hard you taste blood. He tells you to be silent unless told to speak, and you nod and stare at the bare floorboards, your feet, his boots. This is nothing you haven't earned, by your own shortcomings, your own devotion to the path of least resistance. You're temptation's bitch and won't ever argue otherwise.

"I've seen more comely bogarts," he whispers, leaning close. His breath smells of dying roses. "I've seen cowslug sprites with a more rightful claim to beauty. But even the foulest clay may be fashioned into an exquisite simulacrum, in the hands of a skillful artist." Then he paints you with a glamour so that he might spend the next hour or two pretending you're not the aging, corporeal woman who has come to beg a good turn. You become the image of his lost queen. You are clothed in her chartreuse and malachite complexion and a gown woven from dew and spider silk (which your lover tears away). You take him inside of you. And you suffer the violence and gentle moments of Pigwidgeon's affections, and deliver all your lines on cue, as scripted fifteen score years before you were born.

You have never yet learned, nor even tried to learn, why the second and third and fourth fairies move about as they do. Why each time you seek the shop, their whereabouts have changed. You suspect, though, that it may not be the fairies who move about, but, rather, the thin places between worlds that shift, those points on the city map where they may be encountered. You also know far too little about the taxonomy of fairies to know, for certain, what the third creature in the chain might be rightly called. You could make guesses, and you have, but they're not educated guesses and you set little stock by them. Were you a betting woman, you'd never play those odds. But she is always called up from water, and like Pigwidgeon and the alley goblin, her price is fixed. You come to her knowing what it's going to cost, knowing exactly what you'll lose and exactly what you'll gain. The hob takes a memory. The elf takes your body and the pretense of passion. And the third fairy, she takes a song. It's a bad joke. You can gain her indulgences for a song, when there's nothing the least bit cheap about the fee.

By the time Pigwidgeon is done with you and has restored your own face, by the time you leave his attic and the house that won't be there the next time you visit Benevolent Street, sleet is falling from the cloudy Providence sky, a sky that glows orange with reflected streetlights and the lights of parking lots and all the bright lights that burn because human beings will never cease to be afraid of the dark. You have a feeling there will be snow before dawn. The air smells like snow.

Last time you sought out the blue lady (you don't even have a name for her), the elf sent you to the old marble drinking fountain (ca. 1813) in front of the Athenaeum. The time before that, he sent you to the muddy banks of the Seekonk River behind Swan Point Cemetery. This time, he says you can find her in the women's restroom of the train depot on Gaspee Street across from the south façade of the capitol building. You catch a taxi, because you're too cold and much too tired to walk all the way from College Hill.

The restroom is all mirrors and white-tiled floors, the stench of disinfectant and the lingering undertone of urine that can't be scrubbed away. But it's empty. No one sees you enter, unless it was whoever sits on the other end of the security cameras. This isn't going to take long. It never does. But there's still the fear that someone will walk in and find you talking to yourself. You do as you've been told and enter the third stall on the left and flush the toilet four times after dropping a sprig of thyme into the bowl (you almost laugh at the undeniable absurdity of the ritual).

Then you return to the long mirror above the row of sinks. Whatever else she might be, she's punctual, and you don't have to wait very long. She appears behind you, and you know better than to turn and look directly at her. Do that, and she'll vanish. Do that, and it'll be as if she were never there, and worse, she'll never come to you again. Usually, you manage this trick with a compact; tonight, she's made it easier.

"I remember you," she says. "You're the poetess."

"I'm not a poet," you reply. "I write novels." And she smiles at that.

"I remember you," she says again. Her voice is all the innumerable sounds that water makes. You could make a list of analogies as long as your arm, and never reach the end. Her voice has been fashioned from all the wet places of the world. Her voice is a prosopoeia of water.

"I need to find the shop again," you tell her. "I need to find the shopkeeper."

She smiles, unhinging her jaw to reveal row upon row of translucent needle teeth that would be better suited to the mouth of some deep-sea fish. Just another wonder in the tedious string of wonders, that she can speak with teeth like that. Her eyes are as black as hot tar, and they gleam and glisten beneath the fluorescent bulbs. Her skin glistens, as well, the deep blue of glass infused with cobalt ions. Her lips are the vivid Majorelle blue of Berber burnouses. Her long wet cerulean hair hangs down about her shoulders and breasts, but doesn't conceal either sapphire nipple. There's webbing between her fingers and toes, and she's never come to you dressed in any garment more modest than her flesh. She drips, and rivulets wind down her legs to puddle at her feet.

"Then you'll sing for me," she says. "You'll sing for me a sweet, sweet song you'll never hear again but that it brings a sense of regret and loss so keen as to be almost unbearable. You'll never hear this song again without weeping. From this night forth it will always be a lament, a requiem, the most sorrowful of threnodies and nothing more, so choose carefully, poetess. And remember, it has to be a song that is dear to you. Dear to you almost as much as the woman you love. Take the time you require. I am patient. I can wait."

But you decided before you left home which song it would be this time. So you answer her immediately. And she licks her narrow lips with a tongue like India ink.

"Now," she says, "you must sing it for me, each and every word, every note. You must sing it with all your heart, understanding this will be the last time you shall take even the meanest portion of joy in the act."

You halfheartedly pray to a god you haven't believed in since childhood that someone will come in and interrupt. You wish someone would. A passenger in a hurry, late for her train. The janitor. Anyone at all would do. But then your weakness passes, and you sing for her, a Kris Kristofferson song your father taught you.

She shuts her black eyes and listens.

The eerie acoustics of the depot's restroom makes something lilting and unfamiliar of your voice. This is a song you love, and now you're letting it go forever.

"Oh," she said: "Casey, it's been so long since I've seen you."
"Here," she said: "just a kiss to make a body smile."
"See," she said: "I've put on new stockings just to please you."
"Lord," she said. "Casey, can you only stay a while?"

When you've finished, she leans forward and whispers the whereabouts of the shop into you ear (always your left ear, never the right). Her teeth click, and her breath smells like seaweed and silt and brine.

"Your voice is lovely," she says before stepping back and fading from view. "You may come sing for me any time."

You stare at your dingy self in the mirror for a while, and splash your face with water so cold it stings. You dry your face with a brown paper towel from the dispenser mounted on the wall.

The green woman didn't give you an address. Instead, she gave you an image, the awareness of a point in space and time, a conjunction where and when the shop will be, very briefly, accessible by any who are trying to find it. Odds are very, very good that you're the only one. You know that, which somehow makes the whole business that much worse. You can't excuse your actions with a simple "Everybody else is doing it, so why shouldn't I?" You attempt to find consolation in the fantasy that there exist a thousand other copouts at least as execrable as whoring oneself out, piece by piece, to a quartet of fay. The attempt fails utterly, but you settle for the meager solace of having tried. After the train station, you walk. The sleet has changed over to enormous snowflakes that spiral lazily down from the orange Rhode Island sky, frosting the city, dusting lawns and rooftops and sidewalks. If it keeps this up, by morning the unsightly crust of the last snowfall will be buried and hidden decently away, and the snowplows will be making the rounds.

You consider catching another taxi. Two or three pass you by, but you don't flag them down. Suddenly, taking a taxi seems like another brand of cheating, that warm, effortless ride for a few dollars. Better the long walk through the night and the gathering storm, better the wind's tiny, invisible knives slicing at your unprotected face. If you can't butch up and withstand the incompleteness of page thirty-four, much less summon the acumen necessary to complete it, you can endure so minor a tribulation. Let the two-mile walk be your halfhearted hairshirt; it's hardly Saint Catherine of Siena with her sackcloth and thrice-daily scourgings. You put one foot in front of the other, leaving tracks in the freshly fallen snow.

Past the Biltmore and the bus mall, you ford the slate-dark Moshassuck River at Kennedy Plaza. Heading east, you cross South Water and South Main and Benefit streets to Waterman, which leads you all the way to Hope Street where you turn north. Your shoes are wet, and your feet are on fire. You grit your teeth so they don't chatter and manage to block out the worst of the chill by counting your footsteps. You wonder if any among the fairies practice mortification of the flesh. But, then, why would they? With no souls to lose, why ever deny or punish themselves the way that women and men do in all their fruitless bids for forgiveness and salvation. The fairies know better. Even Pigwidgeon locked in the cloistered, mock-asceticism of his garret is a decadent, sating his darkest appetites whenever the opportunity arises.

You let Hope Street lead you all the way to the redbrick and silver dome of the observatory. If there's any significance in being treated to two domes in a single night, it's lost on you. All that matters is that the blue woman hasn't led you astray, and waiting between you and the observatory is what could easily, at first glance, be mistaken for a tall, unframed looking glass. It's not a mirror, of course. It reflects nothing at all. It's most decidedly accurate to say that its function is, in fact, the opposite of a mirror's. It wasn't constructed to reflect anything, but to permit entry.

You spare a single glance over your shoulder, at the snow piling up, the dark or glowing windows of houses, the street, the stark, bare branches of trees. Your fingers brush across the photocopied flier stuffed into your coat pocket. And then you hold your breath and step through the quicksilver doorway.

You smell nutmeg, mildew, and ammonia, each in its turn, before you step out into the shop. Then there's only a comfortable, musty smell. Just as its entryway might be mistaken for a looking glass, the dimly lit interior of the fairy shop could be confused with a certain variety of New England antique shop. Not the upscale sort, but the sort that's all clutter and dust, random odds and ends. Odds, mostly. The walls are lined with sagging shelves and wooden red-lacquered apothecary cabinets. On your first visit, you browsed through the drawers of those cabinets. One was stuffed with old theater tickets, the next with doorknobs, a third with bridge and subway tokens, a fourth with skeleton keys, a fifth with the feathers of songbirds, the sixth with a mismatched assortment of chess pieces, and so on and on and on and on. Dried bundles of herbs, peppers, and corn droop from the low ceiling. There are rows of formalin-filled jars, and the milky eyes of countless species of fish, serpents, rats, and indescribable fairy creatures gaze blindly out as you walk down the long aisle that leads to the glass display counter and the hulking cash register that seems to double as a typewriter and telegraph machine.

"Took your own sweet time *this* time, poet," the peddler of endings says from her place at the register. The crone of sticks and warts and pebbles is sitting on an aluminum stool that creaks and wobbles alarmingly whenever she moves, as if it's always poised on the verge of dumping her onto the cold concrete floor. "Thought maybe you'd lost your way, or your nerve, or both."

"It's snowing," you reply.

"Does that, most every winter," she snickers and chews at the stem of her ivory pipe. Opium smoke curls from the bowl, forming question marks in the musty atmosphere of the shop. Where her eyes ought to be, there are fat yellow spiders spinning crystalline webs. She points the seventh finger of her right hand at you, raises a bramble eyebrow, and tilts her head to one side.

"I paid them," you whisper. "I paid them, every one."

"You wouldn't be standing here if you hadn't, now would you? Seems somewhat south of likely, don't it?"

You agree and try hard not to stare too long at anything in particular.

"Put you through the wringer," the crone mutters. "Can see that much. A right wicked lot, those three. Steal the meat off your bones, then complain the marrow's not sweet enough by half. Hardly seems decent after all they done, but now I have my own small query."

"I know."

"Ain't so much, mind you. Not after those three. A formality, and hardly more."

"I'm not complaining," you say.

"Very well," she nods, and you imagine one of the yellow spiders is gazing directly at you. "I'd ask why you do this to yourself?"

"What else would I do?" you answer.

"And is it worth it?" asks the crone, blinking her arachnid eyes. "All this hurt for another puny tale?"

"It's what I do," you say, same as every time before. "I write stories. There's not much else to me. And my stories have to end somewhere, even if the endings escape me." The words tumble like lead from your chapped lips.

"Fair enough," says the crone. "Fair enough."

"I held out as long as I could," you add, though she hasn't asked for more. "This time, I made it a whole week."

"Not my place to judge," she replies, and plucks the pipe from her mouth long enough to spit at a clay bowl on the counter. She misses. "Figure you're gonna do plenty enough of that all on your own, poet."

"I'm not a poet," you say.

"Of course you're not," she grins, then presses a single brass key, and the cash register blares a cacophony of thunderclaps, church bells, and the high, cruel laughter of children. She leans over, reaching beneath the counter and rummaging about for a moment. The stool totters and sways, and she curses in several languages all in a single breath.

When she sits up again, she's holding a small white linen bag, tied at the top with a carmine ribbon.

"This is a fine one," she says. "Don't think you'll have any room for complaints. Best denouement I've dispensed in a hare's age. Won't find none better nowhere, not on earth nor heaven nor anywhere in between."

You thank her, and she spits again, misses the bowl again, and instructs you to think nothing of it.

Next time, I'll make it two weeks, you think.

"Of course you will, baby girl. Now, best be on your way. The wheel's turning." She jabs a twisted, thorny finger back the way you've come, and you turn away from the counter, slipping the linen bag into your pocket.

"Fare thee well, poet," the crone says before you step through the argent roil of the unmirror and out onto the curb outside your house. You almost slip going up the icy steps to the front door, and you have more trouble than usual with the lock. Your lover may have waited up for you, and she may not have. She's grown accustomed to your nocturnal walks, and hardly ever asks where you've been.

You'll untie the crone's bag in the morning, after you've returned the flier to its place between the pages of *Shardik*, after breakfast and coffee and your first cigarette of the day. You won't think about what it's cost you, or how much it'll cost next time, or the time after that. You'll have your ending, guaranteed, and a few days from now you'll loathe every word you've written. There will be no more satisfaction than you find when you take a piss, but none of that matters a whit, not so long as the check clears. You'll email a copy to your editor in Manhattan, print out a copy for yourself, and file it away.

You'll do your best not to dwell on whatever you lost the night before. What's done is done, and regret never paid the bills. You won't worry much what editors or readers will think of the ending.

It only has to tie everything up neat and pretty. You ask no more than that.

ぴ

The *New York Times* recently hailed **Caitlín R. Kiernan** as "one of our essential writers of dark fiction." Her novels include *The Red Tree* (nominated for the Shirley Jackson and World Fantasy awards) and *The Drowning Girl: A Memoir* (winner of the James Tiptree, Jr. Award and the Bram Stoker Award, nominated for the Nebula, Locus, Shirley Jackson, World Fantasy, British Fantasy, and Mythopoeic awards). To date, her short fiction has been collected in thirteen volumes, most recently *Confessions of a Five-Chambered Heart, Two Worlds and In Between: The Best of Caitlín R. Kiernan (Volume One)*, and *The Ape's Wife and Other Stories*. Currently, she's writing the graphic novel series Alabaster for Dark Horse Comics and working on her next novel, *Cherry Bomb.*

The City: *Seattle, Washington.*

The Magic: *When a band of evil witches kidnap a werewolf's brother, he must seek help from witch who, despite the lack of one of her five senses, makes up for it with plenty of magical ability, moxie, and bravery.*

SEEING EYE

PATRICIA BRIGGS

The doorbell rang.

That was the problem with her business. Too many people thought that they could approach her at any time. Even oh dark thirty even though her hours were posted clearly on her door and on her website.

Of course answering the door would be something to do other than sit in her study shivering in the dark. Not that her world was ever anything but dark. It was one of the reasons she hated bad dreams—she had no way of turning on the light. Bad dreams that held warnings of things to come were the worst.

The doorbell rang again.

She slept—or tried to—the same hours as most people. Kept steady business hours too. Something that she had no trouble making clear to those morons who woke her up in the middle of the night. They came to see Glenda the Good Witch, but after midnight they found the Wicked Witch of the West and left quaking in fear of flying monkeys.

Whoever was at the door would have no reason to suspect how grateful she was for the interruption of her thoughts.

The doorbell began a steady throbbing beat, ring-long, ring-short, ring-short, ring-long and she grew a lot less grateful. To heck with flying monkeys, *she* was going to turn whoever it was into a frog. She shoved her concealing glasses on her face and stomped out the hall to her front door. No matter that most of the good transmutation spells had been lost with the Coranda family in the seventeenth century—rude people needed to be turned into frogs. Or pigs.

She jerked open the door and slapped the offending hand on her doorbell. She even got out a "stop that" before the force of his spirit hit her like a physical blow. Her nose told her, belatedly that he was sweaty as if he'd been jogging. Her other senses told her that he was something *other*.

Not that she'd expected him to be human. Unlike other witches, she didn't advertise and so seldom had mundane customers unless their needs disturbed her sleep and she set out one of her "find me" spells to speak to them—she knew when they were coming.

"Ms. Keller," he growled. "I need to speak to you." At least he'd quit ringing the bell.

She let her left eyebrow slide up her forehead until it would be visible above her glasses. "Polite people come between the hours of eight in the morning and seven at night," she informed him. Werewolf, she decided. If he really lost his temper she might have trouble, but she thought he was desperate, not angry—though with a wolf, the two states could be interchanged with remarkable speed. "Rude people get sent on their way."

"Tomorrow morning might be too late," he said—and then added the bit that kept her from slamming the door in his face. "Alan Choo gave me your address, said you were the only one he knew with enough moxie to defy them."

She should shut the door in his face—not even a werewolf could get through her portal if she didn't want him to. But . . . *them*. Her dream tonight and for the past weeks had been about *them*, about *him* again. Portents, her instincts had told her, not just nightmares. The time had come at last. No. She wasn't grateful to him at all.

"Did Alan tell you to say it in those words?"

"Yes, ma'am." His temper was still there, but restrained and under control. It hadn't been aimed at her anyway, she thought, only fury born of frustration and fear. She knew how that felt.

She centered herself and asked the questions he'd expect. "Who am I supposed to be defying?"

And he gave her the answer she expected in return. "Something called Samhain's Coven."

Moira took a tighter hold on the door. "I see."

It wasn't really a coven. No matter what the popular literature said, it had been a long time since a real coven had been possible. Covens had thirteen members, no member related to any other to the sixth generation. Each family amassed its own specialty spells, and a coven of thirteen benefitted from all of those differing magics. But after most of the witchblood families had been wiped out by fighting amongst themselves, covens became a thing of the past. What few families remained (and there weren't thirteen, not if you didn't count the Russians or the Chinese who kept to their own ways) had a bone-deep antipathy for the other survivors.

Kouros changed the rules to suit the new times. His coven had between ten and thirteen members . . . he had a distressing tendency to burn out his followers. The current bunch descended from only three families that she knew of, and most of them weren't properly trained—children following their leader.

Samhain wasn't up to the tricks of the old covens, but they were scary enough even the local vampires walked softly around them, and Seattle, with its overcast skies, had a relatively large seethe of vampires. Samhain's master had approached Moira about joining them when she was thirteen. She'd refused and made her refusal stick at some cost to all the parties involved.

"What does Samhain have to do with a werewolf?" she asked.

"I think they have my brother."

"Another werewolf?" It wasn't unheard of for brothers to be werewolves, especially since the Marrok, He-Who-Ruled-the-Wolves, began Changing people with more care than had been the usual custom. But it wasn't at all common either. Surviving of the Change, even with the safeguards the Marrok could manage, was still, she understood, nowhere near a certainty.

"No," he took a deep breath. "Not a werewolf. Human. He has the *sight.* Choo says he thinks that's why they took him."

"Your brother is a witch?"

The fabric of his shirt rustled with his shrug, telling her that he wasn't as tall as he felt to her. Only a little above average instead of a seven-foot giant. Good to know.

"I don't know enough about witches to know—" he said. "Jon gets hunches. Takes a walk just at the right time to find five dollars someone dropped, picks the right lottery number to win ten bucks. That kind of thing. Nothing big, nothing anyone would have noticed if my grandma hadn't had it stronger."

The *sight* was one of those general terms that told Moira precisely nothing. It could mean anything from a little fae blood in the family tree or full-blown witchblood. His brother's lack of power wouldn't mean he wasn't a witch—the magic sang weaker in the men. But fae or witchblood, Alan Choo had been right about it being something that would attract Samhain's attention. She rubbed her cheekbone even though she knew the ache was a phantom pain touch wouldn't alter.

Samhain. Did she have a choice? In her dreams she died.

She could feel the intensity of the wolf's regard, strengthening as her silence continued. Then he told her the final straw that broke her resistance. "Jon's a cop—undercover—so I doubt your coven knows it. If his body turns up, though, there will be an investigation. I'll see to it that the witchcraft angle gets explored thoroughly. They might listen to a werewolf who tells them that witches might be a little more than the turbaned fortune-teller."

Blackmail galled him, she could tell—but he wasn't bluffing. He must love his brother.

She only had a touch of empathy and it came and went. It seemed to be pretty focused on this werewolf tonight, though.

If she didn't help him, his brother would die at Samhain's hands and his blood would be on her as well. If it cost her death, as her dreams warned her, perhaps that was justice served.

"Come in," Moira said, hearing the grudge in her voice. He'd think it was her reaction to the threat—and the police poking about the coven would end badly for all concerned.

But it wasn't his threat that moved her. She took care of the people in her neighborhood, that was her job. The police she saw as brothers-in-arms. If she could help one, it was her duty to do so. Even if it was her life for his.

"You'll have to wait until I get my coffee," she told him, and her mother's ghost forced the next bit of politeness out of her. "Would you like a cup?"

"No. There's no time."

He said that as if he had some idea about it—maybe the *sight* hadn't passed him by either.

"We have until tomorrow night if Samhain has him." She turned on her heel and left him to follow her or not, saying over her shoulder, "Unless they took him because he saw something. In which case he probably is already dead. Either way there's time for coffee."

He closed the door with deliberate softness and followed her. "Tomorrow's Halloween. Samhain."

"Kouros isn't Wiccan, anymore than he is Greek, but he apes both for his followers," she told him as she continued deeper into her apartment. She remembered to turn on the hall light—not that he'd need it, being a wolf. It just seemed courteous: allies should show each other courtesy. "Like a magician playing slight of hand he pulls upon myth, religion, and anything else he can to keep them in thrall. Samhain, the time not the coven, has power for the fae, for Wicca, for witches. Kouros uses it to cement his own, and killing someone with a bit of power generates more strength than killing a stray dog and bothers him about as much."

"Kouros?" He said it as if it solved some puzzle, but it must not have been important because he continued with no more than a breath of pause. "I thought witches were all women?" He followed her into the kitchen and stood too close behind her. If he were to attack, she wouldn't have time to ready a spell.

But he wouldn't attack, her death wouldn't come at his hands tonight.

The kitchen lights were where she remembered them and she had to take it on faith that she was turning them on and not off, she could never remember which way the switch worked. He didn't say anything so she must have been right.

She always left her coffeepot primed for mornings, so all she had to do was push the button and it began gurgling in promise of coffee soon.

"Um," she said, remembering he'd asked her a question. His closeness distracted her—and not for the reasons it should. "Women tend to be more powerful witches, but you can make up for lack of talent with enough death and pain. Someone else's, of course, if you're a black practitioner like Kouros."

"What are you?" he asked, sniffing at her. His breath tickled the back of her neck—wolves, she'd noticed before, have a somewhat different idea of personal space than she did.

Her machine began dribbling coffee out into the carafe at last, giving her an excuse to step away. "Didn't Alan tell you? I'm a witch."

He followed; his nose touched her where his breath had sensitized her flesh and she probably had goose flesh on her toes from the zing that he sent through her. "My pack has a witch we pay to clean up messes. You don't smell like a witch."

He probably didn't mean anything by it, he was just being a wolf. She stepped out of his reach in the pretense of getting a coffee cup, or rather he allowed her to escape.

Alan was right, she needed to get out more. She hadn't so much as dated in . . . well a long time. The last man's reaction to seeing what she'd done to herself was something she didn't want to repeat.

This man smelled good, even with the smell of his sweat teasing her nose. He felt strong and warm, promising to be the strength and safety that she'd never had outside of her own two hands. Dominant wolves took care of their pack—doubtless something she'd picked up on. And then there was the possibility of death hovering over her.

Whatever the ultimate cause, his nearness and the light touch of breath on her skin sparked her interest in a way that she knew he'd have picked up on. You can't hide sexual interest from something that can trail a hummingbird on the wing. Neither of them needed the complication of sex interfering in urgent business, even assuming he'd be willing.

"Witchcraft gains power from death and pain. From sacrifice and sacrificing," she told him coolly, pouring coffee in two mugs with steady hands. She was an expert in sacrifice. Not sleeping with a strange werewolf who showed up on her doorstep didn't even register in her scale.

She drank coffee black so that was how she fixed it, holding the second cup out to him. "Evil leaves a psychic stench behind. Maybe a wolf nose can pick up on it. I don't know, not being a werewolf, myself. There's milk in the fridge and sugar in the cupboard in front of you if you'd like."

She wasn't at all what Tom had expected. Their pack's hired witch was a motherly woman of indeterminate years who wore swami robes in bright hues and smelled strongly of patchouli and old blood that didn't quite mask something bitter and dark. When he'd played her Jon's message, she'd hung up the phone and refused to answer it again.

By the time he'd driven to her house, it was shut up and locked with no one inside. That was his first clue that this Samhain Coven might be even more of a problem than he'd thought and his worry had risen to fever pitch. He'd gone down to the underpass where his brother had been living and used his nose through the parks and other places his brother had drifted through. But wherever they were holding Jon (and he refused to believe that he was dead) it wasn't anywhere near where they kidnaped him.

His alpha didn't like pack members concerning themselves with matters outside of the pack ("Your only family is your pack, son"). Tom didn't even bother contacting him. He'd gone to Choo instead. The Emerald City pack's only submissive wolf, Alan worked as an herbalist and knew almost everyone in the supernatural world of Seattle. When he told Alan about the message Jon had left on his phone, Alan had written this woman's name and address and handed it to him. He'd have thought it was a joke but Alan had better taste than that. So Tom had gone looking for a witch named Wendy—Wendy Moira Keller.

He'd been disappointed at his first look. Wendy the witch was five-foot nothing with rich curves in all the right places and feathery black hair that must have been dyed because only black labs and cats are that black. The stupid wrap-around mirrored glasses kept him from guessing her age exactly, but he'd bet she wasn't yet thirty. No woman over thirty would be caught dead in those glasses. The cop in him wondered if she was covering up bruises—but he didn't smell a male in the living-scents in the house.

She wore a gray T-shirt without a bra and black pajama pants with white skull-and-crossbones wearing red bows. But despite all that he saw no piercings or tattoos—like she'd approached mall-goth culture, but only so far. She smelled of fresh flowers and mint. Her apartment was decorated with a minimum of furniture and a mishmash of colors that didn't quite fit together.

He didn't scare her.

Tom scared everyone—and he had even before their pack had a run-in with a bunch of fae a few years ago. His face had gotten cut up pretty badly with some sort of magical knife and hadn't healed right afterward. The scars made him look almost as dangerous as he was. People walked warily around him.

Not only wasn't she scared, but she didn't even bother to hide her irritation at being woken up. He stalked her and all she'd felt was a flash of sexual awareness that had come and gone so swiftly that if he'd been younger he might have missed it.

Either she was stupid or she was powerful. Since Alan had sent him here, he was betting on powerful. He hoped she was powerful.

He didn't want the coffee, but he took it when she handed to him. It was black and stronger that he usually drank it, but it tasted good. "So why don't you smell like other witches?"

"Like Kouros, I'm not Wiccan," she told him, "but 'an it harm none' seems like a good way to live to me."

White witch.

He knew that Wiccans consider themselves witches—and some of them had enough witchblood to make it so. But witches, the real thing, weren't witches because of what they believed, but because of genetic heritage. A witch was born a witch and studied to become a better one. But for witches, real power came from blood and death—mostly other people's blood and death.

White witches, especially those outside of Wicca (where numbers meant safety) were weak and valuable sacrifices for black witches who didn't have their scruples. As Wendy the Witch had noted—witches seemed to have a real preference for killing their own.

He sipped at his coffee and asked, "So how have you managed without ending up as bits and pieces in someone else's cauldron?"

She snorted a laugh and set her coffee down abruptly. Grabbing a paper towel off its holder she held it to her face as she gasped and choked coffee, looking suddenly a lot less than thirty. When she was finished she said, "That's awesome. Bits and pieces. I'll have to remember that."

Still grinning she picked up the coffee again. He wished he could see her eyes, because he was pretty sure that whatever humor she'd felt was only surface deep.

"I tell you what," she said, "why don't you tell me who you are and what you know. That way I can tell you if I can help you or not."

"Fair enough," he said. The coffee was strong and he could feel it and the four other cups he'd had since midnight settle in his bones with caffeine's untrustworthy gift of nervous energy.

"I'm Tom Franklin and I'm second in the Emerald City Pack." She wasn't surprised by that. She'd known what he was as soon as she opened her door. "My brother Jon is a cop and a damn fine one. He's been on the Seattle PD for nearly twenty years and for the last six months he's been undercover as a street person. He was sent as part of a drug task force: there's been some nasty shit out on the street lately and he's been looking for it."

Wendy Moira Keller leaned back against the cabinets with a sigh. "I'd like to say that no witch would mess with drugs. Not from moral principals, mind you, witches, for the most part, don't have moral principles. But drugs are too likely to attract unwanted attention. We never have been as deep in secrecy as you wolves used to be, not when witches sometimes crop up in mundane families—we need to be part of society enough that they can find us. Mostly people think we're a bunch of harmless charlatans—trafficking in drugs would change all that for the worse. But the Samhain bunch is powerful enough that no one wants to face them—and Kouros is arrogant and crazy. He likes money and there is at least one herbalist in his followers who could manufacture some really odd stuff."

He shrugged. "I don't know. I'm interested in finding my brother, not in finding out if witches are selling drugs. It sounded to me like the drugs had nothing to do with my brother's kidnaping. Let me play Jon's call and you make the determination." He pulled out his cell phone and played the message for her.

It had come from a pay phone. There weren't many of them left, as cell phones had made it less profitable to keep repairing the damage of vandals. But there was no mistaking the characteristic static and hiss as his brother talked very quietly into the mouthpiece.

Tom had called in favors and found the phone Jon had used, but the people who took his brother were impossible to pick out from the scents of the hundreds of people who had been there since the last rain—and his brother's scent stopped right at the pay phone, outside of a battered convenience store. Stopped as if they'd teleported him to another planet—or, more prosaically, thrown him in a car.

Jon's voice, smoker-dark though he'd never touched tobacco or any of its relatives, slid though the apartment. "Look, Tom. My gut told me to call you tonight—and I listen to my gut. I've been hearing something on the street about a freaky group are calling themselves Samhain—" He spelled it, to be sure Tom got it right. "Last few days I've had a couple of people following me that might be part of Samhain. No one wants to talk about 'em much. The streets are afraid of these . . . "

He didn't know if the witch could hear the rest. He'd been a wolf for twenty years and more so his judgment about what human senses were good for was pretty much gone.

He could hear the girl's sweet voice clearly though. "Lucky Jon?" she asked. "Lucky Jon, who are you calling? Let's hang it up, now." A pause, then the girl spoke into the phone, "Hello?" Another pause. "It's an answering machine, I think. No worries."

At the same time, a male, probably young, was saying in a rapid, rabid flow of sound, "I feel it . . . Doncha feel it? I feel it in him. This is the one. He'll do for Kouros." Then there was a soft click as the call ended.

The last fifty times he'd heard the recording he couldn't make out the last word. But with the information the witch had given him, he understood it just fine this time.

He looked at Choo's witch but he couldn't tell what she thought. Somewhere she'd learned to discipline her emotions so he could only smell the strong ones—like the flash of desire she'd felt as he'd smelled the back of her neck. Even in this situation it had been enough to raise a thread of interest. Maybe after they got his brother back they could do something about that interest. In the meantime . . .

"How much of the last did you hear, Wendy?" he asked.

"Don't call me Wendy," she snapped. "It's Moira. No one called me Wendy except my mom and she's been dead a long time."

"Fine," he snapped back before he could control himself. He was tired and worried, but he could do better than that. He tightened his control and softened his voice. "Did you hear the guy? The one who said that he felt *it* in him—meaning my brother, I think. And that he would do for Kouros?"

"No. Or at least not well enough to catch his words. But I know the woman's voice. You're right, it was Samhain." Though he couldn't feel anything from her, her knuckles were white on the coffee cup.

"You need a Finder and I can't do that anymore. Wait," she held up a hand before he could say anything. "I'm not saying I won't help you, just that it could be a lot simpler. Kouros moves all the time. Did you trace the call? It sounded like a pay phone to me."

"I found the phone booth he called from, but I couldn't find anything except that he'd been there." He tapped his nose, then glanced at her dark glasses and said, "I could smell him there and back trail him, but I couldn't trail him out. They transported him somehow."

"They don't know that he's a cop, or that his brother is a werewolf."

"He doesn't carry ID with him while he's undercover. I don't see how anyone would know I was his brother. Unless he told them, and he wouldn't."

"Good," she said. "They won't expect you. That'll help."

"So do you know a Finder I can go to?"

She shook her head. "Not one who will help you against Samhain. Anyone, *anyone* who makes a move against them is punished in some rather spectacular ways." He saw her consider sharing one or two of them with him and discard it. She didn't want him scared off. Not that he could be, not with Jon's life at stake. But it was interesting that she hadn't tried.

"If you take me to where they stole him, maybe I can find something they left behind, something to use to find them."

Tom frowned at her. She didn't know his brother, he hadn't mentioned money and he was getting the feeling that she could care less if he called in the authorities. "So if Samhain is so all-powerful, how come you, a white witch, are willing to buck them?"

"You're a cop, too, aren't you?" She finished her coffee, but if she was waiting for a reaction, she wasn't going to get one. He'd seen the "all-knowing" witch act before. Her lips turned up as she set the empty cup on the counter. "It's not magic. Cops are easy to spot—suspicious is your middle name. Fair enough."

She pulled off her glasses and he saw that he'd been wrong. He been pretty sure she was blind—the other reason women wore wraparound sunglasses at night. And she was. But that wasn't why she wore the sunglasses.

Her left eye was Swamp Thing-green without pupil or white. Her right eye was gone and it looked as though it had been removed by someone who wasn't too good with a knife. It was horrible—and he'd seen some horrible things.

"Sacrifice is good for power," she said again. "But it works best if you can manage to make the sacrifice your own."

Jesus. She'd done it to herself.

She might not be able to see him, but she read his reaction just fine. She smiled tightly. "There were some extenuating circumstances," she continued. "You aren't going to see witches cutting off their fingers to power their spells—

it doesn't work that way. But this worked for me," she tapped the scar tissue around her right eye. "Kouros did the other one first. That's why I'm willing to take them on. I've done it before and survived—and I still owe them a few." She replaced her sunglasses and he watched her relax as they settled into place.

Tom Franklin hadn't brought a car and, for obvious reasons, *she* didn't drive. He said the phone was only a couple of miles from her apartment and neither wanted to wait around for a cab. So they walked. She felt his start of surprise when she tucked her arm in his but he didn't object. At least he didn't jump away from her and say, "ick" like the last person who'd seen what she'd done to herself.

"You'll have to tell me when we come to curbs or if there's something in the way," she told him. "Or you can amuse yourself when I fall on my face. I can find my way around my apartment, but out here I'm at your mercy."

He said, with sober humor, "I imagine watching you trip over a few curbs would be a good way to get you to help Jon. Why don't you get a guide dog?"

"Small apartments aren't a good place for big dogs," she told him. "It's not fair to the dog."

They walked a few blocks in silence, the rain drizzling unhappily down the back of her neck and soaking the bottoms of the jeans she'd put on before they started out. It didn't always rain in Seattle, despite its reputation. He guided her as if he'd done it before, unobtrusively but clearly, as if they were waltzing instead of walking down the street. She relaxed and walked faster.

"Wendy." He broke the companionable silence with the voice of One Who Suddenly Comprehends. "It's worse than I thought. I was stuck on Casper the Friendly Ghost and Wendy the Good Little Witch. But Wendy Moira . . . I bet it's Wendy Moira Angela isn't it?"

She gave him a mock scowl. "I don't have a kiss for you and I can't fly, not even with fairy dust. And I *hate Peter Pan*, the play, and all the movies."

His arm moved and she could tell he was laughing to himself. "I bet."

"It could be worse, Toto," she told him. "I could belong to the Emerald City Pack."

He laughed out loud at that, a softer sound that she'd thought he'd have from the rough grumble of his voice. "You know, I've never thought of it that way. It seemed logical, Seattle being the Emerald City."

She might have said something, but he suddenly picked up his pace like a hunting dog spotting his prey. She kept her hand tight on his arm and did her best to keep up. He stopped at last. "Here."

She felt his tension, the desire for action of some sort. Hopefully she'd be able to provide him the opportunity. She released his arm and stepped to the side.

"All right," she told him, falling into the comfortable patter she adopted with most of her clients—erasing the odd intimacy that had sprung up between them. "I know the girl on your brother's phone—her name used to be Molly, but I think she goes by something like Spearmint or Peppermint something-mint. I'm going to call for things that belong to her—a hair, a cigarette—anything will do. You'll have to do the looking. Whatever it is will glow, but it might be very small, easy to overlook."

"What if I don't see anything?"

"Then they didn't leave anything behind and I'll figure out something else to try."

She set aside her worries, shedding them like a duck would shed the cool Seattle rain. Closing her senses to the outside world, she reached into her well of power and drew out a bucketful and threw it out in a circle around her as she called to the essence that was Molly. She hadn't done this spell since she could see out of both eyes—but there was no reason she couldn't do it now. Once learned, spells came to her hand like trained spaniels and this one was no exception.

"What do you see?" she asked. The vibration of power warmed her against the cold fall drizzle that began to fall. There was something here, she could feel it.

"Nothing," his voice told her that he'd put a lot of hope into this working.

"There's something," she said, sensations crawling up her arms and over her shoulders. She held out her right hand, her left being otherwise occupied with the workings of her spell. "Touching me might help you see."

Warmth flooded her as his hand touched hers . . . and she could see the faint traces Molly had left behind. She froze.

"Moira?"

She couldn't see anything else. Just bright bits of pink light sparkling from the ground, giving her a little bit of idea what the landscape looked like. She let go of his hand and the light disappeared, leaving her in darkness again.

"Did you see anything?" she asked, her voice hoarse. The oddity of seeing anything . . . she craved it too much and it made her wary because she didn't know how it worked.

"No."

He wanted his brother and she wanted to see. Just for a moment. She held her hand out. "Touch me, again."

. . . and the sparkles returned like glitter scattered in front of her. Small bits of skin and hair, too small for what she needed. But there was something . . .

She followed the glittering trail and, as if it had been hidden, a small wad of something blazed like a bonfire.

"Is there a wall just to our right?" she asked.

"A building and an alley." His voice was tight, but she ignored it. She had other business first.

They'd waited for Tom's brother in the alley. Maybe Jon came to the pay phone here often.

She led Tom to the blaze and bent to pick up it up: soft and sticky, gum. Better, she thought, better than she could have hoped. Saliva would make a stronger guide than hair or fingernails. She released his hand reluctantly.

"What did you find?"

"Molly's gum." She allowed her magic to loosen the last spell and slide back to her, hissing as the power warmed her skin almost to the point of burning. The next spell would be easier, even if it might eventually need more power. Sympathetic magic, which used the connections between like things—was one of those affinities that ran through her father's bloodlines into her.

But before she tried any more magic, she needed to figure out what he'd done to her spell. How touching him allowed her to *see.*

She looked unearthly. A violent wind he had not felt, not even when she'd fastened onto his hand with fierce strength, had blown her hair away from her face. The skin on her hands was reddened, as if she held them too close to a fire. He wanted to soothe them—but he firmly intended never to touch her again.

He had no idea what she'd done to him while she held on to him and made his body burn and tremble. He didn't like surprises and she'd told him that he would have to look, not that she'd use him to *see.* He especially didn't like it that as long as she was touching him, he hadn't wanted her to let him go.

Witches gather more power from hurting those with magic, she'd said . . . more or less. People just like him—but it hadn't hurt, not that he'd noticed.

He wasn't afraid of her, not really. Witch or not she was no match for him. Even in human form it would be only a matter of moments before he broke her human-fragile body. But if she was using him . . .

"Why are you helping me?" he asked as he had earlier, but the question seemed more important now. He'd known what she was, but witch meant something different to him now. He knew enough about witches not to ask the obvious question though, like what it was she'd done to him. Witches, in his experience, were secretive about their spells—like junk-yard dogs are secretive about their bones.

She'd taken something from him by using him that way . . . broken the trust he'd felt building between them. He needed to reestablish what he could expect out of her. Needed to know exactly what she was getting him into, beyond rescuing his brother. Witches are not altruistic. "What do you want out of this? Revenge for your blindness?"

She watched him . . . appeared to watch him anyway as she considered his question. There hadn't been many people who could lie to Tom before he Changed—cops learn all about lying the first year on the job. Afterwards . . . he could smell a lie a mile away an hour before it was spoken.

"Andy Choo sent you," she said finally. "That's one. Your brother's a policeman, and an investigation into his death might be awkward. That's two. He takes risks to help people he doesn't know, it's only right someone return the favor. That's three."

They weren't lies, but they weren't everything either. Her face was very still, as if the magic she'd worked had changed her view of him, too.

Then she tilted her head sideways and said in a totally different voice, hesitant and raw. "Sins of the fathers."

Here was absolute truth. Obscure as hell, but truth. "Sins of the fathers?"

"Kouros's real name Lin Keller, though he hasn't used it in twenty years or more."

"He's your father." And then he added two and two. "Your *father* is running Samhain's Coven?" Her father had ruined her eye and—Tom could read between the lines—caused her to ruin the other? Her own father?

She drew in a deep breath—and for a moment he was afraid she was going to cry or something. But a stray gust of air brought the scent of her to him and he realized she was angry. It tasted like a werewolf's rage, wild and biting.

"I am not a part of it," she said, her voice a half octave lower than it had been. "I'm not bringing you to his lair so he can dine upon werewolf, too. I am here because some jerk made me feel sorry for him. I am here because I want both he and his brother out of my hair and safely out of the hands of my rat-bastard father so I won't have their deaths on my conscience, too."

Someone else might have been scared of her, she being a witch and all. Tom wanted to apologize—and he couldn't remember the last time that impulse had touched him. It was even more amazing because he wasn't at fault: she'd misunderstood him. Maybe she'd picked up on how appalled he was that her own father had maimed her—he hadn't been implying she was one of them.

He didn't apologize, though, or explain himself. People said things when they were mad that they wouldn't tell you otherwise.

"What was it you did to me?"

"Did to you?" Arctic ice might be warmer.

"When you were looking for the gum. It felt like you hit me with a bolt of lightning." He was damned if he'd tell her everything he felt.

Her right eyebrow peaked out above her sunglasses. Interest replaced coldness. "You felt like I was doing something to you?" And then she held out her left hand. "Take my hand."

He looked at it.

After a moment she smiled. He didn't know she had a smile like that in her. Bright and cheerful and sudden. Knowing. As if she had gained every thought that passed through his head. Her anger, the misunderstanding between them was gone as if it had never been.

"I don't know what happened," she told him gently. "Let me try recreating it and maybe I can tell you."

He gave her his hand. Instead of taking it, she put only two fingers on his palm. She stepped closer to him, dropped her head so he could see her scalp gleaming pale underneath her dark hair. The magic that touched him this time was gentler, sparklers instead of fireworks—and she jerked her fingers away as if his hand were a hot potato.

"What the heck . . . ?" She rubbed her hands on her arms with nervous speed.

"What?"

"You weren't acting as my focus, I can tell you that much."

"So what was going on?"

She shook her head, clearly uncomfortable. "I think I was using you to *see*. I shouldn't be able to do that."

He found himself smiling grimly. "So I'm your seeing-eye wolf?"

"I don't know."

He recognized her panic, having seen it in his own mirror upon occasion. It was always frightening when something you thought was firmly under control broke free to run where it would. With him it was the wolf.

Something resettled in his gut. She hadn't done it on purpose, she wasn't using him.

"Is it harmful to me?"

She frowned. "Did it hurt?"

"No."

"Either time?"

"Neither time."

"Then it didn't harm you."

"All right," he said. "Where do we go from here?"

She opened her right hand, the one with the gum in it. "Not us. Me. This is going to show us where Molly is—and Molly will know where your brother is."

She closed her fingers, turned her hand palm down, then turned in a slow circle. She hit a break in the pavement and he grabbed her before she could do more than stumble. His hand touched her wrist and she turned her hand to grab him, as the kick of power flowed through his body once more.

"They're in a boat," she told him and went limp in his arms.

She awoke with the familiar headache that usually accompanied the overuse of magic and absolutely no idea of where she was. It smelled wrong to be her apartment, but she was lying on a couch with a blanket covering her.

Panic rose in her chest—sometimes she hated being blind.

"Back in the land of the living?"

"Tom?"

He must have heard the distress in her voice because when he spoke again, he was much closer and his voice was softer. "You're on a couch in my apartment. We were as close to mine as we were to yours, and I knew I could get us into my apartment. Yours is probably sealed with hocus-pocus. Are you all right?"

She sat up and put her feet on the floor and her erstwhile bed proved itself to be a couch. "Do you have something with sugar in it? Sweet tea or fruit juice?"

"Hot cocoa or tea," he told her.

"Tea."

He must have had water already hot because he was quickly back with a hot cup. She drank the sweet stuff down as fast as she could and the heat did as much as the sugar to clear her headache.

"Sorry," she said.

"For what, exactly," he said.

"For using you. I think you don't have any barriers," she told him slowly. "We all have safeguards, walls that keep out intruders. It's what keeps us safe."

In his silence she heard him consider that.

"So, I'm vulnerable to witches?"

She didn't know what to do with her empty cup, so she set it on the couch beside her. Then she used her left hand, her seeking hand, to *look* at him again.

"No, I don't think so. Your barriers seem solid . . . even stronger than usual as I'd expect from a wolf as far up the command structure as you are. I think you are only vulnerable to me."

"Which means?"

"Which means when I touch you I can see magic through your eyes . . . with practice I might even be able just to see. It means that you can feed my magic with your skin." She swallowed. "You're not going to like this."

"Tell me."

"You are acting like my familiar." She couldn't feel a thing from him. "If I had a familiar."

Floorboards creaked under his feet as his weight shifted. His shoulder brushed her as he picked up the empty cup. She heard him walk away from her and set the cup on a hard surface. "Do you need more tea?"

"No," she said, needing, suddenly to be in a familiar place. Somewhere she wasn't so dependent upon him. "I'm fine. If you would call me a taxi, I'd appreciate it." She stood up, too. Then realized she had no idea where the door was or what obstacles might be hiding on the floor. In her own apartment, redolent with her magic, she was never so vulnerable.

"Can you find my brother?"

She hadn't heard him move, not a creak, not a breath, but his voice told her he was no more than a few inches from her. Disoriented and vulnerable, she was afraid of him for the first time.

He took a big step away from her. "I'm not going to hurt you."

"Sorry," she told him. "You startled me. Do we still have the gum?"

"Yes. You said she was on a boat."

She'd forgotten, but as soon as he said it, she could picture it in her head. That hadn't been the way the spell was supposed to work. It was more of a "hot and cold" spell, but she could still see the boat in her mind's eye.

Nothing had really changed, except that she'd used someone without asking. There was still a policeman to be saved and her father to kill.

"If we still have the gum, I can find Molly—the girl on your brother's phone call."

"I have a buddy whose boat we can borrow."

"All right," she told him after a moment. "Do you have some aspirin?"

She hated boating. The rocking motion disrupted her sense of direction, the engine's roar obscured softer sounds, and the scent of the ocean covered the subtler scents she used to negotiate everyday life. Worse than all of that, though, was the thought of trying to swim without knowing where she was going. The damp air chilled her already cold skin.

"Which direction?" said Tom over the sound of the engine.

His presence shouldn't have made her feel better—werewolves couldn't swim at all—but it did. She pointed with the hand that held the gum. "Not far now," she warned him.

"There's a private dock about half mile up the coast. Looks like it's been here a while," he told me. "There's a boat—*The Tern*, the bird."

It felt right. "I think that must be it."

There were other boats on the water, she could hear them. "What time is it?"

"About ten in the morning. We're passing the boat right now."

Molly's traces, left on the gum, pulled toward its source, tugging Moira's hand toward the back of the boat. "That's it."

"There's a park with docks about a mile back," he said and the boat tilted to the side. "We'll go tie up there and come back on foot."

But when he'd tied the boat up, he changed his mind. "Why don't you stay here and let me check this out?"

Moira rubbed her hands together. It bothered her to have her magic doing something it wasn't supposed to be and she'd let it throw her off her game: time to collect herself. She gave him a sultry smile. "Poor blind girl," she said. "Must be kept out of danger, do you think?" She turned a hand palm up and heard the whoosh of flame as it caught fire. "You'll need me when you find Molly—you may be a werewolf, but she's a witch who looks like a pretty young thing." She snuffed the flame and dusted off her hands. "Besides, she's afraid of me. She'll tell me where your brother is."

She didn't let him know how grateful she was for the help he gave her exiting the boat. When this night was over he'd go back to his life and she to hers. If she wanted to keep him—she knew that he wouldn't want to be kept by her. She was a witch and ugly with scars of the past.

Besides, if her dreams were right, she wouldn't survive to see nightfall.

She threaded through the dense underbrush as if she could see every hanging branch, one hand on his back and her other held out in front of her. He wondered if she was using magic to see.

She wasn't using him. Her hand in the middle of his back was warm and light, but his flannel shirt was between it and skin. Probably she was reading his body language and using her upraised hand as an insurance policy against low-hanging branches.

They followed a half-overgrown path that had been trod out a hundred feet or so from the coast which was obscured by ferns and underbrush. He kept his ears tuned so if they started heading away from the ocean he'd know it.

The Tern had been moored in small natural harbor on a battered dock next to the remains of a boathouse. A private property rather then the public dock he'd used.

They'd traveled north and were somewhere not too far from Everett by his reckoning. He wasn't terribly surprised when their path ended in a brand new eight foot chain link fence. Someone had a gold mine on their hands and they were waiting to sell it to some developer when the price was right. Until then they'd try to keep out the riffraff.

He helped Moira over the fence, mostly a matter of whispering a few directions until she found the top of it. He waited until she was over and then vaulted over himself.

The path that they'd been following continued on, though not nearly as well traveled as it had been before the fence. A quarter mile of blackberry brambles ended abruptly in thigh-deep, damp grasslands that might once have been a lawn. He stopped before they left the cover of the bushes, sinking down to rest on his heels.

"There's a burnt-out house here," he told Moira, who had ducked down when he did. "It must have burned down a couple of years ago because I don't smell it."

"Hidden," she commented.

"Someone's had tents up here," he told her. "And I see the remnants of a camp fire."

"Can you see the boat from here?"

"No, but there's a path I think should lead down to the water. I think this is the place."

She pulled her hand away from his arm. "Can you go check it out without being seen?"

"It would be easier if I do it as a wolf," Tom admitted. "But I don't dare. We might have to make a quick getaway and it'll be a while before I can shift back to human." He hoped Jon would be healthy enough to pilot in an emergency—but he didn't like to make plans that depended upon an unknown. Moira wasn't going to be piloting a boat anywhere.

"Wait," she told him. She murmured a few words and then put her cold fingers against his throat. A sudden shock, like a static charge on steroids, hit him and when it was over her fingers were hot on his pulse. "You aren't invisible, but it'll make people want to overlook you."

He pulled out his HK and checked the magazine before sliding it back in. The big gun fit his hand like a glove. He believed in using weapons, guns or fangs, whatever got the job done.

"It won't take me long."

"If you don't go you'll never get back," she told him and gave him a gentle push. "I can take care of myself."

It didn't sit right with him, leaving her alone in the territory of his enemies, but common sense said he'd have a better chance of roaming unseen. And no one tackled a witch lightly—not even other witches.

Spell or no, he slid through the wet overgrown trees like a shadow, crouching to minimize his silhouette and avoiding anything likely to crunch. One thing living in Seattle did was minimize the number of things that could crunch under your foot—all the leaves were wet and moldy without a noise to be had.

The boat was there, bobbing gently in the water. Empty. He closed his eyes and let the morning air tell him all it could.

His brother had been in the boat. There had been others, too—Tom memorized their scent. If anything happened to Jon he'd track them down and kill them, one by one. Once he had them, he let his nose lead him to Jon.

He found blood where Jon had scraped against a tree, crushed plants where his brother had tried to get away and rolled around in the mud with another man. Or maybe he'd just been laying a trail for Tom. Jon knew Tom would come for him—that's what family did.

The path the kidnappers took paralleled the waterfront for a while and then headed inland, but not for the burnt-out house. Someone had found a better hideout. Nearly hidden under shelter of trees, a small barn nestled snugly amidst broken pieces of corral fencing. Its silvered sides bore only a hint of red paint, but the aluminum roof, though covered with moss, was undamaged.

And his brother was there. He couldn't quite hear what Jon was saying, but he recognized his voice . . . and the slurring rapid rhythm of his schizophrenic-mimicry. If Jon was acting, he was all right. The relief of that settled in his spine and steadied his nerves.

All he needed to do was get his witch . . . movement caught his attention and he dropped to the ground and froze, hidden by wet grass and weeds.

Moira wasn't surprised when they found her—ten in the morning isn't a good time to hide. It was one of the young ones—she could tell by the surprised squeal and the rapid thud of footsteps as he ran for help.

Of course if she'd really been trying to hide, she might have managed it. But it had occurred to her, sometime after Tom left, that if she wanted to find Samhain—the easiest thing might be to let them find her. So she set about attracting their attention.

If they found her, it would unnerve them. They knew she worked alone. Her arrival here would puzzle them, but they wouldn't look for anyone else—leaving Tom as her secret weapon.

Magic calls to magic, unless the witch takes pains to hide it, so any of them should have been able to feel the flames that danced over her hands. It had taken them longer than she expected. While she waited for the boy to return, she found a sharp edged rock and put it in her pocket. She folded her legs and let the coolness of the damp earth to flow through her.

She didn't hear him come, but she knew by his silence who the young covenist had run to.

"Hello, Father," she told him, rising to her feet. "We have much to talk about."

She didn't look like a captive, Tom thought, watching Moira walk to the barn as if she'd been there before, though she might have been following the sullen-looking, half-grown boy who stalked through the grass ahead of her. A tall man followed them both, his hungry eyes on Moira's back.

His wolf recognized another dominant male with a snarl, while Tom thought the man was too young to have a grown daughter. But there was no one else this could be than Lin Keller—that predator was not a man who followed anyone or allowed anyone around him who might challenge him. He'd seen an Alpha or two like that.

Tom watched them until they disappeared into the barn.

It hurt to imagine she might have betrayed him—as if there were some bond between them, though he hadn't known her a full day. Part of him would not believe it. He remembered her indignation when she thought he believed she was part of Samhain and it comforted him.

It didn't matter, couldn't matter. Not yet. Saving Jon mattered and the rest would wait. His witch was captured or had betrayed him. Either way it was time to let the wolf free.

The change hurt, but experience meant he made no sound as his bones rearranged themselves and his muscles stretched and slithered to adjust to his new shape. It took fifteen minutes of agony before he rose on four paws, a snarl fixed on his muzzle—ready to kill someone. Anyone.

Instead he stalked like a ghost to the barn where his witch waited. He rejected the door they'd used, but prowled around the side where four stall doors awaited. Two of them were broken with missing boards, one of the openings was big enough for him to slide through.

The interior of the barn was dark and the stall's half-walls blocked his view of the main section where his quarry waited. Jon was still going strong, a wild ranting conversation with no one about the Old Testament, complete with quotes. Tom knew a lot of them himself.

"Killing things again, Father?" said Moira's cool disapproving voice, cutting though Jon's soliloquy.

And suddenly Tom could breathe again. They'd found her somehow, Samhain's Coven had, but she wasn't one of them.

"So judgmental." Tom had expected something . . . bigger from the man's voice. His own Alpha, for instance, could have made a living as a televangelist with his raw fire-and-brimstone voice. This man sounded like an accountant.

"Kill her. You have to kill her before she destroys us—I have seen it." It was the girl from Jon's message, Molly.

"You couldn't see your way out of a paper bag, Molly," said Moira. "Not that you're wrong, of course."

There were other people in the barn, Tom could smell them, but they stayed quiet.

"You aren't going to kill me," said Kouros. "If you could have done that you'd have done it before now. Which brings me to my point, why are you here?"

"To stop you from killing this man," Moira told him.

"I've killed men before—and you haven't stopped me. What is so special about this one?"

Moira felt the burden of all those deaths upon her shoulders. He was right. She could have killed him before—before he'd killed anyone else.

"This one has a brother," she said.

She felt Tom's presence in the barn, but her look-past-me spell must have still been working because no one seemed to notice. And any witch with a modicum of sensitivity to auras would have felt him. His brother was a faint trace to her left—which his constant stream of words made far clearer than her magic was able to.

Her father she could only follow from his voice.

There were other people in the structure—she hadn't quite decided what the cavernous building was: probably a barn, given the dirt floor and faint odor of cow—but she couldn't pinpoint them either. She knew where Molly was, though. And Molly was the important one, Kouros's right hand.

"Someone *paid* you to go up against me?" Her father's voice was faintly incredulous. "Against us?"

Then he did something, made some gesture. She wouldn't have known except for Molly's sigh of relief. So she didn't feel too badly when she tied Molly's essence, through the gum she still held, into her shield.

When the coven's magic hit the shield, it was Molly who took the damage. Who died. Molly, her little sister whose presence she could no longer feel.

Someone, a young man, screamed Molly's coven name—Mentha. And there was a flurry of movement where Moira had last sensed her.

Moira dropped the now-useless bit of gum on the ground.

"Oh, you'll pay for that," breathed her father. "Pay in pain and power until there is nothing left of you."

Someone sent power her way, but it wasn't a concerted spell from the coven and it slid off her protections without harm. Unlike the fist that struck her in the face, driving her glasses into her nose and knocking her to the ground—her father's fist. She'd recognize the weight of it anywhere.

Unsure of where her enemies were, she stayed where she was, listening. But she didn't hear Tom, he was just suddenly there. And the circle of growing terror that spread around him—of all the emotions possible, it was fear that she could sense most often—told her he was in his lupine form. It must have been impressive.

"Your victim has a brother," she told her father again, knowing he'd hear the smugness in her tones. "And you've made him very angry."

The beast beside her roared. Someone screamed . . . even witches are afraid of monsters.

The coven broke. Children most of them, they broke and ran. Molly's death followed by a beast out of their worst nightmares were more than they could face, partially-trained, deliberately crippled fodder for her father that they were.

Tom growled, the sound finding a silent echo in her own chest as if he were a bass drum. He moved, a swift silent predator, and someone who hadn't run died. Tom's brother, she noticed had fallen entirely silent.

"A werewolf," breathed Kouros. "Oh, now there is a worthy kill." But she felt his terror and knew he'd attack Tom before he took care of her.

She reached out with her left hand, intending to spread her own defenses to the wolf—though that would leave them too thin to be very effective—but she hadn't counted on the odd effect he had on her magic. On her.

Her father's spell—a vile thing that would have induced terrible pain and permanently damaged Tom had it hit—connected just after she touched the wolf. And for a moment, maybe a whole breath, nothing happened.

Then she felt every hair under her hand stand to attention and Tom made an odd sound and power swept through her from him—all the magic Kouros had sent—and it filled her well to overflowing.

And she could see. For the first time since she'd been thirteen she could see.

She stood up, shedding broken pieces of sunglasses to the ground. The wolf beside her was huge, chocolate-brown, and easily tall enough to leave her hand on his shoulder as she came to her feet. A silvery scar curled around his snarling muzzle. His eyes were yellow-brown and cold. A sweeping glance showed her two dead bodies, one burned the other savaged; a very dirty, hairy man tied to a post with his hands behind his back who could only be Tom's brother Jon.

And her father, looking much younger than she remembered him. No wonder he went for teens to populate his *coven*—he was stealing their youth as well as their magic. A coven should be a meeting of equals, not a feeding trough for a single greedy witch.

She looked at him and saw that he was afraid. He should be. The werewolf had frightened him, too, no matter how calm he'd sounded. He'd used all of his magic to power his spell—he'd left himself defenseless. And now he was afraid of her.

Just as she had dreamed. She pulled the stone out of her pocket—and it seemed to her that she had all the time in the world to use it and cut her right hand open. Then she pointed it, her bloody hand of power at him.

"*By the blood we share,*" she whispered and felt the magic gather. "*Blood follows blood.*"

"You'll die, too," Kouros said frantically as if she didn't know.

Before she spoke the last word she lifted her other hand from Tom's soft fur so that none of this magic would fall to him. And as soon as she did, she could no longer see. But she wouldn't be blind for long.

Tom started moving before her fingers left him, knocking into her with his hip and spoiling her aim. Her magic flooded through him, hitting him instead of the one she'd aimed all that power at. The wolf let it sizzle through his bones and returned it to her, clean.

Pleasant as that was, he didn't let it distract him from his goal. He was moving so fast that the man was still looking at Moira when the wolf landed on him.

Die, he thought as he buried his fangs in Kouros's throat, drinking his blood and his death in one delicious mouthful of flesh. This one had moved against the wolf's family, against the wolf's witch. Satisfaction made the meat even sweeter.

"Tom?" Moira sounded lost.

"Tom's fine," answered his brother's rusty voice, he'd talked himself hoarse. "You just sit there until he calms down a little. You all right, lady?"

Tom lifted his head and looked at his witch. She was huddled on the ground looking small and lost, her scarred face bared for all the world to see. She looked fragile, but Tom knew better and Jon would learn.

As the dead man under his claws had learned. Kouros died knowing she would have killed him.

He had been willing to give her that kill—but not if it meant her death. So Tom had the double satisfaction of saving her and killing the man. He went back to his meal.

"Tom, stop that," Jon said. "Ick. I know you aren't hungry. Stop it now."

"Is Kouros dead?" His witch sounded shaken up.

"As dead as anyone I've seen," said Jon. "Look, Tom. I appreciate the sentiment; I've wanted to do that any time this last day. But I'd like to get out of here before some of those kids decide to come back while I'm still tied up." He paused. "Your lady needs to get out of here."

Tom hesitated, but Jon was right. He wasn't hungry anymore and it was time to take his family home.

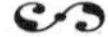

Patricia Briggs is the author of the #1 *New York Times*-bestselling Mercedes Thompson series, the eighth of which—*Night Broken*—was published earlier this year. She lives with six horses, a dog, three cats, snakes, birds, kids, and a very awesome and tolerant husband in a home that resembles a zoo crossed with a library. The horses live outside.

The City: *Nameless, but typical, American city.*

The Magic: *You are told you are a wizard, but wizardry is nothing at all like TV or the movies. Plus there's an "Other Side" out to harm the world . . . and you. But it's all crap—right?*

STONE MAN

NANCY KRESS

Jared Stoffel never even saw the car that hit him. He ollied off the concrete steps of the Randolph Street Rec Center down onto the street and was coming down on his skateboard when *wham!* his butt was smacked hard enough to rattle his teeth and Jared went down. A second before the pain registered, he threw up his arms to shield his face. The Bird-house went flying—he saw it in the air, wheels spinning, a moment before his body hit the street. All at once he was smothered under *a ton of stones he couldn't breathe he was going to die and someone was screaming but it was mostly the rocks —God the boulders flying to land on top of him, under him, everywhere . . .* Everything went black.

"You with us yet, child?"

"Rocks." It came out "bogs." Jared put his hand to his face. The hand stopped an inch away on his swollen mouth.

"How many fingers am I holding up?"

"Who."

"What day is it?"

"Breeday."

"Just rest a while. You took a nasty fall." The blurry old nurse dressed in some stupid pants with yellow ducks on them stuck a needle in Jared's arm and went away.

When he came to again, everything was clearer. A TV on a shelf high up near the ceiling droned out some news about an earthquake someplace. An old man in a white coat sat in a chair by Jared's bed, reading. Jared tried to sit up, and the man rose and eased him back down. "Just stay quiet a little longer."

"Where am I?"

"Perry Street Medical Center. You got hit by a car while skateboarding, but you have nothing more than two fractured ribs and a lacerated hand. You're a very lucky young man."

"Oh, right. Just lousy with luck." The words came out correctly; his lips weren't nearly as swollen. The tiny room had no windows. How long had he been in here?

"I'm Dr. Kendall and I need some information. What's your name, son?"

"I'm not your son." Jared lay trying to remember this accident. Shawn—he'd been skateboarding with Shawn. Shawn had yelled when Jared got hit. "Shawn?"

"Your name's Shawn? Shawn What?"

"I'm not Shawn, dumb-ass. He's my friend, with me. Where's Shawn?"

The doctor grimaced. "Some friend. He took off running as soon as the ambulance arrived. What were you two doing that he didn't want to get caught? Never mind, I don't want to know. But I do need to know your name."

"Why?"

"To notify your parents, for one thing."

"Forget it. She won't come."

Something moved behind the doctor's eyes. He glanced up at the TV, still showing pictures of an earthquake, then returned to watching Jared closely. Too closely. The guy was maybe fifty, maybe sixty, with white hair, but that didn't mean he couldn't be a—was he even really a doctor? Jared said, "Hey, stop staring like that, sicko."

"Ah," the doctor said sadly. "I see. Damn. But I still need to know your name. For the records we—"

"I don't got any insurance. So you can just let me out of here now." Again Jared tried to sit up.

"Lie down, son. We can't release you yet. Now please tell me your name."

"Jared."

"Jared What?"

"None of your business." If he didn't say any more, maybe they'd throw him out. The doc said he wasn't hurt bad. He could crash at Shawn's. If Ma saw him like this, she'd smash the Birdhouse for sure. She— "Hey! Where's my deck?"

"Your what?"

"My deck! The Bird! My skateboard!"

"Oh. I'm afraid I don't know."

"You mean you just left it in the *street?*" Gone now, for sure. And it had been a huge set of trouble to steal it!

Again that strange expression in Kendall's eyes. He said quietly, "Jared, I will personally replace your skateboard, buy you a brand-new and very good one, if you will answer some questions for me first."

"You? Buy me a new deck? For giving you what?"

"I already told you. All you need do is answer some questions."

"Nobody gives away new decks for free!"

"I will, to you." Kendall's eyes, Jared saw, were light brown, full of some emotion Jared didn't understand. But he wasn't picking up rip-off vibes from the man. Hope surged through him. A new deck . . . maybe an Abec four . . . He squashed the hope. Hope just got you hurt.

Kendall reached into his pocket and drew out a wad of bills. "How much does a good skateboard cost?"

Jared's eyes hung on the money. He could get a Hawk deck . . . good trucks and wheels . . . "Two hundred dollars." Maybe the old guy didn't know what stuff cost.

Kendall counted ten twenties and held them out in his closed hand. "After you answer three questions."

"Just three? Okay, but better not try anything perv."

"First, your name and address."

"Jared Parsell, 62 Randolph."

Kendall withdrew his hand. "You're lying."

How did the old bastard *know?* "Wait, don't put the money away . . . I'm Jared Stoffel, and I live at 489 Center Street." When he lived anywhere at all. Ma, strung out on crystal most of the time, only noticed when he screwed up, not when he stayed away. She was pretty lame about time.

Kendall said, "When were you born?"

"April 6, 1993."

Closing his eyes, Kendall moved his lips silently, as if figuring something. Finally, he said, as if it mattered, "Full moon."

"Whatever."

"Now the last question: How did all those stones get around you during the hit-and-run?"

"What?"

"When the ambulance arrived, you were lying on, and were covered with, small stones. They appear to have come from a flowerbed on the other side of the Recreation Center. How did they get with you?"

A vague memory stirred in Jared's mind. Rocks—he was being smothered with rocks, and someone—him—said "bogs." And Shawn yelled something as Jared fell, something Jared couldn't remember now . . .

Jared had thought the rocks were in his mind—something from, like, the pain of the accident. Not real. But maybe . . .

Kendall was watching him sadly. Why sad? This old psycho gave Jared the creeps.

"I don't know anything about any stones."

"You and Shawn weren't playing some game involving the stones? Throwing them at cars or something?"

"Jesus, man, I'm thirteen, not eight!"

"I see," Dr. Kendall said. He handed the two hundred dollars to Jared, who seized it eagerly, even though leaning forward caused pain to stab through his torso. Jared moved his legs toward the end of the bed.

Kendall eased them back. "Not yet, son, I'm afraid." He looked even sadder than before.

"Get your hands off me! I answered your stupid questions!"

"Yes, and the money is yours. But you can't leave yet. Not until you see one other person."

"I don't want to see any more doctors!"

"It's not a doctor. *I'm* a doctor. Larson is a . . . well, you'll see. Larson!"

The door opened and another man entered. This one was young, big, tough-looking, with long hair and a do-rag. He wore a leather jacket and gold necklace, serious gold. A dealer, maybe a gangbanger, maybe even a leader. Or a narc. He stood at the end of Jared's bed, big hands resting lightly on the metal railing, and stared unsmiling. "So is he, Doc?"

"Yes."

"You sure? Never mind, I know you don't make mistakes. But, God . . . *look* at him."

"Look at your dumb-ass self," Jared said, but even to him the words sounded lame. Larson scared him, although he wasn't going to admit that.

"Watch your mouth, kid," Larson snarled. "I don't like this any better than you do. But if you are one of us, then you are. The doc doesn't make mistakes. Damn it to hell anyway!"

"If I'm what? What am I?" Jared said.

"A wizard," Dr. Kendall said. "You're a wizard, Jared. As of now."

Larson left the explanations to Kendall. With a disgusted look over his shoulder at the hospital bed, Larson stormed out, slamming the door. Jared caught the scandalized look of a passing nurse just before the door shook on its hinges.

"A wizard. Yeah, right," Jared said. "Any minute now I'm gonna turn you into a pigeon. No, wait—you're already a pigeon if you believe that crap."

"I'm afraid it's true," Kendall said. "During your accident you summoned those rocks. The smoothest stones from the flowerbed flew through the air and landed on you, under you, around you. You skidded across the pavement on them as if on ball bearings. That broke your fall, maybe saved your life."

"Right. Anything you say."

"You were born under the full moon, also a requirement, although we don't know why. You—"

"And you're a wizard, too, huh?"

"No," Kendall said sadly, "I'm not. I can spot one is all, and so the Brotherhood uses me."

"Uh-huh. So you can't, like, show me something wizardy right now, and Larson left before he had to. Convenient."

"Nothing 'wizardy' could be done here anyway. Not here, in the presence of metal. Not by any wizard now living." Kendall leaned forward, his hands on his knees. "Magic is very old, Jared, much older than even the most primitive civilization. It governs only the things found in nature, and it cannot operate near to the things that are not. The only reason you could summon those stones at all is because your skateboard went flying, you weren't carrying a cell phone, and you had on pull-on running shorts with no zipper."

"You leave my shorts out of this," Jared said. "How come I never did any magic before, huh? You tell me that?"

"That's easy. Your accident. The ability to do magic, among those who possess it at all, is only released in the presence of pain."

"Pain?"

"Yes, Jared," Kendall said quietly. "Everything in life costs, even magic. The price is pain."

This was the first thing the old man had said that made any sense to Jared. He knew things cost. He knew about pain.

But the rest of it was pure psycho bull. And bull with a reason. He said, "So now you tell me I'm going to one of those wizard schools, huh? Like in that book? Only guess what—it'll really turn out to be just another lock-down, like Juvie."

"There is no such thing as a wizard school. All we have is the Brotherhood, and that all too inadequate to its task."

"Listen, this sucks. I'm outta here, man. What do I gotta sign?"

"You're a minor. A parent must sign your release forms."

"Like that's gonna happen. My mom's strung out most of the time and my dad's long gone. You wait on a parent, I'll be here forever. Where's my clothes?"

"You can't—"

"Watch me. I ain't waiting here for Child Services to stick me in a foster home. And I ain't listening to no more of your bull, neither."

"You can talk better than that when you want to," Kendall said. "I've heard you do so. Here, if you're really going—no, your shoes are in that cupboard over there—take this. It's my home address. You can come see me anytime you want, Jared. For any reason."

"Don't hold your breath." He found the shoes, finished dressing, and walked out of the medical center. He had to lean twice against walls to do it, breathing deeply and fighting his own stomach, but he did it.

"Welcome to the Brotherhood, Jared," Kendall said sadly.

"Forget you," Jared said.

It was a week before he could make it out of the house. He lay in his bedroom, fighting the pain, distracting himself with the songs on the radio and with the Game Boy he'd stolen three months ago. Ma had sold the Xbox, but he'd hidden the Game Boy and the radio behind the broken dishwasher, and she hadn't found them. He should have gotten painkillers before he left the clinic. The old doc would probably have given him some, but Jared hadn't thought of it. Fortunately, it was one of the times when there was food in the house. Ma's new guy, whom Jared encountered in the kitchen in his underwear, liked to eat well.

After a week the bedclothes, not too clean to begin with, stank, but Jared felt better. He knew he was better because he was bored. The day after that he dressed and went out. He didn't find anybody on the street. Then he remembered that school had started.

He walked to Benjamin Franklin Middle School, scowled at the security guard, and passed through the metal detector. When classes changed, kids flooded into the halls.

"Hey! Shawn!"

Shawn Delancey glanced up from the girl he was talking to, and a strange expression crossed his face. He nodded coolly. Jared hobbled over to him.

"I'm back, man."

"Yeah, I see."

"So what you doing here? In school?"

Shawn didn't answer. He turned back to the girl, without introducing her. Jared felt his face grow hot.

"Hey, you dissing me, Shawn?"

"I'm busy right now. Can't you see that?"

This had never happened before. He and Shawn were *tight,* had always been tight. The girl snickered. Jared limped away.

The prick, the bastard . . .

But he couldn't let it go. He caught Shawn later, leaving school after fourth period, carrying his deck. Jared stepped out from an alley and said, "Shawn. What's wrong, man?"

"Nothing. I gotta go."

Anger and hurt made him desperate. "Dude, it's me! Me!"

Shawn stopped, turning from embarrassment to anger. Maybe, Jared suddenly thought, they were the same thing. "Just leave me alone, Jared, okay? I don't need you and your lame crap!"

His crap. He didn't have any crap except . . . it was weird and stupid, but he couldn't think of anything else. He said quietly, testing, "The stones?"

"I don't know how you did that, but . . . just leave me alone!" Shawn hurried off.

So it had been the stones. And the stones had happened. They really had. Only it had been some kind of freak accident, wind devil or something, not any freaking magic.

"Forget you!" he yelled after Shawn, but Shawn was already on his board, skimming lightly out of Jared's sight.

With Kendall's two hundred dollars, Jared bought a new deck, a deluxe Hawk, plus awesome trucks and wheels. He spent every day alone, in another neighborhood, painfully regaining his mobility and skill. After what happened with Shawn, he didn't want to approach his other friends, and anyway he didn't have too many other friends. Mostly it had been him and Shawn.

Ma's boyfriend broke up with her, and Jared didn't want to be home with her much; she was always wailing, or else out scoring. When the boyfriend's food was gone, she barely bought more. Sometimes Jared's stomach growled while he practiced, over and over, ollies and kickflips and fifty-fifty grinds and even a few hardflips. He sped around the neighborhood, a better one than his own, past trees turning from green to red and gold, past little kids on trikes, past bright flowers in beds edged with stones.

All the stones stayed where they were supposed to.

It was hunger and cold that finally made him pull out the card Dr. Kendall had given him at the clinic. Hunger, cold, and maybe loneliness, although he didn't like to admit that. The address was not far away, on Carter Street. Jared skated over, preparing an excuse in his mind.

Kendall's house wasn't much, a small two-story—weren't doctors supposed to make a lot of money? Neat bushes surrounded it, and the porch light shone cheerfully in the October dusk. Jared rang the bell and scowled.

"Hi, Doc, something's wrong with my hand. You must not've fixed it right."

"Come in, Jared," Kendall said. Why did the guy always look so sad to see him? What a crock. But the house was warm and smelled of meat roasting. Jared's mouth filled with sweet water. "Let me see your hand . . . you had slight damage to your left transverse ligament from the stones, but it looks all right now. Would you like to stay to dinner?"

"I already ate," Jared said, scowling more deeply. His stomach growled.

"Then have a second dinner just to keep me company. My housekeeper just left, and she cooks a lot on Mondays so she doesn't have to do much the rest of the week." Kendall led the way to the tiny dining room without giving Jared a chance to answer, so he followed. The room had a big table, real curtains, a china chest filled with dishes. Kendall set a second place.

Roast beef and mashed potatoes and peas and a pudding that tasted of apples. Jared tried not to gobble too hard. When he finished, he glanced out the window. A cold rain fell. That sucked—it was too easy to snap a board in the rain, and, anyway, the wood got all soggy.

Kendall, who had been silent throughout dinner, said, "How about a game of *Street Fighter*?"

"You play *Street Fighter*? You? I know it's an old game and everything, but . . . you?"

Kendall had a new Nintendo for the vintage game. He wielded the controllers pretty well for an old guy. Jared beat him, but only barely. As they played, Kendall said casually, "So how's everything going?"

"Like what . . . got you!"

"Like, have you attempted any wizardry?"

"Cut the crap, man."

"All right. How's school?"

He said it in such a fake, prissy tone that Jared had to laugh. Then he didn't. Throwing down the controller in midgame, abruptly he stood. "I gotta go."

"School's not going well?"

"Nothing's going well, thanks to you guys," Jared shouted, before he knew he was going to say anything at all. "Shawn won't hang with me and the rest is just crap and—"

"Shawn is avoiding you?" Kendall said. "What about the other kids?"

"None of your business! Now let me outta here!"

"The door is that way," Kendall said calmly. "And you're welcome for dinner," but Jared was already halfway out the front door, yanking up his collar against the rain, furious at . . . something.

Everything.

"Come back whenever you like," Kendall called after him. "I've got *Super Smash Brothers*, too."

He went back. The first time back, he planned on breaking in and stealing the Nintendo. But Kendall was there, so he didn't, and they had dinner again, and played the Nintendo, and after that Jared didn't pretend there was still something wrong with his hand. Pretty soon he was there nearly every night. During the day he skated if the weather was sunny, hung out aimlessly at the mall if it wasn't, or watched TV at home if Ma wasn't there. Kendall never mentioned wizard stuff again. The food was always good. After a few weeks, Jared started doing the dishes. Sometimes they played Nintendo; sometimes Jared watched TV while Kendall read. Jared wasn't much of a reader. The house was warm.

At six thirty, they always had to stop and watch the news on TV. If there was an earthquake or a flood or a story about some farming problem, Kendall leaned forward intently, his hands on his knees.

On a cold night in November, when Jared knew the heat was off at home, he stayed the night in the guest room. At four a.m., with Kendall asleep, Jared prowled the house. Not to steal anything, just to look for . . . something.

In a drawer of the dining room china cabinet, under a pile of tablecloths, he found the picture. It was totally weird: a group of seventeen people who didn't look like they belonged together. A heavy, middle-aged woman in brown stretch pants and a pink top. A man in a blue uniform with a square badge like a security guard. Two kids, seven or eight, who looked like twins, in miniature gang clothing. An old woman in some kind of long gown. A black man in a gray suit, holding a briefcase. A guy in one of those lame Hawaiian shirts, grinning like an idiot. An Asian kid holding an armful of books.

And Shawn.

Jared stared at the picture. It really was Shawn. But what was this group? It sure as hell wasn't Shawn's family.

"Would you like some coffee?"

Jared whirled around. Kendall stood in the doorway in some old-guy pajamas. He didn't look mad, just that sad-thing, which was getting really old.

"Who are these guys? Why is Shawn here?"

"I just put the water on, Jared. Come into the kitchen."

Jared stood beside the kitchen table, refusing to sit down, while Kendall puttered with teakettle and instant coffee. "I asked you a question—who are those people? Is that your dumb-ass 'Brotherhood'?"

"You remembered that I mentioned them," Kendall said with pleasure. "I didn't know if you would. You were still on painkillers."

"I'm not stupid, man!"

"I know you're not. And no, that's not the Brotherhood. That's the Other Side."

"Other side of *what?* Make sense!"

Kendall poured hot water into his cup, stirred it, and sat across the table. "Jared, didn't you think it odd that Shawn avoided you after your accident? Instead of thinking it rather cool that you could command rocks?"

"'Rather cool,'" Jared mocked viciously. "'Command rocks.' C'mon, give me an answer! What's Shawn doing with those people?"

"He's one of them. And he had no idea you were a wizard, too, until the car hit you. And now he's staying away from you so you won't inadvertently discover what he is. You see, that's our main advantage over the Other Side. We know a lot more about them than they know about us."

"'Us'? I thought you said you wasn't a wizard!"

"I'm not. But I work with them. Pain releases the power, remember. I'm a doctor. I see a lot of pain. Sometimes it brings us one of our own, sometimes one from the Other Side. My position at the Medical Center is how we've been able to identify so many of them."

"I don't believe any of this crap."

"Fortunately, your believing or not believing does not change the reality." Kendall sipped his coffee. "I wish belief was all it took to make the Other Side disappear."

"'The Other Side.' Give me a break. And what are they supposed to be doing that's so bad? What you got against Shawn? You think he's going to set off a bomb or something?"

"I already told you, magic doesn't operate in the presence of metal, which bombs require. Magic is considerably older than that. It belongs to the sphere of nature, of grass and wind and animals and plants. And rocks, the oldest of all nature."

"Right. Sure. So Shawn's gonna mess up the world by growing the wrong grass? Get real!"

Abruptly Kendall leaned forward. "*You* get real, Jared. Your ignorance is appalling—what are they teaching you in that school? Yes, the Other Side might 'mess up the world' by growing the wrong grass, if there's profit in it. Money or power profit. Don't you know that there's money to be made from drought, from famine, from hurricanes, from killer bees, from mutated plants? There's always money to be made in disasters. You cause them, then you charge heavily to clean them up, as just one example. You're poised and ready with whatever is needed, because you know exactly when and where the disaster will occur. And no one ever suspects you caused it, because hurricanes and volcanoes and droughts and invasive plant species are all *completely natural.* Plus, no one in the developed countries, where money flows like green water, even believes in magic anyway. Now do you get it?"

"No," Jared shouted. "You telling me Shawn is rich from this magic? Man, he don't even have a decent deck!"

"No, because riches now would draw attention to the Other Side. And it takes a lot of international coordination to pull off a big profit from a major disaster. They've already managed a couple of small ones—did you read in the paper about that unexpected flood, along the Big Thompson River in Colorado? No, of course you didn't, you don't read the papers. But we think that flood was one of theirs. We're still organizing, too. One day Shawn will be very rich, and very powerful, although most of the world will never know how he did it. The FBI will assume drugs and spend futile years trying to prove it."

"So now you can see the future, too!"

"No, of course not, I just—"

"You're just full of crap! You're crazy, man, you know that? The biggest loser ever, and this sucks!" Jared jerked at the locks on the kitchen door, yanked it open, and bolted outside.

"Jared . . . wait . . . don't—"

He was already gone, skimming along the cold sidewalk in the dark. The man was more than crazy, he was totally gone. Psycho. Loony-bin. Jared was never going back there.

Where else was he going to go?

Jared shivered. Last evening's rain had stopped, but it was really cold out. His hoodie wasn't enough for this weather. He had to move faster, stay warm, get home.

Home. The heatless apartment where Ma and her new boyfriend would be sleeping under all the blankets, including Jared's, or—worse—up fighting, strung out on crystal. And getting home alone, this time of almost morning when only the gangbangers were out on the streets . . .

He stopped under a streetlight. For one terrible minute, he thought he might cry.

Bag that. And bag all the psycho stuff Kendall had been telling him, too. The old man had been kind to him. So what if he was crazy? He wasn't dangerous, and it wasn't like Jared hadn't dealt with worse. He could deal with anything he had to. And Kendall's place was warm, and had food.

Why *had* Shawn reacted so weird to Jared's accident?

He spun his board around and skated back to Kendall's, thinking hard.

The back door to Kendall's house still stood wide open. In the kitchen, the chairs were knocked over, and Kendall's coffee sloshed all over the floor. Blood smeared the table. Jared searched the whole house; Kendall was gone.

He found a flashlight in a kitchen drawer and took it outside. Fresh tire marks slashed across a corner of the soggy lawn. They led down Carter Street—but where after that?

He should call the cops.

Oh, like cops would believe in the kidnapping. If an adult went missing, they wouldn't even start looking for him for a couple of days. And they certainly wouldn't believe Jared, who had a bunch of citations, unpaid, for illegal skating at the Civic Center and the library.

It was only after he thought all this that Jared saw what it meant: that *he* believed Kendall had been kidnapped, and by the so-called "Other Side." The second he realized this, he started shaking. *Cold,* he thought. It was just the cold. Just the cold.

In the dark he skated to one end of the block, peered down it. Nothing. The other end of the block—also nothing.

No one else had been as good to him as Kendall had. Nobody, not ever.

There was no way to know which way the psychos had taken Kendall. No real way. Unless . . .

Jared looked around with his flashlight. The house next door to Kendall had a flowerbed edged with stones. Feeling like the biggest lamebrain in the whole crappy world, Jared picked up three of the rocks and thought, *Which way?*

Nothing happened, so he said it out loud: "Which way?" Nothing happened.

He stepped away from his deck, with its metal trucks, and tried again. Nothing.

His hoodie had a metal zipper, so, shivering, he took it off and laid it on top of the deck, twenty feet away. "Which way, you psycho stones?" Nothing.

His jeans had a metal zipper and studs. "No way," Jared said aloud, but a second later, shivering, he stripped them off and put them on top of his hoodie. In his underwear, shoes and socks, and T-shirt, he scanned the street. Nobody there—it was four-thirty in the morning. He picked up the rocks again. "Which way, you little bastards?"

The rocks grew warm in his hand.

Jared shrieked and dropped them. A sharp pain shot through his wrist, gone in a moment. The stones fell in a straight line toward the north end of Carter Street. Jared stared, disbelieving. He did it again, this time facing south. The rocks got warm, he dropped them, and they swirled around his body to form a line going north. The sharp pain hit his wrist.

He closed his eyes. No way. *This psycho stuff doesn't happen.* All at once he would have given anything, anything in the entire world, to be back skating at the Civic Center with Shawn, ollieing off the steps and trying to do grinds down the rail, trying to land a 540 flip.

Instead, he picked up his clothing and the three rocks, got on his deck, and skated north.

At the next intersection, he again walked away from the board and jeans and hoodie, and said, "Which way?" The rocks pointed east.

Two more turns and he was glad to see the interstate, no turns off it for a long ways. His wrist throbbed from the repeated flashes of pain. Jared put his jeans and hoodie back on. His legs felt like ice—not a good way to skate. But he wasn't going to do any tricks, just straight skating, and the speed would warm him. He skated up the on-ramp, then along the highway, dodging the trucks that blatted angry horns at him, keeping a sharp eye out for cops.

At the first exit, he got off the highway and did the stones thing. They told him to get back on. Jared glanced at the sky, worried; already it was starting to get red in the east. He put on his clothes and skated back onto the highway. His stomach grumbled and he cursed at it, at Kendall, at the world.

At the next exit, the stones told him to follow a deserted stretch of country road. Jared noted its name: *County Line Road.*

The house wasn't far, fortunately: the third house, set back in the woods. A white van with muddy tires sat in the driveway. The van said McCLELLAN SECURITY. Jared remembered the man in the blue uniform in the picture.

He crept up to the house. All the curtains were shut and the basement windows painted black, but when he put his ear to the grimy glass, Jared could hear noises in the basement.

A thud. A groan. Then, "Once more, Doctor—all the names, please. Now. This is getting boring."

Silence. Then Kendall screamed.

They were torturing him to get the Brotherhood names! Including Jared's name. *"You see, that's our main advantage over the Other Side. We know a lot more about them than they know about us."* That's what Kendall had said. But now—

No, not Jared's name. They already had Jared's name, thanks to Shawn. And if Jared had stayed five minutes longer at Kendall's house, they'd have had him down in that basement, too.

He could skate away. Get back on the highway, never go home again, go . . . where?

Kendall screamed again.

A rage filled Jared. He thought he'd been angry before—at Shawn, at his mother, at the cops, at the crap that happened and went on happening and never seemed to stop. But it hadn't been anger like this. This was the mother of angers, the huge one, the serious-hang-time-in-orbit of anger.

Woods bordered the back of the house. Jared thrashed a little way into them, shoved his deck under some bushes, added his jeans and hoodie. Then he stood there, twigs scratching his bare legs and some kind of insects biting at his face, and closed his eyes. He pictured rocks. All kinds of rocks, all sizes, pointy and smooth and rough, smashing through the black-painted basement windows and into the heads of every single bastard down there except Kendall. He pictured the blood and the wounds and the—

Jared screamed. Pain tore through his whole body, dropping him into the bushes. His arms and legs were on fire, he was going to die, he would never skate again—

The pain vanished, leaving him gasping. He staggered to his feet, just in time to see the rocks homing in on the house, flying in from every direction like fighter jets on some video game, but real and solid as Jared himself. All the painted windows smashed, and Jared heard yells and screams from the house. Then silence.

It couldn't have happened. It did happen.

He struggled out of the bushes and ran to the front door. It was locked, and so was the back door. Finally, he ran to the closest busted window, knocked out the glass still stuck around the edges, and slid into the basement, careful to land on his sneakers amid the shards and splinters of glass.

Two men and a woman lay bleeding on the floor, covered with stones. Kendall was tied to a chair, gaping at him. The old man had a gash on his forehead and serious blood on the arm of his pajamas. Jared picked up the knife somebody had dropped and cut Kendall's ropes. He doubled over, gasping, and Jared was afraid Kendall was having a heart attack or something. But then he straightened and staggered to his feet.

"Jared . . . I'm all . . . right . . . "

"Sure you are. Never better, right? C'mon." Jared helped him up the stairs, but then didn't know what to do next.

Kendall did. He gasped, "Go back downstairs and get a cell phone from anybody who has one. Be careful—they're not dead. Don't kill anybody, Jared—we don't want a murder investigation. Then come back up here and lock the door at the top of the stairs."

Jared did as he was told, a sudden sick feeling in his stomach. It fought with a feeling of unreality—*this can't be happening*—that only got stronger when he again saw all the stones lying around the basement.

He'd done that. Him, Jared Stoffel.

Kendall called somebody on the cell, said, "Code blue. The address is . . . " and he looked at Jared. Jared gave it to him. They only had to wait a few minutes before a car screeched up and they went out to meet it. A silver Mercedes S, at least seventy grand. Jared blinked. A pretty black girl jumped out. She had on a school uniform like rich girls wore, green skirt and jacket and a little green tie on a white blouse. Ordinarily Jared hated kids like that, rich snobs, but now was different.

"He did it?" she said, talking to Kendall but staring at Jared, her eyes wide. "How did—"

"I don't know yet," Kendall said. "How much—"

"I hadn't yet told them anything. But I would have, Denise." She nodded, grimaced, and tenderly helped Kendall into the car, apparently not caring that he got blood on the leather seat. Jared climbed into the back. Denise must be old enough to drive, he figured, but she didn't look it. Was the Mercedes hers, or her family's, or maybe stolen?

She pulled the car onto the road and accelerated hard. Over her shoulder Denise threw Jared a glance at once respectful and a little scared. He sat up straighter in the backseat. She said, "Stones?"

"Yeah," Jared said.

"We don't have anybody that can do stone."

He liked the tone of her voice. It let him say, "What do you do?"

"Wind. But strictly small-time. You're *gifted,* dude."

"You ain't seen nothing yet. You should see me skate."

In the front seat, one arm cradled carefully in the other, Kendall smiled.

"No," Larson said. "Absolutely not." He wore his do-rag again and it looked, Jared thought, just as dumb as the first time. Larson himself looked furious.

"I don't think we have a choice," said the older woman in a business suit. Probably she'd been getting dressed for work when they pulled up, just like Denise had been getting ready for school. This house must be the woman's—it looked like something a business lady would have, nice but really boring. Light brown rugs, brown furniture, tan curtains. The lady acted like she was in charge. Trouble was, Larson acted in charge, too. Jared thought they'd square off for a fight, but things didn't work like that around here.

"We do have a choice, Anna," Larson said. That was her name—Anna. "There's a number of cities we could send them to."

Jared said sharply, "Send? You mean me and the doc? Nobody's sending me no place!"

Anna said, "I'm afraid we have to, Jared. The Other Side now knows about both of you. They'll eliminate you if they can, and we might not be able to protect you."

"Oh, right. You can't just put a spell around my house or something? No? I guess you're not real wizards after all!"

A voice behind him said, "I'm afraid it doesn't work that way," and Jared spun around. Denise, back from parking the car someplace. If he'd known she was coming back, he wouldn't have sounded so snotty.

She said to Jared, "I can do wind magic, and Anna can communicate with wild animals, and so on, but only when we're present at the scene, Jared. There's no such thing as a spell that can just be left in place to guard someone. I wish there was."

If anybody else had explained it like that to Jared, he wouldn't have felt so stupid now. Kendall was off in a back room of this house, getting patched up or something. Jared crossed his arms over his chest and scowled. "I can't just leave and, like, move to some other city! I've got Ma and school and crap!"

Larson said brutally, "If you don't go, you're dead. And some of us, the ones you can identify, will be with you."

"But my ma—"

"Will be told that you've been taken away from her by Child Protective Services. She'll believe that."

Jared felt hot blood rush into his face. So Larson knew all about his mother! Furious and embarrassed, he turned to slam out of the room, but Denise blocked the doorway.

Larson said, "We don't need to send him to Tellerton. Send him somewhere else, to a nonactive cell. We don't need a kid this angry in the very center of the Brotherhood."

"I disagree," Anna said.

"No one will be able to control him. He'll endanger everybody there."

"I won't endanger nobody I don't want to!" Jared said.

Anna said, "I think that's true, Larson. And Nick will be with him."

Denise, still standing in the doorway, spoke in a low voice that only Jared could hear. "I know it's hard to be sent away. But Anna's right—you'll have Dr. Kendall with you. And the place you're going . . . I know for a fact that it has an awesome skate park."

"It does?"

"The best."

He blurted, "Will you come there to see me skate?" and instantly hated himself. She was too old for him, she would think he was a little kid, she'd shame him in front of Larson—

"Sure. I think that one way or another, we'll end up working together, anyway. Things are going to get much more serious soon, we'll need every wizard we can get, and we don't have a good stone man. You're really talented."

That was the second time she'd said that. Jared turned back to Anna, ignoring Larson. "Okay. I'll go. Where is this Tellerton?"

"In Virginia."

Jared blinked. "I—"

"Zack will drive you both down there this afternoon. The sooner you get out, the better."

"My stuff! I have—"

"It has to stay here. They'll get you new belongings in Tellerton. Don't worry, Jared, you're one of us now." Anna left. Larson said, "Wait a minute, Anna, I want to talk more with you about the hurricane." He strode after her.

Jared was left alone with Denise. He blinked, scowled, and said, to say something, "What hurricane?"

"It was on the early-morning news," Denise said somberly. "A big hurricane suddenly changed direction and came ashore in Florida, and the hurricane season is supposed to be over. Eight people dead so far. At least one big warehouse was destroyed that we found out had just been bought by the Other Side. Now they'll file all kinds of insurance claims on the stuff inside. Anna, one of our lawyers, just tracked the purchase and the warehouse insurance yesterday, but she hasn't had time to follow through."

Jared tried to understand. Denise was smart; all these people were smart. And wizard stuff seemed to involve nonmagic things like insurance claims, which Jared had never thought about. But one thing was clear to him, the part about eight people dead. So far.

He said, "They'd really do that? Kill, like, innocent people just to make money?"

"They would. They do."

He felt a little dizzy. Too much stuff, too fast. Wizards and magic and moving away and stones . . . He could still feel the rocks warm in his hands, ready to tell him things. Him, Jared Stoffel, who nobody except Shawn ever told anything.

And Shawn . . . the so-called friend he'd trusted like a brother . . . "Shawn is gonna pay," he said to Denise.

"Yes," Denise said, and *that* was what decided him. No lame bull about not being into revenge, or calming himself down, or being too angry a kid to be useful. Just: *Yes.* She understood him.

All at once, Jared felt like he'd just ollied off a twelve-set and was doing serious hang time in the air.

A wizard. He was a wizard. He didn't want to be, but he was. A stone man. And everything was different now.

Maybe that was a good thing.

He could learn about insurance claims or whatever. He wasn't dumb. He had learned to do a Back-180 down a four-set; he could learn what he needed to. He could.

"Welcome to the Brotherhood, Jared," Denise said softly. "Thanks," Jared said.

❧

Nancy Kress's fiction has won four Nebulas (for "Out of All Them Bright Stars," "Beggars in Spain," "The Flowers of Aulit Prison," and "Fountain of Age"), two Hugos (for "Beggars in Spain" and "The Erdmann Nexus"), a Sturgeon (for "The Flowers of Aulit Prison"), and a John W. Campbell Memorial Award (for novel *Probability Space*). She is the author of more than thirty books. Her most recent collection of short fiction is *Fountain of Age: Stories*; her latest novels are *After the Fall, Before the Fall, During the Fall* (2012) and *Flash Point.* Kress lives in Seattle with her husband, writer Jack Skillingstead, and Cosette, the world's most spoiled toy poodle.

The City: *The fantasy city of Hazar (a.k.a. The City of Distractions).*

The Magic: *Four aspiring wizards' final exam—returning grimoires to the proper places in the Living Library, a collection of thaumaturgical knowledge capable of killing anyone who enters it unprepared—requires a large vocabulary and swords as well as sorcery.*

IN THE STACKS

SCOTT LYNCH

Laszlo Jazera, aspirant wizard of the High University of Hazar, spent a long hour on the morning of his fifth-year exam worming his way into an uncomfortable suit of leather armor. A late growth spurt had ambushed Laszlo that spring, and the cuirass, once form-fitted, was now tight across the shoulders despite every adjustment of the buckles and straps. As for the groinguard, well, the less said the better. Damn, but he'd been an idiot, putting off a test-fit of his old personal gear until it was much too late for a trip to the armory.

"Still trying to suck it in?" Casimir Vrana, his chambers-mate, strolled in already fully armored, not merely with physical gear but with his usual air of total ease. In truth he'd spent even less time in fighting leathers than Laszlo had in their half-decade at school together. He simply had the curious power of total, improbable deportment. Every inch the patrician, commanding and comely, he could have feigned relaxation even while standing in fire up to his privates. "You're embarrassing me, Laszlo. And you with all your dueling society ribbons."

"We wear silks," huffed Laszlo, buckling on his stiff leather neck-guard. "So we can damn well move when we have to. This creaking heap of boiled pigskin, I've hardly worn it since Archaic Homicide Theory—"

"Forgot to go to the armory for a re-fit, eh?"

"Well, I've been busy as all hells, hardly sleeping—"

"A fifth-year aspirant, busy and confused at finals time? What an unprecedented misfortune. A unique tale of woe." Casimir moved around Laszlo and began adjusting what he could. "Let's skip our exam. You need warm milk and cuddles."

"I swear on my mother, Caz, I'll set fire to your cryptomancy dissertation."

"Can't. Turned it in two hours ago. And why are you still dicking around with purely physical means here?" Casimir muttered something, and Laszlo yelped in surprise as the heat of spontaneous magic ran up and down his back—but a moment later, the armor felt looser. Still not a good fit, but at least not tight enough to hobble his every movement. "Better?"

"Moderately."

"I don't mean to lecture, *magician*, but sooner or later you should probably start using, you know, *magic* to smooth out your little inconveniences."

"You're a lot more confident with practical use than I am."

"Theory's a wading pool, Laz. You've got to come out into deep water sooner or later." Casimir grinned, and slapped Laszlo on the back. "You're gonna see that today, I promise. Let's get your kit together so they don't start without us."

Laszlo pulled on a pair of fingerless leather gauntlets, the sort peculiar to the profession of magicians intending to go in harm's way. With Casimir's oversight, he filled the sheathes on his belt and boots with half-a-dozen stilettos, then strapped or tied on no fewer than fourteen auspicious charms and protective wards. Some of these he'd crafted himself; the rest had been begged or temporarily stolen from friends. His sable cloak and mantle, lined in aspirant gray, settled lastly and awkwardly over the creaking, clinking mass he'd become.

"Oh damn," Laszlo muttered after he'd adjusted his cloak, "where did I set my—"

"Sword," said Casimir, holding it out in both hands. Laszlo's wire-hilted rapier was his pride and joy, an elegant old thing held together by magesmithery through three centuries of duties not always ceremonial. It was an heirloom of his diminished family, the only valuable item his parents had been able to bequeath him when his mild sorcerous aptitude had won him a standard nine-year scholarship to the university. "Checked it myself."

Laszlo buckled the scabbard into his belt and covered it with his cloak. The armor still left him feeling vaguely ridiculous, but at least he trusted his steel. Thus protected, layered head to toe in leather, enchantments, and weapons, he was at last ready for the final challenge each fifth-year student faced if they wanted to return for a sixth.

Today, Laszlo Jazera would return a library book.

The Living Library of Hazar was visible from anywhere in the city, a vast onyx cube that hung in the sky like a square moon, directly over the towers of the university's western campus. Laszlo and Casimir hurried out of their dorm and into the actual shadow of the library, a darkness that bisected Hazar as the sun rose toward noon and was eclipsed by the cube.

There was no teleportation between campuses for students. Few creatures in the universe are lazier than magicians with studies to keep them busy indoors, and the masters of the university ensured that aspirants would preserve at least some measure of physical virtue by forcing them to scuttle around like ordinary folk. Scuttle was precisely what Laszlo and Casimir needed to do, in undignified haste, in order to reach the library for their noon appointment. Across the heart of Hazar they sped.

Hazar! The City of Distractions, the most perfect mechanism ever evolved for snaring the attention of young people like the two cloaked aspirants! The High University, a power beyond governments, sat at the nexus of gates to fifty known worlds, and took in the students of eight thinking species. Hazar existed not just to serve the university's practical needs, but to sift heroic quantities of valuables out of the student body by catering to its less practical desires.

Laszlo and Casimir passed whorehouses, gambling dens, fighting pits, freak shows, pet shops, concert halls, and private clubs. There were restaurants serving a hundred cuisines, and bars serving a thousand liquors, teas, dusts, smokes, and spells. Bars more than anything—bars on top of bars, bars next to bars, bars within bars. A bar for every student, a different bar for every day of the nine years most would spend in Hazar, yet Laszlo and Casimir somehow managed to ignore them all. On any other day, that would have required heroic effort, but it was exams week, and the dread magic of the last minute was in the air.

At the center of the eastern university campus, five hundred feet beneath the dark cube, was a tiny green bordered with waterfalls. No direct physical access to the Living Library was allowed, for several reasons. Instead, a single tall silver pillar stood in the middle of the grass. Without stopping to catch his breath after arrival, Laszlo placed the bare fingers of his right hand against the pillar and muttered, "Laszlo Jazera, fifth year, reporting to Master Molnar of the—"

Between blinks it was done. The grass beneath his boots became hard tile, the waterfalls become dark wood paneling on high walls and ceilings. He was in a lobby the size of a manor house, and the cool, dry air was rich with the musty scent of library stacks. There was daylight shining in from above, but it was tamed by enchanted glass and fell on the hall with the gentle amber color of good ale. Laszlo shook his head to clear a momentary sensation of vertigo, and an instant later Casimir appeared just beside him.

"Ha! Not late yet," said Casimir, pointing to a tasteful wall clock where tiny blue spheres of light floated over the symbols that indicated seven minutes to noon. "We won't be early enough to shove our noses up old Molnar's ass like eager little slaves, but we won't technically be tardy. Come on. Which gate?"

"Ahhh, Manticore."

Casimir all but dragged Laszlo to the right, down the long circular hallway that ringed the innards of the library. Past the Wyvern Gate they hurried, past the Chimaera Gate, past the reading rooms, past a steady stream of fellow Aspirants, many of them armed and girded for the very same errand they were on. Laszlo picked up instantly on the general atmosphere of nervous tension, as sensitive as a prey animal in the middle of a spooked herd. Final exams were out there, prowling, waiting to tear the weak and sickly out of the mass.

On the clock outside the gate to the Manticore Wing of the library, the little blue flame was just floating past the symbol for high noon when Laszlo and Casimir skidded to a halt before a single tall figure.

"I see you two aspirants have chosen to favor us with a dramatic last-minute arrival," said the man. "I was not aware this was to be a drama exam."

"Yes, Master Molnar. Apologies, Master Molnar," said Laszlo and Casimir in unison.

Hargus Molnar, Master Librarian, had a face that would have been at home in a gallery of military statues, among dead conquerors casting their permanent scowls down across the centuries. Lean and sinewy, with close-cropped gray hair and a dozen visible scars, he wore a use-seasoned suit of black leather and silvery mail. Etched on his cuirass was a stylized scroll, symbol of the Living Library, surmounted by the phrase *Auvidestes, Gerani, Molokare.* The words were Alaurin, the formal language of scholars, and they formed the motto of the Librarians:

RETRIEVE. RETURN. SURVIVE.

"May I presume," said Molnar, sparing neither Aspirant the very excellent disdainful stare he'd cultivated over decades of practice, "that you have familiarized yourselves with the introductory materials that were provided to you last month?

"Yes, Master Molnar. Both of us," said Casimir. Laszlo was pleased to see that Casimir's swagger had prudently evaporated for the moment.

"Good." Molnar spread his fingers and words of white fire appeared in the air before him, neatly organized paragraphs floating vertically in the space between Laszlo's forehead and navel. "This is your Statement of Intent; namely, that you wish to enter the Living Library directly as part of an academic requirement. I'll need your sorcerer's marks *here.*"

Laszlo reached out to touch the letters where Molnar indicated, feeling a warm tingle on his fingertips. He closed his eyes and visualized his First Secret Name, part of his private identity as a wizard, a word-symbol that could leave an indelible imprint of his personality without actually revealing itself to anyone else. This might seem like a neat trick, but when all was said and done it was mostly used for occasional bits of magical paperwork, and for bar tabs.

"And here," said Molnar, moving his own finger. "This is a Statement of Informed Acceptance of Risk . . . and here, this absolves the custodial staff of any liability should you injure yourself by being irretrievably stupid . . . and this one, which certifies that you are armed and equipped according to your own comfort."

Laszlo hesitated for a second, bit the inside of his left cheek, and gave his assent. When Casimir had done the same, Molnar snapped his fingers and the letters of fire vanished. At the same instant, the polished wooden doors of the Manticore Gate rumbled apart. Laszlo glanced at the inner edges of the doors and saw that, beneath the wooden veneer, each had a core of some dark metal a foot thick. He'd never once been past that gate, or any like it—aspirants were usually confined to the reading rooms, where their requests for materials were passed to the library staff.

"Come then, " said Molnar, striding through the gate. "You'll be going in with two other students, already waiting inside. Until I escort you back out this Gate, you may consider your exam to be in progress."

Past the Manticore Gate lay a long, vault-ceilinged room in which Indexers toiled amongst thousands of scrolls and card-files. Unlike the Librarians, the Indexers preferred comfortable blue robes to armor, but they were all visibly armed with daggers and hatchets. Furthermore, in niches along the walls, Laszlo could see spears, truncheons, mail vests, and helmets readily accessible on racks.

"I envy your precision, friend Laszlo."

The gravelly voice that spoke those words was familiar, and Laszlo turned to the left to find himself staring up into the gold-flecked eyes of a lizard about seven feet tall. The creature had a chest as broad as a doorway under shoulders to match, and his gleaming scales were the red of a desert sunset. He wore a sort of thin quilted armor over everything but his muscular legs and feet, which ended in sickle-shaped claws the size of Laszlo's stilettos. The reptile's cloak was specially tailored to part over his long, sinuous tail and hang with dignity.

"Lev," said Laszlo. "Hi! What precision?"

"Your ability to sleep late and still arrive within a hair's breadth of accruing penalties for your tardiness. Your laziness is . . . artistic."

"The administration rarely agrees." Laszlo was deeply pleased to see Inappropriate Levity Bronzeclaw, "Lev" to everyone at the university. Lev's people, dour and dutiful, gave their adolescents names based on perceived character flaws, so the wayward youths would supposedly dwell upon their correction until granted more honorable adult names. Lev was a mediocre sorcerer, very much of Laszlo's stripe, but his natural weaponry was one hell of an asset when hungry weirdness might be trying to bite your head off.

"Oh, I doubt they were *sleeping*." Another new voice, female, smooth and lovely. It belonged to Yvette d'Courin, who'd been hidden from Laszlo's view behind Lev, and could have remained hidden behind a creature half the lizard's size. Yvette's skin was darker than the armor she wore, a more petite version of Laszlo and Casimir's gear, and her ribbon-threaded hair was as black as her aspirant's cloak. "Not Laz and Caz. Boys of such a *sensitive* disposition, why, we all know they were probably tending to certain . . . extracurricular activities." She made a strangely demure series of sucking sounds, and some gestures with her hands that were not demure at all.

"Yvette, you gorgeous little menace to my academic rank," said Casimir, "that is most assuredly not true. However, if it were, I reckon that would make Laszlo and myself the only humans present to have ever seen a grown man with his clothes off."

Laszlo felt a warm, unexpected sensation in the pit of his stomach, and it took him a moment of confusion to identify it. Great gods, was that relief? Hope, even? Yvette d'Courin was a gifted aspirant, Casimir's match at the very least. Whatever might be waiting inside the Living Library, some bureaucratic stroke of luck had put him on a team with two natural magicians and a lizard that could kick a hole through a brick wall. All he had to do to earn a sixth year was stay out of their way and try to look busy!

Yvette retaliated at Casimir with another series of gestures, some of which might have been the beginning of a minor spell, but she snapped to attention as Master Molnar loudly cleared his throat.

"When you're all *ready*, of course," he drawled. "I do so hate to burden you with anything so tedious as the future of your thaumaturgical careers—"

"Yes, Master Molnar. Sorry, Master Molnar," said the students, now a perfectly harmonized quartet of apology.

"This is the Manticore Index," said Molnar, spreading his arms. "One of eleven such indices serving to catalog, however incompletely, the contents of the Living Library. Take a good look around. Unless you choose to join the ranks of the Librarians after surviving your nine years, you will never be allowed into this area again. Now, Aspirant Jazera, can you tell me how many catalogued items the Living Library is believed to contain?"

"Uh," said Laszlo, who'd wisely refreshed his limited knowledge of the library's innards the previous night, "About ten million, I think?"

"You think?" said Molnar. "I'll believe that when further evidence is presented, but you are nearly correct. At a minimum, this collection consists of some ten million scrolls and bound volumes. The majority of which, Aspirant Bronzeclaw, are what?"

"Grimoires," hissed the lizard.

"Correct. Grimoires, the personal references and notebooks of magicians from across all the known worlds, some more than four thousand years old. Some of them quite famous . . . or infamous. When the High University of Hazar was founded, a grimoire collection project was undertaken. An effort to create the greatest magical library in existence, to unearth literally every scrap of arcane knowledge that could be retrieved from the places where those scraps had been abandoned, forgotten, or deliberately hidden. It took centuries. It was largely successful."

Molnar turned and began moving down the central aisle between the tables and shelves where Indexers worked, politely ignoring him. No doubt they'd heard this same lecture many times already.

"Largely successful," Molnar continued, "at creating one hell of a mess! Aspirant d'Courin, what is a grimoire?"

"Well," she began, seemingly taken aback by the simplicity of the question. "As you said, a magician's personal reference. Details of spells, and experiments—"

"A catalog of a magician's private *obsessions*," said Molnar.

"I suppose, sir."

"More private than any diary, every page stained with a sorcerer's hidden character, their private demons, their wildest ambitions. Some magicians produce collections, others produce only a single book, but nearly all of them produce *something* before they die. Chances are the four of you will produce *something*, in your time. Some of you have certainly begun them by now."

Laszlo glanced around at the others, wondering. He had a few basic project journals, notes on the simple magics he'd been able to grasp. Nothing that could yet be accused of showing any ambition. But Casimir, or Yvette? Who could know?

"Grimoires," continued Molnar, "are firsthand witnesses to every triumph and every shame of their creators. They are left in laboratories, stored haphazardly next to untold powers, exposed to magical materials and energies for years. Their pages are saturated with arcane dust and residue, as well as deliberate sorceries. They are magical artifacts, uniquely infused with what can only be called the divine madness of individuals such as yourselves. They evolve, as many magical artifacts do, a faint quasi-intelligence. A distinct sort of low cunning that your run-of-the mill chair or rock or library book does not possess.

"Individually, this characteristic is harmless. But when you take grimoires . . . powerful grimoires, from the hands and minds of powerful magicians, and you store them together by the hundreds, by the thousands, by the tens of thousands, by the *millions* . . . "

This last word was almost shouted, and Molnar's arms were raised to the ceiling again, for dramatic effect. This speech had lost the dry tones of lecture and acquired the dark passion of theatrical oration. Whatever Master Molnar might have thought of the aspirants entrusted to his care, he was clearly a believer in his work.

"You need thick walls," he said, slowly, with a thin smile on his lips. "Thick walls, and rough Librarians to guard them. Millions of grimoires, locked away together. Each one is a mote of quasi-intelligence, a speck of possibility, a particle of magic. Bring them together in a teeming library, in the stacks, and you have . . . "

"What?" said Laszlo, buying into the drama despite himself.

"Not a mind," said Molnar, meeting his eyes like a carnival fortune-teller making a sales pitch. "Not quite a mind, not a focused intelligence. But a jungle! A jungle that *dreams*, and those dreams are currents of deadly strangeness. A Living Library . . . within our power to contain, but well beyond our power to control."

Molnar stopped beside a low table, on which were four reinforced leather satchels, each containing a single large book. Pinned to each satchel was a small pile of handwritten notes.

"A collection of thaumaturgical knowledge so vast and so deep," said Molnar, "is far, far too useful a thing to give up merely because it has become a magical *disaster area* perfectly capable of killing anyone who enters it unprepared!"

Laszlo felt his sudden good cheer slinking away. All of this, in a much less explicit form, was common knowledge among the aspirants of the High University. The Living Library was a place of weirdness, of mild dangers, sure, but to hear Molnar speak of it . . .

"You aspirants have reaped the benefit of the library for several years now." Molnar smiled and brushed a speck of imaginary dust from the cuirass of his Librarian's armor. "You have filed your requests for certain volumes, and waited the days or weeks required for the library staff to fetch them out. And, in the reading rooms, you have studied them in perfect comfort, because a grimoire safely removed from the Living Library is just another book.

"The masters of the university, as one of their more commendable policies, have decreed that all aspirant magicians need to learn to *appreciate* the sacrifices of the library staff that make this singular resource available. Before you can proceed to the more advanced studies of your final years, you are required to enter the Living Library, just once, to assist us in the return of a volume to its rightful place in the collection. That is all. That is the extent of your fifth-year exam. On the table beside me you will see four books in protective satchels. Take one, and handle it with care. Until those satchels are empty, your careers at the High University are in the balance."

Lev passed the satchels out one by one. Laszlo received his and examined the little bundle of notes that came with it. Written in several different hands, they named the borrower of the grimoire as a third-year aspirant he didn't know, and described the process of hunting the book down, with references to library sections, code phrases, and number sequences that Laszlo couldn't understand.

"The library is so complex," said Molnar, "and has grown so strange in its ways that physical surveillance of the collection has been impractical for centuries. We rely on the index enchantments, powerful processes of our most orderly sorcery, to give us the information that the Indexers maintain here. From that information, we plan our expeditions, and map the best ways to go about fetching an item from the stacks, or returning one."

"Master Molnar, sir, forgive me," said Casimir. "Is that a focus for the index enchantments over there?"

Laszlo followed Casimir's pointing hand, and in a deeper niche behind one of the little armories along the walls, he saw a recessed column of black glass, behind which soft pulses of blue light rose and fell.

"Just so," said Molnar. "Either you've made pleasing use of the introductory materials, or that was a good guess."

"It's, ah, a sort of personal interest." Casimir reached inside a belt pouch and took out a thick hunk of triangular crystal, like a prism with a milky white center. "May I leave this next to the focus while we're in the stacks? It's just an impression device. It'll give me a basic idea of how the index enchantments function. My family has a huge library, not magical, of course, but if I could create spells to organize it—"

"Ambition wedded to sloth," said Molnar. "Let no one say you don't think like a true magician, Aspirant Vrana."

"I won't even have to think about it while we're inside, sir. It would just mind itself, and I could pick it up on the way out." Casimir was laying it on with, Laszlo saw, every ounce of obsequiousness he could conjure.

But what was he talking about? Personal project? Family library? Caz had never breathed a word of any such thing to him. While they came from very different worlds, they'd always gotten along excellently as chambers-mates, and Laszlo had thought there were no real secrets between them. Where had this sprung from?

"Of course, Vrana," said Master Molnar. "We go to some trouble to maintain those enchantments, after all, and today is *all about* appreciating our work."

While Casimir hurried to emplace his little device near the glass column, Molnar beckoned the rest of them on toward another gate at the inner end of the Manticore Index. It was as tall and wide as the door they'd entered, but even more grimly functional—cold dark metal inscribed with geometric patterns and runes of warding.

"A gateway to the stacks," said Molnar, "can only be opened by the personal keys of two Librarians. I'll be one of your guides today, and the other . . . the other should have been here by—"

"I'm here, Master Librarian."

In the popular imagination (which had, to this point, included Laszlo's), female Librarians were lithe, comely warrior maidens out of some barbarian legend. The woman now hurrying toward them through the Manticore Index was short, barely taller than Yvette, and she was as sturdy as a concrete teapot, with broad hips and arms like a blacksmith's. Her honey-colored hair was tied back in a short tail, and over her black Librarian's armor she wore an unusual harness that carried a pair of swords crossed over her back. Her plump face was as heavily scarred as Molnar's, and Laszlo had learned just enough in his hobby duels to see that she was no one he would ever want to annoy.

"Aspirants," said Molnar, "allow me to present Sword-Librarian Astriza Mezaros."

As she moved past him, Laszlo noticed two things. First, the curious harness held not just her swords, but a large book buckled securely over her lower back beneath her scabbards. Second, she had a large quantity of fresh blood soaking the gauntlet on her left hand.

"Sorry to be late," said Mezaros, "Came from the infirmary."

"Indeed," said Molnar, "and are you—"

"Oh, I'm fine. I'm not the one that got hit. It was that boy Selucas, from the morning group."

"Ahhhh. And will he recover?"

"Given a few weeks." Mezaros grinned as she ran her eyes across the four aspirants. "Earned his passing grade the hard way, that's for sure."

"Well, I've given them the lecture," said Molnar. "Let's proceed."

"On it." Mezaros reached down the front of her cuirass and drew out a key hanging on a chain. Molnar did the same, and each Librarian took up a position beside the inner door. The walls before them rippled, and small keyholes appeared where blank stone had been a moment before.

"Opening," yelled Master Molnar.

"Opening," chorused the Indexers. Each of them dropped whatever they were working on and turned to face the inner door. One blue-robed woman hurried to the hallway door, checked it, and shouted, "Manticore Gate secure!"

"Opening," repeated Molnar. "On three. One, two—"

The two Librarians inserted their keys and turned them in unison. The inner door slid open, just as the outer one had, revealing an empty, metal-walled room lit by amber lanterns set in heavy iron cages.

Mezaros was the first one into the metal-walled chamber, holding up a hand to keep the aspirants back. She glanced around quickly, surveying every inch of the walls, floors, and ceiling, and then she nodded.

"In," said Molnar, herding the aspirants forward. He snapped his fingers, and with a flash of light he conjured a walking staff, a tall object of polished dark wood. It had few ornaments, but it was shod at both ends with iron, and that iron looked well-dented to Laszlo's eyes.

Once the six of them were inside the metal-walled chamber, Molnar waved a hand over some innocuous portion of the wall, and the door behind them rumbled shut. Locking mechanisms engaged with an ominous series of echoing clicks.

"Begging your pardon, Master Molnar," said Lev, "not to seem irresolute, for I am firmly committed to any course of action which will prevent me from having to return to my clan's ancestral trade of scale-grooming, but merely as a point of personal curiosity, exactly how much danger are we reckoned to be in?"

"A good question," said Molnar slyly. "We Librarians have been asking it daily for more than a thousand years. Astriza, what can you tell the good aspirant?"

"I guard aspirants about a dozen times each year," said Mezaros. "The fastest trip I can remember was about two hours. The longest took a day and a half. You have the distinct disadvantage of not being trained Librarians, and the dubious advantage of sheer numbers. Most books are returned by experienced professionals operating in pairs."

"Librarian Mezaros," said Lev, "I am fully prepared to spend a week here if required, but I was more concerned with the, ah, chance of ending the exam with a visit to the infirmary."

"Aspirant Inappropriate Levity Bronzeclaw," said Mezaros, "in here, I prefer to be called Astriza. Do me that favor, and I won't use your full name every time I need to tell you to duck."

"Ah, of course. Astriza."

"As for what's going to happen, well, it might be nothing. It might be pretty brutal. I've never had anyone get killed under my watch, but it's been a near thing. Look, I've spent months in the infirmary myself. Had my right leg broken twice, right arm twice, left arm once, nose more times than I can count."

"This is our routine," said Molnar with grim pride. "I've been in a coma twice. Both of my legs have been broken. I was blind for four months—"

"I was there for that," said Astriza.

"She carried me out over her shoulders." Molnar was beaming. "Only her second year as a Librarian. Yes, this place has done its very best to kill the pair of us. *But the books were returned to the shelves.*"

"Damn straight," said Astriza. "Librarians always get the books back to the shelves. *Always.* And that's what you *browsers* are here to learn by firsthand experience. If you listen to the Master Librarian and myself at all times, your chances of a happy return will be greatly improved. No other promises."

"Past the inner door," said Molnar, "your ordinary perceptions of time and distance will be taxed. Don't trust them. Follow our lead, and for the love of all gods everywhere, stay close."

Laszlo, who'd spent his years at the university comfortably surrounded by books of all sorts, now found himself staring down at his satchel-clad grimoire with a sense of real unease. He was knocked out of his reverie when Astriza set a hand on the satchel and gently pushed it down.

"That's just one grimoire, Laszlo. Nothing to fear in a single drop of water, right?" She was grinning again. "It takes an ocean to drown yourself."

Another series of clicks echoed throughout the chamber, and with a rumbling hiss the final door to the library stacks slid open before them.

"It doesn't seem possible," said Yvette, taking the words right out of Laszlo's mouth.

Row upon row of tall bookcases stretched away into the distance, but the farther Laszlo strained to see down the aisles between those shelves, the more they seemed to curve, to turn upon themselves, to become a knotted labyrinth leading away into darkness. And gods, the place was vast, the ceiling was hundreds of feet above them, the outer walls were so distant they faded into mist . . .

"This place has weather!" said Laszlo.

"All kinds," said Astriza, peering around. Once all six of them were through the door, she used her key to lock it shut behind them.

"And it doesn't fit," said Yvette. "Inside the cube, I mean. This place is much too big. Or is that just—"

"No, it's not just an illusion. At least not as we understand the term," said Molnar. "This place was orderly once. Pure, sane geometries. But after the collection was installed the change began . . . by the time the old Librarians tried to do something, it was too late. Individual books are happy to come and go, but when they tried to remove large numbers at once, the library got angry."

"What happened?" said Casimir.

"Suffice to say that in the thousand years since, it has been our strictest policy to never, *ever* make the library angry again."

As Laszlo's senses adjusted to the place, more and more details leapt out at him. It really was a jungle, a tangled forest of shelves and drawers and columns and railed balconies, as though the Living Library had somehow reached out across time and space, and raided other buildings for components that suited its whims. Dark galleries branched off like caves, baroque structures grew out of the mists and shadows, a sort of cancer-architecture that had no business standing upright. Yet it did, under gray clouds that occasionally pulsed with faint eldritch light. The cool air was ripe with the thousand odors of old books and preservatives, and other things—hot metal, musty earth, wet fur, old blood. Ever so faint, ever so unnerving.

The two Librarians pulled a pair of small lanterns from a locker beside the gate, and tossed them into the air after muttering brief incantations. The lanterns glowed a soft red, and hovered unobtrusively just above the party.

"Ground rules," said Astriza. "Nothing in here is friendly. If any sort of *something* should try any sort of *anything*, defend yourself and your classmates. However, you *must* avoid damaging the books."

"I can only wonder," said Lev, "does the library not realize that we are returning books to their proper places? Should that not buy us some measure of safety?"

"We believe it understands what we're doing, on some level," said Molnar. "And we're quite certain that, regardless of what it understands, it simply can't help itself. Now, let's start with your book, Aspirant d'Courin. Hand me the notes."

Molnar and Astriza read the notes, muttering together, while the aspirants kept an uneasy lookout. After a few moments, Molnar raised his hand and sketched an ideogram of red light in the air. Strange sparks moved within the glowing lines, and the two Librarians studied these intently.

"Take heed, aspirants," muttered Molnar, absorbed in his work. "This journey has been loosely planned, but only inside the library itself can the index enchantments give more precise and reliable . . . ah. Case in point. This book has moved itself."

"Twenty-eight Manticore East," said Astriza. "Border of the Chimaera stacks, near the Tree of Knives."

"The tree's gone," said Molnar. "Vanished yesterday, could be anywhere."

"Oh *piss*," said Astriza. "I really hate hunting that thing."

"Map," said Molnar. Astriza dropped to one knee, presenting her back to Molnar. The Master Librarian knelt and unbuckled the heavy volume that she wore as a sort of backpack, and by the red light of the floating lanterns he skimmed the pages, nodding to himself. After a few moments, he re-secured the book and rose to his feet.

"Yvette's book," he said, "isn't actually a proper grimoire, it's more of a philosophical treatise. Adrilankha's *Discourse on Necessary Thaumaturgical Irresponsibilities*. However, it keeps some peculiar company, so we've got a long walk ahead of us. Be on your guard."

They moved into the stacks in a column, with Astriza leading and Molnar guarding the rear. The red lanterns drifted along just above them. As they took their first steps into the actual shadows of the shelves, Laszlo bit back the urge to draw his sword and keep it waiting for whatever might be out there.

"What do you think of the place?" Casimir, walking just in front of Laszlo, was staring around as though in a pleasant dream, and he spoke softly.

"I'm going to kiss the floor wherever we get out. Yourself?"

"It's marvelous. It's everything I ever hoped it would be."

"Interested in becoming a Librarian?" said Yvette.

"Oh no," said Casimir. "Not that. But all this power . . . half-awake, just as

Master Molnar said, flowing in currents without any conscious force behind it. It's astonishing. Can't you feel it?"

"I can," said Yvette. "It scares the hell out of me."

Laszlo could feel the power they spoke of, but only faintly, as a sort of icy tickle on the back of his neck. He knew he was a great deal less sensitive than Yvette or Casimir, and he wondered if experiencing the place through an intuition as heightened as theirs would help him check his fears, or make him soil his trousers.

Through the dark aisles they walked, eyes wide and searching, between the high walls of book-spines. Tendrils of mist curled around Laszlo's feet, and from time to time he heard sounds in the distance—faint echoes of movement, of rustling pages, of soft, sighing winds. Astriza turned right, then right again, choosing new directions at aisle junctions according to the unknowable spells she and Molnar had cast earlier. Half an hour passed uneasily, and it seemed to Laszlo that they should have doubled back on their own trail several times, but they were undeniably pressing steadily onward into deeper, stranger territory.

"Laszlo," muttered Casimir.

"What?"

"Just tell me what you want, quit poking me."

"I haven't touched you."

Astriza raised a hand, and their little column halted in its tracks. Casimir whirled on Laszlo, rubbing the back of his neck. "That wasn't you?"

"Hells, no!"

The first attack of the journey came then, from the shadowy canyon-walls of the bookcases around them, a pelting rain of dark objects. Laszlo yelped and put up his arms to protect his eyes. Astriza had her swords out in the time it took him to flinch, and Yvette, moving not much slower, thrust out her hands and conjured some sort of rippling barrier in the air above them. Peering up at it, Laszlo realized that the objects bouncing off it were all but harmless—crumpled paper, fragments of wood, chunks of broken plaster, dark dried things that looked like . . . gods, small animal turds! Bless Yvette and her shield.

In the hazy red light of the hovering lanterns he could see the things responsible for this disrespectful cascade—dozens of spindly-limbed, flabby gray creatures the rough size and shape of stillborn infants. Their eyes were hollow dark pits and their mouths were thin slits, as though cut into their flesh with one quick slash of a blade. They were scampering out from behind books and perching atop the shelves, and launching their rain of junk from there.

Casimir laughed, gestured, and spoke a low, sharp word of command that stung Laszlo's ears. One of the little creatures dropped whatever it was about to throw, moaned, and flashed into a cloud of greasy, red-hot ash that dispersed like steam. Its nearby companions scattered, screeching.

"You can't tell me we're in any actual danger from these," said Casimir.

"*We're tell me can't,*" whispered a harsh voice from somewhere in the shelves, "known, known!"

"*Any actual you*, known, *from these in danger*," came a screeching answer. "Known, known, known!"

"Oh, hell," shouted Astriza, "Shut up, everyone shut up! Say nothing!"

"Known, known, known," came another whispered chorus, and then a dozen voices repeating her words in a dozen babbled variations. "Known, known, known!"

"They're vocabuvores," whispered Master Molnar. "Just keep moving out of their territory. Stay silent."

"Known," hissed one of the creatures from somewhere above. "All known! New words. GIVE NEW WORDS!"

Molnar prodded Lev, who occupied the penultimate spot in their column, forward with the butt of his staff. Lev pushed Laszlo, who passed the courtesy on. Stumbling and slipping, the aspirants and their guides moved haltingly, for the annoying rain of junk persisted and Yvette's barrier was limited in size. Something soft and wet smacked the ground just in front of Laszlo, and in an uncharacteristic moment of pure clumsiness he set foot on it and went sprawling. His jaw rattled on the cold, hard tiles of the floor, and without thinking he yelped, "Shit!"

"Known!" screeched a chorus of the little creatures.

"NEW!" cried a triumphant voice, directly above him. "New! NEW!"

There was a new sound, a sickly crackling noise. Laszlo gaped as one of the little dark shapes on the shelves far above swelled, doubling in size in seconds, its grotesque flesh bubbling and rising like some unholy dough. The little claws and limbs, previously smaller than a cat's, took on a more menacing heft. "More," it croaked in a deeper voice. "Give more new words!" And with that, it flung itself down at him, wider mouth open to display a fresh set of sharp teeth.

Astriza's sword hit the thing before Laszlo could choke out a scream, rupturing it like a lanced boil and spattering a goodly radius with hot, vomit-scented ichor. Laszlo gagged, stumbled to his feet, and hurriedly wiped the awful stuff away from his eyes. Astriza spared him a furious glare, then pulled him forward by the mantle of his cloak.

Silently enduring the rain of junk and the screeching calls for new words, the party stumbled on through aisles and junctions until the last of the hooting, scrabbling, missile-flinging multitude was lost in the misty darkness behind them.

"Vocabuvores," said Master Molnar when they had stopped in a place of apparent safety, "goblin-like creatures that feed on any new words they learn from human speech. Their metabolisms turn vocabulary into body mass. They're like insects at birth, but a few careless sentences and they can grow to human size, and beyond."

"Do they eat people, too?" said Laszlo, shuddering.

"They'd cripple us," said Astriza, wiping vocabuvore slop from her sword. "And torture us as long as they could, until we screamed every word we knew for them."

"We don't have time to wipe that colony out today," said Molnar. "Fortunately, vocabuvores are extremely territorial. And totally illiterate. Their nests are surrounded by enough books to feed their little minds forever, but they can't read a word."

"How can such things have stolen in, past your gates and sorcery?" asked Lev.

"It's the books again," said Molnar. "Their power sometimes snatches the damnedest things away from distant worlds. The stacks are filled with living and quasi-living dwellers, of two general types."

"The first sort we call *externals*," said Astriza. "Anything recently dumped or summoned here. Animals, spirits, even the occasional sentient being. Most of them don't last long. Either we deal with them, or they become prey for the other sort of dweller."

"Bibliofauna," said Molnar. "Creatures created by the actions of the books themselves, or somehow dependent upon them. A stranger sort of being, twisted by the environment and more suited to survive in it. Vocabuvores certainly didn't spawn anywhere else."

"Well," said Astriza, "We're a bit smellier, but we all seem to be in one piece. We're not far now from twenty-eight Manticore East. Keep moving, and the next time I tell you to shut up, Laszlo, please shut up."

"Apologies, Librarian Mezar—"

"Titles are for outside the library," she growled. "In here, you can best apologize by not getting killed."

"Ahhh," said Molnar, gazing down at his guiding ideogram. The lights within the red lines had turned green. "Bang on. Anywhere on the third shelf will do. Aspirant d'Courin, let Astriza handle the actual placement."

Yvette seemed only too happy to pass her satchel off to the sturdy Librarian. "Cover me," said Astriza as she moved carefully toward the bookcase indicated by Molnar's spells. It was about twelve feet high, and while the dark wood of its exterior was warped and weathered, the volumes tucked onto its shelves looked pristine. Astriza settled Yvette's book into an empty spot, then leapt backward, both of her swords flashing out. She had the fastest over-shoulder draw Laszlo had ever seen.

"What is it?" said Molnar, rushing forward to place himself between the shelf and the four aspirants.

"Fifth shelf," said Astriza. She gestured, and one of the hovering lanterns moved in, throwing its scarlet light into the dark recesses of the shelves. Something long and dark and cylindrical was lying across the books on that shelf, and as the lantern moved Laszlo caught a glimpse of scales.

"I think—" said Astriza, lowering one of her swords, "I think it's dead." She stabbed carefully with her other blade, several times, then nodded. She and Molnar reached in gingerly and heaved the thing out onto the floor, where it landed with a heavy smack.

It was a serpent of some sort, with a green body as thick as Laszlo's arm. It was about ten feet long, and it had three flat, triangular heads with beady eyes, now glassy in death. Crescent-shaped bite marks marred most of its length, as though something had worked its way up and down the body, chewing at leisure.

"External," said Astriza.

"A swamp hydra," said Lev, prodding the body with one of his clawed feet. "From my homeworld . . . very dangerous. I had night terrors of them when I was newly hatched. What killed it?"

"Too many possible culprits to name," said Molnar. He touched the serpent's body with the butt of his staff and uttered a spell. The dead flesh lurched, smoked, and split apart, turning gray before their eyes. In seconds, it had begun to shrink, until at last it was nothing more than a smear of charcoal-colored ash on the floor. "The Tree of Knives used to scare predators away from this section, but it's uprooted itself. Anything could have moved in. Aspirant Bronzeclaw, give me the notes for your book."

"*Private Reflections of Grand Necrosophist Jaklur the Unendurable*," said Astriza as Molnar shared the notes with her. "Charming." The two Librarians performed their divinations once again, with more urgency than before. After a few moments, Astriza looked up, pointed somewhere off to Laszlo's left, and said: "Fifty-five Manticore Northwest. Another hell of a walk. Let's get moving."

ꕥ

The second stage of their journey was longer than the first. The other aspirants looked anxious, all except Casimir, who continued to stroll while others crept cautiously. Caz seemed to have a limitless reserve of enchantment with the place. As for Laszlo, well, before another hour had passed the last reeking traces of the vocabuvore's gore had been washed from his face and neck by streams of nervous sweat. He was acutely aware, as they moved on through the dark canyons and grottos of the stacks, that unseen things in every direction were scuttling, growling, and hissing.

At one point, he heard a high-pitched giggling from the darkness, and stopped to listen more closely. Master Molnar, not missing a step, grabbed him firmly by his shoulders, spun him around, and pushed him onward.

They came at last to one of the outer walls of the library, where the air was clammy with a mist that swirled more thickly than ever before. Railed galleries loomed above them, utterly lightless, and Astriza waved the party far clear of the spiral staircases and ladders that led up into those silent spaces.

"Not much farther," she said. "And Casimir's book goes somewhere pretty close after this. If we get lucky, we might just—"

"Get down," hissed Molnar.

Astriza was down on one knee in a flash, swords out, and the aspirants followed her example. Laszlo knelt and drew his sword. Only Molnar remained on his feet.

The quality of the mist had changed. A breeze was stirring, growing more and more powerful as Laszlo watched. Down the long dark aisle before them the skin-chilling current came, and with it a fluttering, rustling sound, like clothes rippling on a drying line. A swirling, nebulous shape appeared, and the mist surged and parted before it. As it came nearer, Laszlo saw that it was a mass of papers, a column of book pages, hundreds of them, whirling on a tight axis like a tornado.

"No," shouted Molnar as Casimir raised his hands to begin a spell. "Don't harm it! Protect yourselves, but don't fight back or the library will—"

His words were drowned out as the tumbling mass of pages washed over them and its sound increased tenfold. Laszlo was buffeted with winds like a dozen invisible fists—his cloak streamed out behind him as though he were in free-fall, and a cloud of dust and grime torn from the surfaces nearby filled the air as a stinging miasma. He barely managed to fumble his sword safely back into his scabbard as he sought the floor. Just above him, the red lanterns were slammed against a stone balcony and shattered to fragments.

From out of the wailing wind there came a screech like knives drawn over slate. Through slitted eyes Laszlo saw that Lev was losing his balance and sliding backward. Laszlo realized that Lev's torso, wider than any human's, was catching the wind like a sail despite the lizard's efforts to sink his claws into the tile floor.

Laszlo threw himself at Lev's back and strained against the lizard's overpowering bulk and momentum for a few desperate seconds. Just as he realized that he was about to get bowled over, Casimir appeared out of the whirling confusion and added his weight to Laszlo's. Heaving with all their might, the two human aspirants managed to help Lev finally force himself flat to the ground, where they sprawled on top of him.

Actinic light flared. Molnar and Astriza, leaning into the terrible wind together, had placed their hands on Molnar's staff and wrought some sort of spell. The brutal gray cyclone parted before them like the bow-shock of a swift sailing ship, and the dazed aspirants behind them were released from the choking grip of the page-storm. Not a moment too soon, in fact, for the storm had caught up the jagged copper and glass fragments of the broken lanterns, sharper claws than any it had possessed before. Once, twice, three times it lashed out with these new weapons, rattling against the invisible barrier, but the sorcery of the Librarians held firm. It seemed to Laszlo that a note of frustration entered the wail of the thing around them.

Tense moments passed. The papers continued to snap and twirl above them, and the winds still wailed madly, but after a short while the worst of the page-storm seemed to be spent. Glass and metal fragments rained around them like discarded toys, and the whole screaming mess fluttered on down the aisle, leaving a slowly falling haze of upflung dust in its wake. Coughing and sneezing, Laszlo and his companions stumbled shakily to their feet, while the noise and chaos of the indoor cyclone faded into the distant mist and darkness.

"My thanks, humans," said Lev hoarsely. "My clan's ancestral trade of scale-grooming is beginning to acquire a certain tint of nostalgia in my thoughts."

"Don't mention it," coughed Laszlo. "What the hell was that?"

"Believe it or not, that was a book," said Astriza.

"A forcibly unbound grimoire," said Molnar, dusting off his armor. "The creatures and forces in here occasionally destroy books by accident. And sometimes, when a truly ancient grimoire bound with particularly powerful spells is torn apart, it doesn't want to *stop* being a book. It becomes a focus for the library's unconscious anger. A book without spine or covers is like an unquiet spirit without mortal form. Whatever's left of it holds itself together out of sheer resentment, roaming without purpose, lashing out at whatever crosses its path."

"Like my face," said Laszlo, suddenly aware of hot, stinging pains across his cheeks and forehead. "Ow, gods."

"Paper cuts," said Casimir, grinning. "Won't be impressing any beautiful women with those scars, I'm afraid."

"Oh, I'm impressed," muttered Yvette, pressing her fingertips gingerly against her own face. "You just let those things whirl around as they please, Master Molnar?"

"They never attack other books. And they uproot or destroy a number of the library's smaller vermin. You might compare them to forest fires in the outside world—ugly, but perhaps ultimately beneficial to the cycle of existence."

"Pity about the lamps, though," said Yvette.

"Ah. Yes," said Molnar. He tapped the head of his staff, and a ball of flickering red light sprang from it, fainter than that of the lost lamps but adequate to dispel the gloom. "Aspirants, use the empty book satchel. Pick up all the lantern fragments you can see. The library has a sufficient quantity of disorder that we need not import any."

While the aspirants tended their cuts and scoured the vicinity for lantern parts, Astriza glanced around, consulted some sort of amulet chained around her wrist, and whistled appreciatively. "Hey, here's a stroke of luck." She moved over to a bookcase nestled against the outer library wall, slid Lev's grimoire into an empty spot, and backed away cautiously. "Two down. You four are halfway to your sixth year."

"Aspirant Vrana," said Molnar, "I believe we'll find a home for your book not a stone's throw along the outer wall, at sixty-one Manticore Northwest. And then we'll have just one more delivery before we can speed the four of you on your way, back to the carefree world of making requests from the comfort of the reading rooms."

"No need to hurry on my account," said Casimir, stretching lazily. His cloak and armor were back in near perfect order. "I'm having a lovely time. And I'm sure the best is yet to come."

It was a bit more than a stone's throw, thought Laszlo, unless you discarded the human arm as a reference and went in for something like a trebuchet. Along the aisle they moved, past section after section of books that were, as Master Molnar had promised, completely unharmed by the passage of the unbound grimoire. The mist crept back in around them, and the two Librarians fussed and muttered over their guidance spells as they walked. Eventually, they arrived at what Molnar claimed was sixty-one Manticore Northwest, a cluster of shelves under a particularly heavy overhanging stone balcony.

"Ta-daaaaaa," cried Astriza as she backed away from the shelf once she had successfully replaced Casimir's book. "You see, children, some returns are boring. And in here, boring is beautiful."

"Help me!" cried a faint voice from somewhere off to Laszlo's right, in the dark forest of bookcases leading away to the unseen heart of the library.

"Not to mention damned rare." Astriza moved out into the aisle with Molnar, scanning the shelves and shadows surrounding the party. "Who's out there?"

"Help me!" The voice was soft and hoarse. There was no telling whether or not it came from the throat of a thinking creature.

"Someone from another book-return team?" asked Yvette.

"I'd know," said Molnar. "More likely it's a trick. We'll investigate, but very, very cautiously."

As though it were a response to the Master Librarian's words, a book came sailing out of the darkened stacks. The two Librarians ducked, and after bouncing off the floor once the book wound up at Yvette's feet. She nudged it with the tip of a boot and then, satisfied that it was genuine, picked it up and examined the cover.

"What is it?" said Molnar.

"*Annotated Commentaries on the Mysteries of the Worm*," said Yvette. "I don't know if that means anything special—"

"An-no-tated," hissed a voice from the darkness. There was a strange snort of satisfaction. "New!"

"Commentaries," hissed another. "New, new!"

"Hells!" Molnar turned to the aspirants and lowered his voice to a whisper. "A trick after all! Vocabuvores again. Keep your voices down, use simple words. We've just given them food. Could be a group as large as the last one."

"Mysteries," groaned one of the creatures. "New!" A series of wet snapping and bubbling noises followed. Laszlo shuddered, remembering the rapid growth of the thing that had tried to jump him earlier, and his sword was in his hand in an instant.

"New words," chanted a chorus of voices that deepened even as they spoke. "New words, new words!" It sounded like at least a dozen of the things were out there, and beneath their voices was the crackling and bubbling, as though cauldrons of fat were on the boil . . . many cauldrons.

"All you, give new words." A deeper, harsher voice than the others, more commanding. "All you, except BOY. Boy that KILL with spell! Him we kill! Others give new words!"

"Him we kill," chanted the chorus. "Others give new words!"

"No way," whispered Astriza. "No gods-damned way!"

"It's the same band of vocabuvores," whispered Molnar. "They've actually followed us. Merciful gods, they're learning to overcome their instincts. We've *got* to destroy them!"

"We sure as hell can't let them pass this behavior on to others," whispered Astriza, nodding grimly. "Just as Master Molnar said, clamp your mouths shut. Let your swords and spells do the talking. If—"

Whatever she was about to say, Laszlo never found out. Growling, panting, gibbering, screeching, the vocabuvores surged out of the darkness, over bookcases and out of aisles, into the wan circle of red light cast by Molnar's staff. Nor were they the small-framed creatures of the previous attack—most had grown to the size of wolves. Their bodies had elongated, their limbs had knotted with thick strands of ropy muscle, and their claws had become slaughterhouse implements. Some had acquired plates of chitinous armor, while others had sacks of flab hanging off them like pendulous tumors. They came by the dozens, in an arc that closed on Laszlo and his companions like a set of jaws.

The first to strike on either side was Casimir, who uttered a syllable so harsh that Laszlo reeled just to hear it. His ears rang, and a bitter metallic taste filled his mouth. It was a death-weaving, true dread sorcery, the sort of thing that Laszlo had never imagined himself even daring to study, and the closest of the vocabuvores paid for its enthusiasm by receiving the full brunt of the spell. Its skin literally peeled itself from the bones and muscles beneath, a ragged wet leathery flower tearing open and blowing away. And instant later the muscles followed, then the bones and the glistening internal organs; the creature exploded layer by layer. But there were many more behind it, and as the fight began in earnest Laszlo found himself praying silently that words of command, which were so much babble to non-magicians, couldn't nourish the creatures.

Snarling they came, eyes like black hollows, mouths like gaping pits, and in an instant Laszlo's awareness of the battle narrowed to those claws that were meant to shred his armor, those fangs that were meant to sink into his flesh. Darting and dodging, he fought the wildest duel of his career, his centuries-old steel punching through quivering vocabuvore flesh. They died, sure enough, but there were many to replace the dead, rank on writhing rank, pushing forward to grasp and tear at him.

"New words," the creatures croaked, as he slashed at bulging throats and slammed his heavy hilt down on monstrous skulls. The things vomited fountains of reeking gore when they died, soaking his cloak and breeches, but he barely noticed as he gave ground step by step, backing away from the press of falling bodies as new combatants continually scrambled to take their places.

As Laszlo fought on, he managed to catch glimpses of what was happening around him. Molnar and Astriza fought back to back, the Master Librarian's staff sweeping before him in powerful arcs. As for Astriza, her curved blades were broader and heavier than Laszlo's—no stabbing and dancing for her. When she swung, limbs flew, and vocabuvores were laid open guts to groins. He admired her power, and that admiration nearly became a fatal distraction.

"NEW WORD!" screeched one of the vocabuvores, seizing him by his mantle and forcing him down to his knees. It pried and scraped at his leather neck-guard, salivating. The thing's breath was unbelievable, like a dead animal soaked in sewage and garlic wine. Was that what the digestion of words smelled like? "NEW WORD!"

"Die," Laszlo muttered, swatting the thing's hands away just long enough to drive his sword up and into the orbless pit of its left eye. It demonstrated immediate comprehension of the new word by sliding down the front of his armor, claws scrabbling at him in a useless final reflex. Laszlo stumbled up, kicked the corpse away, and freed his blade to face the next one . . . and the next one . . .

Working in a similar vein was Lev Bronzeclaw, forgoing his mediocre magic in order to leap about and bring his natural weaponry into play just a few feet to Laszlo's left. Some foes he lashed with his heavy tail, sending them sprawling. Others he seized with his upper limbs and held firmly while his blindingly fast kicks sunk claws into guts. Furious, inexorable, he scythed vocabuvores in half and spilled their steaming bowels as though the creatures were fruits in the grasp of some devilish mechanical pulping machine.

Casimir and Yvette, meanwhile, had put their backs to a bookshelf and were plying their sorceries in tandem against a chaotic, flailing press of attackers. Yvette had conjured another one of her invisible barriers and was moving it back and forth like a tower shield, absorbing vocabuvore attacks with it and then slamming them backward. Casimir, grinning wildly, was methodically unleashing his killing spells at the creatures Yvette knocked off-balance, consuming them in flashing pillars of blue flame. The oily black smoke from these fires swirled across the battle and made Laszlo gag.

Still, they seemed to be making progress—there could only be so many vocabuvores, and Laszlo began to feel a curious exaltation as the ranks of their brutish foes thinned. Just a few more for him, a few more for the Librarians, a few more for Lev, and the fight was all but—

"KILL BOY," roared the commanding vocabuvore, the deep-voiced one that had launched the attack moments earlier. At last it joined the fight proper, bounding out of the bookcases, twice the size of any of its brethren, more like a pallid gray bear than anything else. *"Kill boy with spells! Kill girl!"*

Heeding the call, the surviving vocabuvores abandoned all other opponents and dove toward Casimir and Yvette, forcing the two aspirants back against the shelf under the desperate press of their new surge. Laszlo and Lev, caught off guard by the instant withdrawal of their remaining foes, stumbled clumsily into one another.

The huge vocabuvore charged across the aisle, and Astriza and Molnar moved to intercept it. Laszlo watched in disbelief as they were simply shoved over by stiff smacks from the creature's massive forelimbs. It even carried one of Astrizas's blades away with it, embedded in a sack of oozing gristle along its right side, without visible effect. It dove into the bookcases behind the one Casimir and Yvette were standing against, and disappeared momentarily from sight.

The smaller survivors had pinned Yvette between the shelf and her shield; like an insect under glass, she was being crushed behind her own magic. Having neutralized her protection, they finally seized Casimir's arms, interfering with his ability to cast spells. Pushing frantically past the smoldering shells of their dead comrades, they seemed to have abandoned any hope of new words in exchange for a last act of vengeance against Casimir.

But there were only a bare dozen left, and Laszlo and Lev had regained their balance. Moving in unison, they charged through the smoke and blood to fall on the rear of the pack of surviving vocabuvores. There they slew unopposed, and if only they could slay fast enough . . . claws and sword sang out together, *ten*. And again, *eight*, and again, *six* . . .

Yvette's shield buckled at last, and she and Casimir slid sideways with vocabuvore claws at their throats. But now there were only half a dozen, and then there were four, then two. A triumphant moment later Laszlo, gasping for breath, grabbed the last of the creatures by the back of its leathery neck and hauled it off his chambers-mate. Laszlo drove his sword into the vocabuvore's back, transfixing it through whatever approximation of a heart it possessed, and flung it down to join the rest of its dead brood.

"Thanks," coughed Casimir, reaching over to help Yvette sit up. Other than a near-total drenching with the nauseating contents of dead vocabuvores, the two of them seemed to have escaped the worst possibilities.

"Big one," gasped Yvette. "Find the big one, kill it quickly—"

At that precise instant the big one struck the bookcase from behind, heaving it over directly on top of them, a sudden rain of books followed by a heavy dark blur that slammed Casimir and Yvette out of sight beneath it. Laszlo stumbled back in shock as the huge vocabuvore stepped onto the tumbled bookcase, stomping its feet like a jungle predator gloating over a fresh kill.

"Casimir," Laszlo screamed. "Yvette!"

"No," cried Master Molnar, lurching back to his feet. "No! Proper nouns are the most powerful words of all!"

Alas, what was said could not be unsaid. The flesh of the last vocabuvore rippled as though a hundred burrowing things were about to erupt from within, but the expression on its baleful face was sheer ecstasy. New masses of flesh billowed forth, new cords of muscle and sinew wormed their way out of thin air, new rows of shark-like teeth rose gleaming in the black pit of the thing's mouth. In a moment it had gained several feet of height and girth, and the top of its head was now not far below the stones that floored the gallery above.

With a foot far weightier than before, the thing stomped the bookcase again, splintering the ancient wood. Lev flung his mighty scarlet-scaled bulk against the creature without hesitation, but it had already eclipsed his strength. It caught him in mid-air, turned, and flung him spinning head-over-tail into Molnar and Astriza. Still dull from their earlier clubbing, the two librarians failed spectacularly to duck, and four hundred pounds of whirling reptilian aspirant took them down hard.

That left Laszlo, facing the creature all alone, gore-slick sword shaking in his hand, with sorcerous powers about adequate, on his best day, to heat a cup of tea.

"Oh, *shit*," he muttered.

"Known," chuckled the creature. Its voice was now a bass rumble, deep as oncoming thunder. "Now will kill boy. Now EASY."

"Uh," said Laszlo, scanning the smoke-swirled area for any surprise, any advantage, any unused weapon. While it was flattering to imagine himself charging in and dispatching the thing with his sword, the treatment it had given Lev was not at all encouraging in that respect. He flicked his gaze from the bookshelves to the ceiling—and then it hit him, a sensation that would have been familiar to any aspirant ever graduated from the High University. The inherent magic of all undergraduates—the magic of the last minute. The power to embrace any solution, no matter how insane or desperate.

"No," he yelled. "No! Spare boy!"

"Kill boy," roared the creature, no more scintillating a conversationalist for all its physical changes.

"No." Laszlo tossed his sword aside and beckoned to the vocabuvore. "Spare boy. I will give new words!"

"I kill boy, *then* you give new words!"

"No. Spare boy. I will give many new words. I will give *all* my words."

"No," howled Lev, "No, you can't—"

"Trust me," said Laszlo. He picked a book out of the mess at his feet and waved it at the vocabuvore. "Come here. I'll *read* to you!"

"Book of words . . . " the creature hissed. It took a step forward.

"Yes. Many books, new words. Come to me, and they're yours."

"New words!" Another step. The creature was off the bookcase now, towering over him. Ropy strands of hot saliva tumbled from the corners of its mouth . . . good gods, Laszlo thought, he'd really made it hungry.

"Occultation!" he said, by way of a test.

The creature growled with pleasure, shuddering, and more mass boiled out of its grotesque frame. The change was not as severe as that caused by proper nouns, but it was still obvious. The vocabuvore's head moved an inch closer to the ceiling. Laszlo took a deep breath, and then began shouting as rapidly as he could:

"Fuliginous! Occluded! Uh, canticle! Portmanteau! Tea cozy!" He racked his mind. He needed obscure words, complex words, words unlikely to have been uttered by cautious librarians prowling the stacks. "Indeterminate! Mendacious! Vestibule! Tits, testicles, aluminum, heliotrope, *narcolepsy*!"

The vocabuvore panted in pleasure, gorging itself on the stream of fresh words. Its stomach doubled in size, tripled, becoming a sack of flab that could have supplied fat for ten thousand candles. Inch by inch it surged outward and upward. Its head bumped into the stone ceiling and it glanced up, as though realizing for the first time just how cramped its quarters were.

"Adamant," cried Laszlo, backing away from the creature's limbs, now as thick as tree trunks. "Resolute, unyielding, unwavering, reckless, irresponsible, foolhardy!"

"Noooo," yowled the creature, clearly recognizing its predicament and struggling to fight down the throes of ecstasy from its unprecedented feast. Its unfolding masses of new flesh were wedging it more and more firmly in place between the floor and the heavy stones of the overhead gallery, sorcery-laid stones that had stood fast for more than a thousand years. "Stop, stop, stop!"

"Engorgement," shouted Laszlo, almost dancing with excitement, "Avarice! Rapaciousness! Corpulence! Superabundance! *Comeuppance*!"

"Nggggggh," the vocabuvore, now elephant-sized, shrieked in a deafening voice. It pushed against the overhead surface with hands six or seven feet across. To no avail—its head bent sideways at an unnatural angle until its spine, still growing, finally snapped against the terrible pressure of floor and ceiling. The huge arms fell to the ground with a thud that jarred Laszlo's teeth, and a veritable waterfall of dark blood began to pour from the corner of the thing's slack mouth.

Not stopping to admire this still-twitching flesh edifice, Laszlo ran around it, reaching the collapsed bookcase just as Lev did. Working together, they managed to heave it up, disgorging a flow of books that slid out around their ankles. Laszlo grinned uncontrollably when Casimir and Yvette pushed themselves shakily up to their hands and knees. Lev pulled Yvette off the ground and she tumbled into his arms, laughing, while Laszlo heaved Casimir up.

"I apologize," said Caz, "for every word I've ever criticized in every dissertation you've ever scribbled."

"Tonight we will get drunk," yelled Lev. The big lizard's friendly slap between Laszlo's shoulders almost knocked him into the spot previously occupied by Yvette. "In your human fashion, without forethought, in strange neighborhoods that will yield anecdotes for future mortification—"

"Master Molnar!" said Yvette. In an instant the four aspirants had turned and come to attention like nervous students of arms.

Molnar and Astriza were supporting one another gingerly, sharing Molnar's staff as a sort of fifth leg. Each had received a thoroughly bloody nose, and Molnar's left eye was swelling shut under livid bruises.

"My deepest apologies," hissed Lev. "I fear that I have done you some injury—"

"Hardly your fault, Aspirant Bronzeclaw," said Molnar. "You merely served as an involuntary projectile."

Laszlo felt the exhilaration of the fight draining from him, and the familiar sensations of tired limbs and fresh bruises took its place. Everyone seemed able to stand on their own two feet, and everyone was a mess. Torn cloaks, slashed armor, bent scabbards, myriad cuts and welts—all of it under a thorough coating of black vocabuvore blood, still warm and sopping. Even Casimir—no, thought Laszlo, the bastard had done it again. He was as disgusting as anyone, but somewhere, between blinks, he'd reassumed his mantle of sly contentment.

"Nicely done, Laszlo," said Astriza. "Personally, I'm glad Lev bowled me over. If I'd been on my feet when you offered to feed that thing new words, I'd have tried to punch your lights out. My compliments on fast thinking."

"Agreed," said Molnar. "That was the most singular entanglement I've seen in all my years of minding student book-return expeditions. All of you did fine work, fine work putting down a real threat."

"And imparting a fair amount of new disorder to the stacks," said Yvette. Laszlo followed her gaze around the site of the battle. Between the sprawled tribe of slain vocabuvores, the rivers of blood, the haze of thaumaturgical smoke, and the smashed shelf, sixty-one Manticore Northwest looked worse than all of them put together.

"My report will describe the carnage as 'regretfully unavoidable,' said Master Molnar with a smile. "Besides, we've cleaned up messes before. Everything here will be back in place before the end of the day."

Laszlo imagined that he could actually feel his spirits sag. Spend all day in here, cleaning up? Even with magic, it would take hours, and gods knew what else might jump them while they worked. Evidently, his face betrayed his feelings, for Molnar and Astriza laughed in unison.

"Though not because of anything *you* four will be doing," said Molnar. "Putting a section back into operation after a major incident is Librarian's work. You four are finished here. I believe you get the idea, and I'm passing you all."

"But my book," said Laszlo. "It—"

"There'll be more aspirants tomorrow, and the next day, and the day after that. You've done your part," said Molnar. "Aspirant Bronzeclaw's suggestion is a sensible one, and I believe you deserve to carry it out as soon as possible. Retrieve your personal equipment, and let's get back to daylight."

If the blue-robed functionaries in the Manticore Index were alarmed to see the six of them return drenched in gore, they certainly didn't show it. The aspirants tossed their book-satchels and lantern fragments aside, and began to loosen or remove gloves, neck-guards, cloaks, and amulets. Laszlo released some of the buckles on his cuirass and sighed with pleasure.

"Shall we meet in an hour?" said Lev. "At the eastern commons, after we've had a chance to, ah, thoroughly bathe?"

"Make it two," said Yvette. "Your people don't have any hair to deal with."

"We were in there for four hours," said Casimir, glancing at a wall clock. "I scarcely believe it."

"Well, time slows down when everything around you is trying to kill you," said Astriza. "Master Molnar, do you want me to put together a team to work on the mess in Manticore Northwest?"

"Yes, notify all the night staff. I'll be back to lead it myself. I should only require a few hours." He gestured at his left eye, now swollen shut. "I'll be at the infirmary."

" Of course. And the, ah . . . "

"Indeed." Molnar sighed. "You don't mind taking care of it, if—"

"Yes, if," said Astriza. "I'll take care of all the details. Get that eye looked at, sir."

"We all leaving together?" said Yvette.

"I need to grab my impression device," said Casimir, pointing to the glass niche that housed a focus for the index enchantments. "And, ah, study it for a few moments. You don't need to wait around for my sake. I'll meet you later."

"Farewell, then," said Lev. He and Yvette left the Manticore Index together.

"Well, my boys, you did some bold work in there," said Molnar, staring at Laszlo and Casimir with his good eye. Suddenly he seemed much older to Laszlo, old and tired. "I would hope . . . that boldness and wisdom will always go hand in hand for the pair of you."

"Thank you, Master Molnar," said Casimir. "That's very kind of you."

Molnar seemed to wait an uncommon length of time before he nodded, but nod he did, and then he walked out of the room after Lev and Yvette.

"You staying too, Laz?" Casimir had peeled off his bloody gauntlets and rubbed his hands clean. "You don't need to, really."

"It's okay," said Laszlo, curious once again about Casimir's pet project. "I can stand to be a reeking mess for a few extra minutes."

"Suit yourself."

While Casimir began to fiddle with his white crystal, Astriza conjured several documents out of letters that floated in the air before her. "You two take as long as you need," she said distractedly. "I've got a pile of work orders to put together."

Casimir reached into a belt pouch, drew out a small container of greasy white paint, and began to quickly sketch designs on the floor in front of the pulsing glass column. Laszlo frowned as he studied the symbols—he recognized some of them, variations on warding and focusing sigils that any first-year aspirant could use to contain or redirect magical energy. But these were far more complex, like combinations of notes that any student could puzzle out but only a virtuoso could actually play. Compared to Laszlo, Casimir was such a virtuoso.

"Caz," said Laszlo, "what exactly are you doing?"

"Graduating early." Casimir finished his design at last, a lattice of arcane symbols so advanced and tight-woven that Laszlo's eyes crossed as he tried to puzzle it out. As a final touch, Casimir drew a simple white circle around himself—the traditional basis for any protective magical ward.

"What the hell are you talking about?"

"I'm sorry, Laszlo. You've been a good chambers-mate. I wish you'd just left with the rest." Casimir smiled at him sadly, and there was something new and alien in his manner—condescension. Dismissal. He'd always been pompous and cocksure, but gods, he'd never looked at Laszlo like *this*. With pity, as though he were a favorite pet about to be thrown out of the house.

"Caz, this isn't funny."

"If you were more sensitive, I think you'd already understand. But I know you can't feel it like I do. *Yvette* felt it. But she's like the rest of you, sewn up in all the little damn rules you make for yourselves to paint timidity as a virtue."

"Felt *what*—"

"The magic in this place. The currents. Hell, an ocean of power, fermenting for a thousand years, lashing out at random like some headless animal. And all they can do with it is keep it bottled up and hope it doesn't bite them too sharply. It needs a *will*, Laszlo! It needs a mind to guide it, to wrestle it down, to put it to constructive use."

"You're kidding." Laszlo's mouth was suddenly dry. "This is a finals-week joke, Caz. You're kidding."

"No." Casimir gestured at the glass focus. "It's all here already, everything necessary. If you'd had any ambition at all you would have seen the hints in the introductory materials. The index enchantments are like a nervous system, in touch with everything, and they can be used to communicate with everything. I'm going to bend this place, Laz. Bend it around my finger and make it something new."

"It'll kill you!"

"It could win." Casimir flashed his teeth, a grin as predatory as any worn by the vocabuvores that had tried to devour him less than an hour before. "But so what? I graduate with honors, I go back to my people, and what then? Fighting demons, writing books, advising ministers? To hell with it. In the long run I'm still a footnote. But if I can seize *this*, rule *this*, that's more power than ten thousand lifetimes of dutiful slavery."

"Aspirant Vrana," said Astriza. She had come up behind Laszlo, so quietly that he hadn't heard her approach. "Casimir. Is something the matter?"

"On the contrary, Librarian Mezaros. Everything is better than ever."

"Casimir," she said, "I've been listening. I strongly urge you to reconsider this course of action, before—"

"Before *what*? Before I do what you people should have done a thousand years ago when this place bucked the harness? Stay back, Librarian, or I'll weave a death for you before your spells can touch me. Look on the bright side . . . anything is possible once this is done. The University and I will have to reach . . . an accommodation."

"What about me, Caz?" Laszlo threw his tattered cloak aside and placed a hand on the hilt of his sword. "Would you slay me, too?"

"Interesting question, Laszlo. Would you really pull that thing on me?"

"Five years! I thought we were friends!" The sword came out in a silver blur, and Laszlo shook with fury.

"You could have gone on thinking that if you'd just left me alone for a few minutes. I already said I was sorry."

"Step out of the circle, Casimir. Step out, or decide which one of us you have time to kill before we can reach you."

"Laszlo, even for someone as mildly magical as yourself, you disappoint me. I said I checked your sword personally this morning, didn't I?"

Casimir snapped his fingers, and Laszlo's sword wrenched itself from his grasp so quickly that it scraped the skin from most of his knuckles. Animated by magical force, it whirled in the air and thrust itself firmly against Laszlo's throat. He gasped—the razor-edge that had slashed vocabuvore flesh like wet parchment was pressed firmly against his windpipe, and a modicum of added pressure would drive it in.

"Now," shouted Casimir, "Indexers, *out*! If anyone else comes in, if I am interfered with, or knocked unconscious or by any means further *annoyed*, my enchantment on that sword will slice this aspirant's head off."

The blue-robed Indexers withdrew from the room hastily, and the heavy door clanged shut behind them.

"Astriza," said Casimir, "somewhere in this room is the master index book, the one updated by the enchantments. Bring it to me now."

"Casimir," said the Librarian, "It's still not too late for you to—"

"How will you write up Laszlo's death in your report? 'Regretfully unavoidable?' Bring me the damn book."

"As you wish," she said coldly. She moved to a nearby table, and returned with a thick volume, two feet high and nearly as wide.

"Simply hand it over," said Casimir. "Don't touch the warding paint."

She complied, and Casimir ran his right hand over the cover of the awkwardly large volume, cradling it against his chest with his left arm.

"Well then, Laszlo," he said, "This is it. All the information collected by the index enchantments is sorted in the master books like this one. My little alterations will reverse the process, making this a focus for me to reshape all this chaos to my own liking."

"Casimir," said Laszlo, "Please—"

"Hoist a few for me tonight if you live through whatever happens next. I'm moving past such things."

He flipped the book open, and a pale silvery glow rippled up from the pages he selected. Casimir took a deep breath, raised his right hand, and began to intone the words of a spell.

Things happened very fast then. Astriza moved, but not against Casimir—instead she hit Laszlo, taking him completely by surprise with an elbow to the chest. As he toppled backward, she darted her right arm past his face, slamming her leather-armored limb against Laszlo's blade before it could shift positions to follow him. The sword fought furiously, but Astriza caught the hilt in her other hand, and with all of her strength managed to lever it into a stack of encyclopedias, where it stuck quivering furiously.

At the same instant, Casimir started screaming.

Laszlo sat up, rubbing his chest, shocked to find his throat uncut, and he was just in time to see the *thing* that erupted out of the master index book, though it took his mind a moment to properly assemble the details. The silvery glow of the pages brightened and flickered, like a magical portal opening, for that was exactly what it was—a portal opening horizontally like a hatch rather than vertically like a door.

Through it came a gleaming, segmented black thing nearly as wide as the book itself, something like a man-sized centipede, and uncannily fast. In an instant it had sunk half-a-dozen hooked foreclaws into Casimir's neck and cheeks, and then came the screams, the most horrible Laszlo had ever heard. Casimir lost his grip on the book, but it didn't matter—the massive volume floated in midair of its own accord while the new arrival did its gruesome work.

With Casimir's head gripped firmly in its larger claws, it extended dozens of narrower pink appendages from its underside, a writhing carpet of hollow, fleshy needles. These plunged into Casimir's eyes, his face, his mouth and neck, and only bare trickles of blood slid from the holes they bored, for the thing began to pulse and buzz rhythmically, sucking fluid and soft tissue from the body of the once-handsome aspirant. The screams choked to a halt, for Casimir had nothing left to scream with.

Laszlo whirled away from this and lost what was left of his long-ago breakfast. By the time he managed to wipe his mouth and stumble to his feet at last, the affair was finished. The book creature released Casimir's desiccated corpse, its features utterly destroyed, a weirdly sagging and empty thing that hung nearly hollow on its bones and crumpled to the ground. The segmented monster withdrew, and the book slammed shut with a sound like a thunderclap.

"Caz," whispered Laszlo, astonished to find his eyes moistening. "Gods, Caz, why?"

"Master Molnar hoped he wouldn't try it," said Astriza. She scuffed the white circle with the tip of a boot and reached out to grab the master index book from where it floated in mid-air. "I said he showed all the classic signs. It's not always pleasant being right."

"The book was a trap," said Laszlo.

"Well, the whole thing was a trap, Laszlo. We know perfectly well what sort of hints we drop in the introductory materials, and what a powerful sorcerer could theoretically attempt to do with the index enchantments."

"I never even saw it," muttered Laszlo.

"And you think that makes you some sort of failure? Grow up, Laszlo. It just makes you well adjusted. Not likely to spend weeks of your life planning a way to seize more power than any mortal will can sanely command. Look, every once in a while, a place like the High College is bound to get a student with excessive competence and no scruples, right?"

"I suppose it must," said Laszlo. "I just . . . I never would have guessed my own chambers-mate . . . "

"The most dangerous sort. The ones that make themselves obvious can be dealt with almost at leisure. It's the ones that can disguise their true nature, get along socially, feign friendships . . . those are much, much worse. The only real way to catch them is to leave rope lying around and let them knot their own nooses."

"Merciful gods." Laszlo retrieved his sword and slid it into the scabbard for what he hoped would be the last time that day. "What about the body?"

"Library property. Some of the grimoires in here are bound in human skin, and occasionally need repair."

"Are you *kidding*?"

"Waste not, want not."

"But his family—"

"Won't get to know. Because he vanished in an unfortunate magical accident just after you turned and left him in here, didn't he?"

"I . . . damn. I don't know if I can—"

"The alternative is disgrace for him, disgrace for his family, and a major headache for everyone who knew him, especially his chambers-mate for the last five years."

"The Indexers will just play along?"

"The Indexers see what they're told to see. I sign their pay chits."

"It just seems incredible," said Laszlo. "To stand here and hide everything about his real fate, as casually as you'd shelve a book."

"Who around here *casually* shelves a book?"

"Good point." Laszlo sighed and held his hand out to Astriza. "I suppose, then, that Casimir vanished in a magical accident just after I turned and left him in here."

"Rely on us to handle the details, Laszlo." She gave his hand a firm, friendly shake. "After all, what better place than a library for keeping things hushed?"

Scott Lynch was born in Minnesota in 1978. His first novel, *The Lies of Locke Lamora*, was released in 2006 and was a finalist for the World Fantasy Award. His latest novel, *The Republic of Thieves*, hit the *New York Times* and *USAToday* bestseller lists. Scott moonlights as a volunteer firefighter and spends several months of each year in Massachusetts, the home of his partner, SF/F writer Elizabeth Bear.

The Cities: *Sacramento and Bordertown.*

The Magic: *On the border between our human world and the elfin realm there's a city runaways from both sides often seek out. They never find what they expect—neither magic nor technology work predictably there—but there* is *magic, and that's what counts . . .*

A VOICE LIKE A HOLE

CATHERYNNE M. VALENTE

The trouble is, I ran away when I was fifteen. Everyone knows you run away when you are sixteen. That's the proper age. At sixteen, a long golden road opens up before you, and at the end of it is this amazing life. A sixteen-year-old runaway walks with an invisible crown—boys want to rescue her and they don't even know why. Girls want her to rescue them. She smells like peaches or strawberries or something. She's got that skittish, panicky beauty that makes circuses spontaneously sprout in the tomato field outside of town, just to carry her off, just to be the thing she runs away to. Everyone knows: you run away at sixteen, and it all works itself out. But I couldn't even get that right, which is more or less why I'm sitting here telling you all this, and more thanks to you for the ear.

My name is Fig. Not short for anything, just Fig. See, in eighth grade my school did *A Midsummer Night's Dream*, and for some reason Billy Shakes didn't write that thing for fifty overstimulated thirteen-year-olds, so once all the parts were cast, the talent-free got to be nonspeaking fairies. I'm not actually talent-free. I could do Hermia for you right now. But I was so shy back then. The idea of auditioning, even for Cobweb, who barely gets to say "Hail!" felt like volunteering to be shot. Auditioning meant you might get chosen or you might not, and some kids were always chosen and some weren't, and I knew which one I was, so why bother?

I asked the drama teacher: "What can I be without trying out?"

She said: "You can be a fairy."

So to pass the time while Oberon and Titania practiced their pentameters, the lot of us extraneous pixies made up fairy names for each other like the ones in the play: Peaseblossom and Mustardseed and Moth. I got Fig. It stuck. By the time I ran away, nobody called me by my real name anymore.

Talking to a runaway is a little like talking to a murderer. There was a time before you did it and a time after and between them there's just this space, this monstrous thing, and it's so heavy. It all could have gone so differently, if only. And there's always the question haunting your talk, the rhinoceros in the room: *Why did you do it?*

Because having a wicked stepmother isn't such a great gig, outside of fairy tales. She doesn't lay elaborate traps involving apples or spindles. She's just a big fist, and you're just weak and small. In a story, if you have a stepmother, then you're special. Hell, you're the protagonist. A stepmother means you're strong and beautiful and innocent, and you can survive her—just until shit gets real and candy houses and glass coffins start turning up in the margins. There's no tale where the stepmother just crushes the girl to death and that's the end. But I didn't live in a story and I had to go or it was going to be over for me. I can't tell you how I knew that. I just did. The instinctive way a kid knows she doesn't really love you because she's not really your mother—that's how the kid knows she'll never stop until you're gone.

So I went. I hopped a ride with a friend across the causeway into the city. The thing I like best about Sacramento is that I don't live there anymore, but I'll tell you, crossing the floodplain in that Datsun with a guy whose name I don't even remember now—it was beautiful. The slanty sun and the water and the FM stuck on mariachi. Just beautiful, that's all.

My remaining belongings sat in a green backpack wedged between my knees: an all-in-one *Lord of the Rings*; the *Complete Keats*; a thrashed orange and white Edith Hamilton; a black skirt that hardly warranted the title, little more than a piece of fabric and a safety pin; two shirts, also black: $10.16; and a corn muffin.

Yes, this represented the sum total of what I believed necessary for survival on planet Earth.

I forgot my toothbrush.

So here's *Fig's Comprehensive Guide for Runaways and Other Invisibles*: during the day, sleep in libraries. If questioned, pretend to be a college student run ragged by midterms or finals or whatever. I've always looked older, and libraries have couches or at least an armchair to flop on. I flopped in shifts, so as not to arouse suspicion. Couple of hours asleep, an hour of reading, rinse, repeat. I got through *Les Misérables*, *Madame Bovary*, and *Simulacra and Simulation* before anyone even asked me what school I went to. Don't just drop out—if you bag one life, you have to replace it with something. And when it comes to filling your head, those dead French guys usually have the good stuff: R-rated for nudity and adult concepts.

It's best to stay off email and computers. They can find you that way. Just let it go, that whole world of tapping keys and instant updates: poof. Like dandelion seeds. I could say: *Don't do drugs; don't do anything for money you wouldn't have done before you ran away.* But the truth is, drugs are expensive, and you kind of have to want to crack your head open with those things, to get in trouble. You have to set out to do it. Save your pennies, like for the ice cream man. And hell, I just didn't have the discipline.

At night, I stayed up. All things considered, as a teen wastrel you could do worse than Sacramento, California: warm, lots of grass and trees and open spaces. But not if you run away in February, like I did. Then you're stuck with cold and rain and nowhere to go.

So I went where everyone my age ends up: Denny's.

See, Denny's won't kick you out, even if you're obviously an undesirable—making it the beloved haunt of goths, theater kids, and truckers alike. You're always welcome under the big, benevolent yellow sign—so long as you don't fall asleep. If you nod off, you're out. So I availed myself of their unlimited $1.10 coffee and stayed awake, listening to conversation rise and fall around me, writing on the backs of napkins and in the blank pages in the backs of Tolkien, Keats, Hamilton. I never understood those pages, why they left them blank. Seemed like such a waste. But I filled them up with line after line. Songs. Poems. Anything.

I fit in; before I left home I had the means to dye my hair a pretty choice shade of deep red-purple, and nobody looks twice at a girl in black with Crayola hair scribbling in a Denny's booth. But as time went by, my roots took over. My hair is naturally kind of a blah dark brown, and it kept on growing all dark and ugly on top of my head, like a stair back down to home, getting longer and longer, more and more impossible to take.

Around six a.m., the commuter light rails start running and back then you could get on without a ticket and dodge the hole-punch man from car to car. Or if you don't give a shit and are a somewhat pretty girl who doesn't look like trouble, just sleep by the heater and take the fine the man gives you. It's not like I was ever going to pay it. He could write out all the tissuey pink violation tickets he wanted. The morning March light came shining through the windows, through the rose-colored paper, and the train chugged and rattled along, and even though I was always so hungry it took my breath, I thought that was beautiful, too. Just beautiful.

That's all.

And so I went, day in and day out. Eventually my $10.16 ran out, and I was faced with the necessity of finding some other way to pick up that $1.10 for the bottomless coffee cup, sitting there like a ceramic grail night after night on my Formica diner table—*drink of me and never sleep, never die*. At sixteen, you can get a work permit. At fifteen, you're out of luck.

I didn't want to do it, but sometimes a girl doesn't have any nice choices. Remember—I said I wasn't talent-free.

I could always sing.

Not for a teacher, not in front of parents at talent night, not for Oberon and Titania. For a mirror, maybe. For an empty baseball diamond after school. For a forest. And when I say I could sing, I don't mean I could sing like a Disney girl, or a church choir. No chipmunks and doves alighted at my feet when I sang. I mean I could sing like I was dying and if you got just close enough you could catch my soul as I fell. It's not a perfect voice, maybe not even a pretty one. A voice like a hole. People just toppled in. I stood outside the Denny's, and god, the first time it was so hard, it hurt so much, like a ripping and a tearing inside of me, like the hole would take me, too, my face so hot and ashamed, so afraid, still Fig the nonspeaking fairy, can't even say hail, can't even talk back, can't even duck when she sees a fist coming down.

But I opened my mouth, and I turned my face up to the sunset, and I sang. I don't even know what I sang about. I just made it up, brain to mouth to song. Seemed better than singing some love song belonging to somebody else. I don't know anything about music in a technical sense, and I hated the jolt of it, hearing my own voice break the air, to stand up there and sing down the streetlights like I was better than them, like it mattered, like I deserved to be heard at all. So I just kind of went somewhere else when I sang. Somewhere dark and safe and quiet, and when I came back the song was over and my feet were covered in coins.

Usually. Sometimes I got a dollar or two.

That was my life. Sleep, read, sing, stay awake, stay awake, stay awake. Ride the train, all the way around the circuit and back to Starfire Station. I'm not even kidding—that's what it was called, the station nearest my Denny's and my library. I'd get on the train with the morning sun all molten and orange on a beat-up blue sign: "Starfire Station." The rails glowed white. I thought: *Maybe something wonderful will happen here, and I could tell people about it later, but no one would believe me, because who names a train station that?*

I didn't talk to other runaways much. It was always awkward, dancing around how bad you had it in some kind of gross Olympic event. And even if I made a friend, we're sort of a transitory race by nature. It got repetitive:

"Fig. That's a stupid name."

"Thank you."

"Where'd you come from?"

"Over the causeway."

"Where're you going?"

"I don't know."

I didn't see the point. I had my routine.

But I heard about it.

Of course I heard about it. There used to be a place for kids like us. Some kind of magical city half full of runaways, where anything could happen. Elves lived there. Wizards. Impossible stuff: unicorns and rock singers with hearts of gold. A girl told me about it at this shelter once—and let me tell you, shelters are fucking mousetraps. A warm bed and a meal and a cage overhead.

All they want is to send you back to your parents on the quick, so they rate your crisis level and if you're below their threshold they up and call the cops on you. I went to one called Diogenes. I liked the name. I knew it from books—I'd moved on to philosophy by then. Diogenes searched the world for one good soul. Never found one, but that's not the part that matters. It's the looking, not the finding.

They called my stepmother. I didn't have bruises anymore. Not bad enough. But she didn't come to get me. No one ever came for me. She thanked them and hung up the phone, and the next morning they sent me on my way. I guess I wasn't their one good soul.

But the night before my expulsion from particleboard paradise, this girl Maria talked to me, bunk to bunk, through the one a.m. shadows.

"It's like this place between us and the place where fairies come from," she said dreamily, looking up at me from her thin bottom bunk. She had black curly hair all over the place, like wild thorny raspberry vines. Her eyes were kind of hollow, but they just looked delicate and wounded in that way that makes everyone want to rent a white horse just to save you. She wound one finger in her hair while she went on about this obviously ridiculous thing.

"And there's, like, rock bands with elves in them and no one gives you any shit just for *being*, and there's *real magic*. Okay, supposedly it's kind of broken and doesn't work right, but still, if it's not working right, that still means it works, right?" She sighed like a little kid, even though I knew she was sixteen—I'd seen her file while I stood in the office and they called the candy house and took the witch's advice on child welfare. Maria emphasized her words like she was underlining them in a diary. How did this kid last five minutes out of a pink bedroom? Whatever happened to her must have been really bad—I don't even know what kind of bad—to make some girl still drawing unicorns in her spiral notebooks take off. She sighed dramatically, enjoying the luxury of being the source of information. "But it disappeared or something, years ago. No one's been there in ages. Sometimes I think the city ran away, just like me. Something happened to it and it couldn't bear anything anymore, and so one night it just took off without leaving a note. But I'll get there, somehow. I will. And I'll dance, you'll see. I'll dance with the fairies."

And for a second I could see it like she saw it, all the colors, and Maria dancing in the town square with bells in her hair. It struck me just then: she was really beautiful. Actually beautiful, not like an actress, but like the characters actresses play. Like Titania. I just wanted to keep looking at her all night. I guess that's what you look like when you do it right, when you're sixteen and on the road, and you don't write poems, but poems get written about you. I was already writing one in my head. I figured I could fit it in the margins of J. R. R.'s appendices.

One of the other kids hissed at her from the second bunk in our four-loser room. "They don't like to be called that. Fairies."

"What do you know about it, Carmen? Fuck off," Maria spat, all the pink bedroom gone from her voice. And all the colors, too.

She had me for a second, but I know better. In the end, I always know better than to believe anything.

"More than you," snarled the older girl. "Hey, chica," she said to me, chucking her hair back. "You know how in school they said we'd never get social security, because by the time we get old, our parents will have used it all up?"

"Sure," I said. Carmen was seventeen, too late, where I was too early. Too old.

"Well, it's like that." She sighed, and I could almost see her frown in the dark. "It's all used up. Nothing left for us kittens."

"You don't really believe this stuff, do you? I mean, it sounds great, but it doesn't pay for coffee, you know?"

Maria scowled up at me. It hurt, that scowl. After a long, pointed silence, she said: "Fig is a stupid name."

I rolled back over on my miserable striped mattress.

"I wish I could be like you," I whispered, but not soft enough that the whole room couldn't hear. "I wish I could believe, just like I wish I could believe the church kids when they say they can save me. But no power on this earth, girl. No power on this earth." No one said anything. They ignored me. I had broken the spell they'd worked so hard to cast. I'd ruined it. Only the quiet of all of them breathing and angry was left.

I didn't believe even half of it. Remember when those homeless kids in Florida started talking crazy about the Blue Lady and how she'd come and save them? I thought it was like that. Something pretty to think about when you're cold and hungry. It's nice to think someone beautiful is protecting you. It's nice to think there's a place you can go if you want it bad enough. A place where everything you ever read about is real.

And of course it went away. Of course it did. I mean, that's like the job of magical places, to vanish. Atlantis. Avalon. Middle Earth.

And even if it was real for someone, sometime, it wouldn't be real for me. I ran away when I was fifteen. When Bordertown had already run away itself. I did it all wrong. Maybe other people could go there, but not me. That kind of shit is for Oberon and Titania. Not Fig, shuffling in the background with paper leaves glued to her T-shirt. I don't live in a world with places like that. I live on the train, and in Denny's, and in the Citrus Heights Public Library, and that's all.

Spring came, dry and full of olive pollen. No one came looking for me. I kept singing and reading (*Les Fleurs du Mal* in May, and my Keats for the millionth time). Any time I managed to eat meat I just went wolf-blind with starving for it. I had become completely nocturnal, sleeping through the whole route from Starfire Station out to the suburbs and back again, my green backpack nicely padded with no-fare fines. *Light rail. Rails of light. That's me, speeding along toward Starfire on a rail of light.* I rode longer and longer into the day, chasing the sun, and maybe I wanted to get caught. My roots got longer and I didn't know where I was going, I just wanted to go somewhere.

I can't say it was lonely—it's more like you flip inside out. Everyone can see your business on the outside—too thin, hollow, bruised eyes, clothes worn into oblivion and on the inside you just go hard and impenetrable, like metal. I stopped talking when I didn't need to—that's for social animals, and boy, I just wasn't one anymore. I was something else, not a girl, not a wolf, something blank-eyed, tired, running after meat, running after trains.

One time, just before it happened, the ticket taker shook me awake.

"Kid," he said. "Come on. Wake up. You gotta go somewhere else. I see you here every day. You can't stay. You gotta go somewhere else."

He had blue eyes. With the seven a.m. sunlight shining slantwise through them, they looked silvery, like crystals.

"I'm going, I'm going," I grumbled, and stretched. I wasn't really listening. I was thinking about how totally amazing breakfast was, I mean, as an invention. Bacon and bread. I only thought about food abstractly anymore. The way you think about paintings. Anything I got I just tore through so fast, it didn't really seem to exist in a cosmic sense. Hungry before, hungry after. I frowned at the fine-dispensing man. I didn't hate the guy—adults just lived in this other world, this forbidden world, and in that world I only looked like a problem. Not his fault. Not mine. You can't see one world from where you're standing in the other, that's all.

But he didn't shove me off at the next station. Nobody else was in the car, and the sun gleamed on everything, glittering on the chrome like little supernovas. I settled back into my seat, hunching down so anyone who did come in would know to leave me alone. It's an easy psychic telegraph: Keep out. Like a body is a clubhouse.

And that morning, when a grayish lump of girl got on, hauling a stiff rider of morning wind, she did leave me alone. She dropped into a heap in a seat on the far side of the car, and I was pretty sure she didn't have a ticket either. Her clothes were thrift-store mishmash, green skirt, dingy tank top under a ragged coat with a furry, matted hood. As the train got up to speed, her head dipped back and she started to snore. The hood slid off.

It was Maria.

I mean, you wouldn't have recognized her. But I have a memory for faces. Everyone, all the time. If I've seen you, I've seen you forever. And it was Maria, beautiful Maria, the girl who knew everything. But she was messed up, a hundred years older. Her cheekbones were cutting shards, one eye swollen like she'd been hit. Her skin was half-sunburned, half-clammy, and she had hacked all her hair off, shaved her head. It had grown back a fuzzy, uneven half inch, a thin black cloud. She had sores on her arms; her lips were cracked and bleeding. My lips peeled back like a dog's. Her whole body was like a threat, a ransom note that said: Fast-forward, and this is you.

"Hey," I whispered. She stirred sleepily. I felt awake all of a sudden, sharp. "Maria?"

I went to the girl and slid into the plastic seat beside her. Her eyes slitted up at me.

"Lemmelone, I gotta ticket," she mumbled.

"Maria, it's me. Fig. Diogenes, remember?" One good soul.

Her eyes rolled, unfocused. I could see the ridges in her sternum, like a bone ladder. "Fig's a stupid name," she slurred.

"Yeah," I said. "It is."

I didn't ask her what happened to her, why she didn't just go home if she was so busted. It's not polite. Her breathing got shallow and she fell asleep again. Maria smelled—kind of sweet, and kind of rotten, and kind of sour. Like meat. She slumped against me and started coughing, spattering my arm with gooey strands streaked with pink. Not coughing blood like some movie girl with one big number left in her, but just about as bad.

"God, I fucking told you, Maria!" I yelled at her suddenly. "There's no such thing as fairies or magic, and there is no city waiting for you at the end of this train. Look at you, puking your guts out on my arm. Where's your magic? Where is it?" I was almost crying, shaking her. She promised me that stuff was real. She said we could go there. How could she do this to me? Her head flopped back and I caught it up, like a baby's. I could see the whites of her eyes, and it just stopped me cold. Like a fist.

"Hey, hey," I said, softer. "I'm sorry." I tried to push her upright.

"Wake up, Maria. I didn't mean it. Wake up and tell me what a bitch I am. Come on. Don't put this on me. I can't take it. Wake up." But she didn't. Her heart was racing, but her skin was cold. he just sagged into my arms like a puppy. I kept thinking: *Oh god, oh god, have a seizure, whatever, just don't die on me here, I cannot handle this. This is a safe place. Bad things don't happen on the train. What did you take, what did you do, what was so bad you couldn't dream about magic anymore?*

"Maria, sweetie," I said, and held her. I kissed her forehead. I couldn't say it, but my heart filled up with the image of her glowing, pink-bedroom face below me on the bottom bunk, in the dark. *This wasn't supposed to happen to you. The beautiful one. Titania.*

And under that thought, the next one, black and ugly: *It was supposed to happen to me.* "Baby girl, just open your eyes. Like in the story. Just open your eyes and wake up." She moaned a little and put out her hand to find my face. Housing developments with red roofs whispered by outside the windows—she coughed again, greenish, specks of dark, ugly blood in it this time.

"Okay, Maria, okay." I shifted to hold her better and started rocking. *Shit, just stay awake till the next stop. Just don't die. Come on, kid, you gotta go somewhere else.*

"Just listen to me. Remember that place you wanted to go? Think about that place; think about the elves and the magic and you dancing with the fairies who don't like to be called fairies. You can't go there like this; they'd never let you in. You gotta wake up. Listen, listen."

And I sang to her. The words just came and I sang them into her ear, her shorn head, her phlegm and her sternum and her unicorns and her wizards, and my voice came rough and quiet but it came, and I hoped I wasn't singing her death, I hoped I was singing something better, for both of us, my broken voice and her broken body. I sang because if she could get that far gone, I could; if she wasn't a good-enough soul for Diogenes, I never would be; if she could die, I would never get to be old. The panic in me was like a spider, a crawling, hungry thing. I rocked her and went to that other place I go to when I sing, and the song poured out of me into her. *Think about that place, that place, that place. Let's run away. That other place. Nothing bad ever happened to you. Nothing bad ever happened to me. We're just two girls taking the train to school. We'll go to class and talk about Grecian urns. You can copy off my homework. We'll have lunch in the grass.* I sang and sang, and my voice got big in me, big enough to hurt, big enough to echo. Big enough for her. A voice like a hole. I pressed my forehead to hers and the world went away.

The sky shuddered from full daylight to stars and black and no moon at all with a hard lurch and a snap, like blinds zipping down.

Come on, kid. You gotta go somewhere else.

Nothing left for us kittens.

The train car was gone, and I was sitting on a long bench with a red cushion, with Maria in my lap. We rattled along on some part-stagecoach, part-city bus beast, something out of an old movie, like we'd jumped frames. Jangling silver and bone bells hung from several posts of some kind of twisted black horn; nodding black flowers drooped from their crowns. Several long benches stretched behind me, with some folk asleep, some awake.

A woman was knitting quietly in the starlight. I sat up front, Maria's legs curled on the seat, her head in my arms. The driver wore a top hat covered in living moss with tiny clovers and thistles growing in it. The coach heaved and jerked as though horses were pulling it, and I could hear the clop-clop of hooves, but even in the dim light I could see that no animal pulled us along.

I started shaking—I didn't mean to, but my body rejected what it saw, what it felt, and I couldn't think of anything to do or say, with this girl in my lap and this utterly wrong thing happening.

There was no horse pulling the carriage-trolley, but I could hear the hoofbeats, and like a kid I seized on that, that one thing wrong out of everything, everything wrong.

I cleared my throat. I felt unused to talking to adults. "Sir," I said to the driver. "There's no horse."

"This is Bordertown's own Ye Olde Unicorn Trolley. Famous, like. I'm Master Wallscrew, at yours."

I laughed a little, nervous. "Where's the unicorn?" The driver turned to grin at me from under his fuzzy green hat.

"You're it, kid. It only works with a virgin on board. Sure and it's not me."

I blushed deeply, and at the same moment it hit me, hard as a broken bone: He said *Bordertown*.

I shook, and felt cold, and felt hot, and my hands were clamped so tight in Maria's coat, my fingers got fuzzy with lost circulation. I had been wrong. There was a moon out, low in the sky, almost spent, a slim rind left, hanging there like a smile. I laughed. Then I put my face in Maria's neck and cried.

"What is it, girl?" gruffed the trolley master. "I can't abide girls crying, I'll warn you. Shows a fragile disposition, and brings amorous types to wipe tears away, which would pretty much sort our whole conveyance issue. Sniffle up, before some silver-haired Byron gets your scent."

"It's a mistake," I said quietly.

"What's 'it,' now?"

"A mistake. I'm . . . I'm nobody. I'm nobody. I'm not supposed to be here. It's for her."

I had made it and didn't even audition. Maria auditioned with her whole heart. She had the discipline. She went down into the dark, where I was never brave enough to go. I was supposed to mess around in the back and say nothing. I wasn't supposed to suddenly have to function in Athens, with a lost kid in my skirts. This was Maria's place, and she couldn't even see it.

"Wake up, Maria, wake up," I sobbed. "Wake up. There's unicorns, like you said, sort of, and magic, and . . . "

She didn't stir. But her breathing was better, deep and even, and she had locked her arms around my waist.

"Well. Nobody," the driver said softly, "where to?" I rubbed my nose, flowing with snot and tears.

"What about these people? Don't they need to get . . . places? Go where they want to go. We don't care."

"Tourists." He shrugged. "They wait for the . . . uh . . . fuel stop, and go where the trolley goes. It's exciting—they never know what they might see. Besides, the old monster's not too reliable as a method of mass transit. The kids come on sometimes, to haze each other—if it goes, well, they're not as tough as they say. But mostly we just *glide*, child. It's part magic and part machine and neither of the parts work quite right, so sometimes you'll say, 'Dinner at Café Cubana, hoss,' and it'll take you pert as a duck to Elfhaeme Gate and you'll be dining on fines and forms. Sometimes it's nice as you please, right up to the door at Cubana and no fuss. Not its fault, you understand. The magic wants to go Realmward and the machine wants to go Worldward, and in a mess like that you can't ask for any straight lines."

"Then why ask where we're going?"

The driver looked down at me, his blue eyes dark in the starlight, like crystals.

"It don't run without desire, kid. Nothing does."

Well, what do you do when you don't know what to do? What you've been doing. I wanted somewhere for Maria to get well, to get fed, to get happy again. Something like a benevolent golden Denny's, something I could sing in front of, somewhere with coffee all night for $1.10 in a cup like a grail and just a little more room on the blank pages in the backs of my books. Just a little more room.

I didn't say it. I didn't say anything. But the Unicorn Trolley veered off sharply into the shadows and light of the city, into the sound of it like a wall.

And I looked over my shoulder, back toward the moon and the gnarled, thorny weeds of the road. Something banged there, hanging from an iron pole, banged in the wind and the night. On a scrap of tin that might have once been painted blue, I read: "Starfire Station."

And just then, just then, Maria opened her eyes, bright and deep as a fairy's.

And that's my story, Mr. Din. If you don't mind I'll take that beer now. I still need a little something to be brave. I guess that's better than not being brave at all. It's Titania's world and I'll never be Hermia, and not Helena either. Just Fig, but not in the background. Not anymore. I still stand with the fairies with glued-on leaves, but oh, you'd better believe I've got lines to sing. Hail, mortals, we attend. Well met, and what ho, and all that jazz, every word, down to the last verse.

Now, I see a microphone up there, and my girl and I are hungry.

May I?

❦

Catherynne M. Valente is the *New York Times* bestselling author of over a dozen works of fiction and poetry, including *Palimpsest*, the Orphan's Tales series, *Deathless*, and the crowdfunded phenomenon *The Girl Who Circumnavigated Fairyland in a Ship of Her Own Making*. She is the winner of the Andre Norton, Tiptree, Mythopoeic, Rhysling, Lambda, Locus, and Hugo awards. She has been a finalist for the Nebula and World Fantasy Awards. She lives on an island off the coast of Maine with a small but growing menagerie of beasts, some of which are human.

The City: *Las Vegas—a place where illusion is common.*

The Magic: *We think real magic, not the type of tricks that entertainers fool us with on stage, is a rare, exotic thing. But, really, it isn't . . . if you know what to look for.*

THE ARCANE ART OF MISDIRECTION

CARRIE VAUGHN

The cards had rules, but they could be made to lie.

The rules said that a player with a pile of chips that big was probably cheating. Not definitely—luck, unlike cards, didn't follow any rules. The guy could just be lucky. But the prickling of the hairs on the back of Julie's neck made her think otherwise.

He was middle-aged, aggressively nondescript. When he sat down at her table, Julie pegged him as a middle-management type from flyover country—cheap gray suit, unimaginative tie, chubby face, greasy hair clumsily combed over a bald spot. Now that she thought about it, his look was so cliché it might have been a disguise designed to make sure people dismissed him out of hand. Underestimated him.

She'd seen card-counting rings in action—groups of people who prowled the casino, scouted tables, signaled when a deck was hot, and sent in a big bettor to clean up. They could win a ridiculous amount of money in a short amount of time. Security kept tabs on most of the well-known rings and barred them from the casino. This guy was alone. He wasn't signaling. No one else was lingering nearby.

He could still be counting cards. She'd dealt blackjack for five years now and could usually spot it. Players tapped a finger, or sometimes their lips moved. If they were that obvious, they probably weren't winning anyway. The good ones knew to cut out before the casino noticed and ejected them. Even the best card counters lost some of the time. Counting cards didn't beat the system, it was just an attempt to push the odds in your favor. This guy hadn't lost a single hand of blackjack in forty minutes of play.

For the last ten minutes, the pit boss had been watching over Julie's shoulder as she dealt. Her table was full, as others had drifted over, maybe hoping some of the guy's luck would rub off on them. She slipped cards out of the shoe for her players, then herself. Most of them only had a chip or two—minimum bid was twenty-five. Not exactly high rolling, but enough to make Vegas's middle-America audience sweat a little.

Two players stood. Three others hit; two of them busted. Dealer drew fifteen, then drew an eight—so she was out. Her chubby winner had a stack of chips on his square. Probably five hundred dollars. He hit on eighteen—and who in their right mind ever hit on eighteen? But he drew a three. Won, just like that. His expression never budged, like he expected to win. He merely glanced at the others when they offered him congratulations.

Julie slid over yet another stack of chips; the guy herded it together with his already impressive haul. Left the previous stack right where it was, and folded his hands to wait for the next deal. He seemed bored.

Blackjack wasn't supposed to be boring.

She looked at Ryan, her pit boss, a slim man in his fifties who'd worked Vegas casinos his whole life. He'd seen it all, and he was on his radio. Good. Security could review the video and spot whatever this guy was doing. Palming cards, probably—though she couldn't guess how he was managing it.

She was about to deal the next hand when the man in question looked at her, looked at Ryan, then scooped his chips up, putting stack after stack in his jacket pockets, then walked away from the table, wearing a small, satisfied grin.

He didn't leave a tip. Even the losers left tips.

"Right. He's gone, probably heading for the cashiers. Thanks." Ryan put his radio down.

"Well?" Julie asked.

"They can't find anything to nail him with, but they'll keep an eye on him," Ryan said. He was frowning, and seemed suddenly worn under the casino's lights.

"He's got to be doing something, if we could just spot it."

"Never mind, Julie. Get back to your game."

He was right. Not her problem.

Cards slipped under her fingers and across the felt like water. The remaining players won and lost at exactly the rate they should, and she collected more chips than she gave out. She could tell when her shift was close to ending by the ache that entered her lower back from standing. Just another half hour and

Ryan would close out her table, and she could leave. Run to the store, drag herself home, cobble together a meal that wouldn't taste quite right because she was eating it at midnight, but that was dinner time when she worked this shift. Take a shower, watch a half an hour of bad TV and finally, finally fall asleep. Wake up late in the morning and do it all again.

That was her life. As predictable as house odds.

There's a short film, a test of sorts. The caption at the start asks you to watch the group of people throwing balls to one another, and count the number of times the people wearing white pass the ball. You watch the film and concentrate very hard on the players wearing white. At the end, the film asks, how many times did people wearing white pass the ball? Then it asks, Did you see the gorilla?

Hardly anyone does.

Until they watch the film a second time, people refuse to believe a gorilla ever appeared at all. They completely failed to see the person in the gorilla suit walk slowly into the middle of the frame, among the ball-throwers, shake its fists, and walk back out.

This, Odysseus Grant knows, is a certain kind of magic.

Casinos use the same principles of misdirection. Free drinks keep people at the tables, where they will spend more than they ever would have on rum and Cokes. But they're happy to get the free drinks, and so they stay and gamble.

They think they can beat the house at blackjack because they have a system. Let them think it. Let them believe in magic, just a little.

But when another variable enters the game—not luck, not chance, not skill, not subterfuge—it sends out ripples, tiny, subtle ripples that most people would never notice because they're focused on their own world: tracking their cards, drinking free drinks, counting people in white shirts throwing balls. But sometimes, someone—like Odysseus Grant—notices. And he pulls up a chair at the table to watch.

The next night, it was a housewife in a floral print dress, lumpy brown handbag, and over-permed hair. Another excruciating stereotype. Another impossible run of luck. Julie resisted an urge to glance at the cameras in their bubble housings overhead. She hoped they were getting this.

The woman was even following the same pattern—push a stack of chips forward, hit no matter how unlikely or counterintuitive, and win. She had five grand sitting in front of her.

One other player sat at the table, and he seemed not to notice the spectacle beside him. He was in his thirties, craggy-looking, crinkles around his eyes, a serious frown pulling at his lips. He wore a white tuxedo shirt without jacket or bow tie, which meant he was probably a local, someone who worked the tourist trade on the Strip. Maybe a bartender or a limo driver? He did look familiar, now that she thought about it, but Julie couldn't place where she might have seen him. He seemed to be killing time, making minimum bets, playing conservatively. Every now and then he'd make a big bet, a hundred or two hundred, but his instincts were terrible, and he never won. His stack of chips, not large to begin with, was dwindling. When he finally ran out, Julie would be sorry to see him go, because she'd be alone with the strange housewife.

The woman kept winning.

Julie signaled to Ryan, who got on the phone with security. They watched, but once again, couldn't find anything. Unless she was spotted palming cards, the woman wasn't breaking any rules. Obviously, some kind of ring was going on. Two unlikely players winning in exactly the same pattern—security would record their pictures, watch for them, and might bar them from the casino. But if the ring sent a different person in every time, security would never be able to catch them, or even figure out how they were doing it.

None of it made sense.

The man in the tuxedo shirt reached into his pocket, maybe fumbling for cash or extra chips. Whatever he drew out was small enough to cup in his fist. He brought his hand to his face, uncurled his fingers, and blew across his palm, toward the woman sitting next to him.

She vanished, only for a heartbeat, flickering in and out of sight like the image on a staticky TV. Julie figured she'd blinked or that something was wrong with her eyes. She was working too hard, getting too tired, something. But the woman—she stared hard at the stone-faced man, then scooped her chips into her oversized handbag, rushing so that a few fell on the floor around her, and she didn't even notice. Hugging the bag to her chest, she fled.

Still no tip, unless you counted what she dropped.

The man rose to follow her. Julie reached across the table and grabbed his arm.

"What just happened?" she demanded.

The man regarded her with icy blue eyes. "You saw that?" His tone was curious, scientific almost.

"It's my table, of course I saw it," she said.

"And you see everything that goes on here?"

"I'm good at my job."

"The cameras won't even pick up what I did," he said, nodding to the ceiling.

"What *you* did? Then it did happen."

"You'd be better off if you pretended it didn't."

"I know what I saw."

"Sometimes eyes are better than cameras," he said, turning a faint smile.

"Is everything all right?" Ryan stood by Julie, who still had her hand on the man's arm.

She didn't know how to answer that and blinked dumbly at him. Finally, she pulled her arm away.

"Your dealer is just being attentive," the man said. "One of the other players seemed to have a moment of panic. Very strange."

Like he hadn't had a hand in it.

Ryan said, "Why don't you take a break, Julie? Get something to eat, come back in an hour."

She didn't need a break. She wanted to flush the last ten minutes out of her mind. If she kept working, she might be able to manage, but Ryan's tone didn't invite argument.

"Yeah, okay," she murmured, feeling vague.

Meanwhile, the man in the white shirt was walking away, along the casino's carpeted main thoroughfare, following the woman.

Rushing now, Julie cleaned up her table, signed out with Ryan, and ran after the man.

"You, wait a minute!"

He turned. She expected him to argue, to express some kind of frustration, but he remained calm, mildly inquisitive. As if he'd never had a strong emotion in his life. She hardly knew what to say to that immovable expression.

She pointed. "You spotted it—you saw she was cheating."

"Yes." He kept walking—marching, rather—determinedly. Like a hunter stalking a trail before it went cold. Julie followed, dodging a bachelorette party—a horde of twenty-something women in skin-tight mini-dresses and over-teased hair—that hadn't been there a moment ago. The man slipped out of their way.

"How?" she said, scrambling to keep close to him.

"I was counting cards and losing. I know how to count—I don't lose."

"You were— She shook the thought away. "No, I mean how was she doing it? I couldn't tell. I didn't spot any palmed cards, no props or gadgets—"

"He's changing the cards as they come out of the shoe," he said.

"What? That's impossible."

"Mostly impossible," he said.

"The cards were normal, they felt normal. I'd have been able to tell if something was wrong with them."

"No, you wouldn't, because there was nothing inherently wrong with the cards. You could take every card in that stack, examine them all, sort them, count them, and they'd all be there, exactly the right number in exactly the number of suits they ought to be. You'd never spot what had changed because he's altering the basic reality of them. Swapping a four for a six, a king for a two, depending on what he needs to make blackjack."

She didn't understand, to the point where she couldn't even frame the question to express her lack of understanding. No wonder the cameras couldn't spot it.

"You keep saying he, but that was a woman—"

"And the same person who was there yesterday. He's a magician."

The strange man looked as if he had just played a trick, or pushed back the curtain, or produced a coin from her ear. Julie suddenly remembered where she'd seen him before: in a photo on a poster outside the casino's smaller theater. The magic show. "You're Odysseus Grant."

"Hello, Julie," he said. He'd seen the nametag on her uniform vest. Nothing magical about it.

"But you're a magician," she said.

"There are different kinds of magic."

"You're not talking about pulling rabbits out of hats, are you?"

"Not like that, no."

They were moving against the flow of a crowd; a show at one of the theaters must have just let out. Grant moved smoothly through the traffic; Julie seemed to bang elbows with every single person she encountered.

They left the wide and sparkling cavern of the casino area and entered the smaller, cozier hallway that led to the hotel wing. The ceilings were lower here, and plastic ficus plants decorated the corners. Grant stopped at the elevators and pressed the button.

"I don't understand," she said.

"You really should take a break, like your pit boss said."

"No, I want to know what's going on."

"Because a cheater is ripping off your employer?"

"No, because he's ripping off *me.*" She crossed her arms. "You said it's the same person who's been doing this, but I couldn't spot him. How did you spot him?"

"You shouldn't be so hard on yourself. How would you even know what to look for? There's no such thing as magic, after all."

"Well. *Something's* going on."

"Indeed. You really should let me handle this—"

"I want to help."

The doors slid open, and Julie started to step through them, until Grant grabbed her arm so hard she gasped. When he pulled back, she saw why: the elevator doors had opened on an empty shaft, an ominous black tunnel with twisting cable running down the middle. She'd have just stepped into that pit without thinking.

She fell back and clung to Grant's arm until her heart sank from her throat.

"He knows we're on to him," Grant said. "Are you sure you want to help?"

"I didn't see it. I didn't even look."

"You expected the car to be there. Why should you have to look?"

She would never, ever take a blind step again. Always, she would creep slowly around corners and tread lightly on the ground before her. "Just like no one expects a housewife or a businessman from the Midwest to cheat at table games in Vegas."

"Just so."

The elevator doors slid shut, and the hum of the cables, the ding of the lights, returned to normal. Normal—and what did that mean again?

"Maybe we should take the stairs," Julie murmured.

"Not a bad idea," Grant answered, looking on her with an amused glint in his eye that she thought was totally out of place, given that she'd almost died.

Down another hallway and around a corner, they reached the door to the emergency stairs. The resort didn't bother putting any frills into the stairwell, which most of its patrons would never see: the tower was made of echoing concrete, the railings were steel, the stairs had nonskid treads underfoot. The stairs seemed to wind upward forever.

"How do you even know where he is? If he knows you're looking for him, he's probably out of town by now."

"We were never following *him*. He's never left his room."

"Then who was at my table?"

"That's a good question, isn't it?"

This was going to be a long, long climb.

Grant led, and Julie was happy to let him do so. At every exit door, he stopped, held before it a device that looked like an old-fashioned pocket watch, with a brass casing and a lumpy knob and ring protruding. After regarding the watch a moment, he'd stuff it back in his trouser pocket and continue on.

She guessed he was in his thirties, but now she wasn't sure—he seemed both young and old. He moved with energy, striding up the stairs without pause, without a hitch in his breath. But he also moved with consideration, with purpose, without a wasted motion. She'd never seen his show, and thought now that she might. He'd do all the old magic tricks, the cards and rings and disappearing box trick, maybe even pull a rabbit from a hat, and his every motion would be precise and enthralling. And it would all be tricks, she reminded herself.

After three flights, she hauled herself up by the railing, huffing for air. If Grant was frustrated at the pauses she made on each landing, he didn't let on. He just studied his watch a little longer.

Finally, on about the fifth or sixth floor, he consulted his watch and lifted an eyebrow. Then he opened the door. Julie braced for danger—after the empty elevator shaft, anything could happen: explosions blasting in their faces, ax-wielding murderer waiting for them, Mafioso gunfight—But nothing happened.

"Shall we?" Grant said, gesturing through the doorway as if they were entering a fancy restaurant.

She wasn't sure she really wanted to go, but she did. Leaning in, she looked both ways, up and down the hallway, then stepped gingerly on the carpet, thinking it might turn to quicksand and swallow her. It didn't. Grant slipped in behind her and closed the door.

This wing of the hotel had been refurbished in the last few years and still looked newish. The carpet was thick, the soft recessed lighting on the russet walls was luxurious and inviting. In a few more years, the décor would start to look worn, and the earth tones and geometric patterns would look dated. Vegas wore out things the way it wore out people. For now, though, it was all very impressive.

They lingered by the emergency door; Grant seemed to expect something to happen. Consulting his watch again, he turned it to the left and right, considering. She craned her neck, trying to get a better look at it. It didn't seem to have numbers on its face.

"What's that thing do?" she asked.

"It points," he said.

Of course it did.

He moved down the hallway to the right, glancing at the watch, then at doorways. At the end of the hall, he stopped and nodded, then made a motion with his hands.

"More magic?" she said, moving beside him.

"No. Lockpick." He held up a flat plastic key card. "Universal code."

"Oh my God, if the resort knew you were doing this—and I'm right here with you. I could lose my job—"

"They'll never find out."

She glanced to the end of the hallway, to the glass bubble in the ceiling where the security camera was planted.

"Are you sure about that? Am I supposed to just trust you?"

His lips turned a wry smile. "I did warn you that you probably ought to stay out of this. It's not too late."

"What, and take the elevator back down? I don't think so."

"There you go—you trust me more than the elevator."

She crossed her arms and sighed. "I'm not sure I agree with that logic."

"It isn't logic," he said. "It's instinct. Yours are good, you should listen to them."

She considered—any other dealer, any sane dealer, would have left the whole problem to Ryan and security. Catching cheaters once they left the table was above her pay grade, as they said. But she wanted to know. The same prickling at her neck that told her something was wrong with yesterday's businessman and today's housewife, also told her that Odysseus Grant had answers.

"What can I do to help?" she asked.

"Keep a look out."

He slipped the card in the lock, and the door popped open. She wouldn't have been surprised if an unassuming guest wrapped in a bath towel screamed a protest, but the room was unoccupied. After a moment, Grant entered and began exploring.

Julie stayed by the door, glancing back and forth, up and down the hallway as he had requested. She kept expecting guys from security to come pounding down the hallway. But she also had to consider: Grant wouldn't be doing this if he didn't have a way to keep it secret. She couldn't even imagine how he was fooling the cameras. *The cameras won't even pick up what I did*, he'd said. Did the casino's security department even know what they had working under their noses?

She looked back in the room to check his progress. "You expected that watch, that whatever it is, to lead you right to the guy, did you?"

"Yes, it should have," Grant said, sounding curious rather than frustrated. "Ah, there we are." He opened the top bureau drawer.

"What?" She craned forward to see.

Using a handkerchief, he reached into the drawer and picked up a small object. Resting on the cloth was a twenty-five dollar chip bound with twine to the burned-down stub of a red candle. The item evoked a feeling of dread in her; it made her imagine an artifact from some long-extinct civilization that practiced human sacrifice. Whatever this thing was, no good could ever come of it.

"A decoy," Grant said. "Rather clever, really."

"Look, I can call security, have them check the cameras, look for anyone suspicious—they'll know who's been in this room."

"No. You've seen how he's disguising himself; he's a master of illusion. Mundane security has no idea what they're looking for. I'll find him." He broke the decoy, tearing at the twine, crumbling the candle, throwing the pieces away. Even broken, the pieces made her shiver.

Then they were back in the hallway. Grant again consulted his watch, but they reached the end of the hallway without finding his quarry.

They could be at this all day.

"Maybe we should try knocking on doors. You'll be able to spot the guy if he answers."

"That's probably not a good idea. Especially if he knows we're coming."

"How long until you give up?" she said, checking her phone to get the time. The thing had gone dead, out of power. Of course it had. And Grant's watch didn't tell time.

"Never," he murmured, returning to the emergency stairs.

She started to follow him when her eye caught on an incongruity, because the afternoon had been filled with them. A service cart was parked outside a room about halfway down the hallway. Dishes of a picked-over meal littered the white linen tablecloth, along with an empty bottle of wine, and two used wine glasses. Nothing unusual at all about seeing such a thing outside a room in a hotel. Except she was absolutely sure it had not been there before.

"Hey—wait a minute," she said, approaching the cart slowly. The emergency stair door had already shut, though, and he was gone. She went after him, hauling open the door.

Which opened into a hallway, just like the one she'd left.

Vertigo made her vision go sideways a moment, and she thought she might faint. Shutting the door quickly, she leaned against it and tried to catch her breath. She'd started gasping for air. This was stupid—it was just a door. She'd imagined it. Her mind was playing tricks, and Grant was right, she should have stayed back in the casino.

No, she was a sensible woman, and she trusted her eyes. She opened the door again, and this time when she saw the second, identical—impossible—hallway through it, she stayed calm, and kept her breathing steady.

Stepping gently, she went through the door, careful to hold it open, giving her an escape route. Her feet touched carpet instead of concrete. She looked back and forth—same hallway. Or maybe not—the room service cart wasn't here.

"Odysseus?" she called, feeling silly using the name. His stage name, probably, but he hadn't given her another one to call him. His real name was probably something plain, like Joe or Frank. On second thought, considering the watch, the universal lockpick, his talk of spells, his weird knowledge—Odysseus might very well be his real name.

"Odysseus Grant?" she repeated. No answer. Behind one of the doors, muted laughter echoed from a television.

She retreated to the original hallway and let the door close. Here, the same TV buzzing with the same noise, obnoxious canned laughter on some sitcom. She could believe she hadn't ever left, that she hadn't opened the door and seen another hallway rather than the stairs that should have been there. This was some kind of optical illusion. A trick done with mirrors.

The room service cart was gone.

She ran down the hall to where it had been, felt around the spot where she was sure she had seen it—nothing. She continued on to the opposite end of the hallway, past the elevators which she didn't dare try, to the other set of emergency stairs. Holding her breath, she opened the door—and found herself staring into another hallway, identical to the one she was standing in. When she ran to the opposite end of *that* corridor, and tried the other door there, she found the same thing—another hallway, with the same numbers outside the rooms, the same inane voices from the television.

Bait. The room service cart had been bait, used to distract her, to draw her back after Grant had already left. And now she was trapped.

Casinos, especially the big ones at the mega resorts on the Strip, are built to be mazes. From the middle of the casino, you can't readily find the exit. Sure, the place is as big as a few football fields lined up, the walkways are all wide and sweeping to facilitate ease of movement. The fire codes mean the casino can't actually lock you in. But when you're surrounded by ringing slot machines and video poker and a million blinking lights, when the lack of windows means that if you didn't have your watch or phone you'd have no way to tell the time, when the dealer at the blackjack table will keep dealing cards and taking your chips as the hours slip by—you leave by an act of will, not because the way out is readily apparent.

More than that, though, the resort is its own world. Worlds within worlds. You enter and never *have* to leave. Hotel, restaurants, shopping, gaming, shows, spas, all right here. You can even get married if you want, in a nice little chapel, tastefully decorated in soft colors and pews of warm mahogany, nothing like those tawdry places outside. You can get a package deal: wedding, room for the weekend and a limo to the airport. The resort makes it easy for you to come and spend your money. It's a maze, and as long as your credit card stays good they don't much care whether you ever get out.

That, too, was a certain kind of magic.

Grant climbed two flights of stairs, the single hand on his pocket watch giving no indication that anything untoward lay beyond the door at each landing, before he noticed that the earnest blackjack dealer was no longer with him.

He paused and called down, "Julie?" His voice echoed, and he received no response. He thought he'd been cautious enough. He looked around; the staircase had suddenly become sinister.

One of the notable characteristics of a very tall staircase like this one was that it all looked the same, minimalist and unwelcoming. This landing was exactly like the last, this flight of stairs like the first six he'd climbed up.

The number painted on the door at this landing was five. He turned around, descended a flight, looked at the door—which also read five. And the one below it. Climbing back up, he returned to where he'd stopped. Five again, or rather, still. Five and five and five. Somewhere between this floor and the last, his journey had become a loop. Which meant he was in trouble, and so was Julie.

There were still doorways, which meant there was still a way out.

Five was one of the mystic numbers—well, any number could be mystic to the right person under the right circumstances. Go to the casino and ask people what their lucky numbers were, and every number, up to a hundred and often beyond, would be represented. But five—it was a prime number, some cultures counted five elements, a pentagram had five points. It was the number of limbs to the human body, if you counted the head. A number of power, of binding.

What kind of power did it take to bend a stairwell, Escher-like, upon itself? This magician, who'd orchestrated all manner of tricks and traps, was drawing on an impressive source of it. And that's why the culprit hadn't fled—he'd built up a base of power here in the hotel, in order to initiate his scheme. He was counting on that power to protect himself now.

When turning off a light without a switch, unplugging the lamp made so much more sense than breaking the light bulb. Grant needed to find this magician.

He pocketed his watch and drew out a few tools he had brought with him: a white candle, a yard of red thread, and a book of matches.

Julie paced in front of the doorway. She thought it was the first one, the original one that she and Grant had come through, but she couldn't be entirely sure. She'd gotten turned around.

How long before Grant noticed she was missing? What were the rules of hiking in the wilderness? Stay still, call for help, until someone finds you. She took out her phone again and shook it, as if that kind of desperate, sympathetic magic would work. It didn't. Still dead. She'd be trapped here forever. She couldn't even call 911 to come and rescue her. Her own fault, for getting involved in a mess she didn't know anything about. She should never have followed Grant.

No, that hadn't been a mistake. Her mistake had been panicking and running off half-cocked. This—none of this could be real. It went against all the laws of physics. So if it wasn't real, what was it? An illusion. Maybe she couldn't trust her eyes after all, at least not all the time.

She closed her eyes. Now she didn't see anything. The TV had fallen silent. This smelled like a hotel hallway—lint, carper cleaner. A place devoid of character. She stood before a door, and when she opened it, she'd step through to a concrete stairwell, where she'd walk straight down, back to the lobby and the casino, back to work, and she wouldn't ask any more questions about magic.

Reaching out, she flailed a bit before finding the doorknob. Her hand closed on it, and turned. She pushed it opened and stepped through.

And felt concrete beneath her feet.

She opened her eyes, and was in the stairwell, standing right in front of Odysseus Grant. On the floor between them sat a votive candle and a length of red thread tied in a complicated pattern of knots. Grant held a match in one hand and the book it came from in the other, ready to light.

"How did you do that?" he asked, seeming genuinely startled. His wide eyes and suspicious frown were a little unnerving.

She glanced over her shoulder, and back at him. "I closed my eyes. I figured none of it was real—so I just didn't look."

His expression softened into a smile. "Well done." He crouched and quickly gathered up items, shoving thread, candle, and matches into his pockets. "He's protecting himself with a field of illusion. He must be right here—he must have been here the whole time." He nodded past her to the hallway.

"How do you know?"

"Fifth floor. It should have been obvious," he said.

"Obvious?" she said, nearly laughing. "Really?"

"Well, partially obvious."

Which sounded like "sort of pregnant" to her. Before she could prod further, he urged her back into the hallway and let the door shut. It sounded a little like a death knell.

"Now, we just have to figure out what room he's in. Is there a room five fifty-five here?"

"On the other end, I think."

"Excellent. He's blown his cover." Grant set off with long strides. Julie scurried to keep up.

At room 555, Grant tried his universal key card, slipping it in and out of the slot. It didn't work. "This'll take a little more effort, I think. No matter." He waved a hand over the keycard and tried again. And again. It still didn't work.

A growl drew Julie's attention to the other end of the hallway, back the way they'd come.

A creature huddled there, staring with eyes that glowed like hot iron. At first, she thought it was a dog. But it wasn't. This thing was slate gray, hairless, with a stout head as big as its chest and no neck to speak of. Skin drooped in folds around its shoulders and limbs, and knobby growths covering its back gave it an armored look. Her mind went through a catalog of four-legged predators, searching for possibilities: hyena, lion, bear, badger on steroids, dragon.

Dragon?

The lips under its hooked bill seemed to curl in a smile.

She could barely squeak, "Odysseus?"

He glanced up from his work to where she pointed. Then he paused and took a longer look.

"It's a good sign," Grant said.

"How is that a good sign?" she hissed.

"A guardian like that means we've found him."

That she couldn't argue his logic didn't mean he wasn't still crazy.

"Can you distract it?" he said. "I'm almost through."

"Distract it? How on Earth—"

"This magician works with illusions. That thing is there to frighten us off. But mostly likely it's not even real. If you distract it, it'll vanish."

"Just like that, huh?"

"I imagine so."

He didn't sound as confident as she'd have liked.

She tried to picture the thing just vanishing. It looked solid enough—it filled most of the hallway. It must have been six feet tall, crouching.

"And you're absolutely sure it's not real." She reminded herself about the hallways, the room service cart. All she had to do was close her eyes.

"I'm reasonably sure."

"That's not absolutely."

"Julie, trust me." He was bent over the lock again, intent on his work.

The beast wasn't real. All right. She just had to keep telling herself that. Against her better judgment, Julie stepped toward the creature.

"Here, kitty kitty—" Okay, that was stupid. "Um, hey! Over here!" She waved her hands over her head.

The beast's red eyes narrowed; its muscles bunched.

"Remember, it's an illusion. Don't believe it."

The thing hunched and dug in claws in preparation of a charge. The carpet shredded in curling fibers under its efforts. *That* sure looked real.

"I—I don't think it's an illusion. It's *drooling*."

"Julie, stand your ground."

The monster launched, galloping toward her, limbs pumping, muscles trembling under horny skin. The floor shook under its pounding steps. What did the magician expect would happen? Was the creature supposed to pass through her like mist?

Julie closed her eyes and braced.

A weight like a runaway truck crashed into her, and she flew back and hit the floor, head cracking, breath gusting from her lungs. The great, slathering beast stood on her, kneading her uniform vest with questing claws. Its mouth opened wide, baring yellowing fangs as it hissed a breath that smelled like carrion. Somehow, she'd gotten her arms in front of her and held it off, barely. Her hands sank into the soft, gray flesh of its chest. Its chunky head strained forward. She punched at it, dug her fingernails into it, trying to find some sensitive spot that might at least make it hesitate. She scrabbled for its eyes, but it turned its head away, and its claws ripped into her vest.

She screamed.

Thunder cracked, and the creature leaped away from her, yelping. A second boom sounded, this time accompanied by a flash of light. Less like a lightning strike and more like some kind of explosion in reverse. She covered her head and curled up against the chaos of it. The air smelled of sulfur.

She waited a long time for the silence to settle, not convinced that calm had returned to the hallway. Her chest and shoulders were sore, bruised. She had to work to draw breath into complaining lungs. Finally, though, she could uncurl from the floor and look around.

A dark stain the size of a sedan streaked away from her across the carpet and walls, like soot and ashes from an old fireplace. The edges of it gave off thin fingers of smoke. Housekeeping was going to love this. The scent of burned meat seared into her nose.

Grant stood nearby, hands lifted in a gesture of having just thrown something. Grenade, maybe? Some arcane whatsit? It hardly mattered.

She closed her eyes, hoping once again that it was all an illusion and that it would go away. But she could smell charred flesh, a rotten taste in the back of her throat.

From nearby, Grant asked, "Are you all right?"

Leaning toward the wall, she threw up.

"Julie—"

"You said it was an illusion."

"I had every—"

"I trusted you!" Her gut heaved again. Hugging herself, she slumped against the wall and waited for the world to stop spinning.

He stood calmly, expressionless, like this sort of thing happened to him every day. Maybe it did.

She could believe her eyes. Maybe that was why she didn't dare open them again. Then it would all be real.

"Julie," he said again, his voice far too calm. She wanted to shake him.

"You were right," she said, her voice scratching past her raw throat and disbelief. "I should have stayed behind."

"I'm glad you didn't."

When she looked up, the burned stain streaking across the hall and the puddle of vomit in front of her were still there, all too real. Grant appeared serene. Unmoved.

"Really?"

"You have a gift for seeing past the obvious. You were the kid who always figured out the magic tricks, weren't you?"

She had to smile. For every rabbit pulled out of a hat there was a table with a trapdoor nearby. You just had to know where to look.

"You *are* all right?" he asked, and she could believe that he was really concerned.

She had to think about it. The alternatives were going crazy or muddling through. She didn't have time for the going crazy part. "I will be."

"I'm very sorry," he said, reaching out to help her up. "I really wasn't expecting that."

She took his hand and lurched to her feet. "You do the distracting next time." She didn't like the way her voice was shaking. If she thought about it too much she'd run screaming. If Grant could stand his ground, she could, too. She was determined.

"I was so sure it was an illusion. The players at your table—they had to have been illusions."

"The guy from yesterday was sweating."

"Very good illusions, mind you. Nevertheless—"

She pointed at the soot stain. "That's not an illusion. Those players weren't illusions. Now, maybe they weren't what they looked like, but they were *something.*"

His brow creased, making him look worried for the first time this whole escapade. "I have a bad feeling."

He turned back to the door he'd been working on, reaching into both pockets for items. She swore he'd already pulled out more out of those pockets than could possibly fit. Instead of more lockpicks or key cards or some fancy gizmo to fool the lock into opening, he held a string of four or five firecrackers. He tore a couple off the string, flattened them, and jammed them into the lock on the door.

Her eyes widened. "You can't—"

"Maybe the direct approach this time?" He flicked his hand, and the previously unseen match in his fingers flared to life. He lowered to the flame to the fuse sticking out of the lock.

Julie scrambled back from the door. Grant merely turned his back.

The black powder popped and flared; the noise seemed loud in the hallway, and Julie could imagine the dozens of calls to the hotel front desk about the commotion. So, security would be up here in a few minutes, and one way or another it would all be over. She'd lose her job, at the very least. She'd probably end up in jail. But she'd lost her chance to back out of this. Only thing to do was keep going.

Grant eased open the door. She crept up behind him, and they entered the room.

This was one of the hotel's party suites—two bedrooms connected to a central living room that included a table, sofa, entertainment center, and wet bar. The furniture had all been pushed to the edges of the room, and the curtains were all drawn. Light came from the glow of a few dozen red pillar candles that had been lit throughout the room. Hundreds of dull shadows seemed to flicker in the corners. The smoke alarms had to have been disabled.

The place stank of burned vegetable matter, so many different flavors to it Julie couldn't pick out individual components. It might have been some kind of earthy incense.

A pattern had been drawn onto the floor in luminescent paint. A circle arced around a pentagram and dozens of symbols, Greek letters, zodiac signs, others that she didn't recognize. It obviously meant something; she couldn't guess what. Housekeeping was *really* not going to like this.

Two figures stood within the circle: a man, rather short and very thin, wearing a T-shirt and jeans; the other, a hulking, red-skinned being, thick with muscles. It had a snout like an eagle's bill, sharp reptilian eyes, and wings—sweeping, leathery-bat wings spread behind it like a sail.

Julie squeaked. Both figures looked at her. The bat-thing—another dragon-like gargoyle come to life—let out a scream, like the sound of tearing steel. Folding its wings close, it bowed its head as a column of smoke enveloped it.

Grant flipped the switch by the door. Light from the mundane incandescent bulbs overpowered the mystery-inducing candle glow. Julie and the guy in the circle squinted. By then, the column of smoke had cleared, and the creature had disappeared. An odor of burning wax and brimstone remained.

The guy, it turned out, was a kid. Just a kid, maybe fifteen, at that awkward stage of adolescence, his limbs too long for his body, acne spotting his cheeks.

"You've been summoning," Grant said. "It wasn't you working any of those spells, creating any of those illusions—you summoned creatures to do it for you. Very dangerous." He clicked his tongue.

"It was *working*," the kid said. He pointed at the empty space where the bat-thing had been. "Did you see what I managed to summon?"

He was in need of a haircut, was probably still too young to shave, and his clothes looked ripe. The room did, too, now that Julie had a chance to look around. Crumpled bags of fast food had accumulated in one corner, and an open suitcase had been dumped in another. The incense and candle smoke covered up a lot of dorm-room smells.

On the bed lay the woman's purse with several thousand dollars in casino chips spilled around it.

"I think you're done here," Grant said.

"Just who *are* you?" the kid said.

"Think of me as the police. Of a certain kind."

The kid bolted for the door, but Julie blocked the way, grabbing his arm, then throwing herself into a tackle. He wasn't getting away with this, not if she could help it.

She wasn't very good at tackling, as it turned out. Her legs tangled with his and they both crashed to the floor. He flailed, but her weight pinned him down. Somebody was going to take the blame for all this, and it wasn't going to be her.

Finally, the kid went slack. "It was *working*," he repeated.

"Why would you even try something like this?" she said. "Cheating's bad enough, but . . . this?" She couldn't say she understood anything in the room, the candles or paint or that gargoylish creature. But Grant didn't like it, and that was enough for her.

"Because I'm underage!" he whined. "I can't even get into the casino. I needed a disguise."

"So you summoned demon doppelgangers?" Grant asked. Thoughtfully he said, "That's almost clever. Still—very dangerous."

"Screw you!"

"Julie?" Grant said. "Now you can call security." He pulled the kid out from under Julie and pushed him to the wall, where he sat slouching. Grant stood over him, arms crossed, guard-like.

"Your luck ran out, buddy," Julie said, glaring at him. She retrieved her phone from her pocket. It was working now, go figure.

Grant said, "His luck ran out before he even started. Dozens of casinos on the Strip, and you picked mine, the one where you were most likely to get caught."

"You're just that stupid stage magician! Smoke and mirrors! What do you know about anything?" He slumped like a sack of old laundry.

Grant smiled, and the expression was almost wicked. The curled lip of a lion about to pounce. "To perform such summonings as you've done here, you must offer part of your own soul—as collateral, you might think of it. You probably think you're strong enough, powerful enough, to protect that vulnerable bit of your soul, defending it against harm. You think you can control such monstrous underworld creatures and keep your own soul—your own self—safe and sound. But it doesn't matter how protected you are, you will be marked. These creatures, any other demons you happen to meet, will know what you've done just by looking at you. *That* makes you a target. Now, and for the rest of your life. Actions have consequences. You'll discover that soon enough."

Julie imagined a world filled with demons, with bat-wing creatures and slavering dragons, all of them with consciousness, with a sense of mission: to attack their oppressors. She shivered.

Unblinking, the kid stared at Grant. He'd turned a frightening, pasty white, and his spine had gone rigid.

Grant just smiled, seemingly enjoying himself. "Do your research. Every good magician knows that."

Julie called security, and while they were waiting, the demon-summoning kid tried to set off an old-fashioned smoke bomb to stage an escape, but Grant confiscated it as soon as the kid pulled it from his pocket.

Soon after, a pair of uniformed officers arrived at the room to handcuff the kid and take him into custody. "We'll need you to come with us and give statements," one of them said to Julie and Grant.

She panicked. "But I didn't do anything wrong. I mean, not really—we were just looking for the cheater at my blackjack table, and something wasn't right, and Grant here showed up—"

Grant put a gentle hand on her arm, stopping her torrent of words. "We'll help in any way we can," he said.

She gave him a questioning look, but he didn't explain.

The elevators seemed to be working just fine now, as they went with security to their offices downstairs.

Security took the kid to a back room to wait for the Las Vegas police. Grant and Julie were stationed in stark, functional waiting room, with plastic chairs and an ancient coffee maker. They waited.

They only needed to look at the footage of her breaking into the rooms with Grant, and she'd be fired. She didn't want to be fired—she liked her job. She was good at it, as she kept insisting. She caught cheaters—even when they were summoning demons.

Her foot tapped a rapid beat on the floor, and her hands clenched into fists, pressed against her legs.

"Everything will be fine," Grant said, glancing sidelong at her. "I have a feeling the boy'll be put off the whole idea of spell-casting moving forward. Now that he knows people are watching him. He probably thought he was the only magician in the world. Now he knows better."

One could hope.

Now that he'd been caught, she didn't really care about the kid. "You'll be fired too, you know, once they figure out what we did. You think you can find another gig after word gets out?"

"I won't be fired. Neither will you," he said.

They'd waited for over half an hour when the head of security came into the waiting room. Grant and Julie stood to meet him. The burly, middle-aged man in the off-the-rack suit—ex-cop, probably—was smiling.

"All right, you both can go now. We've got everything we need."

Julie stared.

"Thank you," Grant said, not missing a beat.

"No, thank *you*. We never would have caught that kid without your help." Then he shook their hands. And let them go.

Julie followed Grant back to the casino lobby. Two hours had passed, for the entire adventure, which had felt like it lasted all day—all day and most of the night, too. It seemed impossible. It all seemed impossible.

Back at the casino, the noise and bustle—crystal chandeliers glittering, a thousand slot and video machines ringing and clanking, a group of people laughing—seemed otherworldly. Hands clasped behind his back, Grant regarded the patrons filing back and forth, the flashing lights with an air of satisfaction, like he owned the place.

Julie asked, "What did you do to get him to let us go?"

"They saw exactly what they needed to see. They'll be able to charge the kid with vandalism and destruction of property, and I'm betting if they check the video from the casino again they'll find evidence of cheating."

"But we didn't even talk to them."

"I told you everything would be fine."

She regarded him, his confident stance, the smug expression, and wondered how much of it was a front. How much of it was the picture he wanted people to see.

She crossed her arms. "So, the kind of magic you do—what kind of mark does it leave on your soul?"

His smile fell, just a notch. After a hesitation he said, "The price is worth it, I think."

If she were a little more forward, if she knew him better, she'd have hugged him—he looked like he needed it. He probably wasn't the kind of guy who had a lot of friends. But at the moment he seemed as otherworldly as the bat-winged creature in that arcane circle.

She said, "It really happened, didn't it? The thing with the hallway? The . . . the thing . . . and the other . . . " She moved her arms in a gesture of outstretched wings. "Not smoke and mirrors?"

"It really happened," he said.

"How do you do that? Any of it?" she said.

"That," he said, glancing away to hide a smile, "would take a very long time to explain."

"I get off my second shift at eleven," she said. "We could grab a drink."

She really hadn't expected him to say yes, and he didn't. But he hesitated first. So that was something. "I'm sorry," he said finally. "I don't think I can."

It was just as well. She tried to imagine her routine, with a guy like Odysseus Grant in the picture . . . and, well, there'd be no such thing as routine, would there? But she wasn't sure she'd mind a drink, and a little adventure, every now and then.

"Well then. I'll see you around," she said.

"You can bet on it," he said, and walked away, back to his theater.

Her break was long over and she was late for the next half of her shift. She'd give Ryan an excuse—or maybe she could get Grant to make an excuse for her.

She walked softly, stepping carefully, through the casino, which had not yet returned to normal. The lights seemed dimmer, building shadows where there shouldn't have been any. A woman in a cocktail dress and impossible high heels walked past her, and Julie swore she had glowing red eyes. She did a double take, staring after her, but only saw her back, not her eyes.

At one of the bars, a man laughed—and he had pointed teeth, fangs, where his cuspids should have been. The man sitting with him raised his glass to drink—his hands were clawed with long, black talons. Julie blinked, checked again—yes, the talons were still there. The man must have sensed her staring, because he looked at her, caught her gaze—then smiled and raised his glass in a salute before turning back to his companion.

She quickly walked away, heart racing.

This wasn't new, she realized. The demons had always been there, part of an underworld she had never seen because she simply hadn't been looking. Until now.

And once seen, it couldn't be unseen.

The blackjack dealer returned to the casino's interior, moving slowly, thoughtfully—warily, Grant decided. The world must look so much different to her now. He didn't know if she'd adjust.

He should have made her stay behind, right from the start. But no—he couldn't have stopped her. By then, she'd already seen too much. He had a feeling he'd be hearing from her again, soon. She'd have questions. He would answer them as best he could.

On the other hand, he felt as if he had an ally in the place, now. Another person keeping an eye out for a certain kind of danger. Another person who knew what to look for. And that was a very odd feeling indeed.

Some believe that magic—real magic, not the tricks that entertainers played on stage—is a rare, exotic thing. Really, it isn't, if you know what to look for.

Carrie Vaughn is the author of the *New York Times* bestselling series of novels about a werewolf named Kitty, the most recent installment of which is *Kitty in the Underworld.* She's written several other contemporary fantasy and young adult novels, as well as upwards of seventy short stories. She's a contributor to the Wild Cards series of shared world superhero books edited by George R. R. Martin and a graduate of the Odyssey Fantasy Writing Workshop. An Air Force brat, she survived her nomadic childhood and managed to put down roots in Boulder, Colorado. Visit her at www.carrievaughn.com.

The City: *What is left of one—perhaps in the near future after war and greed have destroyed much; perhaps in an alternate world where the same has happened.*

The Magic: *A girl might take the shape of fox; powerful men might be crows . . . or any sufficiently advanced technology might be indistinguishable from magic.*

THE THIEF OF PRECIOUS THINGS

A. C. Wise

Their shadows are crows.

They are two men, standing at the mouth of an alleyway, watching the night with dark, guarded eyes. Their long, black coats flap in the wind, and their shadows have wings. They have feathers and beaks and claws.

When the moon reaches the apex of the sky, they crush their cigarettes against the bricks. Their shadows break into a dozen birds each and take flight.

They have been waiting for her.

She is a fox-girl, running swift over the close rooftops. Up here, the world smells of dust and feathers. Fresh-washed laundry hangs from obsolete radio relays, satellite dishes, and cell phone towers, which sprout like mushrooms atop every building. Sheets and shirts flap in the wind, flags to mark her passing.

Her paws—black as burnt wood—fly over shingle, tile, brick, and tar. The birds follow, floating on silent, star-lined wings. She stole something from them, something precious. They want it back.

When the roof ends, there is nowhere else to run. She jumps, changes in mid-air, and lands on two feet on the cracked pavement. The smells between the buildings are wet—all puddles, garbage, and food left to rot. She longs for the dry smells of the world near the sky. Neon turns the alley the color of blood. She is on four paws again, running.

The fox-girl can almost remember what she stole. She remembers a stone on her tongue. Images tumble through her mind: an unearthly blue glow, a chair, leather straps around her wrists, a needle in her arm. There was a woman, a human woman, and she buried something under the fox-girl's skin. It burns.

Sheltering against the side of a dumpster, she snaps fox-teeth at her own flank, tastes blood, and spits fur and flesh onto the wet ground. Something catches the light, gleaming in the patch of bitten-free skin. It is a small square of plastic, patterned with silver.

She stole it from the men in the tower; she can almost remember why. The crows want it, the humans want it; it is precious. She picks it up between careful teeth, and tucks it in her cheek.

A door opens onto the alleyway, spilling yellow light and the scent of noodles and cooked vegetables. A young man stands framed against the light, holding a bulging, plastic bag full of wasted food. Her eyes meet his, but before he can speak, four and twenty black birds fall from the sky.

The crows fold their wings tight, diving for her eyes. She whirls, snapping and snarling at the storm of feathers. The precious plastic thing scrapes her gums raw. She leaps, twists—a war dance. She is all fox now, her animal heart beating hard inside a cage of burning bones, wrapped in fur the color of coal.

"Hey! Leave it alone!"

Amidst the chaos of wings, she hears the young man drop the swollen bag of trash. It splits, spilling new scents into the alley—meat and sauce, cooling in the night air.

He runs to her side, arms beating the feathered whirlwind. She could slip away, now that the birds' attention is divided. A sharp beak draws blood from his arm, and he cries out. He is nothing to her, this young human, but she stays.

The crows are distracted, and she leaps, snatching a bird from the air. Her jaws close, crunching hollow bones. Liquid shadow slides down her throat, tasting of primordial tar, tasting of the decayed flesh of a million dead things from the beginning of time.

Twenty-three birds lift, wheeling in the sky. They scream, and fall together again at the far end of the alley, coalescing into shadows where two men wait and watch with hard, dark eyes.

One man is missing a piece of the ragged blackness spread beneath him, cast by the alley's light. His eyes meet hers, full of pain and surprise. He limps as he and his brother walk away.

A hand touches her back. The young man's voice is soft. "Are you okay?"

She's still postured to fight. Instinct snaps her teeth; the man yelps and pulls away. She tastes blood—his and hers—mingled with the lingering taste of crow-shadow oil.

She changes and lifts her head. She is a woman now, naked, crouched on blood-colored pavement that remembers the rain. She is bleeding, shaking, and tired to the bone.

The young man stares at her, open-mouthed, wide-eyed, cradling his wounded hand. She tries to speak, fails, and spits blood and plastic into her palm before trying again.

"Sorry," she says.

She collapses, but not before closing the precious, stolen thing that the crows and the humans want tightly in her hand.

She wakes on a pallet in a strange room. The scent of noodles, cooked meat, and vegetables, has sunk deep into the walls. A thin blanket lies draped over her. When she shifts, its rough weave catches on her torn skin.

The young man from the alleyway enters carrying a tray holding a bowl of water, a bowl of soup, and a roll of gauze. He sets the tray down and backs away. His hand is wrapped; two spots of crimson have soaked through the white.

He could have run, too. He could have left her in the alley on the blood-colored ground. Why bring her here? Perhaps she reminds him of someone.

She sits up, letting the blanket fall, and reaches for the gauze. He watches, wide-eyed, as she licks the wounds she can reach with her tongue, and cleans the ones she can't with water from the bowl. The young man is too frightened, too stunned, to look away.

After she wraps the last of the bandages, he shakes himself and hands her a shirt from a pile draped over the back of a chair. She catches his scent—sweat, laced with pheromones, but mostly with fear.

The shirt is clean. It reminds her of the wind on the rooftops. She pulls it on. Only now that she has covered herself does the young man blush, as though his skin has just remembered shame. He looks away.

She reaches for the soup and drinks, swallowing until she almost washes away the taste of crow-oil and shadows and blood. The young man looks back at her as she sets the bowl down; she smiles—a fox-grin.

"What's your name?" he asks. He watches her as though he believes she will bite him again, or worse.

"I don't know." As she speaks them, the fox-girl realizes the words are true. "I don't remember."

She lifts the plastic square, which she held tight even as she slept, letting the young man see.

"I stole this. Do you know what this is?"

Fear flickers through his eyes. "I think so."

He perches on the edge of the pallet, rigid. He doesn't meet her fox-eyes straight on, but looks at her from the side.

"My name is Yuki. If you don't have a name, what should I call you?"

She shrugs. She isn't interested in names, only the patterned plastic in her hand.

"Ani. I'll call you Ani."

The way he speaks the name makes her look up. He holds the name on his tongue like it's a precious thing, one he's afraid of breaking. The name has a physical weight; it changes the air in the room and leaves it tasting of ghosts. That he has given her this name frightens her. Once she had a name that meant something. Names have power, and this heavy name, fallen from his lips and soaking into her skin, might change her if she lets it. Maybe it already has.

She pushes the thought away. "Tell me about this." She holds up the stolen plastic again.

"It's a computer chip, from before the war. Everyone used to have them, but now they only exist in the tower." He points to the window. "I used to deliver food there, but not anymore."

Ani looks. The tower glitters. A thousand windows catch the setting sun and turn it into a column of living light twisting up from the scrub-brush of the city surrounding it.

"I carried a stone on my tongue," she says.

"What does that mean?"

"I don't know." She closes fox-eyes. "Except sometimes, I do."

She remembers.

Before the glass tower there was a tower of stone. It is nothing like the glittering tower outside Yuki's window. It has no windows, but it is open to the sky, and it rustles with the sound of restless wings.

In the central courtyard, a line of men with cold, hard eyes stand on a raised platform. If the fox looks straight ahead, she can only see their shoes. Even if she changed, they would still look down on her. She is less than nothing in the Crow Lords' eyes—all foxes are. So she stands with her head held high, just to show them she can.

Above the hard-eyed men, hundreds of crows line the tower's edge. The fox-girl holds her tail erect; she does not show her throat; she does not bow.

"Why are you here?" one of the Crow Lords asks.

"I've heard you need a thief. I'm the best there is."

She meets their eyes, bird and human both. Her tongue lolls, a fox-grin. She speaks truth.

Powerful and ancient as they are, there are places no Crow Lord can go.

They were tricksters once, but they've forgotten the old ways, or let them go. Fox-girls were born to steal, and no fox-girl is quicker or cleverer than she.

"Cocky child." Another Crow Lord speaks, and the fox-girl turns to him. His eyes are cold, harder than those of his brothers, filled with contempt.

"You must learn your place," the Crow Lord continues. "I will take your name to teach you respect."

Every fox-girl earns her name. It is a battle, hard-won with teeth and claws, with wit, and cunning, and quickness. But with a thought the Crow Lord rips her name away, leaving a hole where a thing she can't even remember anymore used to be. The hole fills with ice; it slows her blood and threatens to stop her breath. She shivers as though at winter's deepest cold.

The Crow Lord steps down from the platform and crouches. She could reach his throat, tear it out. The cold spreading from the place where her name used to be keeps her from doing anything at all. He laughs—a sound like rustling wings.

He grabs her muzzle, forcing open her jaws. Her needle-sharp teeth are so close to his skin, but she cannot close them while he holds her.

"I could snap your neck," he says in a voice like feathers brushed against fur. "I could rip your lower jaw from your skull and leave you broken and bleeding on the floor."

With his free hand the Crow Lord takes a smooth stone from the pocket of his long, black coat. He places it on her tongue. She expects it to be cold—and maybe it is—but it also burns.

"Your name belongs to me until the moment I choose to return it, if I ever do."

He lets her go. She wants to retch. She wants to whimper and yip, but she won't give him the satisfaction. He watches her with hard, empty eyes. She does not look away. The shadow of a smile lifts the edges of the Crow Lord's mouth.

She knew when she walked into the Crow Lords' hall that this could happen, but she came anyway, because no other fox-girl would. When the Crow Lords fly, her sisters lower their eyes. They keep their places, the places the Crow Lords give them. They whine and show their bellies. And if the Crow Lords' sharp beaks seek their lights and their livers, they hold their teeth, and whimper as they die.

So for the sake of her sisters, she refuses to look down. She needs to show the crows that at least one fox-girl is not afraid. She bares her teeth, trapping a growl at the back of her throat. A name is a small price to pay.

"What would you have me steal?" she asks, and she does not say, *my lord.*

"The humans in the tower are trying to resurrect their old magic, their circuits and wires. This time they are trying to infuse it with Crow Lord magic. They have forgotten their old ways, and they have forgotten their place in the world. They seek to steal from the oldest and the highest. We would have you steal from them what they stole from us first."

"Then it is done." The fox-girl grins, showing sharp teeth.

She will steal this precious thing for them, not because they asked her to, not for their favor, but because she *can*.

Ani wakes with the moon and stars still bright in the sky. Even now, shadows and oil linger on her tongue. She slips from the bed, and tiptoes past Yuki, who lies snoring on the floor.

The night air is cold, raising goose bumps. It hardens her nipples, making them stand out against the fabric of her borrowed shirt, fabric so thin that it shows the thatch of hair between her legs—dark as burnt wood.

A man waits beside the dumpster with its peeling paint. The chill in the air dampens the smell of rotting food. A rat squeaks its fear at Ani's approach, turning tail and running. Ani faces the hard-eyed man, waiting for him to speak.

"You took something from me," the Crow Lord says.

There is pain in his voice where she expected cold anger. She meets his eyes, which are crow-black and hard, but not as hard as before. The moonlight throws his shadow over the cracked pavement. Ani sees the jagged hole where her teeth tore part of that shadow away.

She can taste him, even after a day and a night, she can taste him. He tastes like the sky, like the wind and the stars. He tastes like freedom.

With a suddenness that stuns her, Ani understands. It's no wonder the Crow Lords look down on her kind. The entire world is a blanket spread beneath them. They speak with the dead; they know each current of air by its secret name. Humans read their flight to augur the future, and everything that walks the earth, or swims the seas must look up to them.

Ani understands, and she hates the understanding. She wants to vomit up his shadow—feathers, beak, and all—and force him to take it back, covered in her bile. But she can't. It's in her blood; it beats in her heart. It is part of her.

"You took something from me first," she says, thinking of the stone and her name.

"You walked into our house." Light shines in his eyes. Is he the one who placed the stone on her tongue? All Crow Lords look the same.

"He is my brother." The Crow Lord reads her mind. "All Crow Lords are brothers."

As all fox-girls are sisters, she thinks. But she is different now. There is crow-shadow in her blood; she has no name—or rather she has a name given to her by a human man.

She is part anger, part defiance, as she was when she walked into the Crow Lords' tower. Yet now she is something more. She has tasted crow-shadow and human blood. She looks at the jagged shadow on the ground.

"I could eat more," she says.

The Crow Lord's eyes widen. The memory of shadow tastes of power, *his* power. She wants to turn away, but emptiness gnaws in the pit of her stomach—a craving for freedom. The world has been still too long, crows above, foxes below, and men somewhere in between. She growls, a low animal sound.

The Crow Lord doesn't move. She catches his scent—cold wind, silver stars, and empty sky as black as her fur.

She threads fingers through the Crow Lord's hair—dark as feathers—and pulls his face close. She kisses him, lip bruising lip in a hungry kiss. It tastes like freedom.

Sharp, white teeth nip fragile skin. The Crow Lord tries to pull back, but the fox-girl holds him tight, licking his broken lip with her long tongue before she lets go. Her eyes glow, fox-fire bright in the dark, and she whispers, "I could eat more."

Yuki brings her white rice and strips of cooked meat, which Ani wishes he had left raw. There is something so earnest and sweet about Yuki. She thought she understood the world of men, but he is different. The more she doesn't ask of him, the more he gives. In time, will he learn to read her mind? Will he feed her meat, bloody and raw, and let her lick red juices from his fingertips, flavored with salt from his skin?

He watches her as she eats rice and meat with her bare hands, looking for someone beneath her skin. Ani—the name comes back to her, weighing heavy in the air between them.

"Tell me about her," the fox-girl says.

Yuki looks up, startled. His eyes are the color of good, clear tea, shining in the sunlight falling through the window. For a moment Ani wants to taste them. She imagines Yuki's tears would be just like that hot, strong drink. She imagines they could wash away even the taste of shadows and oil and blood.

Ani sees the question of how she knew to ask about a girl die on Yuki's tongue. He shakes his head and turns away, looking out the window at the glittering tower rising above the waking city.

"Her name was Ani," he says, which she already knew.

The fox-girl looks at the tower, reflected in Yuki's gaze. The thousand glass eyes that make up its infinite sides are formed of all the things that people have lost, left behind, and given up by going inside.

"She worked in the tower. When they ordered food, she was always the one who met me at the door to take the delivery. She smiled at me, every time. Sometimes, when she gave me my tip, I think she put in a little extra, even if her co-workers were cheap, so it would seem like more. It's stupid, but I thought I was in love with her."

"What happened to her?"

"I don't know." Yuki sighs. "She called me . . . the last time she called, she sounded scared. She didn't order any food. She couldn't catch her breath, and it sounded like she was crying. I think her hands were shaking, because the phone kept moving away from her lips and back, her voice going in and out like the wind.

"Then she was gone. The people in the tower stopped ordering food. I called every number in their directory and asked about her, but every person I talked to told me they'd never heard of her. I'm afraid she might be dead."

Ani can't bear to tell him that the name of the girl he thought he loved tasted like ghosts when he first spoke it aloud. She sets aside the empty bowl and picks up the plastic chip marked by her teeth and stained with her blood. She traces the frozen quicksilver patterns.

A memory shivers across her skin, fleeting and quick. In a moment of stillness, she might even catch it.

"If I could get you inside the tower to look for her, would you go?" she asks.

"Yes." Yuki looks like he might cry, spilling good, hot tea down his cheeks. "But how could you get me inside?"

Ani grins. "I'm a fox-girl."

Ani sits on Yuki's pallet, while he sleeps on the floor. Her knees are drawn up to her chest, her arms wrapped around them, her mind seeking after the fragment of memory buried under her skin.

Yuki's dreaming helps. He is dreaming *his* Ani, dreams strong enough to conjure her into the room. Fox-Ani remembers the girl, remembers where she has seen her before. She looks at the rising spire of glass through Yuki's window, and remembers being inside.

She remembers.

ᔓᔕ

The city's nighttime glow falls through a thousand panes of glass. It patterns the floor so she walks through pieces of light, like fallen leaves. Her bare feet pad, silent as paws. The hallways are empty; all the humans have gone home for the night. They are so confident, or so few, that they don't even bother to leave guards behind.

The fox-girl winds along the hall until she find a door leading deeper into the tower's insides. She drops four paws onto the ground for a moment before rising on her hind legs and bracing her front feet against the door. She puts her muzzle to the lock, licks it once to bind it to her, and calls a high, sharp yip into the keyhole. Crow Lords may know the secret name of the winds, but fox-girls know the way to make any door open.

She changes again, two feet on the ground, and twists the knob. She steps into one of the few rooms inside the tower without windows. The room is lit by the glow of machinery, the salvaged scraps of humanity's one-time glory. Some screens shed an eerie luminescence. Others are cracked, broken, long fallen into disuse and disrepair. Outside, the tower is beautiful. At its heart, it is rotten and sad.

A shadowed form moves, illuminated by the half-light. It is a woman with long, black hair. The fox-girl has stayed so quiet that the woman doesn't hear her, doesn't turn.

From the set of the woman's shoulders, hunched protectively forward, the fox-girl recognizes a kindred spirit. This woman is a thief, too, creeping through the shadows after dark, snooping where she shouldn't. The fox-girl slips up behind her, places her teeth next to the woman's throat, and breathes hot against her skin. Even in girl form she could tear through this soft, human throat before the woman could scream.

"Hello," the fox-girl whispers.

The woman doesn't scream, but she goes tense, her body rigid against the fox-girl's naked flesh.

"Who are you?" The woman's voice is almost steady. There is only the faintest tremor, matched by the faintest whiff of fear sweat prickling her skin. The woman's fingers tense on the keyboard in front of her, skritching softly. Now that she has been caught out, the fox-girl wonders, will the woman fight or flee?

"I have no name, not anymore. I came here to steal what you stole from the Crow Lords," the fox-girl says. She sees no harm in honesty; there is nothing the woman can do to stop her.

The woman surprises her with a sound like laughter. The fox-girl can only see part of the woman's face, a half-moon, tinted blue in the monitor-light.

"If I turn around, will you bite me?"

The fox-girl steps back, and lets the woman turn. The woman looks at her, takes in the fox-girl's nakedness, and the corners of her lips lift in a bemused smile. She shakes her head, as if at a wayward child. The fox-girl suddenly feels young, foolish, and she bares her teeth. But she holds her ground, waiting for the human woman to speak.

"Do you really think we could steal from the Crow Lords?" the woman asks. "Think about it, and look at this place. We're just starting to rebuild, re-learn everything we've lost. How could we take anything from them? We have no magic of our own. That's why we built all this." She waves her hand at the machines around them. "And look where it got us."

War. The fox-girl nods, but says nothing aloud. The tower, beautiful on the outside, isn't a stronghold. It's only the gathering place where the shattered remnants of humanity have come to try to put back together what their greed tore apart.

The fox-girl sees now what she should have seen the moment she walked into the Crow Lord's tower. The Crow Lords, tricksters still, are playing a long game, setting humanity and the fox-girls against each other in the hopes they will wipe each other out. They didn't send her here to steal; they sent her hoping she would be captured, tortured, broken, the secrets of fox-girl magic ripped from her skin. They sent her here to make her less, and make the humans more, tipping the balance just enough to start another war.

"What were you doing here?" The fox-girl points at the monitors behind the woman, speaking to hide her shame.

"Trying to wipe out the old programs before our people can unravel them. These machines did us no good the first time. I don't want to see she same mistakes made again."

The fox-girl grins, sudden and quick in the half-light.

"I think I can help you. Can you get me the chip out of one of those?"

The woman looks at her askance, but after a moment she turns and opens a panel beneath the desk. As the woman digs within the machine, nimble fingers working, the fox-girl wonders if her trust is bravery or stupidity. She decides on bravery, holding on to the image of the woman as a kindred spirit, a fellow thief.

"What's your name?" the fox-girl asks. She doesn't think humans earn their names the way fox-girls do, but she would still like to know.

"Ani."

The woman straightens and holds up the thing she has dug out from the heart of the machine. Blue radiance slides across a pattern of frozen quicksilver printed on a small square of plastic. She holds it out to the fox-girl, but the fox-girl shakes her head.

"I want you to cut me open and stitch it up inside my skin."

Yuki turns, snorting in his sleep before moving on to another dream. The fox-girl remembers the chafe of leather against her wrists, the prick of the needle going into her skin. She remembers the look of fear and doubt in Ani's eyes, the salt-tang scent of fox blood, a moment of hot pain, then drifting into the dark.

She glances down at the chip in her hand, flecked with rust-colored flakes. She remembers everything now. She meant to change the programming, re-write it with her being, imprint her memory on its quick-silver patterns and give it back to Ani: a fox-girl virus, thief quick, spreading throughout the human machines and bringing the tower crashing down.

She meant to infect the humans themselves, instilling them with defiance against the Crow Lords, starting a war of her own. She turns the chip, studying it in the light. But now, she is different. The fox-girl she was, all cocky anger and defiance, lives only in the chip. The self that came out of the tower has changed, gentled by eyes like tea, illuminated by a human thief in a tower, and darkened by a crow shadow that tastes like oil on her tongue.

Something brushes against the window, a feathered wing. Ani opens the window and leans out. The sloped roof isn't so far that she can't catch hold as she turns her back to the tower and wiggles out into the cold night air. She pulls herself up, nails scrabbling on the tile, and then she stands on four paws on the roof. Eleven crows circle against the stars before dropping to join the shadow of a man whose eyes are no longer as hollow and hard as they used to be.

The light in his gaze speaks of fear. He doesn't belong with his brothers anymore, as she no longer belongs with her sisters.

"You took something from me." He echoes his words from the night before. "I want it back."

Ani cocks her head, ears alert, eyes bright.

"Give it back!" He lunges for her. His voice breaks, becoming a crow's call.

She sidesteps, and eleven ragged birds rise into the air, maddened by pain. His shadow swarms, but doesn't dive, doesn't strike. His birds beat at her with their wings, and she feels the answering stir of shadow-slick feathers under her skin. She tastes oil at the back of her throat. She can read his mind now, a Crow Lord trick.

He wants her to take away the pain, and he hates himself for wanting it. He wants to roll, like her sisters, whine and show his belly. He hates what he has become, but even more, he hates what he has been. He wants—he needs—to feel her teeth in his skin.

Ani jumps, catching a shadowed bird. She holds it gently between her jaws, a precious thing. He doesn't fight her. Above her, ten crows scream their confusion and speak their divided minds. She bites down, exquisite needle teeth piercing feathers, bone and skin. The shadow slides down her throat. She savors it—Crow Lord power running through her veins.

A truth beats in time with her heart, one half-felt in the moment she tasted the first piece of his shadow, but fully realized now. She owns him. This Crow Lord is hers, and it doesn't matter that she is on all fours on the ground; he can't look down on her, not anymore.

Ten birds coalesce beneath the man crouching on the red roof tile, holding himself against the pain. He looks up, and his eyes aren't hollow, and they never will be again. They shine, heavy with tears.

Ani pads forward, burnt-black paws hushing over the tile. The Crow Lord doesn't move. He whines a little in the back of his throat; he raises his head, baring skin. It is not a crow gesture; it is a fox gesture—submission.

She licks his throat, but doesn't nip. He lowers his face. Her long tongue cleans his cheeks, tasting his tears. Salt mingles with the shadows and blood as she swallows them down. When he stops crying, she sits back on her haunches and looks up at him.

"I'm going into the tower," she says. "Tomorrow. Tonight, I'm going hunting."

She turns, tail blurring in the moonlight. She jumps, changing before she hits the ground. Two feet land, then four paws run over the broken asphalt. She glances back, grinning, tongue lolling, devouring the night air.

"There's blood on your mouth," Yuki says, waking her.

Ani looks up. Yuki stands over the pallet with a tray of plain rice and steamed vegetables. She sits up and the sheet slides away, revealing naked skin. She pushes a hand through her tangled hair, and then licks her lips clean. Blood flakes onto her tongue, cold and dry.

Yuki looks at her sadly, but he doesn't turn away anymore. She isn't his Ani, and it breaks his heart.

"I could be," Ani says, reading his thoughts. "I could be her." She rises, and takes the tray from him, setting it down. She takes his hand. His skin is cool, and she presses it to her breast, over her heart. Her nipple is hard beneath his palm.

"There," she whispers. "Can you feel it? She's inside my skin."

Ani is hungry. The fox in her, the crow in her, she struggles to hold onto to them, because part of her knows she is still changing. Before Yuki can pull away, she digs her nails into his hand, holding it against her sleep-warm flesh. She catches his hair with her other hand, pulls him close. She tastes his mouth. Unlike the Crow Lord, he doesn't respond. Like the Crow Lord, she tastes his tears. They taste just as she imagined.

Ani lets go. Yuki's eyes are infinitely sad.

"What do you want from me?" Yuki's voice is hoarse, heavy with salt.

She reads his mind again. He is thinking about the old tales of fox-maidens seducing young men and stealing their souls. Like the fox-girls who roll over for the crows, Yuki is ready to roll over for her. He thinks he has lost everything that matters, and that there is nothing left to care about anymore. He tried to help her, and she threw it back in his face—taking the last thing that was *his*, the last thing that matters, his kind heart.

"I'm sorry." Fox-Ani means the words, and they surprise her. She is a fox, a thief. She bows to no one, not even the Crow Lords. She takes what she wants because she *can*, but looking at Yuki, all she wants to do is give.

"I'm sorry. I'll take you into the tower, if you still want me to. Then you'll never have to see me again." She smiles—a true smile. Strangely, she doesn't feel weak, laying her words at his feet, showing her throat. She feels strong.

"Put on some clothes," Yuki says. "Let's go."

Inside, darkness swallows the stairwell. A scent pulls her up, a thread of pain. Fox-Ani changes, shedding clothes like skin. Four paws hit the ground, and she sprints up the cold metal steps, her nails clicking as she runs. Yuki's labored breath follows behind.

She stops in front of a metal door, halfway up the tower, and presses her paws to either side of the lock. She speaks her fox-word, a high, eerie sound that echoes in the silence, then she changes again, standing to open the door with human hands. She hears Yuki coming up behind her, still breathing hard.

They step into the hall. The glow of the city spills through the windows, dappling the floor in fallen-leaf patterns of silver and blue and neon-red. Ani walks through them, barefoot, and the light slides across her skin.

"Here." Yuki holds out the fallen robe she left behind in her sprint up the stairs. Ani slips it on, a skin over her skin, and belts it tight.

"It's this way." Ani beckons him down the hall, memory and scent guiding her back to the room filled with half-broken computers.

Outside, she pauses. She opens her mouth, about to tell Yuki to go back. She knows, without a doubt, what they will find inside. She can smell it—strength and pain. He shouldn't have to see this.

As though reading the words on her face, Yuki lifts his chin, defiant. Tea-colored eyes shine in the dark.

"Open it."

Ani doesn't bother to change. The door is unlocked and she pushes it open. The first Ani, the real Ani, is waiting inside for them.

She rises stiffly from the bank of computers. Fox-Ani braces herself, but behind her, unprepared, Yuki gasps. Human-Ani's left eye is swollen shut, the skin around it deepened with purple bruises, fading to sick yellow. She holds one arm against her side, wincing in pain as she steps forward. A hairline fracture in her rib, Fox-Ani thinks. She can smell sickness, infection, a wound improperly cleaned and struggling to heal.

Still, the human Ani's eyes are bright. They defy any offer of sympathy. She holds her chin high, and speaks through cracked lips, her voice almost without inflection.

"They found out I helped you and tried to kill me. I escaped. I've been hiding out in the ventilation system and the basement. There's so few of them in the tower now, they can't cover enough ground. If I keep moving, they'll never find me."

Ani takes a labored breath, and Fox-Ani winces.

"I've been waiting for you to come back. Every night, I sneak up here and wait."

Fox-Ani nods and swallows hard around a sudden thickness in her throat. She reaches up and unknots the leather cord she has tied around her neck, carrying the silver-patterned chip. Ani's eyes gleam, and she holds out her hand, but the fox-girl pulls back.

"Don't touch it, unless . . . unless . . . " She takes a deep breath, and forces herself to look Ani in the eye. "You have a choice. I can destroy the computers, bring the whole system crashing down. But if you touch this chip, you'll be infected with my memories, with the fox-girl I used to be. You can help me spread the disease, bring war to the Crow Lords one human at a time."

Behind her, Fox-Ani feels Yuki stiffen, understanding her betrayal. The real

Ani's bruised face doesn't change, her eyes still shine and she lifts her chin a little higher.

"No more war."

Fox-Ani nods. "Then you should leave now. I'll come find you when it's done."

She turns, unable to bear the human woman's eyes any longer. If she saw anger there, she would understand, but there is only a kind of sadness, and the fox-girl feels young and foolish again. How is it that she, who walked the earth for ages before the first humans ever raised their heads to look up at the stars, could be so much less wise than them?

The fox-girl hears the humans retreat, footsteps soft on the carpeted floor. She counts them along with her breath and her heartbeats, waiting until she can't hear them anymore, and kneels. She opens the panel beneath the desk, seeing where the chip fits back into the computer. The next time one of the humans tries to access something from the chip's memory, the essence of everything she was will infect the system, wipe it clean.

A sound that isn't a sound makes Ani's head snap up. Crow Lords—she can feel them coming, she can smell them on the air, a scent like oil and shadows and blood. She snaps the panel closed and rises, running for the hall.

Ani climbs, spiraling up into the dark. At the top of the stairs, she steps out onto the roof. Crows fall from the sky, screaming at her. Ten of them, whose taste she knows, throw their bodies between her and the bodies of their brothers, fighting beak and claw. She beats his brothers back, snapping with human teeth, trying to gather the birds belonging to her Crow Lord.

All around the edges of the roof, men with hollow eyes watch her while their shadows do battle. Only one does not have hollow eyes. His eyes are full of fox-light. He trembles.

Her gaze fixes on him, ignoring the feathers that snap against her skin and the beaks that draw blood.

"Trust me," she whispers.

Ani holds up cupped palms. She can feel hot, sticky blood, running down her skin. She won't fight the Crow Lords, not here, not now, not like this. Her war will be a quiet war, infecting the Crow Lords from within as she would have infected the humans. One of her birds lands, awkwardly in her out-stretched hands. She draws it close and holds it against her heartbeat. Then she lifts it to her lips.

Across the rooftop, the man with full eyes twitches. His Crow Lord shadow melts between her lips, sliding down her throat. He surrenders. The nine birds remaining flock to her. She opens her arms wide, opens her jaws, and devours them all.

When she has swallowed the last of her Crow Lord's shadow, Ani screams at his brothers. "I'm one of you now! Your Fox Brother, your Crow Sister."

The Crow Lords shriek their rage. They slash at her with beak and claw. Twelve birds lift, swirling around one of the hollow eyed men at the corner of the rooftop. They coalesce, and his shadow lies long beneath him. He steps forward.

"We still have your name." His chuckle becomes a crow-caw. Ani answers with a fox-grin.

"I don't need it anymore."

She turns towards her Crow Lord. He is on his knees now, but he raises his head. His eyes are full of light. Even though he is shaking, she feels his shadow inside her, stronger than ever. He knows her name, and he will whisper it to her in the dark. His eyes are a promise. It is all she needs.

He grits his teeth, and speaks. "Trust me. Jump."

She drops four paws onto the ground and runs for the edge of the roof. She leaps, trusting the shadow beneath her skin. She falls and the city streaks towards her from below. In the screaming wind, her shadow shreds, tatters, and spreads impossible wings. She soars.

She bares fox-teeth, laughing, and tasting the stars. She is free, and she is alive.

After an eternity of flight, of devouring the moonlight and drinking the world, she touches down. Four paws come to rest on dirty asphalt in an alley that smells of rotten food. Red neon spreads puddles of light beneath her feet. When she rises to stand on two legs, she is clothed in a coat as black as a crow's wing. It hides her torn and bloodied skin.

Yuki steps out of the doorway where the fox-girl first saw him, the human Ani behind him. She looks smaller away from the glow of the machines, half-broken by all that has been done to her.

Fox-Ani closes her eyes and places her hand to her mouth. She tastes the stone, Crow Lord magic, smooth and cool on her tongue. It has been there the whole time, but she can touch it now. She pushes it onto her palm and opens her eyes, holding out her hand.

Ani looks at her, questioning. "What is it?"

"Forgetting. If you want, you can start over again."

Ani considers a moment, then holds out her hand. The Fox-Crow-Girl tips the stone onto the human woman's palm. The woman considers it a moment, weighing it, then slips the stone into her pocket.

"Thank you."

She turns away. Yuki moves after her. "Ani! Wait!"

The human woman turns, a sad smile moving cracked lips, pulling bruised flesh tight around her eye. "That's not my name anymore. I'm no one, now. A ghost."

She turns again and walks away. This time Yuki doesn't try to stop her. Fox-Ani steps close and slips her hand into his, pressing warm skin against skin. "I'm sorry."

"Don't be," he answers, but she can feel the sorrow rolling off him. The air around him smells like tea and tears. "I never really knew her. I only had an image of her in my head that I wanted to love. Now there isn't enough of her left to know."

"Maybe she'll come back one day."

"Maybe." Yuki shrugs. He turns to look at Ani, his tea-brown eyes clear. "What are you going to do now?"

"Run. Fly." She lets go of his hand and whirls, changes, a blur of fur and feathers, then she is a girl again.

"Thank you for everything." Her voice is soft in the neon-tinted dark. She means the words more than she has ever meant any words before. Though it was the Crow Lord's shadow she devoured, Yuki has changed her, too.

"We'll see each other again," she says. "If you want. We can eat noodles on the rooftops, up under the sky. The world is going to change soon. I'll tell you what it looks like from above."

A smile touches Yuki's lips, shadowed with pain, but still a smile. "I'd like that."

He lifts his hand to wave goodbye, and she is flying, fox and crow and girl, lifting up above the city to taste the light of the stars.

∽

A. C. Wise is the author of numerous short stories, which have appeared in *Clarkesworld, Halloween: Magic, Mystery & the Macabre, Shimmer,* and *The Best Horror of the Year Volume 4,* among other places. In addition to her fiction, she is the co-editor of *Unlikely Story.* For more information, visit her online at www.acwise.net.

The City: *New York City—again, Manhattan.*

The Magic: *Lords of fairie sometimes walk among us. Even in places stinking of cold iron, up broken concrete steps to tiny apartments, or through the park and into odd little coffee shops . . .*

THE LAND OF HEART'S DESIRE

Holly Black

If you want to meet real-life members of the Sidhe—real faeries—go to the café Moon in a Cup, in Manhattan. Faeries congregate there in large numbers. You can tell them by the slight point of their ears—a feature they're too arrogant to conceal by glamour—and by their inhuman grace. You will also find that the café caters to their odd palate by offering nettle and foxglove teas, ragwort pastries. Please note too that foxglove is poisonous to mortals and shouldn't be tasted by you.

—posted in messageboard www.realfairies.com/forums by stoneneil

Lords of fairie sometimes walk among us. Even in places stinking of cold iron, up broken concrete steps, in tiny apartments where girls sleep three to a bedroom. Faeries, after all, delight in corruption, in borders, in crossing over and then crossing back again.

When Rath Roiben Rye, Lord of the Unseelie Court and Several Other Places, comes to see Kaye, she drags her mattress into the middle of the living room so that they can talk until dawn without waking anyone. Kaye isn't human either, but she was raised human. Sometimes, to Roiben, she seems more human than the city around her.

In the mornings, her roommates Ruth and Val (if she's not staying with her boyfriend) and Corny (who sleeps in their walk-in closet, although he calls it "the second bedroom") step over them. Val grinds coffee and brews it in a French press with lots of cinnamon. She shaved her head a year ago and her rust-colored hair is finally long enough that it's starting to curl.

Kaye laughs and drinks out of chipped mugs and lets her long green pixie fingers trace patterns on Roiben's skin. In those moments, with the smell of her in his throat, stronger than all the iron of the world, he feels as raw and trembling as something newly born.

One day in midsummer, Roiben took on a mortal guise and went to Moon in a Cup in the hope that Kaye's shift might soon be over. He thought they would walk through Riverside Park and look at the reflection of lights on the water. Or eat nuts rimed with salt. Or whatsoever else she wanted. He needed those memories of her to sustain him when he returned to his own kingdoms.

But walking in just after sunset, black coat flapping around his ankles like crow wings, he could see she wasn't there. The coffee shop was full of mortals, more full than usual. Behind the counter, Corny ran back and forth, banging mugs in a cloud of espresso steam.

The coffee shop had been furnished with things Kaye and her human friends had found by the side of the road or at cheap tag sales. Lots of ratty paint-stained little wooden tables that she'd decoupaged with post cards, sheets of music, and pages from old encyclopedias. Lots of chairs painted gold. The walls were hung with amateur paintings, framed in scrap metal.

Even the cups were mismatched. Delicate bone china cups sitting on saucers beside mugs with slogans for businesses long closed.

As Roiben walked to the back of the shop, several of the patrons gave him appraising glances. In the reflection of the shining copper coffee urn, he looked as he always did. His white hair was pulled back. His eyes were the color of the silver spoons.

He wondered if he should alter his guise.

"Where is she?" Roiben asked.

"Imperious, aren't we?" Corny shouted over the roar of the machine. "Well, whatever magical booty call the king of the faeries is after will have to wait. I have no idea where Kaye's at. All I know is that she should be here."

Roiben tried to control the sharp flush of annoyance that made his hand twitch for a blade.

"I'm sorry," Corny said, rubbing his hand over his face. "That was uncool. Val said she'd come help but she's not here and Luis, who's *supposed* to be my boyfriend, is off with some study partner for hours and hours and my scheme to get some more business has backfired in a big way. And then you come in here and you're so—you're always so—"

"May I get myself some nettle tea to bide with?" Roiben interrupted, frowning. "I know where you keep it. I will attend to myself."

"You can't," Corny said, waving him around the back of the bar. "I mean, you could have, but they drank it all, and I don't know how to make more."

Behind the bar was a mess. Roiben bent to pick up the cracked remains of a cup and frowned. "What's going on here? Since when have mortals formed a taste for—"

"Excuse me," said a girl with long wine-colored hair. "Are you human?"

He froze, suddenly conscious of the jagged edges of what he held. "I'm supposing I misheard you." He set the porcelain fragment down discreetly on the counter.

"You're one of them, aren't you? I knew it!" A huge smile split her face and she looked back eagerly toward a table of grinning humans. "Can you grant wishes?"

Roiben looked at Corny, busy frothing milk. "Cornelius," he said softly. "Um."

Corny glanced over. "If, for once, you just act like my best friend's boyfriend and take her order, I promise to be nicer to you. Nice to you, even."

Roiben touched a key on the register. "I'll do it if you promise to be more afraid of me."

"I envy what I fear and hate what I envy," Corny said, slamming an iced latte on the counter. "More afraid equals more of a jerk."

"What is it you'd like?" Roiben asked the girl. "Other than wishes."

"Soy mocha," said the girl. "But please, there's so much I want to know."

Roiben squinted at the scrawled menu on the chalkboard. "Payment, if you please."

She counted out some bills and he took them, looking helplessly at the register. He hit a few buttons and, to his relief, the drawer opened. He gave her careful change.

"Please tell me that you didn't pay her in leaves and acorns," Corny said. "Kaye keeps doing that and it's really not helping business."

"I knew it!" said the girl.

"I conjured nothing," Roiben said. "And you are not helping."

Corny squirted out Hershey's syrup into the bottom of a mug. "Yeah, remember what I said about my idea to get Moon in a Cup more business?"

Roiben crossed his arms over his chest. "I do."

"I might have posted online that this place has a high incidence of supernatural visitation."

Roiben narrowed his eyes and tilted his head. "You claimed Kaye's coffee shop is haunted?"

The girl picked up her mocha from the counter. "He said that faeries came here. Real faeries. The kind that dance in mushroom circles and—"

"Oh, did he?" Roiben asked, a snarl in his voice. "That's what he said?"

Corny didn't want to be jealous of the rest of them.

He didn't want to spend his time wondering how long it would be before Luis got tired of him. Luis, who was going places while Corny helped Kaye open Moon in a Cup because he had literally nothing else to do.

Kaye ran the place like a pixie. It had odd hours—sometimes opening at four in the afternoon, sometimes opening at dawn.

The service was equally strange when Kaye was behind the counter. A cappuccino would be ordered and chai tea would be delivered. People's change often turned to leaves and ash.

Slowly—for survival—things evolved so that Moon in a Cup belonged to all of them. Val and Ruth worked when they weren't at school. Corny set up the wireless.

And Luis, who lived in the dorms of NYU and was busy with a double major and flirting with a future in medicine, would come and type out his long papers at one of the tables to make the place look more full.

But it wouldn't survive like that for long, Corny knew.

Everything was too precarious. Everyone else had too much going on. So he made the decision to run the ad. And for a week straight, the coffee shop had been full of people. They could barely make the drinks in time. So none of the others could be mad at him. They had no right to be mad at him.

He had to stay busy. It was the only way to keep the horrible gnawing dread at bay.

Roiben listened to Corny stammer through an explanation of what he had done and why without really hearing it.

Then he made himself tea and sat at one of the salvaged tables that decorated the coffeehouse. Its surface was ringed with marks from the tens of dozens of watery cups that had rested there and any weight made the whole thing rock alarmingly. He took a sip of the foxglove tea—brewed by his own hand to be strong and bitter.

Val had come in during Corny's explanation, blanched, and started sweeping the floor. Now she and Corny whispered together behind the counter, Val shaking her head.

Faeries had, for many years, relied on discretion. Roiben knew the only thing keeping Corny from torment at the hands of the faeries who must have seen his markedly indiscreet advertisement was the implied protection of the King of the Unseelie Court. Roiben knew it and resented it.

It would be an easy thing to withdraw his protection. Easy and perhaps just.

As he considered that, a woman's voice behind him rose, infuriating him further. "Well, you see, my family has always been close to the faeries. My great great great great grandmother was even stolen away to live with them."

Roiben wondered why mortals so wanted to be associated with suffering that they told foolish tales. Why not tell a story where one's grandmother died fat, old, and beloved by her dozen children?

"Really?" the woman's friend was saying. "Like Robert Kirk on the faerie hill?"

"Exactly," said the woman. "Except that Great Grandma Clarabelle wasn't sleeping outdoors and she was right here in New York State. She got taken out of her own bed! Clarabelle had just given birth to a stillborn baby and the priest came too late to baptize her. No iron over the doors."

It happened like that sometimes, he had to concede.

"Oh," her friend said, shaking her head. "Yes, we've forgotten about iron and salt and all the other protections."

Clara. For a moment, thoughts of Corny and his betrayal went out of Roiben's head completely. He knew that name. And dozens upon dozens of Claras who have come into the world, in that moment, he knew the women were telling a true story. A story he knew. It shamed him that he had dismissed them so easily for being foolish. Even fools tell the truth. Historically, the truth belongs especially to fools.

"Excuse me," Roiben said, turning in his chair. "I couldn't help overhearing"

"Do you believe in faeries?" she asked him, seeming pleased.

"I'm afraid I must," he said, finally. "May I ask you something about Clara?"

"My great great aunt" the woman said, smiling. "I'm named after her. I'm Clarabella. Well, it's really my middle name, but I still—"

"A pleasure to make your acquaintance" he said, extending his hand to shake hers. "Do you happen to know when your Clara went missing?"

"Some time in the eighteenth century, I guess," she said. Her voice slowed as she got to the end of the sentence, as though she'd become wary. Her smile dimmed. "Is something the matter?"

"And did she have two children?" he asked recklessly. "A boy named Robert and a girl named Mary?"

"How could you have known that?" Clarabella said, her voice rising.

"I didn't know it," Roiben said. "That is the reason I asked."

"But you—you shouldn't have been able to—" Everyone in the coffee shop was staring at them now. Roiben perceived a goblin by the door, snickering as he licked chocolate icing from his fingers.

Her friend put a hand on Clarabella's arm. "He's one of the fair folk," she said, hushed. "Be careful. He might want to steal you, too."

Roiben laughed, suddenly, but his throat felt full of thorns.

It is eternal summer in the Seelie Court, as changeless as faeries themselves. Trees hang eternally heavy with golden fruit and flowering vines climb walls to flood bark-shingled roofs with an endless rain of petals.

Roiben recalled being a child there, growing up in indolent pleasure and carelessness. He and his sister Ethine lived far from the faeries who'd sired them and thought no more of them than they thought of the sunless sky or of the patterns that the pale fishes in the stream made with their mad darting.

They had games to amuse themselves with. They dissected grasshoppers, they pulled the wings from moths and sewed them to the backs of toads to see if they could make the toads fly. And when they tired of those games they had a nurse called Clara with which to play.

She had mud brown hair and eyes as green as wet pools. In her more lucid moments, she hated her faerie charges. She must have known that she had been stolen away from home, from her own family and children, to care for beings she considered little better than soulless devils. When Ethine and Roiben would clamour for her lap, she thrust them away. When they teased her for her evening prayers, she described how their skin would crackle and smoke, as they roasted in hell after the final judgment day.

She could be kind, too. She taught them songs and chased them through meadows until they shrieked with laughter. They played fox and geese with acorns and holes dug by their fingers in the dirt. They played charades and forfeits. They played graces with hoops and sticks woven from willow trees. And after, Clara washed their dirty cheeks with her handkerchief, dipped in the water of the stream, and made up beds for them in the moss.

And when she kissed their clean faces and bid them goodnight, she would call them Robert and Mary. Her lost children. The children that she had been enchanted to think they were.

Roiben did not remember pitying Clara then, although thinking back on it, he found her pitiable. He and Ethine were young and their love for her was too selfish to want anything more than to be loved best. They hated being called by another's name and pinched her in punishment or hid from her until she wept.

One day, Ethine said that she'd come up with a plan to make Clara forget all about Robert and Mary. Roiben gathered up the mushrooms, just as his sister told him.

He didn't know that what was wholesome to him might poison Clara.

They killed her, by accident, as easily as they had pulled the wings from the moth or stabbed the grasshopper. Eventually, their faerie mother came and laughed at their foolishness and staged a beautiful funeral. Ethine had woven garlands to hang around the neck of Clara's corpse and no one washed their cheeks, even when they got smeared with mud.

And although the funeral was amusing and their faerie mother an entertaining novelty, Roiben could not stop thinking of the way Clara had looked at him as she died. As if, perhaps, she had loved her monstrous faerie children after all, and in that moment, regretted it. It was a familiar look, one that he had long thought was love but now recognized as hatred.

Corny watched Val foam milk and wondered if he should go home. The crowd was starting to die down and they could probably close in an hour or two. He was almost exhausted enough to be able to crawl into bed and let his body's need for sleep overtake his mind's need to race around in helpless circles.

Then Corny looked up and saw Roiben on his feet, staring at some poor woman like he was going to rip off her head. Corny had no idea what the lady had said, but if the girl at the counter was any indication, it could have been pretty crazy. He left a customer trying to decide whether or not she really wanted an extra shot of elderflower syrup to rush across the coffee shop.

"Everything okay over here?" Corny asked. Roiben flinched, like he hadn't noticed Corny getting so close and had to restrain some violent impulse.

"This woman was telling a story about her ancestor," Roiben said tightly, voice full of false pleasure. "A story that perhaps she read somewhere or which has been passed down through her family. About how a woman named Clarabelle was taken away by the faeries. I simply want to hear the whole thing."

Corny turned to the woman. "Okay, you two. Get out of here. Now." He pushed her and her friend toward the door.

They went, pulling on their coats and looking back nervously, like they wanted to complain but didn't dare.

"As for you," Corny said to Roiben, trying to keep from seeming as nervous as he now felt. His hands were sweating.

"People are idiots. So she made up some ridiculous story? It doesn't matter. You don't need to do . . . whatever it is you're thinking of doing to her."

"No," Roiben said and Corny cringed automatically.

"Please just let—" Corny started, but Roiben cut him off.

His voice was steely and his eyes looked like chips of ice.

"Mortal, you are trying my patience. This is all your doing. Were I to merely turn my back, they would come for you, they would drag you through the skies and torment you until madness finally, mercifully robbed you of your senses."

"You're a real charmer," Corny said, but his voice shook.

The door opened, bell ringing, and they both half-turned toward it. *He's looking for Kaye,* Corny thought. If she came through the door, she could charm Roiben into forgetting to be angry.

But it wasn't Kaye. Luis walked through the door with three college guys, backpacks and messenger bags slung over their shoulders. Luis took a quick look in Corny's direction, then walked to the table with them, dumped his bag.

"Come with me," Roiben said quietly.

"Where are we going?" Corny asked.

"There are always consequences. It's time for you to face yours."

Corny nodded, helpless to do anything else. He took a deep breath and let himself be guided to the door.

"Leave him alone," Luis said. Corny turned to find that Luis was holding Roiben's wrist. The welts in Luis's brown skin where the Night Court had ripped out his iron piercings, loop by loop, had healed to scars, but Luis's single cloudy eye, put out by a faerie because Luis had the Sight, would never get better.

Roiben raised one pale brow. He looked more amused than worried. Maybe he was angry enough to hope for an excuse to hurt someone.

"Don't worry about me," Corny told Luis stiffly. "I'll be right back. Go back to your friends."

Luis frowned and Corny silently willed him to go away. There was no point in both of them getting in trouble.

"You're not getting him without a fight," Luis said quietly.

"I mislike your tone," said Roiben, pulling his wrist free with a sudden twist of his arm. "Cornelius and I have some things to discuss. It's naught to do with you."

Luis turned to Corny. "You told him about the ad? Are you an idiot?"

"He figured it out for himself," Corny said.

"Is that all, Luis? Have we your permission to go outside?" Roiben asked.

"I'm going with you," Luis said.

"No you're not." Corny shoved at Luis' shoulder, harder than he'd intended. "You're never around for anything else, why be around for this? Go back to your friends. Why don't you go study with them or whatever you do? Go back and admit you're sick of me already. I bet you never even told them you had a boyfriend."

Luis blanched,

"That's what I thought," Corny said. "Just break up with me already."

"What's wrong with you?" asked Luis. "Are you really going to be pissed off at people who you've never met—just because I go to school with them? You hate them, that's why I don't tell them about you."

"I hate them because they're what you want me to be," Corny said. "Nagging me to register for classes. Wanting me to stay clear of faeries even though my best friend is one. Wanting me to be someone I'm never going to be."

Luis looked shocked, like each word was a slap. "All I want is for you not to get yourself killed."

"I don't need your pity," Corny said and pushed through the door, leaving Roiben to follow him. It felt good, the adrenaline rushing through his veins. It felt like setting the whole world on fire.

"Wait," Luis called from behind him. "Don't go."

But it was too late to turn back. Corny walked out of the warm coffee shop, onto the sidewalk and then turned into the mouth of the dark, stinking alley that ran next to Moon in a Cup. He heard Roiben's relentless footsteps approaching.

Corny leaned his forehead against the cold brick wall and closed his eyes. "I really screwed that up, didn't I?"

"You said that you envied what you feared and hated what you envied." Roiben rested his long fingers on Corny's shoulder.

"But it is as easy to hate what you love as to hate what you fear."

Roiben leaned against the wall of the alley, unsure of what else to say. His own rage at himself and his memories had dulled in the face of Corny's obvious misery. He had already come up with a vague idea for a fitting punishment, but it seemed cruel to do it now. Of course, perhaps cruelty should be the point.

"I don't know what's wrong with me," Corny said, head bent so that Roiben could see the nape of his neck, already covered in gooseflesh. Corny had left

Moon in a Cup without his jacket and his thin T-shirt was no protection against the wind.

"You were only trying to keep him safe," Roiben said. "I think even he knows it."

Corny shook his head. "No, I wanted to hurt him. I wanted to hurt him before he got a chance to hurt me. I'm ruining our relationship and I just don't know how to stop myself."

"I'm hardly the person to advise you," Roiben said stiffly. "Recall Silarial. I have more than once mistaken hate for love. I have no wisdom here."

"Oh, come on," Corny said. "You're my best friend's boyfriend. You must talk to her sometimes—you must talk to her like this."

"Not like this," Roiben said, not without irony. But in truth the way that Corny was speaking felt dangerous, as though one's feelings might only continue to work if they remained undisturbed.

"Look, you seem grim and miserable most of the time, but I know you love her."

"Of course I love her," Roiben snapped.

"How can you?" Corny asked. He took a deep breath and spoke again, so quickly that the words tumbled over one another.

"How can you trust someone that much? I mean, she's just going to hurt you, right? What if someday she just stops liking you? What if she finds someone else—" Corny stopped abruptly, and Roiben realized he was frowning ominously. His fingers had dug into the pads of his own palms.

"Go on," Roiben said, deliberately relaxing his body.

Corny ran a hand through his dyed black hair. "She's going to eventually get tired of putting up with you never being around when the important stuff is going on, never changing while she's figuring out her own life. Eventually, you'll just be a shadow." Roiben found that he'd been clenching his jaw so tightly that his teeth ached. It was everything he was afraid of, laid before him like a feast of ashes.

"That's what I feel like I'm like. Going nowhere while Luis has gone from living on the street to some fancy university. He's going to be a doctor someday—a real one—and what am I going to be?"

Roiben nodded slowly. He'd forgotten they were talking about Corny and Luis.

"So how do you do it?" Corny demanded. "How do you love someone when you don't know if it's forever or not? When he might just leave you?"

"Kaye is the only thing that saves me from myself," Roiben said.

Corny turned at that and narrowed his eyes. "What do you mean?"

Roiben shook his head, unsure of how to express any of his tangled thoughts. "I hadn't recalled her in a long time—Clara. When I was a child, I had a human nurse enchanted to serve me. She couldn't love me," Roiben hesitated. "She couldn't love me, because she had no choices. She wasn't free to love me. She never had a chance. I too have been enchanted to serve. I understand her better now."

He felt a familiar revulsion thinking of his past, thinking of captivity with Nicnevin, but he pushed past it to speak. "After all the humiliations I have suffered, all the things I have done for my mistresses at their commands, here I am in a dirty human restaurant, serving coffee to fools. For Kaye. Because I am free to. Because I think it would please her. Because I think it would make her laugh."

"It's definitely going to make her laugh," Corny said.

"Thus I am saved from my own grim self," Roiben said, shrugging his shoulders, a small smile lifting his mouth.

Corny laughed. "So you're saying the world is cold and bleak, but infinitesimally less bleak with Kaye around? Could you be any more depressing?"

Roiben tilted his head. "And yet, here you are, more miserable than I."

"Funny." Corny made a face.

"Look, you can make someone appear to love you," Roiben said as carefully as he had put the jagged piece of broken china on the counter. "By enchantment or more subtle cruelties. You could cripple him such that he would forget that he had other choices."

"That's not what I want," Corny said.

Roiben smiled. "Are you sure?"

"Are *you*? Yes, I'm sure," Corny said hotly. "I just don't want to keep anticipating the worst. If it's going to be over tomorrow, then let it be over right now so I can get on with the pain and disappointment."

"If there is nothing but this," Roiben said. "If we are to be shadows, changeless and forgotten, we will have to dine on these memories for the rest of our days. Don't you want a few more moments to chew over?"

Corny shivered. "That's horrible. You're supposed to say that I'm wrong."

"I'm only repeating your words." Roiben brushed silver hair back from his face.

"But you believe them," said Corny. "You actually think that's what's going to happen with you and Kaye."

Roiben smiled gently. "And you're not the fatalist you pretend. What was it you said? *More afraid equals more of a jerk*. You're afraid, nothing more."

Corny snorted a little when Roiben said *jerk*.

"Yeah, I guess," he said, looking down at the asphalt and the strewn garbage. "But I can't *stop* being afraid."

"Perhaps, then, you could address the jerk part," Roiben said. "Or perhaps you could tell Luis, so he could at least try to reassure you."

Corny tilted his head, as if he was seeing Roiben for the first time. "You're afraid, too."

"Am I?" Roiben asked, but there was something in Cornelius's face that he found unnerving. He wondered what Corny thought he was looking at.

"I bet you're afraid you'll start hoping, despite your best intentions," Corny said. "You're okay with doom and gloom, but I bet it's really scary to think things might work out. I bet it's fucking terrifying to think she might love you the way you love her."

"Mayhaps." Roiben tried not to let anything show on his face. "Either way, before we go back inside I have a geas to place on you. Something to remind you of why you ought keep secrets secret."

"Oh come on," said Corny with a groan. "What about our meaningful talk? Aren't we friends now? Don't we get to do each other's nails and overlook each other's small, amusing betrayals?"

Roiben reached out one cold hand. "Afraid not."

Kaye was sitting on the counter of Moon in a Cup, looking annoyed, when Corny and Roiben walked back through the doors. Catching sight of them, her expression went slack with astonishment.

Luis, beside her, choked on a mouthful of hot chocolate and needed to be slapped several times on the back by Val before he recovered himself.

Cornelius's punishment was simple. Roiben had glamoured him to have small bone-pale horns jutting from his temples and had given his skin a light blue sheen. His ears tapered to delicate points. The glamour would last a single month from one fat, full moon to the next. And when he made coffee, he would have to face all those hopeful faerie seekers.

"I guess I deserve this," Corny said to no one in particular.

"Why did I even try to save you?" Luis said. Though his friends had gone, he was still there, still patiently waiting. Roiben hoped that Corny noticed that before all else.

Kaye walked toward Roiben. "I bet I know what you've been thinking," she said, shaking her head. "Bad things."

"Never when you're here," he told her, but he wasn't sure she heard as her arm wrapped around his waist so she could smother her helpless giggling against his chest. He drank in the warmth of her and tried, for once, to believe this could all last.

ᔕ

Holly Black is the author of bestselling contemporary fantasy books for kids and teens. Her latest novel for teens, *The Coldest Girl in Coldtown*, was named an NPR Great Read of 2013, an Amazon Best Teen Book of 2013, and *School Library Journal* Best Book of the Year. Her middle grade novel, *Doll Bones*, received a Newbery Honor and was named a best book of the year by *Publishers Weekly*, *Kirkus Reviews*, *School Library Journal*, and *Booklist*. Her other titles include The Spiderwick Chronicles (with Tony DiTerlizzi), The Modern Faerie Tale series, and the Curse Workers series. She has been a finalist for the Mythopoeic Award, a finalist for an Eisner Award, and the recipient of the Andre Norton Award. She currently lives in New England with her husband, Theo, in a house with a secret door. Visit her at BlackHolly.com.

The City: *A noir-ish Detroit.*

The Magic: *More than a touch of Voudou-style magic, but human grief and revenge possess mighty power too—and pain is usually the price one pays for either.*

SNAKE CHARMER

Amanda Downum

The dragon is dying.

The city feels it in bones of stone and iron, in scabby concrete skin. The *otherkind* feel it in their blood. Even Simon feels it, mortal as he is. The city waits.

The dragon will die, of age or violence, and another will take its place. Someone will eat the dragon's heart and take its power. A lot of people are interested in the dragon's demise.

Some are less patient than others.

Simon crouches in a narrow alley that smells of blood and piss and damp brick. Dark clouds scrape their bellies across the rooftops overhead, heavy with unshed rain and ash from fires that raged the night before. He tastes char with every breath.

A sacrifice. Everyone knows you have to bleed for the dragon, or burn. Simon's already burned; now he sheds blood.

The man at his feet gurgles one last time and falls silent. He's spoken all he needed to. Simon wipes his knife clean on the dead man's shirt. Chance's knife, silver on one side, cold iron on the other—it works on humans too.

He's going for the dragon tonight, the man said. And, *Mary Snakebones.*

Simon uncoils from his crouch, knife vanishing into his coat. He's not done with blood yet. Maybe not ever.

And he still needs to find a costume.

In the Garden of Eden every day is Halloween. Freaks, geeks, and tattooed women.

Tonight isn't much different, except for the costumed crowd and the orange and black streamers hanging from the ceiling, flickering like flames in the draft of the overburdened AC. Dancers writhe in pits and cages, the bass throb of the music drowning a dozen conversations, a dozen propositions and transactions. The air is solid with smoke.

A woman crawls across the main stage, wearing vinyl boots and fingerless lace gloves, a witch's hat balanced on her hair. Not much else. Simon watches her flirt with the crowd and smiles. Chance always loved costumes, fancy dress. She'd have liked his outfit tonight.

His smile turns bitter and falls away. Chance is gone, and the woman he wants tonight won't be on stage.

He slides through the crowd, a colder, cleaner thread twining through the murk of sweat and spilled liquor. Just another costumed schmuck, but elbows and shoulders move aside for him. He rides the current, lets it spit him out in a shadowed back corner where Mary Snakebones holds court.

She's enthroned in a wide, shallow booth, surrounded by pretty hangers-on. Mostly goths and would-be witches. He catches the scent of fae, but it's faint, half-breed at best. Sometimes she runs with a dangerous crowd, but not tonight. Mary's danger enough on her own.

He walks up slow, hands loose at his sides. Sweat trickles down his neck; the holster chafes the small of his back. He should have worn a shirt under the tailcoat. Mary's courtiers barely notice him. They'd all be dead, if that was his business tonight.

Mary notices. She watches him approach, eyes dark as sin under a weight of kohl. Waxy black lips curl. "Hello, Baron."

He tips his top hat, looks down over the tops of his dark round glasses. "Good evening, Marie."

She doesn't wear a costume. She doesn't have to. She's Mary Snakebones, Mojo Mary. The dragon's child. People would dress as her if they could pull it off.

She cocks one black brow. "Are you here for me, Baron?"

What would happen if he said yes? She looks so soft, so young, all trussed up in velvet and vinyl. Her smile isn't soft, nor her eyes young. He's almost tempted to find out.

"We need to talk."

Her eyes narrow, gaze burning through greasepaint and flesh. She's never seen this face before, but she nods. Maybe she can read his mind, or his soul, or invisible omens spinning around him. She waves a hand and the baby-bats scatter from the booth. "Sit with me."

"I was hoping for a more private conversation."

"Maybe later." She nods toward the stage. "My sister is dancing tonight."

He slides into the booth—easier than arguing. Leather creaks as he settles on her right. He keeps his eyes on the crowd, but the most dangerous thing in the room sits beside him.

"The ghost of Simon Magus." She studies him with a smile. "You're a boogeyman now, the thing waiting in the dark. They say you died too, that night."

He swallows. "I did."

"I like this face."

Whether she means the painted face or the one the surgeons gave him, he doesn't know. Doesn't want to know. "Sal is coming for you tonight."

Her smile widens. "Let him." Under the table she takes his left hand, her flesh warm through the leather of his glove. One sharp nail traces the underside of his ring finger, snags on the metal of his wedding band. "Poor Simon. Still wearing your grief like a brand."

Sweat pricks his scalp, trickles greasy through the white paint on his face. His scars tingle. She moves closer, velvet coat rustling against his shoulder, breath tickling his ear. "You've killed someone tonight."

Their lips nearly brush as he turns to face her, bittersweet perfume filling his nose—almond and clove and autumn leaves. "Only one." His fingers tighten around hers. "Sal is after the dragon."

Black eyes narrow. "And death comes to tell me this."

"This?" He touches the brim of his hat. "It's just a costume."

"No, it isn't." Her left hand rises to touch his cheek, thumb trailing whisper-soft over his cheekbone. "This face is very real tonight, Simon Magus."

"Don't call me that. I was never the one—"

Her hand trails down his chest, to the slick, ridged scar tissue over his heart. "I know a true name when I hear it, Simon."

He shudders, and wonders what else she knows. If she can read his heart, he's a dead man. She's too close, dizzying him—he could never draw in time.

The music stops, leaving only the ocean-murmur of the crowd and the surf of blood in Simon's ears. Mary shifts her attention to the stage and he fights a sigh of relief.

"And now—" the DJ's voice echoes over the speakers "—Eve and the snake."

A new song starts, slow and deep, and a woman glides onto the stage. Henna-red hair in wild gorgon braids, skin like cream and cinnamon. Her hair matches the python draped over her shoulders.

Someone in the crowd gasps. Simon sucks a breath through his teeth. The snake is longer than she is, its muscle-fat tail wrapped around her waist. Garnet and cinnabar scales shine under the lights, shimmering with dusty yellow-and-black whorls.

Her name isn't Eve, of course, but Helene Dimanche. The dragon's priestess.

Beautiful as her sister, though they don't look like the twins they claim to be. Mary leans forward, her hand still tight around Simon's, eyes trained on the dance.

It's a real dance—Helene doesn't touch the pole, or leave her feet. Muscles play in her arms as she lifts the snake and twirls. Henna swirls across her back and breasts and belly, patterns rippling as she sways to the beat.

I've got something you can never eat.

She doesn't play to the crowd, either. No flirting or winking—she only makes eye contact with the snake. Money flutters onto the stage, but she doesn't touch it.

I've got something you can never eat.

Mary's chest rises and falls, cafe creme flesh constrained by her tight-laced bodice. Not the woman undulating on stage that affects her so, no matter what the rumors say, but the power Helene raises with her dance. It whispers over Simon's skin like electric wind. He learned to feel those things around Chance.

"We should go," he says. "It isn't safe here."

"This is my place. They wouldn't dare."

A rueful smile tugs at his mouth. She's young after all, young and cocky. "They came to my place, Chance's place. They dared, and now she's dead."

Her thumb strokes his palm, tingling through the leather to the roots of his teeth. "And you're here to protect me? My white knight."

"I want Sal."

"What else do you want?"

His stomach clenches. She'll know if he lies. "I want to rest," he says after a moment. Some of the truest words he's ever spoken. "And I want to see the dragon." Chance always wanted to see one. He can almost hear her voice, feel her drowsing in his arms—but he can't bear to remember it now, not here, not with this witch.

"Are you willing to pay the price?"

She strikes as the last breath of assent leaves his lips, her fingers tangling in his hair. He stiffens, hand twitching toward his gun, but she's pulling his head toward hers, her lips pressing his till he feels her teeth, till he lets her tongue against his and the rum-sugar taste of her fills his mouth and he can't breathe.

She's strong—he can't break her grip, not without hurting her. Her hand presses against his scars again, against his heart. He hasn't kissed a woman since Chance; he's never kissed a woman like Mary. Her teeth sink into his lower lip and he tastes blood.

He pushes her away and she lets him. The rush of air between them raises goosebumps. His chest and lip sting.

"Damn it, Mary . . . "

She wipes a drop of blood off her mouth, licks her finger clean. "You have to bleed."

His ears are ringing, and the shouts across the room register a heartbeat too late.

The crowd parts, dodging away from men with guns in their hands. Simon draws, but they've already got the drop on him. Muzzles raise, take aim, and the look on Mary's face nearly makes him laugh as he grabs her and pulls her over the side of the booth with him.

The world shatters into screams and thunder. Bullets thump into leather and wood, whistle over their heads. The air reeks of fear and bitter gunpowder.

"They are dead men," Mary says. The words are lost in the cacophony, but Simon reads them on her lips and smiles.

"That's the plan, yeah." He leans around the edge of the booth and squeezes the trigger. Bad angle, and a man falls with a hole in his thigh, still alive. Someone else shoots back. The crowd swarms; glass shatters as a waitress drops a tray and lunges for the emergency exit. There's a commotion on the stage.

Then a woman screams Mary's name.

"Helene!" Her coat billows as she runs for the stage. Simon curses and lunges after her, gun kicking in time with his heartbeat as he lays down cover. Patrons shriek and dodge, clogging the front door. Pain like a wasp sting in his left arm and someone behind him screams and chokes.

He tackles Mary, knocking her into the sheltering T-intersection of the stage. Heat soaks his sleeve.

"Mary!" The cry is fainter now, closer to the door.

"They've got her." She struggles against Simon's grip, and he wonders if he'll have to hit her.

He hears the flames first, a crackling rush that floods adrenaline through him. Then the wave rolls over the ceiling, liquid and beautiful. Streamers rain down in sparks and ashes.

Sal's work. Simon's pulse stutters triple-time; a burning scrap of paper brushes his cheek and panic threatens to swallow him. He fights it down, prays for the ice to take it away. A woman twitches on the floor, blood bubbling from her mouth and chest. Lung shot—Simon contemplates a mercy kill, but doesn't want to waste a bullet.

"Back door," he shouts at Mary.

"They've got my sister!"

"And we can't get her back if we're dead." Already smoke sticks in his throat and his eyes water. Eyeliner bleeds ashen tears down Mary's cheeks. After a second she nods.

He pushes Mary ahead of him and slides along the side of the stage. The shooting's stopped. The woman on the floor lifts a pleading hand toward them. Simon pauses for an instant, then gives her what he can. Blood halos beneath her head.

Something hisses angrily in his ear, a second's warning. His left arm screams as he raises it, screams again as his hand closes around Helene's striking snake. The force jars through him and he barely holds on as its jaws gape in front of his face. Needle teeth glint, dark tongue flickering.

Its body writhes against his arm, looking for a grip to crush. A tube of heavy muscle, covered in oiled leather; his skin crawls at the touch. His hand tightens, glove blood-slippery, thumb squeezing under its jaw—

And Mary appears, black-nailed hands scooping up the python, cooing as she drapes its massive coils over her shoulders. It hisses at Simon as he lets go, then settles onto Mary, pacified by a familiar person.

"Follow me." Her heels beat a staccato rhythm as she darts for the door behind the stage.

Smoke billows after them into the raw cement hallway, grey tendrils eddying in their wake. "They'll use Helene to find the dragon," Simon says as they run.

"She won't tell them."

"Then Sal will kill her, and spread her guts out to learn the way."

Mary flinches, and for a second he thinks she'll turn and run back into the inferno. He grabs her arm. "Can you talk to her?"

"Yes," she says after a minute.

"Then tell her to take them to the dragon, and not to fight. We'll meet them there."

She nods, sucks in a deep breath; the python rises with the swell of her chest. Her eyes roll back in her head for a moment and she sways. Simon steadies her, blood dripping off his hand. She's back in heartbeats and the fear eases around her eyes.

She touches his hand, frowns at the blood. He cranes his neck, sees entrance and exit. The bullet went through the meat of his upper arm; not too serious, though it burns like hell. Blood soaks his sleeve shiny, drips in fat drops off his knuckles.

"That should have been mine," she says. She tastes his blood again, but she's not flirting now.

"Let's go, Mary."

He's afraid the gunmen will have the back covered, but the parking lot and alley are empty. Sal got what he came for. Simon's blood cools in the evening chill, and goosebumps crawl over his chest. The air still tastes like char. Sirens scream in the distance, getting closer.

Simon holsters his gun, wipes sweat out of his eyes. Somehow he's managed not to lose the hat.

Mary grins, sallow and tear-streaked in the sodium glow. "I told you it was a true face. I'll dress that for you"—she nods toward his arm—"then we'll see the dragon."

Mary drives, her sleek black car purring through the crumbling streets. Buildings rise like rotted teeth around them, tearing at the clouds. The city is dying, slow and broken.

The streets are nearly empty tonight—smart residents know when to stay inside and lock their doors. Halloween is dangerous enough, without a dragon's death for *lagniappe*.

And the dragon dies tonight, one way or another. Simon feels it in his scars.

The car reeks of blood and rum, both soaking the bandages under Simon's sleeve. It hurts, but he can use the arm. A crust of blood dulls his ring. He slides a fresh clip home, chambers a round.

Mary nearly hums with power, the electric smell of it tingling in his sinuses. They surprised her in the Garden—she won't let it happen again. Streetlights spark and die as they pass; maybe Mary's work, but he doesn't ask. They head for the docks and darkness follows in their wake.

"Is Sal the last?" Mary asks.

They walk now, the car and the snake abandoned in a dark alley. Simon hears water nearby, and the clang of train canisters loading and unloading. Thunder snarls in the distance, but still no rain.

"No," he finally answers. She'll know a lie. Long practice keeps his voice and pulse calm, but his stomach twists. Tonight will end ugly, one way or another. He touches his tongue to his swollen lip. "Sal's the last of the ones who killed Chance, but he didn't give the orders. His boss dies too."

"That's a lot of death for one man."

Too much for any man. "I'll manage."

"Sal is trying to break away," she says after a moment. "That's why he's after the dragon. He wants free of his masters."

Simon frowns. "He should have tried sooner."

Sal never set foot in their house that night, never fired a shot. Chance took two bullets, Simon three, but it was the fire that killed her. The fire that brought the ceiling down, costing Simon half his face and very nearly his left arm. Chance died screaming his name.

"What will you do when you're done?"

He sighs. "Rest."

"You don't have to waste yourself on revenge."

"If they die, it's not wasted. I don't have anything left, anyway."

Mary touches his arm, soft enough to make him shiver. "I can give—" She stops, hand tightening. "They're coming. And we're here."

Simon looks up at the building—five stories, cement and brick. A parking garage once, now walled in. Heavy wood-and-iron doors stand where the ticket booth should have been.

Simon's hand tightens on his gun, and he double-checks the weight of the knife in his pocket.

Lights cut through the night as three cars pull up to the curb. Simon presses against the alley wall, pushing Mary back.

She hums under her breath as she balances on one foot, tugging off her boot. Simon frowns, glances at the glitter of broken glass on the ground. She's moved easily enough in heels so far. "Are you sure that's a good idea?"

Her smile makes his shoulder blades prickle; she slips her other foot free. "I walk on pins and needles, I walk on gilded splinters. I want to see what they can do." Her voice is lower, throatier. The air smells of rum and cinnamon and Simon's skin tightens. She shrugs free of her coat, vinyl corset shining red as heart's blood.

Car doors open and men emerge. Simon recognizes Sal's scimitar-nosed profile in a brief flicker of light.

Dominic Salieri. Nicky the Salamander, though never to his face. The whisper-stream says he's part ifrit. To Simon, he's just another dead man.

But not yet, because Sal reaches into the car and pulls out Helene. She's wrapped in a man's jacket, doesn't look hurt. Sal handles her gently enough, but Simon can see her tremble. He could shoot past her, but not fast enough to take down the dozen thugs before one of them could kill her.

She doesn't fight. She's waiting for Mary.

Simon's not sure Mary's here anymore.

Two men open the doors, another two rolling in to secure the room. Nothing happens, and Sal escorts Helene into the darkness of the dragon's lair.

Mary turns to Simon, pinning him to the wall. "A kiss for luck, Baron."

His swollen lip throbs and he braces for the pain. But she doesn't bite this time.

Her tongue burns against his, heat rushing through him, drawing out the pain, melting the ice. It hurts like something tearing inside, and he wants to push her away, but somehow his arms are around her, gun hand pressing the small of her back, crushing her to him. He hasn't ached for anyone like this since . . .

She pulls away, cheeks flushed, eyes shining. The hair on the back of his neck stands up as he realizes he just kissed a goddess. Or something close to one.

"Mary—"

"Not quite."

"Erzulie."

Her smile is fierce and bloodthirsty, flashing bright as the knives in her hands. "Come on, Baron. The dragon wants blood."

She steps out of the alley.

Six of Sal's guards wait by the door and they all turn, guns rising. Simon's stomach clenches. She's blocking his shot, drawing their fire. He can already imagine the sight of her blood on the pavement.

But Mary starts to dance.

And Simon's jaw drops as he remembers who she is.

She writhes serpent-lithe, daggers like steel fangs. Her sister's dance was just a shadow of this. At first the guards can only stare as she swirls toward them, barefoot on the pitted, glass-strewn street.

Someone breaks the spell and fires.

But Mary isn't there, spinning out of the bullet's path like she could pluck it out of the air if it suited her. Then she's on the man and his throat opens in a red-black spray.

Simon's gun roars and men fall, one, two, three. Mary's heel catches one in the gut as her knife comes down on the other's gun arm. Simon aims and she slides out of the way, letting him finish the one doubled over retching.

She knows just where to cut as she opens the last man's chest. Simon's guts turn to ice water as she straightens, red to the elbows, blood dripping down her cheek. Her eyes flash like coals in the streetlight.

The smell inside the temple fills Simon's nose, makes his flesh crawl. Smoke and ash and something musky and autumnal, like snakes. His stomach cramps with atavistic terror, balls trying to crawl into his torso. He blows a long breath out his nose, wrestling the need to flee. He has to see this through.

Mary, or Erzulie, takes his arm, turns him toward her. She traces a wavy line on his forehead with one bloody finger and the fear recedes. He almost misses it.

Dim lamplight spills across the wide room, throws long shadows across the cement floor. Open spaces, wide ramps. Enough room for a bus to maneuver. Or a dragon.

"Which way?" he asks.

Mary's nostrils flare as she scans the room. "Down."

The air warms as they descend, and the smell worsens. Not just the reptile reek, but the smell of age, or illness. Of a dying beast.

A shadow flickers at the edge of his vision and bullets crack against the wall behind them. Simon dodges behind a pillar, but Mary's moving in a blood-streaked blur, bare feet silent on the floor. An instant later he hears a gurgle and a heavy thump.

"Follow me, boy," she calls. "Try to keep up."

Simon's face feels strange; it takes a second to realize he's grinning. Then Mary gasps in pain.

He rounds the corner to find two men bleeding all over the floor and Mary leaning against the wall, a hand pressed against her stomach.

"He had a knife." Her voice is mortal again, and strained.

Vinyl gapes and curls like skin, a wide gash above her navel. Her corset stays took the worst of it, at least, and nothing's punctured. Blood wells dark as pomegranate juice in the shadows.

"I'm fine," she says, waving him off.

It would be easier without her, but he nods. She keeps up, though sweat slicks her face and her lips pinch pale.

Shots echo below them, followed by a sound that curdles Simon's blood. Not a hiss, not a roar, not a volcano's belch, but all of them at once. The screams don't last long. They round the last corner and enter the dragon's chamber.

A blur of fire and ash, of smoke and embers. Red and gold and black and gray, cracking, shifting, seething. Winged and scaled and feathered and furred and Simon can't make sense of it. He staggers, goes to one knee.

The dragon.

Chance's voice in his head, soft and resonating. *Beautiful. So beautiful.* For an instant he can feel her beside him, smell her skin. Tears stream down his face.

He climbs to his feet. Sweat slicks his palm, slippery against the rough-hatched gun grip.

Sal stands in front of them, silhouetted against the dragon's glow. He's still got Helene, and Simon won't risk the shot.

"Sal!" His voice cracks, rough with smoke. "Let her go."

Sal turns, dragging Helene around. He's got a gun in his free hand; the muzzle gleams as he levels it at Simon.

And pauses. His face is in shadow, but Simon feels the weight of his stare.

"What's the matter, Sal? Don't you recognize me?" He strips off the torn and bloody coat, one sleeve at a time, tosses hat and glasses aside. Pink and white scars shine in the firelight. "Recognize your work?"

"Simon Marin?" Sal laughs. "So it has been you—the ghost, the thing that's got everyone jumping at shadows. You've done me a lot of favors in the past few months."

"I'll do one more. Let the girl go."

"What is this—revenge? You should know better. It was just a job, Simon."

"It was my wife."

"After tonight, I'll never work for Manny again. Hell, I'll turn him to ash. That was what Chance wanted, wasn't it?"

Simon fights the urge to spit. "Don't worry, that will still happen."

Behind him, Mary's breath hisses. Simon's chest tightens; she's finally read his heart.

He's starting to wonder how long they'll stand here like this, guns pointed, when Helene decides it for them. She slams a foot into Sal's knee and throws herself down.

Simon dodges, pulling the trigger. Both guns flash. Sal falls, but his bullet catches Simon's left shoulder like a white-hot hammer. His vision washes red as he stumbles against a pillar.

His chest heaves, pulse echoing in his ears, louder than the dragon's rasping breath. His left arm hangs nearly useless at his side—pity it's not numb. So tired, but he can't rest, not yet.

He pushes himself up. Confirm the kill, but Mary's standing in front of him, black eyes narrow.

"You came for the dragon."

"I did. I have to."

"Do you even know what he is? Do you understand, or is this just another death?"

"That's what I do, Mary. The dragon is power—I can't take out Manny like this, as a man. I'll kill until there's no one left. If you want to cut my heart out then, I won't stop you."

"That's not how it works. My sister is the priestess, the chosen child. This city has enough killers, Simon. It needs new life."

His eyes sag shut for a heartbeat. "I don't have anything to do with life anymore."

She moves closer and he flinches, but she only lays a hand over his heart. "It's not too late. We can give you something more."

"I just want to rest. But I have to keep going. I promised Chance . . . " Strength drips out of him in crimson streams. Already his vision is dark around the corners.

He straightens, steps past Mary. "I promised."

She grabs his arm, nails gouging. "Simon, I won't—"

He punches her in the gut, gun still in his hand. She makes a noise like a run-over cat and falls, face draining grey.

"Sorry," he whispers as he turns away.

Helene lifts her head from where she kneels naked beside the dragon. Tears shine on her cheeks. "It's time. He's dying."

Simon staggers closer, heat washing over him in waves. He can see the beast now, massive head on the ground beside Helene, body long as a train car sprawled limp across the ground. Its chest heaves, dark smoke curling from its nostrils. One lantern eye shines, half-slitted. The other is sunken and swollen shut, leaking black blood and clear fluids. Its forked purple tongue flickers amid broken bone-needle teeth.

Its hide is rough, dark as coal, but as it moves sparks of red and gold writhe through the black like falling embers. Even dying, it's beautiful. Chance always wanted to see a dragon.

Simon brushes its snout with his left hand, hisses as his fingers blister. His blood bubbles as it drips on the dragon's nose. The dragon exhales a steaming sigh and Simon's skin tingles.

Helene looks at him, hazel eyes shining by dragonlight. "I have to eat his heart." Tears drip off her lashes, evaporating before they reach her chin.

Mary staggers closer, limping now, hunched over her bleeding stomach. "You don't have to do it, Simon. You think we won't take care of this? You think you and yours are the only ones Manny's ever hurt? There will be vengeance, all you could ever want, and you don't have to die for it."

"Yes I do."

He holsters the gun and draws his knife. Silver and steel gleam like a flame in his hand as he stands over the dragon. Mary curses softly; Helene watches him with eerie golden eyes.

The dragon doesn't fight, just rolls, baring the hollow of his breast. The hide is softer here, like oiled leather.

The knife slides home and Helene lets out a strangled scream. Then Simon can't hear anything but the roar of his own heart.

Blood like boiling oil. Clinging. Burning. The pain is worse than anything he's ever imagined, until it simply stops, too much for his body to hold and it rolls over him. His vision tunnels until all he can see is the ruin of flesh in front of him, the blackened skin of his arms.

The blade melts as he cuts, barely lasts long enough to sever the great throbbing veins. The gush of blood sears half his face, blinds his right eye. The fluid dripping down his cheek is too thick to be tears.

And then the heart is free, pulsing in his hands. Fire ripples blue-green, washing up his arms. Consuming him. His own heart is failing.

He turns, sees Helene and Marie Dimanche watching him, wide-eyed. Helene has her arm over Mary's shoulder, and they really do look like sisters.

He raises the dragon's beating heart. His hands are twisted char and bone. He'll be dead in seconds if he doesn't eat.

He's been dead for a year.

The city needs new life. He can't give it that.

All he wants is rest.

He steps forward, ribbons of melting rubber trailing from his boot soles. He falls to his knees in front of Helene and offers her the burning heart.

Chance. I'm sorry.

As she takes it from him Simon collapses, his wreck of a body giving out at last, and hot concrete rushes up to meet him, drives the last breath from his lungs.

Simon dies.

Simon burns.

Not the torturous fires of a hell he's never believed in. Not even the fire of his own hell, all too real. This is clean.

No smoke, no soot, just white heat dissolving him. He wishes he could cry for the sheer relief of it.

The dragon is there, inside him, surrounding him. It eats his heart.

He failed, broke his promise, but this isn't so bad. This is a better death than he ever imagined for himself.

And then it's over.

Simon gasps, chest hitching painfully. His face is wet, the taste of blood and tears thick on his tongue. He opens his eyes—both of them—and stares at the soot-scarred ceiling of a parking garage. His gun gouges the small of his back.

He lifts his hands. Whole, clean. He sits up, and nothing hurts, but the skin on his chest pulls oddly as he moves.

His scars are gone.

He touches his chest, his arms, his face. Burn scars, blade scars, bullet wounds, the scars the surgeons' scalpels left. Everything gone.

His breath leaves him on a sob.

"Welcome back, Simon Magus."

Mary sits a few yards away, Helene draped motionless over her lap. No cleansing fire for her—she's still ash-streaked and bruised. The dragon is gone, leaving only pools of blood flickering with green-gold flames.

Sal is gone too, and bloody footprints lead up the ramp.

Simon pushes himself to his knees and stares at Helene's still form. "Is she—"

"She's resting."

"She's not . . . "

"A dragon?" She smiles her wicked smile. "She is, just a baby one. These things take time." She strokes her sister's Medusa braids with a gentle hand.

"Why am I still alive?"

"The dragon must like you. And my sister will need help, as she grows. She has a lot of work to do."

Simon runs a weary hand over his face. "I just wanted to rest."

"We rarely get what we want." Her smug smile belies the words; Mary is used to getting what she wants. "Besides, a lot of people will need killing before this is over." She shifts her weight and winces. "Help me get her home."

Simon sighs and obeys, crouching to take Helene into his arms. Her skin is feverishly hot.

Mary catches his hand before he can stand, nails piercing skin. "If you ever hit me like that again, I'll have your balls for a *gris gris* bag."

He just nods, face carefully flat, and lifts Helene.

Outside it's raining, the sky opened up to wash the city clean. Mary limps beside him as he carries the newborn dragon into the world.

Amanda Downum lives in a garret in Austin, Texas, where she drinks absinthe but tries not to die of consumption. Her day job involves silverfish, scorpions, and the rare snake. Sometimes she gets to dress up as a giant worm. She is the author of the Necromancer Chronicles—*The Drowning City*, *The Bone Palace*, and *Kingdoms of Dust*—published by Orbit Books. Her short fiction has appeared in *Strange Horizons*, *Realms of Fantasy*, *Weird Tales*, and in the anthologies *Lovecraft Unbound*, *Brave New Love*, and *A Fantasy Medley 2*. Her novel *Dreams of Shreds & Tatters* is forthcoming from Solaris.

The City: *New York City—more exactly: Greenwich Village in Lower Manhattan.*

The Magic: *A Faerie Wild Hunt leaves frightened mortals, flattened cars, and pavement glowing with hoofprints in its path. It's up to the Archmage of New York and a few others—including a werewolf drag queen—to stop the Hunt.*

THE SLAUGHTERED LAMB

ELIZABETH BEAR

The smell of the greasepaint was getting to Edie.

"Oh my *god*, sweetheart, and then she says to me, 'Honey, I think you'd look fabulous with dreads,' and I swear I stared at her for ten whole seconds before I managed to ask, 'Do you think I'm a fucking Jamaican, bitch?' I mean, can you believe the gall of . . . "

Nor the mouths on some others, Edie thought tiredly, pressing a thumb into the arch of her foot and trying to massage away the cramp you got from a two-hour burlesque in four-inch stilettos. They were worth the pain, though: *hot* little boots with the last two inches of the dagger heel clad in ferrules of shining metal. When you took them down the runway, they glittered like walking on stars.

She looked in her makeup mirror, still trying to tune out Paige Turner's fucking tirade about fucking Jamaicans, which wasn't getting any more interesting for its intricacy. Edie's vision was shimmering with migraine aura—full moon tonight—and the smell of makeup and scorched hair was making her nauseated. The fucking cramp wasn't coming out of her fucking foot. No way she could walk in flats like this.

She didn't want to go home: there was nothing in her apartment except three annoying flatmates—one of whom had an incontinent cat—and a telephone that wasn't going to ring. Not for her, anyway.

She wanted a boyfriend. A family. Somebody who would help her get rid of this fucking headache, and treat her like a person rather than a sideshow. Somebody who wouldn't spout bigoted shit at her. She didn't get that from her father's family, and she certainly didn't get it here.

"Fuck." She dropped her foot to the floor, arching it up so only the ball and toes touched. "I'm fucking fucked."

"Aw, sweetie," somebody said in her ear—a lower voice than Paige's, and a much more welcome one. "What's wrong?"

Somebody was trying to distract Paige by asking her if she was staying up for the lunar eclipse. It wasn't working. Edie wondered if a punch in the kisser would do it.

She looked up to see Mama Janeece leaning over her, spilling out of her corset in the most convincing manner imaginable.

"I gotta get out of here," Edie said. "You know, I'm just gonna walk to the subway now."

She jammed her foot back into the boot. The support eased the cramp temporarily, but she knew there'd be hell to pay all night. *So be it.*

"It's fifteen degrees," Janeece said. "You're going to go out there in high heels and a wig and four inches of fabric?"

"I've got a coat. And a bottle of schnapps back at my place." Edie stood. She smiled to take the sting out of it, then made sure her voice was loud enough for Paige to overhear as she gathered her coat. "Besides, if I have to listen to any more racist bullshit from Miss Thing over there, I'm going to be even colder in a jail cell all night. Somebody ought to tell her that it ain't drag if you look like Annie Lennox."

She sashayed out, letting the door swing shut behind her. Not quite fast enough to cut short the cackles of outraged queens.

Halfway down the corridor, she realized she'd left her cellphone behind. It wasn't worth ruining a good exit for. She would get it tomorrow. Anyway, she didn't have anybody to call.

The coat wasn't long enough to cover her knees and the cold burned through those hot little boots. After ten steps, Edie regretted her decision. But going back now would be a sure way to convert triumph into ignominy, so she soldiered on, sequined spandex stretching around her thighs with each swinging stride as she click-clacked up Jane Street toward 8th Avenue. Sure, it was cold, but she could take it. Sure, her feet hurt—but she could take that, too. She was probably less miserable than the gaunt black hound with his hide tented over his hipbones that she glimpsed slinking aside at the first intersection.

The cold deadened her sense of smell. Manhattan's rich panoply of scents gave way to ice, cold concrete, and leaden midwinter. The good news was it deadened her incipient migraine, too. And in the freezing dark of the longest night of the year, there weren't many people hanging around to hassle her.

Of course, she'd no sooner thought that than the purr of an eight-cylinder engine alerted her—seconds before the car glided up beside her. Somebody rolled down the window, releasing warm air and the scent of greasy bodies. A simpering catcall floated through the icy night. A male voice, pitched singsong. "Hey lady. Hey lady. I like your big legs, lady. You want a ride?"

The car was a beige American land yacht from the 1980s, rusty around the wheel wells. There were four guys in it, and the one in the front passenger seat was the one purring out the window. From the look on his face, his friends had put him up to it, and he was a little horrified by his own daring.

Edie turned, flipped the skirts of her coat out, and planted both hands on her snake-slender hips. She drew herself up to her full six-foot-eight in those stilettos. Something smelled mushroomy; she hoped it wasn't the interior of that car.

"I ain't no lady," she said definitively. "I'm a *queen*."

The car slowed, easing up to the curb. The front and rear passenger doors opened before it had coasted to a stop. Three men climbed out—one must have slid across the rear bucket seat to do so—and then the driver's door opened and the fourth man stood up on the far side of the car.

Edie brazened it out with a laugh, but her hand was in her purse. She didn't have a gun—this was New York City—but she had a pair of brass knuckles and a can of pepper spray. And other advantages, but she'd hate to have to use those. For one thing, she'd ruin her blouse.

The throbbing behind her eyes intensified. She kept her hand in her purse, and was obvious about it. *They* wouldn't know she didn't have a gun. And now that they were standing up beside the car, it was obvious that she had a foot on the tallest of them.

I'm not easy prey, she thought fiercely, and tried to carry herself the way her father would have—all squared shoulders and Make-My-Day. Thinking of him made her angry, which was good: being angry made her feel *big*. The car was still running, albeit in "park." That was a good sign they weren't really committed to a fight, and she could pick out the pong of fear on at least two of them.

She smiled through the blood-red lipstick and said, "What say we part friends, boys?"

They grumbled and shifted. One of them looked at the driver. The driver rolled his eyes and slid back behind the wheel—and that was the signal for the other three to pile back into the car with a great slamming of doors. Predators preferred to deal from a position of strength.

"Fucking faggot," one shouted before leaning forward to crank the window up. Edie didn't quite relax, but her fingers eased their deathgrip on her mace.

Oh, bad boys, she thought. *You never got beat up enough to make you learn to get tough.*

She hadn't had time to come down off the adrenaline high when a shimmering veil of colors wavered across the width of the street, right in front of the beige Buick. The car nosed down as the driver braked hard; that mushroomy smell intensified. The veil of light had depth—beyond it, Edie glimpsed a woodland track, the green shadows of beech leaves, the broken ways of a brilliant sun. She heard a staccato sound, as of drumbeats, echoing down the street. She took an involuntary step forward and then two back as something within the aurora lunged.

A tall pale horse, half-dissolved in light, lurched through the unreal curtain. It stumbled as its hooves struck sparks from the pavement, reins swinging freely from a golden bridle, then gathered itself and leaped. Its hooves beat a steel-drum tattoo on the hood and roof of the Buick. The men within cringed, but though the windshield starred and spiderwebbed, the roof held. It smelled of panicked animal, sweat, and—incongruously—lily of the valley, with overtones of hungry girlchild.

The horse pelted down the street, leaving Edie with a blurred impression of quivering nostrils, ears red as if blood-dipped, and white-rimmed eyes—and of something small and delicate clinging to its back with inhumanly elongated limbs.

The veil still hung there, rippling in the darkness between streetlamp pools. Edie could see the full moon riding high beyond it, and the sight made her migraine come back in waves. She wanted nothing so much as to put her head down to her knees and puke all over the gutter. That sweetly fungal aroma was almost oppressive now, clinging, reminding Edie of stepping in a giant puffball in the Connecticut woods as a boy. The drumming of hooves had faded as the white horse vanished down the street. Now it multiplied, echoing, and over it rang a sound like the mad pealing of a carillon in a hurricane.

Edie dropped her purse and sprinted into the street, so hasty even she tottered on her heels. She yanked open the front passenger door and pulled the abusive one out by his wrist, shouting to the others to get out and run. *Run.*

The thunder of hooves, the clangor of bells, redoubled.

The driver listened, and one of the passengers in the rear—and he had the presence of mind to drag his friend after. The man she was hauling out of the car looked at her wild-eyed and seemed about to struggle. She grabbed the doorframe with one hand and threw him behind her with the other, sending him stumbling to his knees on the sidewalk when he fell over the curb. When she turned to throw herself after him, her heel skittered out from under her. She only saved herself from falling by clutching the car's frame and door.

Edie had half an instant during which to doubt her decision. Then she dropped to the ground and wriggled under the car, aware that she'd never wear these stockings again. She just made it; her coat snagged on the undercarriage a moment before the clatter of dog nails on pavement reached her ears, and she tore it loose with a wince. Then the swarming feet of hounds were everywhere around her, their noses thrust under the car, their voices raised in excited yips. Some were black, a dusty black like weathered coal. Some were white as milk, with red, red ears hung soft along their jowls and pink, sniffing noses. But they sniffed for only a moment before moving on, baying in renewed vigor. Edie was not their prey.

Close behind them came the crescendo of that hoofbeat thunder. Edie cringed from the judder of the car she sheltered beneath as horse after horse struck it, hurtled over, and landed on the far side. The horses also ran to the left and the right, and all their legs, too, were black as coal or white as milk. The car shook brutally under the abuse, a tire hissing flat. The undercarriage pressed her spine. She was realizing that maybe this hadn't been her best idea ever when she heard human voices shouting. Something broke the wave of horses before her, so now they thundered only to the left and the right. The belling of the hounds was not lessened, except in that it receded, and nor was the pounding of hooves—but the stampede flowed around her now, rather than over. It felt like minutes, but Edie was sure only seconds had passed when the sounds faded away, leaving behind the raucous yelps of car alarms and the distant wail of a police siren.

She wriggled against the undercarriage like a worm between stones. The pavement smelled of old oil, vomit, and gasoline, so cold it burned against her cheek. She pressed against it with her elbows, inching forward, kicking with her feet. So much for the hot boots.

Doc Martens appeared at street level, followed by a young olive-skinned woman's inverted face. She was crowned in a crest of black-and-blond streaks and framed by the sagging teeth of a leather jacket's zipper.

"Hi," she said. "I'm Lily Wakeman. You look like you could use a hand."

"Or two," Edie said, extending hers gratefully.

The woman and a slight white guy wearing a sword pulled her from beneath the car. It was pancaked—the roof crushed in, the suspension broken.

Edie shook herself with wonder that she hadn't been smashed underneath. She turned to her rescuers—the punky girl, that slight man, who had medium-dark hair and eyes that looked brown by streetlight, except the right one seemed to catch sparkles inside it in a way that made Edie think it might be glass—and a second man: a butchy little number with his slick blond hair pulled back into a stubby ponytail, who wore a tattered velvet tailcoat straight out of *Labyrinth.*

"Oh, my shoes. Do you know what these *cost*?"

"Matthew Szczgielniak," said the bigger and butcher of the two white guys. She didn't miss his nervous glance in the direction the hunt had run, or the way his weight shifted.

"Edith Moorcock," she said haughtily, smoothing her torn coat.

He stared at her, eyebrows rising. He wasn't bad, actually, if you liked 'em covered in muscles and not too tall. She was waiting for—she didn't know what. Scorn, dismissal.

Instead, the corners of his mouth curved up just a little. "That's rather good."

Edie sniffed. "Thank you."

Then she realized why his face seemed so familiar. "You're that guy. The Mage." He'd been all over the news for a while, after the magic finally burst through in big ways as well as small, enchanting all of New York City. He was supposed to be some sort of liaison between the real world and the *otherwise* one; the one Edie's people came from. The one she couldn't go back to unless she was willing to lie about who she was.

She tried to remember details. There'd been a murder . . . But if this was Matthew Magus, that meant his companions were people Edie should have recognized too. The woman was supposed to be Morgan le Fey's apprentice. And that meant the little guy was . . . oh *shit.*

Edie stole a glance at Matthew's right hand, but he was wearing black leather gloves.

"From the comic book," she said.

Matthew covered half his face with the left hand, then let it drop. "Guilty. And you're my responsibility, aren't you? You're a werewolf."

"Don't be silly," Edie said, swallowing a surge of bitterness. She dismissed the whole thing with a calculated hand-flip. "Werewolf is an all-boys club. Queens need not apply. Besides, since when was the rest of Faerie ready to write us a certificate of admission?"

Lily and the other man—who Edie also recognized, now that she had context—were already jogging away down Jane Street after the vanished Faerie hunt. Matthew turned to follow, and Edie trotted after him in her ruined shoes.

She couldn't let it go. "How did you know I was a werewolf?"

Matthew shrugged. "I've met a few. Never a drag queen before, I admit—" He waved back at the flattened Buick. "That was very brave. Did you stop to think you could have shifted? It's a full moon; it would have been easy."

Edie tossed her wig away, since it was a mess anyway. She wasn't going to tell them that it had been a dozen years since she'd used her wolf-shape. That lupines were pack-beasts, and it hurt too much being alone in that form.

She said, "Turn back into a wolf? Are you kidding? You know we regenerate when we do that? You know how long it takes to wax this shit?"

They were catching up to the others quickly now. "Did you call up that hunt?"

"Just happened to be standing by when it broke through," Edie admitted between breaths. "Lunar eclipse on Solstice night. Is it any wonder if the walls of the world get a little thin?"

"That's why we're on patrol," Matthew said. "Solstice night. Full moon. And a lunar eclipse. Let's catch them before they flatten any pedestrians."

They caught up to the others. The little guy favored them with a sideways glance as they all slacked stride for a moment. "You brought the wolf along."

"The wolf brought herself," Edie said.

Lily chuckled.

"Welcome to the party. I'm Kit," the little guy said.

Edie snorted to cover exactly how impressed she was. Him, she still cringed with embarrassment for not having recognized immediately: Christopher Marlowe, late of London, late of Faerie, late of Hell. "Hel-*lo*, Mister Queer Icon. *I* know who you are. Don't *you*?"

"Oh, he knows," said Matthew, breathing deeply. "He just likes the fussing. Edith, I don't suppose you got a look at what they were after, did you?"

Edie remembered the first white horse, the thing wadded up on its shoulders, face buried in its flowing mane. "A little girl," she said. "On an elven charger. She looked terrified."

"Shit!" Matthew broke into a jouncing, limping run. The other three fell in behind him.

The cramp in her foot was back, and now her toes were jammed up against the toes of her boots with every stride. She started to run with a hitching limp of her own, accompanied by a breathy litany of curses.

Here, there were no destroyed vehicles or shattered pavement. It was as still and dark as Manhattan ever gets—the streets quiet and cold, if not quite deserted. The scent pulled her down Washington to West 10th Street, and then she tottered to a stop beneath a denuded tree.

"My feet," she said, leaning on a wall.

"Let me see," said Matthew. He crouched awkwardly, one leg thrust off at an angle like an outrigger, and put his hands on her ankle. She could feel through the soft leather that one of them was misshapen, and did not grip.

"Hey," Edie said. "No peeking up my skirt." She gave him the foot as if she were a horse and he the farrier. When she felt him pressing his hands together over her anklebone, she glanced back over her shoulder. "You can't see anything with the boot on."

"Hush," he said. "I'm talking to your shoes."

When he put the foot down, it did feel easier. The incipient blood blisters on her soles hadn't healed, but something was easing the cramp in her instep, and the toes felt like they fit better. Matthew touched the other ankle, and Edie lifted the foot for him.

A moment later, and she was offering him a hand up. As he pushed himself to his feet she saw him grope his own knee, revealing the outline of metal and padding through the leg of his cargo pants.

She blurted, "You're kicking ass in a knee brace? Hardcore."

"If the team needs you, you play through the injury," he said. "Ow!"

That last because Lily had thumped him with the back of her hand.

"I need a new knee," Matthew said apologetically, as they limped along a street lined with parked cars and brick-faced buildings. "I'm trying to put it off as long as possible. The replacements are only good for fifteen years or so."

"Ouch," Edie said, even as he picked up the pace. "Ever consider a less physical line of work?"

"Every day," he said.

It wasn't too hard to follow the hunters—the flattened cars and glowing hoofprints pounded in pavement were a clear trail, and there was always the wail of car alarms and police sirens to orient by. The sounding of the hounds carried in the cold night as perfectly as the distant ring of a ship's bell over water. The air still reeked with the scents of hunters and hunted. Before long, Edie was running at the front of the pack, directing the others.

Matthew limped up beside her, the chains and baubles hung from his coat jangling merrily. Despite the awkwardness of his stride, his breath still wreathed him in easy clouds.

He reached out one hand and tugged her sleeve, slowing her. "Can we get ahead of them? Being where they've been isn't helping us at all."

"It's been a long time since I hunted, sugar, and the rest of the pack never thought me much of a wolf." Edie skimmed her hands down her sides and hips as explanation.

Drawing up beside them, Kit said, "You should talk to the Sire of the Pack. Things have changed in Faerie—"

"How much can they have possibly changed? The Pack doesn't want me, and I don't want them." Edie made a gesture with her left hand that was meant to cut off discussion.

A prowl car swept past, its spotlight briefly illuminating their faces, but they must not have looked like trouble—at least by Village standards—because the car rolled by without hesitation. Distant sirens still shattered the night, a sort of a directional beacon if you could pick the original out of the echoes.

Edie saw Matthew's crippled hand move in the air as if he were conducting music—or, more, actually, as if he were plucking falling strands of out of the air. He frowned with concentration. *Magi*, she thought tiredly.

Just out of range of a kicked-over hydrant spouting water that splashed and rimed on the street, Edie paused to consult her mental map of the Village's tangle of streets. The middle and northern parts of Manhattan were a regular grid, but this was the old part of the city, where the roads crossed each other like jackstraws.

Edie raised her head and sniffed to the four directions. "Let's double back and head south on Washington. I think they've headed that way."

"I'm pushing them that way." Matthew fell in behind her, and Kit and Lily followed. Edie's palms were wet inside her gloves: nervousness. The nose didn't lie, but it could be tricked—and it had been a long time since Edie ran with a pack.

Off to the left, Kit cried "Hark!" and slowed his pace to a walk. Edie cupped her hands to her ears. The scent was strong again, and growing stronger. At the end of the block, Hudson was still moderately busy with cars, and the noise could have confounded her. But there was the trembling of hooves through the street—

The first horse and rider burst into sight around the oblique corner of West 10th and Hudson. Sparks flew from beneath the hooves. Matthew's hand moved again, and down the street, a pedestrian, distracted by her phone, chose that minute to jaywalk. A panel van swerved to avoid her, cutting off the horse and rider. Edie found herself slowing as the animal raced toward her, running against traffic. She could smell its sweat, its exhaustion and terror.

From behind it, she heard the baying of the hounds.

"Stand aside," Kit said, and took Edie by the wrist to pull her onto the sidewalk, amid the shelter of trees and light poles. Matthew stood firmly in the middle of the street, his back to traffic, his velvet coat catching winey highlights off the streetlamps. Edie pulled against Kit's grip; Lily was suddenly there beside her, restraining her as well.

"He's the Archmage," Kit said. "If he doesn't know what he's doing, it's his own fool fault."

The Faerie steed bore down on him, and Matthew drew himself up tall. At the corner of a red brick building whose ground floor façade was comprised of grilled Roman arches, the horse reached him. She was going to run him down, Edie saw. She reached out a futile hand—

The horse gathered itself to leap, and as it did, Matthew threw out his arms. "Hold!" he cried, in a voice that shook the windows and rattled the fire escapes against the brick faces of the buildings. "In the names of the City that Never Sleeps—New York, New Orange, New Amsterdam, Gotham, the Big Apple, and the Island of Manhattan—I bid you stand fast!"

Edie would have expected flares of light, shivers of energy running across the pavement—something from a movie or a comic book. But it wasn't there: all she saw was the man in the tatterdemalion dark red coat, his hands upraised.

And the lather-dripping mare planting her heels and stopping short before him. Her head hung low, her throat and barrel swelling with each great heaving gasp of air. She swayed, and for a moment, Edie thought she would collapse.

The girl on her back, all snarled pale hair and twig-limbs, raised her head painfully from where it had rested, face pressed into the mare's mane. Edie gasped.

Here was no elf-child, moving as stiffly as an old woman: just a human girl of eleven years, or twelve.

The hounds rounded the corner in full cry, surging like a sea around the knees of the running horses. Matthew sprinted forward, arms still outstretched, and put himself between the hunt and the girl. Edie shook off Kit's hand and ran to stand beside him, aware that Kit and Lily were only a step or two back—and that only because Edie's legs were longer. When she drew up, Matthew snaked out a hand and clasped hers, and then she was grabbing Lily's hand on the other side while Lily linked arms with Kit. They stood so, four abreast, and Matthew again raised his voice and shouted, "Hold!"

Edie felt the power through her fingertips, this time, like a static charge. She imagined a barrier sweeping across West 10th from building to building, towering high overhead. She imagined it thick and strong, and hoped somehow she was helping.

Whether she had any effect on it or not, the hounds quit running. They circled back into the pack, their belling turned to whining, a churn of black bodies and white ones dotted with red. The horses drew up among them, harness-bells shivering and hooves a-clatter. At the forefront, on a tall gelding, sat an elf-lord who smelled of primroses and prickles. He had cropped hair as red as his white horse's ears, shot through with streaks of black where a mortal man would show graying. He wore a blousy silken shirt, heavily embroidered, and a pair of skinny black jeans stuffed into cowboy boots.

"Matthew Magus," he said, casting a green-gray eye that seemed to gather light across Edie, Kit, and Lily. His harness did not creak as he shifted his weight, but the bells tinkled faintly—rain against a glass wind-chime. "And companions."

"I do not know you," Matthew said. "How are you styled?"

"I am a lord of the Unseelie Court, and I would not extend my calling to one so ill-met."

Matthew sighed. "Must we be ill-met?"

"Aye," said the anonymous lord, "if you would keep a thief from me."

Now police cars were filling the intersection, and both ends of the block. Edie looked nervously one way and another, waiting for men and women with guns to start piling out of the vehicles and charging forward, but for now they seemed content to wait.

New York's Finest knew better than to get between a magician and an elf-lord.

"A thief?" Matthew asked, with an elaborate glance over his shoulder. Edie could still hear the heaving breaths of the horse, smell the sweat and fear of the girl. "I see someone who has sought sanctuary in my city. And as you owe fealty to King Ian, you are bound by my treaty with him. What is she accused of stealing . . . Sir Knight?"

"What's there before your eyes," the Faerie answered, as his companions of the hunt—men and women both—ranged themselves around him. "That common brat has stolen the great mare Embarr from my stables, and I will have her back. And the thief punished."

The mare snorted behind them, her harness jangling fiercely as she shook out her mane. "He lies!"

At first, Edie thought the child had spoken, and admired her spunk. But when she turned, she realized that the high, clear voice had come from the horse, who pricked her ears and continued speaking. "If anything, t'was I stole the child Alicia. And my reasons I had, mortal Magus."

"The mare," said the elf-lord, "is mine."

Matthew did not lower his hands. "Be that as it may," he said. "I cannot have you tearing my city apart—and it is *my city*, and in it I decree that no one can own another. The girl and the horse are under my protection, and if you wish to have King Ian seek their extradition, he is welcome to do so through official channels. Which do *not*—" Matthew waved his hands wide "—include a hunt through Greenwich Village."

The Faerie Lord sniffed. "I have come here, where iron abounds, and where your mortal poisons burn inside my breast with every breath, to reclaim what is rightfully mine. By what authority do you deny me?"

He stood up in his stirrups. His gelding took a prancing, curveting step or two, crowding the horses and hounds on his right. They danced out of the way, but not before Edie had time to wrinkle her nose in the human answer to a snarl. "This is going to come to a fight," she whispered, too low for anyone but Lily and Matthew to hear. The whisk of metal on leather told her that Kit had drawn his sword.

"Why doesn't the girl speak for herself?" Matthew asked.

"Because," the mare answered, "His Grace had her caned and stole her voice from her when one of his mares miscarried. But it wasn't the girl's fault. And I'll not see my stablehands mistreated."

Lily squeezed Edie's hand and leaned close to whisper. "Edith? Shift to wolf form."

Edie shook her head. "I told you, it's been—"

"Do it," she said, and gave her a little push forward from the elbow.

Edie toed out of her boots and stood in stocking-feet on the icy pavement. She ripped her blouse off over her head and kicked down the stockings and the sequined skirt.

Everyone was staring, most especially the Faerie lord. Lily, though, stepped forward to help Edie with her corselet and gaff. She handled the confining underclothes with the professionalism of a seasoned performer, folding them over her arm before stepping back. Edie stood there for a moment, naked skin prickling out everywhere, and raised her eyes to the Faerie lord.

"Well, I'll be a codfish," he said callously. He looked not at Edie, but at Matthew. "The bitch has a prick. Is that meant to upset me?"

"The bitch has teeth, too," Edie said, and let the transformation take her.

She'd thought it would be hard. So many years, so many years of enduring the pain, of resisting, of petulant self-denial. Of telling herself that if she wasn't good enough for the Pack to see her as a wolf, then she didn't want to be one.

Once she managed to release her death-grip on the self-denial, though, her human form just fell away, sheeting from the purity of the wolf like filth from ice. Edie's hands dropped toward the pavement and were hard, furred paws before they touched. Her muzzle lengthened; what had been freezing cold became cool comfort as the warmth of her pelt enfolded her. The migraine fell away as if somebody had removed a clamp from her temples, and the rich smells of the city—and the horse manure and dog piss of the hunt—flooded her sinuses.

She snarled, stalking forward, and saw the Faerie hounds whine and mill and cringe back among the legs of the horses. She knew the light rippled in her coat, red as rust and tipped smoke-black, and she knew the light glared in her yellow eyes. She knew from the look the Faerie lord shot her—fear masked with scorn—that the threat was working.

"So you have a wolf," the Faerie lord said, though his horse lowered his head to protect his neck and backed several steps.

"And your high king is a wolf," Matthew said. "You know how the pack sticks together."

This time, the gelding backed and circled because the Faerie lord reined him around. When he faced Edie and the others again, he was ten feet further back, and his pack had fallen back with him.

"I don't understand why the horse didn't kill you," he called to the girl, over Matthew's head. "They don't let slaves ride."

He yanked his horse's mouth so Edie could smell the blood that sprang up, wheeling away.

"Oh," said the mare, "is *that* why you never dared get up on me?"

As the lord rode off, spine stiff, the rest of the hunt fell in behind him. Edie was warm and at ease, and with the slow ebb of adrenaline, swept up in a rush of fellow-feeling for those with whom she had just withstood a threat.

A veil opened in the night as before, shimmering across the pavement before the phalanx of squad cars. Edie and her new allies stood waiting warily until the Faerie lord and his entourage vanished back behind it. The mare eyed Matthew quite cunningly. *She planned this*, the wolf thought. But the mare said nothing, and Edie would have had to come back to human form to say it—and what good would it do at this point, anyway?

"Well, I guess that's that," Matthew said, when they were gone.

He made a hand-dusting gesture and turned away, leaving Kit to handle the girl and the mare who had stolen each other while he walked, whistling, up the road to speak with the assembled police. Edie went and sat beside Lily, tail thumping the road. Lily reached down and scruffled her ruff and ears with gloved fingers.

"Good wolf," she cooed. "Good girl."

In New York City's storied Greenwich Village, on the Island of Manhattan, there is a tavern called the Slaughtered Lamb. A wolf howls on its signboard. In one corner lurks a framed photo of Lon Chaney as the Wolf Man. The tavern is cramped and dark and the mailbox-sized bathroom—beside the grilled-off stair with a sign proclaiming the route to The Dungeon closed for daily tortures—is not particularly clean.

The Slaughtered Lamb (of course) is the favored hangout of Lower Manhattan's more ironic werewolves. Edie hadn't been there even once since she came to New York City. She'd been an outcast even then.

Now she strode west on 4th Street from Washington Square, her high-heeled boots clicking on the preternaturally level sidewalks of Manhattan. Her feet still hurt across the pads, but the worst was healed. She wore trousers to hide her unshaven legs. A cold wind curled the edges of damp leaves, not strong enough to lift them from the pavement.

Fourth was wider and less tree-shaded than most of the streets in the famously labyrinthine Village, but still quiet—by Manhattan standards—as she made her way past the sex shops, crossing Jones in a hurry. An FDL Express truck waited impatiently behind the stop sign, rolling gently forward as if stretching an invisible barrier when the driver feathered the clutch.

She hopped lightly up one of the better curb cuts in the Village and crossed the sidewalk to the Slaughtered Lamb's black-and-white faux-Tudor exterior. Horns blared as she let herself inside. A reflexive glance at her watch showed 4:59.

Rush hour.

"And so it begins," she muttered to no one in particular, and let the heavy brown nine-panel door fall between her and the noise.

There was noise inside, too, but it was of a more welcoming quality. Speakers mounted over the door blared Chumbawamba; two silent televisions shimmered with the sports highlights of the day. A gas fire roared in the unscreened hearth behind the only open table. Edie picked her way through the darkness to claim it quickly, sighing in relief. It might roast her on one side, but at least it would be a place to sit.

She slung her damp leather coat over the high back of a bar stool and jumped up. She was barely settled, a cider before her, when the door opened again, revealing Matthew Magus and a tall, slender young man with pale skin and black hair that touched his collar in easy curls.

They sat down across from Edie. She shifted a little further away from the fire. "Edith Moorcock," Matthew said, "His Majesty Ian MacNeill, Sire of the Pack and High King of Faerie."

"Charmed," Edie said, offering the king a glove. To her surprise, he took it.

"Edie is a New World wolf," Matthew said. "Apparently, your grandfather did not find her . . . acceptable . . . to the Pack."

"Oh, yes," Ian said tiredly. "It's about time the Pack got itself out of the twelfth century." He steepled his fingers as the server came over, and both he and Matthew ordered what Edie had. "I can't imagine what you would want with us at this point, though—"

Edie's heart fluttered with nervousness. "An end to exile?"

"Consider it done. Do you plan to remain in New York?"

Edie nodded.

"Good. The Mage here needs somebody to look after him. Somebody with some teeth." Ian paused as his cider arrived, then sipped it thoughtfully. Matthew coughed into the cupped palm of his glove. "The better to eat you with, my dear," he muttered.

The king regarded him, eyebrows rising as he tilted his head. "I beg your pardon?"

"Nothing, your Majesty."

Ian smiled, showing teeth. If Edie's were anything to go by, he had very good ears. He drank another swallow of cider, wiped his mouth on the back of his hand, and said, "Now, about that changeling girl and the horse that stole her—"

Elizabeth Bear was born on the same day as Frodo and Bilbo Baggins, but in a different year. When coupled with a childhood tendency to read the dictionary for fun, this led her inevitably to penury, intransigence, and the writing of speculative fiction. She is the Hugo, Sturgeon, Locus, and Campbell Award winning author of twenty-five novels (The most recent is *Steles of the Sky*, from Tor) and almost a hundred short stories. Her dog lives in Massachusetts; her partner, writer Scott Lynch, lives in Wisconsin. She spends a lot of time on planes.

The City: *An American city, perhaps one fairly near Philadelphia.*

The Magic: *At night, nothing is quite the same as it is during the day in Mari June's neighborhood. But even she doesn't know just how "different" Miz Willow and her dogs are.*

THE WOMAN WHO WALKED WITH DOGS

Mary Rosenblum

"You be in this house by dark."

Mama's words were always the same, a parting benediction as she left for her job at the nursing home. "I don't work for no daughter of mine to be out on the street at night. I'll call you."

The street at night . . . "Yes, Mama," Mari June would say. "I got homework to do." Sometimes she wondered if Mama really knew.

"Good girl, you do that." And then Mama would close the door firmly, with a bang of decision, as if by that single definite slam she could seal the door airtight against the dark seductive dangers of nighttime on the streets of their crummy city neighborhood.

Nah, Mari June thought. Mama didn't know. Mostly, she was afraid of boys.

Don't you have any boys in this house while I'm out workin' my fingers to the bone for you, she'd say. *I find out you actin' slutty, you hav'n boys droppin' in like you're trash, and you'll be out on the street so fast your ears'll flap.*

She didn't know about the street.

Silly, too, because Mari June didn't like boys. They stared at her in school, but their stares stopped short at her skin, sliding over her like sticky fingers. They looked at her breasts—those strange and uncontrollable twin magics that swelled and itched and sometimes seemed like alien flesh, changing the sleek way she slid through the grimy city air, making her clumsy. Sometimes her nipples hurt and when they did, a strange creature moved deep in her belly. It was dark and furry and lived between her hips and when it moved, it made her breathless, her skin cold and hot at the same time.

Mari June let Mama's slam keep the door tight shut against boys and did her homework because she had a 4.0 this year again, so far, and she was going to keep it. But Mama didn't have a cell, which meant she had to wait for her breaks to call home on the pay phone in the lobby. Because of Miz Bellamy, the Supervisor from Hell, Mama called her. And her breaks came at six and eleven p.m. So there was plenty of time to do her homework and answer Mama's six PM call. If she was careful, she could still get out and back in by eleven. Mari June locked the front door and took her English book and algebra to the dining room table to finish the stupid story problems (a snap, she had done them all in sixth grade) and work on her report on *Romeo and Juliet.*

It's not really about them falling in love and dying, like most people think, she wrote in her long narrow handwriting. *It's about families and how stupid they are, how they only see what they want to see, instead of what's really in front of them.* Then she stopped and chewed on the end of her number two pencil, thinking about that. Might not be a good thing to turn in.

She'd already gotten in trouble with Mrs. Roberts when she had written about Columbus landing for Columbus Day. Mrs. Roberts didn't like her title—"There Goes the Neighborhood"—to start with. "We're celebrating our history," she had scolded Mari June in front of the class, handing back the pages marked with a big, red C-. "We're proud of our country and our heritage in this class." For her next assignment . . . Thanksgiving . . . Mari June had written two pages of drivel copied straight from the newspaper about Family Turkey Values. For that, she got an A. Obviously Mrs. Roberts didn't read the paper.

Mari June erased those first sentences about Romeo and Juliet and changed the title to Young Love. *Romeo and Juliet is a classic tale of tragic and unrequited love,* she wrote. The "unrequited" alone should get her an A, she figured. Mari June bent over her notebook, looping her p's and f's carefully, because she only planned on writing this crap once, thank you. Timed it perfectly. The phone rang just as she finished the last syrupy sentence with a flourish, poked that final period into place.

"Hi, Mama." She picked up the phone, gathering the pages with the other hand. "Still working on it. Won't finish before bedtime, no that's fine, I'll still be up when you call." Mama would still call anyway, even if she said she'd be asleep. "Too bad Lori called in sick. Maybe you could make Dragon Lady empty a few for a change? Sorry, Mom." Mari June rolled her eyes. "I didn't mean to be rude about Ms. Bellamy . . . I was kidding. Yeah. 'Night, Mom." And she hung up thinking that if she had to work for Ms. Bellamy, Dragon Lady, she'd starve first. And Dragon Lady wasn't what she'd call her, either.

She put her books in her back pack for the morning, mussed up her bed and left the toothbrush, wet, beside the soap dish in the bathroom and dampened the towel, just in case she had to race Mom into the house. (Had happened). Mom noticed those kinds of details.

Safeguards in place, she went out.

The moon floated overhead in the darkening sky, almost full, a pale, lopsided sphere like an orange fallen out of Mr. Schwartz's wire shopping cart when he bumped it up and over the curb. School had started four weeks ago. New friendships had been forged, boundaries freshly drawn between the gangs, teachers tried and tested. Everyone knew what was what. Summer was a nostalgic memory, routines as familiar now as the cicadas' end-of-summery monotony.

But tonight a hint of fall edged the air, a tiny tweak of chill, a promise of red leaves, pumpkins, Halloween, a gorge of candy, never mind Mama's threats every year to drag her off to the Halloween Party at Saint Sebastian's where you had to wear costumes of the Virgin Mary or Cinderella (who should have sold the stupid carriage for a good price and caught a plane to one of those white sandy islands you saw in the magazines), and only got lame treats like stale oatmeal cookies with bright orange icing and plastic-wrapped popcorn balls that stuck to your teeth and pulled out fillings.

Halloween, that chill breath promised. *The real thing, with good candy, and scary things in the dark that want to suck your breath. Then Christmas, then Easter eggs, and pretty soon it will be summer again.* The night-air tickled her and she giggled, pausing on the sidewalk in the streetlight's yellow pool to check the watch Mama gave her for First Communion. Six twenty. Plenty of time. She stepped off the white sidewalk, out of the nice safe pool of streetlight yellow and into . . . the night.

By day the street was safe, boring, a sunny reality defined and bounded by the iron rules of the known—stop signs, neatly painted siding, mowed lawns, and the mail man. *A good neighborhood*, Mama always said when she whined about the bills. *It's worth whatever it costs so you can grow up in a good neighborhood.* And she would level a hard, accusing stare at Mari June. *Even if I have to go without new clothes or those cute shoes I saw at Kaufmann's, it's worth it to give you a good place to grow up. You listenin', girl?*

Yes, ma'am. Why adults seemed to equate *good* with *boring*, Mari June had never been able to figure out.

But by night . . .

By night, Elm Street was another world, with different rules.

By night, Mr. Kingston, who yelled at you if you stepped off the sidewalk onto his perfect lawn, wore a red ball gown and a blond wig and sometimes spit champagne at his image in the full length mirrors that lined one wall of his downstairs rec room. Mrs. Silvano, who swept her sidewalk every day and always asked you if you had said your rosary sang to her dead husband at her big black piano that took up her living room. He sat right next to her on the piano bench with his hand on her butt. In between numbers she told him about her day, laughing, answering him, and tossing her head, really young and sexy, not all shriveled up and old.

Ms. Johnson, who was really a vampire, waited for the young men who arrived every night, parking their cars around the corner on Maple Street, across from the empty lot where the boys rode their bikes. She would greet them at the door all dressed in black and usher them inside, pausing to peer past the screen door, eyes searching the night street like laser beams before closing the door. Once or twice, up early with the sun, Mari June had seen them stumble out again, white as the grubs you find under the bark on dead trees, or maybe something that lives in a cave. Then there was Miz Willows who walked her invisible dogs, chirping at them, babytalking to them, commanding them to get off that lawn right now, don't you pee on that nice lily plant you big lunks. Her yard was all beaten dust and scraggly old rhododendrons with burnt up drooping leaves and straggling weeds that struggled and sometimes bloomed along the rusty chain link fence that bordered the sidewalk. Muddy brown rawhide bones and old sun-bleached rubber toys lay here and there. No dogs. Some of the boys threw stones into her yard and pretended to hit the nonexistent dogs. Then Miz Willows would come out the front door, yelling and waving a broom, threatening to call the cops, threatening to let her dogs loose to chew on their butts, her gray hair standing up all over her head, her Hawaii-print dress as faded as the rubber toys in the dusty yard and about ten sizes too large. The boys would run away laughing and she would babytalk to the dogs, hushing their inaudible barking, telling them it was okay, not to kill the boys 'cause they were just babies, before retreating to the house again.

Mari June liked Miz Willows. Mom wouldn't let her have a dog and so she pretended—something she wouldn't admit to if they tore her tongue out, like Sister Martha described when she read to them in Sunday School from the really cool, gross book about all the things people did to the saints. She'd created Shep when she was little, scared of the dark, and Mom wouldn't let her have a nightlight because everybody knew that they were a fire danger. Shep was a big German shepherd that slept on the foot of her bed and would tear out the throat of anybody who tried to hurt her. So she felt a certain kinship with Miz Willows, even though her hair was pretty awful. But she was old anyway, so it didn't matter.

And besides, Miz Willows was the only one on the street who was the same in the daytime as she was at night. Mari June slipped across the street in the narrow crevice of shadow between the streetlights in the middle of the block. If Mrs. Silvano or Ms. Johnson saw her, they'd tell Mama, and then she'd send Mari June to stay nights with Aunt Susanna over in Lents who had ten kids and lived in a house with three bedrooms. So she slipped across the narrow crack of shadow like a ghost and onto the sidewalk in front of Mr. Kingston's house. Sure enough, there he was, down in his rec room, back arched, head tilted like the old pictures of Marilyn Monroe in the history books, right down to the blond wig and the black spot (that was supposed to be pretty but just looked just like a black spot to Mari June) by his mouth. His breasts were about the same size as the movie star's, too, which really made her curious. She hoped to run into him on the sidewalk one day . . . literally . . . see if they were padding or if they might be real.

He had a thick green champagne bottle as usual, and he tossed his head back, tilted the bottle to his lips, then faced the mirror. Liquid sprayed out, spattering the glass, running down in long streaks. Fascinated, Mari June crouched by the blooming rose of Sharon, peering raptly between the branches. Maybe he filled the bottles with ginger ale, she thought. Mom said champagne cost a lot. But he sold cars. Mrs. Silvano had said something about that once, how that was why he always drove a shiny new car, that's why he parked it in the back yard, inside the tall board fence with the big padlock on the gate. Because it didn't really belong to him. He was just putting on airs, she had said and sniffed.

She watched him for a little while, but that hint of fall breathed on the back of her neck and filled her with a winey, cidery tingle of excitement. Mr. Kingston with his jowly, Marilyn Monroe face and stained dress was . . . old. Mari June drifted across the limp fall grass, letting the beams from the squashed-orange moon push her along, restless as the first fall leaves skittering along the sidewalk. Mrs. Silvano's high, shrill soprano seeped through her cracked-open windows. *Beautiful dreamer, dream of my heeaartt . . .* Ms. Johnson leaned against the front door of her house, watching for her next victim, her eyes reflecting the red glow of her cigarette.

All old tonight. All boring. Mari June crossed the street, cut through the vacant lot with the bags of garbage and lawn clippings burst and spilling on the rough clay like cut open stomachs she thought, like scenes from the book on the saints Sister Martha read. The yard on the far side didn't have a fence and Mari June crossed it, navigating around flowerbeds, the grass a weird washed out gray in the squashed-orange moonlight. Across the street, barricaded by a fence of nose-to-tail beater cars loomed . . . The Park.

Mari June always thought of it in capitals, the way her mother spoke of it. *Don't you set a foot in The Park, girl. You-know-who hangs out there! You know what They'll do to you!* And when Mari June had once said that no, she didn't know, and asked for clarification, Mama had delivered a stinging slap and a sharp admonition to *watch your mouth, girl, don't you get smart with me.* Adult speak for "I don't know."

But she paused at the sidewalk, eyeing the dark bulk of the cars, an occasional bit of chrome reflecting the moonlight like animal eyes. Waiting. She imagined them snapping their hoods like cartoon alligator jaws as she squeezed between them, lunging at her with sharp chrome teeth and glaring headlight eyes. Enough time? She checked her watch and hesitated.

The moon laughed at her and fall tweaked her hair, teasing her, daring her.

Mari June lifted her chin and marched across the empty street, I'm not scared of you, you're just empty metal like old oil drums and that's all. She stared at the wide dark snouts of the cars, teeth hidden behind painted bumper lips. They stared back at her, eyes dull and smug. *We choose to let you pass*, they whispered in the hiss and skitter of the dry leaves on the blank black asphalt. *This time we choose to let you passss.*

She walked between them, head still high, the skin on her thighs quivering, hairs erect, wary of movement, aware of the soft scrape of jeans against metal, faint heat leaking from the car-snout like dragon breath.

They let her pass and she didn't run as she stepped up onto the curb, didn't change the rhythm of her walk one beat as she stepped into the grass on the far side, hairs prickling on the backs of her legs, tiny antennae trained on the sleeping cars . . .

Maybe next time . . . they whispered behind her.

The air changed as she stepped off the sidewalk, as if she had passed through an invisible door. The chill in the air intensified, breathing down her neck, making her nipples hurt. She crossed her arms on her chest, squeezing those swollen not-quite-part-of-her breasts against her rib cage until they ached. Leaves swirled around her feet like puppies and she hesitated, back to the streetlight glow, facing darkness beneath the trees. A deeper darkness than the darkness in her back yard, it pooled like a brooding creature between the trees.

Ordinary maples by day, in the dark their branches stretched out, gathering the darkness to them, whispering together beneath that squashed moon.

For just a moment, Mari June hesitated. Behind her, the cars tittered. Then she put her arms down at her sides and walked resolutely into the pooled darkness. It swallowed her and then parted like a curtain. Ahead she saw the swing set and jungle gym, bright with graffiti like Christmas lights in glowing red, green, blue, empty and strange in the moonlight, like the ruins of a civilization that had flourished and died right here in the city and nobody ever noticed. Beyond it lurked the benches, not the benches that old men sat on by day, drowsing and staring at the squirrels, or hard tired-eyed women yelling at kids on the swing set not to pull Jamie's hair, or stop throwing sand. Nobody had ever sat on *these* benches and Mari June edged around them, sheltered by the thick darkness, not willing to step into the empty space beneath the moon's stare. A bird called, a hollow questioning sound and the trees answered, whispering their answer in a rustle of leaves.

Time to go home, she told herself. Got to be there for sure when Mama called, let the empty-oil-drum-cars giggle and laugh! But as she turned, she heard them. Loud voices hard and bruising, not-caring. The darkness thickened and retreated, leaving behind the kind of darkness you saw at the edges of the streetlights, tame darkness, submissive. *Yah, you wish, dude. Boobie's asking a dime, the slut. And then she did me and . . .*

Mari June shrank back into the darkness of the night maples, wanting to pull it around her, hide in it. But instead, she felt the darkness pulled from around her the way someone might pull the blanket off you in the middle of the night, leaving you cold and naked. Visible. They drifted into the orange-moonlight, tall and gray, dodging, pushing each other, laughing. One of them leaped to catch the top arch of the jungle gym, swinging out, feet arcing down to a perfect landing, spinning to punch another's shoulder.

She wanted to run, but her body had frozen, stiff as one of the mannequins in the Nordstrom's windows downtown, shoulders, ribs, hips, legs all hard plastic, her shirt hanging on its hard ridges and curves, jeans slack around her plastic legs. Not thinking. Frozen.

They danced closer, walking weird, legs almost stiff, every pelvis thrust out, going first. Leading. She tried to swallow but her throat was dry and they heard it . . . the rasping of it. All looked.

"Hey." Tallest one moved forward, bending a little at the knees now, his eyes on her like the headlight glare of the tittering cars. "What have we here?" The others were moving now, spreading out, making a fence between her and the cars, street, home. The playground wall crowded her back. Strange yards beyond it with fences to stop her, clotheslines to catch her.

"It's a chick."

"Whatcha doin' out here, little girl?"

"I got what you need, honey."

They moved closer, lithe, sinuous shadows, their faces blurred by orange moonlight, hair black as night, clothes baggy, gang uniform. She'd know them, if it was morning. If they were lounging here, laughing and spitting, hassling the younger boys, hitting them up for their lunch money, their iPods—yeah she'd know them. Put a name to them, a street, a family. Littl Big, his dad's in jail for dealing crack, mom's a hooker, that's Brushy, been kicked out twice, this time's his last chance, Spell Boy, he was maybe the one who let the oil out of Principal's car, wrecked the engine . . .

Not tonight. Tonight they had no names.

They were staring at her. Like the boys at school.

Only . . . hungry. Like the kids who got free lunch at school. Staring at the gray meat loaf and drooling.

She backed up one step, two. They moved with her, faces sharp and feral in the orangey moon glow. Their eyes gleamed like cats in the dark, and the thing in her belly moved, like a cat waking up, full of hunger. She hated them for waking it.

Hated it for waking for them.

Hard cold bumped her back. The wall, the brick wall layered with graffiti and white paint like some kind of urban lasagna. The thing in her belly writhed, and heat and cold buzzed in her ears.

"Hey, baby," one of them said. "Don't be scared, baby."

The others laughed, the sounds sawing at her brain. They moved closer, faces identical, shark-grinning, feral eyes speaking to the thing in her belly, calling it by name.

"Now don't you go peein' on those bushes, you hear? You mind your manners, you dogs." The voice cut through the orange moon glow and they all looked, faces turning in perfect unison.

Miz Willows stepped out from nowhere, wearing the darkness like a hem of black cats, prowling feral around her feet as she stepped into the orange moonlight, walking straight up to Mari June as if *they* weren't there at all, as if it was just the two of them in the park. *They* didn't really move aside for her. But somehow she walked through them. "You're out late, Mari June." She smiled, her face as clear as if it was noon, like a private spotlight shone down to illuminate it. "You go out late, don't you leave Shep home. You bring him with you."

"Hey, old woman. Get the hell out of here."

"Not your bizness, bitch."

The tallest one reached for her, grabbed for her arm, like you'd reach for a left-behind newspaper on the daytime benches, toss it on the ground before you sat down. Mari June cringed.

Miz Willows turned around, a look of mild surprise on her face. She didn't say anything, but the hem of darkness like black, feral cats, grew, rising up like ebony fog, taking shape—legs and wide chests, thick necks, blunt, wide muzzles. White teeth gleamed and the growl seemed to come from the ground, the trees, the thick, feral darkness itself. A cloud slid across the squashed moon like someone covering their eyes with both hands.

"Hey." Tallest one stepped back. "What the hell . . . "

Black as the dark, they edged forward, heads low, white gleam of teeth like exposed bone. Mari June tried to count them, but when she looked straight at them, she saw nothing but darkness and the shape of benches, trees, the colorless poles of the play structure. *They* took a step back, but not all together, not in unison, not any more. "Bitch," the tallest one hissed, but behind him, one of them broke. Ran.

The dark surged forward, razored with teeth, and the night growled.

They all ran, not yelling, silent as the torrent of shadow surging at their heels, toward the street, toward the cars, toward the safety of the yellow street-lamp glow beyond.

A metallic banging like car hoods and trunks slamming echoed through the night. A car alarm went off, shrill shrieking and beeping, splitting the night like an axe blade.

It stopped.

The cloud slid timidly way and the squashed orange moon peeked out. Miz Willow smiled at Mari June, her hair tufted, dry and ugly, her eyes bright, brighter than the orange moon's feeble glow. The breeze frisked around her and Mari June rubbed her arms, goosebumps speckling her skin. The shadows were slinking back, sliding silently across the moon-washed grass, glints of white light like splinters of razor blades here and there. Grinning. Licking shadow chops.

"You shouldn't be out here without Shep." Miz Willow wagged a finger at her. "Don't you go leavin' him home. Bad things out here in the night. You need your dog."

"Yes, Miz Willow." Mari June could only whisper.

"That's better. You promise?"

"Yes, Miz Willow." And Mari June squeaked as something cold poked her hand. She looked down. Shadow streaked the ground, but right there, by her left knee, it kind of lifted, almost like a low bank of black fog with the shape of a dog. A big dog, maybe a German shepherd. The cold poked her again, moist, like a dog's nose. "Shep?" She whispered it, felt Miz Willow's eyes on her, felt the night tapping an inky toe, waiting. "Good boy." She swallowed, what the hell, said it out *loud*. "Good boy, Shep, good boy for coming. I won't leave you home again. I promise."

When she looked up again, Miz Willows was clear across the park, striding along like a man, like she always did, the shadows swirling around her legs. And if she looked at them sideways, didn't really *look*, you know, she could almost, almost see rottweilers and furry malamutes, boxers, German shepherds, and even a border collie or two. They melted into line of scrawny elms at the far edge of the park and . . . vanished.

"Good boy, Shep." She almost-looked at him, admired the upright ears, the fine head. "You're really handsome, you know? Let's go home. Quick before Mama gets there."

She walked straight back, right between the cars that looked at the asphalt with their bright, headlight eyes. *You can pass*, the night breeze whispered in their grilles. *You can pass with him.* And she wasn't afraid.

They just made it.

She stripped off her clothes as Mama's key turned in the locks, pulled the covers up as her footsteps creaked down the hall, breathed slow and even as Mama peeked in the door. "You're a good girl, baby," Mama murmured low and soft. "You sleep well, honey." At the foot of the bed, Shep watched her and didn't growl, but after Mama closed the door, his bright golden eyes filled the room with a dim, warm light.

All kinds of rumors went around in the next few days . . . Littl Big, Brushy, Spell Boy, Breaker, Fireball, they got busted for dealing, got offed by the Ninth Street Knights, were robbing banks in Philly. Mari June listened to the "I heard they . . . " whispers and nodded and didn't tell anybody that she'd heard anything at all. And her mom threw a fit because some punk had gone down the line of cars parked on the block and had banged up every one. "You tell me what the cops want a raise for when they can't even catch a bunch of hoodlums out smashing up cars with a hammer, huh? You wanna tell me?"

And Mari June didn't tell her it wasn't a hammer that made those dents. Shep went everywhere with her, just like she'd promised. He curled up under her chair and stared at Tim Pollack when he stared at her and he stopped. He slipped through the lunchtime crush in the halls by her side, and not one person stuck her with a pin or tried to grope her. He lay under the table at lunch while she ate her peanut butter sandwich and one day Emiline Jackson and Sheraline Brown came over to sit down, and they were pretty nice, and popular, too, not cheerleader popular but pretty cool. They were nice. Shep thumped his tail at them.

She took Shep out for a walk every night after Mama made her check up call, even if she wasn't done with her homework. They watched Mr. Kingston dance in his prom dress and listened to Mrs. Silvano sing with Mr. Silvano, which made Shep put his head back and howl like a wolf. Mari June howled with him, and they both ran away, her giggling, Shep panting, as Ms. Johnson came out of her house looking thoughtful, peering after them as she lit her cigarette and settled down to wait.

Then they went to the park and the cars looked down at the asphalt and not at Mari June, and they walked through the darkness and the moon said polite nothings in the vault of its sky and nobody bothered them. And sometimes they saw Miz Willow and Mari June always waved.

Politely.

ꟹ

Mary Rosenblum has been publishing her fiction since 1988, when she graduated from the Clarion West Writers Workshop with a sale to *Asimov's*, and has been a finalist for both Hugo and Nebula awards, as well as a winner of the Sideways in Time Award and the Compton Cook Award for Best First Novel. She writes speculative fiction as Mary Rosenblum and mystery as Mary Freeman, with eight novels out from New York publishers and dozens of published short stories. She has returned to Clarion West twice as an instructor, and divides her time between writing and working as a "literary midwife" (see www.newwritersinterface.com) for new authors. When she's not working with words, she's flying a small plane as an instrument-rated pilot.

The City: *An ordinary city—probably somewhere in Australia—with comfortable suburban neighborhoods.*

The Magic: *"Words and magic were in the beginning one and the same thing, and even today words retain much of their magical power."*—Sigmund Freud, *Introductory Lectures on Psychoanalysis*

WORDS

Angela Slatter

She was a writer, once, before the words got out of hand.

She would read aloud what she'd written that day, dropping sounds into the night, into the sometimes balmy, sometimes frosty air. After a while, she noticed that the words seemed to warm her no matter what the season.

Her voice became stronger, so soon she could read for longer. The sentences took on a life of their own, prancing and weaving themselves into the shapes of the things they described. She was always busy concentrating on those words that stayed obediently on the page, but one night, something caught her eye. A flowing diphthong movement, the graceful pivot of an elision as they wrapped themselves around each other and turned into a small, pale pink dragon, which then disappeared with a slight pop.

She knew, then, that she'd become something other than a writer. The word *wordsmith* had hidden itself away in protest against misuse about three hundred years ago and refused to come out. The word *witch* appeared but she ignored it, thinking it best.

Her house and the house next door were quite close—you could look out the window of one almost into the window of the other. Three children lived there, two little girls and a boy. They knew about the words before she did, had been watching nightly for some time. Their parents had been pleased—indeed so relieved as to not be pricked by suspicion—when they started going to bed at the prescribed hour without protest.

It gave the children time to brush their teeth, struggle into their pajamas, get tucked in by their parents, and for George to sneak out of his room, across the hallway into his sisters' and for them all to take their places on the edge of Sally's bed just before the writer settled down on the old green velvet couch in her living room. Rose would hand out the hard sweets, the fruity ones that could be sucked on for almost an hour before they dissolved into a sugary puddle in the mouth. Unless Sally crunched down on hers (which she frequently did); then, she would chew noisily on the friable shards and beg Rose for another, promising not to do it again.

It may have gone on for years, until the children grew sick of enchantment or the writer died or someone moved away. It might have gone on forever if it hadn't been for the wolf. The writer rewrote "Little Red Riding Hood," which was Rose's favorite story and the one that frightened Sally the most, so when the wolf swirled into being in the middle of the sitting room, gray and shaggy and rather larger than the word-creatures usually were, Sally screamed.

It still could have been okay had their parents not been walking past the bedroom. Their father flung open the door before the children had a chance to get away from the window, before George could duck under a bed, and before the word-wolf had time to dissipate with a half-hearted snarl.

The parents put their children to bed, all in George's room on the other side of the house. They held a discussion. They went next door and knocked.

"We don't like it," said the mother.

"We don't like what you do," the father said.

"They're fairy tales," explained the writer.

"They're not . . . " hissed the mother, "not normal! Stop or we'll tell."

"Tell whom?" asked the writer. "And what would they do? It's a long time since the age of torches and pitchforks."

The parents didn't think this was funny at all. The mother rang the Neighborhood Watch chairman, Mrs. Finnerty, who was also on a Committee for Moral Hygiene (though no one seemed to know what that was).

The mother told Mrs. Finnerty what they'd seen; she also said that the writer walked around naked a lot. Mrs. Finnerty (whose husband had run away with a young nudist) found her doubts about the word-creatures overcome when she heard about the nakedness.

Letters began to arrive for the writer, insisting she desist. She read the first two; tore up the rest as soon as she drew them out of the letter box, recognized the stiff, off-white envelopes, ripped them up right in her front yard so the whole neighborhood could see. She threw the pieces into the air and even if it were a still day, a breeze would start up and carry the pieces of torn envelope and letter into the gardens of her neighbors. The ones that wafted to Mrs.

Finnerty's always managed to land on her doormat and spell out rude words. In spite of herself, Mrs. Finnerty started yelling some of those rude words back, coupling them with *witch*.

The writer kept reading out her stories, the word-creatures becoming more and more realistic, staying longer before the inevitable pop. She started concentrating on landscapes, too, and buildings, so small villages would spring up on the carpet in her living room, with tiny people wandering the cobbled streets, carts pulled by donkeys, vendors arguing with customers in the markets; and all making a tremendous noise for their size until they disappeared.

The police were called but they weren't sure what they could do. They (a fat sergeant and two thin young constables) spoke with the writer and she smiled and laughed and refused to stop. She wasn't disturbing the peace, she was in her own home, and as far as they were aware, there was no legislation against writing this way. To the disappointment of his companions, the sergeant reluctantly refused her offer of coffee and cake and went next door.

They watched from Sally and Rose's bedroom window, with the neighborhood parents and Mrs. Finnerty all crowded in behind them. One of the young policemen found the discarded bag of candy under Sally's pillow (where Rose had stuffed it on that fateful night), surreptitiously put one in his mouth, and sucked at it.

As they watched, the clock clicked over to eight-thirty and a chime sounded, deep and sonorous. The writer came into her living room, gave the audience a small smile and shuffled the papers in her hands, rather like someone preparing to give a speech at a hostile debating society. She wore a long dress, green and flowing—the young policeman sucking on his sweet rather hoped it was a bathrobe that she would discard fairly soon—and her hair was caught up and covered by a scarf.

She turned her back to the window and began to murmur; this evening she did not use her clear reader's voice to project the story, but the word-creatures came all the same. Fairies, dragons, wolves, striped sheep and tuxedoed bears, candy-covered trees, men made of tin and women of cloud, and finally, a door.

It was a perfectly normal door if a little ornate, dark-wooded and banded with iron engraved with stylized holly. It was stout and it stayed. The neighbors and police saw her reach for the handle and turn it. The door opened and they could all see hills, sky, apple trees, and a cottage with many windows, many rooms. The writer turned and smiled and as she did so they saw their children—twenty-seven in all, from teenagers to babies, with Sally and Rose and George in the forefront.

The children waved to their parents and stepped through the door, one by one until only the writer remained. Parents screamed.

Soon, police and parents were battering at the writer's house. She heard the windows break, the wood tear as men as angry as bears broke through the door. She saw the young policeman still sitting on the edge of Sally's bed, his mouth slightly open, the candy wet and just visible between his lips. She stepped through the door and closed it just as the first parent staggered into the room.

In their rage, they burned the house, but some nights you can see shades and shadows dance around the big tree in the yard. And the young policeman comes by sometimes, to sit beside the blackened ruins and watch in hope of a door.

Specializing in dark fantasy and horror, **Angela Slatter** is the author of the Aurealis Award-winning *The Girl with No Hands and Other Tales*, the World Fantasy Award finalist *Sourdough and Other Stories*, and the Aurealis finalist *Midnight and Moonshine* (with Lisa L. Hannett). She is the first Australian to win a British Fantasy Award (for "The Coffin-Maker's Daughter" in *A Book of Horrors*, Stephen Jones, ed.). Forthcoming in 2014 will be *The Bitterwood Bible and Other Recountings*, *Black-Winged Angels*, and *The Female Factory* (with Lisa L. Hannett). In 2013 she was awarded one of the inaugural Queensland Writers Fellowships. She has an MA and a PhD in Creative Writing, and is a graduate of Clarion South 2009 and the Tin House Summer Writers Workshop 2006. She blogs at www.angelaslatter.com about shiny things that catch her eye.

The City: *The fictional Santo del Vado Viejo, a city in Arizona.*

The Magic: *When gang members resort to* brujería *and go after the new kid in town, its a good thing he knows some local Kikimi tribal members with special powers of their own.*

DOG BOYS

Charles de Lint

I hate this place. Hate the heat and the dust. Hate this stupid chi-chi gated community. And I so hate my new high school. You really have to wonder what my parents were thinking. They move us to Desert View with its walls and patrols, and a security checkpoint to get in, but they send me to Rose Creek High, a public school. Hello? Filled with the people a gated community keeps out.

Don't get me wrong. I don't judge. Most of the kids are Mexicans or Indians with a few blacks, Asians and, white kids like me, but I'm cool with that. We had a wide racial mix at my old high school and I got along fine with just about everybody. But here, the Mexicans run in serious gangs and the Indians look at me like I'm supposed to constantly apologize for what my ancestors did to theirs, except my ancestors only got to North America in the fifties.

I was online with my best friend Ronnie last night looking for advice, but he just gave me the same drill he did before my parents pulled us out of the good life in Atlanta and dumped us here: *Keep your head down until you get the lay of the land. Don't make waves, but don't take any shit.*

Today is the first day of week three and I've already decided to treat this school like jail. Just keep out of trouble and do my time until I can graduate. Except in the middle of the afternoon I've got a hall pass to go to the can and I come across some big Mexican dude pushing around a little Indian girl in the stairwell.

Keep your head down. Don't make waves.

Sure. Good advice. But you've also got to do the right thing.

"Hey," I call to him. "Leave her alone."

Cold eyes rise to meet mine. I can tell he's memorizing my face. "You going to make me?"

"If I have to."

For a long moment, it could go either way, but then he shoves the girl hard enough to knock her off her feet.

"This isn't finished, *amigo*," he says as the stairwell door slams behind him.

I help the girl up, give her space once she's on her feet. She straightens her shirt, but she doesn't thank me.

"You shouldn't have done that," she says instead. "Now we're both dead."

She's probably right. The bandas—the local gangs—don't wear their colors at school, but everybody knows who they are. Except for the new guy. Which would be me. The dude I told off is probably one of them.

Too late to do anything about it now.

"My name's Brandon," I tell her.

"I know. The new kid. I'm Rita."

"What was that guy's deal, anyway?"

She shrugs. Up close she's really cute and curvy. Her skin's a warm coffee brown, hair black, eyes like a deer, soft and dark. She's dressed in jeans and sneakers with a rose-colored T-shirt under a gray hoodie.

"He's just trying to wind up my brother," she says.

"Why? What did he do?"

"Nothing. The rez boys just naturally piss everybody off—but especially the 66 Bandas."

From walking through the halls and listening to the other kids talk, I've already learned enough to know that the 66ers are the biggest of the Mexican gangs here in Santo del Vado Viejo.

"Great."

She nods. "And seeing how that was Bambino Perez—Big Chuy's little brother—now they're all pissed off at you—and me, too."

"So can't we—I don't know. Go to someone and get help? The office? The cops?"

"What universe did you beam in from? You haven't seen what the bandas do to snitches."

"Right. That was stupid. But everything's so different here from back home."

Her eyebrows go up.

"Well, for one thing," I tell her, "back there you stood a pretty good chance of getting through a day without being knifed or shot."

"Welcome to your new world."

"Why do you put up with it?" I have to ask.

"I'm not going to be the reason there's a war between the rez boys and the bandas. So Bambino knows he can yank my chain and I'm not going to tell anybody about it. But now you've stood up to him and I was there, so all bets are off. His pride's going to demand payback."

What have I gotten myself into?

"The real problem," she says, "is that in the eyes of the law, the only thing lower than a Mexican is an Indian. If there's trouble, we never come off well."

"So what do we do?" I ask.

"Do you have a car?"

"If you can call it that."

Dad bought me a beat-up old Toyota that doesn't have much pep. Hell, I'm happy when it starts in the morning. But so far it's gotten me back and forth to school.

"Then let's get out of here," she says. "Drive me back to the rez and we'll see if we can get some help there."

It's only my third week in the new school. Do I really want to start skipping classes? I'm hoping to get on the basketball team, but that's not going to happen if they think I'm a troublemaker.

"Is that really the best idea?" I ask.

"You'd rather stick around to see what the bandas have planned for you?"

I think of the stretcher I saw leaving the campus the first week I was here.

"No, but I can't just quit school. I've got to deal with this sometime."

"Exactly. I need to finish school, too. It's my only way off the rez and away from all this crap."

"Okay."

"So unless you've got a better idea," she says, "we should get going."

I let her lead me down the stairs and outside to the parking lot. I keep expecting a teacher to stop us. Or a gang of Mexican boys with knives and chains. But we make it to my car in one piece.

"Sorry about the ride," I say.

"Are you kidding? You should see the dust buckets on the rez."

The Toyota starts first try. I decide to take that as a good sign instead of having used up my luck for the day.

"Which way?" I ask.

She points down Leawood Road, which runs in front of the Rose Creek High School campus.

"Take Leawood down to Mohave," she says, "and hang a left on Jacinto. After that, it's straight all the way."

She settles in her seat as we pull out onto Leawood. Opening the window, she adjusts the side mirror to check the road behind us.

"So," I say. "If we get through this in one piece, you want to go for a coffee or something sometime?"

"Seriously? You're hitting on me in the middle of this?"

I glance at her, already shaping an apology, except she's smiling.

"Sure," I say. "I haven't had the chance to meet many people since I got here."

She laughs. "You know, I think Jack's actually going to like you."

"Who's Jack?"

"My brother. Oh crap."

The sudden switch catches me off guard until I realize it's something she sees in the side mirror. I look in the rearview. There's a lowrider muscle car coming up fast behind us. Flames on the hood, the chassis about two inches from the ground.

"How fast can you go?" she asks.

"Not very."

"Then we're screwed."

"Not necessarily."

I stomp on the gas and the Toyota picks up some speed.

"Are there any rougher roads around here?" I ask.

"Why would you—oh, I get it. Take your next left, and then the first right."

I follow her directions. The second street is perfect. Full of uneven pavement and potholes. The guys chasing us are going to bottom out if they don't slow down. They've probably got a hydraulic suspension system to change the height of the car, but by the time they do that, we'll be long gone.

And sure enough, we make a couple more turns and we've lost them.

I let Rita direct me back onto Jacinto Road and open the Toyota up. I actually get it to twenty miles above the posted speed limit. I'm not worried about cops. I'd much rather get stopped for a ticket than get my skull bashed in by a bunch of crazy headbangers.

"Nice," Rita says. "Maybe we've got a clear run to the rez."

She bumps a fist against my shoulder and I give her a grin.

Jacinta Road takes us out of town, west to the mountains. After awhile we leave behind the last few fast food joints and gas stations, and it turns into a rural highway. Now it's just ranches and desert scrub. In other words, a whole lot of dusty nothing.

I keep checking the rearview, but all that's back there is a white SUV and a beat-up old pickup truck that turned onto the road after we left town—nothing any self-respecting gangbanger would be caught dead in.

"What happens when we get to the rez?" I ask after we've been driving for a while.

"We'll talk to my uncle Reuben. I need to figure out a way to get the bandas off our backs without letting my brother know. If anyone can figure something out, it's Reuben."

I don't ask the question, but she sighs and answers me anyway.

"Jack just got out of juvie," she says. "I can't take the chance of him doing something stupid and going right back in."

"Like taking on this gang."

She nods. "But I also don't want my parents to pull me out of school—which they'll do if they find out how bad it's getting there with the stupid bandas. The whole reason I'm going to Rose Creek is because it's my only chance to get into a decent university. The school on the rez is crap."

"University's expensive."

"Tell me about it. But I work evenings and weekends at the Rosalinda House Café and I've been saving my money. Plus I've got a good chance at a scholarship."

I'm about to ask her what she's going to major in, when I see something on the road far ahead of us. I can't quite figure out what it is, but it looks like a bunch of cars parked across the highway.

"Is that some kind of blockade?" I ask.

But Rita's already sitting up, hands on the dash as she stares down the road.

"It's the damn bandas," she says. "They must have figured we'd head for the rez, so some of them got here ahead of us."

I start to brake.

"What do we do now?" I ask her.

"Make our peace with *los santos*?"

"What?"

"We're dead," she says. "What else can we do? And we were so close. The border of the rez is just on the other side of their blockade."

"And they can't follow us onto the rez?"

"They can if they want a full-out war with the Warrior Society, but it doesn't matter. We're not on the rez." She shakes her head. "We are so screwed."

"Okay, then."

I take my foot off the brake and push the gas pedal to the floor. The Toyota starts to pick up speed.

"Whoa, cowboy," Rita says.

"Hang on," I tell her.

I know the Toyota's not like the dirt bikes that Ronnie and I used to ride at his grandparents' place outside of Atlanta, but some of the physics are the same. The bandas are watching us approach and I can guess what they're thinking: I've got to slow down and then they'll have me.

But I keep my foot on the gas until the last minute, then brake and haul on the wheel. The Toyota skids on the pavement, burning rubber. Now we're coming at them sideways. I think I hear a gunshot, but it must have gone wild, the same way those gangbangers are scrambling to avoid being hit.

Just before we slam into their cars my foot's back on the gas. I haul the wheel again. We skid on the dirt verge, wheels spinning until they catch, and we shoot past the cars. There's a bad moment when I almost lose control, but I finally get us back onto the highway. We pass the "Welcome to Kikimi Reservation" sign and leave the bandas eating our dust.

"Holy crap," Rita says. "Where'd you learn to do that?"

Her phone rings before I can answer. I glance at the screen as she lifts the phone to see who it is. Caller blocked. She pushes *talk.*

"Hello?" she says.

She listens for a moment, then cuts off the call and gives me a worried look.

"That was Bambino," she tells me. "Says he knows where we live and to tell you that a gated community's not going to keep you safe." She waits a beat, then adds, "You live in a gated community?"

"Desert View."

"If your parents can afford that, why the hell are you going to Rose Creek?"

I shrug. "Ask them."

"Huh. And seriously. Where'd you learn to drive like that?"

"That was my first time."

She shakes her head. "God, you're as crazy as my brothers."

"Is that a good or a bad thing?"

"I'll get back to you on that. See that place coming up on the left?"

It's an adobe building, surrounded by mesquite trees and cacti, and a dusty parking lot. There are a couple of beat-up pickups and a jeep out front. The sign on the roof is missing a couple of letters, but it's still easy to make out: *Little Tree Trading Post.*

"Pull in here," Rita says.

I park beside the jeep. We get out and walk to the door.

Inside, it's like an old general store. There's a big wooden counter with souvenirs and jewelry with cigarettes shelved on the wall behind the cash register. A half-dozen Indians dressed like cowboys sit around a pot-bellied stove. The rest of the store is a mix of food staples and dry goods.

One of the guys at the stove stands up when we come in. He's tall and good-looking, with a long black braid. He wears a flannel shirt, jeans, and boots, same as his companions. I get a curious once-over before he turns his attention to Rita. He looks happy to see her, but a little puzzled as well.

"Aren't you supposed to be in school?" he asks.

She nods. "Is Jack around?

"Naw," the man says. "He's on a run to Phoenix with Petey to pick up a part for that damn truck of his. Do you need to talk to him? I've got Petey's cell number."

"What I need is for Jack not to hear any of this," Rita says. She gives the guys by the stove a warning look. "And that goes for you gossiping hens as well. This gets out and there'll be hell to pay."

"What's going on?" the standing man asks.

"Uncle Reuben," Rita says, "this is my new friend Brandon."

And then she relates everything that's happened from when I first met her in the stairwell. Her uncle's face darkens with anger.

"So you see why Jack can't know about this," Rita finishes. "He'll go after the 66ers and end up right back in county."

"Someone still needs to go after Bambino and pound some manners into his head."

Rita waves off the suggestion. "You know that's just going to make things escalate into a full-out war. I was hoping we could figure out a more practical—and legal—solution."

"Well, for starters, you're not going back to your grandmother's. And we should send somebody 'round her place to make sure she's okay."

"I'm not dropping out of school."

"I know what it means to you," Reuben says, "but school won't mean anything if you're dead."

Rita shakes her head. "Dropping out's not an option."

I think about our new house in Desert View. It's big with lots of room. My parents might be a little freaked, but they're not the kind to turn their backs on anyone in need. And it wouldn't be forever. Just until this blows over.

"They could stay with me," I say. "Rita and her grandmother."

Reuben's eyebrows go up.

"He lives in a gated community," Rita explains. "Desert View." Then she turns to me. "But you heard what Bambino told me. He's gunning for you. No place is safe."

"Maybe not," Reuben says. "But a place like that is contained. They'll have to keep their numbers down. They come after you there and we can deal with them. I like it."

Rita gives a slow nod. "Maybe it's time they got a taste of their own medicine."

I look from one to the other. "Um, what, exactly, are you talking about here?"

"Don't worry," Rita says. "You and your parents won't be involved."

"Involved in what?"

"This is tribal stuff," Reuben says. "It's not something we can talk about with outsiders."

My head's full of questions, but I can tell by the look on his face that he won't give me any more explanation than that.

"We'll put together an escort," Reuben says. "First, we'll pick up Gabriella."

"My grandmother," Rita explains.

"And we'll bring you all to Desert View," he goes on, as though she hasn't spoken. "The bandas will see us leave and after that—well, if they don't make a play tonight, we'll figure out what to do next. But bottom line, we're putting an end to this crap."

Out in the parking lot, Rita's uncle stops me as I'm getting into the Toyota.

"I appreciate you stepping up the way you did to help my niece," he says. "What I can't figure out is why you got involved."

"It was the decent thing to do," I tell him.

"Yeah, I know that. It's just, most people wouldn't bother."

"I guess I'm not most people."

He studies me for a moment, then smiles.

"I guess you're not," he says. "I just want you to know—however this turns out, our family's in your debt."

I shake my head. "It doesn't work like that."

"Maybe not in the white man's world," he says, "but here on the rez, that's how we roll."

He claps a hand on my shoulder, then heads off to his jeep.

"It's just a thing," Rita says when I get into the car. "It's a way of saying he's grateful."

"Okay. But I just want you to know I did it because it was the right thing to do. You do something like that, you don't expect a medal—not where I come from."

She smiles. "But maybe a date for coffee?"

I feel the heat rush up my neck.

She bumps her fist against my shoulder.

"Joking," she says. Then she nods out the front window. "They're waiting on you."

I start the Toyota and follow Reuben's jeep down the highway back to town. He's got one of the men from the trading post riding shotgun. The two pickups follow behind us with the rest of the guys. When we get to where the blockade was there's a Mexican guy sitting on a chopper at the side of the road. He watches us go by without expression.

A few moments later I hear the roar of his motorcycle and he passes our little convoy.

After we pick up Señora Young Deer and Rita packs a bag with some clothes and toiletries, our escort brings us to the front gate of Desert View. Before I can pull in, Reuben gives a honk. I wait while he gets out of his jeep and comes over to my side of the Toyota.

"When you get home," he tells me, "just stay inside. Hang tight and let us do our thing. This'll all be over come morning."

"Do you really think they'll try to break into here?" I ask.

Reuben nods down the street where a familiar lowrider with the flames on its hood is parked by the curb. Bambino Perez's ride.

"Once it gets dark, they'll come over the walls," Reuben says. "But don't worry. We'll be waiting for them."

How are you going to get in? I want to ask, but I don't want to sound like a wuss.

"Sure," I tell him. "We'll lock the doors and stay inside."

He waits until we get past the guardhouse before he returns to his jeep. As I wind through the streets to my house, I try to figure out what I'm going to tell my mom.

Back in Atlanta, she was used to me bringing home strays, like when Bobby Newton's dad lost his job and started taking it out on him. She let Bobby stay with us for a couple of weeks, no questions asked. Same with Susie and Rick Healey after their house fire. The insurance company put their family up in a motel that was so far away it made it really hard for them to get to school, so my folks suggested the kids come stay with us, instead.

A sixty-year-old Native woman and her granddaughter is a new one, even for me, and I have no idea how to begin to explain the mess I'm in.

But when we get inside the house, no one is there. Mom's left a note on the kitchen counter telling me that her friend Judy sprained her ankle, so she's gone over to Judy's ranch to help look after the horses and stuff. Dad's working late, and she left me money to order a pizza.

"That will make it easier," Señora Young Deer says when I read the note to them.

She's pretty cool for a grandmother. Actually, she doesn't look at all like a grandmother. She's got long greying hair that she wears in a braid, and she's dressed in jeans, a white T-shirt, fringed buckskin jacket, and cowboy boots. And she doesn't look lame—like she's pretending to be young.

"How so?" I ask.

"Perhaps we can get this done before they return," she replies, "which will save having to explain ourselves."

I nod. I'd be relieved to leave my parents out of this.

"So, should I order a pizza?" I ask.

"Let me see what's in your fridge," Señora Young Deer says. "If that's all right with you."

"Sure. I just don't want you to go to any trouble."

"Are you kidding?" Rita says. "Indian women love to nurture." Then she adds to her grandmother, "How can we help?"

"I'm fine. Don't you have homework?"

"Yes, but we'll do it after dinner," Rita says, then adds to me: "I noticed a hoop hanging above your garage door. I also had to miss basketball practice and I'd love to blow off some steam."

"You play basketball?"

She frowns at me. "Why are you so surprised?"

"It's just . . . you know. You're kind of . . . well . . . "

"Short?"

"Well, sort of. For a basketball player."

Rita grins. "Let's play some one-on-one. Maybe we can make it interesting—say, a quarter a point?"

"Don't be foolish, Brandon," Señora Young Deer says. "The girl's a shark."

"Aita!" Rita says. "Don't give away all my secrets."

Her grandmother laughs. "Go ahead. Have some fun. But be back inside before the sun sets."

"We will."

Rita and I leave the kitchen through the door into the garage. I grab my basketball.

"Does she always treat you like a little kid?" I ask.

"What do you mean?"

"You know. Be in before dark."

"Have you already forgotten the bandas?" she says.

"No."

But I kind of had. I'd rather pretend none of that is happening because it makes me feel like throwing up.

"Let's shoot some hoops," I say.

I pass her the ball and she dribbles it like a pro. Once we start playing one-on-one, she cleans up. She might be small, but I've never seen anybody so fast, on or off the court.

If she's any indication of what the kids are like here, I don't think I'll be making the team any time soon.

Of course, first I have to make it through tonight in one piece.

Señora Young Deer put together an amazing meal. It's just a vegetable stew, but it's like nothing I'm used to. Fiery, but so flavorful. She must have a stash of special spices in that backpack of hers because I've never tasted anything like them in Mom's cooking.

It's almost dark by the time we've cleaned up and Señora Young Deer says we have to go upstairs.

"There are no bars on your windows," she says when I give her a puzzled look. "If we hold the upper level they can only come at us one at a time, by the stairs."

"But I thought Reuben was taking care of them."

She nods. "My boys will do their best, but there's no guarantee that they will be successful. We have to be prepared for any circumstance."

So, as the night comes washing down the tidy streets of Desert View, we're camped upstairs in my bedroom. Señora Young Deer and Rita are sitting on the bed, leaning back against the headboard. Rita's doing some homework while her grandmother is reading a book. I'm in a chair by the window, also doing homework, or at least trying to. I'm worried about what's on the other side of the glass.

I keep looking outside, except there's nothing to see. Not Rita's uncle and her friends. Not the bandas, either. For now.

"You know," I finally say, "there's so much security in this place that as soon as one of the neighbors sees a bunch of gangbangers skulking about, they're going to call the police."

Señora Young Deer smiles and nods. "We can hope."

By which I take it she means, fat chance. But I think she's underestimating the people who live in Desert View. Okay, so places like this aren't exactly known for their sense of community, but I'm pretty sure anybody living here would be on the phone in a second if they saw gangbangers creeping around. They'd do it if they saw Reuben's people, too, for that matter.

I look out the window again. It's full dark now, but the streetlights are bright and the street's well lit. Some of the houses don't have floods, though, and there are pools of shadow lying up against their walls. I'm studying the skirt of darkness around the house across the street when suddenly all the lights go out. I mean *everywhere*. Here in the house and outside. Up and down the street, everything's gone dark.

Señora Young Deer makes a hissing sound and jumps up from the bed.

"Aita?" Rita says.

I turn back to look at their shadow shapes.

"*Brujería*," the older woman says. "Can't you smell it in the air?"

"Come again?" I say.

"Magic," Rita whispers.

I don't know about magic, but this has gone far enough. I take out my phone to call 911, but even my phone's dead. I don't mean I'm not getting a signal. The phone won't even turn on.

"They've laid a veil over us," Señora Young Deer says. "We're no longer a part of the world. They've pushed us outside it."

"But that means . . . " Rita starts.

Señora Young Deer nods. "We're on our own. The boys won't be able to get to us."

"Wait a minute," I say. "You're not making any sense. This is just a power failure. The bandas must have cut the power lines coming into Desert View. What we have to do is call the police."

"The police can't reach us any more than Reuben and the boys can," Señora Young Deer says.

I decide to ignore her and turn to Rita. My eyes are adjusting to the poor light. She looks as freaked as I'm feeling. Maybe more.

"My phone's dead," I tell her. "Use yours to call out."

She shakes her head. "It won't work any better than yours."

I look from Rita to her grandmother.

"Come on," I say. "You guys are starting to creep me out."

"I'm sorry," Señora Young Deer says, "but this is not our doing. The bandas must have hired a *brujo*."

"I don't know what that means."

"It means they're using witchcraft against us," Rita says.

"Get real."

Except I can see from the way she's looking at me that she *does* believe it's real. I shake my head.

"Am I being punked?" I say. "I'm being punked, aren't I? Did this start back in school, when I first saw you in the stairwell?"

Rita shakes her head. "Brandon—"

"Because you guys are really good. So where's the camera crew? Ronnie's going to never stop ragging me about this once it airs."

I'm babbling. I can hear myself doing it, but I can't seem to stop. Panic is jumping around in my chest.

Rita leans over and grabs me by the shoulder, her faces inches from my own.

"Brandon!" she says. Her voice is firm. "This isn't a game. It's not a joke or some stupid TV show."

"But . . . but . . . "

"It's for real. Think about it. How likely is it for us to lose all electrical power at the same time that both our cell phones stop working?"

She looks dead serious. I turn toward her grandmother. Señora Young Deer also has a grave expression. She nods.

"I'm afraid it's true," she says.

Rita steps back and I push my hands against my face, then slide off the chair onto the floor. I don't know whether I'm kneeling here to pray, or what. I just wish none of this were happening.

"You'd better pull yourself together," Señora Young Deer tells me. "Without your help, we won't survive this attack."

That pulls me back. "Me? What are you talking about?"

"Reuben and the other dog boys can't get through the enchantment by themselves," she explains. "But if one of their own is inside, he becomes a means through which they can enter."

"One of their own? You mean like another Kikimi?"

She nods. "But it has to be a male. In our tribe, the men are the dog boys. We women have different strengths."

I think I read something about this in some history class.

"Dog soldiers," I say. "Isn't that an Apache thing?"

"Historically, Cheyenne," Señora Young Deer says, "but we're talking about Kikimi dog boys here. They're as much a warrior society as the dog soldiers were, but when ours run in a pack, it's more literal."

I blink. "What do you mean by 'literal'?"

"She means they take animal shapes," Rita says.

I look at her. I feel like I'm going crazy, but they're both so serious.

"I still don't see what I can do," I tell them. "I'm not Kikimi. I don't have any kind of Native American blood, so far as I know."

Señora Young Deer takes a sheathed knife out of her backpack. I stare at the blade when she removes it from the leather casing.

"There's an easy ritual that can fix that," she says. "But we have to do it quickly. The bandas will soon be here."

"You're going to—what? Cut me with that?"

"We will share blood. The women of our tribe carry the gift of life within us. We make the connections between the newborn, our ancestors and the Great Spirit."

I stopped listening at "share blood." I flash on health class and how we were told that diseases like HIV and hepatitis can be spread through blood from open wounds or by having sex.

"It's perfectly safe," Señora Young Deer says. "But it will change you and there will be no going back."

My mouth is dry. I swallow.

"Change me how?" I say.

"You'll become one of the dog boys," Rita says.

I hear an echo of the other thing she said a moment ago.

They can take animal shapes.

"You must do this willingly," Señora Young Deer says, "or it can go bad."

"You want me to become some kind of werewolf?"

"No," she says. "You will become a shape-changer—they are not remotely the same thing."

"And if I don't do it?"

"Reuben won't be able to help us and we'll probably die." She hesitates, then adds, "Not right away, but knowing the bandas, we'll wish that we had died quickly."

I swallow again. My mouth is like sandpaper. I feel a little dizzy.

"Okay," I say. My gaze goes to Rita and I stand up, hoping I won't faint or something equally stupid.

"But if we get out of this," I tell her, "we're definitely going out for a coffee."

I say it to lighten the mood. But she smiles, steps up close and kisses me. Long and hard.

"Definitely," she says a little breathlessly when she breaks it off.

My heart's beating so fast I've forgotten to be scared.

"What do we do?" I manage to get out.

In response, Señora Young Deer takes the knife and slices lightly across her palm. Then she hands the knife to me.

"Left palm," she says. "And take care not to cut too deeply. That knife's sharp."

My hand's trembling as I hold the knife. I feel like I'm going to cut my hand off.

"Here," Rita says turning my left palm up and cupping it inside hers. Her hand feels so warm and steady.

She takes the knife from me and without hesitation cuts across my palm. Her touch is so light I don't even feel it, but when the knife comes away, blood wells up from the long thin cut.

"Brandon," Señora Young Deer says. She takes my left hand in her own and our blood mingles. "Our ancestors welcome you."

Beside me, Rita murmurs, *"Hey ya, hey ya, yi yi."*

When Señora Young Deer lets go of my hand, I hold it palm up and so that it won't drip on the rug. Except there's no blood. No cut. Just a long, thin white star.

"Okay," I say. "That's weird. But I don't feel any different. Is that all there it to it?"

Señora Young Deer smiles. "Some rituals are fueled more by intent than trappings. My focus has always been sharp."

"Yeah, but—"

But then I hear a voice I recognize as Reuben's.

Brother? it says. *I don't recognize you, but I know we're kin. Can you let us in*?

I can't tell where it's coming from. It sounds like it's right in my head.

I guess I look pretty freaked because Rita grabs my arm.

"Brandon," she says. "Are you okay?"

I shake my head. "I don't know. Did you hear that?"

"Hear what?"

"There was this voice. It sounded like Reuben."

Brother?

"There it is again."

"I don't hear anything," Rita says.

"The dog boys are all connected," Señora Young Deer says. "It's part of what makes them so formidable in battle. Reuben is using that connection to contact you. What does he say?"

"He wants me to let him in."

Right then there's a loud bang on the front door below. Somebody else wants in. Not into this magical whatever that Rita's grandmother is talking about, but into my house. Nobody has to tell me that the bandas are here. It's like I suddenly have this radar in my head. I can feel them out there in the night—a dozen or so.

Why won't you answer me? the voice in my head asks.

"Then do it," Señora Young Deer says. "Let him in. We don't have much time. The bandas are already here and Reuben's still outside of Desert View."

"I don't know *how!*"

There's more banging on the door downstairs. Then I guess the bandas decide to find an easier way inside because I hear the crash of the front window being smashed in.

"Of course you don't," Señora Young Deer says. "How could you?" She stands in front of me and takes my hands. "Find that connection to Reuben's voice inside yourself, then follow it back until you can feel him. As soon as you do, you can talk to him the same way he's talking to you. And you'll be able to bring him through, despite the spell the bandas have laid upon us."

I don't know how she expects me to do that. All I know is that the bandas are in my living room. I haven't a clue how to find any connection inside myself. I don't even know where to start.

Rita goes over and grabs my baseball bat where it's leaning in a corner and takes it to the door. She looks scared, but determined.

I need to be determined, too, but just wanting something doesn't make it happen.

Except now Reuben's in my head again.

Is this Brandon? he asks. *Can you hear me?*

I just latch on to the sound of his voice and think back as hard as I can: *Yes, yes! I can hear you! I—um, I'm letting you in.*

Perfect. Hang tight, kid, we're on our way.

I guess it worked because now that weird radar in my head is aware of a handful of figures racing through the dark streets of Desert View, heading for my house. The problem is the bandas are already here inside. Coming up the stairs.

I pull my hands from Rita's grandmother and move past her to take the bat from Rita.

"Reuben's on the way," I say as I jerk the door open. "Push the bed against the door or something."

"Brandon, you can't—"

But I've already stepped through. I pull the door closed behind me, keeping my gaze on the top of the stairs.

I know it's stupid to go out and face the bandas with only my bat. But there's a *need* in me to protect Rita and her grandmother. I can't explain it. It's burning inside me. I have to protect them. To protect the house.

A suicide mission—yeah, I know. But this is *my* territory.

I have no idea where that's coming from. I just know it's true.

The first of the gangbangers to reach the top of the stairs is Bambino. A couple more that I don't recognize are right behind him. I hear something growling, but I'm not sure if it's in the hallway with me, or in my head.

Bambino grins as he lifts the gun in his hand.

I don't even think about it. I raise the bat and charge him. But then the bat falls out of my hand and I feel as if my whole body is being torn apart. Just for a moment, it's like I'm here and not here at the same time. Bambino's eyes go big. His gun fires. The boom is like a clap of thunder in the confined space. The bullet whistles by my ear.

I launch myself toward him with all four paws, my teeth bared and intent on decimating his shocked face.

What the hell—?

There's not even time to think about what's happening. I land on him and the force of my impact drives him back. He falls onto the other two guys and we all go tumbling down the stairs in a mess of flailing limbs.

There's this horrible growling—now I know it's me. The bandas are screaming. I'm snapping and lunging at their throats, but only get mouthfuls of arm as they try to defend themselves. My jaws break bones. My mouth fills with blood. It's horrible and wonderful all at the same time.

They scramble away from me at the bottom of the stairs. One of them knocks a chair in my way and it throws me off long enough for them to go leaping back out through the big picture window they smashed to get in. I recover quickly. I can feel the broken glass cutting the pads of my paws as I cross the living room, but I ignore the pain. I launch myself out the window and take the nearest bandas down by leaping onto his back.

He falls to the ground and the next second my jaws are around his throat. I'm about to snap his neck when someone pulls me off. I turn to snarl at the stranger, but I can't move because of the grip he has on me.

"Easy, brother," he says. "Easy now."

The protest dies in my throat as I'm finally able to turn and look into Reuben's eyes.

"We can take it from here," he tells me.

Then everything goes black.

When I come to, I'm lying on my back on something soft. I'm so disoriented that I panic and lunge up off what turns out to be the couch in my own living room. I blink in the bright light at all the people moving around. It takes me a moment to realize that they're trying to clean up the mess the bandas left.

"Hey," a voice says.

I turn in Reuben's direction.

You okay? he asks.

The voice is in my head now and it all comes back. The bandas attacking our house. Me turning into—what? Some kind of wolf or dog? Chewing on the gangbangers' arms. The taste of their blood . . .

"Going . . . to be . . . sick . . . "

"Johnny?" Reuben says.

"On it."

A tall Kikimi I don't know hoists me to my feet and walks me fast down the hall to the bathroom. The bottoms of my feet hurt with every step, but I feel weirdly comforted by his arm around my shoulders. Like I'm safe.

I lose that stew Rita's grandmother made for us.

I hear running water and Johnny hands me a wet washcloth. I clean my mouth. He leaves me to brush my teeth.

When I limp out of the bathroom, Rita's leaning against the wall. She pushes away from it.

"I'm so sorry you got involved in all of this." she says. "If I'd had any idea . . . "

I make a vague wave with my hand.

"I involved myself," I say. "You couldn't have known what would happen."

"You're taking it really well."

I give her a weak smile. "Tell me that tomorrow, when it's all had a chance to sink in."

I start to hobble back to the living room. Rita steps up and puts her arm under mine and around my waist to help support me. I get a different kind of comfort from the press of her body against mine. I guess I'm projecting what I feel because Reuben looks up when I come in and grins knowingly.

I pretend to ignore him.

"My parents are going to kill me," I say instead.

Reuben, Señora Young Deer and their friends have done a really good job cleaning things up, but there's no ignoring the missing picture window, nor the broken coffee table that one of the bandas must have damaged in their mad effort to escape—me, I realize.

I sit down in the nearest chair. The weight of everything that's happened is too much to carry, standing on my cut feet.

"So what am I now?" I ask the room in general.

Johnny and the other Indians all look to Reuben.

"One of us," Reuben says. "A dog boy. Is that such a bad thing?"

"I don't know. Am I going to pull a Hulk every time I get mad and turn into a dog?"

Everybody laughs, but Reuben answers me seriously.

"This isn't some little favor you did for us," he says. "It's major. You saved my niece and my aunt. And you've become one of us. We'll take care of you. We'll teach you how to control the dog under your skin. Anything you need, we're here to help."

I give a slow nod. "Because it's a pack thing."

"A tribe within the tribe," Reuben agrees.

I look around at the other dog boys. "And everybody's okay with that, me being—you know, not born into the tribe?"

"You're our brother now," Johnny says. "How would it not be okay?"

He's got such a big, easy smile I can't help but return it.

"But what about my parents?" I ask Reuben. "It's not just explaining the mess in here. How do I tell them what's happened to me? *Can* I even tell them?"

"I would never advise a son to lie to his parents," he says. He waits a beat, then adds, "But I might recommend that you edit your story a little. Tell them what happened at school and how, when the bandas threatened to come after the two of you, you brought Rita and Gabriella here because you thought it would be safer in a gated community. There was a power failure. The bandas broke in and you held them off long enough for me to arrive."

"But nothing about this . . . other thing that happened to me."

"It's your call, son. You will need to spend some time on the rez with us to get a handle on things, and for that we're going to need your parents' permission. We can tell them that you're taking a desert survival course with the tribe, which won't exactly be a lie. You will be in the desert and we will be teaching you how to survive. But if they know the truth and blame us for what's happened to you, it could cause problems."

"Oh boy."

Reuben nods. "The biggest one being trying to figure it out on your own. Learning to control the dog that's now sitting under your skin."

I glance at Rita and she gives me a sympathetic look.

"Last question," I say, turning back to Reuben. "For now, anyway. What happens with the bandas? I didn't—I didn't *kill* any of them, did I?"

Reuben shakes his head. "The funny thing is, they probably won't even remember all the details. They'll remember us, but not the dogs. People tend to ignore anything that doesn't fit into their world view."

"But they used magic themselves."

"Yeah," Reuben says. "There's that."

"Are they still going to be coming after us?"

"Not with magic, they won't. Turns out they didn't hire a *brujo*. One of the gang was messing with spells and got lucky."

"What's to stop him from getting lucky again?" I have to ask.

"Gabriella put him under a compulsion. Now whenever he even thinks of magic, he'll break out in hives. If he keeps at it, he blacks out."

I rub my head, trying to be cool about all of this. But I can't pretend it doesn't freak me out. I shoot Señora Young Deer a quick look.

"So you guys do this broo-ha, too?" I ask.

"*Brujería*," Señora Young Deer says. "But ours is different. We work with spirit guides. We try not to upset the natural order of things."

"Don't worry," Reuben says. "The kid won't be bothering you anymore. Gabriella can be very persuasive."

"Okay," I say, like I understand. "So, what about school? What happens with us there?"

"Getting there in the morning shouldn't be a problem," Reuben says. "I'll take you myself. But be careful during the day. Don't get caught alone anywhere. Some of the boys will meet you after school to make sure nobody starts anything."

I look at Rita and she shrugs, but I can tell she's no happier that I am with the idea of having to constantly be on guard.

"I know," Reuben says. "It's not ideal. But before we do anything I have to have a sit down with Big Chuy and see if he even knows what his kid brother was up to. He's smart. He knows a war with the dog boys isn't in his best interest, so I'm sure we'll work something out. But it might take a couple of days. Can you hang in that long?"

"I guess. I think I'll go clean up these cuts on my feet."

But when I stand up there's hardly any pain. I pull off the slippers I'm wearing and look at the soles of my feet. They're crisscrossed with lots of tiny white scars.

"We tend to heal quickly from little wounds," Reuben says.

I remember the cut on my palm from when I shared blood with Señora Young Deer. There's no sign of it now.

"Yeah," I say. "I can see that."

Except for Reuben, the dog boys clear out, and Dad comes home not long after that. Naturally, he's freaked. The first thing he wants to know is where's Mom and am I okay. I tell him that Mom is still at Judy's, then I relate the story we agreed on. It sounds preposterous to me as I'm explaining what happened, but he buys it completely. He even tells me he's proud of me, which makes me feel a little like an imposter, except I guess I did try to do the right thing. Everything just got way out of hand.

"Have you called your mother yet?" he asks.

"No, we were just trying to clean stuff up," I say. "I knew you were coming home soon and I didn't want her to worry and feel like she has to leave Judy on her own."

"Good thinking," Dad says. "I'll call her." He looks over to Señora Young Deer and Rita. "You're welcome to stay until this blows over."

Rita's grandmother starts to say no, but Reuben interrupts her.

"Maybe that's a good idea," he says. "I can pick you all up here in the morning."

"I still don't understand why we're not calling the police," Dad says.

Reuben lifts his hands, palms up. "I certainly won't stop you if that's what you feel you have to do. But when it comes to the gangs—I won't say the police are helpless. They're simply not as effective as we might like, and the bandas always find ways to punish those who report them."

"But you can clear this up?"

"Absolutely."

"Because . . . ?"

"In a situation such as this, the Kikimi Warrior Society has more flexibility than the police department. The 66ers know that when we make a statement we're not just blowing smoke. We'll back it up."

I can tell Dad doesn't like this. But he knows he's out of his depth, so finally he just nods and goes off to call Mom.

The morning goes just the way Reuben said it would. He drives us to school and we get through homeroom and our first classes without incident. I meet up with Rita between each class and we stick to the crowded hallways.

At noon, Rita and I go out into the schoolyard with the lunches her grandmother made for us this morning. She leads me to a free picnic table under the mesquite trees where there's some shade. There are kids all around us, but that's where Bambino decides to make his play.

He swaggers over to where we're sitting, a half-dozen guys following in his wake. I stand up and put myself between him and Rita.

"You and me," Bambino says. "We've got business."

"Are you sure you want to get into that right now?" I ask.

I'm talking a lot braver than I feel, but at least I don't see any knives. Yet.

I wonder if he remembers what happened back at my house last night, how he and his crew ran like little girls from the big pissed-off dog I became. I wonder if I can call that dog up again. I know it's a terrible idea. I don't need anyone to tell me that the dog boys are something that needs to be kept out of the public eye. But I need some kind of edge.

"Why?" Bambino asks. "You think I'm scared of you?"

"Okay," I tell him. "You and me. Let's go."

He's pretty much my size. Probably a little stronger. But I'm fast and I'm not going to get into a clinch.

He laughs. "That's not how it works, *puto*. You disrespect me, you disrespect my crew. Everybody's going to need a piece of you."

"How about *me* needing a piece of *you?*" an unfamiliar voice asks.

I turn to see a tall Indian boy has stepped up beside me. He's got shoulder-length black hair, held back from his face by a thin strip of leather around his forehead. He reminds me of the coyotes I've seen running in the desert. Smart and lean.

"*No me chingues,* Joaquin," Bambino says. "This isn't Yaqui business."

Rita told me yesterday that only a couple of kids from the rez go to school at Rose Creek. The other Indians are all from the local Yaqui pueblo, although there are a few Apache and Tohono O'odham, too.

"And you know that—how?" Joaquin asks.

Bambino shakes his head. "I'm serious, man. Back off now or you're next on my list."

"What list is that? The guys you want to blow in this school?"

Bambino takes a step, cocking a fist, but one of his friends grabs his arm. Bambino starts to shake off the grip, but then he realizes what everybody does. A dozen or so big Indian boys have drifted over to where we're standing, outnumbering the bandas two-to-one.

Bambino lets his hand drop. "This isn't over," he says.

I'm not sure if he's talking to Joaquin or me.

He stalks away, his crew fanned around him. Beside me, Joaquin laughs. When I turn to him he lifts a fist. I hesitate a moment, then bump fists with him.

"Back where you come from," he says, "do they all have big *cojones* like you?"

"Back where I come from we don't need them. Thanks for stepping in with Bambino."

"*De nada*. Rita tells me you play a little ball."

"I used to be on the team at my old school."

"She says you're pretty good. You should try out for our team."

I glance at Rita with raised eyebrows and she just smiles.

"Did she tell you we played a little one-on-one yesterday," I say, "and she totally wiped me out?"

Joaquin nods. "Yeah, but she says you stopped maybe a third of her shots. You know how many people can do that?"

I shake my head.

He gives me a grin. "You have no idea who she is, do you?"

"Sure. She's Rita Young Deer."

"Yeah. She's also captain of the girl's team. State champions last year because of her scoring. Seriously, try out for our team. Why let the girls have all the glory? We could use a good defenseman. We have a practice tomorrow after school."

"I'll be there."

If I'm still alive, I think. I guess he reads it on my face.

"Don't worry about the 66ers. They'll be waiting for you after school, but we'll be there, too."

"Reuben's picking us up," Rita says.

"We'll still be there," Joaquin tells her. He nods at me. "Later."

I turn to Rita. "Captain of the team, huh? No wonder your grandmother told me not to bet with you."

I look at her, thinking, here's a smart competitive girl who's good at sports, takes her studies seriously, and nobody thinks it's weird. I amend that to: nobody I know thinks it's weird. I've never understood how so many other kids act like underachieving is something cool. But the best thing is that I think she kind of likes me.

A cute girl kind of likes me. People are talking to me. I got asked to try out for the basketball team.

I should probably thank Bambino for being such an asshole because, without him, none of this would be happening.

"What are you smiling about?" Rita asks.

"I'm just in a good mood."

"Almost getting beat up puts you in a good mood?"

"Sure."

She shakes her head. "You're weird."

It feels a bit like some western movie when Rita and I leave school at the end of the day. You know, the big showdown scene. It's hot and dusty. Bambino and his crew are waiting for us, strung out in a line just off school property. Joaquin and his friends fall into step on either side of us as we walk in their direction. I look for Reuben, but I don't see his jeep. I don't see any of the dog boys. There's only the 66ers. I just hope they're not carrying guns.

With the Yaqui beside us, we now outnumber the 66ers, but people are still going to get hurt.

"You ever fight a guy with a knife?" Joaquin asks me.

I shake my head.

"Here, do this," he says.

He takes off his hoodie and holds it loosely in his left hand.

"Wait for the right moment," he goes on, "then trap the knife hand with your jacket. Try to get it wrapped around at least a couple of times."

"Sure," I say without an ounce of his confidence.

We stop while I take off my backpack and then my jacket. I put my backpack on again. My jacket feels useless in my hand, but what he said makes sense. Whether I can pull it off—well, that's a whole other matter.

"Do you have your phone?" Joaquin asks Rita. When she nods he tells her, "Get a video of everything. If they pull weapons we want proof they started it so that it's not our asses that get dragged off to jail."

He looks at me and his friends.

"Everybody ready?" he asks. "Then let's do this."

We start moving again. In my head I hear the themes of one of those spaghetti westerns that Ronnie and I used to watch back home. I'm not feeling confident, but at least there are more of us than them. Then a black Hummer comes up the street and stops near the bandas. A Mexican guy gets out. He's covered in tattoos—they're even all over his shaved head.

Joaquin puts up a hand and we all stop.

The bandas perk up. A couple of them give each other high fives as a half-dozen more guys join the first one. Of course they're happy. They just got serious reinforcements.

"Crap," Joaquin says.

"What?" I ask. "Who is that guy?"

"Big Chuy. Bambino's older brother. He and Crusher run everything in this part of town."

"Maybe forcing a face-off with those losers today wasn't such a great idea," one of the other Yaquis says.

Joaquin grunts. I can't tell if he's agreeing or not.

For my part, I never thought it was. But I don't say anything. Beside me, Rita is still taking the video. I don't know what use it'll be if we're all dead.

Where the hell is Reuben?

Big Chuy walks up to his brother. He yells something in Spanish, then gives him an open-handed slap on the back of the head. I say slap, but it's hard enough to almost knock Bambino off his heat.

"Oh, this is good," Joaquin says. "You keep shooting that video, Rita."

Bambino says something back and Big Chuy slaps him again. Then he glares at the other 66ers who were lined up with his brother.

"What are they saying?" I ask. "What's going on?"

Joaquin grins. "Big Chuy's tearing a strip off of them. Man, is he pissed."

"About what?"

"About starting something with the rez boys. Rita, put the camera down," he adds when Big Chuy turns in our direction. "But save that file, girl."

Bambino's friends take off, heads down, not looking anywhere but at the ground. Bambino starts to follow them, but his brother slaps him again and says something to one of the men that came with him. This guy is huge, all shoulders and arms. He grabs Bambino by the arm and hauls him back to the Hummer. Pushing him inside, he closes the door and leans against the side of the Hummer, arms folded across his massive chest.

Just as Big Chuy turns to us again, Reuben finally shows up. He parks his jeep behind the Hummer. Johnny's sitting in the shotgun seat, but he stays in the jeep while Reuben gets out and saunters towards us. He's walking at an angle to Big Chuy, who's also approaching. They reach us at the same time. I glance at Rita to see she's palmed her phone and stuck it back in her pocket.

"Everybody okay?" Reuben asks.

"We are now," Rita says. "What took you so long?"

Reuben jerks a thumb in Big Chuy's direction.

"I was having a conversation with Mr. Perez," he says. "Chuy, this is my niece Rita and her friend Brandon."

Big Chuy frowns as his gaze rests on me. "He's Anglo."

"Is he? I hadn't noticed. All anyone needs to know is that he's one of my people."

Big Chuy nods.

"So we're good?" he asks Reuben. "This stops here and there won't be any retaliation?"

"Not so long as you keep your boys in line."

"That isn't going to be a problem," Big Chuy says.

He gives us all another considering look, then turns and walks back to his Hummer.

"How the hell did you pull that off?" Joaquin asks when Big Chuy is out of hearing.

Reuben shrugs. "There's a lot of desert between Mexico and here. Lot of places where a car could be ambushed. That wouldn't be good for some people's business. Expensive, too, with all the extra guards you'd have to hire."

"Sweet," Joaquin says.

"You kids still want a ride?" Reuben asks Rita and me.

I leave the decision to Rita. She shakes her head.

Reuben points a finger at me. "I need you on the rez this weekend."

"Sir, yes sir," I say.

"Piss off," he tells me, but he's laughing as he turns away and heads back to the jeep.

Joaquin bumps my shoulder with his fist. "Basketball practice. Tomorrow. You're in, right?"

"Yeah, sure. And listen, thanks for—"

He waves it off. "Later."

He and his boys take off and then it's just Rita and me standing there in front of the school.

"I've still got an hour before I need to get work," she says.

I nod, even though I don't see where this is going.

She shakes her head. "So, are you going to ask me to have a coffee with you?"

That takes me off guard, but I catch up quickly.

"Absolutely," I tell her. "Do you know a good place?"

She takes me by the hand and leads me off toward Mission Street.

Have I mentioned how much I love this place?

ഗ

Charles de Lint is an award-winning full-time writer who lives in Ottawa, Canada. With thirty-nine novels and thirty-five books of short fiction published, he is known as a master of the contemporary fantasy genre. Recent books include *Seven Wild Sisters*, a novel for middle-grade readers published in February 2014 by Little, Brown; and young adult novels *Under My Skin* and *Over My Head*, published by Penguin Canada in 2012 and 2013, respectively. A proverbial Renaissance man, de Lint also loves to paint, and has been a professional musician for many years, writing original songs and performing with his wife, MaryAnn Harris. For more information, visit his personal website at www.charlesdelint.com. He's also on Facebook, Tumblr and Twitter.

The City: *Ancient Babylon, some time after 1760 BCE and before 1595 BCE.*

The Magic: *A creature who could be a guardian angel, but is equally capable of the demonic, enters a woman's life.*

ALCHEMY

Lucy Sussex

Three figures walked in single file in the evening heat haze besides the Euphrates River, heading homewards.

All women, shawled, hunched by the baskets on their backs. The last, youngest and smallest, was further slouched by the year-old baby riding on her hip.

As if the sun had blinked, now an extra figure suddenly appeared, appended to their procession. Where day met night, before the sun god disappeared through the doors to the underworld, can be a time where strange things happen. The three women had taken a risk staying so late to gather sweet rushes outside the city gates. Now returning with their baskets dripping and laden, they knew that they must hurry, lest something untoward sneak into the city with them.

The third woman, her nostrils full of the scent of leaves and rhizomes on her back, her mind occupied by the problem of how to preserve that smell, nonetheless heard behind her the extra set of shuffling footsteps. Some field worker, some beggar? Though very tired, and with extra work ahead of her that night, the processing of the sweet flag besides cooking the evening meal, she let her mind fix on the sound.

Suddenly she realized what about it was so strange—it was an exact copy of her own footsteps.

She reeled in a turn, saw the bent figure, the shawled head—and *nothing* beneath the fringes of woven wool. For a moment she and the demon were face to face, his disguise rumbled. Then in a flap of confusion, shawl transmogrifying from fronds of hair to great feathery wings, he shot away and up.

Her mouth opened wide—she could scream, but that would wake her baby. Worse, it would alert her companions, her censorious sisters-in-law, that she had somehow, by her actions, drawn the attention of the spirit world. She closed her mouth, turned again, as the three trudged towards the city gates, the watching guards, the safety of a walled city state, a relatively new thing in the world: Babylon.

From above, the demon watched her, biding his time. His name was Azubel, a name not written in cuneiform on the clay tablets kept by the priests in the temples of Babylon, and before that, old Sumer. He was not part of their spirit world as they perceived it—or, more to the point, as they had shaped it, like they took the Mesopotamian clay and made it into bricks, jugs, writing tablets, everything useful to an aspiring civilization. He might be useful to the Babylonians, he knew that. But it would require a transaction, something in return. Something that would make it worthwhile that he, an immortal, should invest his time and power in these creatures doomed to die amongst their clay-dust. Whatever that something might be, he had a notion it could be in that hindmost woman, shuffling along with her load of reeds and drowsing baby.

He had not meant to scare her, merely to get closer, to get a sense of her thoughts. They had a special savor, distinct as musk: an unusual mind was here, working on a different level from those around her. She had been acute enough to detect his presence despite the crude disguise. That was interesting. Enough to keep him from the immortal's curse, that of being eternally bored? Possibly. But he would have to proceed carefully, he could tell that. He would watch invisibly, and then reveal himself slowly, to see how she would react.

Over the next moon, he followed her, as focused as a hunting bird on its prey.

He observed her at the street markets, among all the other good housewives. Accompanied by her shadows, the watchful sisters-in-law, she bought her family's daily provisions, or ordered delivery of larger purchases: a new water barrel, a load of straw for fuel. She sat at a market stall herself, in the perfumer's quarter, in front of her many stoppered jars. She was not a good saleswoman, her mind puzzling over the details of perfume-making even as the customers filled her ears with trivial questions. Which suited them best, the myrtle-wash, or the honeysuckle? He overheard their chatter and also the deeper, unvoiced questions: Will this keep my husband home at night? Will this keep him interested in me? She was even oblivious to the outstretched hands, clutching items of barter, the customers finally paying, until a sister-in-law pinched her into alertness, once even openly slapped her.

He nearly slapped back, because he was beginning to realize how important were the thoughts behind those dark-brown eyes: their brown study so easily turned towards something darker, which would come to be called the black arts. Her thoughts made a beginning, no more than her baby's stumbling steps, towards his special interests, for which no word yet existed in all of Babylonia. It did in Egypt, the land where he had spent the last thousand years. He could trace the lines of the hieroglyphs that spelled it out: *Khemeia*. The word meant black, a good thing, named from the soil alongside the Nile, and by extension, as surely the floodwaters spread over the delta, to the land of Egypt itself. Black earth, fertile as an enquiring mind, into which ideas could be seeded, notions of a dark, powerful art.

He vocalized the word, a soft breath: *Khemeia!* What might it be in translation to Babylonian? The more he looked at her, the more he had a sense that he was about to find out. He had assayed the minds around her, and knew now she was the most intelligent person in Mesopotamia, a civilization bursting with new ideas, unlike static Egypt.

So he watched, amassing information. She was good at her perfumer's craft, for despite the apparent absent-mindedness, the inattention to social chit-chat, the customers kept returning. That slap had been powered by genuine anxiety: her sisters-in-law knew her skills, and were even a little in awe of her. Afraid of her, even?

He tracked her to her home, the typical mud brickwork of Mesopotamia forming a house of the poorer sort: one storey, the streetfront blank wall. She worked in her courtyard, the household's center. Here was domesticity: fowls fussing and clucking in their pen, sacks of lentils or barley, a child's leather ball, its stitching half unpicked. Her trade was also carried out in this space, with myrtle leaves steeping in a clay trough, a well-used mortar and pestle, flower petals drying in the shade on wicker racks. No husband, he observed, but small children. A widow, as ripe as a fresh date, dark, small, and rounded. The eyes she circled with kohl each morning were almond-shaped, as lustrous as her hair in its long plaits. She looked ready for love, for another marriage?

Slowly, gradually, he let her sense his presence. A flash of a wing in the corner of an eye, a shadow, as he flew overhead in the full sun. She showed no sign of fear after that first encounter; she even seemed not particularly surprised at his return. He *habituated* her to seeing him, and soon they were, if not nodding acquaintances like the market stallholders she greeted every day, approaching a familiarity. She knew him by sight; and also that nobody else around her had this privilege, this special visitant. So, as a Babylonian woman would not do with any other male who was not a relation, even though this male had wings and a raptor's head, she twitched aside her shawl and met his gaze. It was an unspoken communication, a glance that held, but never approached the contest of a stare. Moreover, it coolly appraised; much like his own.

On one rare occasion when she was alone, without infants, or her attendant chaperones, he followed her. She wore her best beads and carried a basket of wares. Her destination? The temple of Aruru, the mother goddess, the maker goddess, a fashioner equally of children and clay. Even the holy places of this city needed perfumes, incense, to mask the foul stench that any human settlement creates. In Babylon as in Egypt, to be sweet-smelling was considered next to godliness. And, like many things in this supremely practical culture, incense could have another function.

In a quiet back courtyard of the temple, she met with a priestess at once motherly and gauntly ascetic. There she presented a package wrapped in leaves. The priestess unwrapped it, put it to her nose and sniffed: incense, top quality, and so reserved for libanomancy, divination from smoke. Then, as he watched, a ritual progressed, culminating with a handful of incense being scattered into a small brazier. A cloud of sweet-smelling smoke ascended to the heavens, in a cluster: a favorable divination. As she left the temple, smiling to reveal one crooked tooth, he let himself become visible to her for a moment. Her jaw set, but she did not look surprised.

This coy flirtation had to stop. Tonight, to meet with her, and put forward his proposition.

Late on that warm night in old Babylon, she tended the *tinuru*, the household clay oven. The embers were banked, and a pot seethed above them, boiling the day's harvest of delicate petals. Peripherally she registered the scents of her surroundings: the fresh straw from the pen where the fowls dozed; the clay water tubs full of steeping myrtle leaves; the powdered sweetbark, the labor of her mortar and pestle. All seemed safe, cozy—except for the monstrosity, a man with wings and a falcon's head, watching from atop the encircling brick wall.

She eyed him as she worked, noting that he had not flickered out of vision, as previously, but remained, a silent presence. Wanting: what? Without being too specific, like those customers of hers who really wanted love potions, she had queried the priestess about her visitant. From the equally guarded reply she knew he could be a demon, or an *ilum*, a personal protective spirit. Such was small wonder in Babylon, where, as befitted the greatest city in the world, three worlds co-existed: heaven, earth, and the afterlife.

That was one thought in her mind, amongst so many others. She was a mother, a businesswoman, with continual demands on her time. Of most immediate concern to her now were her experiments in perfumery. It is easy to steep the perfume out of flowers, and so make a wash for the hair. But can you capture the essence of those flowers more permanently, fix the fragrance? The pot wobbled and spat, and temporarily she forgot her visitant. She lifted the lid, sniffed at the condensate. How best to collect it, concentrate it? Through her eyelids she saw his head move slightly, following her action intently. To herself she voiced: Ah! Whatever he wanted, it involved her, and the experiments of her perfumery.

A child's moan came from the rooms opening onto the courtyard, its door a dark cave in the firelight: "Ummum." [Mother].

She answered, softly, reassuringly: "Martum." [Daughter].

Her shawl stirred, and the baby woke briefly, reaching for one soft breast. He took a mouthful, drowsed on the nipple.

Both children subsided before she spoke again, quietly, as if to herself: "I know you have not come for my children." The demon on the wall nodded, as if she were not speaking to him for the first time.

"You have been watching every move I make. You had the opportunity to take them, but no."

The raptor head nodded again.

"And demons carry off virgins or princesses, not humble housewives, mothers . . . "

Her tone was deprecating, as if to say: Desirable? Me? Her hair was tousled in its plaits after a long working day, and the kohl she applied this morning had surely faded. But as she spoke she knew well that he had not followed her through Babylon for an idle reason. Desirable? Of course she was, somehow, to this strange, unknowable male.

"You watch my perfume-making as closely as I do . . . so do you want my recipes then? My fine scents, my salves?"

"Well-observed . . . " he finally said. To her his voice sounded not like the harsh cry of a hawk, but rather soft and hissing, like a resinous log in flame. "Tapputi-Belatekallim, of the perfumers."

Now that he had finally greeted her, she made the formal obeisance of response. And added: "Also daughter of Tapputi, herself a perfumer."

"With brewers and bakers of uncommon ability in your family too! People who take materials, observe them, mix them, watch them transform, then refine the results."

"Isn't that what a good artisan should do?"

"Others think differently, they follow tradition. Your lineage has enquiring minds. You promise to be the greatest of them."

Her head was bowed, but she listened intently, though she suspected these flattering lines were a lure. "Really?"

"One day the King of Babylon will want your perfumes."

"Says who?" She tried to sound unconcerned, but she was as hooked now as an Euphrates perch.

"My name is Azubel."

"Are you a demon or an *ilum*?" she shot back, though from the priestess she knew the distinction between the two could be small, the categories of godliness and demonic being fluid.

"A *lamassu*."

She drew in her breath quietly. An *ilum* was merely a spirit of varying power. A *lamassu* was something stronger: a guardian angel. Tread carefully, she thought. A wrathful *lamassu* was equally capable of the demonic, with worse consequences.

"A *lamassu*? Mine?"

"If you will have me."

"I have a choice? To your proposal, that sounds like a marriage proposal?"

"It is . . . if you want it."

She poked the fire, added more fuel, temporizing whilst thinking hard.

"You must know I am a widow. Do you also know my sisters-in-law want me to marry again within their family? They have a cousin already picked out—a lout and dolt." She spat into the embers. "A young girl never has a choice in her husband. My family decided for me, as is the custom. So I got a man fiery and raging, and babies all the time—until the river fever took him. Do you think I want that again?"

"Your husband's family aim to keep your perfumery for themselves. They love your knowledge."

"You observe well," she said. "But did you also see my gift of incense to the priestess? It was large, because it paid for two divinations. The first, for my enterprise. The smoke clustered as it rose: that is the sign I will succeed."

"I saw the priestess throw a generous handful of incense into the brazier, on a windless day—it could hardly do else but cluster."

She touched the amulet of Aruru at her neck. "If the goddess thought otherwise, she would have sent the smoke to the left, and so indicated a bad omen."

"Of course she would. And what about the second divination?"

"A more expensive one, for when my in-laws come, and seek the omens for their marriage proposal."

"Let me predict," he said. "The brazier will just happen to be placed near a draft, that day? Or the incense scattered scantily?"

"It is not for me to question the diviner's art," she said piously.

He laughed. "You are clever—and also practical."

"Is it too much to want a good husband?"

"It is all you deserve. And more. That I can give you. Do you want to know how to solve the problems with your perfumery, so that its products will be the greatest ever produced in Babylon, and the world?"

Although she was really flattered now, she kept her tone slightly mocking, unbelieving.

"You do not offer me jewels?"

"Because that is not your bride-price. Your price is knowledge. *Khemeia*, as the Egyptians call it. It is up to you to supply the Babylonian name."

She stood, awkwardly, dropping her poker. From the top of the wall, he launched himself down, landing silently as an owl, his great wings near spanning the little courtyard. She looked at the feathers, imagined the touch of them on her bare skin, then met his gaze, the unblinking golden eyes above that hooked beak, fashioned for tearing, maiming, killing.

Unbidden a memory surfaced for her like a dumpling in a boiling cook pot.

"That ragged, foreign prophet!" she cried. "The one the priests threw out of the city five summers back! He prophesied bad angels seeking mortal women for their wives, offering them occult knowledge, and breeding giants on them! Isn't an ordinary baby big enough, when you're kneeling on the birth-bricks, feeling as if you're about to split open?"

She clutched her infant to her, and ducked under his wing towards the house, shouting: "Begone! Begone!" The poker out of reach, she threw the nearest possible weapon, a pot containing vinegar. It smashed against the brick wall as Azubel flapped upwards and out of the way.

Pandemonium!—the baby wailed, the hens clucked hysterically, the older children woke, shrieking. On the wall was now a stain, spreading like blood.

"Go to sleep," she said to all and general, including her nosy neighbors. "It was just a nightmare."

From far above, Azubel watched the scene in the courtyard, like a common Babylon market toy, a child's clay model of a house, in miniature. Why did these mortals get things so wrong? He could have had her then and there, but for the wretched, flea-bit, self-styled prophet Enoch, for whom stoning out of Babylon was clearly too good.

Nonetheless, he would return.

Immortals being somewhat careless with time, the waiting period he allowed for her to reflect on his offer stretched into years. When he found Tapputi again, there were silver strands in her hair, and gold hung from her ears and neck. Her mortar and pestle were metal now, high quality. Even her house was in a better quarter, larger, with extra rooms built onto the roof and courtyard. For extra children, he supposed. He tallied her offspring, noting a difference between the older ones, lanky and half-grown, alike as lentils except for their slight differences in height. The younger were chubby, unformed, but cast from a slightly different mold. He guessed she had not married again for looks, and these additions were cute in the way of all small children, but distinctly homely. And there were only two of them, spaced well apart. A plain but considerate man sired them?

In the market, her former sisters-in-law sold her perfumes, from a larger, well-situated stall, helped by her eldest son. She had clearly kept them on her side, yet out of her hair. Most days she worked at home, except when making special deliveries, not only to the temple of Aruru, but also the major houses of worship of Marduk and Ishtar. The reason why occupied most of her courtyard: a huge *tinaru* with appendages of copper and glass.

Behold a new thing in the world—a distillery, for taking the raw matter of flowers, boiling them, condensing the vapor and extracting the essential oils. And she had done it all by herself! Azubel felt a glow of pride at the aptness of his choice, the untutored intelligence of his prospective pupil. What else might she be capable of, when bonded with him? The possibilities stretched out in his mind: alternate Babylons, a Mesopotamian empire that would never fall. Yes, that was one way he could buy this woman, so capable at abstract as well as practical thought. But also he knew he had to engage her feelings, be personal, for a true marriage of minds and much more.

Alchemical, he nearly added, though that word will not come into existence for over a thousand years, and not in all the possible timelines that stretch like a web from Babylon to the future. The Arabic article added to the ancient Egyptian word *khem*, its hieroglyph recurring through papyrus tracts on the arcana of embalming, glass and dye making, metallurgy, all practices which mingled heavily with magic. From *al-chemy* derived, eventually, chemistry, Azubel's specialty, the art of elements and their interactions. A great knowledge, two-edged, dangerous: it could reveal the secrets of the cosmos, or turn humans destructively on each other. The choice was theirs—the temptation of power, the real story behind Adam and Eve.

They got it badly wrong there, he thought, *as humans always seemed to do.* Consider the prophet Enoch and his fable of giant babies, which had so unnerved Tapputi. Catching a rumor, a whisper, of Azubel and his fellows, during his mad wanderings through the Middle East, he wove a tale from it. Enoch's words gained currency, were recorded in writing, part of the swirling mass of words slowly forming what would someday become the Bible. Through the luck of history and its stories, the book of Enoch failed to become part of the Biblical canon, though it had more than a grain of truth to it, unlike most tales of gods and men. Enoch raved of a host of fallen angels teaching women secret knowledge, black arts: the manufacture of cosmetics to enhance sexual allure; enameling; dye making. In return the angels gained sexual favors, human wives. Enoch was a misogynist, forever blaming women for his misfortunes, his impotence. Azubel knew better: temptations were for either gender, and women were not particularly easy. In his chance rare encounters with other spirits, he had heard far more boasts about beautiful bright boys.

Alchemical marriage: where two elements unite, or the earthly and the spiritual, to produce something much, much finer—like gold. What might he and Tapputi make together, if she would just give in to him, accept his proposal?

As he had done before, he watched and followed her, waiting for the chance to reveal himself. It came on a day she had dressed with particular care, with a basket prepared of wares for her best clients, the temples. Her older children were capable enough to mind the youngsters, but as she was almost outside the house, the littlest girl threw herself at her mother, insisting on accompanying her. Tapputi could have disentangled herself with a slap, leaving someone else to deal with the ensuing tantrum. Instead she let the little hands stay clinging to her skirts, the chubby feet follow her.

Her destination was the great temple of Ishtar, goddess of love and war, perched atop its *ziggurat*, an artificial mountain reaching for the sky. He watched from above as she entered, climbing the steps slowly, her speed hampered by her child. Finally she stopped on a flat mezzanine that was slowly being turned into a garden space. Here she set down her basket, and engaged in a long negotiation with a young, fat, bedizened priestess. The little girl first sat by, docile, then wandered off to investigate the green waving plants. Azubel plucked a small feather from the underside of his wing, and blew it into the child's path. As she stretched her hand out for it, he blew again, sending it out of reach. So ensued a pouncing, leaping chase. Tapputi could hardly stop it, as the haggling had reached its critical phase. Even the priestess was beginning to look puzzled: where did that raptor feather come from, and on a still day, too! Until came the moment when he sent the feather soaring over a thick cluster of infant date palms. The child leapt to catch it, tripped on landing—and fell headlong over the edge.

It was not far to fall, but enough to break young unformed bones, leave a cripple.

He soared downwards, and just as the child was about to hit the hard courtyard bricks, scooped her up in his arms—And hovered, just above the ground, giving Tapputi and the priestess, who had rushed to the edge and stood peering agonizedly over, a full view.

He dropped the child, who landed on her two bare feet, and immediately burst into ear-splitting wails. Stray worshippers and temple slaves rushed toward her, oblivious to him. Such a lucky child, to fall and not be hurt! He trod air, above the cries and coos. Up above, Tapputi would be rushing too, except that the priestess had fainted heavily into her arms. All she could do was glare at him.

Her gaze mingled anguish and fury but part of it said: You again!

Working at night had started for Tapputi from dire need: child-free time! Then it had become habit, a time and place that was hers alone, where she could think and experiment. So as usual, that night, under the bowl of moon and stars, Tapputi tended her still. Beside her sat her eldest daughter, old enough now to watch and learn—until the long hours of darkness became too much for her, and her head drooped onto her mother's knee.

"Now we can talk," she said, to the creature again watching from her wall.

The great bird-head inclined softly in agreement. She could nearly have fainted herself, to see her child in the arms of the demon; although her mother-love was powerful enough to propel her over the roof herself, to grapple with the creature, even if she fell in a heap of shattered bones. Instead she had been forced to attend to an arm-load of heavy priestess. She had half-expected the demon to shoot up and away, stealing the child as a delayed revenge for her refusal. But to deposit her safely, before making his exit? Beware of the supernatural granting favors, for something is always asked in return.

It was like her haggling with the priestess all over again, she thought. An introductory offer had been made, a show of apparent good faith. Now she would have to respond, counter if necessary.

"Am I in debt to you since you rescued my child?"

"Assuredly," came that voice, never unpleasant in her ears, and even more so now she had reason to feel gratitude to it.

"I am married again, you know."

"That I know." It was hard to read that voice, but it sounded amused.

"Does not the code of Hammurabi the all-wise decree that an adulteress be thrown in the Euphrates, tied to her lover? You with your wings could just fly away, and I would drown."

"If tied to me, you would rise on my wings . . . "

With anyone else, she would snort: a likely story! But she had seen those wings in action, their strength and, she imagined, their softness, like a scentless petal.

"I believe you," she finally responded.

"In any case, my proposal is not for an earthly marriage."

She almost laughed. "Thank the gods for that! What would a woman do with two husbands at once? Double the trouble and never any peace!"

She cocked her head, listening to the sound of breathing from the room with the marriage bed, where her husband lay alone. "Men get jealous. Old as he is, he would fight you, though he could not put up more than a child's fight."

"So you did get the good husband you deserved? A Dumuzi for your Ishtar?"

"Divine love is for the gods. Or for your children." She reached down and stroked her daughter's hair.

His head turned, he preened a wing feather with his beak.

Male vanity! she thought.

"I got a man quiet and calm. Kind, even. A coppersmith—he made the retort."

"And I thought it all your own work."

"Oh Tapputi, my grandmother, had some ideas in that line, experimented, as did Tapputi, my mother. And a cousin of mine, dead several summers back, got closer. But yes, mostly my own work, to make the most beautiful perfume."

She knew she sounded prideful, but rightly so.

"Just as well—my husband can do little work now. He gets sore, can barely move some days. I make him salve, and I'm getting better with each batch I distill."

"But not good enough," he said.

The words hung in the air between them. In the silence, she listened to her husband again. She felt affection—but nothing more, not like in the hymns of Enheduanna that the Ishtar devotees sang.

"You mean, to cure him? Is that what you offer?"

"I can offer you an empire of knowledge."

Tapputi knew haggling. At a crucial point the negotiator must show their goods, to prove their worth before any contract is entered into, even the *riksum* [marriage contract]. Very slowly, she edged her daughter's head off her knee and onto a pillow of sacking stuffed with wool for carding and spinning.

"Show me! And then see if I'll buy!"

"Bring your best incense, then!"

She darted to her storeroom, finding the leaf-wrapped packet by feel and smell in the darkness. Pausing only to throw her shawl over her head, she rejoined him. He swooped down, took her hand in his: a cool, dry, strong yet gentle grasp. Then he shot upwards again, she with him. Her plaits whipped around her, the fringes of shawl blew into her eyes, but she held her fragrant package tight. Their passage negotiated the lazy night breezes to the temple atop the *ziggurat* of Marduk, the chief god, the highest point in Babylon. Alighting on the flat roof he released her. Spread out before them was the city, the walls, the slow coils of the Euphrates, but also the darkness of the Mesopotamian plains.

"Why are we here?" she asked, adjusting her shawl.

"To see the future."

"Divination?" She held the packet out to him.

"But not like any you know." He was glancing down intently, and now he swooped again to the lower levels of the *ziggurat*. When he returned, he carried a brazier in one unprotected hand, the embers still glowing a dull red. Although her fingers were shaking, she had undone the leaves; now he took the incense from her, and threw all of it into the brazier. Dense, sweet-smelling smoke surrounded them, obscuring the stars above them, and below, all the world she knew, her Babylon. He took her hand again, and as if the moon had risen, the smoke lightened around them, to daylight, though it was hours away. His other hand moved as if he wove, like a woman at her loom.

"What are you doing?"

"There are lines here that lead to Babylon's futures. But they break, fork, rejoin . . . "

Futures, she thought. *More than one*. From the look of it, his weavings were not easy work. His muscles tensed, he clicked his beak irritably. Slowly around them shapes formed, at first as inchoate as any smoky whorl that a diviner could read to have meaning. Then she gasped, as the shapes suddenly solidified into the clarity of the experienced, either in the waking world or in the dream. They looked down on Babylon in dawn light, its great gates closed, the walls bristling with armed men. Towards the city advanced the chariots and spears of an advancing army.

"As beautiful as an army with banners," he said. "Except if they are someone else's army. Have you ever heard of King Sennacherib of the Assyrians? Your children's children's children will. He will come like a wolf upon the sheepfold, to sack and burn Babylon."

She flinched a moment, yet kept her grip on his strong hand.

"Now watch what you could do about it, if you had the power of *Khemeia*."

A crack, as from the walls, lightning struck, again and again, at the Assyrian king in the leading chariot. It knocked him sideways and onto the earth, scorched and dead.

"Tapputi, you could command that lightning, if you say the word. You have all the ingredients here for it, if you knew how to mix them, make the transformation into exploding fire."

"War is the goddess Ishtar's work," she said.

"She is also the goddess of love."

Tapputi hesitated. Under their feet was the temple roof. They were within the confines of a holy place, and any apparent impiety could be fatal, even with a *lamassu* at her side.

"I worship the gods of Babylon, that is only right. I sell my incense in the temples of Ishtar and Marduk, to glorify their names. But I wear the talismans of Aruru, the divine Mother and Maker."

"So?"

"So war is not for me. And my perfumes are not made as love-charms, either."

"What do you want, then?"

"Show me your salves instead! Show me how I can cure my husband, save my daughters from the pains of childbirth, stop the river fever!"

He could have thrown his raptor head back and screamed, but that would have alerted her to the difficulty of her request. Teaching her how to make gunpowder to use against the Assyrians was easy in comparison: the Babylonians already refined one necessary ingredient, saltpeter. But medicine of the sort Tapputi craved—anesthetics, the antibiotics that would cure her husband, or the quinine to prevent Babylon's epidemics of malaria—would happen nearly two millennia in the future. The timelines were, as much as they could be, consistent as to the date. To summon such far visions would be to negotiate a web of possibilities, in which each year created more complexity: anything could happen, mostly disastrous for his purposes.

He probed, near the limits of his abilities, and struck gold: a hospital in Babylon that he could show Tapputi. It was far in the future, but a facility fully equipped, at the cutting edge of its times' medicine. Though he could only dimly perceive it, he pulled as hard as he could, bringing the vision into view. The mists re-formed, and the Mesopotamian plain came into view again, this time in the glare of midday. Now they seemed to hang in open air, no *ziggurat* below them, nor a city. Instead was desert, a mix of ruins and furious activity, as an army made a semi-permanent camp.

"Tents," she said. "Like the desert nomads."

To one side was what had drawn him to this future, the mobile field hospital, but her gaze had seized on the great war-vehicles, bigger than elephants, that propelled themselves across the sand. Ancient paving and brickwork cracked beneath them. Others, equipped with shovels at their fronts, dug into the ruins with the force of a hundred laborers, instantly making trenches, defensive positions. Men wearing clothes as pied as beasts—ochre, brown, sandy—rode the war-vehicles, shouted directions.

"These are soldiers? No armor, and dressed like barbarians! And so pale, like those slaves sent in tribute from the north, whose language nobody could understand."

As if in response, a soldier below took off his helmet, to reveal bronze-colored hair, and skin as pale as fresh milk. He wiped his brow, kicked a pebble at his feet. It flipped, revealing bird-scratches of text: cuneiform.

Tapputi drew her breath in a hard gasp. "Where are we?"

"On the site of Hammurabi's Babylon."

"Have they no respect for the law? For the great law-giver?"

"About as much as the Assyrians."

She had closed her eyes tight. "I don't want this vision! Send it away!"

Easier said than done, he thought, for the waft and web of the far future entangled them in a complex knot, from which numberless possibilities diverged. He tried to feel his way back, cautiously, but the scene of martial desecration remained fixed in front of them. He let go of Tapputi, to use both his hands; she opened her eyes, staring at him. It felt as if he, a divine being, had no more power than a fly caught in a spider's snare. Angry, he struggled, at first cautiously, then desperately, with all his strength.

A line snapped, freeing them, but at the same time sending them tumbling through clouds of incense and fleeting visions. He was just able to grab Tapputi's shawl, pulling her into his arms as they flapped through scene after scene of this unwanted future Mesopotamia.

—Another of the huge war-vehicles, attached with rope to the enormous statue of a broad shouldered, mustached man, pulling at it, trying to drag it down. A small crowd watched: recognizably Mesopotamian, with their dark hair and eyes, their olive skin.

"Why do these men look like Babylonians but dress like barbarians?" Tapputi cried.

With a crash the statue toppled, falling to the paving and cracking.

"Their god must have abandoned the city, to allow such impiety! Pulling down his statue!"

"He was . . . their king."

Same thing, her gaze said. He dipped his wings, towing her away from this vision and straight into another, in which a convoy of war-vehicles lumbered along a narrow city street. From an alleyway shot a smaller vehicle, small as a chariot, in it a young man, silent, intent, his lips moving in prayer. He struck the leading war vehicle head-on, and moments later both ignited in a massive explosion, a fiery cloud that mixed with the holy incense so densely it even obscured the tips of Azubel's wings. Tapputi screamed and Azubel turned, desperate to get them away from this malign future. He saw a gap in the smoke, a point of what might be starlight, and headed for it as fast as he could fly. Night, blessed peace, and old Babylon— prosperous, intact, and sleeping.

At the top of the *ziggurat* of Marduk again, he released her. The brazier had been kicked over, igniting the trailing fringes of Tapputi's skirt. She snuffed out the smoldering wool, her eyes wide with the witnessed horror.

"That chariot, the one that charged. The young man in it looked like my eldest son, grown into adulthood."

Down the generations, Azubel knew, Tapputi's line would persist in Mesopotamia. But better for her not to think her distant descendant might have exploded into flame before her eyes.

"And what happened to him! It was worse than the Assyrian! Was it your *Khemeia* too?"

"Its descendant." Petrochemicals . . . She was silent, biting her lip.

"Take me home," she said. "To my house, before the sun rises. I must tend my still, and when my children wake, make their breakfast. You can keep your lightning and your *Khemeia*. I want nothing of it."

He had hoped for a bridal flight from her. Now, her hand in his again, he flew her down to her home, the courtyard. She lifted her daughter to her feet, holding the half-awake child, her eyes still drooping, in a fierce embrace. And watched him as he flew away.

He did not forget Tapputi the remaining decades of her life, but kept his distance from Babylon. He returned to Egypt, tried to shake their obsession with embalming without success. Then, because she would always be a wavelength, be attuned to him, he heard an unmistakable call from her.

He found her this time in the royal palace, in a room of her own, the door guarded by courtiers and her zealous female descendants. In the anteroom mourners were preparing for a major funeral, in rehearsal. They prostrated themselves as the King of Babylon was ushered out, having made his farewell to the greatest perfumer in the world.

He slipped past, and into her presence. She lay on a simple bedstead, but wearing all her gold jewelry. She was old now, but like a date, the wrinkles were merely a surface decoration for the great sweetness within.

He sat beside the bed, folding his wings neatly behind him.

"I did tell you the King of Babylon would want your perfumes."

She smiled, that crooked tooth again.

"Better than any divination. I even was appointed palace overseer for perfume. With an assistant to help me."

Though there never was the meeting of two minds between them, still they were pleased to see each other.

"Did anybody buy your lightning?"

"Not in this time. There was, Tapputi, nobody like you."

"I was widowed several summers after I last saw you. He died in great pain, with my hand in his."

He reached out, similarly took her withered little paw.

"He said I was the best wife a Babylonian could have. Because I was faithful when I could have saved him?"

"I could have given you more than lightning. You know that."

"But then I would not have done what I did all by myself!"

"And you did achieve much. Your fame will last forever." He will ensure—as Babylon is burnt by the Assyrians, and built up again, to face yet another set of conquerors—that in the mess of cuneiform tablets one will survive, with the name of Tapputi, the perfumer. The first distiller, and thus, the first chemist.

"It was all I wanted." She breathed, her voice becoming tired. "Not that I wasn't tempted by your knowledge. Or you. You were ever the most beautiful thing I saw."

A long silence, her breaths coming far apart now, and shallow.

"Can I touch your wing?"

In answer, he stroked it across her face. That smile again.

"Now that I have no time to use it, can I know about the lightning? And other, more peaceful knowledges you might know?"

"Is this a proposal?"

"If you want it to be so, from an old woman, then yes." Even near extremis, she could surprise him. He wrapped his wings around her, moving so that his beak was just above her own hooked nose, and her open lips. She gazed up into his eyes, gave a faint nod. He put his beak to her lips, then struck deep into her mind. In this deep kiss, the real alchemical marriage, the union of minds, knowledge passed between them, his *tirhatum* [bride price], her *sheriqtum* [dowry]. She gave him her life, in ancient Mesopotamia, the transient—yet because of that, the most intense—joy: a small girl gazing into the heart of her first flower and inhaling its scent; running alongside the Euphrates, her shawl flowing behind her like a sail; the sight of her firstborn's wet, wrinkled face; the moment of pure pleasure when her distillery began to work. He in turn gave her what it would take nearly two millennium to discover, the intricate sequence of the elements: hydrogen, helium, all the way to thorium, uranium, and beyond. A great knowledge given freely to the only mind of her era that could appreciate it.

One of these elements could have been named after Tapputi. No matter, too late now. There was a little blood on her lips, but her expression was peaceful, replete. He laid her small, heavy head down, the eyes closed, and took his leave.

Much later, the High Priestess of Ishtar—fat no longer, and also an old woman—found, when preparing the body of her friend, the great perfumer, for burial, a feather clasped in Tapputi's hand. It had a faint, indefinable, sweet, even heavenly scent. And as the priestess gaped at it, the feather vanished from view.

ꙮ

Lucy Sussex was born in New Zealand. She has edited four anthologies, including *She's Fantastical* (1995), shortlisted for the World Fantasy Award. Her award-winning fiction includes books for younger readers, and the novel, *The Scarlet Rider* (1996, to be reprinted 2014). She has five short story collections, *My Lady Tongue*, *A Tour Guide in Utopia*, *Absolute Uncertainty*, *Matilda Told Such Dreadful Lies* (a "best of"), and *Thief of Lives*. Currently she reviews weekly for the *Age* and *Sydney Morning Herald*. Her latest project is *Victorian Blockbuster: Fergus Hume and "The Mystery of a Hansom Cab"* (forthcoming).

The City: *Chicago, Illinois.*

The Magic: *When a curse lasts as long as this one—and matters to so many fans—it's time to bring in a wizard.*

CURSES

Jim Butcher

Most of my cases are pretty tame. Someone loses a piece of jewelry with a lot of sentimental value, or someone comes to me because they've just moved into a new house and it's a little more haunted than the seller's disclosure indicated. Nothing Chicago's only professional wizard can't handle—but the cases don't usually rake in much money, either.

So when a man in a two-thousand-dollar suit opened my office door and came inside, he had my complete attention.

I mean, I didn't take my feet down off my desk or anything. But I paid attention.

He looked my office up and down and frowned, as though he didn't much approve of what he saw. Then he looked at me and said, "Excuse me, is this the office of—"

"Dolce," I said.

He blinked. "Excuse me."

"Your suit," I said. "Dolce and Gabbana. Silk. Very nice. You might want to consider an overcoat, though, now that it's cooling off. Paper says we're in for some rain."

He studied me intently for a moment. He was a man in his late prime. His hair was dyed too dark, and the suit looked like it probably hid a few pounds. "You must be Harry Dresden."

I inclined my head toward him. "Agent or attorney?"

"A little of both," he said, looking around my office again. "I represent a professional entertainment corporation, which wishes to remain anonymous for the time being. My name is Donovan. My sources tell me that you're the man who might be able to help us."

My office isn't anything to write home about. It's on a corner, with windows on two walls, but it's furnished for function, not style—scuffed-up wooden desks, a couple of comfortable chairs, some old metal filing cabinets, a used wooden table, and a coffeepot that is old enough to have belonged to Neanderthals. I figured Donovan was worried that he'd exposed his suit to unsavory elements, and resisted an irrational impulse to spill my half-cup of cooling coffee on it.

"That depends."

"On what?"

"What you need and whether you can afford me."

Donovan fixed me with a stern look. I bore up under it as best I could. "Do you intend to gouge me for a fee, Mr. Dresden?"

"For every penny I reasonably can," I told him.

He blinked at me. "You . . . you're quite up front about it, aren't you?"

"Saves time," I said.

"What makes you think I would tolerate such a thing?"

"People don't come to me until they're pretty desperate, Mr. Donovan," I said, "especially rich people and hardly ever corporations. Besides, you come in here all intriguey and coy, not wanting to reveal who your employer is. That means that in addition to whatever else you want from me, you want my discretion, too."

"So your increased fee is a polite form of blackmail?"

"Cost of doing business. If you want this done on the down low, you make my job more difficult. You should expect to pay a little more than a conventional customer when you're asking for more than they are."

He narrowed his eyes at me. "How much are you going to cost me?"

I shrugged a shoulder. "Let's find out. What do you want me to do?"

He stood up and turned to walk to the door. He stopped before he reached it, read the words HARRY DRESDEN, WIZARD backward in the frosted glass, and eyed me over his shoulder. "I assume that you have heard of any number of curses in local folklore."

"Sure," I said.

"I suppose you'll expect me to believe in their existence."

I shrugged. "They'll exist or not exist regardless of what you believe, Mr. Donovan." I paused. "Well. Apart from the ones that *don't* exist except in someone's mind. They're only real *because* somebody believes. But that edges from the paranormal over toward psychology. I'm not licensed for that."

He grimaced and nodded. "In that case . . . "

I felt a little slow off the mark as I realized what we were talking about. "A cursed local entertainment corporation," I said. "Like maybe a sports team."

He kept a poker face on, and it was a pretty good one. "You're talking about the Billy Goat Curse," I said.

Donovan arched an eyebrow and then gave me an almost imperceptible nod as he turned around to face me again. "What do you know about it?"

I blew out my breath and ran my fingers back through my hair. "Uh, back in 1945 or so, a tavern owner named Sianis was asked to leave a World Series game at Wrigley. Seems his pet goat was getting rained on and it smelled bad. Some of the fans were complaining. Outraged at their lack of social élan, Sianis pronounced a curse on the stadium, stating that never again would a World Series game be played there. Well, actually he said something like, 'Them Cubs, they ain't gonna win no more,' but the World Series thing is the general interpretation."

"And?" Donovan asked.

"And I think if I'd gotten kicked out of a Series game I'd been looking forward to, I might do the same thing."

"You have a goat?"

"I have a moose," I said.

He blinked at that for a second, didn't understand it, and decided to ignore it. "If you know that, then you know that many people believe that the curse has held."

"Where the Series is concerned, the Cubbies have been filled with fail and dipped in suck sauce since 1945," I acknowledged. "No matter how hard they try, just when things are looking up, something seems to go bad at the worst possible time." I paused to consider. "I can relate."

"You're a fan, then?"

"More of a kindred spirit."

He looked around my office again and gave me a small smile. "But you follow the team."

"I go to games when I can."

"That being the case," Donovan said, "you know that the team has been playing well this year."

"And the Cubs want to hire yours truly to prevent the curse from screwing things up."

Donovan shook his head. "I never said that the Cubs organization was involved."

"Hell of a story, though, if they were."

Donovan frowned severely.

"The *Sun-Times* would run it on the front page. CUBS HIRE

PROFESSIONAL WIZARD TO BREAK CURSE, maybe. Rick Morrissey would have a ball with that story."

"My clients," Donovan said firmly, "have authorized me to commission your services on this matter, if it can be done quickly—and with the utmost discretion."

I swung my feet down from my desk. "Mr. Donovan," I said. "No one does discretion like me."

Two hours after I had begun my calculations, I dropped my pencil on the laboratory table and stretched my back. "Well. You're right."

"Of course I'm right," said Bob the Skull. "I'm always right."

I gave the dried, bleached human skull sitting on a shelf amidst a stack of paperback romance novels a gimlet-eye.

"For *some* values of right," he amended hastily. The words were conciliatory, but the flickering flames in the skull's eye sockets danced merrily.

My laboratory is in the subbasement under my basement apartment. It's dark, cool, and dank, essentially a concrete box that I have to enter by means of a folding staircase. It isn't a big room, but it's packed with the furnishings of one. Lots of shelves groan under the weight of books, scrolls, papers, alchemical tools, and containers filled with all manner of magical whatnot.

There's a silver summoning circle on the floor, and a tiny-scale model of the city of Chicago on a long table running down the middle of the room. The only shelf not crammed full is Bob's, and even it gets a little crowded sometimes. Bob is my more-or-less-faithful, not-so-trusty assistant, a spirit of intellect that dwells within a specially enchanted skull. I might be a wizard, but Bob's knowledge of magic makes me look like an engineering professor.

"Are you sure there's nothing you missed?" I asked.

"Nothing's certain, boss," the skull said philosophically. "But you did the equations. You know the power requirements for a spell to continue running through all those sunrises."

I grunted sourly. The cycles of time in the world degrade ongoing magic, and your average enchantment doesn't last for more than a few days. For a curse to be up and running since 1945, it would have had to begin as a malevolent enchantment powerful enough to rip a hole through the crust of the planet. Given the lack of lava in the area, it would seem that whatever the Billy Goat Curse might be, I could be confident that it wasn't a simple magical working.

"Nothing's ever simple," I complained.

"What did you expect, boss?" Bob said.

I growled. "So the single-spell theory is out."

"Yep," Bob said.

"Which means that either the curse is being powered by something that renews its energy—or else someone is refreshing the thing all the time."

"What about this Sianis guy's family?" Bob said. "Maybe they're putting out a fresh whammy every few days or something."

I shook my head. "I called records in Edinburgh. The wardens checked them out years ago when all of this first happened, and they aren't practitioners. Besides, they're Cub-friendly."

"The wardens investigated the Greek guy but not the curse?" Bob asked curiously.

"In 1945 the White Council had enough to do trying to mitigate the bad mojo from all those artifacts the Nazis stockpiled," I said. "Once they established that no one's life was in danger, they didn't really care if a bunch of guys playing a game got cursed to lose it."

"So what's your next move?"

I tapped my chin thoughtfully with one finger. "Let's go look at the stadium."

I put Bob in the mesh sack I sometimes tote him around in and, at his petulant insistence, hung it from the rearview mirror of my car, a battered old Volkswagen Beetle. He hung there, swinging back and forth and occasionally spinning one way or the other when something caught his eye.

"Look at the legs on that one!" Bob said. "And whew, check *her* out! It must be chilly tonight!"

"There's a reason we don't get out more often, Bob," I sighed. I should have known better than to drive through the club district on my way to Wrigley.

"I love the girls' pants in this century," Bob said. "I mean *look* at those jeans. One little tug and off they come."

I wasn't touching that one.

I parked the car a couple of blocks from the stadium, stuck Bob in a pocket of my black leather duster, and walked in. The Cubs were on the road, and Wrigley was closed. It was a good time to knock around inside. But since Donovan was evidently prepared to deny and disavow all knowledge, I wasn't going to be able to simply knock on the door and wander in.

So I picked a couple of locks at a delivery entrance and went inside. I didn't hit it at professional-burglar speed or anything—I knew a couple of guys who could open a lock with tools as fast as they could with a key—but I wasn't in any danger of getting a ticket for loitering, either. Once I was inside, I headed straight for the concourses. If I mucked around in the stadium's administrative areas, I would probably run afoul of a full-blown security system, and the only thing I could reliably do to that would be to shut it down completely—and most systems are smart enough to tip off their home security company when that happens.

Besides. What I was looking for wouldn't be in any office.

I took Bob out of my pocket so that the flickering golden-orange lights of his eyes illuminated the area in front of me. "All right," I murmured. I kept my voice down, on the off chance that a night watchman might be on duty and nearby. "I'm angry at the Cubbies and I'm pitching my curse at them. Where's it going to stick?"

"There's really no question about that, is there?" Bob asked me.

"Home plate," we said together.

I started forward, walking silently. Being quiet when you sneak around isn't difficult, as long as you aren't in any rush. The serious professionals can all but sprint in perfect silence, but the main thing you need isn't agility—it's patience and calm. So I moved out slowly and calmly, and it must have worked, because nobody raised a hue or a cry.

The empty, unlit stadium was . . . just wrong. I was used to seeing Wrigley blazing with sunlight or its lights, filled with fans and music and the smell of overpriced, fattening, and inexplicably gratifying food. I was used to vendors shouting, the constant sea-surge of crowd noise, and the buzz of planes passing overhead, trailing banners behind them.

Now Wrigley Field was vast and dark and empty. There was something silently sad about it—acres of seats with no one sitting, a green and beautiful field that no one was playing on, a scoreboard that didn't have anything on it to read or anyone to read it. If the gods and muses were to come down from Olympus and sculpt unfulfilled potential as a physical form, they wouldn't get any closer than that hollow house did.

I walked down the concrete steps and circled the infield until I could make my way to the seats behind home plate. Once there, I held Bob up and said, "What have we got?"

The skull's eyelights flared brighter for a second, and he snorted. "Oh, yeah. Definitely tied the curse together right there."

"What's keeping it going?" I asked. "Is there a ley line passing underneath or something?"

"That's a negative, boss," Bob said.

"How fresh is it?"

"Maybe a couple of days," the skull replied. "Maybe more. It's an awfully tight weave."

"How so?"

"This spell resists deterioration better than most mortal magic. It's efficient and solid—way niftier than you could manage."

"Gee. Thanks."

"I call 'em like I see 'em," Bob said cheerfully. "So either a more experienced member of the White Council is sponsoring this curse, and refreshing it every so often, or else . . . "

I caught on. "Or else the curse was placed here by a nonmortal being."

"Yeah," Bob said. "But that could be almost anything."

I shook my head. "Not necessarily. Remember that the curse was laid upon the stadium during a game in the 1945 World Series."

"Ah, yes," Bob said. "It would have been packed. Which means that whatever the being was, it could blend in. Either a really great veil or maybe a shapeshifter."

"Why?" I asked. "What?"

"Why?" I repeated. "Why would this theoretical being have put out the curse on the Cubs?"

"Plenty of beings from the Nevernever really don't need a motivation."

"Sure they do," I said. "The logic behind what they do might be alien or twisted beyond belief, but it makes sense to them." I waved my hand at the stadium. "This being not only laid a curse on a nexus of human emotional power, it kept coming back week after week, year after year."

"I don't see what you're driving at, boss."

"Whoever's doing this is holding a grudge," I said thoughtfully. "This is vengeance for a genuine insult. It's personal."

"Maybe," Bob said. "But maybe the emotional state of the stadium supercharged Sianis's curse. Or maybe after the stadium evicted Sianis, who didn't have enough power to curse anybody anyhow, someone decided to make it stick."

"Or maybe . . . " My voice trailed off, and then I barked out a short bite of laughter. "Oh. Oh, that's *funny*."

Bob spun in my hand to look up at me.

"It wasn't *Sianis* who put the whammy on the Cubs," I said, grinning. "It was the *goat*."

The Llyn y Fan Fach Tavern and Inn was located down at the lakeside at the northern edge of the city. The place's exterior screamed "PUB" as if it were trying to make itself heard over the roar of brawling football hooligans. It was all whitewashed walls and heavy timbers stained dark. The wooden sign hanging from a post above the door bore the tavern's name, and a painted picture of a leek and a daffodil crossed like swords.

I sidled up to the tavern and went in. The inside matched the outside, continuing the dark-stained theme on its wooden floors, walls, and furnishings. It was just after midnight, which wasn't really all that late, as bar scenes went, but the Llyn y Fan Fach Tavern was all but empty.

A big red-haired guy sitting in a chair by the door scowled at me. His biceps were thick enough to use steel-belted radials as armbands. He gave me the fisheye, which I ignored as I ambled on up to the bar.

I took a seat on a stool and nodded to the bartender. She was a pretty woman with jet-black hair and an obvious pride in her torso. Her white renaissance shirt had slipped entirely off both of her shapely shoulders and was only being held up by her dark leather bustier. She was busy wiping down the bar. The bustier was busy lifting and separating.

She glanced up at me and smiled. Her pale green eyes flicked over me, and the smile deepened. "Ah," she said, her British accent thick and from somewhere closer to Cardiff than London. "You're a tall one, aren't you?"

"Only when I'm standing up."

Her eyes twinkled with merry wickedness. "Such a crime. What are you drinking, love?"

"Do you have any cold beer?" I asked.

"None of that colonial piss here," she replied.

"Snob," I said, smiling. "Do you have any of McAnally's dark? McAnally's anything, really."

Her eyebrows went up. "Whew. For a moment, there, I thought a heathen walked amongst us." She gave me a full smile, her teeth very square and straight and white, and walked over to me before bending over and drawing a dark bottle from beneath the bar.

I appreciated her in a polite and politically correct fashion. "Is the show included in the price of the drink?"

She opened the bottle with an expert twist of her wrist and set it down in front of me with a clean mug. "I'm a generous soul, love," she said, winking. "Why charge when I can engage in selfless charity?"

She poured the beer into the mug and set it on a napkin in front of me. She slid a bowl of bar nuts down my way. "Drinking alone?"

"That depends on whether or not you'll let me buy one for you."

She laughed. "A gentleman, is it? Sir, you must think me all manner of tart if you think I'd accept a drink from a stranger."

"I'm Harry," I said.

"And so we are strangers no longer," she replied, and got out another bottle of ale. She took her time about it, and she watched me as she did it. She straightened, also slowly, and opened her bottle before putting it gently to her lips and taking a slow pull. Then she arched an eyebrow at me and said, "See anything else you like? Something tasty, perhaps?"

"I suppose I am kind of an aural guy at the moment," I said. "Got a minute to talk to me, Jill?"

Her smile faded swiftly. "I've never seen you in here before. How is it you know my name?"

I reached into my shirt and tugged out my pentacle, letting it fall down against my T-shirt. Jill studied that for a few seconds, then took a second look at me. Her mouth opened in a silent "ah" of understanding. "The wizard. Dresden, isn't it?"

"Harry," I said.

She nodded and took another, warier sip of her beer.

"Relax," I said. "I'm not here on Council business. But a friend of mine among the Fair Folk told me that you were the person to talk to about the Tylwyth Teg."

She tilted her head to one side, and smiled slightly. "I'm not sure how I could help you, Harry. I'm just a storyteller."

"But you know about the Tylwyth Teg."

"I know stories of them," she countered. "That's not the same as knowing them. Not in the way that your folk care about."

"I'm not doing politics between members of the Unseelie Accords right now," I said.

"But you're one of the magi," she said. "Surely you know what I do."

"I'm still pretty young, for a wise guy. And nobody can know everything," I said. "My knowledge of the Fair Folk pretty much begins and ends with the Winter and Summer Courts. I know that the Tylwyth Teg are an independent kingdom of the Wyld. Stories might give me what I need."

The sparkle returned to her eyes for a moment. "This is the first time a man I've flirted with told me that *stories* were what he needed."

"I could gaze longingly at your décolletage while you talk, if you like."

"Given how much trouble I go to in order to show it off, it would seem polite."

I lowered my eyes demurely to her chest for a moment. "Well. If I must."

She let out a full-bodied laugh, which made attractive things happen to her upper body. "What stories are you interested in, specifically?"

I grinned at her. "Tell me about the Tylwyth Teg and goats."

Jill nodded thoughtfully and took another sip of beer. "Well," she said. "Goats were a favored creature among them. The Tylwyth Teg, if treated with respect by a household of mortals, would often perform tasks for them. One of the most common tasks was the grooming of goats—cleaning out their fur and brushing their beards for Sunday morning."

I took a notebook from my duster's pocket and started making notes. "Uh-huh."

"The Tylwyth Teg were shapeshifters," Jill continued. "They're a small folk, only a couple of feet tall, and though they could take what form they wished, they usually changed into fairly small animals—foxes, cats, dogs, owls, hares, and—"

"And goats?"

She lifted her eyebrows. "And goats, aye. Though the stories can become very odd at times. More than one Welsh farmer who managed to capture a bride of the Tylwyth Teg found himself waking up to a goat beside him in his bed, or took his wife's hand only to feel the shape of a cloven hoof beneath his fingertips."

"Weregoats," I muttered. "Jesus."

"They're masters of deceit and trickery," Jill continued. "And we mortals are well advised to show them the proper respect, if we intrude upon them at all."

"What happens if we don't?"

Jill shook her head. "That would depend upon the offense, and which of the Tylwyth Teg were offended. They were capable of almost anything if their pride was wounded."

"The usual Fair Folk response?" I asked. "Bad fortune, children taken, that sort of thing?"

Jill shook her head. "Harry, love, the Queens of Winter and Summer do not kill mortals, and so frown upon their followers taking such action. But the high folk of the Tylwyth Teg have no such restrictions."

"They'd kill?" I asked.

"They can, have, and will take life in acts of vengeance," Jill said seriously. "They always respond in balance—but push them too far and they will."

"Damn," I said. "Those are some hard-core faeries."

Jill sucked in a sharp breath and her eyes glittered brightly. "What did you say?"

I became suddenly aware of the massive redhead by the door rising to his feet.

I swigged a bit of beer and put the notebook back in my pocket. "I called them faeries," I drawled.

The floorboards creaked under the weight of Big Red, walking toward me. Jill stared at me with eyes that were hard and brittle like glass. "You of all, wizard, should know that word is an insult to . . . them."

"Oh, right," I said. "*They* get real upset when you call them that." A shadow fell across me. I sipped more beer without turning around and said, "Did someone just put up a building?"

A hand the size of a Christmas ham fell onto my shoulder, and Big Red growled, "You want me to leave some marks?"

"Come on, Jill," I said. "Don't be sore. It's not as though you're trying all that hard to hide. You left plenty of clues for the game."

Jill stared at me with unreadable eyes and said nothing.

I started ticking off points on my fingers. "Llyn y Fan Fach is a lake sacred to the Tylwyth Teg over in the Old World. You don't get a lot more Welsh than that leek-and-daffodil emblem. And as for calling yourself 'Jill,' that's a pretty thin mask to cover the presence of one of the Jili Ffrwtan." I tilted my head back to indicate Big Red. "Changeling, right?"

Big Red's fingers tightened enough to hurt. I started to get a little bit concerned.

Jill held up a hand and Big Red let go of me at once. I heard the floor creaking as he retreated. She stared at me for a moment more, then smiled faintly and said, "The mask is more than sufficient when no one is looking for the face behind it. What gave us away?"

I shrugged. "Someone has to be renewing the spell laid on Wrigley Field on a regular basis. It almost had to be someone local. Once I remembered that the Fair Folk of Wales had a rather singular affinity with goats, the rest was just a matter of legwork."

She finished off the beer in a long pull, her eyes sparkling again. "And my own reaction to the insult was the cherry on top."

I drained my mug and shrugged modestly. "I apologize for speaking so crudely, lady. It was the only way I could be sure."

"Powerful, clever, *and* polite," she murmured. She leaned forward onto the bar, and it got really hard not to notice her bosom. "You and I might get along."

I winked at her and said, "You're trying to distract me, and doing it well. But I'd like to speak to someone in authority over the enchantment laid on Wrigley."

"And who says our folk are behind such a thing?"

"Your cleavage," I replied. "Otherwise, why try to distract me?"

She let out another laugh, though this one was softer and more silvery, a tinkling and unearthly tone that made my ears feel like someone with fantastic lips was blowing gently into them. "Even if they are, what makes you think that we would alter that weaving now?"

I shrugged. "Perhaps you will. Perhaps you won't. I only request, please, to speak to one with authority over the curse, to discuss what might be done about it."

She studied me through narrowed eyes for another silent moment. "I said please," I pointed out to her. "And I did buy you that beer."

"True," she murmured, and then gave me a smile that made my skin feel like I was standing close to a bonfire. She tossed her white cloth to one side and said, toward Big Red, "Mind the store for a bit?"

He nodded at her and settled back down into his chair.

The Jili Ffrwtan came out from behind the bar, hips swaying in deliciously feminine motion. I rose and offered her my arm in my best old-fashioned courtly style. It made her smile, and she laid her hand on my forearm lightly, barely touching. "This," she said, "should be interesting."

I smiled at her again and asked, "Where are we going?"

"Why, to Annwn, my love," the Jili Ffrwtan said, pronouncing it *ah-noon.* "We go to the land of the dead."

I followed the Jili Ffrwtan into the back room of the pub and down a narrow flight of stone stairs. The basement was all concrete walls and had a packed-earth floor. One wall of the place was stacked with an assortment of hooch. We walked past it while I admired the Jili Ffrwtan's shape and movement, and wondered if her hair felt as soft as it looked.

She gave me a sly look over one bare shoulder. "And tell me, young magus, what you know of my kind."

"That they are the high ladies of the Tylwyth Teg. And that they are surpassingly lovely, charming, and gracious, if you are any example, lady." *And that they could be psycho bitches from hell if you damaged their pride.*

She laughed again. "Base flattery," she said, clearly pleased. "But at least you do it well. You're quite articulate—for a mortal."

As we got farther from the light spilling from the staircase, the shadows grew thick, until she made a negligent gesture with one hand, and soft blue light with no apparent source filled the room around us. "Ah, here we are."

She stopped beside a ring of large brown mushrooms that grew up out of the floor. I extended my otherworldly senses toward the ring and could feel the quiver of energies moving through the air around the circle like a silent hum of high-tension electrical lines. The substance of mortal reality was thin here, easily torn. The ring of mushrooms was a doorway, a portal leading to the Nevernever, the spirit world.

I gave Jill a little bow and gestured with one hand. "After you, lady."

She smiled at me. "Oh, we must cross together, lest you get lost on the way." She slid her fingertips lightly down my forearm. Her warm fingers intertwined with mine, and the gesture felt almost obscenely intimate. My glands cut my brain out of every decision-making process they could, and it was an effort not to adjust my pants. The part of my head that was still on the job got real nervous right about then: There are way too many things in the universe that use sexual desire as a weapon, and I had to work not to jerk my hand away from the Jili Ffrwtan's.

It would be an awful idea to damage her pride with that kind of display.

And besides, my glands told me, *she looks great. And smells even better. And her skin feels amazing. And . . .*

"Quiet, you," I growled at my glands under my breath. She arched an eyebrow at me.

I gave her a tight smile and said. "Not you. Talking with myself."

"Ah," she said. She flicked her eyes down to below my waist and back, smirking. Then she took a step forward, drawing me into the ring of mushrooms, and the basement blurred and went away, as if the shadow of an ancient mountain had fallen over us.

Then the shadow lifted, and we were elsewhere.

It's at this point that my senses pretty much broke down.

The darkness lifted away to light and motion and music like nothing I had ever seen before—and I've been to the wildest spots in Chicago and to a couple of parties that weren't even being held inside our reality.

We stood inside a ring of mushrooms and in a cave. But that doesn't really cover it. Calling the hall of the Tylwyth Teg a cave is about the same as calling the Taj Mahal a grave. It's technically accurate, but it doesn't begin to cover it.

Walls soared up around me, walls in the shape of natural stone but somehow surfaced in the polished beauty of marble, veined with threads of silver and gold and even rarer metals, lit by the same sourceless radiance the Jili Ffrwtan had summoned back in Chicago. They rose above me on every side, and since I'd just been to Wrigley, I had a fresh perspective with which to compare them: If Wrigley was any bigger, it wasn't by much.

The air was full of music. I only call it "music" because there aren't any words adequate to describe it. By comparison to any music I'd ever heard played, it was the difference between a foot-powder jingle and a symphony by Mozart, throbbing with passion, merriment, pulsing between an ancient sadness and a fierce joy. Every beat made me feel like joining in—either to weep or to dance, or possibly both at the same time.

And the dancers . . . I remember men and women and silks and velvets and jewels and more gold and silver and a grace that made me feel huge and awkward and slow.

There aren't any words.

The Jili Ffrwtan walked forward, taking me with her, and as she went she changed, each step leaving her smaller, her clothing changing as well, until she was attired as the revelers were, in a jeweled gown that left just as much of her just as attractively revealed as the previous outfit. It didn't seem strange at the time that she should grow so much smaller. I just felt like I was freakishly huge, the outsider, the intruder, hopelessly oversized for that place. We moved forward, through the dancers, who spun and flitted out of our path. My escort kept on diminishing until I was walking half hunched over, her entire hand covering about half of one of my fingers.

She led me to the far end of the hall, pausing several times to call something in a complex, musical tongue aside to one of the other Fair Folk. We walked past a miniature table laid out with a not-at-all-miniature feast, and my stomach suddenly informed me that it had never once taken in an ounce of nutrition, and that it really was about time that I finally had something. I had actually taken a couple of steps toward the table before I forced myself to swerve away from it.

"Wise," said the Jili Ffrwtan. "Unless, of course, you wish to stay."

"It smells fine," I replied, my voice hoarse. "But it's no Burger King."

She laughed again, putting the fingers of one hand to her still proportionately impressive bosom, and we passed out of the great hall and into a smaller cavern—this one only the size of a train station. There were guards there—guards armored in bejeweled mail, faces masked behind mail veils, guards who barely came up over my knee, but guards nonetheless, bearing swords and spears and bows. They stood at attention and watched me with cold, hard eyes as we passed them. My escort seemed delightedly smug about the entire affair.

I cleared my throat and asked, "Who are we going to see?"

"Why, love, the only one who has authority over the curse upon Wrigley Field," she said. "His Majesty."

I swallowed. "The king of your folk? Gwynn ap Nudd, isn't it?"

"His Majesty will do," rang out a voice in a high tenor, and I looked up to see one of the Fair Folk sitting on a throne raised up several feet above the floor of the chamber, so that my eyes were level with his. "Perhaps even, His Majesty, sir."

Gwynn ap Nudd, ruler of the Tylwyth Teg, was tall—for his folk, anyway—broad shouldered, and ruggedly handsome. Though dressed in what looked like some kind of midnight-blue fabric that had the texture of velvet but the supple sweep of silk, he had large-knuckled hands that looked rough and strong. Both his long hair and beard were streaked with fine, symmetrical lines of silver, and jewels shone on his fingers and upon his brow.

I stopped at once and bowed deeply, making sure my head went lower than the faerie king's, and I stayed there for a good long moment before rising again. "Your Majesty, sir," I said, in my politest voice. "You are both courteous and generous to grant me an audience. It speaks well of the Tylwyth Teg as a people, that such a one should lead them."

King Gwynn stared at me for a long moment before letting out a grunt that mixed disbelief with wry satisfaction. "At least they sent one with half a sense of manners this time."

"I thought you'd like that, sire," said the Jili Ffrwtan, smiling. "May I present Harry Dresden, magus, a commander of the Order of the Grey Cloak, sometime mortal Champion of Queen Mab and Esquire of the Court of Queen Titania. He begs to speak to you regarding the curse upon the Field of Wrigley in the mortal citadel of Chicago."

"We know who he is," Gwynn said testily. "And we know why he is here. Return to your post. We will see to it that he is safely returned."

The Jili Ffrwtan curtsied deeply and revealingly. "Of course, sire." Then she simply vanished into a sparkling cloud of lights.

"Guards," King Gwynn called out. "You will leave us now."

The guards looked unhappy about it, but they lined up and filed out, every movement in sync with the others. Gwynn waited until the last of them had left the hall and the doors boomed shut before he turned back to me.

"So," he said. "Who do ye like for the Series this year?"

I blinked my eyes at him several times. It wasn't one of those questions I'd been expecting. "Um. American League, I'm kind of rooting for Tampa Bay. I'd like to see them beat out the Yankees."

"Aye," Gwynn said, nodding energetically. "Who wouldn't. Bloody Yankees."

"And in the National League," I said, "the Cubs are looking good at the moment, though I could see the Phillies pulling something out at the last minute." I shrugged. "I mean, since the Cubbies are cursed and all."

"Cursed?" Gwynn said. A fierce smile stretched his face. "Cursed, is it?"

"Or so it is widely believed," I said.

Gwynn snorted then rose and descended from his throne. "Walk with me."

The diminutive monarch walked farther back into the cavern, past his throne, and into what resembled some kind of bizarre museum. There were rows and rows of cabinets, each with shelves lined in black velvet, and walls of crystalline glass. Each cabinet had a dozen or so artifacts in it: ticket stubs were some of the most common items, though there were also baseballs here and there among them, as well as baseball cards, fan booklets, team pennants, bats, batting gloves, and fielders' gloves.

As I walked beside him, careful to keep my pace slow enough to let him dictate how fast we were walking, it dawned on me that King Gwynn ap Nudd of the Tylwyth Teg was a baseball fan—as in *fanatic*—of the original vintage.

"It was you," I said suddenly. "You were the one they threw out of the game."

"Aye," King Gwynn said. "There was business to attend, and by the time I got there the tickets were sold out. I had to find another way into the game."

"As a goat?" I asked, bemused.

"It was a team-spirit thing," Gwynn said proudly. "Sianis had made up a sign and all, proclaiming that Chicago had already gotten Detroit's goat. Then he paraded me and the sign on the field before the game—it got plenty of cheers, let me tell you. And he did pay for an extra ticket for the goat, so it wasn't as though old Wrigley's successors were being cheated the price of admission. They just didn't like it that someone argued with the ushers and won!"

Gwynn's words had taken on the heat that you can only get from an argument that someone has rehearsed to himself about a million times. Given that he must have been practicing it since 1945, I knew better than to think that anything like reason was going to get in the way. So I just nodded and asked, "What happened?"

"Before the game was anywhere near over," Gwynn continued, his voice seething with outrage, "they came to Sianis and evicted him from the park. Because, they said, his goat smelled too awful!"

Gwynn stopped in his tracks and turned to me, scowling furiously as he gestured at himself with his hands. "Hello! I was a *goat*! Goats are *supposed* to smell awful when they are rained upon!"

"They are, Your Majesty, sir," I agreed soberly.

"And I was a *flawless* goat!"

"I have no doubts on that account, King Gwynn," I said.

"What kind of justice is it to be excluded from a Series game because one has flawlessly imitated a goat!?"

"No justice at all, Your Majesty, sir," I said.

"And to say that I, Gwynn ap Nudd, I the King of Annwn, I who defeated Gwythr ap Greidawl, I the counselor and ally to gods and heroes alike, *smelled!*"

His mouth twisted up in rage. "How *dare* some jumped-up mortal ape say such a thing! As though mortals smell any *better* than wet goats!"

For a moment, I considered pointing out the conflicting logic of Gwynn both being a perfect (and therefore smelly) goat and being upset that he had been cast out of the game for *being* smelly. But only for a second. Otherwise, I might have been looking at coming back to Chicago about a hundred years too late to grab a late-night meal at BK.

"I can certainly see why you were upset and offended, Your Majesty, sir." Some of the righteous indignation seemed to drain out of him, and he waved an irritated hand at me. "We're talking about something important here, mortal," he said. "We're talking about *baseball.* Call me Gwynn."

We had stopped at the last display cabinet, which was enormous by the standards of the furnishings of that hall, which is to say, about the size of a human wardrobe. On one of its shelves was a single outfit of clothing; blue jeans, a T-shirt, a leather jacket, with socks and shoes. On all the rest were the elongated rectangles of tickets—season tickets, in fact, and hundreds of them.

But the single stack of tickets on the top shelf sat next to the only team cap I'd seen.

Both tickets and cap bore the emblem of the Cubs.

"It was certainly a serious insult," I said quietly. "And it's obvious that a balancing response was in order. But, Gwynn, the insult was given you unwittingly, by mortals whose very stupidity prevented them from knowing what they were doing. Few enough there that day are even alive now. Is it just that their children be burdened with their mistake? Surely that fact also carries some weight within the heart of a wise and generous king."

Gwynn let out a tired sigh and moved his right hand in a gesture that mimed pouring out water cupped in it. "Oh, aye, aye, Harry. The anger faded decades ago—mostly. It's the principle of the thing, these days."

"That's something I can understand," I said. "Sometimes you have to give weight to a principle to keep it from being taken away in a storm."

He glanced up at me shrewdly. "Aye. I've heard as that's something you would understand."

I spread my hands and tried to sound diffident. "There must be some way of evening the scales between the Cubs and the Tylwyth Teg," I said. "Some way to set this insult to rights and lay the matter to rest."

"Oh, aye," King Gwynn said. "It's easy as dying. All we do is nothing. The spell would fade. Matters would resume their normal course."

"But clearly you don't wish to do such a thing," I said. "It's obviously an expenditure of resources for you to keep the curse alive."

The small king suddenly smiled. "Truth be told, I stopped thinking of it as a curse years ago, lad."

I arched my eyebrows.

"How do you regard it, then?" I asked him.

"As protection," he said. "From the *real* curse of baseball."

I looked from him to the tickets and thought about that for a moment. Then I said, "I understand."

It was Gwynn's turn to arch eyebrows at me. "Do ye now?" He studied me for a time and then smiled, nodding slowly. "Aye. Aye, ye do. Wise, for one so young."

I shook my head ruefully. "Not wise enough."

"Everyone with a lick of wisdom thinks that," Gwynn replied. He regarded his tickets for a while, his hands clasped behind his back. "Now, ye've won the loyalty of some of the Wee Folk, and that is no quick or easy task. Ye've defied Sidhe queens. Ye've even stuck a thumb into the Erlking's eye, and that tickles me to no end. And ye've been clever enough to find us, which few mortals have managed, and gone out of your way to be polite, which means more from you than it would from some others."

I nodded quietly.

"So, Harry Dresden," King Gwynn said, "I'll be glad t'consider it, if ye say the Cubs wish me to cease my efforts."

I thought about it for a long time before I gave him my answer.

Mr. Donovan sat down in my office in a different ridiculously expensive suit and regarded me soberly. "Well?"

"The curse stays," I said. "Sorry."

Mr. Donovan frowned, as though trying to determine whether or not I was pulling his leg. "I would have expected you to declare it gone and collect your fee."

"I have this weird thing where I take professional ethics seriously," I said. I pushed a piece of paper at him and said, "My invoice."

He took it and turned it over. "It's blank," he said. "Why type it up when it's just a bunch of zeroes?"

He stared at me even harder.

"Look at it this way," I said. "You haven't paused to consider the upside of the Billy Goat Curse."

"Upside?" he asked. "To losing?"

"Exactly," I said. "How many times have you heard people complaining that professional ball wasn't about anything but money these days?"

"What does that have to do—"

"That's why everyone's so locked on the Series these days. Not necessarily because it means you're the best, because you've risen to a challenge and prevailed. The Series means millions of dollars for the club, for businesses, all kinds of money. Even the fans get obsessed with the Series, like it's the only significant thing in baseball. Don't even get me started on the stadiums all starting to be named after their corporate sponsors."

"Do you have a point?" Donovan asked.

"Yeah," I said. "Baseball is about more than money and victory. It's about facing challenges alone and on a team. It's about spending time with friends and family and neighbors in a beautiful park, watching the game unfold. It's . . . " I sighed. "It's about fun, Mr. Donovan."

"And you are contending that the curse is fun?"

"Think about it," I said. "The Cubs have the most loyal, diehard fan following in Major League ball. Those fans aren't in it to see the Cubs run rampant over other teams because they've spent more money hiring the best players. You know they aren't—because they all know about the curse. If you *know* your team isn't going to carry off the Series, then cheering them on becomes something more than yelling when they're beating someone. It's about tradition. It's about loyalty to the team and camaraderie with the other fans, and win or lose, just enjoying the damned game."

I spread my hands. "It's about *fun* again, Mr. Donovan. Wrigley Field might be the only stadium in professional ball where you can say that."

Donovan stared at me as though I'd started speaking in Welsh. "I don't understand."

I sighed again. "Yeah. I know."

My ticket was for general admission, but I thought I'd take a look around before the game got started. Carlos Zambrano was on the mound warming up when I sat down next to Gwynn ap Nudd.

Human size, he was considerably over six feet tall, and he was dressed in the same clothes I'd seen back at his baseball shrine. Other than that, he looked exactly the way I remembered him. He was talking to a couple of folks in the row behind him, animatedly relating some kind of tale that revolved around the incredible arc of a single game-deciding breaking ball. I waited until he was finished with the story, and turned back out to the field.

"Good day," Gwynn said to me.

I nodded my head just a little bit deeply. "And to you."

He watched Zambrano warming up and grinned. "They're going to fight through it eventually," he said. "There are so many mortals now. Too many players and fans want them to do it." His voice turned a little sad. "One day they will."

My equations and I had eventually come to the same conclusion. "I know."

"But you want me to do it now, I suppose," he said. "Or else why would you be here?"

I flagged down a beer vendor and bought one for myself and one for Gwynn.

He stared at me for a few seconds, his head tilted to one side.

"No business," I said, passing him one of the beers. "How about we just enjoy the game?"

Gwynn ap Nudd's handsome face broke into a wide smile, and we both settled back in our seats as the Cubs took the cursed field.

ᔓ

Jim Butcher, a *New York Times* bestselling author, is best known for his The Dresden Files series. *Skin Game*, the fifteenth in the series, was published last year. He's also the author of the six-book Codex Alera epic fantasy series. A new steampunk series, the Cinder Spires, is also slated. His resume includes a laundry list of skills which were useful a couple of centuries ago, and he plays guitar quite badly. An avid gamer, Butcher plays tabletop games in varying systems, a variety of video games on PC and console, and LARPs whenever he can make time for it. Jim currently resides mostly inside his own head, but his head can generally be found in his hometown of Independence, Missouri.

The City: *Los Angeles, California.*

The Magic: *A mortal hitman serves one side murderously well in a magical war . . . until he meets the enemy.*

DE LA TIERRA

EMMA BULL

The piano player drums away with her left hand, dropping all five fingers onto the keys as if they weigh too much for her to hold up. The rhythms bounce off the rhythms of what her right hand does, what she sings. It's like there's three different people in that little skinny body, one running each hand, the third one singing. But they all know what they're doing.

He sucks a narrow stream of Patrón over his tongue and lets it heat up his mouth before he swallows. He wishes he knew how to play an instrument. He wouldn't mind going up at the break, asking if he could sit in, holding up a saxophone case, maybe, or a clarinet. He'd still be here at 3:00 a.m., jamming, while the waiters mopped the floors.

That would be a good place to be at 3:00 a.m. Much better than rolling up the rug, burning the gloves, dropping the knife over the bridge rail. Figuratively speaking.

They aren't that unalike, she and he. He has a few people in his body, too, and they also know what they're doing.

The difference is, his have names.

"*¿Algo mas?*" The wide-faced waitress sounds Salvadoran. She looks too young to be let into a bar, let alone make half a bill a night in tips. She probably sends it all home to *mami*. The idea annoys him. Being annoyed annoys him, too. No skin off his nose if she's not blowing it at the mall.

He actually *is* too young to legally swallow this liquor in a public place, but of course he's never carded. A month and a half and he'll be twenty-one. Somebody ought to throw a party. "*Nada. Grácias.*"

She smiles at him. "Where you from? Chihuahua?"

"Burbank." Why does she care where he's from? He shouldn't have answered in Spanish.

"No, your people—where they from? My best friend's from Chihuahua. You look kinda like her brother."

"Then he looks like an American."

She actually seems hurt. "But everybody's from someplace."

Does she mean *everybody*, or *everybody who's brown like us?* "Yep. Welcome to Los Angeles."

He and the tequila bid each other goodbye, like a hug with a friend at the airport. Then he pushes the glass at the waitress. She smacks it down on her tray and heads for the bar. There, even the luggage disappears from sight. He rubs the bridge of his nose.

Positive contact, Chisme answers from above his right ear. Chisme is female and throaty, for him, anyway. *All numbers optimal to high optimal. Operation initialized.*

He lays a ten on the table and pins the corner down with the candle jar. He wishes it were a twenty, for the sake of the Salvadoran economy. But big tippers are memorable. He stands up and heads for the door.

Behind him he hears the piano player sweep the keys, low to high, and it hits his nerves like a scream. He almost turns—

Adrenal limiter enabled. Suppression under external control.

Just like everything else about him. All's right with the world. He breathes deep and steps out into the streetlights and the smell of burnt oil.

The bar's in Koreatown. The target is in downtown L.A. proper, in the jewelry district. Always start at least five miles from the target, in case someone remembers the unmemorable. Show respect for the locals, even if they're not likely to believe you exist.

He steps into the shadow that separates two neon window signs and slips between, fastlanes. He's down at Hill and Broadway in five minutes. He rubs the bridge of his nose again. *Three percent discharge*, says Chisme. After three years he can tell by the way it feels, but it's reflex to check.

The downtown air is oven-hot, dry and still, even at this hour, and the storm drains smell. They'll keep that up until the rains come and wash them clean months from now. He turns the corner and stops before the building he wants.

There's a jewelry store on the first floor. Security grills lattice the windows, and the light shines down on satin-upholstered stands with nothing on them. Painted on the inside of the glass is *Gold Mart/Best prices on/Gold/Platinum/ Chains & Rings*. Straight up, below the fifth floor windows, there's a faded sign in block letters: *Eisenberg & Sons.*

Time to call another of the names. He massages his right palm with his left thumb.

Magellan responds. Not with words, because words aren't what Magellan does. Against the darkness at the back of the store, white lines form like a scratchboard drawing. He knows they're not really inside the store, but his eye doesn't give a damn. The pictures show up wherever he's looking. This one is a cutaway of the building: the stairwell up the left side, the landings, the hallways on each floor. And the target, like a big lens flare . . . at the front of the fourth floor.

They're always on the *top* floor. Always. He focuses on the fifth floor of the diagram and massages his hand again. The zoom-in is so fast he staggers. *Vertical axis restored*, Chisme murmurs.

The fifth floor seems to be all storage; the white lines draw wire-frame cartons and a few pieces of broken furniture in the rooms.

Not right, not right. Top floor makes for a faster getaway, better protection from the likes of him. Ignoring strategy can only mean that the strategy has changed. He probes his upper left molar with his tongue, and Biblio's sexless whisper, like sand across rock, says, *Refreshing agent logs. Information updated at oh-two-oh-three.*

Fifteen minutes ago is good enough. He thinks through the logs, looking for surprises, new behaviors, deviations in the pattern. *Nada.* His fourth-floor sighting will be in the next update as an alert, an anomaly. He's contributed to the pool of knowledge. Whoopee for him.

He stands inside the doorway, trying to look like scenery, but every second he waits makes it worse. If the target gets the wind up, a nice routine job will have gone down the crapper. And if the neighborhood watch spooks and the LAPD sends a squad, the target will for sure get the wind up.

But it's not routine. He knows it, he's made and trained to know it. The target is not where it ought to be. The names are no help: they follow orders. Just as he does. *No te preocupes, hijo.* Do the job until it does for you; then there'll be another just like you to clean up the mess, and you'll be a note in the logs.

Blood pressure adjusted, Chisme notes. Not an admonishment, just a fact. The names give him facts. It's up to him what to do with them. To hell with the neighborhood watch. He touches thumb to middle finger on each hand, stands still, breathes from the belly. Chisme isn't the only one who can do his tune-up.

He takes the chameleon key from his pocket, casual as any guy who's left something on his desk at work—oops, yeah, officer, the wife'll kill me if I don't bring those tickets home tonight. The key looks like a brass Schlage; he could hand it to the cop and smile. But when it goes in the lock—

He feels it under his fingers, like a little animal shrugging. It's changing shape in there, finding the right notches and grooves and filling them. When it feels like a brass key again, he turns it, and the lock opens easy as a peck on the cheek.

Thirty seconds on the alarm, according to the documents in the archives of the security service that installed it. Biblio tells him what to punch on the keypad, and the display stops flashing ENTER CODE NOW and offers him a placid SYSTEM DISARMED. This part is never hard. If a target showed up in one of the wannabe mansionettes on Chandler at four in the morning, he could walk right in and the homeowner would never know.

If nothing went wrong after the walking-in part, of course.

The stairs in front of him are ill-lit, sheathed in cracked linoleum and worn rubber nail-down treads. He smells dust, ammonia, and old cigarette smoke. But not the target, not yet.

He starts up toward the next floor.

The evening before, he got an official commendation for his outstanding record. He had to go to Chateau Marmont, up the hill from Sunset, to get it, and on a Friday, too, so he had to pay ten dollars for valet parking to get his head patted. Good dog. If he could fastlane on his own time, it would solve so many problems. But hey, at least there was still such a thing as "his own time."

She was out on the patio by the pool, stretched in a lounge chair. From there a person could see a corner of the Marmont bungalow where Belushi had overdosed. He was pretty sure she knew that; they liked things like celebrity death spots.

Some of them almost anyone could recognize—if almost anyone knew to look for them. They're always perfect, of their kind. That's why so many of them like L.A., where everybody gets extra credit for looking perfect. Try going unnoticed in Ames, Iowa, looking like that.

She had wavy golden hair to her shoulders, and each strand sparkled when the breeze shifted it. She wore a blue silk halter-top, and little white shorts that showed how long and tan her legs were. She could've been one of those teen-star actresses pretending to be a forties pin-up, except that she was too convincing. She sipped at a *mojito* without getting any lipstick on the glass.

For fun, he jabbed his molar with his tongue to see if Biblio could tell him anything about her—name, age, rank. *Nada, y nada mas.* None of them were ever in the database. Didn't hurt to try, though.

"Your disposal record is remarkable," she said, with no preface.

"I do my job." He wondered what other agents' records were. He was pretty sure there were others, though he'd never met them. She didn't ask him to sit down, so he didn't.

"A vital one, I assure you." She gazed out at the view: the L.A. basin all the way to Santa Monica, just beginning to light up for the night, and a very handsome sunset. No smog or haze. Could her kind make that happen, somehow? They'd more or less made him, but he was nothing compared to a clear summer evening in Los Angeles.

She turned to look at him fully, suddenly intent. "You understand that, don't you? That your work is essential to us?"

He shrugged. A direct gaze from one of them had tied better tongues than his.

"You're saving our way of life—even our lives themselves. These others come from places where they're surrounded by ignorant, superstitious peasants. They have no conception of how to blend in here, what the rules and customs are. And their sheer numbers . . . " She shook her head. "A stupid mistake by one of them, and we could all be revealed."

"So it's a quality-of-life thing?" he asked. "I thought the problem was limited resources."

She pressed her lips together and withdrew her gaze. The evening seemed immediately colder and less sweetly scented. "Our first concern, of course. We're very close to the upper limit of the carrying capacity of this area. Already there are . . . " (she closed her tilted blue eyes for a moment, as if she had a pain somewhere) " . . . empty spots. We are the guardians of this place. If we let these invaders overrun it, they'll strip it like locusts, as they strip their native lands."

A swift movement in the shrubbery—a hummingbird, shooting from one blossom to another. She smiled at it, and he thought, *Lucky damned bird*, even though he didn't want to.

"I still don't get it," he said, his voice sounding like a truck horn after hers. "Why not help them out? Say, '*Bienvenidos*, brothers and sisters, let's all go to Disneyland?' Then show them how it's done, and send them someplace where they can have their forty acres and a mule? They're just like you, aren't they?"

She turned from the bird and met his eyes. If he thought he'd felt the force of her before, now he knew he'd felt nothing, nothing. "Have you seen many of them," she asked, "who are just like me?"

He's seen one or two who might have become like her, in time, with work. But none so perfect, so powerful, so unconsciously arrogant, so serenely *sure*, as she and the others who hold his leash.

He's on the first landing before he remembers to check the weapon. Chisme monitors that, too, and would have said something if it wasn't registering. But it's not Chisme's ass on the line (if, in fact, Chisme *has* one). Trust your homies, but check your own rifle.

He holds his left palm up in front of him in the gloom and makes a fist, then flexes his wrist backward. At the base of his palm the tiny iron needles glow softly, row on row, making a rosy light under his skin.

He used to wonder how they got the needles in there without a scar, and why they glow when he checks them, and how they work when he wants them to. Now he only thinks about it when he's on the clock. Part of making sure that he can still call some of the day his own.

When he finishes here, he'll be debriefed. That's how he thinks of it. He'll go to whatever place Magellan shows him, do whatever seems to be expected of him, and end by falling asleep. When he wakes up the needles will be there again.

He goes up the stairs quiet and fast, under his own power. If he fastlanes this close, the target will know he's here. He's in good shape: he can hurry up three flights of stairs and still breathe easy. That's why he's in this line of work now. Okay, that and being in the wrong place at the right time.

Introspection is multitasking, and multitasking can have unpleasant consequences. That's what the names are for, *hijo*. Keep your head in the job.

Half the offices here are vacant. The ones that aren't have temporary signs, the company name in a reasonably businesslike typeface, coughed out of the printer and taped to the door. Bits of tape from the last company's sign still show around the edges. The hallway's overhead fluorescent is like twilight, as if there's a layer of soot on the inside of its plastic panel.

At least it's all offices; one less problem to deal with, *grácias a San Miguel*. Plenty of the buildings on Broadway are apartments above the first two floors, with Mom and Dad and four kids in a one-bedroom with not enough windows and no air conditioning. People sleep restless in a place like that.

Which makes him wonder: why *didn't* the target pick a place like that? Why make this easier?

On the fourth floor, the hall light buzzes on and off, on and off. He feels a pre-headache tightness behind his eyebrows as his eyes try to correct, and his heart rate climbs. Is the light the reason for this floor? Does the target know about him, how he works, and picked this floor because of it?

Chisme gives his endocrine system a twitch, and he stops vibrating. He's a well-kept secret. And if he isn't, all the more reason to get this done right.

He walks the length of the hallway, hugging the wall, pausing to listen before crossing the line of fire of each closed door. He doesn't expect trouble until the farthest door, but it's the trouble you don't expect that gets you. Even to his hearing, he doesn't make a sound.

Beside the last door, the one at the front of the building, he presses up against the wall and listens. A car goes through the intersection below; a rattle on the sidewalk may be a shopping cart. Nothing from inside the room. He breathes in deep and slow, and smells, besides the dry building odors, the scent of fresh water.

He probes his right palm with his thumb, and when Magellan sends him the diagram of the fourth floor, he turns his head to line it up with the real surfaces of the building. Here's the hall, and the door, and the room beyond it. There's the target: shifting concentric circles of light, painfully bright. Unless everything is shot to hell, it's up against the front wall, near the window. And if everything *is* shot to hell, there's nothing he can do except go in there and find out.

At that, he feels an absurd relief. *We who are about to die.* From here on, it's all action, as quick as he can make it, and no more decisions. Quick, because as soon as he fastlanes the target will know he's here. He reaches down inside himself and makes it happen.

He turns and kicks the door in, and feels the familiar heat in nerve and muscle tissue, tequila-fueled. He brings his left arm up, aims at the spot by the window.

Fire, his brain orders. But the part of him that really commands the weapon, whatever that part is, is frozen.

The *coyotes* mostly traffic in the ones who can pass. After all, it's bad for business if customers you smuggle into the Promised Land are never heard from again by folks back in the old 'hood.

But sometimes, if cash flow demands, they make exceptions. *Coyotes* sell hope, after all. Unreasonable, ungratifiable hope just costs more. The *coyotes* tell them about the Land of Opportunity and neglect to mention that there's no way they'll get a piece of it.

Then the *coyotes* take their payment, dump them in the wilderness, and put a couple of steel-jackets in them before leaving.

He's done cleanup in the desert and found the dried-out bodies, parchment skin. and deformed bone, under some creosote bush at the edge of a wash. The skin was often split around the bullet holes, it was so dry. Of course, if they'd been dead, there wouldn't have been anything to find. Some that he came across could still open their eyes, or speak.

Maybe in the dark this one can pass. Maybe she looks like an undernourished street kid with a thyroid problem. In the pitch-dark below an underpass from a speeding car, maybe.

She should never have left home. She should be dying in the desert. She should be already dead, turned to dust and scattered by the oven-hot wind.

Her body looks like it's made of giant pipe cleaners. Her long, skinny legs are bent under her, doubled up like a folding carpenter's ruler, and the joints are the wrong distance from each other. Her ropy arms are wrapped around her, and unlike her legs, they don't seem jointed at all—or it's just the angle that makes them seem to curve like tentacles.

And she's white. Not Anglo-white or even albino-white, but white like skim milk, right down to the bluish shadows that make her skin look almost transparent. Fish-belly white.

Her only clothing is a plaid flannel shirt with the sleeves torn off, in what looks like size XXL Tall. It's worn colorless in places, and those spots catch the street light coming through the uncovered window. The body under the shirt is small and thin and childlike. Her head, from above, is a big soiled milkweed puff, thin gray-white hair that seems to have worn itself out pushing through her scalp.

The office is vacant. An old steel desk stands on end in the middle of the room. Empty filing cabinet drawers make a lopsided tower in a corner. Half a dozen battered boxes of envelopes are tumbled across the floor, their contents spilled and stained. But the room's alive with small bright movements.

It's water—trickling down the walls, running in little rivulets across the vinyl flooring, plopping intermittently in fat drops from the ceiling. Water from nowhere. From her.

He hears the words coming out of his mouth even as he thinks, *This isn't going to work.* "I'm here to send you back." Once one of the poor bastards becomes his job, there's no "sending back." His left arm is up, his palm turned out. He should fire.

The milkweed fluff rocks slowly backward. Her face is under it. Tiny features on an out-thrusting skull, under a flat, receding brow, so that her whole face forms around a ridge down its middle. Only the eyes aren't tiny. They're stone-gray without whites or visible pupils, deep-set round disks half the size of his palm.

She opens her little lipless mouth, but he doesn't hear anything. She licks around the opening with a pale-gray pointed tongue and tries again.

"*Eres un mortal.*"

You're a mortal. A short speech in a high, breathy little-girl voice, but long enough to hear that her accent is familiar.

He's lightheaded, and his ears are ringing. He needs adjusting. Damn it, where's Chisme?

Wait—he knows what this is. He's afraid.

She's helpless, not moving, not even paying attention. All he has to do is trigger the weapon, and she'll have a hundred tiny iron needles in her. Death by blood poisoning in thirty seconds or less—quicker and cleaner than the *coyote's* steel-jacketed rounds would have been. Why can't he fire?

He tries again, in Spanish this time—as if that will make it true. "I'm sending you back."

Something around her brows and the corners of her eyes suggests hope. She rattles into speech, but he can't make out a word of it. He recognizes it, though. It's the *Indio* language his grandmother used. He doesn't know its name; to his *abuela*, it was just speaking, and Spanish was the city language she struggled with.

He can't trust his voice, so he shakes his head at her. Does she understand that? His left arm feels heavy, stretched out in front of him.

Suddenly anger cuts through his dumb-animal fear. She's jerking him around. She found out somehow where his mother's family is from, and she's playing him with it. He doesn't have to make her understand. All he has to do is shoot her.

"You are not of the People, but you are of the land." She's switched back to Spanish, and he hears the disappointment in her voice. "You cannot send me back to something that is not there."

"Whose fault is that?" *Don't talk to her!* But he's angry.

"I do not know who it was." She shakes her head, less like a "no" than like a horse shaking off flies. "But the spring is gone. The water sank to five tall trees below the stone. The willows died when they could not reach it."

Willows and cottonwoods mark subsurface water like green surveyor's flags all through the dry country. He remembers willows around the springs in the hills behind his grandmother's village. "So you're going to move north and use up everything here, too?"

"¿*Que*?" Her white, flattened brow presses down in anger or confusion, or both. "How can I use up what is here? Is it so different here, the water and the land and the stone?"

There has to be a correct answer to that. Those who sent him after her probably have one. But he's not even sure what she's asking, let alone what he ought to answer. *Nothing, you moron.* And what did he expect her to say? "Sí, sí, I'm here to steal your stuff"? They both know why she's here. If she'd just make a move, he could trigger the weapon.

"We keep, not use. How to say . . . " She blinks three times, rapidly, and it occurs to him that that might be the equivalent, for her, of gazing into space while trying to remember something. "Protect and guard. Is it not so here? Mortals use. We protect and guard. They ask for help—water for growing food, health and strength for their children. They bring tobacco, cornmeal, honey to thank us. We smell the presents and come. Do the People not do this here?"

He tries to imagine that piece of blond perfection by the Chateau Marmont pool being summoned by the smell of cornmeal and doing favors for *campesinos*.

The word triggers his memory, like Chisme toggling his endocrine system. He recalls his last visit to his *abuela's* house, when he was eight. She was too weak to get out of bed for more than a few minutes at a time. She was crying, yelling at his mom, saying that somebody had to take the tamales to the spring. His mom said to him, as she heated water for his bath, "You see what it's like here? When your cousins call you *pocho*, you remember it's better to be American than a superstitious *campesino* like them."

He'd grown up believing that, until *they* found him, remade him, and sent him out to do their work. In that hot, moist room he feels cold all over. To hide it, he laughs. "Welcome to the Land of the Free, *chica*. No handouts, no favors, no fraternizing with the lower orders."

Her eyes darken, as if a drop of ink fell into each one. Fear surges in him again. *You should have shot her!* But tears like water mixed with charcoal well up, spill over, draw dark gray tracks on her white, sloping cheeks. "Please—it is not true, tell me so. I have nowhere to go. The machines that are loud and smell bad come and tear the trees from the soil, break mountains and take them away. They draw the water away from the sweet dark places under the earth. Poison comes into the water everywhere, how I do not know, but creatures are made sick who drink it. I tried to stay by the spring, but the water was gone, and the machines came. There was no room for me."

"There's no room for you here," he snaps. But he thinks, *You're so skinny,* Jesucristo, *you could live in a broom closet. There must be some place to fit you in.*

She shakes her head fiercely, smears the gray tears across her cheeks with her fingers. "Here there are places where the machines do not go. I know this. The People here are *inmigrantes* from the cold lands—they must know how it is. They will understand, and let us help them guard the land."

Already there are . . . empty spots, the blonde by the pool had said. But just this one little one? Would she be so bad?

No. All of his targets were each just one. Together they were hundreds. "They're guarding it from all of you, so you don't use everything up. Like locusts."

She goes still as a freeze-frame. "Mortals use. The People guard and protect. Surely they know this!"

What is she saying? "The power. Whatever it is, in the land. It's drying up."

"The People let the magic run through us like water through our fingers. We do not hoard it or hide it or wall it in. If we did, it would dry up, yes. Who told you this lie?"

"They did. The ones like you." *Have you seen many who are just like me?* he hears the blonde saying, in that voice that made everything wise and true.

She hasn't moved, but she suddenly seems closer, her eyes wider, her hair shifting like dry grass in the wind. There's no wind. He wants to back away, run.

And he remembers that night in his grandmother's house, after the fight about the tamales. He remembers being tucked up in blankets on the floor, and not being able to sleep because it stayed in his head—the angry voices, his *abuela* crying, his *mamá* cleaning up after dinner with hard, sharp movements. Nobody's mad at you, he'd told himself. But he'd still felt sick and scared. So he was awake when the *tap, tap, tap* sounded on the window across the room. On the glass bought with money his mother had sent home. And he'd raised his head and looked.

The next morning he'd told his mother he'd had a bad dream. That was how he'd recalled it ever since: a bad dream, and a dislike for the little house he never saw again. But now he remembered. That night he saw the Devil, come to take his mother and grandmother for the sin of anger. He'd frozen the scream in his throat. If he screamed, they would wake and run in, and the Devil would see them. If it took him instead, they would be safe.

What he'd seen, before he'd closed his eyes to wait for death, was a white face with a high, flattened forehead, gray-disk eyes, and a lipless mouth, and thin white fingers pressed against the glass. It was her, or one of her kind, come down from the spring looking for the offering.

"It is not true," she hisses, thrusting her face forward. "None of my kind would say that we devour and destroy. This is mortals' lies, to make us feared, to drive us away!"

He *is* afraid of her. He could snap those little pipe cleaner arms, but that wouldn't save him from her anger. It rages in the room like the dust storms that can sand paint off a car. She has to be wrong. If she isn't, then for three years he has—He had no choice. Did he? Three years of things, hundreds of them, that should have lived forever. "Your kind want you kept out," he spits back at her. "You don't get it, do you? They sent me to kill you."

He'd thought she was still before. Now she's an outcrop of white stone. He can't look away from her wide, wide eyes. Then her mouth opens and a sound comes out, soft at first, so he doesn't recognize it as laughter. "You will drive us back or kill us? You are too late. Jaguars have come north across the Rio Grande. The wild magic is here. We will restore the balance in spite of the ignorant *inmigrantes*. And when we are all strong again, they will see how weak they are alone."

She moves. He thinks she's standing up, all in one smooth motion. But her head rises, her arms shrink and disappear, her bent legs curve, coil. He's looking into her transformed face: longer, flatter, tapered, serpentine. The flyaway hair is a bush of hair-thin spines. Rising out of it are a pair of white, many-pronged antlers.

Their points scrape the ceiling above his head. The cloud of tiny iron needles fills the air between him and her and he thinks, *Did I fire?*

But by then she's behind him. There's a band of pressure around his chest. He looks down to see her skin, silver-white scales shining in the street light, as the pressure compresses his ribs, his lungs. She's wrapped around him, crushing him.

Chisme will know when he stops breathing. When it's too late. The room is full of tiny stars. She's so strong he can't even struggle, can't cry because he can't breathe. He wants so much to cry.

The room is black, and far, far away. He feels a lipless mouth brush his forehead, and a voice whisper, "*Duermes, hijo, y despiertas a un mundo mas mejór.*" The next world is supposed to be better. He hopes that's true. He hopes that's where he's going.

He lies with his eyes closed, taking stock. His ribs hurt, but he's lying on something soft. Hurt means he's not dead. Soft means he's not on the floor of that office in the jewelry district, waiting for help.

He listens for the names. Nothing. He's alone in his head.

He opens his eyes. The light is low, greenish and underwatery, and comes from everywhere at once. He's back in their hands, then.

At the foot of whatever he's lying on, a young guy looks up from a sheet of paper. Brown hair, hip-nerd round tortoiseshell glasses, Oxford-cloth button-down under a cashmere sweater under a reassuring white coat. For a second he thinks he was wrong and this is a hospital, that's a doctor.

"Hey," says the guy. "How do you feel?"

Come on, lungs, take in air. Mouth, open. "Crummy." He sounds as if his throat's full of mud.

The guy draws breath across his teeth—a sympathy noise. "Yeah, you must have caught yourself a whopper."

This one's remarkably human, meaning damned near unremarkable. But the lenses in the glasses don't distort the eyes behind them, because of course, they don't have to correct for anything. He's never seen one of them so determined to pass for normal. Is there a reason why this one's here now? Are they trying to put him at ease, off his guard?

"Actually," he answers, "it was a little kid who turned into a big-ass constrictor snake."

"Wow. Have you ever gotten a shape-changer before?"

Bogus question. The guy knows his whole history, knows every job he's done. But there's no point in calling him on it. "Yeah."

A moment of silence. Is he supposed to go on, talk it out? Is this some kind of post-traumatic stress therapy they've decided he needs? Or worse—is he supposed to apologize now for screwing up, for letting her get by him?

The guy shrugs, checks his piece of paper again. "Well, you're going to be fine now. And you did good work out there."

Careful. "Any job you can walk away from."

"Quite honestly, we weren't sure you had. Your 'little kid' put out enough distortion to swamp your connection with us. As far as we can tell it took almost thirty minutes for it to dissipate, after you . . . resolved the situation. Until then, we thought you'd been destroyed. Your handlers were beside themselves."

Handlers—the names. He wonders what "beside themselves" looks like for Chisme and Biblio and Magellan, or whatever those names are when they aren't in his head. He's never heard emotion out of any of them.

He stares at the young guy, handsome as a soap-opera doctor. He starts to laugh, which hurts his ribs. Has he dealt with shape-changers before? Hell, which of them *isn't* a shape-changer? However they do it, they all look like what you want or need to see. Except the ones, bent and strange, who can't pass. "I wasn't sure I killed her."

The young guy winces. *Killed* is not a nice word to immortals, apparently. "The site was completely cleansed. Very impressive. And I assure you, I'm not the only one saying so."

"That's nice." He's never failed to take out his target before this. He doesn't know what punishment it is that he seems to have escaped. For this one moment, he feels bulletproof. "I talked to her, before I did it."

Surprise—and alarm?—on the young guy's face. "By the green earth! Are you nuts? You must have been warned against that."

"She said her kind—your kind—aren't a drain on the local resources. Or aren't supposed to be. She implied you'd forgotten how it's done."

The soap-opera features register disgust. "Just the sort of thing one of them would say. They're ignorant tree-dwellers. They have no idea how complex the modern world is. You know what they're like."

He doesn't, actually. He's supposed to kill them, not get acquainted with them. "Her folks were here first," he says, as mildly as he can.

The young guy frowns, confused. "What does that have to do with it?" He shakes his head. "Don't worry, we understand these things. We know what we're doing. You can't imagine what it would be like if we let down our guard."

Pictures come into his head—from where? A picture of jaguars, glimmering gold and black like living jewelry, slipping through emerald leaves; of blue-and-red feathered birds singing with the sweet, high voices of children; of human men and women sitting with antlered serpents and coyote-headed creatures, sharing food and stories in a landscape of plenty; of the young white-coated guy, on a saxophone, jamming with the piano player in the Koreatown bar while a deer picked its way between the tables.

"You'll be fine now," the young guy repeats. "Get some sleep. When you wake up you'll be back home. I think you can expect a week or two off—go to Vegas or something, make a holiday of it."

Of course, "get some sleep" is not just a suggestion. The guy makes a pressing-down motion, and the greeny light dims. He can feel the magic tugging at his eyelids, his brain. The young guy smiles, turns away, and is gone.

It's a good plan—but not Vegas, oh, no. He'll wake up in his apartment. He'll get up and pack . . . what? Not much. Then he'll head south. Past the border towns and the *maquiladoras*, past the giant commercial fields of cotton and tomatoes scented with chemicals and watered from concrete channels. He wonders if they'll be able to track him, if they'll even care that he's gone. For them, the world must be full of promising, desperate mortals. He'll lose the names, the senses, the fastlane, but he'll be traveling light; he won't need them. Eventually he'll get to the wild places, rocky or green, desert or forest or shore. Home of the ignorant, superstitious peasants. That's where he'll stop. He'll bake tortillas on a hot, flat stone, lay out sugar cane and tobacco.

Maybe nothing will come for them. Maybe he won't even be able to tell if anything's there. But just in case, he'll tell stories. They'll be about how to get past people like him, into the land where the magic is dying because it can't flow like water.

Then he'll move on, and do it again. Nothing makes up for the ones he's stopped, but he can try, at least, to replace them.

Sleep, child, she'd said, *and wake to a better world*. He'd thought then she'd meant the sleep of death, but if she'd wanted to kill him, wouldn't he be dead? He relaxes into the green darkness, the comforting magic. When he wakes this time, it'll be the same old world. But some morning, for someone, someday, it will be different.

Emma Bull is a science fiction and fantasy author whose best-known novel is *War for the Oaks*, one of the pioneering works of urban fantasy. She has participated in Terri Windling's Borderland shared universe, which is the setting of her novel *Finder*. Her post-apocalyptic science fiction novel *Bone Dance* was nominated for the Hugo, Nebula, and World Fantasy Awards. Bull and her husband, Will Shetterly, created the shared universe of Liavek, for which they have both written stories. There are five Liavek collections extant. Her most recent novel is Territory. Bull and Shetterly live in Minnesota.

The City: *An American city where there are animals in need of rescue. In other words:* any *American city.*

The Magic: *Malou loves animals, but she makes a connection with one lost dog that's truly magical. Unfortunately, she only has three days to find the canine's master . . . or else.*

STRAY MAGIC

DIANA PETERFREUND

You can't have this job unless you love animals, but if you love animals, it's hard to have this job. We're a no-kill shelter, but all that means is that there are some animals who are stuck here for life, wasting away in their little cages. And sometimes we're too full and we have to turn animals away, knowing they'll be taken to the county shelter, where they'll be put down after seventy-two hours.

Three days. That's how long they give them at county. Three days for their owners to find them if they're lost (which, trust me, they usually aren't), or for them to find a new home. Jeremy, my buddy over there, sends me likely candidates for adoption whenever we have space. Good dogs, adorable puppies that all have the potential to be great companions, if only they get the chance to try.

I don't know what he's thinking with this latest one, though.

There has to be some sort of mix-up. Jeremy's voice mail described her as a young golden retriever mix, but when I arrive at the shelter, the crate waiting for me outside the back door does not have a golden inside. What it contains is the most bedraggled, patchy-coated, pathetic creature I've ever seen. The dog's twelve if she's a day. What's left of her fur is a stained and dingy white.

Her eyes are bloodshot, her chocolate-and-pink nose is dry and cracked, some kind of mite's been gnawing on her floppy ears, and she's got a big old infected scrape on her belly oozing pus into the remaining mats of her hair.

Adoptable? Not in this state. I wonder what Jeremy was thinking, sending along a hopeless case like her.

I grab a leash and open up the crate door. "So you're the one who they caught out wandering on the highway, huh?" Highway dogs are the worst. This one was probably dumped by her owner because she was too old, or because she was diagnosed with some terminal illness and they didn't have the heart or the money to watch her get put down. Happens all the time out here. I guess people just delude themselves into thinking their pets are going to live out their days in a nice country farmhouse. People think this is the land of milk and honey for unwanted dogs.

Wrong. It's the land of roadkill and pound euthanasia.

The dog crushes itself against the far corner of the crate.

Typical. I see a dozen cases like this a week. Usually they're terrified, and they have a right to be.

"I'm just going to take you inside and get you some nice kibble." I grab her by the scruff of the neck and tug her out into the light.

And darn it if she's not a golden retriever. I'm so shocked, I let go of her, and she shoots off. Or tries to, anyway, as I know that trick well. I snatch up the end of the leash before it disappears, and her flight stops short. She whimpers as I haul her back, and I blink my eyes to clear them, for she's the old white dog again. Strangest thing ever.

She slumps and stops struggling as I lead her inside. The dogs in the cages start up the second I flick on the lights. I lead the newcomer to crate nineteen. "Welcome to Shelter from the Storm. I'm your host, Malou."

She beelines for the blanket in the darkest corner of the kennel and curls up, resting her head on her paws and looking at me dejectedly. Those big brown eyes are just about the saddest I've ever seen—and I work in a pet shelter, so that's saying something. Must be the eyes that got to Jeremy, though he's a pretty tough sell after eight months volunteering at county.

He fits there, though. He wants to be a vet, and they've already taught him how to spay kittens. I just do this to get my dog fix—we can't have pets at home since Carson's allergic. At least, that's what Cynthia, my stepmother, says, but my baby half brother never sneezes when I come home from the kennel covered in fur. I appealed to my dad, but since he's gone most of the time, he lets Cynthia have the final say in all home matters. So if I want to play with puppies, I have to do it at the shelter.

I guess it's better this way. I know if she'd let me I'd bring them all home. "You're going to be fine here," I say to the new dog in that high, soft voice they all like.

No I'm not. I'm doomed.

She might as well have spoken the words aloud. I swear some days I can read their thoughts—not that most of them have thoughts other than "play with me, pet me, feed me." Dogs aren't simple, but their needs are. They don't ask for much, and even then most people let them down.

"I know what will make you feel better."

Doubt it.

"Some kibble." I wonder what brand Libby, the shelter manager, managed to find on sale at the supermarket this week. The food here's not great, but it's better than nothing—which is what a lot of these dogs are used to getting.

I fill a bowl for the newcomer, then start the routine of changing papers and feeding the others. I let the socialized ones out to run around in the yard for a bit while I process our latest arrival. Libby says they adopt better with a cute name, rather than something like "Old white dog" or "Crate #19." I check on the new dog, who hasn't eaten her kibble yet. Sometimes they come in starving and will wolf down whatever they can get, and sometimes they come in too scared or too depressed to eat, especially if they think you're watching.

"What would be a good name for you?" I tap my fingers on my mouth, considering.

My name is Goneril.

The dog doesn't lift her head, but her eyes are glued to me.

"Pearl?" I ask. Something stately, I think. This is not a goofball dog.

Goneril. The thought's more insistent this time. *Goneril Aurelia Boudicca Yseult, to be exact.*

I write "Gaby" on the chart and hang it from the hook at the top of the crate.

The dog lifts her head. *Wait . . . Gaby?*

I swear, sometimes it's like they're really talking to you. "You should have seen some of the names they gave you guys before I came along. Really cheesy stuff. Cuddles. Punkin. You probably would have ended up a Snowball. I guess it helps to get you adopted, but you're too dignified for a name like that, aren't you? No matter what you're looking like now."

Wait, you can see me? The real me? She stands and bats her paw against the bars.

"Are you thirsty, girl?" I kneel to undo the crate door and grab her water dish. Gaby throws herself against it, but I hold it closed. See? I know all their tricks.

You understand me! She sits and her whiplike tail flops once on the concrete floor. I let go of the door. There's something seriously weird going on with this dog . . .

And you see the real me, too. Gaby stands now and moves into the thin shaft of sunlight that slices across the back corner of the crate.

I fall back on my butt. This can't be real. There's the old white dog, but then, in flickers like a broken filmstrip, I can see bits of golden retriever, hanging in scraps. I watch in shock as the dog hoses her golden flank back into place. As soon as she moves, it slips again.

It's the glamour. It's fading. Every spell my master put on me is breaking.

"The glamour?" I whisper, hardly believing the words coming out of my mouth. I am answering the dog. Because . . . she's talking to me.

Gaby bounds back over to the door. Her tail comes out from between her legs, and her eyes aren't quite as filled with despair.

"What are you, Gaby?" I ask.

Goneril.

"Goneril."

I'm a dog.

A talking dog. A talking dog who sometimes looks like a young, well-groomed golden retriever, and sometimes . . . doesn't. "You're not like most dogs I know."

I'm my master's dog. His . . . special dog.

Poor, deluded pooch. They all think they're special, until they're dumped on the side of the road.

And I've lost him.

"You mean you're lost? You wandered off?"

No! One second I was in the car with him . . . and then I wasn't.

A highway dump. I knew it.

I lost him.

And I might just have lost my mind. "How are you doing this?"

The dog—Goneril—snorts. *I told you. It's a glamour. I have all these pieces of magic I got from my master. But now that we're separated, they're falling to pieces.*

I crawl toward the kennel, too flabbergasted to speak. The dogs nearby are transfixed, too. None of the usual barking, whining, scratching, or even snoozing. Whatever's happening here, they're witnesses, too. At least the dogs prove I'm not hallucinating.

And when they're gone, Goneril continues, *I'll die.*

"Mary Louise," Jeremy singsongs into the phone when I call.

"What can I do you for?"

"What kind of game are you playing?" I snap.

Goneril paces at my feet, jabbering away. *My master—he's been using his magic to keep me alive for a good fifteen years.*

"What do you mean?" Jeremy asks. "Didn't you pick up the golden?"

“There’s no golden.” I watch as another shred of the weird golden-retriever filmstrip disintegrates off Goneril’s back.

“It’s . . . something else. And if this is some kind of practical joke, it’s cruel.”

Without him I’m done for.

Jeremy sighs. “Not another one of your ‘No pit bull’ speeches. Because first of all, you sound like a broken record, and second, there’s no way that’s a pit mix. Golden and collie maybe, or golden and spaniel—”

“It’s not a golden at all!” I cry. “And it’s not my fault that Libby is prejudiced against pits.”

Would you believe I’m thirty?

I press the mute button on my phone and look down at Goneril. “Really? That you’re two hundred and ten in dog years—*that’s* the part you think it’s hard for me to believe?”

Good point.

Jeremy’s still on mute, so I feel free to talk to the dog. “You’re saying all this stuff—the talking, the golden retriever disguise—it’s a result of some kind of spell your owner put on you? ”

Goneril starts to pant. Her tail flops twice. *My master, yes. He’s a witch.*

“I thought witches kept cats.”

She snorts. *Not mine! Cats suck.*

“Whatever breed it is,” Jeremy is saying, sounding annoyed. I turn back to the phone. “She has a sweet disposition, responds well to voice commands—seems like an excellent adoption candidate.”

The talking 210-year-old dog is still going strong. *I need to find my master to mend the spells. The glamour is unimportant—what I really need is to make sure the spell on my heart is still working. This is why you need to let me out.*

I shake my head at her. I’m not about to let this dog back on the streets—Jeremy would have my head. “I’m sorry,” I say aloud. “There’s no way that can happen.”

Goneril sighs.

So does Jeremy. “If you don’t think you can place her, I’ll take her back to the pound . . . ”

Is that manipulative or what? Jeremy knows darn well that I won’t give up a dog I can save.

But I have to get back to my master! At the rate this magic’s failing I’d guess I only have about three days.

“But you know what that means. She’ll only have three days.”

“Three days,” I say to both of them. “That’s a tall order.”

❧

That afternoon, I focus on making Goneril look as good as possible, cutting the mats out of her hair, smearing ointment on that scrape on her belly, and cleaning up her paws.

She's unimpressed. *This is a waste of time. I can't be adopted by just anyone. I need my master. My master fixed my leg, he propped up my heart, he stalled this tumor I've got in my neck.* She blinked her eyes at me. *See these peepers? No cataracts, thanks to my master's magic.*

Dogs have the most ridiculously misplaced sense of loyalty.

Libby was on a raid with Animal Services last month and she brought back horror stories. A bunch of abused animals, starving, with broken bones and open sores, and they *still* responded to their master's call.

I want to tell Goneril that her precious master dumped her by the side of the road, but I don't have the heart. If she really is going to die in three days, isn't it better that she dies thinking he loved her?

It's tough to groom her, because I keep catching sight of her glamour. It's hanging in strips all over her body. I wonder if there's some way I can arrange it better. I reach for a strip, but it slides through my fingers like smoke. I try again and just barely manage to catch hold of the end. As gently as I can, I twist it with another strip of glamour, hoping to conceal the gaps and make it look smooth and unbroken again.

Goneril watches me, her eyes narrowed. *You shouldn't be able to do that.*

I mend another shred. This would be better. All the grooming in the world wasn't going to make her real skin look right.

"Do what?"

Manipulate my glamour. I wonder if that's what happens when the magic breaks down.

"You don't know?"

Goneril hangs her head. *I never bothered much with anyone who wasn't my master. He was all I ever needed.*

I bite my tongue. What a jerk her master is, throwing her away like garbage. I always suspected that the dogs who came in here depressed or despondent knew they'd been abandoned.

I always wondered if every time their ears perked up or their tails started going at the sound of a car on the driveway, it was because they hoped it was their owners coming back for them.

Now I know for sure.

I sit back and study my handiwork. She looks a little worse for wear, but at least now she resembles the young golden retriever Jeremy said she was. "This is as good as it's going to get," I say. "Try not to move around too much. I don't want it to slip off again."

Goneril plops down. *Okay, but I'm hungry.*

"Because you didn't eat your kibble."

She cocks her head. *Kibble? Oh, you mean those desiccated little brown pebbles of meat-scented grain? I wasn't aware that was food.*

"What did you think it was?"

She considers this for a moment. *Potpourri?*

I shake my head. "No, it's kibble, and it's all we can afford around here." I wonder what her precious master had been feeding her. T-bones?

Oh. Her head goes back down. *Well, perhaps I can wait to eat until I reunite with my master.*

When pigs fly. Then again, if dogs can talk, who knows what else is out there?

She covers her nose with her paws. *And if that doesn't happen, I won't live long enough to starve.*

Libby's out of town for the weekend, so it's just me holding down the fort. It's fine, though. Gets me out of the house and away from Cynthia's lectures. By the time I return to the kennel the next day, Goneril's nearly frantic. She paws at the cage, her eyes wide with a mix of terror and hope.

Did you find my master? I've been calling for him all night but he won't come.

I rub my temples. Judging from the way the dogs in the crates nearby are hugging the sides farthest away from Goneril, it's been a tough night for everyone. "Look, Goneril, I think it's possible that you might not ever be reunited with your master."

All four paws hit the floor and she droops her head.

I can't stand it. "What about another witch? What if we found a witch to help you?"

Until my master comes back for me? Her tail starts wagging.

"Sure," I lie.

That would work. Wag, wag. *For a little while at least. You know any witches?*

Not really.

After I do some socialization work with the puppies, give a few unfortunates their baths, check on the stitches of some of our recently spayed inmates, and redistribute the chew toys in the common space, I sit down at our ancient hulk of a computer and try to write up a description for Goneril.

Naturally, I call her Gaby. The name of a murderous Shakespearean princess just doesn't scream "adopt me" to your average pet lover. And then my hands hover over the keyboard. Breed? Should I say golden retriever? I squint at Goneril, trying to guess what lies beneath the age and glamour.

Age? If I put thirty, people will just think it's a typo. Height and weight are easy enough to fill in, and I upload the picture I took right after I arranged her glamour. But then I get to the description, and I pause again.

Finally I type:

> A very special dog in need of a good home. Gaby is quite affectionate, and seems to have been much loved by her previous owner. She is well trained, responds amazingly to voice commands, and is in search of a new owner as special and unique as she is. Please contact ASAP as Gaby cannot stay in the kennel much longer.

"Much loved," that is, until he dumped her. I scroll back to *unique*. Should I just lay my cards out on the table and write *magical?*

"Hey, Goneril, is there a word witches use when they mean magical?"

She cocks her head to the side. Her tongue's hanging out a bit. *They just say magical.*

"I mean when they're trying to keep it a secret. That they use in front of nonmagical people."

She scratches at her ear, which just has the effect of messing up her glamour again.

Right, because she never spent much time dealing with anyone who wasn't her master. I feel a fresh wave of rage at her cruel owner as I start over:

> Gaby is the most unusual animal we've ever had in this kennel. It's almost like she can communicate with you.

Exactly like it, in fact.

> Well trained, with excellent response to all voice commands.

And a few voice commands of her own.

> She needs a very special owner who can attend to her unique—

Particular? Peculiar? Extraordinary?

> —needs. If you can help Gaby, please respond ASAP.

What are you writing about me? Goneril puts her front paws up on my legs and arches to see the screen.

"Hey!" I say. "Off." She hops back down. "Besides, it's not like you can read."

Her tail stands straight in the air, indignant. *Of course I can! What good would I be to my master if I couldn't read?*

I stare at her, agog. "What do you mean? Were you a service dog? Was he blind or something?"

She cocks her head at me. *Not blind. But yes, I was in service to my master. I explained that part to you.*

"Explain it again."

She stretches her front legs out before her, sticking her butt in the air, then lies down, her head up and alert.

I was my master's special dog. I was his eyes and ears in the outside world. I spied on his neighbors, I gleaned information from his enemies, I walked among his cohorts, unseen and unnoticed, and I observed all. She yawned. *I also fetched his slippers.*

The bell over the door rings and the dogs start barking. I look up to see Jeremy strolling in, his hoodie pulled up underneath his County Animal Shelter jumpsuit. "Hey there, Malou. So where's that golden you say isn't a golden?"

I point at Goneril, who now looks every inch the golden, at least out of the corner of my eye. "Here. Hey, what's the word they use for a witch's cat?"

"Um, 'familiar,' I think?"

I snap my fingers. "Thanks, that was driving me nuts." He leans down and scratches Goneril behind the ear. Her glamour stays firmly put. She edges away from him and bares her teeth. I can only see it underneath the glamour, though. The golden retriever part of her is still panting happily.

This is the guy that put me in the cage.

I position my fingers over the keyboard again.

> Goneril is the most unusual and yet familiar animal we've ever had here at our kennel. She's definitely far more than she appears to be at first glance! A retired service dog, she's beautifully trained. It's almost like she can communicate with you. She requires an extraordinary owner who can attend to her unique needs. If you can help Goneril, please respond ASAP. Time is of the essence!

There. That's the best I can do. Maybe any witch who happens upon this listing will take note of the unusual name and the word familiar and read between the lines.

But though I'll never tell Goneril, the chance that a witch will come looking for an animal on our website is pretty slim.

"You're a real cutie," Jeremy is saying. "How could someone dump you on the side of the road, huh, girl?"

I wasn't left on the side of the road. Goneril's tail thumps in indignation. *My master would never leave me.*

Jeremy leans on the desk. "So, what're you doing tonight, Malou? Couple kids from school are going into town to see that new spy movie. Any interest?"

I put a checkmark next to "housebroken" and another next to "good with kids" on the Web form. "No thanks," I say. "My dad and I are going to go see that next time he comes home."

Jeremy gives me a skeptical glance. "Think it'll still be out then?"

I raise my eyes to his over the top of the monitor. "What are you getting at, Jeremy?"

He steps back, his hands up in surrender. "Nothing. I just hadn't heard any news about him coming home soon."

"Well, he is," I snap. Lordy, I sound like Goneril, whining about her stupid master. My dad's job takes him away from home a lot. It's not his fault he doesn't get back much, and that when he does, he's always really busy with Carson and Cynthia.

After all, Carson's a baby. And a boy. He needs his daddy far more than I do.

"Whatever you say." He sticks his hands in his pockets. "So why you asking about witches?"

"Know where I can find some?"

He grins. "Does your stepmother count?" He does a little drumroll against the desk. "Ba dum bum ching!"

Goneril paws at my leg. *Malou, is your stepmother a witch? Is that why you can touch my glamour? Did she teach you?*

I roll my eyes. "No. What she is starts with a *b*."

Jeremy grins wider. If he got rid of that scraggly soul patch, I'd almost think he was cute.

Suddenly Goneril starts hacking away.

"Got a hairball, pup?" Jeremy asks, but I'm horrified.

Beneath the glamour, I can see she's in real distress. There's bile and pus trailing from her mouth, and her limbs are shaking and seizing.

I scoop her up and carry her back to her crate as she shudders in my arms, gasping for breath. "Here, have some water." But when I set her down, her paws buckle beneath her. She lies on her side, panting, her eyes rolling up in her head.

"Is she choking?" Jeremy appears over my shoulder. "She looks okay to me." Why can't he see through the glamour like I can?

"Shh, it's okay," I say softly, stroking her flank.

Master, Goneril sobs. *Master, where are you? I didn't mean to lose you. Please come back. Please, Master.*

I bite my lip and look away.

Jeremy looks at me and back to Goneril. "Do you think she's sick? Is that an infection on her belly? Want me to call the emergency vet?"

No vets. Goneril gives my hand a pathetic little swipe with her tongue. *I need my master.*

Or a witch. How in the world am I going to find this poor dog a witch? I hate her master. If he didn't want her anymore, couldn't he have just taken her spells off while she slept? Let her die in her home?

"She'll be okay," I say to Jeremy. "I put some ointment on that scrape. I think it was just a hairball, like you said."

Jeremy clucks his tongue. "Poor girl." He's quiet for a moment as I stroke Goneril, who's still trembling. "You know, Malou, we don't have to go to the movies."

"Huh?" Of course we don't. I wonder where witches go.

Renaissance Faires? Magic shops? Is there a solstice or something coming up soon?

"We could do something else," he's saying now. "If you wanted."

I look up at him. "A farmers' market."

Jeremy's eyes widen. "Really?"

"Yeah. They have them in town on Sundays, right?" Witches might go to something like that. They need to buy . . . herbs and stuff. For potions.

"Um . . . yeah. You want to go to a farmers' market?" His tone is incredulous.

"I want to hold an adoption event there," I say. "Tomorrow."

"Oh." Why does he sound so down about the idea? Jeremy loves organizing those things. "Okay. I guess I'll see if my boss can get us some space. And the banner. How many dogs you think you want to bring?"

"Three or four." And Goneril will be one of them. "Thanks, Jeremy," I say, returning my attention to the sick dog. "You're the best."

"Yeah." I don't hear him leave, because in my head, Goneril is crying for her master.

❧

By Sunday morning she's a mess. I sit outside the shelter with my four chosen dogs, waiting for Jeremy to swing by with his van.

Aside from Goneril, I picked an adorable adolescent beagle, a tan hound with sad eyes and a wiggly butt, and a glossy black spaniel mix I think would be perfect for a young family. Aside from Goneril, they're gorgeous, well socialized, and eminently adoptable. They're all wearing bright yellow vests with ADOPT ME! printed on them in blue letters. The three normal dogs are straining at their leashes, excited to be part of our outing.

Goneril is lying on the ground, getting mud on her vest and occasionally letting out a wheezing gasp.

I'm worried about her. She still hasn't eaten, and this morning her water bowl was filled to the brim. There was blood on the blanket in her kennel, and she limps as she walks. I wonder what Jeremy will see when he looks at her. Even if I can find a witch at the farmers' market, will they be willing to fix her master's broken spells and make her well again?

Jeremy pulls round with the van and we load the dogs into the waiting crates. He's brought along two tortoiseshell kittens, a Rottweiler I just know he's going to try to pawn off on our shelter if any of my charges get adopted, and a terrier puppy I bet gets snatched up first out of all of them.

"This one?" he asks as I lift Goneril gingerly into her crate.

"You sure?"

Goneril's glamour is looking raggedy again. "You were the one who said she was such a good adoption candidate." My tone is sharp, and Jeremy just sucks air in between his teeth and finishes fastening the straps to hold the crates in place.

Most of the dogs nap on the way, but Goneril sleeps fitfully, whimpering out loud and calling out for her master in a way that breaks my heart.

"Where did you find that golden again?" I ask Jeremy.

He shrugs. "Out wandering the highway. Another dumped dog. Wonder why—she seems well trained. Came right over to me."

She was probably hoping he'd take her back to her master.

"Bet it was some yuppies who didn't want her after they had kids." Jeremy's voice hisses as he speaks. That's a common excuse, and this is a common game of ours—theorizing about the cavalier actions of our rescue dogs' former owners.

"Maybe it was someone who lost his home and couldn't afford to keep his dog," I suggest. Much as I hate Goneril's old master, I can't help but think he must have been in dire straits to give up on a companion of thirty years.

"Maybe he was sick and couldn't keep her," Jeremy replies.

"Maybe the *dog* is sick," I say. "Maybe she has a terminal illness and he couldn't handle the vet bills."

Jeremy gives me a look. "Maybe you shouldn't take her to an adoption event until we have a vet check her out."

"Too late now," I mumble. He's right, of course. Libby would never allow this—it's completely against shelter policy to put a sick dog up for adoption. But Goneril doesn't need to be adopted—she just needs to find a witch to fix her spells. Like, *now.*

The drive into town is about forty-five minutes, and once we're there we set up shop near the end of a row of vegetable and plant peddlers. Across the aisle from us, someone is selling hand-dyed silk scarves. She's got one wrapped around her head like a fortune-teller. If I'm going to find Goneril a witch, this is the spot. Jeremy sets out the portable dog run and we put a few chew toys and pallets inside. Most of the dogs are happy to stretch their legs and bound around the enclosure, wagging their tails and barking hello at passersby. Goneril slumps, panting hard. Beneath the glamour, I can see that her eyes are clouded over with cataracts. She's frothing at the mouth a bit—it's pink, which makes me think she's coughing up blood again.

I set down a water dish in front of her. "Are you all right?"

She leans hard against my hand for a moment. *This is day three.*

"I know. Don't worry. We'll find someone who can help you." I scratch her behind the ears, and her hair comes off in my hands. She's nearly bald now.

She leans against me even harder. *I wish . . . I just wish I could see my master one more time before I die. I miss him so.*

"You're not going to die," I lie.

I remember when I first became his. She closes her eyes for a moment and her tongue lolls out of the corner of her mouth. *I was just a puppy. Looked a lot more like my glamour, all golden and beautiful.*

She's not white, I realize with a start. She's just older than most dogs ever get a chance to become. I've seen old dogs with white muzzles. Goneril had gone entirely white.

"Just rest," I tell her. "And let me know if you . . . feel any witches nearby."

They'll feel me—they'll notice my glamour. But I can't sense anyone but my master.

If her master dares show his face here after what he did, he'll need all his magic to protect himself from me.

Jeremy and I take our stations. He mans the enclosure, answering questions about the dogs, while I take the beagle for a stroll, distributing brochures and keeping an eye out for anyone who looks particularly witchy.

Problem is, I don't know exactly what I'm looking for. Flowing clothing? A pointed hat? A magic wand? I stop one lady in black with dangly crystal earrings and try to talk her into checking out our dogs, but she insists she's allergic to all animals. I approach a dude trailing a cart piled high with herbs in pots, only to discover he's a horticulture professor at the local college.

Maybe we should have tried a Renaissance Faire after all.

Halfway through the market, I return to the booth to switch places with Jeremy, who's grinning.

"I got the golden to buck up," he says proudly.

I look over at Goneril. She's not exactly bouncy, but she is sitting calmly on a sheepskin pallet near the front of the enclosure, observing the crowd. "How?"

"Picked her up a pig's ear from the butcher three booths down." Jeremy tugs on the string of my jacket. "You can pay me back later."

And then off he goes, armed with a stack of brochures about animal rescue, and the roly-poly terrier. The beagle I was trotting around decides to snooze under my chair.

"Do you feel better?" I ask Goneril.

A little. At least I'll die with a good last meal.

Maybe she was just starving. Maybe all this talk about dying without her master is some kind of doggy hypochondria.

Goneril looks over the other dogs. The poor Rottweiler is standing right at the border of the enclosure, offering a pathetic paw to every person who pauses (and probably freaking a good half of them out). The spaniel is demonstrating her best "roll over" technique.

"Do you know any tricks?"

Like parlor tricks?

"Um, sure."

She yawns. *I can cast a sacred circle, of course. I can go invisible for short periods, especially during the full moon. Let's see . . . I can read divination bones. My master made me learn to keep me from eating them—*

"I mean, can you shake or catch Frisbees or roll over?"

She crosses her front paws. *Well, of course. But where's the difficulty in that?*

Talking dog or not, sometimes trying to communicate with Goneril is very frustrating. "Wait, can you really go invisible?"

Goneril flickers out of existence for an instant, like the air above a hot road. *I can usually go longer, but . . . I'm not feeling up to it right now.*

"That's okay," I say. "Save your strength."

But even that show of her magic appears to be too much for Goneril, since another coughing fit overtakes her a few minutes later.

A young woman looks up from where she's filling out an application for the beagle. "What's wrong with that dog?" she asks, pointing her pen at Goneril in suspicion. "Is she sick? Are you trying to pawn off sick dogs on us?"

"No!" I cry, rushing to Goneril's side. "I think she just ate something . . . " But it's no use. As I watch, tiny cracks begin to shimmer on the surface of Goneril's glamour. They branch and multiply before my eyes, and within moments the whole thing disintegrates like a dried-up leaf. The pretty golden retriever is gone, and in its place is the balding white dog, rheumy and shuddering.

The woman gasps and drops her clipboard. A few people look over to see what's causing the commotion in the enclosure.

I throw a spare blanket over Goneril's back as the crowd looks on in dismay. Some ask questions, but I'm focused on the sound of Goneril wheezing beneath the blanket. I ignore the people crowding around until Jeremy returns, a look of concern painted across his face.

"What happened?" he asks.

"You're right," I say to him. "She's sick. We've got to get her out of here." I keep her covered up as much as possible, but Jeremy still looks suspicious.

We can't leave, Malou, Goneril is protesting weakly from beneath the blanket. *I need to find a witch. I need one now or I'll die for sure.*

"We should take her to the vet," Jeremy says. "What if it's catching? I can't let the other dogs get sick."

I nod enthusiastically. "Yes, okay. Whatever, let's just get out of here."

Goneril's too weak to walk, so I wrap her securely in the blanket and carry her back to the car. We load up the crates again and I climb into the front seat, resting the sick dog as gently as I can in my lap. As we head toward the highway, Jeremy can't stop casting glances at the bundle in my arms. "She looks . . . weird. What if it's some kind of canine Ebola or something?"

I give him a dirty look. "It's not Ebola. And, might I remind you, you were the one who brought her to me."

There's an accident near the on-ramp, so we're forced to detour through town to the next highway entrance. I honestly don't know if Goneril's going to make it back to the shelter.

Her breath is shallow and wheezy, and she's trembling all over.

The dogs in the back are awake but quiet. When I look over my shoulder they are staring at Goneril through their cage doors, their eyes glowing with unspoken knowledge. Is this what it's like at the county shelter—all the dogs in their cages, staring at one another in full awareness as the clock ticks down toward their deadlines?

Master, please. I was such a good dog for you. Where did you go?

I bend my head low and whisper comforting words into her ears. Oh, how I wish I was a witch and could fix all her spells. I'd adopt her right now, and my stepmother could just shove it.

At the next stoplight, Jeremy dares to look over again.

"Malou, it's okay."

That's when I realize I'm crying. "It's not fair," I say softly. "This poor dog never did anything, and now she's being left alone to die among strangers . . . " I look away and wipe the tears from my eyes.

Jeremy's hand is warm on my shoulder. His touch slides down my arm, and then he wraps his fingers around mine and squeezes tight. "You did the right thing," he says. "You tried your hardest. It's not your fault if people are jerks." He takes a deep breath. "There's nothing you can do if they don't realize what they have."

I meet his eyes. "You don't understand. This dog is really special."

"I understand she's really special to you. And that's enough for me."

I blink the tears out of my eyes and look at Jeremy again.

Really look at him, forgetting for a moment the stupid scraggly facial hair and that grin he likes to wear when he's teasing me. I said once that Jeremy's a tough sell when it comes to saving animals, but he arranged this whole event on a moment's notice because I asked him to. He calls about dogs he thinks will fit at the shelter as soon as he can because he knows I hate how quickly they put them down at county.

"Hey, Jeremy?"

"Yeah?"

"Did you go see that movie last night?"

He tightens his grip on the wheel and looks out over the dash. "No."

"Want to go see it with me next weekend?"

He smiles for real this time—not his teasing grin, but a real smile. "Okay," he says as the light turns green. He starts to put his foot on the accelerator again, and that's when Goneril goes nuts.

Master!

She barks. She jumps out of my lap and throws herself, hard, against the window. *MasterMasterMasterMaster*! She starts scrabbling at it, baying at the top of her lungs.

Jeremy slams on the brakes. "Whoa! What's up with her?"

"Pull over!" I shout. I grab the nearest leash and try to clip it onto Goneril's collar, but she's gone totally wild. Jeremy has hardly had a chance to put the van in park when I open the door and Goneril tumbles out, still barking her head off. She pulls me along, across a parking lot and toward a squat white building.

In our hurry, it's all I can do to make out the sign on the sliding front door as we whiz past: MEDICAL CENTER.

Goneril gallops down the corridor. She's panting and limping, but that hardly slows her down. We rush past folks in wheelchairs, doctors and orderlies and nurses. A few of them shout as we pass, but I can hardly hear their protests over the sound of Goneril screaming in my head.

Master! Master! Master! Master! Master! Master! Master! Finally we reach a door that won't open for us. Goneril begins slamming her body against it. A nurse hurries out from behind the nearby desk.

"Young lady! You can't go back there. That's our critical ward—" She stops short when she catches sight of Goneril. "It can't be," she whispers.

"What?" I ask. I try to hold Goneril back, but she's straining so hard I fear she might break the leash. "What is it?"

"It's like she knows he's in there . . . "

But it's hard to hear the nurse over the barking. Goneril's noise is almost deafening.

Let me in! Let me in! Oh please, oh please, oh please let me in!

I turn to the nurse, eyes wide. "Who's in there?"

The nurse is shaking her head in disbelief. "He was brought in last week. Bad car accident out on the highway. He's not awake often, but every time he is, he asks after his dog . . . "

Masterrrrrrrrrrrrrrrrr! The leash slips from my hands and Goneril smashes her head into the glass door, butting it over and over.

"I'm glad she got home safe."

I look at the nurse, dumbstruck. "She didn't. I don't know your patient. I'm from an animal shelter."

Goneril was right all along. She hadn't been abandoned by her owner. They'd been in an accident together, and she'd gotten lost.

The nurse worries her bottom lip. "This is so against the rules," she says, "but I make exceptions for miracles." She presses the buzzer over the door. Goneril slips through the crack. The nurse and I follow.

But she's already found him. The nurse and I hurry to the bed, where a man covered in bandages and hooked up to tubes and wires is smiling and weakly petting Goneril, who stands over him, licking his face with gusto. Her tail is wagging so fast it's a blur, and I watch in amazement as her glamour knits itself back up. In a few moments, it's so thick on her that I can't see the old white dog at all anymore.

Master! Goneril cries in ecstasy. *Master. I found you! I found you!*

"My sweet Goneril," says the man. He's middle-aged, with soft brown eyes and a gentle smile. "Yes, you found me. Good girl. Good, good girl."

The nurse checks the man's vitals, then departs, muttering something about protocol and pulling a tissue out of the pocket of her scrubs.

The man looks up at me. "Thank you for bringing her back to me, young lady." He has an odd accent. I can't quite place it.

Her name is Malou. Goneril curls up against her master. Her snout is spread into a wide doggy smile, her pink tongue lolling out as she looks at me. *She's been trying to help me find a witch to mend my spells. Of course I told her all I needed was you.*

He raises his eyebrows. "You told her?"

Yes. She didn't believe me, though. She's very stubborn, Master. Oh, and she tried to feed me something called kibble. Goneril grimaces.

"You have a way with dogs, do you?" he asks me.

"Yes, but not usually so much as with yours," I admit.

"So you do understand her." He strokes his dog, and color seems to return to his face as I watch. "That's . . . unusual."

"So's your dog."

He nods, his hands buried deep in Goneril's fur. They both look blissful. Maybe it isn't just about him keeping Goneril healthy. Maybe the magic works both ways.

I should go. After all, I've left Jeremy alone in the parking lot. I'm beginning to back away when Goneril pipes up again.

And she fixed my glamour some, Master. She's really good. Her tail flops on the bedcovers.

"She did?" The man's eyes go wide. Strange lights seem to dance inside them. Must be the painkillers. Or something.

"Please, Malou, wait."

I stop.

His stare is unnerving. He doesn't look like a man who belongs in a hospital bed. "You swear you have no . . . experience?"

"With magic?" I laugh. "No, sir."

"Then it's quite extraordinary, what you did. To manipulate another's spells is very advanced magic."

I shrug, sheepish. "I was just trying to help the dog. I'm no witch."

"I'm not so sure about that, my dear." The witch holds tight to his beautiful familiar and studies my face. "Tell me about your family."

Diana Peterfreund is the author of ten novels for adults and teens, including the four-book Secret Society Girl series (Bantam Dell); the "killer unicorn novels" *Rampant* and *Ascendant* (Harper Teen); *For Darkness Shows the Stars*, a post-apocalyptic retelling of Jane Austen's *Persuasion*; and the companion novel *Across a Star-Swept Sea*, a futuristic, gender-switched take on *The Scarlet Pimpernel*. Her critically acclaimed short stories have appeared on *Locus*'s Recommended Reading List and in *The Best Science Fiction and Fantasy of the Year*. Peterfreund lives in Washington, DC. with her family. Learn more at dianapeterfreund.com.

The City: *Chicago . . . and other places between there and Port Harcourt, Nigeria.*

The Magic: *A very unusual cab driver (with an equally unusual cab) gets a lawyer where she needs to go via a most unexpected route.*

KABU KABU

Nnedi Okorafor (Written with Alan Dean Foster)

Ngozi hated her outfit. But it was good for traveling.

Her well-worn jeans had no pockets on the back, thereby accentuating the ass she didn't have. She'd accidentally stained her white T-shirt with chocolate after stuffing too much chocolate doughnut too fast into her mouth while rushing. And she had grabbed the wrong Chuck Taylor's: her black ones would have matched better than the red. She'd overslept. Somehow, she hadn't heard her fucking alarm clock. Now she was going to be late for her plane to New York, which would make her late for her plane to London, which would cause her to miss her connection to Port Harcourt.

"Shit." She fought desperately to hail a cab. "*Shit!*" As a stress reliever, the angry repeating of the word helped to lower her blood pressure about as effectively as it did to draw something yellow with wheels closer to the curb—which was to say, not at all.

The day's disaster didn't end here. The long fingernail of her right index finger had broken and she kept scratching herself with it. Her skin was sandpaper-dry from taking a hot shower and not having time to put on lotion afterward. She had forgotten her antiperspirant. Not only did she feel that she *looked* like a pig, despite the cold outside she was sweating like one. *Wonderful,* she thought. Bronchial pneumonia would give her something to look forward to, as well.

The only saving grace was that she'd had the good sense to pack her things the night before. Her backpack, carry-on, and large suitcase were in far better shape than their owner. She stumbled out of her townhouse and dragged her things down the steps. Outside, the full moon was still visible in the early morning sky. The sun wouldn't be up for a while. Nothing like leaving for another continent after a restful night's sleep.

She saw it then. An unprepossessing vehicular miracle heading up the street in her direction. *Too much to hope for*, she thought wildly. She started jumping up and down, waving wildly and shouting. "Taxi! Oh please God, let it be a taxi!"

As it drew nearer, Ngozi first sensed and then saw that it was traveling too fast, buoyed along by a cushion of heavy-based music. She frowned. Her frantically waving hand dropped to her side and she took a step back. The cab had the sleek but stunned look of a hybrid vehicle. Might be a Toyota or Honda. In the darkness she couldn't see the logo. The car was weirdly striped green and white and lizard-like. Even from a distance she could see that the exterior was pocked with way too many dents and scuffs, like an old boxer past his prime. As it came closer, she hunted in vain for a taxi number or business logo on the passenger-side door. Neither presented itself. Instead, there was a short inscription:

Two footsteps do not make a path.

Standing in front of a fire hydrant, the only open space on the stretch of street, she gawked at the oncoming vehicle. Despite the seriousness of her situation, she made a choice that was as easy as it was quick.

"I am not," she muttered to herself, "going *near* that thing." She glanced down at her watch and bit her lip. She was out of options.

The taxi screeched to a halt, and backed up impossibly fast. Then it zigzagged crazily into the undersized and very illegal parking space before her. It was the most adept bit of parallel parking she had ever witnessed. Not to mention quasi-suicidal. Barely an inch of clearance remained in front of or behind the cab. She shook her head and chuckled. "This guy *must* be Nigerian. Just my luck." In the back of her mind she felt a twinge of caution. But she didn't have time to waste.

The driver turned his music down and jumped out, shrugging a leather jacket over his short-sleeve blue shirt to ward off the chill. He was short, squat, medium brown-skinned, and possibly in his early forties. *Definitely Igbo*, she decided.

"I take you wherever you need to go, madam," he announced grandiosely. His accent immediately confirmed Ngozi's suspicion. It was quite similar to that of her own parents.

"O'Hare," she said.

"No problem."

She hefted her backpack up and stepped to the cab's passenger door as he loaded the rest of her luggage into the trunk. "I'm running late. *Really* late."

"I see," he responded with unexpected solemnity. "Where you headed?"

She was too busy wrestling with the back passenger door to reply. She grew even sweatier. The door wasn't budging at all. Loading a traveler's baggage and taking off before he or she could get in was a widespread taxi scam everywhere in the world. The cab driver shut the trunk and smiled at her. "Let me get that for you," he said. "It doesn't open for just anyone." He was chuckling to himself as he came around and grabbed the handle.

Wrapping his fingers around the worn, smudged metal he gave it a simultaneous twist and tug. The door swung wide with a curious non-metallic *pop*. Her nose was assailed by the unexpected aromatic scent of cedar wood and oil, both in much stronger concentration than was typical for the usual generic, commercial car deodorant. She slid inside. And promptly froze.

Nestled snugly between the front seats was a large leafy potted plant. On the ceiling of the car but presently shut was a slightly askew sliding skylight. A wealth of skillfully hand-wrought rosaries and glistening cowry shell necklaces drooped from the rearview mirror. Most startlingly, the entire interior of the cab was intricately hand-inlaid with thousands upon thousands of tiny, multicolored glass beads.

"Wow," she whispered, running an open palm carefully over the car's interior. The feel was smooth but bumpy, like a golf ball turned inside-out. *This must have cost a fortune*, she thought. It was as if she had stepped inside the world's most elaborate handicraft necklace. Gazing at her unexpectedly ornate surroundings she tried to imagine someone, or even several someones, taking the time and patience to complete the intricate work of art.

Further up front was something that looked decidedly out of place in the bead-encrusted, shell-strung interior. Set into the dash beside the battered heating and air-conditioning controls was what looked like a computer installation. Rotating lazily on the screen was a three-dimensional image of a bushy ceremonial Igbo masquerade mask. At least, that's what Ngozi guessed it to be. As a choice of screensaver, it was a distinctly unsettling one. She shivered. She'd never liked masquerades. Especially the ones at certain parties back home that turned so violent people had to hold back the performers with thick ropes. The damn things were supposed to be manifestations of spirits of dead people and they looked and danced like insane monsters. Serious nightmare material.

The driver got in and slammed his door shut. If he noticed the anxiety in her expression, he chose not to remark on it.

"You never answered my question," he said. Throwing his right arm over the top of the front passenger seat, he twisted to look back at her as he started the cab. Another surprise: despite the vehicle's scruffy appearance, the engine's purr was barely audible. Definitely a hybrid, Ngozi concluded. "How do I know where to take you if you don't tell me where you're going?"

"I did." Ngozi frowned. "Didn't I say O'Hare? United Airlines. I'm, ah, going to New York."

"Got relatives there?" the man inquired. "You visiting your folks?"

"No." She wavered and finally confessed, "I . . . I'm going to Nigeria. Port Harcourt. My sister's getting married."

He grinned. "Thought so. You can't hide where you're from, *O.* Not even with those Dada dreadlocks on your head. You still an Igbo girl."

"Woman," she corrected him, growing annoyed. "Woman in a *big hurry.* I'm a lawyer, you know." *Fuck,* she thought. *Shut up, Ngozi. How much does he need to know to get me to the airport, man? Next thing he'll try to scam me out of all my money in some fiercely tricky specifically Nigerian way.*

"Ah, a big Igbo woman, then," he murmured thoughtfully.

"And I was born and raised here," she added, unable to resist. "So I'm Igbo, Nigerian, and American."

The driver laughed again. "Igbo first," he said as he shifted into drive. Jamming the accelerator, he roared out of the illegal parking space with the same lunatic adeptness with which he had darted into it. Flinching, she grabbed the back of the seat in front to steady herself and held her breath. *Oh my God, I feel like I'm in Nigeria already.*

As they accelerated out onto the street, he turned the music back up. Listening, Ngozi smiled. It was Fela Kuti, Nigeria's greatest rebel musician. She loved the song that was playing . . . "Schuffering and Shmiling." Crooning his unique command of mystery, mastery, and music, Fela spoke to her through the speakers:

"You Africans please listen as Africans
And you non-Africans please listen to me with open mind.
Ahhhh . . . "

Ngozi found herself, as always, lulled into reminiscence by his honeyed words. She thought of her father's village. Where the dirt roads became impassable every rainy season. Where any effort to improve them was thwarted by friendly thievery, lies, and jealousy. Last time she had visited her father's village with her parents and sister and their departure had been marked by a small riot. It was caused by cousins, aunts, uncles, and strangers battling into the rooms the four of them had just left. They hoped to grab whatever the "visitors from America" might have left behind.

Among the desperate, hopeful scavengers had been Ngozi's cousin who was so smart, but unable to afford medical school. And her uncle with the Hausa tribal marks on his cheeks from when he was a little boy. Those three vertical lines on each cheek had served for more than decoration. They were all that had allowed her uncle to survive the civil war of the sixties.

Ngozi let herself slump back against the surprisingly soft seat. She had not been home in three years. Chicago, America was great. But she missed Nigeria.

"I want you all to please take your minds out of this musical contraption and put your minds into any goddamn church, any goddamn mosque, any goddamn celestical, including sera-phoom and cheraboom! Now—we're all there now. Our minds are in those places. Here we go . . . "

She smiled to herself. That was Fela—West Africa's greatest anti-colonialist. Angry, obnoxious, wonderful, and thought-provoking all at the same time.

They turned onto Halsted and headed south, weaving through traffic at a high speed with an intensity and determination that earned the cab several furious honks and not a few Chicago-style curses from the startled drivers they shot past. Ngozi hung on for dear life. What ought to have been an opportunity for her to cool down was instead one for more sweating as the driver skirted airport-bound limos and huge semis by scant inches. She considered telling him to drop her off at the next stoplight. Up front he was swearing and laughing and at times it was impossible to tell one from the other. His hands worked the horn as if it were a second mouth.

Eventually he glanced up at the rearview mirror. She struggled to look back with an expression other than that of sheer terror.

"Why you wear your hair like that?"

Instantly Ngozi's fear turned to exasperation. She wasn't even in Nigeria yet and already she was getting this typical antediluvian macho shit. "Because I like it this way," she snapped. "Why do you wear *your* hair like *that*?"

"Is that any way to speak to your elder?" the cab driver commented, sounding hurt. "Miss big fancy lawyer with no ass."

Ngozi's eyes widened. Her blood pressure, already high, went up another twenty points. "What?"

The man laughed afresh. "Do you even *speak* Igbo?"

"No. Not a damn word. You got a problem with that?"

"*Ewoooo!*" he exclaimed disapprovingly. "Of course I do! You are incomplete, *sha*."

"Oh, give me a break." She rolled her eyes. "You don't know me."

Dodging around a slow bus, he took a wild turn to the left, which threw her sharply to the side. Straightening, she searched the back seat. "How come you don't have any seat belts back here?"

"What you need those for?" he asked, eying her in the mirror. "You in the back."

"Maybe because you drive like a maniac?"

"Don't worry, I get you there alive."

They had turned onto a side road flanked by uniform rows of houses marching in brownstone lockstep. None of the intersections they crossed appeared to have street signs, including the one they were rocketing along.

"Have you ever been to Nigeria, Miss?"

"Many times. A lot of my family is still there. I try to visit as often as I can."

That shut him up. She smiled. *Nigerian men and their bullshit assumptions*, she thought. Her smile vanished when the cab's speakers went *doom*! The entire vehicle shook. She clapped her hands over her ears. "*What the fuck*?" she screamed.

"Watch your language, Miss big lawyer."

"First you criticize my hair, now you criticize my language. Do I look ten years old to you?"

"Got a stop to make," he said. He fiddled with the dashboard computer, where the masquerade mask had given way to an image of a young man. "Don't worry, we won't be late."

Within a minute, they pulled up in front of one of the brownstone buildings. The man whose visage smiled from the screen was standing out front cradling a briefcase. The image on the monitor didn't convey his height and build. The man stepped up to the front window.

"Festus," the driver said. He reached out and slapped hands with the man. "What's up?"

"Can you take me over to Vee-Vee's really quick?" Festus' accent was an intriguing mélange of Nigerian and British English—and something else. Perfectly-styled jeans enveloped his long legs. A finely cut long-sleeved navy shirt could not conceal his muscled chest.

"Vee-Vee's?" Ngozi frowned as she leaned forward. "I know that place. That's too out of the way. I can't miss this flight, man!"

"Relax," the driver urged her. "I said I get you where you need to go."

Bending low, Festus peeked inside the cab. Ngozi had every intention of persuading him to find another taxi. Initially. The soft glow of street lights revealed smooth brown skin, perfect perfect lips, prominent cheekbones. Festus was utterly and unabashedly gorgeous. Her urgency dissolved like a pat of butter in hot broth.

The driver got out and opened the door for his second passenger. Ngozi felt her ears pop. She knew she should slide as far away as possible from this man, but what she wanted to do was slide closer. She swallowed hard, not moving either way.

"Hi," was all she could say.

"Hey." He held her eyes with a gaze that was more than forward. A shiver ran through her from her periwinkle-colored toenails to her "dadalocks." He pulled the door shut as the driver started the car, then turned toward her. "I'm Festus McDaniel."

Despite feeling more than a little overwhelmed, she had to laugh. "Is that your real name?"

"When I need it to be."

"Then my name is Ororo Munroe."

"Ah, an X-Men fan."

She could not have been more surprised if he had announced he was the pilot for her forthcoming flight. "You, too?"

"When I need to be," he repeated, this time punctuating it with an undisguised leer. He scooted closer. Ngozi was annoyed to find that she did not mind, especially after her edgy go-round with the cab driver. What was happening? This was not like her. Her temples were pounding. She felt her eyes closing, her lips parting.

"Hey!" the driver yelled. Her eyes snapped open. "Festus! This is my passenger. *Back off!*"

Ngozi blinked again. Her mind cleared and the throbbing in her blood faded. Festus' face was close enough to hers that she could smell his breath. It was, unexpectedly, slightly fragrant of mint. And a saltiness she could not immediately place. Not only was he the most gorgeous man she had ever seen (and she'd seen plenty), he smelled really really good.

She pressed her temples harder. *What the* hell *was I just doing?* That leer . . . Or had it been a sneer?

Whatever it was, it was still there, plastered across his face as he leaned away and stared at her. Adrift in confusion, Ngozi could have sworn she saw fangs retreating under his upper lip. What the *fuck*? She pressed herself as close to the door and as far away from him as possible.

"What goes on in your head right now?" he asked softly.

"Huh?"

"Don't mind him," the driver advised her. He was scowling at Festus as he tossed something over his right shoulder. Ngozi felt it land in her lap. "Suck on that," the driver said, watching her through his mirror. "It'll make you feel . . . more like yourself."

She looked down, found herself staring at a cherry Jolly Rancher. Her fingers worked mechanically as she unwrapped the candy and popped it in her mouth. Flushed from embarrassment, she turned to the window to avoid the other passenger's unwavering gaze. All sweetness and tartness and fake cherry-ness, the candy dissolved slowly in her mouth. She did feel better.

Having lost her attention, Festus chatted with the driver in rapid Igbo all the rest of the way to Vee-Vee's. Ngozi tried to translate what they were saying but all she caught were bits and pieces like "419," "the money," and "oyibo," which meant either "white person" or "foreigner."

It took much less time to get to Vee-Vee's than she had anticipated and she was more than a little shocked when she checked her watch. Only fifteen minutes. She attributed the accomplishment to the driver's unsurpassed, if wholly maniacal driving skills.

They pulled up to the Nigerian restaurant and the passenger eased out, his movements as supple as a dancer's. As he stepped over the curb he looked back at the cab and blew a kiss in Ngozi's direction. She winced and tried to look away, and instead found herself following him as he strode inside. As he entered, he thrust first one arm and then another into a neatly pressed suit jacket. He slipped it easily over his shoulders. He looked sharp. *Is that Armani?* she wondered. A frown creased her face. *Wait a minute. He wasn't carrying that when he got in the cab.*

"Sorry about that." The driver apologized. "But he tips well."

"Of course, he does," Ngozi mumbled, still confused. "Someone like that . . . " Her voice trailed away.

Once again the driver cranked up the music and, wonder of wonders, both passenger and driver remained silent for the duration of the drive to O'Hare. As the cab pulled up to the United Airlines terminal a check of her watch showed that she had barely a half hour before take-off. The instant the car stopped she jumped out, yanking her pack and purse after her. While the driver was unloading her large suitcase from the trunk, she fumbled in a pocket for her cell phone. It wasn't there. Her heart started pounding. She checked her purse, then her carry-on.

Passport, purse again, backpack. Underwear. Deodorant. All present and more or less accounted for. Only one thing still missing. Only one thing . . .

Obligingly, the driver helped her drag her suitcase into the cab. Then he got in the driver's seat. Soon the security people would shoo them off.

"I'll drive around," he said, when a security guard began yelling at them to move on. "You search."

She quickly unlocked her suitcase and began rummaging frantically within. Futile. She knew damn well that her cell had been in her jacket pocket. She glanced again at her watch. The numbers continued to tick away relentlessly. She had fifteen minutes left—and that is if they didn't lock the boarding gate on her.

"Where the hell?" she asked, rising hysteria in her voice. "Where the hell *is* it? No time to get another boarding pass! I can't miss this flight! I can't miss the wedding! I have to be there for her."

She had a horrible sinking feeling. She grabbed her wallet. "Credit card, credit card, come on," she whispered. She'd need that for her new boarding pass. It wasn't *there*! Her license, library card, office building ID, insurance cards, Sam's Club card, World Wildlife Foundation card, they all sat in their usual slots. Except her credit card. Inside, she screamed and frothed at the mouth. On the outside, she stayed calm.

They arrived back at the terminal and she threw open the rear door of the taxi and began searching. Seat creases, floor, under the front seat. Ten minutes left. Getting back into the car and slamming the door, she tilted her neck forward and rested her forehead against the cold metal of the hood, defeated.

"They do all this stupid crazy traditional shit," she mumbled, talking as much to herself as to the silently staring driver. "My sister was born here like me. I can't let her go through this alone."

He closed his door and looked in the rear-view mirror. "I'm sorry," he murmured. "I truly am." He paused. "The security guy is coming. We go around again?"

"Whatever," she muttered.

They drove away from the terminal. At that moment revelation dawned on her—and it was not pretty. She looked up sharply and when she met his eyes in the mirror, she knew. "You've got to be kidding!"

The driver let out a short sigh and nodded sadly, knowingly. "He isn't common, but he can be a thief."

"Festus." Stupid, she told herself. Big lawyer, she was. Uh-huh, right.

"Yep," the driver confirmed.

"*Dammit*." She screamed. "My own fault, too. I should have left earlier, given myself more time. Skipped the damn make-up."

"I've heard about the hours lawyers have to deal with," he said. "The pressures."

Ngozi couldn't bear it anymore. The tears came. She wasn't thinking about herself. Her mind was full of visions of her sister being toted around like some parcel, being forced to say things she had not been raised to believe. Her sister was marrying an Igbo man she had met in college. Fine. That was her sister's choice. It didn't mean Ngozi had to like him, and she never had. He was always making snide comments about how Ngozi was thirty-five, childless, and unmarried. Once he had even, quite deliberately, called her "Mr. Ngozi." Then he had insisted on a traditional wedding in the village for all his relatives to attend. She didn't really want to go, but she had no choice. She *needed* to be there, for her sister.

The driver continued to stare at her in the mirror, but by now she was too miserable for his steady gaze to make her any more uncomfortable than she already was. He pulled onto the side of the highway and turned around. "Look," he said, "my job is to get you where you need to go. I promised you I would do that. I—know other ways to get you where you need to be."

She wiped her nose on her sleeve, not giving a damn about the hygienic or visual consequences. "What? Like a flight from another airport? Midway?"

He shrugged. "It's sort of a . . . a private transport set-up."

She stared back at him. Heroin drop-offs, 419 scams, and all sorts of other Nigerian-oriented shady business flashed through her mind. Hadn't she already been victimized once this morning? "I'm a lawyer," she reminded him. "It's my duty to uphold the . . . "

"You want to be there for your sister, right?"

Her insides clenched. She was past desperate. "I have to be."

Her answer appeared to resolve something within him. "So we go."

She started to say something. Finally, motivated more by resignation than any real hope, she got in. "Can I use your phone to cancel my credit card and pause my cell service?"

They drove down South Wabash Avenue for ten minutes, exited onto Congress, and turned onto a small commercial road. The increasingly industrial surroundings were unnerving her anew.

"Now then: I only have one request," he told her.

She frowned. "Request? What are you talking about? What kind of 'request'?"

"Stay in my cab."

"Why would I want to . . . ?"

Doom! For the second time that morning Ngozi felt her head rattle. When her vision cleared she found herself looking toward the dashboard computer installation. The picture had reverted back to the image of the disquieting masquerade mask. She felt a fresh jolt of anxiety.

Get a hold of yourself, she thought uneasily. "You aren't picking anyone else up are you?" she asked.

"A man must make his bread," the driver said. "Don't worry. I get you there." Turning down still another side street, he slowed to a halt in front of a carwash. It was operational, but not especially busy.

"Have another passenger to pick up," he declared.

"Oh, whatever." Thoroughly beaten, Ngozi leaned back. She took a deep, deliberate, calming breath. It didn't help. With nothing to do and nothing to look forward to, she peered indifferently at the carwash. A glistening silver Mercedes emerged, paused briefly at the exit, turned left and drove off. Behind it, oversized tan and brown brushes continued to spin. She'd heard of twenty-four hour car washes, but had never had occasion to make use of one.

"So who are we . . . "

"Shhh," the driver hissed. He was staring intently at the car wash. Bemused and exhausted, Ngozi followed his eyes.

She let out a startled gasp. "Oh, great. What now?"

Then she saw. The largest spinning brushes detached itself from the interior of the car wash. Still rapidly spinning, it came toward them, as if it had officially checked out and was leaving work for the day. Ngozi trembled, unable to look away. It whipped water from itself as it approached.

"What's—what is—you see that?" Ngozi babbled. "Are you seeing . . . "

"You better move over," the driver advised her. "It's going to be a tight fit."

She gaped at him. "Say *what*?"

The apparition continued advancing toward the idling cab. Ngozi guessed it to be about seven feet tall, four feet wide. It hadn't looked that huge when it first came out. A giant spinning carwash brush. Oh sure, right, why not? Then she heard it.

"Oh shit, this isn't happening," she heard herself whisper.

Tock, tock, tock—the thumping of a small drum. Frantically she grabbed at her nearest door handle. She no longer cared where she was or where she needed to be. She was going to get the fuck out of that insane cab and away from its crazy driver and make a run for it.

The door would not open. The handle wouldn't even budge.

"Let me out!" She kept her voice as calm as she could. Looking back she saw that the giant brush was almost to the cab. Her eyes blurred with tears of terror and distress. She blinked them away. "Please, sir," she stammered. "Lemme out. *Right now*."

"Now you just take it easy, big lawyer," the driver admonished her. "She won't hurt you. She just needs a ride."

A thousand clashing, conflicting impossibilities were flying through

Ngozi's mind. That that thing approaching the cab was a masquerade. But masquerades were mythical beings. They were the spirits and ancestors. They didn't exist, except in legend.

A remnant of full moon still lingered in the sky, its baleful light now illuminating entirely too many of her surroundings. She was in a part of the city she had never seen before. No street signs. First a strange man steals her emotions and then her cell phone and credit card. And now this *thing* was going to get in the cab. With her.

It stopped outside the passenger window. Up close, so close, too close, she could see its body was a thick column of shredded raffia, pieces of cloth, and strings of red beads. She tried to open the door again. The handle wouldn't move.

"Open!" she heard herself screaming, "Plea . . . !"

A sudden breeze from nowhere filled the interior of the cab with the heady aroma of palm wine. Ngozi pressed herself against the car door, raising a leg and arm up as a shield. The creature standing outside the taxi dissolved into a rose-hued mist and came wafting slowly in through the window. Pressing against the door now, Ngozi started to laugh uncontrollably. Once fully within the cab the being rematerialized, its fragrant bulk completely filling the seat beside her and threatening to spill over onto her cringing lap.

Rough raffia scratched at Ngozi's face. At least it was dry now. The wooden head perched atop the raffia mass had a stern female face. Now it turned, slow and silent, and stared down at her. She felt every hair on her body stand on end.

"Just stay calm," the driver suggested, unperturbed. "It'll be a short ride. She's just another passenger." As he pulled away from the carwash he turned up the music again. Fela sang:

"Ever day na de same thing
Shuffering and Shmiling!"

As they drove, the masquerade shook to the beat of the music, the raffia that composed its body quivering and shaking.

When it got out of the cab ten minutes later in the parking lot of a bookstore that wasn't open for business yet, Ngozi was left half paralyzed and with nothing more to say. Her arms and right cheek sported fine scratches from the brush of the creature's leaves. And the blast of rose-colored mist the masquerade became when it exited the car had left her clothes and hair damp. Fragrant and sweet-scented, but damp.

"Chicago's a big place," the driver declared amiably. "You work graveyard, you pick up *all* kinds of immigrants who work all kinds of jobs."

Clearing her throat, Ngozi managed to find a voice. Though reduced to something like a whimper, it did resemble hers. "I want to go *home*."

The driver smiled, the driver laughed, just as he had before. "You worry too much, girl. Woman," he corrected himself. "I suppose it part of being a big lawyer. I said I'd get you there."

"Home," she croaked weakly, repeating herself. Slouching low in the seat, she grasped her short dreadlocks. *I am seriously screwed*, she thought. They were barely clear of the parking lot when the car shook yet again.

DOOM!

The image on the monitor changed to that of a rotating ax. Immediately, the driver slammed on the brakes and turned around.

"Where are we—who are you picking up now?" Her voice had turned shrill. "When am I going to get priority here? *When are you going to start listening to me?*"

"Sorry," he murmured regretfully. "Gotta pick this one up."

"Why? Why one more? Will there always be 'just one more'?" She was staring fixedly at the rotating ax on the monitor, trying to square the image with everything else that had happened this morning. Thoughts of her sister's missed wedding were receding rapidly into memory. They had been replaced by: *Will I ever be allowed to get out of this cab? And will I get out alive?*

The man stood under a street lamp on the side of Lake Shore Drive. Encouragingly, dawn was not far away, but the city lights were still on. Staring at this latest phantom, Ngozi couldn't understand why people who passed him on the highway did not use their cell phones to call the police. If she saw someone like him, she certainly would have. She started to reach into her pocket. Then she remembered that Festus guy—who was probably some sort of Nigerian vampire—had stolen her cell phone.

Of course, the driver slowed to a stop right in front of the guy on the side of the highway. The door swung open opposite her. After her ears popped, she could hear the big man breathing, even over the increasing roar of early commuters zooming by on the road. Raspy and heavy his respiration was. He was large, African, and clad in jeans and T-shirt. She couldn't tell what color the shirt was because its owner was spattered from head to toe in what could have only been blood. Once more she found herself scrambling to the far side of the seat. Digging into a pocket, she pulled out the only hard object she had in there. A pen.

Bending forward, he peered into the cab. His eyes met Ngozi's. He smirked.

"Hello there and good morning." His voice was exceptionally deep, somewhere down near the lowest register of which a human being was capable. His accent was Nigerian but very slight. His face glistened as he slid in. Ngozi shut her eyes and squeezed her hands into tight fists. The handle on her door still refused to work. She heard the worn leather beneath the beads creak as the passenger dropped his weight onto the seat. The cab filled with the coppery smell of fresh blood. He said something in Igbo to the driver.

"Sure thing," the driver responded in English, maddeningly accommodating as ever.

The man's breathing remained loud and grinding, as if he was trying to digest something in his lungs instead of his stomach. Every so often he grunted to himself. Trapped, weary, frightened, Ngozi wished the driver would turn his music up loud enough to drown out the sound of the new passenger's merciless respiration.

Not long after but far too much later, the cab finally slowed and stopped. She heard the door open and shut. Her ears popped. Cautiously, she opened her eyes. The sun was just starting to lighten the sky. Had she made her plane, she would now have been an hour closer to where she needed to be, instead of stuck and terrified in the confines of a cab not far from her townhouse. No, this wasn't even a cab. The driver didn't have a license displayed anywhere; it was probably illegal. She'd somehow wound up in a *kabu kabu* right here on the streets of greater Chicago.

"Why didn't you call the police?" She didn't have any energy left to shout.

She stared at where the passenger had been sitting. The space was stained with blood. Her stomach rolled.

"For what?" the driver asked innocently.

She managed to muster a little more volume, a smidgen more outrage. "He was covered in blood!"

"Oh, that. That's just the Butcher's preference." He was counting money as he deposited bills into the cab's lockbox.

" 'Butcher'? Butcher of what?"

"Not my place to ask," the driver replied solemnly. "He tips very very well, also. Hates my music, though. Maybe hates all music." He paused. "I take you where you need to go now. No more pick up. It's daytime anyway." He touched the screen and the image changed to that of a waving Nigerian flag.

She had given up trying to predict whether the driver meant anything he said or if she was interpreting his words correctly. She just rolled with it. When he finally slowed to a stop, she wasn't sure if they were still even in Chicago. In front of them were the remnants of what might have been an open flea market a half a century ago.

"My God. A friend of mine told me there were places like this in Chicago, but I've never seen one of them. She calls them 'dead zones.'"

"Ha!" Accelerating slowly, the driver turned the cab into a narrow alley that ran parallel to the ghost market. "Dead indeed, for sure. Lots of *wahala*, places like this. Trouble, trouble, trouble. But plenty useful to folks like me. And today, folks like you."

They drove along flanked by red brick walls. Very red. If Ngozi had not already seen all that she had seen, she would have been sure that this taxi driver, having had his fun, was taking her to a secluded place where he could dismember her at his leisure.

"Why do we have to take this way to get to this mystery airport of yours?" She struggled to keep the shakiness out of her voice.

He opened the cab's skylight. "You see the sky up there?"

It was the first time she had looked up, instead of just out, since she had first entered the cab. "Oh my," she whispered, forgetting her uncertainties. Even as the dawn sky continued to brighten, she could see millions of twinkling stars, with the plump, white, full moon perfectly framed in the rectangular opening. She inhaled sharply as she spotted a shooting star. And then another. And another. Shooting stars at twilight, she thought. What a treat. A large bird soared by, passing low and slow. It was gray with a very large beak. She thought she could see it looking at her, following her with its eyes. Impossible, of course. She was exhausted, and lapsing into anthropomorphization.

"What kind of bird was that?" she asked herself.

Gazing at the expansive, clear, waking sky filled her with more than a little sense of wonder. The weariness dropped away from her like a cheap rapa. The voice of the driver interrupted her unanticipated reverie.

"You might want to hang on for this." It sounded like a warning.

"Huh?"

The car started shuddering as the ground beneath the tires became rugged. With no seatbelt to hold her down she was thrown from side to side, the wind knocked from her lungs.

"*Biko-nu*, just hold on," he shouted over the rumble of the wheels. "It won't last long!"

The bumping became too violent for her to even speak. At any moment she expected the doors to fall off. They would be followed by the floor, the roof, the engine, and finally her seat. In addition to the deafening noise of vibration, the interior of the cab was filled with a rushing sound, as if the earth was whistling in her ears. Above it all she could still hear the rhythmic pounding of the cab's stereo, though she could no longer make out the words of the irrepressible Fela.

Almost as soon as it had commenced, the brutal jouncing stopped. When she had recovered enough to look out the window, she saw that the brick walls had been replaced by trees on both sides of the road. A park. They were driving through one of Chicago's notable parks. At any minute she expected to see the Museum of Science and Industry, or one of the colossally expensive new high-rise condos set in carefully landscaped faux natural grounds.

Up ahead the narrow, badly maintained dirt road joined a paved one. *Must be coming out of the park*, she told herself. As they drew closer she was able to make out the details of the cross traffic. She sank as far down into her seat as her shaking spine would permit.

"Good idea." The driver was watching her in the rearview. "I was going to suggest that you do exactly that."

"S-s-stop the car!"

"Don't worry." He did not slow down. "I'm known here."

The cab's tires screeched as he dug out of the dirt path and pulled onto the main road. A minute later they were stuck in the most bizarre traffic jam Ngozi had ever seen.

Monsters. Insane vehicles. Monsters riding insane vehicles. And every and all things in-between. Creatures sporting every color imaginable, and some that were not. Some insubstantial as mists, their selves half there and half elsewhere. Figments of imagination, fragments of unreality. But not of her mind. She could never have envisioned a fraction of what she was seeing.

They were all traveling, on the move, all heading somewhere. To where exactly was another question to which she did not wish to learn the answer. On the left side of the road they trekked in one direction and on the right in the opposite way. As they moved, they made sounds like the wind in the trees, the water in the river, the bees in their hives. Individual yet uniform buzzing and howling and screeching and whispering that ebbed and flowed to a rhythm only they understood.

She saw a milky gray-skinned humanoid giant walking on all fours. It had very large breasts and what Ngozi thought was a purple vagina. An equally enormous male ghost dragging an immense penis followed her closely. As Ngozi looked on, speechless and frozen by the sight, he thrust into the giant female-thing and the two continued on their way without pause, walk-crawling as they copulated.

Turning away, she found herself gazing at a small truck that looked as if it were fashioned entirely from moist eyes. Each eye stared in a single but different direction from the others. As she looked at it, one after another every one of its intense blue eyes swung around to fixate on her.

"Oh God oh God," she hissed. Shaking, holding herself, she dropped back down on the seat.

It was a position neither her spine nor her curious mind allowed her to maintain for very long. Moments later, she was up again and peeking over the lower edge of the window. Thankfully, the eyeball truck had dropped out of sight. Her cab driver had shifted into a slightly faster interior lane. As he drove on they were surrounded and hemmed in by thousands, by millions of spirits and ghosts and specters.

Some had many legs, some bounced, some drove, some sat inside things that drove. Others crawled or tumbled, flew or dragged themselves along. Shrieking madly, a skeleton woman rode by on a skeleton ostrich. A ghostly man with feet facing the wrong way sprinted swiftly backwards past the cab. A phantom woman walked by on her hands, herding before her a pack of pig-like things that were completely covered with wooly black hair.

"We all must travel," the driver said, keeping his eyes on the way ahead. His hands grasped the wheel firmly. "It is the essence of all things, to move and change and keep going forward and backward and around. Even the spirits and the dead."

He had turned the stereo down low. Clearly, this was not a place where one wanted to aggravate one's fellow travelers. Ngozi tried to concentrate on the muted music as she spoke a silent prayer to whatever gods were hopefully watching over her. She had long since turned her back on Christianity, but she was not an atheist, either. In this moment and in this place, atheism was a joke. She closed her eyes. She didn't want to *see* anymore.

Time passed. Long minutes, or maybe it was a short hour. Unable to keep them closed any longer, she finally opened her eyes. They were on a wide road now.

And alone.

"You see," the driver told her confidently. "We were just passing through." He sighed. "Traffic can be a problem anywhere."

Outside the cab, the terrain looked nothing like Chicago, a city park, or even the far south suburbs. It did not look like any place she had been. The road ahead was old and worn out. The soil on the side of the road was red instead of brown. In place of oak and pine she saw palm, iroko, mahogany, and oboche trees.

Something finally came unhinged in her brain. It was all too much, she'd had more than enough of a morning unreal. Twisting around on the seat, she kicked at the car window as hard as she could. Part of her wanted to stop, but a larger part craved the hopeful tinkle of shattering glass. Her foot merely left a print on the window.

"Ah, what are you doing?" The driver screamed and the cab took a sudden swerve.

"Where are you taking me?" she screamed. "I can't stand this anymore! I'm going crazy! Let me out! Let me out!"

"Where do you think I'm taking you? I'm taking you where you need to be! Are you stupid? Big lawyer?"

Staring wide-eyed at the latest manifestation of impossible surroundings, which happened to be a stretch of palm trees, Ngozi fought to get herself under control. "This can't be," she whimpered. "It can't be."

"If it can't be then how we be here? Lighten up," he instructed her. "I said I get you where you have to go—and I will."

Ngozi shut her eyes. She opened them. "Stop the car."

He glanced at her in the rearview mirror but kept going. She took a very deep breath. "*Stop the fucking car!*" she screamed loud enough to strain the lining of her throat.

He pulled over at a crossroads. Tentatively, she tried the door handle. It turned so easily she almost sprained her wrist. She stared at it.

"It's open." He turned around in his seat. "What did you expect?"

She narrowed her eyes at him. Gripping the handle hard, she pushed. It opened effortlessly. Her ears popped and a rush of warm, humid air caressed her face. Before anything else could happen, she jumped out of the car.

She just stood there.

The sun beat down hard, the heat and light heavy and hot on her skin. A different kind of sun. The air smelled different, too. She sniffed a hint of distant burning wood. A subtle, invisible, but nonetheless very real shift ran through her entire being, like ripples from a stone cast in flat water. She knew where she was.

"But—how . . . ?"

Wordlessly, the driver got out of the cab.

She knelt down and touched the ground. She rubbed the red dirt between her fingers. On the road, occasional cars zoomed by. As if this was all normal.

"Are you coming back in?" He was standing behind her now.

She grabbed a rock, rose, turned, and threw it at him. A part of her wanted the stone to hit him square between the eyes. "All I wanted was a goddamn ride to O'Hare!" she screamed.

"You can't always get what you want." He smiled. That same, damnable smile. "But if you try sometimes . . . "

"Don't you dare finish that . . . "

His smile widening, he sang the last part of the annoying Rolling Stones song, " . . . you get what you nee-eed!"

Bending, she found and threw another stone at him, aiming for the knees. This time she had better luck, and he had less. He let out a yelp and grabbed at himself where the rock had hit. The tide of satisfaction that flowed through her was brief.

"So you do feel pain," she snapped. "Well, that's good. At least you're not some fucking demon."

"Spoken like a true American girl—woman—I must say." He winced, rubbing the bruise he was going to have. "Are you going to get back in the cab, so we can finish this trip and you can pay me?"

"No."

They were silent, staring hard at each other. She felt as if she had just finished two triathlons in a row. Without food. Across Death Valley. Or maybe been chased around the world. Unexpectedly, she found that she had to stifle a sudden urge to laugh.

Cautiously, the driver stepped closer. "Do you trust me?"

Let's see now, she thought. *I got in your cab under the pretense that you would have me at O'Hare airport in half an hour. Instead, I shared the passenger seat with a thieving vampire, a shedding masquerade, some kind of bloody-man butcher, was driven through the traffic of Hell or the Highway Styx or whatever. And now here I am.* Alive. Alive, and more or less well.

"Holy shit, I'm in Nigeria," she said wonderingly.

He held the door open for her as she slowly slid into the back seat. Smiling as he did so, of course. She looked at her watch. The hands pointed to the same time it had been when she left, give or take a half hour. "That can't be right," she mumbled.

Somehow she was not surprised to learn that they were only a short distance from her village. Shouts of joy and wide grins of happiness from three of her aunties greeted her when she stepped out. As the driver unloaded her big suitcase she saw that other guests were also disembarking from cabs similar in appearance to the one that had brought her to the site of her sister's wedding.

Seeing the shock and jubilation on her younger sister's face was worth everything Ngozi had gone through to make it home. Almost. Excusing herself, Ngozi paid the driver.

"Just for the equivalent of the trip to the airport," he told her. "A flat fee. I give you ten percent discount for when I carried other passengers. No charge for the . . . time travel." He smiled that enigmatic smile. "I don't have a meter anyway. No point in putting one in a cab like mine, is there?"

Then other relatives noticed her, and she found herself swarmed with questions, concerns, and love. When she looked back, the cab was gone.

Something on the ground caught her eye. Bending, she picked it up, and grinned. It was a tiny bright red bead. One of the thousands that had decorated the interior of the cab. She doubted the driver would miss it. He seemed to have a good business, and would be otherwise occupied.

"We thought you'd call before you traveled. We were worried about you," her cousin Emeka said as he took her suitcase and carry-on and escorted her to the compound's main house.

"Sorry," she told him. "I got up late and forgot to call before leaving. Then, well, I took some weird Nigerian unlicensed cab, it got kind of crazy."

"Ah, a Naijameican-style kabu kabu." He nodded knowingly. "I hear those can be bad business."

They stopped in the shade of the house. "Emeka, this might sound like a stupid question . . . but am I too late? For the wedding? My watch says . . . well, I don't know how long I was *really* in that, ah, kabu kabu."

Emeka looked at her oddly. "Too late? No, no. The wedding isn't until tomorrow. You are a day early, Ngozi."

She stared at him, then looked down at her watch. So it wasn't broken. That driver. That crazy smiling fucking driver. He was busy, all right. He really had lost track of the time.

∽

Nnedi Okorafor is a novelist of African-based science fiction, fantasy, and magical realism. Her award-nominated and -winning novels include *Who Fears Death*, *Akata Witch*, *Zahrah the Windseeker*, and *The Shadow*. Her children's book *Long Juju Man* is the winner of the Macmillan Writer's Prize for Africa. Her first collection of short fiction, *Kabu Kabu*, was published in 2013. Her science fiction novel *Lagoon*, and young adult novel *Akata Witch 2: Breaking Kola* are scheduled for release in 2014. Okorafor holds a PhD in Literature and is a professor of creative writing at Chicago State University. Find her on Facebook, Twitter and at nnedi.com.

The City: *An American city that resembles Seattle, or perhaps San Francisco, but is neither.*

The Magic: *Personal "Invisibles" guide, even protect, each of a band of homeless kids . . . but can anything save them when unimaginable evil appears and the mean streets of the city turn deadly?*

PEARLYWHITE

MARC LAIDLAW & JOHN SHIRLEY

The boy they called Inchy was on his way to meet his friend Clyde for breakfast down at the City Shelter, when Pearlywhite appeared on his shoulder like a wisp of ivory smoke. "Stop. Go back. Around the block." He'd found his own shelter from last night's rain and fog beneath the thrown-back lid of a dumpster in Longtree Alley, where half a dozen Asian restaurants cast out their scraps and he could usually find something to eat for dinner. Breakfast was a different story though.

Pearlywhite's sudden appearance, in the strong gray light of morning, was startlingly out of place: a small but powerful-looking dragon made of white mist that fairly shone in this light; twisting its body as smoke twists; the smoke writhing as dragons do.

Usually the smokedragon didn't show itself any earlier than twilight—and then only on the darkest days, when three o'clock felt more like dinnertime than it usually did. He wasn't used to talking to Pearlywhite when other people were around. He didn't want to look crazy; but right now no one was looking.

For the first time he noticed the tail end of a prowlcar pulled into the alley up ahead, Naiad Lane, and a muttering gathering of people crowded around the spot. Yellow police tape held them back, aided by a lady cop the kids called Officer Cat (from Catlett). "Everyone get back," she told the crowd, menacingly. It was a different tone of voice than she used on Inchy when she talked to him about getting off the street, into a program. He was always nice to her and pretended to consider her advice, but he always managed to slip away.

She hadn't seen him yet. Pearlywhite's warning had kept him from walking into her view.

"Be very careful, Inchy," said the infinitely soft voice, softer yet more penetrating than the constant rushing noise of traffic. "I want you to go back the way you came, around the block to the corner of Mawkin and Lydell."

"Whuh—" he started to say, and then noticed a pouch-faced man in a business suit staring at him as he walked up the street, away from the crowd. He didn't want to look crazy even in front of this suit-guy. " 'Kay." He stepped back into the entryway of an apartment building, a little stoop reeking of cigarettes and urine, lined with mailbox slots, and waited till the man went by: a businessman passing through the dingy part of town, on his way to buildings where the lobbies smelled of fresh-cut flowers.

Inchy dreamed of someday entering those buildings on real errands. His dream was to be a courier—on bike, skates, or scooter, he didn't care. He would wear a helmet and a leather jacket and a scarf thrown 'round his neck; he'd wear new high-top sneakers and carry important parcels from one office to another, delivering them in person to men like this one, who gave him a chilly blue-eyed look that made Inchy even more determined to accomplish his dream.

Inchy spent some time looking after the man, waiting to see if he'd look back, but he never did.

"Go," Pearlywhite insisted, and Inchy went.

Around the corner and up one block, then down Mawkin to the boarded-up back end of Naiad Lane.

"Now stop here and duck down," Pearly ordered. "There's a loose board. Go through it."

He crouched down, not even daring to see if anyone was looking, for fear that would bring on more attention. Often he hated feeling invisible to the people who passed by, but right now he wished he could have made himself completely transparent. Pretending to stoop for a dropped coin, he reached out a hand and touched the boards until one of them swung aside. There was room to squeeze through, but the cops in Naiad Lane would surely see him.

On the other hand, Pearlywhite had never steered him wrong, and this was no place for an argument. He scrunched through the splintered gap, thankful that Pearly was insubstantial, and came out in a small pile of junk. He was in the alley's blind end now. Trashcans and giant dumpsters were shoved back here, heaped with wooden pallets and tangles of wire.

He checked his pocket to see if the string of pearls were still there. Once they'd fallen out, when he'd bent over to climb through something, and he'd almost lost them forever. Since then, he checked them constantly. His mom's pearls. There were seven and one more on the string. He counted them:

one-two-three-four-five-six-seven and one more. He could only count to seven; he couldn't remember the name of the next number, if he'd ever known it.

He stroked the pearls, wondering what now. A police radio crackled nearby. If he went any farther they'd catch sight of him, and you knew where that could lead. Some of the places they put homeless kids—especially ones without families—were no better than prisons.

"Pearly," he said, slipping the pearls back in his pocket, "Clyde's waiting on me. He's gonna go nuts if I don't get down there soon. You know how he gets when he's starving."

"Quiet, Inchy. We have to see this. We have to be sure."

"We?" he said. "Whatever this is, it's your idea."

"You're doing this for all of us. Now sneak through those bins and put your head out. Not far. Just enough to peek. We have to be sure."

"Sure of what?"

But Pearlywhite wouldn't answer. He could be maddening that way—never answering the most basic questions, leaving Inchy to work things out for himself. Inchy sighed, resigned to it, and got down on all fours. The pavement was oily and cold, as if it had sweat all night in a fever; he could smell fish and rotten vegetables and automotive grease, along with the odor of brewing coffee, which was always everywhere on cold mornings. He put his head down and crept under a snag of wire, between two crumpled metal drums. When he lifted his head again he was staring at a cop. Two cops. Three. Two had their backs to him and the other, the one he'd seen first, was crouching down examining a shape crumpled on the asphalt. What mostly stood out was a pair of small feet, white beneath grime they shared with the pavement.

Two small feet, and one of them, the left one, was missing its little toe.

That was all the detail he noticed. That was enough. His mind stopped after that. He just kept thinking one thing: *Clyde.*

"Get back now," Pearlywhite said. "Inchy, get back."

He wasn't sure how long Pearlywhite had been talking to him. For once the smoky voice didn't reach him—couldn't cut through what he was feeling. What finally prompted him to move was fear that the cops might spot him.

The crouching cop was pointing out things around the body—Inchy couldn't exactly see what. But one of the things started to move. It looked like a ball of ragged bits of string, all different colors collected and tied together and rolled up in a tangle, the sort of thing you'd find in a kid's pocket. And without any of the cops noticing (so far), the ball came rolling slowly down the alley toward Inchy. Maybe one of them had kicked it. All Inchy knew was that it was coming straight at him. Eventually one of the cops was going to notice it out of the corner of an eye and turn and see the ball of string—and beyond it Inchy himself. And then there would be questions and confinement, and he couldn't have that. Not ever again.

He started to scramble back, but he'd only gotten a few inches when Pearlywhite said, "Wait."

"Nooooo." A thin whine.

But Pearlywhite had never been more insistent. Inchy had the feeling Pearly was actually capable of physically stopping him, although the smokedragon never had before. He'd never felt a hint of this much power. This must be important. He stopped. He trusted Pearlywhite and knew Pearlywhite would never do anything to harm or endanger him, unless . . .

Well, he'd never known there was an "unless" until now.

What had changed?

The ball of string touched his fingers. He opened his eyes, not having realized they were shut. His hands closed around the ball.

"Okay," Pearlywhite whispered. "Let's go."

He backed into the cans, bumping them in his anxiety to be away. A piece of crumpled tin came clamoring down, and suddenly there were shouts and whistles blowing, and a whoop of sirens at the far end of the alley. Inchy threw himself free of the garbage, slammed into the board that swung by one nail, and was out on the far side, diving into traffic that somehow couldn't touch him. And not noticing at first that in slamming past the board he'd driven the nail into his arm . . . He felt as if he were made of the same stuff as Pearlywhite. Wispy, weird, and insubstantial, flowing between the cars. And then there were more alleys, more streets, on and on until he came to the invisible edge of his world, the border beyond which he wasn't really welcome, where he was always the opposite of invisible. Even if he passed beyond, into those broader, brighter streets, he carried the barrier with him. He was forever something out of place, out there.

He needed to be invisible now. He needed to blend in. He backed up, thinking of places where he would be safe, where he could think for a while. Pearlywhite was gone now. And he had this ball of twine in his hand. He had a feeling nothing was going to get any clearer until nightfall, when Pearlywhite would certainly return and they could talk openly in the dark. He would just have to hole up and wait it out. And he was used to that.

He barely took notice of the small, perfectly round red-oozing hole punched into his left upper arm.

Inchy sat on the floor of a big circular room—the Thinking Tank—with a high ceiling, under blinking Christmas lights, eating half a stale egg muffin from a dumpster bag. The lights were plugged into a much-taped cord that ran across two roofs to a light socket on the roof of a building that still had electricity.

The nighttime has two personalities; there are two spirits abroad in it, or so it always seemed to Inchy. There was the nighttime that protected, that was like a comforting mother swathed in shadow; there was the nighttime that hunted you. One nighttime tried to protect you from the other.

Right now, Inchy felt he was safe in the arms of night the protector; he knew that Pearlywhite was coiled up in the pearls in his pocket, and the night was curled up around the tank. The Thinking Tank was a dry, busted-open water tank that stood on metal poles atop the defunct Mesmer Brewery. By common agreement, the kids didn't use it for a home—you only slept there in emergencies. Be there too much, and someone would notice. But they met in the tank when they needed advice, or when they just needed to meet up with each other; if you couldn't figure out what to do by yourself, you went to the Tank and waited for someone else who also needed help to come. Answers came more easily when you could talk things over.

The mostly empty, rat-haunted factory below still smelled of moldy hops and grain, though no beer had been made there as long as any of the kids remembered.

Inchy thought about Clyde as he chewed meditatively on the rubbery remnant of fried egg white within the hard crust of the English muffin: Clyde and Inchy at the river, fishing with other people's broken fishing lines, rusty old hooks; Clyde pretending he was going somewhere to piss where he wouldn't drive off the fish, actually crossing the rotting old wharf and climbing down to the support beams below, where he grabbed Inchy's line and tugged on it, in the shadows. "*Clyde—I got a huge one! It's something monster big!*" Then hearing the fish laugh—but recognizing that laugh. Inchy had been annoyed, but now he smiled at the memory.

He scratched at the tingling wound in his arm, and remembered when Clyde had found some arcade tokens, and taken him into the Flashpoint Arcade to play the games—the greatest moment of their lives, until they got chased out by the fat guy with that drippy wad of smokeless in his mouth.

He remembered when Clyde had been attacked by that wild dog in the bushes of the park, and he'd lost a toe to it—how Clyde, once he'd gotten away, had actually laughed, seeing the dog snapping and gulping the toe down.

"Wild dog got to eat too," he said. But then he'd turned white and fainted, and Inchy—acting on a suggestion of Clyde's Invisible, Koil—had to drag him to shelter.

And sometimes, when they slept in the cardboard fort under a bridge near one another, they awakened late at night to hear their Invisibles whispering to one another . . .

"Yes," Pearlywhite said, issuing from his pocket, drifting upwards. "It's good to remember lost friends. It's their real funeral, remembering them; it's the real way to say goodbye."

"What really happened, Pearly?" For the first time since Clyde died, Inchy felt his eyes burning with tears.

Pearlywhite took up his place on Inchy's shoulder, nestled against his ear. Inchy could feel the gentle pressure, just a hint of warm cotton. "I don't know," Pearlywhite said. He was changing colors with the Christmas tree lights. A red Pearly; a blue one. "But there might be enough left of Koil to ask."

Inchy's eyes widened. "I thought he was . . . gone!"

"Let's see. He was homebased in that ball of string."

"He was?" Clyde had never told him what object Koil was homebased in. You didn't usually see them go in and out of their homebases, and most of the kids were secretive about it.

Inchy took the grubby ball of string, a little smaller than a baseball, out of the paper sack and hefted it in his hand. It felt *less* than it looked. Not lighter, but . . . *less*.

He set it on the floor between his outstretched legs, beside his scabbed knees.

Pearlywhite said something in the language of the Invisibles, which sounded like a breeze whistling through a broken bottle. The ball didn't move. Pearlywhite spoke again. The ball rolled—ever so slightly—a quarter-inch one way, then back. Just rocking in place. Then the end of the string lifted up, and from it issued a smoky bluish shape—more like a seahorse than a dragon—made out of strings of mist; the foggy tendrils stretched up and twined, and turned, and coiled, back and forth, looping in the air to make the outline of Koil's body, like a sculpture made entirely of a single strand of wire.

But this time, the living string of mist was broken, here and there—stretched thin and missing in places, fraying to nothingness at the edges. Fading.

"He's weak!" Inchy said in alarm.

"What happened to Clyde?" Pearlywhite asked Koil; in Inchy's language, so he could understand.

Inchy heard Clyde's voice faint and far away in his head, through a cracklyness like the song on the scratched record his dad had played for him when he was little; before the police took his dad away, and his mom died.

"Killed . . . too strong . . . no . . . experience with . . . teeth like the blade of all suffering . . . with what sorrow, he . . . glass three . . . hunter hunted by his hunting . . . "

"His weakness is even in his speech," Pearlywhite said. He whistled another question in his own language.

But a gust of wind seemed to answer from the two-foot-high gap in the rusted metal of the wall, its sharp edges curled back by the kids—and the wind reached into the Thinking Tank to push Koil out of shape, so that he blew into wisps—and then into nowhere.

"Koil!" Inchy shouted, grabbing the ball. There seemed to be a fading bluish light deep in the ball of twine, but then even that ebbed and went out without answering.

"Something's taken them both," Pearlywhite said.

They heard a crunch in the broken glass outside. And Inchy knew from the slightness of the crunch that he didn't have to worry about bolting.

In came Garvey, a black kid who was older and stronger than his small limbs and legs suggested. He wore a brown suit jacket, brown corduroy pants with a seam so sharp it looked like he had just picked it up from the dry cleaner. His shoes were shiny brown, freshly polished and buffed. Beneath the suit jacket, the neck of a frayed yellow T-shirt was just visible. He wore a ring he'd found in the train station bathroom, missing its jewel; there was just a shiny socket. And in the jacket's breast pocket, the pointed tip of a neatly folded bright red handkerchief, vivid as a rose—clean and crisp in appearance, although the kerchief was older than Garvey and had belonged to his father. The kerchief was the one unchanging element of his attire. Garvey had the uncanny ability to delve into masses of dingy rags at the clothing banks and emerge with an outfit that looked as if it had been tailored for him. His father, a Caribbean immigrant who'd sold flowers on street corners, had taken similar pride in his appearance. And even though he'd hardly known his father, Garvey spoke with a hint of the older man's island accent.

"Good," Garvey said, not at all surprised to see him. "You got word of the meeting."

Inchy shook his head. "I've been here all day."

"That's not smart."

"I had—I had to hide."

"Let me in," came a small cracked voice from outside.

Garvey turned and held the ragged metal open behind him, and Mina put her head through, pausing when she saw Inchy getting to his feet. Her eyes slid around, looking scratched and blurred behind her thick eyeglasses. She had hair cut just below her ears, dyed turquoise at the ends, a look at odds with her shyness, since it meant that you couldn't help but look at her, and that always made her nervous. She stood with her back to the curved metal wall, wiping her nose on the thick tattered sweater several sizes too large for her, and pulling on the blue ends of her hair, looking away every time Inchy glanced at her.

After Mina came Vick, a tall boy with wild white hair and skin so pale it seemed to be powdered and eyes of cold blue crystal. Vick stood next to Mina, a few feet away, his back to the wall. Then came the twins, Rosalie and Junebug, and they took their positions. Inchy got up as Cassandra came in, and she was the last one for now. He leaned against the chill metal until it boomed beneath his weight. They all jumped at the sound, and Garvey gave him an irritated look.

"You shouldn't have come so early. We were looking for you." And to the others: "Inchy's been here since daylight."

"Stupid," said Vick, who always had some reason not to like anyone.

"Shut up," Inchy said. "I had to come. They saw me seeing Clyde—the cops did."

"You saw him?" Mina said, holding him in the regard of her blemished spectacles. "After . . . ?"

"Pearlywhite sent me to look at him. Yeah, it was after."

"What happened to him, then?" Cassandra asked. She was a plump, unsmiling girl with stringy brown hair; Clyde had tried many times to make her laugh, even for a moment, and failed. Her face looked broken from inside, more than usual; and Inchy found himself wondering if she had maybe hoped that Clyde would make her really laugh some day . . . and now that far-off hope was gone.

"I don't know. He was on the ground . . . just lying there in Naiad Lane."

"We know where," Vick said. "They took him away and we scouted the place. But we don't know what happened."

"And the cops or somebody got his charm," said Rosalie. "His homebase."

"No," said Inchy. "That's why Pearly sent me. See." He put out his hand. The ball of string lay there, unmoving. "Koil came out. Pearlywhite called him and he came out and said something I couldn't hardly understand, but . . . but whoever hurt Clyde, they got Koil too."

"Clyde's not *hurt*," Vick said savagely. "He's dead."

"K-killed," Inchy said. "I know."

"But . . . but that's impossible," Mina said softly, and they all turned to look at her because she spoke so rarely. "The Invisibles are . . . they can't die. Nothing can hurt them."

"Maybe if they kill *you*, your *Invisible* goes away," Inchy said.

"The hell with maybes," Garvey said. "Why don't we just up and ask 'em?"

They looked from one to the other, there in the gently twinkling light, and reached silent agreement. One by one, each of the children standing ringed around the wall of the tank put out a hand holding his or her homebase, whatever precious object their Invisible had chosen to inhabit.

Inchy pulled the remainders of his mother's pearl necklace from his pocket; the beads dangled from his fingers, in the same hand that held Koil's ragged ball. He felt Pearlywhite stirring. Smoke seeped from the pearls and pooled in the palm of his hand, and the wise dragon eyes blinked open to stare at the other kids.

Next to him, Garvey slowly drew the red handkerchief from his pocket and draped it across his hand. A dark stain muddied the middle of the cloth. The stain never went away, no matter how often Garvey washed it. That was his father's blood, from the chest wound where the bullet went in, when the cop who shot Garvey's father had mistaken a black iris for a gun.

The kerchief seemed to stir, something rising up from the stain, then subsiding. Garvey looked impatient and he took the cloth by a corner and snapped it, then settled it again on his palm. "Come on, Slink!" His Invisible was slow to wake tonight.

Mina took off her glasses, which weren't hers after all, but had belonged to her lost brother. *Her* eyes were 20/20. She wore the thick lenses despite the blurred vision they gave her, the dizzying headaches. They had all stopped trying to talk her out of wearing the things; Garvey sometimes said she ought to at least smash out the lenses, but she would never do that, nor would any of them. Mina's Invisible lived in there somewhere, and now came out in a subtle warping of the ambient light, as if the air itself had turned into a thick lens. This was Glimmish. It flickered up into the air before Mina's eyes, and Inchy gladdened to see her clear-eyed, knowing that for once she was able to see him as well as he saw her. He wished she would look at him the way she looked at Glimmish. But Glimmish, really, was the only thing she trusted anymore.

So it went around the circle. Vick's Invisible, Catseye, sprang from a red and white marble, and it was a thing like a mottled glass eye that spun and stared and sang when it spoke, which was rarely. The twins carried two halves of a golden locket, each half with its own chain, and their Invisible was likewise twinned, so that two shapes sprang from the locket-halves and twisted around each other until the seething shape settled into one form with two faces peering in opposite directions with eyes of emerald and ever-murmuring mouths. Cassandra was the last of them to put out her hand; she did it with a sigh, slowly straightening her fingers until they could see the crucifix with the shortest bit broken off so it now resembled a T. Hers was the only somewhat humanoid Invisible: A luminous, ethereal Christ, dripping crusted blood from hands and feet and brow. The little bearded man, glowing like a night light, stood erect on her palm with a pained expression that mirrored Cassandra's. She called him Jessie.

By then, finally, Slink had taken up the task of animating Garvey's handkerchief. The red cloth sat on his hand like a wrinkled four legged doll, its legs drawn from the corners of the kerchief, its central body a bunched mass marked with the dark bloodstain. The crumpled red doll wriggled and dropped to the floor, freeing itself from Garvey's fingers, then stumped out into the middle of the Thinking Tank. It walked with a scaled-down version of Garvey's swagger.

Pearlywhite swirled down to meet Slink. Catseye whirled toward them, giving off a sound like singing crystal. The other Invisibles joined them, making their own smaller circle at the center of the Tank, taking up positions between the kids.

"Koil no longer manifests," Pearlywhite said. "I tried . . . " Pearly's speech dissolved into susurration, and the other Invisibles merged their comments into the hiss. After a few minutes the sounds became something the children could understand again, mostly.

"One stalks," said Glimmish, in words that flashed along the inner walls of the tank. "Stalks children."

"Children?" said Cassandra. The horror Inchy felt struck all of them; even Vick and Garvey, too tough to show fear in their different ways, seemed to take the news badly. Cassandra clenched tight to the glowing figure in her hand, and they heard it gasp in a smallish voice: *"Calm down, Cass!"*

"But . . . but why?" she said.

"I got another question," Garvey said. "One we could maybe answer. Where's Niall? Where's Leafjacket?"

The kids began to murmur. Niall was missing . . . the only other kid aside from Clyde who had failed to reach the Thinking Tank tonight. He was usually down at the library, hidden in the darkest reaches of the stacks, reading some big old book of useless knowledge. And Leafjacket was his Invisible, a papery rustling thing that lived inside a waterlogged, yellowed paperback with pages so thoroughly stuck together that Niall himself didn't know what was written inside.

The Invisibles began to murmur. The mouths of the Twins' Invisible contorted in something like fear, and Inchy realized he had never known them to show anything of the sort. What could frighten Invisibles?

But then again, they had all thought Invisibles were immortals and apparently that was not the case.

"I thought you were gonna tell Niall about the meeting," Vick told Garvey.

"I was," he said. "Then I ran into the Twins and they were headed toward the library, and they said they'd tell him."

"We did," said Rosalie.

"He said he'd be here," Junebug agreed.

"Then something's happened . . . "

"Yesssssss," sang Catseye. "Happening now. Leafjacket—"

Slink suddenly stiffened. "Leafjacket! Something . . . something!"

They feel it, Inchy thought. They're in touch with Leafjacket. And if something's happening to the Invisible, it's happening to his boy. Niall's in trouble too.

"We gotta find him!" Inchy said. "Where are they? Where's Leafjacket, can you tell us that?"

But even as he threw out the question, the Invisibles were slipping away. The red handkerchief settled to the floor. Catseye dropped and rolled back toward Vick's feet. Pearlywhite leapt catlike back into the string of pearls. All the kids fell quiet, their sense of panic perfectly preserved, and listened to the night.

Something out there—night the stalker now, night with a predator's hunger, sniffing for them.

A footstep on the rooftop, just outside the Tank; a heavier than usual crunch in the glass. And then the soft creak of the metal flap pulling open. Inchy smiled, thinking it must be Niall at last, joining up with them, late as always.

But the Invisibles wouldn't have fled then.

And the person who ducked and came into the Tank was not Niall at all.

"I thought I'd find you here," said Officer Cat.

She straightened up, smiling around at the blinking Christmas lights. She was Chinese—she'd married a white guy and taken his name—but she had no accent, she'd lived here all her life. She had a round face and small eyes and a wide flexible mouth; when she smiled, her whole face moved.

Garvey and Inchy looked at each other; a flicker of mutual understanding. They went to stand in front of Officer Cat, their backs close to the curved, rusty metal wall, to keep her attention focused on them so the others could get away.

"How long you know about this place?" Garvey asked.

"A little while. I looked in once when you guys weren't here." Officer Cat amiably rested a hand on the butt of her gun. Her belt radio crackled and talked to itself. Some numbers and a description of someone on foot on East Third. She didn't seem to pay it any attention; she was absorbed in looking at Garvey and Inchy. "I had a feeling you'd be meeting here tonight. You guys tired of living on the streets yet?"

Inchy glanced past her and saw Mina slip through the door. Vick and the others were going, one by one.

Officer Cat turned her head a little at the sound of their going, but she didn't try to stop them. She probably figured she could only get one or two kids at a time, if that's what she was here for.

"Who's livin' on the streets?" Garvey asked, offended, one hand clasping the lapel of his coat like a politician. "I live with my cousins."

Officer Cat shook her head. "Far as I can find out, you live in that car in Old Mule's Pit, most of the time. Aren't you tired of it? I know the system is a drag for a while but if you're patient they'll eventually find you either an adoption or foster care—"

"Nobody's going to adopt us. They like babies," Inchy said.

"I *done* foster homes. No thanks. That's why I'm—I'm living with my cousins. Don't tell me where I'm living, Officer Cat, I got to have my props."

"Uh huh. Well. I think you might be in danger on these streets, more than usual. There's a guy out there killing kids, we think. We don't think Clyde was the first one. We don't want one of you to be next."

Inchy nodded gravely, but he had no intention of going with her. He knew Pearlywhite wouldn't follow him to any foster home. Like Garvey, he remembered what being in the system was like.

"Is that supposed to be some kind of threat?" Garvey said.

"We can't protect you out here, and you boys are way overdue for . . . Whoa, hold on there now—"

She spread her arms as the two boys started to move away from each other, circling her, in opposite directions, to make a dash for the doorway. "Inchy, Garvey—I mean it! Don't take another step!"

She reached for her walkie-talkie, to call for someone to help her round them up, Inchy guessed. As she pulled the radio out of its belt loop, Garvey slapped it from her hand.

"Damn it, Garvey!" she yelled, as the radio tumbled to bounce low on the wall. Instinctively, she bent to retrieve it, giving the boys the moment they needed to dart past her.

Garvey was hunkered over, scurrying through the crude door, Inchy crowding after—but she caught Inchy by the ankle and held on as she followed onto the roof, dragging him back into her grip.

"Inchy, shit, hold still! I'm trying to save your life, here! Come on!"

He stopped struggling—he didn't want her to put cuffs on him. He might get his chance later, if she didn't do that. Garvey had gotten away, anyhow.

"Okay," she said, turning him to face her. "How about if we get something to eat?"

He shrugged. "I'm not hungry."

"Oh *really*?" She didn't believe him for an instant. "I remember you like fresh hot pizza slices, right? I'll buy you one, any kind you like, and we'll figure out how to get you to someplace safe and warm. And a bath. You could definitely use a bath."

She kept a good strong grip on him down the fire escape, to the street, muttering to herself about what a death trap the fire escape was, with its bolts grinding loose in the powdering concrete sockets as they passed.

He pretended to be eager for the pizza. He would've liked it, too; but if he accepted a slice and then ran away after eating it, he'd feel bad about that, somehow. Pearlywhite wouldn't approve, he knew. Pearly believed in living by a code of honor.

When they got to the sidewalk-service pizza window at Enrico's, he waited till she was giving her order, and then did that twisting-jump that had gotten him loose from so many adult grips. He dodged behind her and slipped down the alley by Enrico's. She shouted but he could already hear the resignation in her voice. She must've known she couldn't catch him once he'd gotten such a start on her. He angled down the narrow passage between two buildings—piled with trash, rotting blankets, and old metal buckets to jump over—and around another turn of the familiar way, gasping when he got to the street, a block from Enrico's. He was surprised to hear pursuit—but turned to see Garvey coming.

Garvey grinned, leaping over a pile of old paintbrushes as he came. Huffing, he skidded to a stop beside Inchy on the sidewalk, both of them looking up and down the street for Officer Cat. "Why you make me run through that trash?" Garvey asked, not really expecting an answer. "Get shit all over my damn clothes. Look at this, scrape up my shoes. Shit, man."

"Yours tell you where she was taking us?" Meaning Garvey's Invisible.

"I was hiding behind the Tank, I heard her talk about it. I don't need Slink to tell me everydamnthing like you and that dragon. Come on, let's find Niall."

Getting past the librarians required a certain strategy—one they had practiced. It was an old library, but it had a modern security gate and a librarian sitting at the checkout desk where she could keep an eye on who went in and out.

Sometimes Inchy came in to get out of the weather and look at picture books. He couldn't read, much. Mina would take off her glasses and read to him now and then.

Inchy was grubby and smelled sour, and he knew it. They had a policy of keeping the homeless out, and he was pretty obvious.

Sometimes he waited till the librarian's back was turned, and vaulted the low railing by the gate, then ducked under a reading table and ran between the stacks. Today, though, they were in a hurry, so they did another bait and switch, with Garvey—who never got stopped—asking the librarian why they didn't have more books on black culture, and her protesting they had a great many of them, and him shaking his head in pretended outrage, waving his arms, to keep her attention on him, so that Inchy could vault the railing without her seeing.

After a minute Garvey said, "Hey—tell you what, white lady, I will check out what you got myself, and then we'll see."

He strutted into the library, heading for the Black History stacks, where he met Inchy as prearranged. They were between a high shelf filled with magazines and slender books, and a silver painted radiator under an old, high, smoked-glass window. The ceilings were high, in here, with dusty glass fixtures, way up there, that were almost spider shaped. "Where you think Niall'd be, Inch?"

"I don't know. Pearly feels distant. Ask yours."

He looked around; they were alone in the stacks. He took out his kerchief and bunched it up in his palm, whispering, "Slink . . . ?"

This time the little red-stained dollshape emerged, translucent and shivering, almost immediately. "What's the matter, Slink?" Garvey asked. "You're shakin'."

"The *fear* . . . like a scent in the air . . . I see books on the ancient gods, there . . . that way . . . " He pointed with a tiny indistinct hand, then surprised them by jumping to the floor and pointing again, urgently.

"Ancient gods," Garvey muttered. "Niall likes to read about mythology and stuff. Greek gods . . . "

They followed Slink, who was running down the aisle like a runaway puppet, ahead of them, pausing now and then to turn and gesture. *Follow, follow . . .*

A middle-aged lady with hair like a dyed-blond helmet turned her quietly angry eyes toward them as they ran past. She couldn't see Slink, but she snorted out a single derisive laugh, shaking her head and muttering something about grungy little urchins running in here, and she seemed happier, Inchy thought, to have something specific to be angry about besides the thing that frightened her that she never let come into the front of her mind—

He knew that view of the lady came to him from Pearly somehow—

Garvey and Inchy left her behind, jogging around a corner after Slink who was leaping and weaving down increasingly dim aisles, between high shelves of musty books; the aisles seemed to get narrower, edging closer and closer, and Inchy felt like they were starting to lean in, toward him; like the books were all going to tumble furiously down like the pictures Mina had shown him of the playing cards coming at Alice in Wonderland, when she'd read the book to him—

(Was Mina safe?)

—and then Slink turned another corner, went down another aisle, turned another corner, they were zigzagging through the library, past a startled black man and a tall man with a beard, and it seemed to Inchy that Slink must be confused, lost, because they were going back the way they'd come, until he realized that they were following some kind of trail in the air itself, a trace left by someone or something that had gone here before . . .

And then Slink skidded to a stop and spun around, like a figure skater in slow motion, and then fell on his miniature behind and stared dazedly at the ceiling, as if trying to understand the spidery light fixtures.

They stopped running, breathing hard. Looking around.

"We're here," Garvey said, gasping, "but I don't see Niall."

The aisle looked normal to Inchy, now, not too dark or narrow or leaning. Just library shelves of books, some of them old and leather-bound and tattered, some of them glossy backed. He saw a picture of a naked flying guy holding up the snake-headed lady, on the spine of one of the books. The myth books, for sure. But Niall wasn't there.

Garvey was staring at Slink. A slender woman with butterfly-type glasses and leopard-pattern pedal pushers, her hair in a retro beehive, was coming down the aisle, smiling at them; one of those hip girls that hang out in front of nightclubs. She said, "You guys lost?"

"Nuh," Inchy said. "Resting. Looking."

"Okay-dokers." She walked on . . . right over Slink, almost stepping on him, not seeing him. He ignored her. She glanced back at Garvey who was staring, as far as she knew, at the empty carpet.

Then Garvey looked up at a top shelf nearby. "He's looking up there. I thought he was looking at the ceiling but . . . "

There was a set of books, on the top shelf, that stuck out a little so you could see the edge of the pages under the spine; and some of them were a wet-red color, that looked new, and some were white. They found a stool with little steps on it in the next aisle, and brought it over, and Inchy stood on it to look. There was a little space between a set of gold-covered numbered books and the wooden shelf-wall. In the space between books and wall, in the shadows behind the books, he could see a small, dirty hand clutching a curling, yellowed paperback book. And he saw there was blood seeping into the books.

He felt like he was going to fall backward off the stool, and had to clutch the back of the books to hold on; they were big books and stayed in place. He reached into the niche and took the book from the little, curled hand, having to pull sharply; the fingers curled up like a dying flower as Niall's charm came free.

As he climbed down off the stool, he felt a series of sensations in his chest. First there was a kind of electrical numbness, then a deep coldness, and then an aching hole. Just a hole that hurt.

Garvey was staring at the old paperback in Inchy's hand.

The retro girl was coming back toward them. She seemed to work here. "You guys sure you're . . . What's the matter?"

Garvey pointed. "We were looking for our friend. Someone left him up there."

"What?" She laughed. "He's in the *Golden Bough*?"

"Behind those books."

"You got a hamster or something in here . . . ?"

She climbed up on the stool, and said, "Oh my god."

Inchy and Garvey ran, while she was up there looking; Inchy stuffing the homebase for Niall's Invisible in his shirt.

As they left the library, he thought he saw the pouchy-faced man with the icy blue eyes; the man was walking around the corner of the building, on his way home from work. Looking at Inchy and Garvey; gone from sight.

∽

Inchy clutched the paperback to his chest, under his shirt, as the wind soughed past him and Garvey, and through them too, it seemed to him. "Garvey . . . I feel like . . . like there's a window in my forehead that's just . . . left open and the wind is blowing right inside my head . . . "

"Yeah well, if it tried to blow through my head it couldn't get in 'cause there's a damn brain in there. Shit, it ain't no cold wind." But he sounded hoarse, scared.

"I got Leafjacket but . . . I don't know if he's in there any more . . . "

"Maybe Pearly can tell you. I got to go home."

Inchy looked at him. Home? "You mean the old car? Why?"

"I just got to think."

"I don't know—I don't think we should be apart. I think we should get all the kids and . . . " He stopped on the corner, dizzy. He felt hot, and then cold, as a ripple of weakness went through him. Was he feverish? His arm ached, where the nail had punched into him.

"I meet you later, man, maybe at the McDumpster. You get 'em together. I got to think. I just . . . I got to think. I got to be alone . . . "

Inchy watched Garvey walk away, and wanted to chase after him. But he felt too sick to do it now. He felt sick about Niall and just sick. One blended into the other.

"Inchy?"

Mina's face hovered in lamplight, just around the corner of the library, her body in shadow. So shy with her bony fingers creeping around the cold gray edge of the building. He looked up at the massive building, thinking it looked like a tomb. He could hear sirens coming to claim Niall. He hurried toward Mina, grateful for her appearance, and took hold of her thin elbow through the ragged sweater.

"Inchy, you're hurting me!"

"We gotta get out of here, Mina. Come on."

"I—I came to find Niall."

His teeth started chattering. "N-Niall . . . "

"Did you tell him? What the Invisibles said, did you tell him?"

"Niall's dead," he spat out. "Garvey and me, we found him in there in the books. He's dead, Mina, killed." He had to bite his tongue; he didn't want to tell her more than that. He could have, he desperately wanted to unburden himself, but it would have been cruel to her. She had loved Niall, Inchy knew, loved him in something like the way Inchy himself loved her. Niall never really noticed Mina, unless they were talking about books; but Inchy had seen the way she looked at him and sometimes let her glasses slide down a fraction of an inch so she could peer at him clearly, shyly, when he wasn't looking.

She didn't ask any questions, he was grateful for that. She just started shaking and sniffing, and he tried to hold her up but suddenly she was down on her knees on the sidewalk, just wailing. He moved her over a little bit, out of the way, back onto the stoop of a massage place. A Korean woman looked out at him, fat and sweaty, fanning herself with a magazine; it felt so cold out here, but warm humid air pushed its way through the iron grating that held the woman. She narrowed her eyes and fanned the kids away with her mouth hardening. "You go!" she said. "You bad for business!"

Mina cried harder. Inchy had to get his hands under her arms and haul her to her feet. There was a park around the corner, a little place that used to be a vacant lot until they put in hedges and grass and benches; but the grass had been pissed on until it was burned yellow, and the hedges were so choked with trash they seemed to have browned scraps of paper for leaves, and the benches were long gone, just uncomfortable metal struts remaining. It was basically a vacant lot again. But he found a dirt knoll and brushed it sort of clean and sat there next to her, taking some comfort when she finally pushed him away from holding and hugging her, because it meant she was finding her strength again. She held her knees up to her face, arms wrapped around her shins, and rocked and moaned until finally she sighed and raised her eyes to him. He saw that she'd taken her glasses off. He thought maybe she was going to call Glimmish. Instead she just stared at him clear-eyed and said, "What now, Inchy? Who's next? Who's hunting us?"

"It's not that," he said. "There's . . . there's so many people out here . . . people getting hurt and killed and just plain lost . . . every day it seems there's someone else missing. Don't you feel that way, Mina?"

"I don't feel any way," she said. "I just know someone took Clyde and now . . . now Niall. And it feels like it's coming for us. And I want to know why."

He nodded, hanging his own head.

And found himself staring at Leafjacket.

The old book seemed to stir, the pages parting like a parched mouth trying to speak.

"Look, Mina!"

She looked at the crumbling paperback, then quickly scanned the street around them. There were people here and there, business on the corner nearby, men arguing up the block, some women leaning in to chatter at the driver of an idling car which pulled away just as a black and white cruised through; but no one was watching the two kids. She ducked her shoulders and huddled in closer to Inchy, as if they were making a barrier around Leafjacket.

Inchy wondered if he should try to pry the pages open with his fingers, but there was no need. For the first time in his memory, Leafjacket opened. The pages crackled and ripples began to spread through the gray smeared ink, greenish-brown stains puddling on the ancient paper like rain or tears. Forming letters . . . words. He could hear the book whispering, but it was too weak to speak. Inchy tried to mouth out the letters, but he only knew a few of them: "I-N . . . N . . . I-S-I . . . D?"

"B," said Mina. "In-vis-i . . . Invisible."

"That's it?"

"That's all," she said. "Look."

Leafjacket cracked open all the way along its spine, sighing away bits of brittle dust. For a moment the letters hung across two smeared pages, then they faded out like the headline of a newspaper taped up in a shop window for years and years. Inchy caught the halves of the book before they could fall apart completely. He dug in his pocket and found a rubber band, snapped it around the remains of Niall's homebase, and shoved the whole wad down into his jacket with the remains of Koil and the warm pearls of his own Invisible.

"Garvey said we should get the others," he said.

"Garvey? Where'd he go?"

"His old car."

"Inchy, that's not a good idea. We shouldn't be apart tonight, we should . . . we should all stick together. It's the only way to get through this, I think."

"Maybe you should tell him that. Could be he'd listen to you."

Garvey would get into strangers' cars if he thought they would drive him a few blocks. "Saves me some wear on these shoes," he'd say when Inchy told him he was crazy. He didn't believe Garvey would take any chances at a time like this, but you never knew. He was suddenly stricken with fear and concern for his friend. Garvey on his own, always acting so fearless, and sometimes so genuinely trusting—sort of an idiot about it, really.

"We should go," he said.

"Yeah."

He was so grateful for Mina's company. They walked close together, stumbling on the uneven sidewalk and bumping up against one another. She was walking more steadily now; she hadn't put her glasses back on yet and he wasn't sure if he should say something about it. Without him even asking she said, "I want to see again. It's making me crazy, seeing everything all bent and foggy. Glimmish will understand."

"Okay," Inchy said. "Sure. Glimmish is probably glad. Makes her job easier."

"You think?"

They came to a stop past the wall of a brick building where the sidewalk just . . . ended. The Pit. For as long as Inchy could remember, there'd been a gaping hole here, all that remained of what had been a hotel or a skyscraper or some building they'd knocked down years ago. The Pit was all that remained of a basement two stories deep. You could see girders and beams down there, where floors used to be. Someone had come along and scooped out the center of the building and left this hollow place to be carpeted with broken glass and weeds and charred wood and cans and trash barrels. Piles of whitish foam and mold and shredded upholstery that one could no longer call furniture. And in the middle of all that, a car. It had crashed into the Pit one night, ending up crumpled like a can someone had stepped on. The glass was smashed from every window; it was rusted and crushed and dangerous to touch. But inside it, Garvey found shelter. It wouldn't keep a grown man dry; but it was barely enough for the boy.

They stood at the edge of the pit and yelled down: "Garvey! Gaaaarvey!"

A siren whooped and startled Inchy into leaping down to the floor below. He held up a hand to Mina, who knelt at the brink and then leapt down with him. They made their way over to the foundation wall of the adjacent building, where some bent prongs of rebar formed steps down into the Pit. At the bottom, they picked their way across the broken glass.

Back in the permanent shadows, Garvey's neighbors laughed and coughed and someone kicked bottle shards toward them.

"Garvey?" Inchy said, stooping toward the car.

"He ain't here," called a hoarse voice. A flame flared up; he saw a hooded figure with milky eyes. Old Mule. He was okay.

"You . . . you seen him tonight?" Inchy asked.

"Not since this morning," the raspy voice replied. "You're welcome to wait, though."

"Sure," said another voice, one they didn't know. "You come on in, and bring that sweet thing of yours."

More laughter. Mina scuffed away in the glass. Inchy had to stop himself from rushing in there, making them stop. Didn't they know what was out here in the night? Maybe they did. Maybe it was one of them.

"You watch out!" he called. "You don't know who you're talking to!"

"Woo-hoo!" called the voices. "Hoo-hoo!"

"Hey!" Old Mule, chastising them. "You watch your mouth around them kids."

"Mule," someone laughed. And then Inchy heard more glass breaking. Someone choked. The laughter got louder. Inchy moved back because he could see them surging forward out of the shadows. Old Mule made a wet broken noise and fell over into the light, his head slamming down on the broken glass.

"Run!" Inchy whispered. "Get out, Mina!"

She was already running, working her way onto the first of the rebar steps. Inchy found himself frozen in place, his fingers working furiously at the pearls in his pocket, squeezing them and clicking them together, *please let Mina get away, please let Mina be okay . . .*

Swirling mist. Pearlywhite cut the air, bridging the gap. The laughing ones hadn't even cleared the shadows before the pearly gray dragon was among them. Inchy knew they would see nothing but a blur, if that. But for Inchy it was clear enough. Pearly seized the darkness and tightened it, made a web and caught the lurkers in it, snarling it over their heads and throwing them backward. He heard them shriek. They didn't have a clue what was happening. He saw the smoky whiteness of his Invisible turn sharp and savage and tear into them like a mass of gnashing knives. Now they were screaming. He didn't care what Pearlywhite did to them . . . they deserved it, for scaring Mina.

"Inchy!" She called him from street level. He spun away, finding the rebar rungs, mounting quickly to the sidewalk. He turned to peer back down into the darkness. Pearlywhite was already drifting back toward him, wrapping around his neck, slithering down his arm. Not a sound came from the Pit.

"Was . . . were they the ones?" Mina said.

Pearly looked at her. Tendrils of fog curled around the smokedragon's broad lips like the catfish whiskers of a Chinese dragon. The fangs no longer visible. A gentle smile hid the dragon's fangs. Its opalescent eyes were heavy-lidded, reassuring.

"No," Pearlywhite whispered. "Not them. They're no danger to any of us. Not now."

"Where . . . but where'd Garvey go?" Inchy said. "He was supposed to come down here."

Pearlywhite reared back, nostrils flaring as it sniffed the air. "I don't smell either of them," said Pearlywhite. "Slink or his boy. Garvey's not here."

"Is that bad?" Mina asked.

Pearly made an urgent sound. Mina understood, and pulled the thick spectacles from somewhere in her pockets. At Pearly's cry, the Invisible unwound from her homebase, glittering up from the warped depths of the lenses. She polished the glasses on her cuff as Glimmish danced in the air. Pearly and Glimmish spoke for a moment, without either human understanding their meaning, and then both grew very still. Glimmish twisted around, said something abrupt to Mina, then swirled like a small storm of sparks and shot off into the night.

"He's going to look," she told Inchy. "He can see farther than Pearlywhite."

"Okay. Good. Should we . . . should we find the others?"

"They come," said Pearly. And at that moment Inchy heard footsteps rushing up the sidewalk, scuffing and slapping steps of bare feet and rotten sneakers bound with duct tape. And here came the pale, excited faces of the others—Vick and Cassandra and the twins. Vick stopped at the edge of the pit, out of breath, and barked out a hoarse cry into the dark maw below: "Garvey! Inch!"

"Psst!" Inchy waved them toward the shadows where he and Mina hid. Rosalie notice them first, tugged Junebug's arm, and then the two of them kicked the back of Vick's heels until he turned. He came stomping toward them, his face so pink from running it looked as if it would burst. Cassandra stood looking back, until the twins grabbed her sleeves and pulled her along.

"We saw . . . oh, man," Vick said suddenly. "Inchy? It's you?"

"Of course," Inchy said. "Who'd you think?"

"We thought . . . we . . . " Vick didn't seem to know how to say it.

Rosalie finished for him: "We thought he got you."

"Who?"

"The big man," said Junebug. "The one who's been doing it."

"—we think—" said Rosalie.

"We figured it out because we saw the same guy this morning, hanging around Naiad Lane, and just little while ago we saw him again with a kid . . . a little kid about as tall as you—"

"—same color hair—" said Rosalie.

"We thought it was you," said Cassandra, and swallowed a lump in her throat. Tears sat on the edge of her eyelids.

"Big man," Inchy repeated. "Was . . . was he in a blue suit?"

Remembering the man at the alley this morning; the man he had seen this evening, walking away from the library. Two places of death, and the man in both of them.

"Yes!" said Rosalie and Junebug, their words blurring together. "Blue!"

"You saw him with another kid?"

"Well, it wasn't you, obviously," Vick said. "But we had to be sure."

"But it was a boy," Cassandra said. "He was walking him down the subway steps—forcing him along. Oh . . . we should have followed. We should have followed but we were scared!"

"*You* were scared," Vick said. "I just didn't want to be stupid."

"Oh, Vick, we should have gone down there! He wouldn't have done anything with all of us watching! And our Invisibles to help us!"

"Vick's right," Inchy said. "The Invisibles aren't enough."

He held out Leafjacket and let them all bear witness to the tattered bloodstained book. There were no questions . . . just shocked silence. "Garvey and I found him in the library. And I saw that man in blue there, too. I think you're right about him."

"Here's what we have to do," Mina said. "First we find Garvey, then together we go after the man."

Her eyes were so bright and clear now. Inchy found himself looking to her for the plan, for real answers. She was so much smarter than he ever felt, but usually she just hid that, pretended she wasn't . . . but she was using it now. He felt proud of her.

"Us?" said Cassandra with audible dread.

"Niall and Clyde are dead," she said. "That's too many already. If this man's hunting us, then only we can stop him."

"Alone?"

"We're not alone. We've got Invisibles. And that makes it our job, because somehow he can kill *them*. How do you make a cop believe that, huh? No, it's up to us."

"What do you think, Inch?" said Vick, staring hard at Inchy. But Inchy looked over at Mina. "I think she's right," he said. "We should listen to her."

Mina looked from face to face, then took out her glasses and gazed into the murky lenses.

"Glimmish?" she called.

The lenses exploded in her hands. Shining dust shattered from the plastic frames. Mina shrieked and dropped them. She stumbled back against the wall and stared at the broken spectacles and wailed: "What's happening?"

At that moment, the Invisibles came unbidden. Pearlywhite sharpened and solidified, bright in the night air. The twins' twinned Invisible climbed from their lockets and clasped itself into a single form. Catseye rose spinning and singing from Vick's pocket, its lighthouse gaze swerving over all of them, casting its rays over the streets and the grimy walls. Cassandra's little deity came out and stood on her shoulder and whispered in her ear and Cassandra's eyes grew even wider and more terrified.

"Children," said Pearlywhite. "There is danger greater than you know. It hunts us all tonight."

"Oh, god," said Cassandra. "Where's Garvey?"

"Glimmish was looking for him," Mina said.

The pain in her face was worse than anything she'd shown on hearing of Niall's death. Inchy could only imagine what it would mean to lose an Invisible after losing everything else in this world. But surely, while Mina still lived, there was some chance of restoring her friend.

Unless, as Pearly said, the lives of the children were of no consequence.

He had assumed the death of the kids had caused the death of the Invisibles. But if it was the other way around? What if the kids were only in danger because something hunted the Invisibles?

The world spun; the fever suddenly gripped him, and he found his teeth chattering so hard that his jaws clenched tight. No one else seemed cold . . . why wasn't anyone else shivering tonight? Chills swept him, and he couldn't separate them from fear. Something was paralyzing him. He fought to shake it off, to take action, but he was having trouble even breathing.

"Inchy, man, come on!" Vick was saying, and Mina was pulling at his hand but he couldn't respond . . . he couldn't come with her. They were all yelling at him to run and he wasn't sure why. He tried to swim up out of the fever dream, but by the time he broke free . . .

They were gone.

They were gone, and Officer Cat was standing over him, holding his arm with one hand, feeling his forehead with the other. "Inchy? Don't run from me, boy. You come with me now and no fooling. This is serious. You come with me for a little while, and if you still don't want my help getting you off the street, well, that's your decision. You need to get in the car right now. I'm taking you to the hospital."

He looked once more to see if there was any trace of the others, to see if they were perhaps peering out at him from the shadows, or up from the Pit, but no—they were gone. Something was very wrong with him, but that was just the tip of it all. The wrongness went deeper than that. It went all the way down.

"Come on." She guided him toward the car. He thought she was going to put him in back, in the cage with no door handles, but she helped him gently onto the front seat, next to her. He sat there listening to her radio going, looking at the shotgun set up in its mount by the steering wheel. And when the lights started streaming across the windows he couldn't tell if they were moving or if it was the fever again.

"You have a seriously high fever, Inchy. There's a virus going around. Leave it untreated a couple days and it could kill you. God only knows what inoculations you ever got. Your mother wouldn't want this for you, Inchy. She'd want someone looking after you, don't you think? Especially now. When none of you should be out there, not with all this evil going on."

"Perhaps that would be best," Pearlywhite murmured, in Inchy's ear. "A doctor."

"No, Pearly—I can't," Inchy said. "I have to help find the man. We have to stop him. Save you and the others. If I go with her, to . . . wherever . . . they might take your homebase away."

There, he'd said it—what he'd never said aloud before. The biggest reason he didn't want to leave the streets: he could lose the pearls and that'd mean losing Pearly.

"What'd you say, hon?" Officer Cat asked.

Inchy didn't reply. She shook her head, thinking he was delirious.

Then she made another noise, deep in her chest, and it filled him with foreboding. He felt Pearlywhite suddenly rearing back, winding up into thick tense coils of smoke that brushed the back of his neck and caused his jaw to clench. The cruiser slowed. Looking up, Inchy saw the lights above the 97th Street subway station, the plaza around the entrance. He peered up over the edge of the window, saw a cluster of cop cars thrashing their lights against the night, beyond a wall of bodies—the crowd that always clotted around the lights as if summoned to an impromptu carnival. Officer Cat rolled down the window to talk to a cop who stood by a taut stretch of yellow police tape. Inchy unbuckled his seat belt and got his knees up on the seat to crane past Officer Cat. The other cop pointed, and the gesture seemed to cause the crowd to part. Suddenly Inchy could see what everyone was looking at.

Three other cops and a woman in an ambulance attendant's uniform were standing over a limp, awkwardly skewed shape that was somehow ground into the pavement. Inchy recognized the suit jacket instantly, although it was hard to make sense of the shape that filled it. The only thing that made any sense was the hand, with upturned fingers, and the golden gleam of a ring with no jewel at its center, which therefore failed to catch the light. Garvey's ring, Garvey's suit . . . Garvey.

Officer Cat got out of the car. "Stay there, Inchy." She said that, but then she made no effort to stop him when he slid after her and slipped out through her door before it slammed. He felt like an Invisible himself at that moment, a wisp of smoke, merged with Pearlywhite. He walked beside her through the crowd, no more noticeable than her shadow.

"Oh my God," she was saying. "Not . . . not another?"

Inchy tried not to look at what was left of Garvey, but there was movement on his friend's body. Life . . . some stirring of life. His heart leapt. Garvey!

A crumpled face of blood-soaked fabric looked at him with hollow mouth, hollow pleading eyes. Slink raised itself slowly from the bloodied jacket, inching down to the ground. For a moment he thought it was coming to him and he knelt to snag it, hoping the detectives wouldn't notice—because there was no way they would let him have it. But instead, Slink seemed to gather itself for a last burst of movement. It pulled itself taut and poked a wadded limb toward the mouth of the subway station, back in the shadows where the lights had been shattered out. It was pointing at . . . at what?

Far back in the shadows, the pouchy face drifted away. The ice-chip eyes glinted and started to fade, but not before he saw the hunger in them.

"There he is!" Inchy burst out, grabbing Officer Cat's wrist.

"Inchy? What are you doing here? Get back to the car! Get back now, I'm telling you!"

"Don't you see him? He's getting away! Oh, he's getting away! That's the man! He's been in all the other places. We seen him all over!"

"Inchy, you're sick, you've got to get back . . . and you shouldn't be seeing this."

"Just look, Cat!"

She glanced back at the subway station, but it was too late . . . the man had been only the dimmest trace if you knew where to look for him, if you'd already seen him before. She thought he was raving from fever. The fever raged in him, true, but her blindness and his frustration were making it worse. His face felt unnaturally smooth and dry, hard and hot. Like burning bones. As if the skull had caught on fire inside him and burned its way out through his skin.

"Listen to her, Inchy," Pearlywhite said quietly. He didn't know what to make of that. Pearly sounded genuinely scared. It was the raw form of what he'd heard in Pearly's voice that morning, when going after Clyde's homebase. What he'd taken for a threatening tone was Pearly being afraid, facing something that could actually end Pearlywhite's existence. He hadn't known there was such a thing, but Pearly had known. The Invisibles weren't what he'd thought them to be. So much had changed in one day.

She looked back at him, and he knew she'd seen nothing.

"There's no entrance there, Inchy," she explained patiently. "This whole side's been closed off for repairs. Gate's closed. Now—"

Her pistol was staring him in the face. Inchy saw his hand going toward it, a slip of pale smoke, invisible.

"—I want you to get back in the car—"

"No . . . " Pearly whispered.

"—and stay there while I get some things straightened—"

" . . . Not alone . . . "

And he flicked up the snap with his thumb, dug in and grabbed the butt, had it out of the holster, still invisible, moving like a breath of hot wind, unstoppable. Or so he felt himself to be, though Officer Cat was screaming at him and grabbing at his arm, already aware that she had lost him. He could feel Pearlywhite frowning down on him. In a way that was the hardest part: doing something against Pearly's wishes. But he was committed now. He was running, stooping to snag Slink as he went, stuffing the bloodied rag down into his pocket. The other cops lunged at him but Inchy was white mist, unstoppable. He flew down the subway entrance, past the point where he'd seen the fat man standing, feeling both strangely energized and as if he might spin into oblivion at any moment.

Behind him, Officer Cat shouted, "Hold your fire, damn it, hold your fire!"

Then Inchy was leaping five stairs at a time down the trashy hole of the subway entrance. The floor-to-ceiling gate was closed and padlocked, just as she'd said—but it was bent back at one corner. There was an opening just big enough for a kid to squeeze through. As Inchy wriggled through, the bars scraped over the inflamed wound in his arm, making him wince. He realized it was somehow connected with his sickness. Something had gotten into him through that little nail hole; it was eating away at him. Another invisible thing.

Pearly tightened around his neck. "Inchy, you must not do this. Go back! This place you are taking us . . . I cannot promise our return."

Inchy made no reply.

The shouting of cops fell farther and farther behind. It would take them a while to find a key to that padlock. Of course, they could go across the street and down the block to the other station entrance, and considering he had a gun they were not going to just let him go. But right now he had freedom, and he would use it. Feet banging out echoes, he ran through the moldy concrete darkness to the subway platform—and there he saw the man. The killer in blue, herding a boy ahead of him, down on the track. The boy might have looked a little bit like him, he supposed. He was about the same age with curly brown hair; but he wore dark blue jeans that looked like they hadn't been worn or washed many times; he also wore expensive hightop sneakers and a blue silk football jacket that was too big for him. Something bulky shifted in the jacket but Inchy couldn't tell what it was. The pouchy-faced man glanced back at the sound of Inchy's steps, and shot him a look that was first furious and then sneering; then he chivvied the boy up the ladder onto the other platform.

Lungs heaving broken glass, Inchy climbed down, jumped over the tracks and the lethal third rail, running to the ladder. Pausing there, Inchy shouted: "Boy—kid! Jump off the platform! I'll shoot him if he follows you! I got a gun! Mister—I'm . . . I'm gonna shoot!"

Pearly appeared, then, between him and the ladder—glimmering ghostly in the murk. "Inchy, let them go. You can give descriptions to the police now. You are a child and weak with fever, and *that one* is too strong. I can't let you go after them."

Inchy hesitated. There was something in Pearlywhite's eyes—was it tears? No, but it was an endless sorrow. As if Pearly had read his heart, already knew his answer. Maybe Pearly was right.

But then Inchy saw Garvey lying crushed into the asphalt, smeared there with incredible force as if dropped from a height and then hammered down. He saw Niall's hand tumbling out above the blood-soaked edges of the books he treasured. He saw Clyde's poor grubby bare defenseless foot. And he thought of Mina. Vick and Cassandra and the twins, sure, and the other kids in the city, so many of them. But especially Mina.

"No," he said. "It has to stop. It's up to us . . . you, too, Pearly. You, too."

He took the pearls from his pocket and held them out in the palm of his hand. Pearlywhite whirled in the air and drained away into the pearls. Inchy heard him whisper, as he went: "We might lose each other . . . we might lose . . . "

When Inchy got to the top of the ladder, a train was raging out of the dusty tunnel. The wind of it flung wax-paper trash as it came, and then it squealed to a stop. A few people idled on the active side of the station, several moved toward the train, but there were still no cops.

Far down the dimly lit platform, the man pushed the boy ahead of him, onto the train.

Inchy hesitated once more. He was suddenly sickeningly tired and thirsty, his mouth paper dry. But the train made a chirping sound that meant the doors were about to close.

Inchy hid the cold metal bulk of the gun in his coat and dodged into the last car just as the doors closed. There was a chunky black lady, a transit cop, sitting across from him. He waited for her to grab him, but she only glanced at him, frowning.

It looked to Inchy like she was going home after a long day on duty. She had her belt radio turned off and zero interest in turning it on. She hadn't heard about the kid who'd swiped a cop's gun and run away. Still, he imagined they'd be searching the stations up ahead, if they had time to organize. He hoped the man wasn't going too far. He had few enough advantages in this chase.

He started to go through the door to the next car, to find the man and the boy up front, but a hard grip on his arm stopped him. "Boy, you stay right in here. We don't want you kids running around between cars now. Jus' sit your ass down and wait for your stop." He nodded. But instead of letting him go, she cocked her head and peered at him. "You okay, boy? You look sick."

"I'm okay. Goin' home."

"That right? Well tell your mama to give you a bath."

A stab of painful sadness went through him at that. "Yes, ma'am. I will." She let go and he went to sit down. To wait.

The train rattled and grumbled through an endless chain of stops. At each, a few people got on or off—but never the big man with his captive boy.

That didn't happen until the end of the line.

He let them get ahead of him, because he felt so vulnerable here—so exposed. No one else had gotten off, and the station was bright enough that he couldn't follow them too soon. Poplar trees poked their swaying feathery heads up beyond the fence at the end of the raised, open air platform. From up here Inchy could see a parking lot, and across from that houses. Endless miles of houses on long regular streets spreading off into darkness toward a line of hills. Low roofs with warm lights glowing out from under them. None of the hulking buildings he was used to. None of the city noises. It was quiet. He stood feeling the cool wind on his cheek, wishing it would take the edge off his fever. Instead, it only made him shiver, and instantly he felt sicker.

Down below, coming out from under the edge of the platform, he saw the man urging the boy ahead of him toward the parking lot. It suddenly occurred to him that they were probably going to get into a car and drive away, and then he'd have lost them for good. In a panic, he hurried down the escalator, leaping steps so fast he felt he was flying. The station was deserted down here, too. Seeing no station agent, he leapt the turnstile and rushed out to the street.

The man and his boy were just passing under the last row of streetlights at the edge of the lot, moving on foot toward the houses. They weren't driving after all. Inchy breathed a sigh of relief, and followed.

It was a pretty house in a street of pretty houses; a two-story white house trimmed with open green shutters. Curtains, soft-looking as cobwebs in the tall windows. Someone hadn't mowed the thatchy lawn in a while, and one of the tires of the station wagon that sat in the driveway was flat. There was a light shining out from around back—the kitchen, Inchy thought, as he walked past the glossy bulk of the station wagon.

His head throbbed, and he felt sort of dreamlike; the gun was heavy against his rib cage. He wanted to see if the car was unlocked, and if it was he wanted to lie down on those wide soft seats. But he kept going, through the open wooden gate into the back yard. Crickets sawed away. A nightbird chattered and fell silent.

There was a fountain in the back, built into a terraced garden; the upper spillway was dry, the pool brackish. Inchy heard an electrical humming from the little black-plastic pump, half hidden in the grass. A pipe in the base of the fountain made a sucking noise as it sipped at the shallow, stagnant puddle where the light from a kitchen window surged and rippled.

Inchy turned his attention to the house. The back door stood ajar, atop a flight of red-painted concrete steps. Another flight of flagstone steps led down to where a second light issued from a white wooden door. Through a pane in the basement door he could see, distorted by the beveled glass, the boy from the subway, crossing a dull gold carpet. He couldn't see anyone else.

"Maybe the man's upstairs," he whispered. "Why doesn't the boy run? Pearly?"

He waited but Pearly neither emerged nor answered.

He started down the steps to the basement—and then dizziness whirled up in him and he had to stop to steady himself on the stairwell wall. Pearly wouldn't abandon him now—wouldn't leave him alone, to this. Maybe Pearly was too scared to come out. He thought of the times Pearlywhite had helped him, had given him the courage he needed to go on.

He wished he could do the same for Pearly now. But the only one he could do it for was himself.

He took a deep breath and reached for the doorknob. It turned in his fingers. Unlocked!

He pushed the door open quietly, searching for the boy, afraid of seeing the man. A fire burned in a black-metal fireplace, but the logs it danced upon were fake, cement. A pool table sat somewhat slanted on the gold carpet; all the balls had gathered in one corner, or fallen into pockets. At the far end of the room was a little cocktail bar; bottles tried to gleam in a glass case under it, but a thin layer of dust seemed to choke them. To the left of the bar, stairs led up to the kitchen.

He took a step into the room, and suddenly heard a gasp.

Inchy stiffened as the boy rose up from behind the padded bar, mouth and eyes wide. His head jerked sideways, toward the stairs, obviously listening and looking for the man. Inchy listened too, but he heard nothing.

"Kid!" Inchy hissed. "Come on! He left the door unlocked!"

The boy had tired brown eyes; he looked as skinny as Inchy, despite having grown up out here where people didn't have just one refrigerator, they had two. Inchy waited for the kid to respond, waited with his head throbbing, wanting to get out of here and take the kid to the cops and lie down somewhere safe. But the boy just looked at him. Too scared to move, maybe.

Inchy decided to help him. He came all the way into the room and edged past the fireplace, past the pool table, circling the bar.

His foot bumped something and he looked down, saw a small wooden baseball bat, the kind you give to preschoolers. He stepped over it and crossed to the boy.

"He left that back door open! Let's go!"

"No," the boy said. "I can't."

"I know all about him," Inchy said. "We can get out of here. I can hide you somewhere he'll never find you, and we'll tell the cops and . . . "

"If I try to leave," the boy said raspily, sounding like he had a bad cold, "he'll come out and get me."

Inchy could see that the boy's nose was running, his eyes red; he'd been crying.

"It's okay, uh—uh—what's your name?" Inchy said.

"Errol."

"It's okay, Errol. I know about him. I know what he's been doing."

"No . . . no you don't. You only think you know, but you were stupid to follow us, now he'll get you. I saw you in the city. By the alley this morning, and at the library, and then at the train station. I thought maybe you would get away, but then you had to go and follow me, so I know he was still using me. And it worked. Other kids, he made me talk to them till they followed. Telling them I had food and stuff. But you . . . he must have known you wouldn't fall for that. You, he had to lead on a chase. Used me again."

"So stop letting him. Get out of his house."

"It's not his house. It's mine. And . . . and hers."

Errol turned and looked for some reason at the bar refrigerator. It was long and white, like a big white coffin, and suddenly Inchy felt Pearlywhite's claws sharpening on his shoulders, underneath his clothes; tightening around his rib cage, right where the gun rode. He thought about reaching for the gun, just as the boy was reaching for the chrome handle of the fridge.

Errol pulled on the handle, hard, and cold mist streamed out of the open case; cold white light streamed out of it. It wasn't a refrigerator, it was a freezer. Full of frozen meat pies and plastic-wrapped steaks and chicken parts all crammed into every last bit of space that wasn't taken up by the two hard-frozen bodies of grown-ups. The stiff wrinkles in their clothes looked like snowy valleys; ice bearded their faces, pressed so close together; bearded the woman's face as well as the man's. One of her eyes was red-crusted shut, her blue lips parted; the frost on her lashes looked like some kind of exotic white makeup. She'd been a smallish, foxy-faced woman, with curly brown hair, closely resembling the boy. Her face was pressed into the man's face. The freezer had turned his pouchy cheeks and jowls into hard, bluish ice. But Inchy knew him at once.

"It's—it's—you killed him!" Inchy looked at Errol in awe, wondering how it was possible—how anything could have frozen so quickly, even in a freezer this size.

"Because he hurt her. Like that, you see?" Errol's voice went flat as his eyes roved the frozen wasteland of her features. "He—he gave me the bat when I was little, and then he used it to hurt me when, when he said I was bad, which was all the time. And then he used it on her." Errol's eyes welled up with tears. "I heard them, I heard it happen, but I . . . I didn't see anything until I came in and saw him next to her, on his knees, drinking from one of his bottles and laughing and sort of crying too. The . . . the bat was there, on the floor, and he didn't hear me pick it up. He didn't hear a thing until I hit him in the head. He didn't see me, but he knew it was me. He had to know. That's why he stayed. He tried to get up but he slipped and I hit him again and he fell and I hit him again and . . . it didn't matter. He still wouldn't go away."

"Inchy . . . " Pearly's voice. Pearly was constricting around his chest, squeezing him so hard he could hear his heart beating louder than Errol's voice. "Inchy get out of here *now.*"

Errol's eyes widened. "What . . . who said that?"

"Move away from him, Errol," came a deep, mocking voice from behind Inchy.

Inchy spun, heart leaping, and saw the man standing there holding the little baseball bat. The man who . . . what was he, the brother of the man in the freezer? A twin?

Inchy pulled out the gun, catching it on his coat-zipper—tore it loose as the man lunged at him, shoving Errol aside. Raised the gun and squeezed the trigger.

Pulling the trigger was harder than he'd thought. He had to use both hands as the man towered over him, raising the little baseball bat to bring it down on Inchy's skull.

The gun went off, dead center into the man's chest.

The man stopped—

—as the bullet splashed into his chest.

Inchy fired again—

—the second bullet making the man's substance splash and swirl so that for a moment Inchy could see right through the hole where the bullet had gone, could see the light from the kitchen and the gas flames flickering on the wall. Then the hole closed, like heavy fog, and re-formed as before.

Inchy staggered back. "You're . . . "

"Invisible," whispered Pearlywhite, slithering up along his back, clawing up to the top of Inchy's skull. And the man caught sight of Pearlywhite, his head literally splitting in a grin obscenely wide. He paused, chuckling, and raised one finger, beckoning. Not only to Inchy, but to Pearly. His pouchy features starting to squirm and tremble and flow into distinct, writhing pockets. The icy eyes began to slip below a surface of bubbling, molten flesh, but the man didn't need eyes to see. He saw with his whole horrible essence, beyond physical form.

Hopelessly, Inchy threw the gun at the man, but of course it passed harmlessly through him.

At that same instant, with a snarl that traveled down Inchy's spine, Pearlywhite tore itself free, leaving stinging gouges in his scalp, and launched itself at the . . . the Invisible who was starting to lose the form of a man. The blue suit of the other Invisible flickered and reformed into some kind of horn, an armored skin. Pearlywhite was a blur of teeth and claws, as Inchy had seen him earlier at the Pit; but this time Pearly could find no purchase on the scaly coat. The smokedragon grew dense and knifelike, striking and plunging repeatedly, but the "man" was nothing like a man now—even his laugh became less and less human as it cackled on and on and on.

Inchy saw Errol sunk to the floor, watching the struggle in terror, his hands clamped over his ears. Pearly was weakening, he saw that now; the poor thing had used up nearly all its strength. As if, somehow, the man-thing was drawing Pearly's power out of it. Every time Pearlywhite flashed into a new form, the enemy Invisible seemed to thrust out some part of itself—a face tendril, an amorphous finger—and wrap it deep in Pearly's misty core and rip out a bit of the stringy stuff that suddenly didn't look so insubstantial. And every time it ripped a bit of Pearly loose, it thrust the filthy finger deep into the writhing pouchy face and sucked at it with a juicy sound that echoed the dry slurp of the evaporated fountain.

Inchy crawled back toward the fire because he had to get away, and there was nothing he could do for Pearlywhite—he knew that with complete certainty. Pearlywhite was giving his essence to save Inchy. The smokedragon whirled for a moment and cast a desperate look back at Inchy, a pleading look, as if warning him to flee while he had a chance. Alone, they had no hope of beating the thing. It fed on Invisibles, sucked them dry, turned itself into this fat, powerful monstrosity. Look how many it already had consumed.

Thinking of the others it had taken, Inchy felt a stirring in his pockets.

"Let . . . us . . . "

The man-thing heard the whisper, just as Inchy did. It slipped its triumphant stranglehold on Pearlywhite and started toward Inchy. But Pearly hissed and slithered, tightening like a bit of moonwhite noose, binding with translucent sinews, throwing the monster back toward the bar where every bottle shattered as they hit it. And Inchy dug his hands deep into his pockets and removed the coiled ball of string, the bloodied paperback, the kerchief freshly steeped in gore.

The man struggled up, tearing Pearly free, shredding Pearlywhite to its last bit of matter—but thankfully not consuming the stuff. Some of it floated free on the air. The monster's arms widened to surround Inchy, but he had already hurled the homebases of his murdered friends. He could see them uncoiling, awakening in the flickering air, rising above the man whose face was no longer a face or anything much at all except a void, a hunger, an absolute emptiness. The man's arms clamped reflexively around Inchy, and his breath was just . . . gone. It was not like the physical touch of another human being—it was like gravity pulling when he jumped from a fast swing, or a heavy wind all compressed into a man-shape. Inchy's life was almost squeezed out in that instant.

Then the man released him. Inchy collapsed on his back, paralyzed and stricken, gasping up at the scene above him. The man stood there, thrashing at the forms of the other Invisibles, snatching at the weakened bits of them. Koil and Slink and Leafjacket and a storm of white froth that seemed to be all that remained of Pearlywhite. They were so weak, so insubstantial, that the man couldn't get a purchase on them. He swatted and they swarmed; he tried to snag them but came up empty and a black rage poured from the vacuum of his mouth.

Inchy saw Errol, then. Errol standing behind the man, with the bat raised as if to try once more to brain the thing. Utterly futile. Errol pulled back and the man thing, Errol's enraged and insane Invisible, turned and took a swipe at the boy but the other Invisibles closed in around the thing's mouth, choking it with themselves.

Inchy felt pearls in his fingers, sensed Pearlywhite whispering something to him, and he managed to choke out to Errol, "Burn it!"

The man-thing struck at Errol, struck him hard in the head, clapped his two massive hands together so hard on either side of the boy's head that his life was extinguished. All the rage he hadn't been able to bring to bear on the elusive Invisibles, spent in a final blow that made of Errol's skull a thing misshapen.

The bat flew. Went spinning. Struck cement with a hard clink, and a moment later Inchy smelled burning wood.

The man let out a roar and tried to rush to the fire. His foot struck Inchy's leg, but the blow felt soft and unreal. The man toppled flat across him, but the weight was almost nothing. The other Invisibles followed him to the ground, harrying and tearing at him, diving into his eye sockets, tearing at the folded flesh. He shredded them with his bare hands, clawing them as a man would wave away cigarette smoke, but they just reformed. He opened his gulf of a mouth to howl and they stuffed themselves inside and allowed nothing out. The Invisibles caught the edges of the man's face and pulled him inward, drawing his extremities down into the hungry maw. The thing was consuming itself, and all of them as well. Inchy prayed that as a result of what the Invisibles had done, they would find another way out, once they had destroyed this one. They deserved something more than the void into which they threw themselves.

The man's fleshy fingers, arms, and thrashing blue limbs all stretched and drew into the center of the blackness, caught by the relentless pull of something graver than gravity, which he had experienced for less than an instant and would never forget. There was no escaping it now, not even for the man itself. The collapse, when it came, came quickly. A sudden indrawing, a quickening, and then an explosion that made Inchy wonder how he could ever have called his friends and guardians "Invisibles." *This* was invisibility. It was an absence of sight—of everything.

They were gone. All of them.

He raised his head weakly. "Pearly?"

White mist still hung in the air, but he couldn't tell if it was Pearlywhite or smoke from the burning bat. He looked at Errol. He was dead, very for-sure dead. Inchy turned away—and almost fell over. The fevered weakness was pulling him down like a drain.

Inchy knew, now, that he needed help—help that Pearly couldn't give him. He needed real help, and he needed to help himself.

The last thing he did, summoning all his strength, was to drag himself behind the bar, where a telephone sat. He picked it up. And although he couldn't remember it later, he must have called a number he had never called before.

Officer Cat was sitting beside him, in a chair, and he was in a bed. A bed with crisp white linen. That was the first thing he noticed: he was lying down in a white bed in a white room, and Officer Cat was sitting beside him. The second thing he noticed was that she wasn't wearing a uniform. She was wearing some white slacks and a soft yellow blouse. He felt weak, but the throbbing was gone. There was a tube going into his arm, he saw then, from a bottle hanging from a metal stand on the side opposite Officer Cat.

She smiled at him. "They said you'd probably feel better this morning. Looks like it's true. They've had you on IV antibiotics for two days. You had a bad infection, on top of everything else."

"Two days?"

"Seemed like longer, to me," Mina said.

She came from a doorway behind him, a half-eaten candy bar in her hand. She was cleaned up, and she had a new blue shift on, and—no glasses.

He looked at her and she shook her head. Glimmish was gone.

Pearly!

He sat up, fumbling in the bedclothes. "You looking for those pearls?" Officer Cat asked. "They're in that drawer by the bed."

There was a little white table next to the bed with a vase of daffodils on it. He opened it and found the pearls, clutched them to him.

"The others?" he asked Mina.

She shrugged. He turned to Officer Cat. "There was a book, and . . . and Garvey's handkerchief, and a ball of string. Where they found me . . . ?"

"I haven't been there, Inchy. But I imagine it's all in Evidence now. What do you need to trouble yourself with that stuff for? I know the history. It all belonged to your friends. But those are morbid memories, Inchy. Bloodstained and all . . . even if you could have them back, why would you want them? Some things you're better off putting away. Believe me."

Beyond her, Mina was nodding slowly, and he knew it was the truth.

"Of course, no one's saying you should throw away those pearls, Inchy. I know what they mean to you."

A beeper sounded from Officer Cat's purse. She opened the purse, looked at the beeper, and said, "Be right back, have to call in." She got up, patted his arm, and went out into the hall.

Mina seemed to know he was thirsty. She poured him a glass of water from a plastic pitcher at the bedside. He drank deeply as she sat on the edge of his bed; she waited. Then he told her what had happened.

"So the man won't be back?" she asked.

"I don't think so. But neither will Errol." He pressed the pearls to his cheek and whispered, "Pearly? Pearlywhite?"

There was no answer. He had known somehow that there wouldn't be. He could feel some sort of difference in the pearls. They didn't seem lighter: they just seemed *less*.

"Glimmish is gone, too," Mina said, looking at her feet. New tennis shoes on them. "I don't know if it's because my brother's glasses broke, or if it's because I . . . I told Cat yes."

"Yes what?"

"She filled out some forms and talked to some office people—asked if we could live with her. They said yes and I said yes. Now it's your turn."

"Me?" His head spun. "I don't know. Pearly . . . "

But Pearly wasn't here to advise him anymore. He had to guide himself now. He remembered how it had felt to know he could do that, could make the hard decisions without looking to someone or something else. He thought, This is the way it's supposed to be—or anyway, the way it's going to be from now on. Pearlywhite had taken him most of the way, past his mother's death, down the hard streets. But the last few steps, well, he'd had to go those alone. And they had brought him to a place where he might not have to be alone any longer.

He closed his hand around the string of pearls and lay there feeling how the warmth in them, now, was simply the warmth his own flesh gave them. Before he realized what was happening, Mina was holding him, and holding his hand around the pearls. He was crying and it was okay, she understood what he had lost. What they had lost.

And when he told her one last thing he had to do, she understood that too.

Three days later, he walked away from Mina and Officer Cat, leaving them standing on the gravel road while he stepped through the wet grass toward a line of graves. He was wearing new clothes, new shoes, and he was surprised at how annoyed he felt when he saw mud splattering the nice new shine. "Damn, these are new shoes!" he thought, then he let out a surprised laugh. It was Garvey's voice, almost. Garvey living on in him.

The rain had been falling steadily all morning, and it didn't let up for a minute as he knelt by the plastic marker. Someday he would replace it with something nice—real stone, something lovely and permanent. But for now, he was already soaked through the shoulders, and he didn't want to ruin the suit Cat had bought for him. She had already told him not to worry about that, but anyway, it didn't take long. Just long enough to push the pearls, and, in a way, Pearly too, down into the soft earth over Mama's grave, and say goodbye to both of them.

Before he became one of the creators and lead writer on the Half-Life videogame series, **Marc Laidlaw** was an acclaimed writer of short stories and novels. His novel *The 37th Mandala* won the International Horror Guild Award for Best Novel. A writer at Valve since 1997, his short fiction continues to appear in various magazines and anthologies.

John Shirley is a prolific writer of novels, short fiction, TV scripts, and screenplays who has published over thirty books and ten collections. His latest novels are *High* and *Doyle After Death*. His first historical novel, *Wyatt in Wichita*, will be published this year. As a musician Shirley has fronted his own bands and written lyrics for Blue Öyster Cult and others. In 2013 Black October Records released a two-CD compilation of Shirley's own recordings, *Broken Mirror Glass: The John Shirley Anthology*. See www.john-shirley for more information.

Acknowledgements

"Paranormal Romance" © 2013 Christopher Barzak. First publication: *Lightspeed Magazine*, June 2013.

"The Slaughtered Lamb" © 2012 Elizabeth Bear. First publication: *The Modern Fae's Guide to Surviving Humanity*, eds. Joshua Palmatier & Patricia Bray (DAW).

"The Land of Heart's Desire" © 2010 Holly Black. First publication: *The Poison Eaters* (Big Mouth House).

"Seeing Eye" © 2009 Patricia Briggs. First publication: *Strange Brew*, ed. P. N. Elrod (St. Martin's Griffin).

"De la Tierra" © 2004 Emma Bull. First publication: *Faery Reel: Tales From the Twilight Realm*, eds. Ellen Datlow & Terri Windling (Viking Juvenile).

"Curses" © 2011 Jim Butcher. First publication: *Naked City: Tales of Urban Fantasy*, ed. Ellen Datlow (St. Martin's Griffin).

"Snake Charmer" © 2006 Amanda Downum. First publication: *Realms of Fantasy*, October 2003.

"Street Wizard" © 2010 Simon R. Green. First publication: *The Way of the Wizard*, ed. John Joseph Adams (Prime Books).

"Dog Boys" © 2012 Charles de Lint. First publication: *Dog Boys* (Triskell Press).

"-30-" © 2010 Caitlín R. Kiernan. First publication: *Sirenia Digest #61*, December 2010.

"Stone Man" © 2007 Nancy Kress. First publication: *Wizards: Magical Tales from the Masters of Modern Fantasy*, eds. Jack Dann & Gardner Dozois (Berkeley).

"Pearlywhite" © 2003 Marc Laidlaw & John Shirley. First publication: *Carved in Rock: Short Stories by Musicians*, ed. Greg Kihn (Thunder's Mouth Press).

"Spellcaster 2.0" © 2012 Jonathan Maberry. First publication: *An Apple for the Creature*, eds. Charlaine Harris & Toni L. P. Kelner (Ace).